Dr Elizabeth Haywood has spent her career in business and has appeared on major TV and radio outlets across the UK. She lives with her husband, Lord Peter Hain, mostly in south Wales. This is her first book, born out of a desire to tell her ancestor's extraordinary story.

For my father Douglas and mother Zaidée, who first told me stories of Sam Lord; for all the current Haywood offspring – Katherine, Richard, Patricia, Andrew, Zoë, Karima, Aisha, Daniel, Isabella, Cameron – and for future generations, so we do not forget our history.

Elizabeth Haywood

LUCY: ULTIMATE SURVIVOR

AUSTIN MACAULEY PUBLISHERS™

LONDON • CAMBRIDGE • NEW YORK • SHARJAH

A CIP catalogue record for this title is available from the British Library.

ISBN 9781528983525 (Paperback)
ISBN 9781528983532 (Hardback)
ISBN 9781528983549 (ePub e-book)

www.austinmacauley.com

First Published (2021)
Austin Macauley Publishers Ltd
25 Canada Square
Canary Wharf
London
E14 5LQ

I would like to thank Harriet Pierce of the Barbados Museum, and Miguel Pena of the Barbados National Trust for being so generous with their time. I am also extremely grateful to the Rector of St Philip's Church Barbados, Rev. Trevor O'Neale; and the Parish Clerk, Mrs Andrea Waithe, for letting nte scour the parish records.

Thanks also to the helpful staff at the Greenwich Maritime Museum and Cardiff Museum.

Particular thanks go to two people: my long-suffering husband, Peter Hain, who has used his long experience of writing books to read, comment and re-read various manuscript drafts and contributed hugely to the final version; and my good friend Christine Warwick, who helped by participating enthusiastically in early research trips, digging out birth and death certificates and a completely illegible will, and editing the final draft.

I would also like to thank the maritime artist Peter Power for guiding me in identifying relevant information on ships and the facilities available to passengers in the early 1800s.

And last but by no means least, I also want to acknowledge the role played by my mother and siblings, whose continual demands of "When can I read it?" kept me going throughout the process and ensured I didn't give up even when I came across facts which contradicted each other or required unravelling to make sense of them.

Elizabeth Haywood
Neath, July 2020

Author's Note

This is the story of my great-great-great-grandmother, Lucy Lord née Wightwick. As far as possible, it is based on fact. But for the sake of the story, I have had to imagine some of the circumstances in which she found herself, and the dialogue throughout, as she left no diary.

A portrait of Lucy Lord appears on page 31 and of Sam Lord on page 57.

Some of the language (such as 'Negro', 'picaninny') will rightly appear racist to a modern audience. And the early 19th century prejudices and violence depicted towards enslaved people will also offend. That will especially be the case as I finalise the text in July 2020 following the powerful, global #BlackLivesMatter movement against deeply rooted, institutionalised racism. But such language and attitudes were typical of that era and are only used where necessary to depict historical reality, ugly warts and all. Similarly, violence towards women and their degrading treatment as chattels were also the norm, and also unacceptable to today's reader.

Prologue

It was dark and clammy. She could hear the wind, or perhaps it was the sea. But it sounded far away. Her arm brushed the wall beside her. Damp. A gust of despair swept over her as she realised where she was. She had been here before, never of her own volition and she hated it.

She tried to sit up and groaned as she felt the ache in her back and legs. Cautiously, she ran her tongue around her mouth. At least her teeth all seemed to be intact. She touched her face, and felt the bruise beginning to form around her left eye.

Slowly, with a rustle of petticoats, she swung her feet round to the floor, her thin slippers feeling the slippery, uneven stone. She moved cautiously, looking for the two buckets she knew from experience should be there somewhere, one full of water, the other for her bodily functions. She stubbed her toe, but her right arm touched the wall and she followed it around, feeling with her foot for the buckets. A hollow clang told her she had found them, but when she bent to scoop water into her parched mouth, she realised only a few inches remained in the bottom. She bit back a sob, knowing it could be many hours before anyone came to replenish the supply. She must ration what she drank and keep her wits about her.

She allowed herself two small mouthfuls of the stale water then groped her way back to the pile of chains where she had lain awkwardly before. A rustling to her left told her the rats were there as usual, and she suppressed a shiver. They had not done her any harm before, but in the dark, she could not help imagining them gnawing at her bare flesh. She fought a rising tide of panic. *Be sensible,* she thought. She would be released, as before, after she had spent enough time in this hateful place to cool her fiery temper.

And then it all came flooding back. This time, there was not a moment to lose. For once this was not just a blazing marital row – of which there had been many. This involved her little girl. She must get out in time to protect her, to prevent her husband placing the child in harm's way by bringing her to this beautiful but dangerous place. Of course she ached to be with their daughter just as he did, but the girl was vulnerable and would die here, like the others.

She got to her feet and groped for the door, banging her fists on the thick wood and crying out for someone, anyone, to respond to her calls. But no one came. They never did at night. She knew that. Finally, exhausted and thirstier than ever, she sank to the floor sobbing. What could she do to save her baby girl? Would tomorrow be too late?

She took a deep breath and steadied herself. Bunching her skirts around her knees, she got to her feet and went back to her perch on the pile of chains she used for a seat, determined to think of a way of resolving her problem, determined not to give in to despair. She sat back and set about weaving her plans.

Part 1
The Early Years, 1785–1807

Chapter 1
Childhood, 1785–1806

"I baptise thee, in the name of the Father, Son and Holy Spirit." The seven-month-old baby named Lucy after her mother wriggled and let out a roar of fury as the cold baptismal water from the fifteenth century font poured over her head. Lucy senior sighed at this lack of female submission from her little namesake and hoped that this was not a sign that she would be a wayward child. The baby's father beamed, delighted at this proof that his daughter had so much liveliness – and, of course, was rejecting Satan and all his works, he thought hurriedly, with a glance at the vicar. He was happy to do his duty and attend church services as required but he was not a devout man, preferring to leave the niceties of religion to his wife while he busied himself with more worldly matters.

Following the ceremony, parents Thomas and Lucy Wightwick stood outside the imposing red sandstone church of St Peter's in Wolverhampton on this cold, blustery day in April 1785 and greeted all their well-wishers before getting into their carriage and driving the short distance home to Wightwick Manor at Tettenhall. Nurse had taken baby Lucy on ahead, to alert the staff to the imminent arrival of the invited guests. As she was handed down from the carriage, Mrs Wightwick cast a harassed glance around and was relieved to see that everything was in order, with the servants moving smoothly to serve the christening tea. Baby Lucy, too, appeared to be on her best behaviour, placed in her cradle in the shade, her white lace christening garments flowing around her (the traditional Stubbs family gown, thought her mother with pride), her deep brown eyes wide open, she stared solemnly about at all the bustling activity, looking remarkably angelic. Mrs Wightwick breathed a sigh of relief and moved gracefully to greet her guests, extended family members and local landed gentry known to the Stubbs family for the most part, and to thank the vicar.

Mrs Wightwick had been brought up in Staffordshire, the youngest daughter of Humphrey Stubbs and was a wealthy woman. She was one of four co-heiresses to the numerous properties of her childless uncle, Matthew Stubbs of Water Eaton, a marching camp in Roman times, and Great Bloxwich. When Thomas asked her father for her hand in marriage, she was not unwilling. It was a good match – the Wightwicks were an old established family able to trace their roots back to the Domesday Book, with properties in Staffordshire and Shropshire and connected to an array of Wightwicks in Surrey, Berkshire and Coventry. Thomas was an only son, and so stood to inherit everything from both his father (another Thomas) and his mother, Margaret Devey.

Her one regret was that she had not – yet – been able to give her husband Thomas the sons (or rather, any which survived infancy) he so wished for, a desire made even stronger by the knowledge that he was the last of his direct line. Still, now that little Lucy had been born strong and healthy, it was to be hoped that it would prove to be the start of a line of little Wightwicks, as many of them as possible boys. There was still time. She and Thomas had only been married two years. She smiled to herself as she moved forward gracefully to greet her guests. Mrs Lucy Wightwick was content with her life.

****

An eight-year-old Lucy woke, and sat up in the same instant. She looked at the sunspots dancing on the ceiling and walls of her room, and decided it was time to get up, even though she could hear no sounds of stirring in the great house. She was always an early riser, but her mother did not like her to wander outside on her own – and certainly not to leave the garden – but how could she lie abed on such a glorious day? Besides, she thought, Papa was away on business in Wolverhampton; Mama had gone to bed early yesterday suffering from a chill. And Nurse could generally be persuaded to hide her peccadilloes if they were not too outrageous…

She jumped up and put on the bare minimum of clothing from the neat heap of petticoats, stockings and over-garments laid out for her to wear and, shoes in hand, ran lightly along the corridor and down the stairs. She slipped into the library, hoping to find it empty of servants because the French windows opened silently onto the garden (which the front door did not), and skipped noiselessly across the path and down the lawn towards the lake. Her heart beat a little faster, because it was expressly forbidden for any child to go anywhere near the water unsupervised, especially since the gardener's boy had drowned there one night a year ago. Papa had said one of the great pike who inhabited its murky depths had probably decided he looked like a tasty meal, but he did not look as though anything had tried to eat him when they found him. Her father had had a fence erected about the lake since then. In any case, she loved sitting under the willow tree and watching the colourful dragonflies dancing on the water like fairies. Surely, they would not hurt her.

She found her favourite spot in the hollow of the old willow and curled up in it, wriggling her bare toes for the sheer pleasure of the sunshine. A thrush was singing its heart out nearby, and a trout jumped lazily from the lake's surface in search of breakfast. The little girl sighed for she was hungry too. If only she had thought about it before leaving the house she would have put an apple in her pocket to stave off the hunger pangs, but as her mother frequently reminded her, she was too impulsive and did not think things through.

The sound of water lapping against the bank, the sunlight dancing on the surface of the lake and through the leaves, lulled her into drowsiness. She had meant to slip back to her room before anyone was aware of her absence, but she must have dozed and awakened with a start to hear her name being called. With a sigh, Lucy stood up, her skirt clinging to her from the dewy grass. She could probably expect a caning for her disobedience, but the day was so lovely she did not regret it. And if Mama was ill, perhaps she would just be reprimanded. She hoped she would not be sent to her room without food, for she was now ravenous.

She slipped out of her hiding place and started towards the house, then saw Betsi, one of the younger maids, hurrying in her direction. She stood still, and Betsi looked at her, hands on her hips and with a broad smile on her face.

"Come along now, Miss Lucy. Let's see if we can get you back to the house without anyone the wiser that you've been disobeying your Papa by coming down to the lake."

Betsi took her hand and pulled her towards the kitchen entrance to the house. Lucy went willingly. At least in the kitchen she could fill her pinafore pockets with food to keep her going if she was to be shut in her room for the rest of the day. When they reached the pantry, the maid silently handed her a peach, and as they moved through the bustling kitchen, Lucy helped herself to some bread and cheese and slipped that into her pocket too. Betsi still had firm hold of her hand, and did not let go until she spied Nurse, who was looking harassed, and to whom she handed Lucy over without a word.

"Where have you been, you naughty girl? Your mother wants you to help her making jelly today and you were nowhere to be found. And look at the state of your dress – we'd best get you changed before you go down to join her." Nurse bustled her away and Lucy for once made no demur. She liked jam-making, and this meant she was not to be punished for going down to the lake.

While Nurse found her clean clothes, Lucy took a bite of her bread and cheese, but hid the peach carefully in a drawer for later. When Nurse returned, she brought a glass of milk too, which Lucy drank gratefully. A short while later, washed, in clean clothes and with her hair combed and tied back demurely, she was ready to join her mother.

"There you are, child! Come – we must finish the currant jelly today before your father returns." Her mother, a notable housewife, oversaw the preparation of all the household preserves made to her own recipes out of produce from Hewelsfield's own gardens.

While the family home remained Great Bloxwich in Staffordshire, the Wightwicks had recently taken a lease on Hewelsfield Court in the Forest of Dean. It was a lovely old sandstone house with an impressive façade, a *garderobe* turret and a beautiful, large, airy first floor room (particularly appreciated by Lucy's mother) which was kept warm even in the long winter months of rain and wind by lateral stack heating from the enormous sixteenth century range in the kitchen.

The Court – which the Wightwicks rented from the owners – was surrounded by hundreds of acres of farmland; the village of Hewelsfield itself was tiny, with only a few small houses and cottages on the lanes approaching the church, but the main road from Chepstow to St Briavels passed nearby to the west, which was an important business consideration for Thomas as he travelled so frequently between Chepstow, Bristol and Wolverhampton. It would also make it easier for visitors to the Wightwick family to reach them. If the Wightwicks decided to spend a large portion of their time in the south – and Mrs Wightwick had a shrewd suspicion that they might, given Thomas' growing business interests in Bristol and Chepstow – it was to be hoped that several times a year members of the Stubbs family might come to spend a week or more at Hewelsfield Court.

Thomas was interested in being more than just a country gentleman and had started using a portion of the rents from all their properties in Staffordshire, most of which had come to him through their marriage, to invest in a variety of enterprises, discovering in himself a real enjoyment of commerce. Gradually these investments took more and more of his time, and since many of them originated in Bristol and Chepstow, Thomas had announced that they should move south, leaving the Staffordshire properties in the hands of a capable agent and travelling north several times a year.

Mrs Wightwick also rather thought she would enjoy entertaining the local gentry such as the Janes of Haresley Court (who were almost their next-door neighbours) or the Wyndhams of Clearwell. She found it satisfying to run a busy household at Hewelsfield, as well as their houses at Tettenhall and Great Bloxwich when they returned north. She also liked the variety of town and country life provided by the two places and was proud that her husband's interests were thriving. And she had been brought up in a family with a strong Protestant work ethic which she channelled into pride in running the perfect household and demonstrating by example how all domestic tasks should be accomplished.

One of those tasks was jam-making, which she thoroughly enjoyed and found soothing. She sat Lucy down with a basket of redcurrants and put her to work pulling them off their stalks in preparation for the pot. The sun was streaming through the window, and Lucy swung her legs on her stool and set to work, enjoying the smell of the sugar and lemons to be used in the process. Other smells wafted from the main kitchen – cloves, cinnamon, nutmeg, used in rare abundance in the Wightwick house because of her father's links with West Indies' merchants. Good, she thought with a smile, there will be apple tart for tea tonight. She knew it was her father's favourite also.

She worked diligently for about an hour, then began to get restless. She finished sorting the contents of her basket and moved to a stool closer to where her mother was stirring the giant jam pan on the stove with a batch of fruit prepared earlier. Lucy watched fascinated as her mother poured a little of the jam onto a dish to test whether it had set. When it had, she put one of the kitchen girls to ladling the steaming mixture into the rows of pots which had been laid out ready, watching closely to ensure she did not overfill them. At last she turned to smile at her daughter.

"There, Lucy. This is a good year for fruit, we shall have a plentiful supply of preserves throughout the winter." She saw her daughter's eyes dwell longingly on the dish on which she had tested the jam. "Yes, you may try it, now that it has cooled. Then you must go and have your lunch with Nurse."

Lucy hugged her mother impulsively, thinking in a little surprise that her arms did not seem to reach as far around her waist as they did normally, then she scooped up the warm jam with her finger and smiled as its sweetness hit her tongue.

Later that afternoon, Lucy spent another hour helping her mother, after which she was released to play outside. She crossed the neat gravel driveway, scrambled over a stile and ran across the field to Hewelsfield Church. Dedicated to St Mary Magdalene, the church, parts of it dating from Saxon times, exuded an air of ancient wisdom. In particular, Lucy liked the way the stone tiled roof swept down from the ridge on the north side almost to the ground, giving the impression that it was curling around the old building to protect it. But she had not come to admire the building today. In the quiet and empty churchyard, she clambered up the thick trunk of her favourite tree which had a convenient view of the road to watch for her father's return and settled into a fork in the branches.

The ancient, hollow yew tree was more than one thousand years old and her perch provided Lucy with an untrammelled view not only of the road, but also of the horse chestnut trees with their gleaming conkers sheathed in a green, prickly shell and the quiet old tombstones around which Lucy enjoyed weaving stories in her head. She loved to intercept her father when she could; if he was in a good mood, he might take her up with him in the carriage or on his saddle and they would go to the stables together, another source of rich sounds and smells which Lucy enjoyed. Then she saw her father's horse rounding the corner of the track leading into the village, picked up her skirts and ran like the wind along the grass verge to meet him. He had been on the lookout for her, stopping his horse and smiling down at the little girl, who was stroking its nose. He reached down and lifted her onto his saddlebow.

"Papa, Papa, there is apple tart for tea and I have been making jam with mother," she told him. "What have you been doing today, Papa?"

"One of my ships came into Bristol laden with spices and cotton from the West Indies, and I have been checking the produce. Do you know where the West Indies are, Lucy?" When the child shook her head, he frowned slightly. "It is time you learned a little more than jam-making," he said. "I will arrange for a governess for you. And if you show an aptitude for geography and arithmetic, I will take you to my offices in Bristol one day so that you can understand the practical use to which such knowledge can be put. Would you like that?"

Lucy, who had begun to look mulish at the suggestion of a governess, brightened. "Indeed I would, Papa. I would like to work with you at the port."

By this time they had reached the stables, and she became so engrossed in greeting the horses by name and then by thoughts of the promised treat of apple tart for tea that she forgot the conversation with her father – until, at the beginning of November, the new governess arrived.

In the meantime, she had another interest to preoccupy her, a baby brother. The family had travelled back to Great Bloxwich several weeks previously, and she had woken one morning to hear a surprising amount of noise around the house at that early hour – people whispering and running feet. Ever curious, the little girl opened her door and peered out, only to see Nurse – who was quite plump – scurrying past her room faster than Lucy had ever seen her move.

"What is happening, Nurse?" she asked.

"Stay in your room, cariad, there's a good girl, and I will send one of the maids to help you. I must tend to your mother and don't have the time to watch over you today as well." She whirled around, arms akimbo, to face Lucy from a little further down the hallway. "If you behave yourself today and give no trouble you shall have a lovely surprise this evening!"

"What sort of surprise?" asked Lucy.

"Why, a baby brother or sister, to be sure," was the response. "Now, I must run along to your mother. Remember – you must be a good girl!" And with that she hurried off towards Mrs Wightwick's room.

Lucy had no intention of waiting in her room for one of the maids. If the house was at sixes and sevens, she could easily slip out unnoticed and visit all her favourite places like the stables, which her mother and Nurse always sighed over because she generally returned with dirty, and frequently torn, clothes. She hobnobbed too closely with the grooms and other lowly persons according to her mother who was worried that she would learn bad habits.

She scrambled into the first clothes she could find and raced down the stairs in stockinged feet, shoes in her hands, in order to make her getaway before anyone came to look for her. She made for the kitchen, where Cook was a great friend, and wheedled some bread and cheese and an apple out of her. With her pinafore pockets bulging with these items, she made her way outside to the walled garden, munching on the apple.

After a while, she went to the stables to stroke the horses and talk to the head groom, John, with whom she was a firm favourite. She was sad that she had not thought to bring any carrots for the horses, but the groom allowed her to dip her hands into a bucket of oats and give these to the animals instead. She spent the most time with her own pony and did her best to groom him as she had seen one of the under-grooms doing to the big, glossy chestnut that her father often rode, but she soon got hot and tired. Seeing this, John lifted her up to sit on the mounting block to eat her bread and cheese.

When she had finished, she hopped down from the block, said her goodbyes to John and the horses, and, swishing a stick she had picked up, walked across the field behind the house towards their nearest neighbours. There was no point in watching out for her father as he had said he would not be back for another two days. At about 4 o'clock, she felt hungry again and decided to make her way home. She looked down ruefully at a torn stocking, dirty pinafore and crushed skirt, and realised she had lost her bonnet somewhere during the day. She would be in for a scold. She walked back along a muddy track, waving in a friendly fashion to two labourers who were plodding in the opposite direction, their farm tools slung over their shoulders, and stopped at a patch of blackberries to ease her hunger – and get red stains down her clothes.

She entered the house as she had left, through the kitchen, and immediately sensed that while the unusual bustle of the morning had vanished, there was an air of suppressed excitement among the staff. Cook smiled at her.

"You have a new brother, dearie. What do you make of that?" she asked.

Lucy remembered Nurse's words before she left the house that morning and clapped her hands. "Where is he? Can I see him now?"

It was Betsi who answered. "You'd best change first, miss. The mistress would have a fit if she saw you looking like the hoyden you are. You come along o'me, seeing as Nurse is busy, and we'll clean you up a bit."

Betsi took the girl's hand and pulled her towards the stairs, Lucy quite willing, wondering what it would be like to have another child in the house. She had been on her own for so long, it would be exciting to have someone else to share her games with.

Washed and re-dressed by Betsi, she approached her mother's room as instructed and knocked on the door. Nurse opened it; her face wreathed in smiles.

"Come in, *cariad*, come in, and take a look at your brother. And a bonny lad he is!"

Lucy walked over to the crib which was next to her mother's bed. Her mother waved a weary hand at her and smiled, and Lucy bent over the crib to take a look. Her brother was asleep on his back. He had a red, wrinkled face and no hair. She inspected his fingers, which lay outside the blankets, and was disappointed that he seemed so small.

"When will he be able to play with me, Mama?" she asked, looking up.

Her mother and Nurse both laughed. "Not for a long time yet, Lucy. He cannot walk, you know – he must grow first."

Lucy sighed. "Bye-bye, baby," she said. "What is his name, Mama?"

"He will be called Stubbs, after my family," Mrs Wightwick answered firmly.

"You run along now, dearie and have your tea in the kitchen. I'll be along later to tuck you in," said Nurse, and Lucy reached up on tiptoe to kiss her mother's cheek then happily headed for the kitchen, for she was starving.

In the weeks that followed, Nurse and Mother seemed always busy with the new baby and Lucy found herself subject to far less supervision than usual, particularly once they returned to Hewelsfield. The little girl was unaware that her mother had already lost one son, John, born when Lucy was only a year old. She revelled in her new-found freedom. She rode her pony all over the surrounding countryside whether at Great Bloxwich or Hewelsfield, tumbling off frequently when she tried to take a jump too big for her and coming home very muddy but happy. She was always accompanied by a groom, for all the stable hands knew that she was reckless and that her father would blame them if she came to any harm. She talked to the labourers in the fields and shared their lunches of bread and cheese. And in the evenings during her mother's lying-in when her father was at home, she would curl up comfortably on the floor at his feet in his study and they would tell each other about their day's activities.

But all that came to an abrupt halt at the beginning of November when her father announced one evening that Miss Priddy, the new governess, would be arriving the next day to begin her lessons.

Lucy was standing before her father at the time, and he looked down at the curly bent head and smiled to himself. "Remember what I said to you, Lucy? That if you work diligently, particularly at geography and arithmetic, I will take you with me to Bristol one day."

Lucy, whose heart had sunk at the warning that her carefree days were over, brightened considerably at that. "I will do well, Papa. I will make you proud!" she declared.

Nurse received instructions to have Lucy ready to meet Miss Priddy when she arrived in the early afternoon. Lucy was allowed to go for a ride on her pony in the morning, but only if she came straight back to wash and dress neatly. Lucy thought this a terrible waste of a bright, sunny day, but she did not dare to disobey because she knew that this order, while it was delivered by her mother, was backed fully by her father. She suffered Nurse's ministrations and tut-tutting but could not help but squeal once or twice when the hairbrush was wielded a little too vigorously in order to tame Lucy's tangled hair. When she was ready, she sat at the top of the staircase, hoping to get a first glimpse of this person who, she was sure, was going to ruin her life, before being summoned to meet her formally.

When she heard the dog-cart – which had been sent to fetch Miss Priddy from the mail-coach in which she had travelled to Chepstow – draw up at the door, she pressed her face against the banisters to see better. The lady who entered was slim and appeared younger than Lucy's mother. She was dressed soberly, as governesses were expected to, in grey kerseymere and wore a modest bonnet tied with dark blue ribbons. As she removed this and handed it to the waiting maid, she glanced up while trying to pat her hair into order and Lucy, still as a mouse, looked into a pair of grey eyes. She could not be sure if Miss Priddy had noticed her, as the governess made no sign, merely inclining her head to show the maid that she was ready to be taken to greet the master or mistress of the house. She turned towards Thomas' study and was gone from view.

Lucy was not summoned for at least half an hour and grew bored. She was just wondering whether to visit the kitchen – for it had been a long time since lunch – and see whether she could wheedle some sweetmeats or a piece of apple tart out of Cook, when she heard Betsi coming towards the stairs. Betsi looked up, and seeing Lucy sitting on the top step beckoned to the girl, saying, "Come, Miss Lucy. The master and mistress wish to see you in the study."

Lucy was on her best behaviour, awed by a sense of occasion. She was rarely the centre of attention except when alone with her father, and she instinctively knew that this was a turning-point in her life. She entered the study and Betsi closed the door behind her from the outside. She went over to her mother who was seated and kissed her cheek, and then to her father who stood by the fireplace and received a little hug. Thomas then turned Lucy gently around to face their visitor.

"Lucy, I want you to meet Miss Priddy. She is the daughter of someone I met in commerce. She will be your governess from now on." Lucy bobbed a reasonably neat curtsey in Miss Priddy's direction. "I have impressed on Miss Priddy that I wish you to become competent in writing, arithmetic and geography, without which you will not understand anything when I introduce you to my business."

At this point, Mrs Wightwick interrupted, "We do not wish her to become too scholarly, you understand. You will need, Miss Priddy, to instil ladylike behaviour into our daughter. She can be somewhat wild and wilful. I wish her to learn French – you do know French, do you not?" Miss Priddy inclined her head politely to signify assent. "Please ensure she can sing and paint and understands etiquette. Later, when she is old enough, I shall engage someone suitable to teach her to dance. Now, Lucy," turning to her daughter, "you must obey Miss Priddy in all things. You will spend your morning on your lessons, such as geography and history, and in the afternoon, you will learn needlepoint and painting."

"But, Mama, when will I ride my pony?" Lucy burst out, unable to contain herself any longer. Her mother frowned at her but answered,

"You like to rise early in the morning. You may ride then – and you must learn to ride side-saddle! Riding astride is indecent for a lady."

Lucy looked mutinous but wisely said nothing. At least her riding was not going to be taken away from her. She stole a cautious look at Miss Priddy, and noticed her lips twitching with suppressed laughter. Perhaps after all things would not be so bad – and she would do anything to impress Papa.

"Now, why don't you take Miss Priddy to her room so she can freshen up after her journey? Then you might take her for a walk in the garden," said her mother.

Obediently, Lucy turned towards the door, looked back to ensure Miss Priddy was following her and marched upstairs to a large, airy, westerly facing room on the second floor. The governess had said nothing, but Lucy noticed that her shoulders seemed to relax as she looked around the pleasant room.

"So, Lucy," she said, smiling. "Would you like to help me to unpack? Then perhaps we could have something to drink – for I am a little thirsty after the journey. And perhaps you might introduce me to some of the servants before we go for that walk in the garden?"

The unpacking was soon done, Miss Priddy did not appear to have brought much. Smoothing out a shawl before placing it in the clothes press, Lucy stole a look at the governess. "Have you been a governess for long, Miss Priddy?"

"I have been working for the last year near Manchester. Do you know where that is, Lucy?"

Lucy nodded. Her father had shown it to her on a big map once, before one of his regular business trips to Wolverhampton, and told her it was the centre of industry. "Did you like it?" asked Lucy.

The governess hesitated. "Not very much. I was brought up in a small town, and Manchester is very big. It is noisy, and dirty too because of the smoke from all the manufactories. The sun doesn't shine there often."

"What is a manu... manu...?" Lucy stumbled over the new word.

"Manufactory. It is where they make everything, using machines. They make cotton and woollen cloth for our dresses; they produce guns and buttons, soap and glass, all of which used to be made slowly by hand but the work is now done by machine."

Lucy nodded gravely but found it difficult to picture the scene Miss Priddy had conjured up, oblivious that her learning process – not all of which would happen in the schoolroom – had already begun.

The unpacking finished, the two descended the stairs once more. Lucy clattered down in a rush; Miss Priddy followed more sedately, head high and holding her skirt up ever so slightly to avoid tripping on it.

"I can see I am going to have my work cut out teaching you deportment and how to walk in a ladylike fashion!" she said.

Lucy looked back up the stairs at her, warily, but then saw she was smiling as she said it. Relieved, Lucy smiled back and then turned to lead her governess towards the kitchen where she planned to ask Cook for a glass of milk and a piece of cake.

"Cook, this is my new governess, Miss Priddy," she announced. "Miss Priddy, this is Cook."

"Mrs Bainham is my name. Very pleased to meet you, I'm sure," sniffed Cook, looking anything but. Lucy hardly noticed, launching immediately into a request for sustenance. Cook patted her on the head and told Lucy to hop up on a stool at the table. Politely, she turned to the governess.

"And you, Miss Priddy? Would you like something after your journey?"

"I would welcome a glass of milk and a piece of cake also. Thank you, Mrs Bainham."

What Miss Priddy knew only too well but Lucy did not was that the position of a governess was a difficult one, neither a member of the family nor, technically, a servant. Generally she was resented by more senior members of the servant hierarchy, such as Cook and Nurse. A paid employee like them (although rarely as well paid), she nevertheless was expected to behave in a ladylike manner to instil this in her charges, and this of necessity included giving orders. In her previous employment, her mistress had also resented her, fearing (rightly) that Miss Priddy was better educated, and she had been allocated a tiny, back boxroom to live in. She had detected no such resentment in Mrs Wightwick and was pleasantly surprised by Mr Wightwick's desire that his daughter receive some genuine learning. Added to that, her room was what she could only have dreamed of. She could cope with the pettiness of the servants as long as she could persuade Lucy to accept her lot and to enjoy some of her lessons at least. Clearly, she was keen to please her father, so this might not be such a difficult task as she had expected, which was heartening because if a governess's charge took against her – and they did, all too frequently – no one would take the governess's part and her life was made intolerable. Miss Priddy was acutely aware that she knew nobody in the vicinity of Hewelsfield and was unlikely to make any friends who could relieve her drab existence in such a small place.

Having finished their milk and cake, Lucy took Miss Priddy into the garden where they went for a decorous walk along the paths, very different from the madcap running about the grass which was what Lucy normally did. Miss Priddy unfurled a very pretty parasol – a present from her father before he fell on hard times – to shield her from the sun, but Lucy was too young to care about such things.

Later, the two ate supper together in Lucy's room and Miss Priddy helped her get ready for bed. It was agreed that they would meet in the breakfast room when Lucy returned from her morning ride and had washed and changed.

A small desk had been set up for Lucy in her father's study, and lessons began in earnest after breakfast. Miss Priddy started teaching her the times tables and tested her reading skills. These were not very advanced. Lucy liked to take down the books on her father's shelves, but she looked at the pictures only. Her writing was also poor, so the governess started from scratch with her letters. When Lucy began to flag, she picked one of the books at random from a shelf and started to read it to her young charge. It happened to be a book about the produce to be found in Africa, and Miss Priddy found that Lucy listened intently and asked to see the pictures. She asked Lucy to point out Africa on her father's globe, which she did with alacrity. Together they identified some of the countries mentioned in the text, then Miss Priddy asked Lucy to tell her what she knew about Africa.

Lucy had picked up a surprising amount of knowledge for one so young, presumably from her father thought Miss Priddy, but she did get some of the facts muddled and the governess had to hide a smile on several occasions. She then led Lucy over to look at Mr Wightwick's collectors' cabinet and pointed to a beautiful butterfly pinned to a board in one of the drawers.

"What can you tell me about this butterfly?" she asked.

What Lucy told her was obviously a mixture of fact and fiction. It was clear that, like most little girls, she liked stories but that – more unusually – she also had the imagination to invent them herself. This was the hook Miss Priddy had been waiting for. From now on she could coax her pupil to read, learn her letters and her geography by showing her how important these were if she wanted to create stories.

After lunch, Miss Priddy gave Lucy a singing lesson, then decided that her charge had had enough for the first day and that they would go outside for the rest of the afternoon. Lucy was happy to demonstrate her knowledge of the plants and birds they saw, and Miss Priddy gently added to that knowledge. Lucy took her to visit the church and was delighted when the governess joined in to help her weave stories about the people buried in the graveyard, hardly noticing that Miss Priddy was still teaching her by telling her about something historical that had happened in the year of the person's birth or death. She admired Lucy's ancient tree but declined to scramble up into its branches, although she did not forbid Lucy to do so even though it meant a torn hem. She would take the dress away to mend after the little girl had gone to bed. All in all, the two were quite pleased with each other at the end of the first day.

Over the years that followed, Lucy gained a reasonable education and showed a remarkable aptitude for painting. Miss Priddy's father had ensured she received an unusually good education for a girl, until he lost his money on a trading deal which went wrong and had to remove her from school and she delighted in being able to pass on her knowledge. They read and discussed *The History of Tom Jones* and *The History of Sir Charles Grandison*; they studied the plays of Shakespeare and the poems of William Wordsworth and Samuel Coleridge; and they worked their way through all four volumes of Goldsmith's *The History of England*. Lucy's behaviour became a little less wild and her deportment improved; however, there were tantrums and tears and she would often kick over the traces and vanish for several hours when she should have been in the schoolroom.

But the biggest fight Lucy had was with her father after her mother forbade her to ride unless she learned to do so in a ladylike fashion, which meant side-saddle. Until that point, at age 13, Lucy had defied every instruction to do so but her father agreed that she must and put his foot down. After a week without riding, she rebelled, took her horse and went off by herself without even a groom in attendance. For such disobedience she was severely thrashed, but she remained mutinous for a further week at which point, unhappy that her father was studiously ignoring her and had gone so far as to sell her horse, she agreed to learn to ride side-saddle. Miss Priddy was unable to help, never having learned to ride, so a suitable instructor was procured.

When Lucy was 16, Miss Priddy left them because Mrs Wightwick wished Lucy to spend her last two years at boarding school to learn to socialise with her peers. It was agreed that Lucy should go to an exclusive seminary for young ladies under the auspices of Mrs Geary at Keynsham, near Bristol. For 30 guineas per year, her education would continue ('under the most approved masters') in English and French, History, Chronology, Mythology, Needle Work, Music, Dancing, Writing, Arithmetic, and Geography with the Use of Globes. Mrs Wightwick was hoping that she would learn to dance well before she was introduced into society, and that a school regime would drum more decorum into her daughter and stifle her impetuosity.

If the weather was kind, the trip to Keynsham was a pleasant one, but in bad weather it could be long and arduous. When Lucy first went to Mrs Geary's school, she and her mother took the dog cart (which could also carry her trunk) to Brockweir where they caught a boat to Chepstow. From there a post-chaise took them with her belongings to the Old Passage at Beachley, where they boarded a small boat for a 15-minute crossing of the River Severn to Aust. Here they stayed overnight at The Boar's Head before setting off, again by post-chaise, for the 30-mile drive to Keynsham. In inclement weather, this one-and-a-half-day journey could take three or four days, with muddy, impassable roads and the river passage too dangerous to contemplate.

Lucy's feelings about her time at school were mixed. With only one, much younger, brother and no sisters at home, she found it strange at first to be constantly with dozens of girls of her own age but quickly made several friends and enjoyed the companionship. Her mother had selected Mrs Geary's establishment because of its emphasis on strict social mores and deportment which tended to bring out Lucy's rebellious streak, but it also had a reputation for encouraging excellence in dancing and music, which Lucy did enjoy, and she received encouragement in her painting from a sympathetic teacher. She was also introduced to the delights of less improving books than those she had studied with Miss Priddy, namely the improbable tales of Gothic terror and sentimental romances which had become all the rage. Naturally these were not approved of in school, but a number of the girls smuggled in copies from home and she borrowed some from the lending library when small groups of pupils were escorted into town.

Once a month if the weather was fine, she was driven home to Hewelsfield for the weekend where she would revel in her morning rides which, other than her father's company, were what she missed most when away at school. Her days of careering across the countryside riding astride were over. She now rode side-saddle, as a young lady should, although she still enjoyed a challenge and frequently pushed both herself and her horse to the limit by jumping fences which most women would have quailed at. She often took home her music book, into which she had carefully copied out her favourite selections, and to please her mother she would play these in the evening while Mrs Wightwick busied herself with some exquisite needlework, a ladylike pursuit Lucy had little patience for.

On several occasions, Mr Wightwick fulfilled his promise to take her into Bristol to visit his place of work and to see the sights. Lucy loved accompanying her adored father, feeling most grown up when he was escorting her. She seemed to have inherited his interest in commerce, and found his business fascinating, finally thankful that she had paid attention to her sums and geography as he had insisted. She enjoyed visiting the New Vauxhall Gardens and the Hotwells at Clifton, both because they were attractive places in themselves but also because she liked to study the fashions being shown off on the promenade. But the war with France had stopped the development of Clifton when it was booming, and Hotwells now looked a little tired and shabby. She thought she would have taken pleasure in the balls, picnics and breakfasts which, her mother told her, had taken place in Hotwells' heyday only a few years previously, but no doubt she would find similar activities in which to participate when Mrs Wightwick introduced her to society in fashionable Bath the following winter.

What Lucy enjoyed rather less were the crush of people and the stench in the streets of Bristol itself.

Built on trade, Bristol had grown rich and powerful in the previous 200 years through its port, playing a key role in the slave trade triangle. Manufactured goods (copper, woollen cloth, trinkets, beads, guns and ammunition) were shipped to West Africa, where they were exchanged for slaves. The slaves were then taken to the Caribbean to be sold to sugar planters (and also to America to be sold to cotton and tobacco planters). The profits from the sale of the slaves were then used to buy sugar, rum and spices from the Caribbean (and tobacco from America) which were shipped to Europe, restarting the cycle. Depending on the weather the triangular round trip could take up to a year.

But Bristol did not just trade, it had a strong manufacturing economy – shipbuilding, glass, chocolate, coal, cannons and brewing. As a result, the population had boomed to almost 70,000 and the city was generally dirty, insanitary and overcrowded. Parts of Bristol contained stately squares of magnificent houses built for the wealthy, but as one drew closer to the water, an overwhelming mingled stench of rotting rubbish, left lying in the narrow streets adjoining the water, the mud of the estuary at low tide, coal dust, tobacco and chocolate made Lucy's gorge rise. She had to fan herself rapidly with one hand and press a handkerchief to her nose and mouth with the other to keep from fainting.

Her father seemed not to notice the smell, and cheerfully pointed out the sights to her as they passed: the Exchange on Corn Street; the Theatre Royal; Bristol Royal Infirmary; the forest of masts, small and large, bobbing and jostling against the quayside – many towering over the tiny, dark, dank houses there – and the new bridge, built only 50 years earlier and which had been the cause of severe rioting in 1793 when a promise to scrap the toll charges with which it had been built was not kept. Mr Wightwick's office was on the second floor of a building situated on Queen Charlotte Street, close to the Landoger Trow public house – in which he spent more of his time conducting his business than in the office – and overlooking the city centre docks. The windows were kept tightly sealed to keep out the noisome smell, for which Lucy was grateful despite the stuffy atmosphere this created. When her father lit up his pipe, she welcomed the scent of tobacco as it smelled far cleaner and more pleasant than the city or the docks.

When she had recovered slightly, Mr Wightwick seated his daughter in the big leather chair behind his desk, on which lay a huge ledger, and began to explain the different entries to her. Lucy was fascinated and quickly forgot the stench of the city as she pictured in her mind's eye the different trades in which her father was involved.

****

It was with some regret that Lucy waved farewell to her schoolfriends in the early summer of 1804, although as they all swore eternal friendship for each other she was confident they would keep in touch. Some were looking forward to being introduced to Society during 'the Season' later in the year; Lucy was among a smaller group whose mothers had decreed they were still too young and – in Lucy's case – should spend another year or more learning how to manage a household and gaining a little polish. Mrs Wightwick would dearly have liked to take her to France to finish her education, but the war with Napoleon Bonaparte made this impossible. Instead, she and Lucy's father had decided that there were plenty of things in Britain to which they could introduce her which would furnish her with the knowledge and confidence to converse sensibly with their acquaintances – without, Mrs Wightwick hoped, appearing too bookish as this might put off any potential suitors.

So Lucy spent another two years learning the intricacies of running two households from her mother, and learning more about her father's businesses (he was thinking about diversifying into coal mining, and she accompanied him on a tour of the south Wales canals which had been built recently to link Swansea, Neath, Cardiff and Newport). They took a day's outing to view the great Pontcysyllte Aqueduct, started in 1795, and Trevithick's Pen-y-Darren steam locomotive at Merthyr Tydfil. She (sometimes with her mother) accompanied her father to the houses of some of his business acquaintances such as Thomas Evans, a Chepstow timber merchant, and Henry Wise of Caldicot – both like her father with shipping interests – where she practised drinking tea and conversing with the ladies of the house.

Lucy also accompanied her father to Whitebrook, where he had an interest in wire manufacturing, and the whole family (including Stubbs, when he was not away at school) went on several outings to Chepstow. To get there, they would ride (or drive, depending on the weather) from Hewelsfield to Brockweir, a busy little village on the River Wye whose population was almost entirely involved in the river trade (principally corn, hoops and faggots), loading, unloading and navigating the trows and sloops from Brockweir to Bristol. Lucy and Stubbs were fascinated to see the tiny, one-man Welsh coracles, rather like a walnut shell, which looked too frail to survive on the busy river, and which could be carried on the owner's back.

At Brockweir, the Wightwicks caught a boat to take them down the river towards Chepstow. Sometimes, if the day was fine, they would go no further than Tintern, where they would wander and picnic among the beautiful ruins of Tintern Abbey – and once their father took both Lucy and Stubbs to visit the nearby ironworks. On other occasions they would take the boat all the way to Chepstow, a bustling town of whitewashed houses situated in a deep hollow surrounded by woody hills, towered over by the rich groves of Piercefield to the north, with what seemed to be hundreds of ships' masts jostling for position in the port. Chepstow with its population of 2,000 contained none of the manufactories that Miss Priddy had so disliked in Manchester but made its living by serving Herefordshire and Monmouthshire's import needs and exporting timber, grain, iron, mill stones, oak bark and cider to Bristol.

Once in Chepstow, they might lunch at the Beaufort Arms on fish, roast veal, cheese and ale or take a picnic to Piercefield to wander in the parkland – a favourite destination for local visitors and tourists alike – with its beautiful views across the valley, its grotto, temple and bathhouse. Mr Wightwick might attend to business on his own, or sometimes Lucy and her mother would accompany him. When Stubbs was with them, the young boy particularly liked to watch for the arrival of the London and Bristol mail coach at 4 p.m., his eyes round with astonishment at the speed with which the ostlers would change the horses.

And all the while Lucy was being taught the domestic arts by her mother so that she might be prepared when she had her own home to manage. Because they were fortunate enough to be wealthy, the servants did the work but the women must still know the detail of how it should be done. So Lucy learned how a room should be cleared out and a floor scrubbed, how to remove stains from polished furniture, how to deter moths, how to clean tarnished silver, how to make preserves to see them through the winter months when fresh fruit was scarce, how to pluck a goose, how to care for bedding and curtains and how to store winter clothes safely during the summer and summer clothing in the winter. In addition, Mrs Wightwick passed on many of her treasured recipes to her daughter, who spent hours copying them out, and Lucy learned which foods went well together and which did not, what wines to serve with different dishes, how to arrange a table of guests and – most importantly – how to keep the household accounts.

Lucy had a chance to put all her learning into practice when the whole family went to the house in Great Bloxwich for several months in the spring of 1806 and her mother had to leave Thomas, Stubbs and Lucy together while she went to care for an elderly relative who was on her deathbed. With a little help from her father, Lucy thoroughly enjoyed herself and did not make too many mistakes. She found she liked being busy and took pride in a job well done. She did feel a little self-conscious instructing Cook, whom she had known for so long and who was the source of many illicit sweetmeats and bits of bread and cheese, but she found that by discussing the dinner menu with Cook rather than simply telling her what to do she felt less uncomfortable and, indeed, often learned new things.

Mrs Wightwick kept a watchful eye on her daughter's social skills during this period also, accompanying her to dances at the houses of their acquaintances and occasionally to some more public entertainment in Chepstow, Bristol, Stafford or Wolverhampton. She wished her daughter to have a comfortable life and move in the best circles possible. She had no illusions that Lucy would sweep an eligible aristocrat off his feet for she recognised that her daughter was no beauty, but she knew that good breeding and upbringing, together with a good dowry, should attract eligible bachelors who could provide Lucy with the desired objective of a good marriage and a house of her own.

Lucy knew what was expected of her and looked forward with great excitement to the time when her mother would deem that she was ready to make her debut into Bath society. This would signal an end to her childhood and her education, and a start to her adult life. She hoped she would not disappoint her parents. She thought it would be enjoyable to be a married woman like Mama, and saw no reason why marriage should curb her activities – indeed, from what she heard in letters from her married friends, she would have more freedom as a young matron.

So when the time finally came in 1806 that her mother decided to take her to Bath for the Society Season, she was over the moon, and threw her heart into choosing a whole new wardrobe of clothes suitable for a débutante with not a care in the world. Aged 20, she was thrust into an unknown and exciting world of dancing, picnics, card parties and the theatre; she met dozens of other débutantes and a similar number of eligible and not-so eligible young men, some keen, others reluctant, to find a suitable wealthy bride with whom to set up their own family household.

She enjoyed the company of most of them – but made absolutely no attempt at all to 'catch' a husband, much to the annoyance and dismay of Mrs Wightwick, who had hoped that the end of one expensive Season would see her only daughter engaged to an eligible young man with good prospects. Lucy therefore ended the Season in Bath, to which she had looked forward so much and for so long, in some disgrace. But she could not really feel guilty about this: not only had she enjoyed herself very much, she still retained a girlhood dream of being swept off her feet by a tall, dark handsome man who would show her London and the world and she could not warm to the notion of marriage to an English country squire or a stolid, wealthy merchant from a northern industrial town.

Lucy Lord, circa 1806

Chapter 2
Sam, 1804-07

The brig Flora rode the waves joyously, dipping and swaying gracefully despite its heavy cargo. They were moving at a fair pace now, and the well-built young man leaning on the railing, straining to make out any sign of land, looked eager. A pod of dolphins was travelling parallel to the ship to starboard, leaping out of the water as though chased by some giant sea creature below. The sound of the wind in the canvas of the sails was loud but steady; several sailors were, as usual, swarming about the rigging as nimble as the green monkeys Samuel Hall Lord saw in abundance at home.

He turned around and, with his back now to the railing, looked towards the top of the tall masts, searching for the gulls he expected to see if they were not too far from land, but sighting only the fluttering pennant. Everyone other than himself was busy about their allotted tasks, cleaning, setting or mending sails, coiling ropes, carrying boxes... He heard the bo'sun bellow at some unlucky crew member and watched as Captain Young snapped his telescope shut and went below. After more than a month at sea, he would be glad to reach journey's end but there was something exhilarating about being on the limitless ocean; perhaps it was knowledge of the danger that lurked beneath the water and in the weather, impossible to forecast accurately, but potentially fatal if the captain was unskilled, the boat not truly seaworthy, or the luck was not with you.

Samuel went below to find out if any of the other passengers wished to play cards. Even though they had had a pretty batch of it the previous night in the captain's quarters, drinking the red wine as though they did not have to eke it out until they reached England, he thought they would be stirring by now. A little self-consciously he smoothed his slightly travel-worn coat and brushed his hair, blown about by the wind, back into place. His fellow passengers were generally older than he, solid merchants for the most part, and he wanted to make a good impression on them – he needed their help when they reached dry land.

As luck would have it, as he rounded the corner at the bottom of the first stairway, he came face to face with Andrew Taviner, the son of a plantation owner from St Kitts who, like Samuel, was on his first trip to England.

"Mr Taviner, good morning. Would you care to take a hand or two at cards to pass the time?" enquired Samuel.

"I was on my way to discover if land was yet in sight," responded Taviner. "Gad, it was a lively night was it not?"

"I have been on deck this past hour and have seen no sign of land. The captain was there a short while but has gone below again. Perhaps we shall find out more at dinner about when we are likely to spy England. What do you say to that game of cards?"

"I am happy to oblige you, sir, though my pockets are all to let, so I fear we must play for penny stakes. Will you join me in my cabin? I will ask the steward to bring ale for us."

Samuel acquiesced – he had no desire to fleece the man when he might need his goodwill, and besides, he wanted to play merely to ease his boredom – and the two turned towards the stern of the ship, where the captain's quarters and most of the passenger cabins were to be found. Taviner shouted for the steward, who promised to bring two tankards of ale to his cabin at once.

Taviner ushered Samuel in, waved him towards the table and went to a small chest of drawers beside his bed to search for a pack of cards. Samuel sat, and took stock of his surroundings. The cabin was somewhat larger than his own, with space for two teakwood chests for a passenger's belongings, a small writing desk, a sea couch and a bookcase as well as the table and chairs, a pewter basin, and a sizeable curtained window looking starboard. The walls were painted pale blue. The Taviner plantation must be a profitable one, Sam thought.

The steward arrived with the ale, and the two men settled down to play at *vingt-et-un* until called to the midday meal. At first, they concentrated on the cards, with little in the way of conversation, but after three or four hands Samuel became bored. He loved to gamble when the stakes were high but playing for chicken stakes was merely a way of whiling away time.

"So tell me, Mr Taviner, are you bound for England on business or pleasure?" he asked.

Taviner hesitated, taking his time to decide his next move. Then he looked up and smiled mischievously. "My father has tasked me with some dealings in Bristol, but I am then free to spend the early part of the Season[1] in London and I plan to enjoy every minute of it. He has arranged for rooms for me in Jermyn Street. He will return to England himself within a few months, but before then I hope to renew my acquaintance with some choice fellows who know how to have a good time. And you, Mr Lord? What are your plans?"

"This is my first visit to England. I have spent all my life in Barbados, so I am looking forward to seeing the sights in London but have no specific plans." Samuel did not mention that his main aim was to identify a wealthy young woman to become his wife. The Lord plantation was not hugely profitable, so as a second son and a young man with expensive tastes he planned to increase his spending power and indulge a desire for a luxurious lifestyle by obtaining a healthy dowry. Taviner could prove a useful guide in England, and introduce him to just the circles he needed to move in. He smiled his charming smile.

"I would welcome any tips you can give me about where to look for rooms and what to see and do. Please, do call me Sam, all my friends do. My father always called me Samuel, but that leads me to expect a thunderous scold!"

---

[1] Late January to early July

"I think we shall deal exceedingly well together. My name is Andrew, by the way. And – you say your father always *called* you Samuel; why the past tense?"

"He passed away some five years ago. He left Long Bay to my elder brother John and I and, once probate was settled, we decided that John should stay in charge of the plantation and I should visit England to engage with our merchant contacts there and take the opportunity to see a bit more of the world."

Sam forbore to mention that he had sold his share to John, which was how he was financing the voyage. He had no desire to play second fiddle to brother John – a position his father had clearly hoped would take some of the fidgets out of him and cure him of his more extravagant tastes and ideas.

"Well, Sam, I think this calls for more ale" said Andrew, and strode to the door of his cabin where he stood and shouted for the steward. The order placed, he sat down again at his ease, and the two settled down to learn more about each other – or rather, Sam sought to garner as much information as he could from his new-found friend while presenting himself in the best possible light.

Sam's family had been in Barbados since the 17th century. His father had a small estate of 145 acres called Long Bay, on the windy east coast, which produced cotton, cloves and aloes, but was unsuitable for sugar production on account of the shallow depth of the soil and the force of the north east trade winds. When Sam's father had died, he left the estate equally divided between him and his elder brother, John, with provision for their three sisters, Mary, Sarah and Elizabeth. The girls and their widowed mother continued to live at Long Bay.

The Taviner sugar plantation on St Kitts was, Sam learned, an altogether larger affair and, as was common on St Kitts, the family spent little time there. Andrew's mother and sister resided near Bath; he had returned to the island following his schooling in England to start learning the plantation trade with a view to succeeding his father, and his brother would probably do the same once his own schooling was finished. Most of the management of the plantation was left in the capable hands of an excellent overseer and his team; Andrew and his father spent only a few months a year on the island, and his father was talking about returning permanently to England once Andrew had sufficient experience to take over the reins. At 22, Andrew was four years younger than Sam but, despite his engaging sense of mischief, the self-confidence born of travel made him seem older than his years. Sam wondered if his sister might prove a suitable marriage prospect and determined to find out more.

By now, it was time for the midday meal, and the two young men headed with the other passengers for the dining cabin. After the storms they had encountered on the early part of the passage, it was a relief to be able to eat without fear of crockery hurtling across the table, or hot food tipping into one's lap. But the food was becoming monotonous, and all would be glad to reach dry land once more. Over luncheon, Sam was seated between a middle-aged solicitor from Bridgetown, Barbados, and the ship's surgeon. The latter was a taciturn man who rarely spoke, but the solicitor was quite ready to engage in small talk about some of their mutual acquaintances.

After the meal, the young men strolled out on deck and smoked two of Sam's cigars. They watched idly as the crew went about their business, trimming sail, painting some weather-beaten areas of the ship, coiling rope, replenishing water supplies in the galley and cabins from the stores in the hold. Andrew complained his head was still sore from the previous night, and went below to catch up on his sleep, and Sam found a secluded corner and sat down to ponder how he could best make use of his new acquaintance when they reached England.

His reverie was interrupted by a scream, a thud and a splash, then the sound of running feet. He followed the noise forward and was pushed somewhat roughly aside by the second mate who ran past him. Several of the crew had stopped what they were doing and were leaning over the rail looking down into the ocean: no-one spoke. He looked up and saw one young sailor clinging to the rigging and looking down, ashen-faced. The second mate had thrown a rope into the water and shouted for all sail to be trimmed so they could come about, but they were too late. One of the crew had slipped from high in the rigging and fallen into the water, and his lifeless body was already floating face down. The captain was called up and offered a brief prayer, then the second mate ordered the subdued crew back to work.

Sam went down to his cabin and lay on his cot, staring at the ceiling. He well knew that death at sea was a common occurrence. Sailors were expendable and the work was dangerous. Surprisingly, this was the first such death he had witnessed. How ironic that it should happen in such clement weather rather than during the storms that had assailed them a week out of Barbados. Idly he wondered if the man had a family and what would happen to them if so, then he gave a mental shrug. No doubt the wife, if there was one, would soon enough find another husband and, since they were so close to home, would receive the man's wages.

He surprised himself with his concern. Accidents were constantly happening to the plantation slaves and he never wasted a moment's thought on them; must be the fact that this poor devil was a white man he thought. He closed his eyes and dozed until it was time to get ready for the evening meal, which was served early at sea. He was dining in the captain's cabin this evening and did not want to alienate the man by arriving late for he wanted to get an answer as to when they would dock at Gravesend.

****

As a result of some contrary winds, it was another week before they heard the welcome shout of "Land ahoy!". All the passengers, including Sam, ran up on deck and were able to make out a smudge on the distant horizon that Captain Young assured them was the green hills of England. Sam leant on the rail for hours as the Flora sailed close by the treacherous Goodwin sands where hundreds of vessels had been shipwrecked and so many unfortunate people had died over the years.

At last they reached the Thames, full of large and small ships and boats either sailing parallel to the Flora or lying at anchor; Sam marvelled at the soft, green hills on either side, and the continuous fertile and cultivated fields. The green cornfields bounded by living hedges and interspersed with the occasional windmill gave to the whole of the distant country the appearance of a large and majestic garden. The neat villages and small towns with large country seats dotted in between suggested a prosperity and opulence beyond his wildest dreams: surely he must be able to achieve his ambitions in a country of such boundless wealth?

Over lunch in the Flora's great cabin, those passengers with experience proposed disembarking shortly before the ship reached Dartford. They explained that this was commonly done to avoid the delays which passengers encountered on the last leg of their journey because the waterway became increasingly crowded as one neared London. This could result in a ship taking many days to travel between Dartford and its final destination, not to mention the likelihood of being dashed against other vessels. Travelling the 16 miles by land, however, was a much speedier option.

So Sam packed and strapped his trunk for later collection in London, threw a few things into an overnight bag and joined the others in a small boat which two of the sailors rowed to shore. As they left the Flora, the remaining crew – as was common – raised three cheers to them. The group of passengers resolved to go on foot to Dartford, keen to stretch their legs after so long at sea. Immediately they landed they had a pretty steep hill to climb, and they were all panting a little by the time they reached the summit. In front of them lay a typical English village, with neat houses generally built of red bricks with flat roofs.

By the time they reached Dartford, several of the group were beginning to flag while Sam and Andrew Taviner, being the youngest, continued to set a brisk pace. They asked for directions to a coaching inn and there procured two post-chaises. Sam was interested to find that there was no haggling over the price which was fixed nationally at a shilling per mile, irrespective of the number of passengers: each post-chaise could carry between one and three. He noticed that the postilions, who were white as they would not have been in Barbados, were dressed smartly and the one accompanying their coach sported a nosegay in his buttonhole.

The roads between Dartford and London were firm and smooth so despite the fact that the rather chubby solicitor had squeezed in with him and Mr Taviner, Sam hardly felt the motion of the coach. While his fellow passengers dozed, he spent the journey staring out of the windows at the view, every now and then catching sight of the Thames – or rather, a little forest of masts above the water – and enjoying the picturesque and amazingly large and varied signs at the entrance to each village. Announcing an inn, these hung in the middle of the street, fastened to large beams extended across the street from one house to another opposite it.

Sam had decided before he left Barbados that London would offer him the most opportunities to achieve his aim. Somehow - he could no longer remember the occasion - he had obtained an ancient copy of *The Rich Ladies' Treasury*. Published in 1742, this listed eligible women by street, rank and fortune. Despite being out of date, Sam hoped it would furnish him with sufficient information to narrow his search for a potential wealthy wife. So when Andrew Taviner suggested he accompany him to the lodgings procured for him in Jermyn Street by his father, Sam went willingly. Taviner had obligingly offered his services to help Sam procure a lodging the next day in the same neighbourhood and invited Sam to stay the night with him.

Somewhat overawed by the sheer size of the city (London, with a population of some 900,000, was the most populous city in Europe), Sam was more cautious and less bombastic than usual, and when he was introduced to the elegance of Jermyn Street he reluctantly decided that his slender funds would not be able to accommodate an apartment there, however much it might be to his taste. The ever-amicable Taviner made no comment when Sam haltingly mentioned this but offered to accompany him in search of lodgings in rather cheaper parts of town once they had consumed the breakfast his landlady made ready for them, consisting of tea and bread and butter.

The two young men set off across town. Sam was struck by the height of the buildings and the narrow streets which seemed likely to create dark and gloomy rooms. In Barbados nothing stood more than one or two stories high, and other than in the poorest parts of towns, the streets were generally wider, if very dusty. In one of the areas they came to – York Buildings on George Street – they procured a comfortable lodging for Sam for 16 shillings a week at the house of a tailor's widow. This consisted of a large room in front on the ground floor, which had a carpet and mats, and was very neatly furnished; the chairs covered with leather, the tables of mahogany which Sam studied with interest, given recent efforts to introduce mahogany to Barbados, and a lockable cupboard in which he could store his own tea, coffee, bread and butter. Adjoining this was another large room. He was pleasantly surprised that in the smaller streets towards the Thames calm reigned, compared to the tumult and bustle of people and carriages and horses that were constantly going up and down the Strand.

Over the next few days, Sam divided his time between getting to know the huge and dirty city and developing a circle of acquaintances who would be able to help him, unbeknown to themselves, to achieve his goal of finding a rich wife.

He first visited Westminster, keen to view for himself the buildings which he had been told were magnificent, but also curious to gain some first-hand knowledge of Parliament, the distant source of Barbadian law, and where there was much heated discussion about abolishing slavery, led mainly by a man named Wilberforce. Sam thought such ideas misguided and unlikely to succeed. How else would the trade on which Britain depended thrive? Every other country in the civilised world used slave labour to produce their goods, surely the Mother of all Parliaments would recognise which side its own bread was buttered.

He looked in awe at Westminster Hall, an enormous Gothic building whose vaulted roof was supported by large unnatural angels' heads, carved in wood. Passing through this long hall, he was directed up a short staircase and led through a dark passage into the House of Commons which, below, had a large double door and above another small staircase to reach the gallery, the place allotted for strangers. Having paid the two shillings entrance fee to a genteel man in black, Sam settled down and looked around him with interest. He thought the House of Commons resembled a rather dingy chapel. The Speaker, an elderly man in a black cloak and an enormous wig with two knotted tresses behind, sat almost opposite Sam on a lofty chair. In front were two clerks also dressed in black. On the table by the side of the great parchment acts lay the huge gilt sceptre which – he was informed in a hushed whisper by the obliging genteel man – was always taken away and placed in a conservatory under the table as soon as the Speaker quit his chair.

Sam was taken aback by the lack of solemnity to proceedings. From what he knew of the Assembly in Barbados, proceedings there were conducted with a great deal more dignity and, indeed, sobriety. At Westminster, Members seemed to go in and out at will; if one wished to speak, all that was necessary was to stand up, take off his hat, turn to the Speaker holding hat and cane in one hand and with the other make any motions that occurred to him to accompany his speech. Many of the speeches were very poor and uninteresting, and far too long, these were greeted by much noise and laughter, with the Speaker crying out unavailingly, "Order, order!" At times of heightened interest it was more like a rowdy tavern than a legislature, Sam thought.

That afternoon he accompanied Taviner to an eating-house, where they paid a shilling each for some roast meat and a salad and a further six pence to the waiter. Taviner assured Sam that this was reckoned a cheap house and to dine out once a day like this was a frugal style of living, and altogether far more pleasant that the meals provided for lodgers which generally consisted of a piece of half-boiled or half-roasted meat and a few cabbage leaves boiled in plain water on which they poured a sauce made of flour and butter.

Sam, thinking his funds might not last as long as he had hoped, made a mental note to visit a merchant contact for whom John had reluctantly provided him a letter of introduction, in order to change some money and ensure the transfer of funds remaining from the sale of his portion of Long Bay had been undertaken satisfactorily.

The real benefit of the time spent in the tavern in Sam's eyes was the fact that his shipboard friend introduced him there to several of his acquaintances. They seemed a pleasant enough group, clearly knew their way around London and would be able to advise him on where to go and how to meet other men, ideally wealthy ones with younger sisters. He covertly eyed their clothes and decided that his most urgent task must be to find a good tailor and ensure he was dressed in the first style of fashion, for he felt somewhat dowdy and shabby.

His initial port of call the following morning was John's merchant contact in Lombard Street. He found the man pleasant and fully ready to exchange some of the bills Sam had with him, as well as agreeing to check up on the transfer of the sale proceeds and happy to advise him on how to invest the money when it arrived. Flushed with success, Sam decided to pay a visit to the Cat & Fiddle Inn close by to fortify himself with a tankard of ale before seeking out the tailor recommended by one of Taviner's friends the previous evening.

Armed with this recommendation, he had no difficulty being seen promptly by a very respectful middle-aged man, exquisitely dressed in an understated way to demonstrate the excellence of the tailoring he provided. It was clearly a popular business and more than a dozen clients came and went during the hours Sam spent that long afternoon being measured for a variety of clothing to wear from morning dress to riding dress to evening wear, and being introduced to the intricacies of Bath coating, merino wool and the like. Sam had always been well-dressed – he was well aware of its value in attracting women's gaze – but he found himself quite dazed by the size and intricacies of his potential wardrobe, which the tailor delicately assured him would be required if he wished to cut a dash in London, at the same time telling him,

"Sir, if I may say so, has a fine pair of legs to set off the current fashion in fitted trousers, and an excellent figure for a waistcoat."

Sam opened his eyes a little when he saw the staggering sum he owed the tailor, but telling himself that it was a worthwhile investment, he put down several bills as deposit and provided his address so that he could be called back for a final fitting. He then asked where he should go to buy other items needed for his toilette, where was a good hatter, where he should go to be measured for a pair of boots? The tailor obligingly suggested he make his first port of call Flint & Palmer, London's first department store, at London Bridge.

By this time it was after three o'clock and Sam was exceedingly hungry. He started out on foot on the route to Flint & Palmer, keeping an eye open for a steakhouse in which to have his dinner. He quickly came across one and entering, sat down with a sigh of relief, calling for a tankard of ale. A slightly sullen waiter approached, gave Sam's section of the trestle table a desultory wipe with the corner of his apron and, upon being asked what was on the menu, grudgingly admitted that the steak and ale pie was very good. Clearly this steakhouse was not up to the standard of the one Taviner had taken him to on his first night in London, but Sam was too hungry to care. He downed his tankard and called for another to go with his pie. Feeling more human once he had eaten, he ordered bread and cheese and some port to finish.

Energised after his meal, Sam threw down a few coins on the table and, settling his hat on his head, hailed a hackney cab to deliver him to the department store, for a grey, persistent rain had begun to fall. He proceeded to spend a further two hours marvelling at the variety of goods available at Flint & Palmer. He purchased several shirts – to augment those he had been measured for by the tailor; socks and garters (less visible than suspenders under the skin-tight breeches and pantaloons being made for him), smallclothes, handkerchiefs, cravats, gloves and several nightshirts. In the end there were far too many packages wrapped up in brown paper and string for him to carry, so an obliging porter carried them out to one of many passing hackneys, deposited them inside, held the door for Sam to climb in behind and gave his direction to the driver.

It had been a good day, if tiring, and Sam was quite glad that he had made no plans for the evening. In the end, he ate a supper of pickled salmon in his lodgings, washed down by a bottle of claret which he sent his landlady's young son out to buy, and fell fast asleep. He awoke with a start at around 11 pm and decided to visit an interesting venue he had heard about, the Folly of the Thames, a floating coffeehouse moored outside Somerset House, where jittery dancers performed waltzes and jigs late into the night. However, he did not find it to his taste; indeed, he thought it rather seedy, and resolved to try the Jamaica Coffee House the next day instead, which Taviner had mentioned to him in passing.

When Sam awoke the following morning late, he found little incentive to go out to see the sights. London was shrouded in what he would quickly learn was its habitual fog. It wreathed its grimy way between the buildings, sapping all colour from the scene, and it was impossible to see anything more than ten yards ahead of your nose. Reluctantly, Sam rose from his bed to drink some small ale and eat some slightly stale bread for his breakfast while he waited for the landlady's boy to bring him hot water for shaving. He still found some difficulty in shaving; a slave had performed this task for him every day since he could remember, and he found it all too easy to cut himself. He thought he might treat himself to a shave at a barber's when his new clothes were delivered.

While he was engaged in the delicate task, the boy returned with a note for Sam. It was the news he had been waiting for – the Flora had safely docked and he could now collect his trunk. So shortly after midday (although it was impossible to tell what time of day it was because of the all-pervading fog) he hailed a hackney and set out for the West India Docks, a journey of some seven or eight miles. He amused himself along the route looking at the myriad signs in large golden characters festooning many of the buildings, advertising "Children educated here", "shoes mended here", "foreign spirituous liquors sold here" (very common), or "funerals furnished here". Since people of different trades inhabited the same house, the signs frequently seemed to jostle for position. In the more salubrious parts of town, he admired the footway, paved with large stones on both sides of the street – an innovation he thought could usefully be applied in Bridgetown – and the large, well-proportioned houses, with lamp-posts at regular intervals.

There were numerous poor people, all white beneath their grime, something he had never seen in Barbados, grubbing among the cobblestones. At first, he could not make out what they were searching for but eventually realised that they were collecting up small coins, rings, shawls or handkerchiefs and, in particular, nails fallen from horseshoes. This, he learned later, was because being of high-quality iron, they could be re-smelted to make gun barrels, for which the seemingly never-ending wars created unceasing demand.

The first part of the route from George Street was bristling with people, on foot, on horseback or in carriages. Their progress was slow – along The Strand, Fleet Street, past St Paul's to Cheapside and Cornhill. It was only once they reached Aldgate that traffic eased and the vista opened out. The hackney turned south towards Commercial Road and the West India Docks.

Sam had been advised not to have his trunk taken to the Custom House but to collect it directly from the ship, as he would have to pay less to the officers and those who came on board the ship to search it. After some haggling, he had to part with two shillings for each of the three officials involved, but it would have cost him still more at the Custom House. A porter then hefted the heavy trunk on his shoulders with astonishing ease, and carried it till they found a hackney coach. This he hired for a further two shillings with no additional cost for the trunk. Sam had already found out that the great advantage of English hackney coaches was that you were permitted to take with you whatever you pleased, whether dozens of packages, pieces of furniture or, as in this case, a large item of baggage.

When they arrived at his lodgings, Sam called over a pair of strong-looking young lads and paid them a penny piece each to carry the trunk to his rooms – a relatively easy task, since they were on the ground floor. He uncorded the trunk and opened the lid but could not summon up any enthusiasm for unpacking his things, and instead reverted to the notion he had had the night before of visiting the Jamaica Coffee House.

The Jamaica Coffee House was situated at St Michael's, Cornhill, and was the main meeting place for merchants engaged in commerce with Madeira and the West Indies. It was said to have been built on the site where one Pasqua Rosée had set up the first coffee shack when the brew was little known in England some 150 years previously. When Sam arrived, it was early afternoon and the place was quiet. The merchants tended to meet there in the morning before going to their counting-houses, or later in the afternoon after leaving the Royal Exchange. Upon explaining that he was a planter from Barbados, he was very civilly welcomed, and offered the subscription book. He entered his name and address in Barbados, together with his lodgings in London, paid his dues and was ushered into the large subscription room. A scattering of men sat around the rectangular wooden tables, which were strewn with newspapers, pamphlets, shipping lists, information relative to the mail packets on the West India station, or the merchant vessels such as those on which Sam had arrived which made these voyages.

Sam sat down at one of the tables chosen at random, stretching his legs out in front of him, and looked around at the wainscoted walls and shaved wooden floors. A young white boy wearing a large, flowing wig approached him and carefully placed a full dish of coffee in front of Sam. It cost him a penny, but the boy assured him that the price covered unlimited refills. He further advised that, should Sam wish for stronger refreshment, wine and other spirituous liquors were available.

Sam pulled a couple of newspapers towards him and flicked through the pages carelessly, keeping one eye open for any news of Barbados. As the place began to fill up, he entered into conversation with several of the other subscribers – merchants and ships' captains for the most part – who were discussing the growing cry led by William Wilberforce for abolition of the slave trade, and the impact this might have on the commerce they were involved in. Since Long Bay, like all plantations on Barbados, was entirely worked by slaves, Sam felt able to add an authoritative voice to the discussion; he noted with satisfaction that not one person there spoke up for Wilberforce's ideas.

In the weeks and months that followed, Sam continued his forays of exploration around the city, taking in St Paul's and the Monument – a stately obelisk erected in memory of the great fire of 1666 – Westminster Abbey, the new, graceful Adelphi buildings surrounded by tree-lined terraces sweeping down to the Thames, and St James's Park, a semicircle formed of an alley of trees enclosing a large green area in the middle of which was a marshy pond. Cows fed on this green turf, and he was amused to see their fresh milk sold there on the spot for far more than its worth to Society ladies who sat on the benches provided to drink it. He soon grew used to the hustle and bustle of London streets, to the way abject poverty and misery lived side by side with opulence and wealth. But it never ceased to amaze him that the Thames with its countless swarms of little boats passing and repassing, many with one mast and one sail (and some with none) which carried persons of all rank from one side to the other, was just as busy and no less crowded than the streets.

The rest of his time he spent cultivating a growing group of acquaintances. His grandiose dreams of being readily accepted into London Society were soundly trounced when he was refused entry to Almack's in King Street, the most exclusive venue in Regency London. Known as 'the Marriage Mart', a ball and an assembly were held there on Wednesdays to provide young ladies and gentlemen with an opportunity to find a suitable partner. Sam knew that the dress code was exceedingly strict and dressed accordingly, but no-one informed him that you could only gain entry if you had a voucher from one of the lady patronesses. As a result, he found himself humiliatingly rejected by a burly and supercilious doorman, discreetly watched by a number of the elite who had procured vouchers and whom he had hoped to impress. Angry and embarrassed, he sought solace in one of the brothels to which he had been introduced by Taviner and his friends and got very drunk. He could not even be sure he had availed himself of the scantily-clad women on offer.

Sam stayed in his lodgings the whole of the following day, in a foul temper, exacerbated by the number of bottles of wine and port he sent the landlady's son out to buy for him, and brooding on the verses he had seen written by the poet and wit, Henry Luttrell,

"All on that magic List depends;
Fame, fortune, fashion, lovers, friends;
'Tis that which gratifies or vexes
All ranks, all ages, and both sexes.
If once to Almack's you belong,
Like monarchs you can do no wrong;
But banished thence on Wednesday night,
By Jove, you can do nothing right."

A short while later, he was politely turned down for membership of White's Club, despite having been put forward by a sponsor. All in all, he found the upper echelons of Regency Society less than welcoming to a young man of obscure origins without title or wealth. But his good looks and usually pleasant manner made it easy for him to strike up friendships on the fringes of Society, with other young bucks who like himself were eager to get on in the world, and he learned from them that while the aristocracy might look at him askance, he would be likely to get a better reception from the wealthy merchant class or the landed gentry away from the metropolis, and also have more luck in finding a bride with prospects. So he spent several months accompanying his new acquaintances, all aspiring Regency Bucks like himself, to boxing matches outside London, to horseracing events and cockfights, to Manton's shooting gallery at Dover Street in Piccadilly, to the Fives Court on St Martin Street to watch and practise boxing, where he watched Bill Richmond (a black man) fight Fighting Youssop (who was Jewish) and win in six rounds.

And he accompanied them on their drinking sprees and to endless coffee and chocolate houses. These were generally smoky and convivial places where strangers would gather around long wooden tables sharing news, gossip and ideas late into the night. Because of the range of backgrounds these people came from, here he met more individuals sympathetic to Wilberforce's ideas who would argue against slavery, and he quickly learned that if he threw back in their faces the plight of children forced down mines, up chimneys and into factories in so-called civilised England, it gave them pause for thought.

It was in one of these coffee houses that he read in the Morning Post in early November 1805,

The celebrated pugilist the Chicken arrived in Town on Saturday last from Somersetshire, where he had been several days in durance vile [prison], by order of the Magistrates of the District charged with attempting to disturb the public peace by the introduction of a prize fight intended to have been fought in the neighbourhood of Bath. Chicken was to have been second to the favourite.

He found no shortage of men among his acquaintance keen to watch the Chicken while he was in London, and they celebrated far into the night when he won – Sam delighted to have won a large sum of money to shore up his dwindling resources by betting heavily on the man.

He went with his friends to Vauxhall, a little village which housed the famous Vauxhall Gardens. They travelled on a crowded boat to dock at the west doors of St Mary's Church, Lambeth. For a shilling entrance fee, you could not only enjoy the beautiful grove and walks and look at statues of the most renowned English poets, philosophers and musicians such as Milton, Thomson and Handel but also enjoy the attentions of some very bold women of the town while ogling the more refined young ladies, seated in small boxes before the orchestra while eating wafer-thin shavings of ham. The highlight of the evening, and the event for which the Gardens were famous, was the raising of a curtain to exhibit a mechanical waterfall, so realistic it appeared entirely natural. The downside to the venue was the proliferation of pickpockets. Sam took particular care to ensure none could steal his pocket-watch.

They also frequented Ranelagh Gardens, again to ogle the ladies. Here the entrance fee was half a crown, but the boxes were far more handsome and refreshments included in the price. All the *beau-monde* of London went there. All the while he was gathering information about the way Society in England worked, the best ways to go about meeting eligible young women, how he should portray himself to appear in the best possible light to them and their fathers.

He learned that it was fashionable, if one could afford it, to 'keep' a dancer or an actress as a mistress, or if not, then at least to spend time at the theatre on the lookout for a shapely ankle (never in short supply among the dancers). Since he was uninterested in serious drama, preferring the farces that generally followed during a performance, Sam found the behaviour of London audiences (particularly in the cheap seats in the upper gallery or 'gods') quite amusing, with so much noise and uproar, including throwing orange peel and other objects, it was a wonder anyone could hear the players or musicians. Only where the best actors played, Covent Garden and Drury Lane – which were only open in the winter, during the Season – was there a little more decorum.

By the time of Admiral Nelson's state funeral at St Paul's in January 1806 Sam was well into his second London Season, having arrived in 1804. Yet he was no nearer achieving the goal he had set himself of finding a rich wife, and his funds were disappearing at an alarming rate. He had had no communication with his family in Barbados since he left and had no intention of asking John to provide him with additional money when he knew he would simply be rebuffed. His cherished copy of *The Rich Ladies' Treasury* had proved of no help. He had asked the merchant he had been introduced to by John if he might put him in the way of meeting a suitable heiress, but the man had failed to come up with anything, so Sam was gambling heavily in the hopes that his gains would outweigh his losses. Generally, he was lucky, and he quite enjoyed the excitement of living on his wits, but he could see no way that his objective would be achieved by continuing to live as he did. His mood veered between optimism and despair, and he frequently drank to excess.

He made inquiries in some of the coffee houses and on the basis of this information, decided on a visit to York or Manchester. In the end he decided on York because a merchant he met at the Jamaica Coffee House provided him with an introduction to a member of the merchants' company there. He had thought to remain in London until the end of the Season and leave before the city became as fetid as parts of Bridgetown with the increasing temperatures, but he left rather more precipitately as a result of several very unpleasant letters from his tailor, demanding payment of a sum of truly staggering proportion which he simply could not meet. Since he had already been cold-shouldered by several of his gaming partners following a couple of embarrassing incidents when he had been unable to honour his debts to them quite as quickly as was expected, he decided to shake the dust from his feet and head north.

His friend Taviner had long since departed for Bristol, but other friends gave him such a rousing send-off that he awoke with an extremely sore head and could only be grateful that some unusual sense of thrift had driven him to purchase an advance ticket on the stagecoach to York rather than the more expensive mail-coach, which left earlier. His trunk, which he had arranged to leave with the landlady for safekeeping, was already corded and he had taken the precaution of paying his shot the night before. All he had to do was toss a few belongings into a smaller valise, dress (somewhat carelessly) and hail a hackney cab to take him to the Black Swan in Holborn to catch the stagecoach.

Once in York he found himself a room at one of the central hostelries and, after a good night's sleep – for he felt battered and jolted by the long hours of travel over three days – he dressed himself soberly and took along his letter of introduction to his merchant contact. But York, although quite attractive, did not match up to his expectations. He had assumed that the place would be full of textile factories as he knew Manchester to be, and planned to use the fact that Long Bay produced cotton as a way to open doors, but he was disappointed. The York merchants' company had lost most of its influence and social importance. Many of its members were by now merely small retail shopkeepers and were unlikely to have the wealth he was looking for as a potential inheritance.

So after a brief stay in York, Sam decided to try his luck in Manchester, despite the fact that he knew no-one there. Manchester had grown rapidly since Richard Arkwright began construction of Manchester's first cotton mill in 1780 and now had around 100,000 inhabitants. Unlike York, it was a thriving industrial city so surely, once he got to know a few wealthy mill-owners he would be bound to meet their daughters socially and finally have a chance to make his dream come true.

As he was driven into the town, he looked around him, initially with interest, then with despair. It was raining and Manchester was, if anything, dirtier and more over-crowded than London; row after row of rather squalid red-brick housing was blackened by coal smoke from the factories' fuel of choice, and a foul-smelling open drain ran down the centre of the street. How he longed for the clean air of Barbados – even during the sugar harvesting season the air never smelled so unpleasant.

The stagecoach deposited him at the Bridgewater Arms on High Street, a large house which had been converted into a coaching inn with accommodation for 100 people and which was, it appeared, the hub of Manchester stagecoach traffic. He took a room there – which he had to share the first night with a man who snored. The following day at breakfast he asked the waiter (who became extremely helpful and friendly once a silver coin was pressed into his hand) where he might find reasonably priced lodgings, together with the whereabouts of the Assembly Rooms and the public library. Armed with this information, he set out on foot on a cold, grey March day to tramp the dirty streets. These were full of pools of standing water containing unmentionable rotting objects and smelling foully of the contents of the occasional public privy which he could glimpse down small alleyways and passages. Sam frequently had to hold his handkerchief to his nose to block out the stench and prevent himself feeling nauseous, and he quickly became resigned to ruining his boots.

He first visited the Portico Library on Mosley Street in order to ferret out some information from the local newspapers on who were the wealthy merchants in the town. He had decided that his best course of action was to introduce himself to several of the cotton factory owners in Manchester, explaining that his plantation in Barbados produced cotton which they might well be using, and that he was interested in understanding the whole manufacturing process in order to make good future investment decisions to improve Long Bay's production.

The Portico, designed in Greek Revival style, was a new building, opened only that year and designed by Thomas Harrison who had earlier successfully completed the Liverpool Lyceum. It was a subscription library, so Sam duly signed the register and paid his fee before making his way to the reading room, which made him open his eyes in astonishment. Sam was used to visiting the coffee houses of London to read the newspapers as well as meeting friends, but this was enormous by comparison, and incorporated an impressive five-bay colonnade. Sam walked slowly around the room, admiring the columns and dreaming of how he might include something similar in the mansion he would one day build on Barbados.

Finally he sat down at one of the long wooden tables in the centre of the great space, and began perusing some of the dozens of newspapers – local and national – displayed there. He glanced cursorily through *The Times*, and rather more carefully through *Lloyd's List*, looking both for news of ships travelling between England and the West Indies, and for any mention of Manchester ship owners. He then turned his attention to the *Manchester Mercury*. Some of the advertisements caused a wry smile of amusement but he was searching primarily for society pages such as *The Times* of London carried, with all the wealth of detail that could be gleaned about individuals from its gossip and innuendo, together with announcements of important upcoming events. Failing that, he hoped to find news stories about key businesspeople in the town. He took a few notes, then stood to stretch his legs and strolled over to the stairs to try the Portico's bar on the first floor, next to the library.

Sam's next port of call was the Assembly Rooms, which hosted balls, tea parties and card-playing. He had been reliably advised by the waiter in the Bridgewater Arms that the purpose-built Assembly Rooms in the Palladian Cotton Exchange at St Mary's Gate had been virtually abandoned because the Exchange was situated in an area which abounded in pickpockets and petty criminals and was notoriously filthy. Idly, Sam wondered how much filthier the area could possibly be than the streets he had already trudged through, but he followed his source's advice and made his way instead to Lady Bland's Assembly Rooms, which were situated above a passage between King Street and St Ann's Square.

The Rooms were not busy when Sam arrived, which was exactly as he had hoped. He once again signed the subscription book and paid his fee, then took some time to study the book in order to cross-reference some of the names he had picked up in the Portico reading-room. He then engaged a very bored young man, responsible for looking after visitors' coats, in a period of discussion only broken by the very occasional duty he had to perform. After asking a range of questions – about forthcoming events, where the best coffee houses were, where he might find a decent lodging – Sam steered the conversation around to what he really wanted information on: which of the wealthy merchants and landed gentry (and/or their wives and daughters) attended the Assemblies regularly, who was in town now and which days of the week he was most likely to catch them.

The young man thought for a while.

"Me sister works at Decker Mill – cotton, you'll understand. That's one of the Murrays' mills. They own at least four or five of the mills, and they're still building now. I don't reckon I've ever seen them here, though. It's two brothers, come from Scotland, are the owners. Then there's Mr McConnel, he comes in and is a real gentleman. He's building a fine new house for himself and his lovely lady wife at Ardwick. She comes in almost every week for the balls, often with Mr McConnel but sometimes with friends. Mr McConnel's just finished building a new manufactory, they'm taking on workers now…"

He named a few other key figures, such as the Ashton brothers (also in cotton), and Thomas Harrison, who had just laid the foundation stone for a new Royal Exchange to be built at the junction of Market and Exchange streets.

Sam returned to the Bridgewater Arms tired from his day of trudging the streets, but well satisfied with the information he had gleaned. He rather thought it would be interesting to develop an acquaintance with Mrs McConnel, particularly if she had sisters. Even if this were not the case, she could introduce him to some of her lady friends. But he did not want to be too obvious; if he could get to meet her husband first, it should only be a matter of timing to get introduced to Mrs McConnel. His acceptance into their circle would, he thought, then be guaranteed.

After quizzing the waiter again the following morning, Sam spent some time penning careful letters to both James McConnel and Adam Murray, introducing himself as a cotton planter from Barbados interested in learning how his product was used in their Manchester mills and discussing what he might do differently with his crop so that it consistently met their highest quality standards, in order to increase his profitability and their satisfaction.

He then donned his hat and coat, picked up his cane and sauntered out to acquaint himself with the streets where, he had been told, the gentry were building new houses for themselves. It turned out that they radiated out from Market Street in Manchester's commercial area, and had names like Princess Street, George Street, Charlotte Street and Hanover Street. Despite being so close to the commercial hub, it was a quiet, leafy part of town, where it was possible to believe that the foul-running kennels and piles of filthy human detritus he had encountered yesterday were nothing but a bad dream. The roads were broad, with raised paved areas on each side for pedestrians, the houses tall and narrow. New houses were still being built, and Sam stopped casually at many of these sites to discover for whom the work was being carried out.

The rain had ceased and the morning mist had lifted, and he quite enjoyed strolling back towards Market Street. By this time he was hungry, so he stopped to refresh himself at Cobden Coffee House on Port Street. He had been advised of possible lodgings nearby and wanted to assess the area before he viewed them. Having eaten his steak pie and swallowed a tankard of ale he headed towards the address, deciding that Port Street was at least less filthy than the area around the Exchange where he had spent the previous day. The rooms (on the second floor) were still available, and he concluded his business quickly, paying a month in advance. He was surprised that the price was little cheaper than his London lodgings had been but at least he would be spending less than he was now at the inn.

He went back to the Bridgewater Arms, packed his bags and gave instructions for them to be delivered to his new lodgings, settled his tab then made his way first to the Portico to glean what information he could about the Murrays and McConnel, then to the Exchange where he struck up a conversation with a group of traders about the price of cotton, and casually introduced the fact that 'his' plantation in Barbados produced the commodity. He found them courteous but terse, entirely focused on their business and with no time or inclination to develop new acquaintances outside their own small circle.

Feeling lonely – a novel sensation for Sam – he decided to dine at the White Bear, another coaching inn at the top of Market Street. He enjoyed watching the hustle and bustle of travellers arriving and departing, the ostlers rushing out to change the horses. He decided he would attend the Assembly Rooms later where he was sure he could join one of the card tables and hoped to encounter a few choice spirits prepared to welcome his participation in their leisure pursuits.

When he arrived back late that night there was a letter addressed to him waiting on the table in the narrow hallway. He lit the candle also awaiting him and carried both to his room. He threw his coat onto the only chair and sat on the bed to haul off his boots, looking at the state of them with distaste. He must find out if there was someone as obliging as his London landlady's son had been, who would clean them for him for a penny. Only then did he take up the letter and open it.

Squinting to try and decipher the handwriting in the poor light offered by the candle, Sam realised with relief that it was from Mr McConnel, who was suggesting that he visit the works at Ancoats in two days' time at two o'clock for a tour of the premises to be conducted by McConnel's foreman; following which he – James McConnel – would join them.

Two days later, boots shining, neatly and quite soberly dressed (to emphasise his business intentions), Sam presented himself at the aptly named New Factory (which, as he was to discover had only opened earlier that year) punctually at two o'clock having walked the short distance from his lodgings. He was clearly expected; a grizzled, bent, elderly man was waiting in the drizzle at the factory entrance once Sam passed through the gate, and ushering him inside asked him to wait 'nary a moment' while he sent a boy with younger legs than his running to fetch the foreman.

Dougal Mackay, the foreman, was a bear of a man with greying sandy hair, probably only about ten years older than Sam himself. He had big, calloused hands from which it seemed he had only perfunctorily wiped the oil before hurrying to meet Mr McConnel's guest, and which gave the distinct impression that he was more at home working on machinery than 'doing the pretty' as he termed it when he confirmed as much to Sam.

After a brief but friendly greeting, Mackay swung on his heel and invited Sam to follow him to the workshop. He was a loquacious man and was keen to apprise his visitor of the points of interest of the new building – at least, that was what Sam thought he was doing, but he found it difficult to understand the man's broad Scottish accent. As they approached the workshop itself, the noise became deafening.

Sam found himself looking down from a viewing platform onto the heads of several hundred workers standing bent over the looms or scurrying around the floor. A number of small children were crawling about, at which he expressed surprise. Surely they must get in the way, and have a propensity to get injured or killed?

Mackay explained that they were collecting up the scraps of cotton yarn which fell to the floor to re-use, and that they did indeed sometimes get injured but that their families were glad of the money they earned, and there were always plenty more bairns to take their place. Puffing out his chest, he explained to Sam that Manchester's growth rested largely on the expansion of the cotton industry, and indeed the town was already being described in 1806 as the 'workshop of the world'.

"Every day people stream in from the surrounding areas, eager to find work in the new factories and mills. We pay good wages – far more than they can get in the countryside as agricultural labourers. And we take on many women whose men have enlisted and who have nowt to feed the bairns with."

He made it seem like a philanthropic exercise but did not find it necessary to explain to Sam that in return for high wages, mill owners exacted a price, long hours, every day, with little time off – some 69 hours per week. And while McConnel's factory was new, in many of the older ones women (and children) often worked in appalling conditions and were subject to severe injuries and death.

Mackay waved his hand over the scene below of seething humanity, noisy machinery and dust, and asked Sam if he had visited any other mills. On hearing that he had not, Mackay led the way down the stairs, and began to explain the process, shouting above the din which got louder and louder as they descended.

"The value of cotton yarn depends upon its length. The machines produce it in hanks. But its quality – and so, its value – is distinguished by how fine the cotton is. A coarse cotton like No. 20 yarn has 20 hanks; No. 100 has 100 in each pound weight. Which means one pound of No. 100 contains 84,000 yards of cotton."

Mackay stopped to inspect the product; the girl working at the spindle did not look up, but Sam saw that she looked pale and undernourished, and probably no more than 14 years old. Satisfied, the foreman moved on.

"Of course, we don't produce coarse cotton, nothing but the best for Mr McConnel. Here we spin fine yarns up to 230 hanks to send back to Scotland for weaving. This is far higher quality than most of the mills in Manchester. Most spin only up to 100."

By this time Sam was heartily bored of the man and although he kept pace with him, his thoughts wandered. He began looking at the girls working the machines, and noticed one who, despite the grime and evident exhaustion, looked remarkably pretty. Regretfully, he decided that it would not help his cause if Mackay saw him propositioning her.

They were now once again at the foot of the stairs leading up to the viewing platform, almost two hours after Sam's arrival.

"… turn off, of a fair average, ten hanks per week," he heard Mackay saying. Sam nodded, and looked up to see a slender man of medium height and much the same age as himself, standing at the top of the stairs.

"Mr McConnel, sir, I have just been giving our visitor a tour of the premises," the foreman said (or rather, shouted) as he climbed, puffing – for he was a little stout.

"So I can see," smiled McConnel. He bowed slightly. "Mr Lord, it is a pleasure to make your acquaintance. I suggest some refreshment. Please join me in my office where it is a little quieter. Mackay, you may join us also."

Turning, he led the way, and they were soon ensconced in a comfortable office with large windows overlooking the canal. Drinks were laid out on a side cabinet. "Will you take a glass of Madeira with me, Mr Lord?" McConnel said. "I know Dougal will not. He favours ale, but I draw the line at keeping a barrel at the ready for him!" He smiled as he said this, and his foreman, clearly uncomfortable in such surroundings, nodded in response.

The three sat down and McConnel, crossing one booted leg over the other, asked Sam,

"Tell us, if you please, Mr Lord, something of your plantation in Barbados. I am interested because the quality of cotton from your island is generally very fine – we certainly use it when we can obtain it, but too many ships are captured or sunk due to these never-ending wars England is engaged in, and I am sure only the half of your product ever arrives at its destination! You wrote in your letter that you were interested in discussing how you might improve your yield without jeopardising quality, I think?" He took a sip of his Madeira.

"I should be happy to do so, sir," replied Sam. "Our plantation, Long Bay, is some 145 acres, and the ground is unsuitable for sugar so we concentrate on cotton, which grows well. Our climate is kind to cotton – unless we suffer hurricanes."

McConnel was frowning. "That is no great size, sir. That will only produce… how much, Mackay? A thousand hundredweight if you are lucky, think you?"

Mackay growled, "Your head is better for doing the sums than mine, sir. I am sure you are right."

"My plan is to expand, by buying adjacent land, but before doing that I wished to see for myself how the process worked once our cotton is shipped, and what might be done – as you recollect, sir – to improve the yield as we grow."

For once, Sam regretted his lack of interest in the details of plantation business; dear John would have been able to corroborate or dispute the figure McConnel suggested and discuss the finer points of production, while Sam had only a hazy idea of them and tried to bluff his way through the conversation.

"Mr McConnel, as you know, size is not everything. We aim to produce high quality cotton – the very best, in fact. That way you can spin the finest yarn – say, a 300 yarn, even more valuable than the yarns you already spin here. Our Sea Island cotton has very long fibres, and produces a wonderfully smooth, silky fabric. I saw in London how sought-after it was by the Society ladies."

Thank God, he thought. Some at least of what his father had tried to instil in him, and John continually droned on about, must have sunk into his brain.

He sat back and waited to see what impact his sudden burst of erudition might have on his host. To his satisfaction, James McConnel was studying him thoughtfully. Sam, although rendered slightly uncomfortable by the direct gaze, was happy to let the silence continue while he savoured the Madeira, which was truly excellent.

At last McConnel spoke, "Away with you, Mackay. You will need to get back to the shop-floor. By the by, I noticed Number Six was sounding rough this morning, I will take a look this evening and fix it."

As Sam was to learn, James McConnel was first and foremost a qualified machine maker, along with his partner John Kennedy; and the two designed and built the textile machines used in their mills and continued to have a hands-on relationship with the factory equipment.

While studying Sam he had been thinking about what his visitor had said on the subject of Sea Island cotton. Since involving himself in the cotton trade, he had learnt that *Gossypium barbadense*, the original Extra Long Staple variety of cotton, was particular to the West Indies, where the tropical climate was responsible for producing some of the most luxurious cotton fibres in the world, known – as Sam had mentioned – as Sea Island cotton. It had been grown in Barbados for more than a hundred years and was highly coveted. If it were possible to do a deal for exclusive trade with Mr Lord, McConnell mills might outstrip all the competition, not on volume but on quality. The notion appealed to his strong sense of business.

"If you will not object to taking pot-luck, come home with me to dine, Mr Lord," he invited as he turned back to his guest. "You should meet my wife, Peggy."

A little startled that things were moving so fast – and in just the direction he had hoped – Sam was careful to hesitate slightly before replying diffidently, "Are you sure it will not be too much trouble, sir?"

51

"Trouble? Why, no. I regularly turn up with one or more guests to dine with us. We have only recently moved into a house I had built out at Ardwick. You shall tell me how the structure would fare in your tropical storms! We dine at six o'clock."

"Then I should be delighted to accept," responded Sam, standing in readiness for their departure and bowing to his host.

Donning his hat and coat – the rain had started again, and a thick mist deadened much of the external sound – and picking up his cane, he accompanied his host out to his carriage. It was not a showy vehicle, but the pair of bay horses harnessed to it were in excellent condition, and when they began to make their way along the unpaved, uneven streets, Sam realised that no expense had been spared on the springing of the carriage, the ride was infinitely more comfortable than the stagecoach bringing him to Manchester.

It took some 20 minutes to reach Ardwick, situated as it was well away from the noxious fumes belched out by mills such as McConnel's own. Indeed, it was surrounded – as far as Sam could tell, for although the mist was lighter here it still lingered – by fields. The front door of the house was flung wide, and the silhouette of a tall, slender woman appeared.

"See, Peggy, I have brought a gentleman home to dine with us," was James McConnel's greeting to his wife as he put an arm gently round her waist. "Let me present you, this is my wife, Margaret, sir. And Peggy, this is Mr Samuel Hall Lord of Barbados."

"Barbados, how exotic!" exclaimed Peggy, laughing. Sam bowed low over her hand and looked up into her beautiful, smiling face. "You shall tell us all about it while we dine. Come in and meet my best friend, Mary Chaworth. We are only six to dine today, so we can all talk together – and the children wish to see you before you before they go to bed, James."

Ushered through the front door, Sam found himself in a matted hall, tastefully decorated in pastel colours and dominated by huge portrait of a haughty-looking man on horseback; through this he was conducted to a large parlour, with a cheerful fire in the grate. A series of pastoral water-colours decked the walls, together with several large portraits in oil. There was a guitar and some music on a sofa; there were cameos and beautiful miniatures scattered on several side-tables, and a set of Grecian-looking vases on the mantelpiece; and there were two elegant bookcases filled with books.

"How many children do you have, ma'am?" asked Sam politely, picking up on his hostess' last comment. As she told him four, he could not take his eyes off her face. She was very lovely, and fleetingly he wondered what might have been if they had met before she and James McConnel did. But he knew he must be on his best behaviour if he wanted Peggy's assistance in introducing him to an unmarried, wealthy young lady, so he was careful to treat her in a friendly yet proper way.

A stately butler was bowing and offering refreshments. While Peggy took a glass of Madeira wine, James ordered a tankard of porter, so Sam followed suit. Meanwhile, he was introduced to two other people in the room, a rather shabby looking, plump curate of uncertain age, and a thin, elderly woman in a severely-cut, high-necked grey dress with no ornamentation, who he took to be some sort of lady's companion. He had just sat down when the door opened once more, and another lady walked in.

As he rose from his chair to greet the new arrival, she immediately drew Sam's eye and claimed all his attention. Her name was Mary Ann Chaworth, and she was very beautiful. Her slender shoulders sloped white from her simple yet elegant dress; her brown eyes were large and almond-shaped, topped by dark, delicate brows; she had a smiling, rosebud mouth and chestnut hair. Peggy McConnel introduced her as her childhood friend and bridesmaid, but by dint of some skilful questioning, Sam learned something far more important: she was heiress to the Chaworth estates in Annesley, Wiverton and Edwalton. So he turned the full power of his charm on her, and was delighted to find her responsive.

At dinner, Sam was placed at the right hand of his hostess, with Miss Chaworth at McConnel's right hand. He found Mrs McConnel lively company and could only regret that he had not met her sooner – but it was clear from the number of children she had that she had been married before Sam ever came to England. He asked if she attended the Assemblies and was gratified to find that the information provided by the young lad at the Assembly Rooms was correct. He expressed a hope to see her at the next Assembly and asked if Miss Chaworth would be accompanying her. Peggy McConnel smiled and glanced in her friend's direction, answering that since Mary Ann was staying at the Polygon for several more weeks she would certainly do so.

Shortly after this the ladies left the table and the men settled down to discuss politics over their port. The main topic was the continuing Orders in Council, which restricted neutral trade and enforced a naval blockade of Napoleonic France and its allies, and France's response. The Berlin Decree of 21 November 1806 forbade the import of British goods into European countries allied with or dependent upon France, and installed the Continental System in Europe. All connections were to be cut, even the mail. Any ships discovered trading with Great Britain were liable to French maritime attacks and seizures.

This, of course, was hurting England's textile trade, since France was its principal cotton export market and McConnel, like all cotton manufacturers, was unhappy with the government of the day. However, he was a thoughtful, warm-hearted man who rarely flew into a rage; not so the curate, who ranted for some 15 minutes on the iniquities such laws produced, and the desperate poverty in which many of his parishioners found themselves owing to loss of employment at the mills and therefore loss of wages to keep their families.

For once, Sam was content to listen to the conversation and contributed little to it – although he did point out that plantation owners in the West Indies frequently suffered heavy losses also as the British ships carrying their entire cotton harvest were seized or sunk by marauding French privateers.

After they had drunk a full bottle of excellent port between them, the gentlemen once again joined the ladies. Peggy and Mary Ann were engaged in singing a duet, while the austere elderly lady accompanied them on the pianoforte. The men immediately joined in, and by the time the party broke up at ten o'clock, Sam decided he had rarely spent a more delightful evening and said as much to his hostess as he bowed over her hand to say farewell. She smiled and said she hoped to see him at the next Assembly; when Mary Ann laid a hand on his arm and supported her friend's comment, he felt his whole body quicken with excitement, hardly daring to believe that he might finally have found an heiress who was both eligible and beautiful, and with whom he thought he could easily fall in love.

James sent Sam back to his lodgings in his own carriage. Lulled to sleep by its gentle rocking, Sam was jerked rudely awake when they arrived in what seemed no time at all. As he entered his rooms, he thought how dreary and unwelcoming they looked compared to the warm and cheerful house he had just left.

Sam spent the next few weeks making himself agreeable to Peggy McConnel and Mary Ann Chaworth whenever he saw them, which he contrived to do frequently. He was invited into their society and made an instant hit with the ladies of all ages, bringing with him an air of sophistication and knowledge of the most recent fashions from his sojourn in London, together with a slight air of mystery and the excitement of a foreign upbringing. He also got on as well with his male contemporaries here as he had in London and listened carefully for the nuggets of gossip which would let him know which of the young ladies – their sisters – were the most promising targets for his attentions should his delicate pursuit of Miss Chaworth fail, although he felt sure it would not.

He haunted the library on days he was confident they might visit; he attended the Assemblies to dance with them and on other evenings, he played cards there to keep his precarious finances afloat. As he had expected, once it was understood that he was known to Mrs McConnel, he was invited to concerts and, once, to see a play at the Theatre Royal on York Street starring the great Welsh-born tragedienne Sarah Siddons. While privately he would much rather have seen a comedy, he expressed enthusiasm for her performance; it would have been churlish to do otherwise when his hosts were so ecstatic over it.

He found Miss Chaworth charming and lively company; she flirted deliciously with him while remaining decorous and within the bounds of propriety. But then suddenly he was to suffer a severe setback. Some three weeks after the pleasant dinner party at the McConnel house, he was fanning a somewhat heated Mrs McConnel during a break in the dancing at one of the Assemblies when she let drop a piece of information he was not expecting.

"I shall be sad to lose Mary Ann; she is always so good humoured and makes the days pass so pleasantly," she said.

Sam briefly ceased fanning her and looked at her in enquiry.

"She will be going back to Chaworth at the end of the week. Her husband is insistent that she has been away quite long enough."

Sam felt the earth fall away beneath his feet and nearly dropped the fan. "But… but… she is the daughter of Viscount Chaworth is she not? I do not understand…" he stammered.

Peggy McConnel laughed, not unkindly. "She has been married more than a year to Jack Musters. Oh – you thought that because she enjoys flirting with you that she was not only an heiress but eligible?" And she laughed again to see him blush. "Oh dear! The confusion probably arose because her husband recently took the surname Chaworth by Royal Licence, so to all intents and purposes she has not changed her name. I am sorry to disappoint you, sir, but you are behind the fair."

Sam recovered himself well, saying how sorry he too would be to lose the pleasure of Mrs Chaworth's company, but went through the rest of the evening in a daze. When he returned to his lodgings that evening it was in a mood of deep gloom and despondency, which quickly turned to anger at having been, as he saw it, deliberately misled. He paid a street urchin loitering at the corner a penny to fetch him a bottle of brandy from one of the gin palaces in the rough neighbourhood near the Exchange and told him to bring it directly to his room. He pulled off his jacket, tossing it into a corner, and threw himself into the only armchair the lodging possessed.

When the boy returned, Sam demanded his help in pulling off his boots and dismissed him. He pulled the stopper from the dark glass bottle and proceeded to make himself extremely drunk and increasingly bad-tempered. The bottle finished, he threw it against the wall in his rage, and staggered to bed without bothering to undress. He awoke late the next morning, his mouth furry, his head pounding, and with a desperate thirst. Having splashed some water on his face from the pitcher the landlady refilled in his room each day, he struggled into his mired, scuffed boots and buttoned a frock coat over his small clothes with a view to going out and finding some porter to drink to ease his raging thirst and, hopefully, his headache.

Such a state of undress was quite commonplace in central London in the morning, but rather less so in Manchester. Sam became aware of some curious stares as he staggered along the street towards the nearest public house, and this lashed him into a renewed sense of fury.

A pint of porter and some bread went some way towards helping him think more clearly. His dreams seemed at an end. He had discovered no other 'eligible' damsel to pay suit to in Manchester and, besides, he had devoted himself so assiduously to Mary Chaworth that he would be looked at askance if he were seen to transfer his affections overnight. In a mood of deep despair, he could think of no way out of his financial difficulties than to beg his brother John to pay for his passage back to Barbados, having gambled away his entire inheritance.

He called for another jug of porter, and just as the waiter – who shuffled along like a man with dropped arches, and sniffed repeatedly – arrived with it, Sam remembered something his shipboard friend, Taviner, had said about Bath. Did he not say he had a sister there?

His naturally mercurial spirits lifted by this shred of opportunity, Sam downed the second pitcher, shouted for his bill and strode towards the door, miraculously recovered. He returned to his lodgings on Port Street and proceeded to dress himself in a way more befitted to a young gentleman, before heading out again to discover what would be the best means of transport to get him to Bath.

He recalled that the stagecoach from London had made its Manchester stop at the Bridgewater Arms when he first arrived, and therefore decided to make his way there to find out the quickest way (within his means) to travel from Manchester to Bath. He walked quickly through the filthy streets to his destination, head held high and swinging his cane almost jauntily – a far cry from his deportment the previous evening. Once he reached his destination, he sought out the waiter who had been so helpful when he was staying there and was given to understand that he was in the right place to find a seat on a stagecoach.

"The London-bound vehicle left at five o'clock this morning, it being a Wednesday; that's why the inn is so quiet, see. The next will leave in two days' time, on Friday. Or if you were in a hurry, sir, you could ask at the White Bear. They have a coach leaving tomorrow, which will arrive on Saturday evening at Lad Lane?"

"I am in search of passage to Bath rather than London and need information on how best to arrive there," responded Sam.

"Bath. Hmm… Bath. I never know'd anyone go to Bath, sir. Is it on the road to London?"

"No. It is only a few hours from Bristol to the west. Who can tell me what route I must take, if there are no vehicles which go directly? And where can I buy my ticket?"

The waiter, disappointed that he was unable to help the young gentleman and would therefore receive no tip, sniffed dolefully and directed Sam towards the large, wood-panelled entry hall where a desk to the left of the main door served as the ticket office for passengers. Here Sam entered into detailed parleying with a red-faced, rotund individual who perched a *pince-nez* on the end of his nose and consulted copious timetables. Eventually he came up with two options. There was, in fact, a mail coach which travelled directly from Manchester to Bath, but Sam was reluctant to pay what seemed like a very large sum for the journey.

"Or you could catch the coach to Birmingham tomorrow afternoon, sir. It leaves at three o'clock and will arrive in time for breakfast at eight o'clock at a fare of £1/5s for a seat inside. From there you will be able to catch another coach either direct to Bath, or else to Bristol and thence to Bath."

"How long will I have to wait in Birmingham before I can catch a Bristol or Bath coach?"

"Oh, you will obtain passage the same day you arrive, I should think, sir. Bath is very well served by coaches and waggons, now the nobs like to go there in the Season."

Sam decided to book his passage on the Birmingham coach (despite the fact that he knew from his previous journeys that the cost would mount as he had to pay the inevitable *douceurs* to the driver, the guard, and any waiters he had to deal with), and returned to his lodgings to pack his bags and inform his landlady that he was leaving.

He decided to dash off a note to Mrs McConnel, advising her that urgent business had called him south and thanking her for her and her husband's attention to him (although he had seen James McConnel but once since that dinner at his house), and that he would be in touch, etc, etc. He felt it prudent to try and produce a face-saving reason for his sudden departure and not to let her have any evidence that he was leaving town so precipitately because he had miscalculated over Mary Ann Chaworth, although no doubt she would suspect it.

Sam Lord, circa 1806

Part 2
Mutual Attraction, 1807-09

Chapter 3
Bath, 1807-08

Lucy was excited, but also a little apprehensive. She sat back against the comfortable squabs of the carriage next to her mother – who was dozing, with her mouth slightly open and her hat a little askew – and gazed out of the window at the passing countryside. Opposite her sat Mrs Podmore, her mother's dresser, an angular, middle-aged woman who had been with Mrs Wightwick for some ten years. On her bony lap she clutched a vanity case containing the Wightwick ladies' jewels, from which she refused to be parted. The remainder of their luggage – contained in several large trunks and smaller valises – was either strapped to the rear of the carriage or following on behind. They were on their way to Bath.

Lucy liked Bath, she enjoyed the activities of the social Season, the dances and promenades, the picnics and visits. She had made a number of friends there the previous year, and looked forward to meeting them again, to swapping stories about the new fashions, to being allowed to walk with them in the gardens. Some, of course, were now married ladies with houses of their own; others, like her, would be returning for their second Season.

And therein lay the cause of her apprehension. Her mother had visited her in her bedroom last night after they had completed preparing their summer gowns for winter storage and made it very clear that Lucy must strain every sinew on this, her second Season, to find herself a husband. Her mother had been very disappointed that she had failed to contract an engagement the previous year, despite no expense being spared on turning her out in style and numerous introductions to eligible young men at the Bath Assemblies. Lucy's liveliness – which her mother frequently condemned as hoydenish – meant that, despite the fact that she was no beauty, she never lacked for dance partners, she had attracted a small group of around half a dozen young men who were happy to spend time with her, but not one had made an offer for her hand despite the fact that it was common knowledge that she would receive a handsome dowry.

Not, of course, that Mrs Wightwick wanted to see her daughter married off to a gazetted fortune hunter, but several of Lucy's 'court' had been perfectly respectable young men who were nevertheless desirous of making a good match with financial benefits. There was one younger son whom Mrs Wightwick had thought quite delightful, with perfect manners, who would have made an excellent son-in-law. Lucy had liked him too, but not enough to marry him, so she was secretly rather pleased that he had given no indication of becoming particularly attached to her – although, of course, it would have been flattering if he had asked her father for her hand.

Lucy sighed. Papa had said nothing when she had finished her enjoyable first Season without any offers of marriage, but she knew that this was one aspect of her life in which her father would defer to her mother. It was easy to wrap Papa around her little finger on most things, but when it came to Lucy's marital future, her mother was in charge. She wanted to be a dutiful daughter, but she would so like to marry for love, just as they did in the novels she had enjoyed borrowing from the library in Bath last year. On the other hand, she was uncomfortably aware that despite her family's wealth, her life might not be very agreeable once her younger brother, Stubbs – still at school – married and her parents were dead.

Dwindling into an old maid dependent on her brother did not appeal to Lucy, who yearned for independence and the ability to throw off the shackles of convention, but despite already having attained her majority (she had been 21 before embarking on her first Bath Season), only if she were herself to marry could she hope to gain even a modicum of autonomy. She would be looked at askance and ostracised by society if she tried, as an unmarried woman, to travel the world. The nearest she would ever get would be visiting the dockside in Bristol or Chepstow with her father when he discussed trade with a ship owner or one of the timber merchants.

Well, even if she did not meet the perfect eligible bachelor in Bath this Season, she must try to encourage the best among them to make an offer for her. She did not think her mother would be prepared to cover all the costs of a third, potentially equally unsatisfactory, Season, and then what would become of her? She would be immured at Hewelsfield Court or Great Bloxwich, where the limited social opportunities had failed to produce any suitors, with little to occupy her other than helping her mother around the house; and no doubt she would be made to feel her mother's disapproval and disappointment keenly. She had always enjoyed her small acts of rebellion in childhood but had come to realise that any similar acts in adulthood would be frowned upon by society. Marriage would, at least, offer her an element of freedom – and she would be assured of her parents' approval. She could only hope she had sufficient address to be sure of receiving a suitable offer.

The carriage slowed as they approached the centre of Bath, making for Pulteney Bridge. Traffic was, as always heavy, and Lucy shook off her thoughts and started looking for familiar faces among the pedestrians walking alongside. She saw no one she knew, but let her gaze rest on the lovely, familiar buildings and determined she was going to enjoy herself to the full over the next few months. She loved the bustle and atmosphere of the city, so different from the rural tranquillity of Hewelsfield – which she loved dearly, of course, but she did enjoy the variety of things to do, of people to see that Bath had to offer. Soon they were crossing the bridge, trotting along Great Pulteney Street towards the pretty townhouse the Wightwicks had once again hired for the Season in Bathwick, a smart new development situated only a few miles from the centre.

The October[2] sunshine lit up the gold Bath stone of the house as they approached, and Lucy smiled. Her mother opened her eyes and straightened her hat as the three women waited for the carriage door to be opened and the steps let down. Lucy shook out her crushed skirts as she alighted and stood looking about her at the elegant surroundings. The front door opened, and she followed her mother up the shallow steps, nodding to the footman with a smile to show she recognised him from their previous visit. Then all was bustle as the valises were carried in and Mrs Podmore followed, still grimly clutching the jewel case. The ladies went upstairs to their bedchambers to refresh themselves and take off their hats and coats. Lucy then ran back downstairs and insisted on visiting every room in the house before sitting down to take a dish of tea with her mother.

The housekeeper, who had arrived the day before from Hewelsfield, came in to discuss arrangements for the evening meal and to enquire if everything was to their liking. In a short while they heard the sounds of the second carriage arriving and the trunks being unloaded, and Mrs Wightwick went out to supervise their disposal. Lucy wandered along to the room her father used as his study whenever he came to stay with them. She loved the big wooden desk, the floor-to-ceiling bookcases and the glass-fronted cabinet – empty now, but which would soon contain some of his precious collection of translucent porcelain from home. She heard her mother calling and accompanied her upstairs again to oversee the unpacking.

Her spirits rose further as she watched the walking dresses, morning dresses and evening dresses being unpacked from the tissue paper in which they had been folded and placed carefully in the clothes press. She was particularly keen to try out a new walking dress of French cambric, trimmed with broad lace, and thought she would wear it accompanied by a delightful chip straw bonnet with orange ribbons the following morning when she would accompany her mother to the Pump Room and try to persuade her to visit the Milsom Street shops. She indicated as much to her maid, Peggy, and helped her finish unpacking all her undergarments and putting them away in drawers. She had bought several pairs of silk stockings, to be worn with her evening dresses, and she stroked them, loving the luxurious feel of the fabric. She left Peggy sorting out her toiletries, and tripped downstairs to join her mother in time for dinner. There was no need to change her dress since it was just to be the two of them this evening, and she thought she would raise the idea at the table of strolling down Milsom Street with Mrs Wightwick, who was just as fond of shopping as her daughter.

The following morning, attired in the French cambric dress, she visited her mother in her bedroom before going down to breakfast. A good night's sleep had fully restored Mrs Wightwick and she confirmed that they would leave for the Pump Room at eleven o'clock. Both were energetic walkers, and since the sun was shining again, they decided to go on foot – always the easiest way to get about the cobbled streets and steep hills of the city.

Lucy was on her best behaviour, treating her mother with great deference and affection and, having slipped on a light, apricot pelisse and tied the orange

---

[2] Bath Season, October to June

ribbons of her hat at one side under her chin, she linked arms with Mrs Wightwick and the two set out. They made their way downhill at a good pace, and soon found themselves crossing the bridge into a throng of people. They made their way along High Street towards the Abbey and from there directly to the Pump Room, stopping to admire the Roman remains which were being slowly and carefully excavated.

On entering, they joined the crowd of ladies intent on putting their names in Mr King's subscription book, to ensure admission during their stay to the New Assembly Rooms where so many Bath activities (balls, card assemblies and concerts) took place.

Mr King had been made Master of Ceremonies at the Upper Rooms in 1805. He was promoted to the role from that of presiding over the long-established Lower Rooms, thus confirming the superiority of the former. Mr King asked of visitors to Bath that "They will on their arrival cause their names, with their places of abode, to be inserted in the book kept at the Pump Room for that purpose, which will afford him such information as will enable him to comply with his own wishes, and the expectations of the public." The cost of a single subscription for the Season was only twelve shillings, a very reasonable sum for a great deal of entertainment.

Mrs Wightwick recognised an acquaintance and Lucy settled the two ladies in chairs to enjoy a gossip while she obtained two glasses of the waters for them to drink. She threaded her way through the throng to where a woman distributed King Bladud's waters from the fountain to all who had paid their subscription. Lucy had tried a glass once last year and found the taste unpleasantly mineral in flavour.

As she waited her turn patiently, she gazed around the spacious hall which had only been built some nine years previously for the specific purpose of providing a promenade for the increasing number of visitors and for drinking the waters. Elegant Ionic pillars soared to the high ceiling; a statue of Beau Nash, the first master of ceremonies, had been placed at one end, and an orchestra constantly played music for the pleasure of the promenaders. She thought once again how unlike Hewelsfield was Bath, with its cheerful cacophony of scores of people talking at once mingling with the music.

Carefully holding the two hot glasses, she made her way back towards where her mother sat with her friend and found herself being hailed. "Lucy, how lovely to see you. I looked for you earlier in the month and was afraid you were not coming again this year! Have you seen Marianne? I think she must be very conscious of her status as a young matron – she is not nearly as lively as she was last Season before her marriage. Have you got a beau? Have you… Oh! I have so much I want to talk to you about! Are you here with your mother?"

Lucy smiled at the vivacious and extremely pretty brunette. "You are the first acquaintance I have seen, Annabel. We only arrived in Bath yesterday evening, Mama had some things she needed to attend to which delayed our arrival. I am just taking a glass of the waters to her and her friend, come with me."

Annabel bobbed a schoolgirl's curtsey to Mrs Wightwick and her companion. "Good gracious, you are not here alone are you?" Lucy's mother asked.

"No, Mrs Wightwick. My mother is somewhere on the other side of the Pump Room, and my maid is just over there keeping some seats for us. May Lucy walk with me, or do you need her here?"

Mrs Wightwick indicated that the girls might go off the length of the building and keep an eye out for any other friends who might be about and – although this would not have received Mrs Wightwick's blessing – any good-looking young men. Annabel had had a great many admirers last Season, and Lucy was surprised that she had not become engaged.

"Well, if Marianne is anything to go by, I wish to stay single as long as possible," she dimpled irrepressibly when Lucy voiced her thoughts. "It's far more fun and although I think Marianne's dress is simply sumptuous, I don't think being able to wear rich dresses is a reason to get married, do you? Papa received no fewer than three offers for me at the end of the Season which was very gratifying, but I didn't care for any of them enough to marry them so was quite happy when Papa didn't approve of them! Did Adrian Letchworth approach your father?"

Mr Letchworth was brother to one of the girls Lucy had struck up a friendship with the previous Season and he had shown her quite a marked degree of attention. Lucy shook her head.

"Did you wish him to?"

Lucy hesitated. "No," she responded slowly, shaking her head, "but…" She hesitated, not wanting to voice the thoughts she had had on the journey in such a public place.

Annabel looked at her sympathetically. "I think we need to make an opportunity to have a long talk, without interruptions," she said. Lucy nodded gravely. "Do you think your mother will allow you to come and visit when I am dressing tomorrow morning, Annabel? If so, I'll mention it to Mama."

Annabel flashed her lovely smile, then her roving eye was caught by a very dapper young gentleman in a maroon coat and fawn breeches. He was clearly equally taken with her, and turned to his companion, perhaps to ask if he knew who the young lady was. Annabel cast down her lashes and arm-in-arm with Lucy sauntered off to find her mother, taking a quick look over her shoulder to make sure the young man was paying attention.

Lucy's mother came up with them at this point, and the daughters, mothers and two other friends engaged in some idle chit-chat about fashions. Just before they parted, Lucy asked if Annabel could visit the following morning and it was agreed that she would be driven to the Bathwick house at an early hour, this being a Tuesday when there would be a card assembly at the New Rooms, which neither of the girls would be permitted to attend and so could have an early night.

The Wightwicks made their way on foot towards Milsom Street and spent a pleasant hour window-shopping and discussing animatedly which shops best deserved their patronage at a future date. They then returned to Bathwick in a hackney carriage. While her mother dozed on the short ride home, Lucy slipped into a reverie about her first Season in Bath, which she remembered as being one of unalloyed pleasure. She had always enjoyed dancing and took every opportunity to do so whether in the Assembly Rooms or, occasionally, when invited to a ball at a friend's house, and she enjoyed country dances just as much as more formal ones such as the quadrille or minuet. The acquaintances made at these events led on to invitations to join groups on picnics (if the weather was fine, which did not happen often, given the time of year) or visits to local landmarks. Lucy spent the rest of the day writing a letter to her father (Annabel was a special favourite of his) and making a new reticule out of cardboard and some gold thread fabric for use with one of her two new ballgowns.

The following morning, as agreed, Annabel arrived early, accompanied by her maid whom Mrs Wightwick sent home saying that she would ensure Annabel was sent back later by carriage. The Wightwick ladies were at breakfast, so Annabel joined them, sipping at a cup of coffee and crumbling a roll on her plate without eating it. Mrs Wightwick seemed a little preoccupied, but smiled at the girls' chatter and, when they had finished, dismissed them to continue their gossiping in Lucy's bedroom, where she had no doubt they would swap views on fashion and Lucy would describe the dresses and hats she had set her heart on the previous day during their stroll along Milsom Street. With this comforting thought, she rang for the housekeeper to discuss what needed to be done that day, before attending to her household accounts.

In fact, Lucy had scarcely closed the door behind the two of them than Annabel demanded to know why Lucy had been so ambivalent when she had raised the subject of Adrian Letchworth during their conversation in the Pump Room. Lucy explained that her mother had made it very clear it was her duty to find a husband this Season.

"You see, Annabel, I am not nearly as pretty as you so I cannot hope to attract a string of beaux to ask for my hand. Adrian Letchworth showed an interest in me, but even he did not make an offer. What if no one does? What is to become of me? Mama will not bring me to Bath for another Season, and I shall dwindle into an old maid, and be seen as of use only as aunt to Stubbs's children!"

Her cheeks were burning red and there were tears in her eyes. Annabel tried to soothe her.

"Don't be upset, Lucy! We will find a gentleman that you can like and who wishes to offer for you, I am sure. I shall make it my project for the Season – to find you a husband. There are plenty of candidates more suitable than Adrian Letchworth."

Lucy hiccoughed on a sob, but allowed her tears to be dried, and soon the two young women had their heads in a book of fashion plates, and Annabel was pirouetting round the floor wearing one of Lucy's hats which she fancied.

Annabel remained with the Wightwicks all through the afternoon. The weather had turned to rain, and the girls entertained themselves by playing the card game known as lottery tickets, singing, playing the piano, and practising the complicated steps of the minuet, squabbling amicably over when to do a *demi-coupé* and when a *demi-jeté*.

Annabel stayed on for dinner, which was enlivened by the arrival of Mr Wightwick who had to be regaled with all that had happened since his wife and daughter had last seen him. He sent Annabel home in the carriage, and the family spent a quiet evening together, curtains closed against the rain, Mrs Wightwick doing some white needlework while Lucy read aloud several chapters of Fanny Burney's *Camilla* to them.

From now on, Lucy was carried away in a whirlwind of social events which she thoroughly enjoyed, and most of the time she managed to forget that she was here for a purpose, that if she failed her mother's ambition to attract a suitable husband, this might well be the last time she would have a chance to taste the gaieties of Bath.

They obtained tickets for the Wednesday evening concert at the Upper Assembly Rooms. The main piece was a Haydn one she had never before heard, the Farewell Symphony. She sat entranced, from the very first note of the first movement, and found her emotions stirred by the yearning she was sure she could hear in the second movement. She was actually moved to tears by the end of the final movement, which was really quite theatrical and very unusual: several of the musicians were given little solos to play, after which they snuffed out the candle on their music stand and took their leave, followed by other musicians without solos. As the musicians and instruments departed, the sound emanating from the orchestra gradually faded to a murmur, with only the first violinists remaining to complete the work pianissimo.

The silence of the audience following the final note seemed almost louder than the music and then they burst into spontaneous applause and shouts of "Bravo!". Lucy turned to her mother, her face wet with tears, and smiled tremulously, sighing. Mrs Wightwick dabbed at her daughter's cheeks with a handkerchief before moving towards the tearoom for the interval. There they met Mr King, who was circulating among the subscribers as was his wont. He bowed to the ladies and enquired how they had enjoyed the symphony. Mrs Wightwick explained that Lucy had been quite overcome by emotion, at which he turned and smiled at her.

"Do you know the history of the piece?" he asked. When she shook her head he explained, "It was written for Haydn's patron, Prince Nikolaus Esterházy, while he, Haydn and the court orchestra were at the prince's summer palace. The stay there was longer than anticipated, and most of the musicians had been forced to leave their wives back at home in Eisenstadt, so in the last movement of the symphony, Haydn subtly hinted that perhaps the prince might allow the musicians to return home. It seems to have worked, apparently the court returned to Eisenstadt the day following the performance."

He then introduced the Wightwick ladies to Signor Rauzzini to convey their enthusiasm for his concert direction, when Lucy spied her friend Annabel talking vivaciously to Adrian Letchworth. The two came across and Adrian bowed to Lucy and her mother while Annabel – who was not in the least musical – thanked

Signor Rauzzini very prettily for providing such a treat for them all. The pale, elderly Italian beamed: he had an eye for a pretty woman.

When his attention was claimed by another group, Annabel took the opportunity to ask Mrs Wightwick if she and Lucy would join their party on a picnic on the Saturday.

"We plan to go to Box Hill, Mrs Wightwick. My mother and father are coming, and my brother. Mr Letchworth has just agreed to come with his sister, and there will be one or two others. Please do say you'll come – and please bring Mr Wightwick also if he is still in Bath." Mrs Wightwick graciously accepted on behalf of all three of them.

As they walked back to their seats for the second half of the concert, Mrs Wightwick said in an under-voice to Lucy, "I make no doubt you noticed that Mr Letchworth appears to have switched his attentions to your friend. Her dowry is not as large as yours, but she is an extremely pretty girl. It is a shame you did not make more effort to attach him to you last year."

Her pleasure in the concert now extinguished, a subdued Lucy answered, "Yes, Mama. I am sorry. I will endeavour to behave just as I ought this year."

Thursday was cotillion day at the Upper Rooms. The cotillion was a French dance for two or four couples in a square formation featuring complex footwork. Cotillions had a standard set of nine "Changes", such as circle to the right and then the left, turn partner by the right and left and so on, and each Change was followed by a complicated "Figure" or chorus that was distinctive to each tune. The Changes included an *allemande* turn where partners crossed hands behind each other's backs, looking at each other over their shoulders.

Since the waltz was still generally frowned upon in polite society – although it was already frequently danced in private houses – this was the closest dance partners physically came to each other. Lucy had felt very embarrassed when she first stepped onto the dance floor at the Assembly Rooms the previous Season, it was one thing to practise the cotillions with her girlfriends and cousins but being so close to a strange man was a novel and not altogether welcome experience. She had quickly grown accustomed, however, and rather enjoyed the complex moves required, and the stately nature of the dance.

Before the evening's entertainment, Lucy assisted her mother with several housekeeping chores including mending a torn flounce. After a light lunch of some cold meat and fruit with Mr Wightwick – who had spent the morning working on something in his study – the two ladies donned their pelisses and decided to walk to the lending library. They skies were leaden, promising more rain, but although the day was blustery the walk was not an unpleasant one. Lucy borrowed two poetry books, *Palmyra* by Thomas Love Peacock, which Annabel had told her was delightful, and *Wild Flowers or Pastoral and Local Poetry* by Robert Bloomfield, both new editions. Her mother borrowed *Thoughts on the education of daughters: with reflections on female conduct, in the more important duties of life* by Mary Wollstonecraft, a domestic conduct book that Mrs Wightwick thought would be an improving manual to read with her daughter during quiet periods together at the Bathwick house.

While her mother engaged in animated conversation with an acquaintance about the benefits of the new-fangled gaslighting, Lucy occupied herself by idly turning the pages of the London newspapers, which were delivered daily by the mail coach. The two of them then made their way to the Upper Rooms where it was usual to practise the cotillion figures in the tea room before dinner, so that when the dancers took to the floor of the ballroom in the evening their dancing would be perfect.

They returned to Bathwick by sedan chair, summoned successfully by an obliging doorman despite the rain now pouring down, and Lucy was urged to rest on her bed for a while before dressing for the evening's ball, which would begin at six o'clock.

When Lucy came downstairs, she was dressed in a ball dress of plain crape, over a white satin slip, with plain back and sleeves, a quartered front, trimmed round the bottom on the waist and sleeves with a white velvet riband thickly spangled with gold. A white satin sash, tied in long bows to the right side, terminated with splendid gold tassels. The *ensemble* was finished with a high gathered tucker of Brussels lace at the top of the bodice, white satin dancing slippers, white gloves and a white velvet riband through her hair.

Mr Wightwick, looking resplendent in evening dress which he rarely wore, was to accompany Lucy and her mother to the Upper Rooms. He assisted the ladies into their waiting carriage, which proceeded to make its careful way along the slippery, cobbled streets. Lucy looked forward to the evening with excitement, tempered with a niggling concern that she might not be able to fill her dance card completely with prospective partners.

As they approached the entrance on Bennett Street, near the Circus, Lucy leaned forward to look out of the window and catch a glimpse of others arriving at the Assembly Rooms. The approach was very congested, thronged with sedan chairs and carriages of all sorts, so that when they did eventually manage to alight Mr Wightwick told their coachman to return to Bathwick and to come again for them at eleven o'clock when the ball would come to an end.

The ballroom was lit by dozens of candles in a series of chandeliers, with rows of red damask benches around the walls, and the musicians in a balcony above. The brilliancy of the lights, the size and proportions of the room filled with graceful dancers in a stately minuet, and the effect of the music made Lucy think of a fairy palace, and she clapped her hands together in excitement as she waited for her father to pay sixpence for each of them to partake of the refreshments to be provided at nine o'clock.

The room was already crowded, and the Wightwicks made their way with some difficulty towards the benches, keeping well away from the dancefloor itself – chalked in many squares – as Mr King was very strict about permitting only dancers to occupy it. They bowed and nodded to a number of acquaintances as they went, and the two ladies eventually managed to find space on one of the benches, there to await potential partners for Lucy. When the minuet finished, there was applause from the spectators standing at the bottom of the room and the dancers moved towards the benches where Lucy and her mother were sitting.

Mr King, who always liked to ensure that the young people who wished to dance had partners and who prided himself on never forgetting a subscriber, came across to greet the Wightwicks and to introduce a quiet, solid looking man by the name of David Copthorne to Lucy, who duly wrote his name on her dance card for the first cotillion. Once they took to the floor they engaged in little conversation: while Lucy was a confident dancer, her partner was clearly watching his steps; and besides, the complexity of a cotillion did not make conversation easy. She thanked him prettily when the music stopped, and he asked if he might have the pleasure of dancing a country dance later in the evening with her. She warmed to him when he apologised disarmingly for being so unsure of himself in the cotillion and hoped she would forgive him, and readily agreed to his request.

She danced the next dance with her father, and another with one of her acquaintances from the previous Season, and then they all went in to tea. Adrian Letchworth approached them in the tearoom, bowed and asked Mrs Wightwick if he might have the pleasure of dancing the next cotillion with Lucy. Mindful of her mother's comment about Mr Letchworth transferring his attentions to Annabel, Lucy blushed, and stammered her acceptance whilst looking up at him under her eyelashes. She looked forward to it, for she knew him to be a much better dancer than Mr Copthorne.

And indeed, she did enjoy it. He quickly put her at her ease, and – when the dance allowed – talked in an amusing way about what he had been doing over the summer months and showed a genuine interest in her activities. He told her that he was looking forward to the picnic arranged for Saturday, and how delighted he was that Lucy would also be attending.

"I only hope it won't be rained off!" he exclaimed. "I believe my sister will be inconsolable if it is, but you know how uncertain the weather is in Bath."

They were performing an *allemande* turn at the time, and Lucy looked laughingly over her shoulder at him, unconsciously coquettish. She thought what a comfortable companion he was and wondered if – should he make an offer for her hand – she could see herself being married to him. She rather thought she could.

When they came off the dancefloor, flushed and panting from their exertions, he escorted her back to her mother who, having danced one country dance with her husband, was now comfortably conversing with two other matrons while all of them kept a watchful eye on their daughters to ensure that they did not overstep the line of decorous behaviour. Adrian's sister Rebecca joined the group, as well as Annabel, and the four young people discussed in animated terms how much they were enjoying themselves, to the accompaniment of much fanning by the ladies. Lucy and Rebecca sat out the next country dance which Annabel danced with Adrian, then Mr Copthorne claimed Lucy's hand for the final dance of the evening.

When he returned Lucy to her mother (Mr Wightwick had retired to the card room some time earlier), Mr King was talking to Mrs Wightwick, accompanied by a tall, handsome man of about 30 years old. As Lucy approached, the two men turned and, once David Copthorne had bowed his thanks and moved away, Mr King spoke to her.

"Miss Wightwick, may I present Mr Samuel Lord to you? He is but newly arrived in Bath on his first visit from the West Indies and asked me to introduce him to you. I made sure you and Mrs Wightwick would help him find his way about." The Master of Ceremonies smiled, bowed and went on his way.

"Miss Wightwick, I am only sorry that I am too late to solicit you for a dance this evening," the young man said with a charming smile, "but I do hope you will not object to my calling upon your mother, and perhaps inviting you to dance the cotillion with me next Thursday?"

Mrs Wightwick watched the scene approvingly, clearly encouraged by what she saw.

"Mr Lord is staying in lodgings in Orange Grove, Lucy, and has expressed an interest in seeing some of the sights around Bath. I think we might invite him to join us on our next expedition."

"By all means, Mama," responded Lucy demurely, thinking she had rarely seen such a handsome man and elated that he seemed to be taking an interest in her.

"We have a number of engagements over the next few days," said her mother, turning to Mr Lord, "but if you would like to pay us a visit next Tuesday morning, we shall be at home in Bathwick."

Too astute to leap at this opportunity, Sam said regretfully that he would be otherwise engaged out of Bath at that time, but that he would certainly attend the next Cotillion Ball. He then bowed to each lady in turn and kissed their hands, turned and walked away.

"Come, Lucy. We must find your father and then John Coachman," said Mrs Wightwick. The Assembly Rooms were emptying rapidly, for Mr King was a stickler for punctuality and all the balls had to end at eleven o'clock – even, as Lucy had discovered the previous year, if the musicians were in the middle of a dance tune.

Her father fell asleep almost immediately he climbed into the carriage, and both Lucy and her mother were uncharacteristically silent, both thinking about Mr Samuel Lord – although the content of their thoughts was rather different. Mrs Wightwick determined to ask her husband to make inquiries into the gentleman's circumstances, for it was not unknown for unscrupulous fortune hunters to try their luck with wealthy young ladies in provincial towns where they were less likely to be exposed for what they were than in London. Lucy, meanwhile, was daydreaming about a love-match with a handsome man, as always seemed to happen in the novels she so enjoyed reading, and tingling with anticipation at the notion of dancing with him the following Thursday.

Mrs Wightwick had purchased tickets to the theatre for Friday evening, and had invited Lucy's friend Marianne with her husband to join the Wightwick family in a box for which she had paid five shillings. At the last moment, as they were due to leave Bathwick, Mr Wightwick announced that he rather thought he would not join them at the theatre but would go to play billiards at the Assembly

Rooms instead. Mrs Wightwick tut-tutted, but there was no moving him, even though Lucy added her pleas to her mother's and shrewdly mentioned that Annabel was also attending the evening's performance of Hamlet.

The Theatre Royal on Beaufort Square was a modern building, designed by George Dance and built just two years previously by John Palmer to replace the earlier theatre of the same name in Orchard Street, which had proved so popular that it became too small. Mrs Wightwick privately thought the exterior over-ornate with its arches, pilasters, garlands and ornaments, but Lucy (and public opinion generally) thought it very fine. She had also been in raptures over the auditorium with its tiers of ornate crimson and gilt plasterwork, *trompe-l'oeil* ceiling and glittering chandelier, when she first visited the theatre during her 1806-07 Season to see Master Betty when he came from Drury Lane to play *The Clandestine Marriage* and *Richard III* in January 1807 – performances which were universally praised by public and journals alike. Lucy was only sorry that Master Betty would not be acting on this occasion, but perhaps it would be interesting to see how different the play was with another principal actor, as she discussed with Marianne on their way upstairs to their box having met up in the foyer.

Mrs Wightwick apologised profusely to Marianne's husband that Mr Wightwick was not, after all, able to be present to provide him with some male company, but he turned it off laughing.

"I believe myself very fortunate, ma'am, to have to myself the company of three such charming ladies!"

During the intermission Annabel, her mother and companions joined the Wightwicks' box over a glass of negus to discuss the play and plans for the picnic the following day. Annabel hoped anxiously that the sun would shine and all agreed that, unless the weather was particularly atrocious, they would go on the outing in any case.

The farce which followed was, in Lucy's indignant opinion, very inferior to the performance of Hamlet, and she was not unhappy when the whole party decided to leave for home before the end. Her mother was sleepy, so having said their goodbyes, Lucy was once again alone with her thoughts on the short journey back. How pleasant it would be if Mr Lord were to join the picnic, but of course he was not invited.

When Lucy woke the following morning, she ran to the window of her bedroom and opened a chink in the curtains to see what the weather was like, breathing a sigh of relief that it was fine, if a little on the chilly side – not surprising for October. Now she could look forward to the picnic outing with unalloyed pleasure. Rain would surely have spoiled the day as there was nothing so unpleasant as wet feet and wet hems, and the views would have been limited.

An enormous raised chicken and ham pie had been prepared on the Friday, and when Lucy entered the kitchen Cook was packing it carefully into a large wicker basket.

"You go and have your breakfast, Miss Lucy. I must finish baking the cherry tart and cool it before you leave. You'll only fluster me if you come in here now."

Lucy smiled at the harassed cook but did as she was bid. There was no real hurry, they would not be leaving for another hour.

They had agreed to meet Annabel's family – who were providing the bulk of the picnic equipment – and the other guests at the foot of Box Hill. The Wightwicks piled several rugs into the carriage as well as the basket containing the food they were supplying, and at the last moment Lucy's mother insisted that one of the servants check in the cellar for any outdoor furniture that might have been left by the owners of the house as she was reluctant to sit on the ground and had convinced herself that Annabel would forget to bring any chairs. Mr Wightwick expostulated,

"Now Lucy, you know that when we joined their picnic last year Annabel – or at least her mother – had organised everything beautifully, and they brought several folding chairs. I am sure they will do so again."

So the search – which was proving abortive – was called off, although Mrs Wightwick did insist on taking a cushion with her, as she feared the chairs might be a little hard to sit on. Finally they set off on the ten-mile drive to Box Hill.

When they arrived at the meeting place Annabel's carriage was already there, together with a wagon full of outdoor furniture, rugs and baskets containing food, cutlery and plates. Two servants were perched precariously amongst it all. Mr Wainwright, Annabel's father, was just giving the order for the wagon to make its ponderous way up the hill.

Annabel clapped her hands with delight when she saw them. "Isn't this the jolliest thing?" she called out. "And the weather is just perfect! We are very lucky, and this may be the last picnic outing we can make this Season."

Mrs Wightwick was renewing her acquaintance with Mrs Wainwright, but Mr Wightwick took Annabel's hand and bowed over it.

"Miss Wainwright, it is a pleasure to renew my acquaintance with you. Thank you for including me in your picnic invitation."

"Oh, please, Mr Wightwick, you always called me Annabel before."

"But you are now a grown-up young lady and it does not seem quite proper…" he said, laughing, "however, if you insist, I shall continue to call you Annabel with pleasure." He turned, with Lucy, to greet Mr Wainwright who had joined them.

The two families conversed as they strolled around the peaceful grassland at the foot of Box Hill, awaiting both the return of the empty wagon and the arrival of the Letchworth siblings, together with Annabel's younger brother Peter. "I did invite Marianne too, but she had another engagement," Annabel explained to Lucy.

Lucy squinted up the hill. "I think I can see the wagon returning," she said.

As the wagon arrived, the last three guests drew up also. Adrian Letchworth jumped down from the carriage and helped Rebecca to alight; the youngest Wainwright, Peter, emerged last, frowning. It was clear that he had a sore head, which was confirmed by Adrian.

"Sorry we are late. Master slug-a-bed here delayed us," pointing to Peter. "It seems he had a pretty batch of it last night!"

It was agreed by all that it was such a pleasant day it would be a shame to waste it, and they decided to walk up Box Hill to the picnic site rather than ride in the wagon. So the last items were loaded into it – the Wightwicks' basket among them – and it set off again, with the party dividing naturally into the four older people, who set off briskly, and the five younger taking a less direct route in order for the young ladies to stop and admire patches of late flowers or, as they climbed higher through the trees (box, yew, beech and oak), views of the surrounding countryside.

The fresh air seemed to revive Peter, and he was soon in animated discussion with Adrian about the merits of a couple of prize-fighters due to hold a boxing match just outside Bath in the next month. Rebecca found a patch of blackberries which they all sampled, with the result that when they arrived, pink and breathless, at the summit their fingers were all stained purple from the fruit.

"Mama," said Lucy when she had got her breath back, "we should pick blackberries on the way back down to make jam and perhaps a blackberry and apple pie."

Mrs Wightwick smiled, but suggested that Lucy was not dressed for blackberrying, and would ruin her muslin dress, but she had little hope of being heeded.

The servants had laid out the rugs, set up some tables and chairs in the shade of two huge oak trees, covered the tables with white cloths and transferred the food from the various baskets to them. A pile of white plates was set next to gleaming silverware and white napkins and – most welcome of all to those who had just walked up the hill – jugs and bottles of lemonade, claret, cider and ale.

They spent a pleasant few hours in the late autumn warmth and ate a great deal of the provisions which included – besides the Wightwicks' pie and tart – a joint of cold beef, an onion pie, some tongue, cheese, bread and jam, syllabub and a plum cake. They frequently got up from the meal to stroll around and look at the views for which Box Hill was rightly famous, before coming back for a further helping.

By four o'clock the air was growing cool, so they helped the servants pack everything into the wagon once more and began the walk back. Lucy had not forgotten about the blackberries. She picked out the least unwieldy of the wicker baskets and with help from her mother, Annabel and Rebecca had soon collected as much as she could carry from the bramble patch they had found on the way up. Adrian insisted on taking the basket from her and carrying it to the bottom, despite teasing from the others that it made him look like some farmer on his way to market.

When they reached the foot of the hill, the servants had almost finished unloading the items belonging to the Wightwicks and the Letchworths and transferring them to their respective carriages. The party said their goodbyes; the young ladies had arranged to walk in Sydney Gardens the following afternoon after attending a service in the Abbey, and there was talk of getting up a party to go to a balloon launch planned for November, although Mrs Wainwright and Mr Wightwick were dubious that the weather would hold for it.

The Wightwicks arrived home pleasantly tired, and spent the evening in, playing cards and talking over the day's events. The fresh air had made Lucy unusually sleepy, and she was happy to go to bed early for once.

The days continued to be crammed with social events, whether it was card parties at noon in the house of an acquaintance, or shopping in Milsom Street, or going to the theatre, or a concert in the Abbey, or taking her mother to drink the waters in the Pump Room, or attending balls in the Upper Assembly Rooms.

By the time Thursday's Ball came around again, Lucy's brief encounter with Sam was, if not entirely forgotten, pushed to the back of her mind, and she had indeed forgotten that he had promised to ask her to dance on the next occasion. But almost as soon as she and her mother had arrived at the Upper Rooms, Sam was standing before them bowing civilly to both ladies, having been on the lookout for them.

"Miss Wightwick, Mrs Wightwick. It is a pleasure to meet you again. I do hope your dance card is not yet full, Miss Wightwick? Would you be kind enough to keep a country dance for me?"

Lucy could feel a blush rising up her neck and into her cheeks, and her heart started beating rather fast. She unfurled her fan and used it to hide her confusion. "We have only this moment arrived, Mr Lord, so my dance card is by no means full. I shall be happy to put you down for the next country dance."

Sam bowed his thanks, then stayed to converse with the ladies until the country dance was called. Mrs Wightwick looked on complacently as he led Lucy onto the dancefloor with its chalked squares.

Lucy enjoyed country dances; she found their liveliness fun. She hoped Mr Lord was a good dancer, but she was not sure whether society in the West Indies was the same as England, or where he might have learned their dances. But she need not have worried. They took their places in the middle of the line, and from the start she noticed that he watched and listened carefully to the lead dancer who called the steps and figures. She relaxed and smiled at him as they took their turn dancing down the line between their fellow dancers, men on one side and women on the other. As it was still early in the evening, there were only some ten couples on the dancefloor, and the session was over in twenty minutes.

Sam walked her back to where her mother waited, asking on the way whether Lucy might favour him with a Scotch Reel later in the evening. When she said yes, he was emboldened to ask Mrs Wightwick if he might take both ladies into tea at nine o'clock. Having secured their agreement he took his leave. Lucy's hand was almost immediately claimed by Adrian, who just reached her before a disappointed David Copthorne, to whom she also granted a later country dance.

When she returned from her dance with Adrian, Annabel (who had just been dancing with her brother Peter) waved her over. Adrian went off in search of another partner and Peter made his escape to the card room. Annabel wasted no time.

"Who is that handsome man you were dancing with? Where did you meet him?" she demanded.

Lucy told her what had occurred the previous Thursday, and Annabel's eyes widened when she heard that Sam had requested an introduction.

"Well, you'd certainly put a few noses out of joint if he makes you an offer!" she said bluntly. "Do you like him?"

"I hardly know yet, Annabel," responded Lucy, laughing. "I have danced with him twice. In fact, I think Mama knows him better than I do."

Having heard that Sam had committed to escorting the Wightwicks in to tea, Annabel resolved to manoeuvre herself close enough to be introduced to him. She towed her faintly protesting mother through the throng making their way towards the refreshments until she could see the Wightwicks ahead of her, then circled round to meet them so that it looked accidental. Mrs Wainwright looked quite bewildered, not knowing why her daughter could not just stand in line and wait like everyone else.

Mrs Wightwick frowned, well aware that her daughter's looks did not shine in the presence of pretty little Annabel. Lucy, knowing her friend was incurably inquisitive, smiled and introduced her. Annabel looked up through her lashes and dimpled, as she curtseyed prettily. Sam bowed and looked at her approvingly. But he had researched the eligible young ladies in Bath before he asked for his introduction to Lucy. Annabel had not yet attained her majority, and her portion was not as large. Although he would have been happy to flirt with such a pretty girl, he knew this could only jeopardise his chances with Lucy – particularly with her mother looking on – so he behaved just as he ought, responding to Annabel politely and then turning his attention once again to Mrs Wightwick.

The two girls had arranged to meet the following day for a walk in Sydney Gardens and when they did, Annabel could scarcely contain herself until they were at a sufficient distance from Lucy's maid or Mrs Wainwright to be able to speak privately.

"Such a gentleman! And what a delightful smile! Not only is he handsome, but he can dance well and has charming manners – so, Lucy, tell me more about the unknown Mr Lord," whispered Annabel excitedly.

"Mr King told Mama that he is only recently arrived from the West Indies," responded Lucy, "but otherwise I know nothing about him. Oh – he has taken lodgings in Orange Grove and wants to get to know Bath."

"Does he own a large plantation? Or is he a younger son? Does he plan to live in England or to return to the West Indies?"

When Lucy shook her head, laughing, Annabel said firmly, "We must invite him on all our outings, and I shall make it my business to find out as much as possible about him and to encourage him to make you an offer."

Lucy blushed, but did not remonstrate with her friend. She, too, was curious about Mr Lord; he was by far the best-looking young man who had shown an interest in her, although rather swarthy, and there was romance and excitement in the fact that he came from the West Indies, about which she had heard so much from her father.

Over the following weeks, Annabel was as good as her word. She persuaded her mother to organise a visit to the theatre and to invite Lucy with her parents, then pressured her brother Peter to attend also and to invite Mr Lord, to whom she had artlessly introduced Peter at one of the Assemblies. After some grumbling, Peter good-naturedly agreed despite having no desire to attend a play.

"I can see you're up to mischief, sister. What's your interest in Mr Lord?"

Annabel explained that she was trying to help Lucy, and begged Peter to find out as much as he could. "Could you not take him to a prize-fight, or a cockfight, or something equally horrid?" she asked.

"I can try, Annabel, but he is much older than me and may see it as an imposition. By the by, is there a good farce along with the play to make this theatre outing bearable? If he's any sense, Lord will run a mile rather than spend such a boring evening when he could be playing cards!"

But to Peter's surprise Sam accepted the invitation and he was able to report success to his sister. And during the interval, Peter mentioned somewhat diffidently that he and some cronies planned to attend the prize-fight he had discussed with Adrian Letchworth at the Box Hill picnic. Would Mr Lord be interested in joining them? Sam responded that he would be delighted, and in an aside to Peter admitted that such an outing would be far more to his taste than a visit to the theatre, at which Peter laughed.

Sam also took up Mrs Wightwick's invitation to visit them in the Bathwick house on a Tuesday and, having sent up his card, stayed just the correct half hour before taking his leave of the ladies. Lucy's mother was delighted with him and wrote to her husband (who had once again departed on business) to put into effect her notion of getting him to make some enquiries into Sam's background, and also to suggest that Thomas might wish to return to Bath soon to make the acquaintance of this promising suitor for Lucy.

By now, Sam had made the acquaintance of all of the small circle of friends of the Wightwicks in Bath, and although he spent as much time in Lucy's company as he deemed sensible (or Lucy's mother deemed proper), he also spent time with other male acquaintances he had met while playing cards, attending cockfights or boxing matches or engaged in other male pursuits. It would not do to look as though he was living in Lucy's pocket – he was well aware that he might not be able to secure her as his wife, and he must have contacts able to introduce him to other suitable girls if this venture failed. Besides, he was enjoying himself, and although the lords and ladies of Bath society were as distant and unfriendly as London society had been to him, wealthy commoners (whether landowners or people in trade) were far more in evidence. That they were also of far more use to him as well as more to his taste was another consideration. Sam was not on the hunt for a title but for the funds to keep him in style and idleness, although of course he would not have put it quite so bluntly himself.

The next big outing – at which the whole of Bath seemed to be present – was the balloon ascent discussed at the October picnic. Adrian and Rebecca Letchworth got up a party with Marianne and Jonathan, her husband, Lucy and Stubbs (who happened to be with them on a break from school). Mrs Wightwick was happy to let Marianne chaperone Lucy as she had no desire to view a balloon ascent.

They took two carriages and a picnic. The ascent was scheduled to take place at noon from Beechen Cliff but Adrian had made some enquiries and learned that, because a successful ascent was so dependent on the wind, it could happen earlier or later. They set off at ten o'clock, and quickly found themselves in a throng of traffic all seemingly headed the same way. It was a beautiful autumn day, with a brisk breeze and the sky almost cloudless. The girls were all dressed in their warmest pelisses, with muffs to keep their hands warm and rugs across their knees.

Stubbs (who had just celebrated his thirteenth birthday) was extremely excited, and had procured a dog-eared copy of Tiberius Cavallo's *The History and Practice of Aerostation*, which, while somewhat out of date, had provided him with sufficient information to be able to pelt the adults with facts and questions about ballooning, such as the valves used to control the craft, the silk used to make the bag's covering and why hydrogen was used to inflate the balloon. When they arrived, he quickly hopped out of the carriage and persuaded Adrian to accompany him to the enclosure where the yet-to-be inflated balloon was tethered.

Jonathan manoeuvred his phaeton closer to the landaulet Adrian had driven, so the party could remain in the warm and talk to each other comfortably while they waited to see the ascent.

"Doubtless Mr Letchworth and Stubbs will return when they are hungry," laughed Lucy to Rebecca. "I would be afraid, I think, to go up in such a flimsy craft, but I should like to see the view. Stubbs has been telling me that towns and cities look like models in motion, and that you can see the horizon always at the level of your eye."

"I should love to watch the sunset whilst floating above the treetops," said Marianne wistfully, surprising her two friends for this was much more like the Marianne they had known at school than the demure matron she had become. They all looked at each other, then laughed, and settled down to enjoy a good gossip while waiting for the action to begin. Jonathan sauntered away to talk to some friends who had just arrived.

After about an hour, Adrian and Stubbs returned, both bubbling with enthusiasm and filling their conversation with so many convoluted explanations of unexpected currents of air at high altitudes, speeds of fifty miles per hour, struggles with the valve and the obstacles in the way of landing safely that the ladies protested, and insisted that, despite it still being early, they unpack the contents of the various picnic hampers and sample them before the ascent.

Stubbs had a typical thirteen-year-old boy's healthy appetite and was more than happy to get stuck into the beef and onion pie – still warm from the oven – provided by Cook. His mouth full, he could only point, and shake his sister's arm, when he noticed the silken bag begin to rise slowly above the heads of the crowd as the balloon crew filled it from their hydrogen gas supply. Like the rest of the crowd, the party all turned to watch as the massive crimson and gold balloon rose up straight, straining at its moorings, then all of a sudden soared upwards, the boat-shaped wicker structure beneath it containing the two aeronauts. The wind helped it to rise rapidly, while pushing it towards the north east over the town. Lucy and her friends remained another half hour watching it drift gently away while tucking into more of the delicious picnic foods, but finally Marianne shivered and suggested they go home before they froze to death, so they packed up and followed the crowd – which had already mainly dispersed – back towards town and, in Lucy and Stubbs' case, back to Bathampton.

The following Sunday the whole Wightwick family (for Lucy's father had returned on a brief visit) attended a service in the Abbey. When they came out into the pouring November rain, Sam came hurrying up with an umbrella, which he gallantly offered the ladies. Mrs Wightwick took the opportunity to introduce him to her husband.

Sam bowed. "It is an honour to meet you, sir. Your family has been very kind to me and introduced me to many people in Bath so I no longer feel I am a foreigner in a strange land." Then he turned to Mrs Wightwick. "Let me see if I can obtain a sedan chair for you to carry you to your next destination or your dresses will be ruined by this rain, ma'am."

"You are very obliging, Mr Lord. We are visiting friends in Bennett Street and you are right, it is by far too wet to walk there today," responded Mrs Wightwick with a smile, casting a speaking glance at her husband.

Sam darted off, taking advantage of what little shelter there was, and after some time managed to secure a chair despite the fierce competition for it caused by the rain. By the time he returned with it, he was dripping from head to toe, and he shook himself like a dog to rid himself of the worst of the wet. He laughed, showing strong, white teeth.

"In Barbados, we have downpours like this during the rainy season, but they generally last ten minutes and then the sun comes out. I still have trouble remembering that here it can rain for days at a time!"

He helped the two ladies into the chair, tipped his hat to Mr Wightwick and waved away the return of his umbrella. "By all means, you and Stubbs use it," he said. "I am already so wet that it cannot make any difference. I shall head back to my lodgings and change." And with that he was off towards Orange Grove.

This event, together with Sam's exquisite manners generally, cemented Mrs Wightwick's warm feelings towards him and made Mr Wightwick inclined to look favourably on him. However, Thomas had already received one slightly disturbing report from a contact with excellent knowledge of the Barbados scene.

Mr Samuel Lord is the younger son of the deceased owner of a small and unprofitable plantation. He was apparently given to some wild excesses and liked to gamble heavily: indeed, he left the island without paying several of his gambling debts, which perforce had to be settled by his elder brother (a sober, well-regarded individual) – to whom, it appears, he had sold his share of the inheritance before he left. I have no wish to pain you, Thomas, but I feel it is also

79

my duty to report that this young man is known to have had several liaisons with married members of island society. The island is an absolute hotbed of intrigue and scandal, but I have no reason to believe that this rumour is untrue. Of course, Mr Lord left Barbados some three years ago and may well have become a more sober person now, and I certainly would not go so far as to suggest he is an out-and-out libertine, but you might wish to learn more about his lifestyle since he arrived in England before deciding what his intentions may be in relation to your delightful daughter.

Thomas had placed the letter in a secret, locked drawer in his desk in Great Bloxwich, but the words were firmly ensconced in his memory. He liked and trusted the individual who had sent it (a shipbuilder from Chepstow with whom he had conducted business on numerous occasions) and had no reason to disbelieve the contents.

If Lucy had been under age, Thomas would have executed a father's right to send Mr Lord packing, but he was well aware that although he could still do so, his daughter was headstrong and might be precipitated into some impetuous and ill-fated action. He was equally aware that Lucy was already almost twenty-three years old and that no one (other than a completely unsuitable, penniless young man in Chepstow) had ever approached him to ask for his daughter's hand in marriage. Knowing that his wife was disposed to look kindly on Sam's suit, Thomas decided to make some more enquiries into Sam's activities since his arrival in England before discussing the contents of the letter with her. It was, after all, entirely possible that the young man had simply been sowing his wild oats in Barbados before he left, but the fact that he had left his gambling debts unpaid bothered Mr Wightwick exceedingly.

He decided that it would be a good idea to get to know Mr Samuel Lord a little better, and to that end invited him to join the Wightwick family on an outing he proposed to Combe Down. This was a village to the south of Bath surrounded by natural woodland and with spectacular views over the Midford Valley, which he knew would please his wife and daughter who might also be interested in the limestone quarries; but Mr Wightwick's real object in going to the village was to visit the new De Montallt paper mill there. The increased demand for paper as a result of an explosion of publishing made him think it might be a good investment.

When he proposed the outing to his wife and daughter, Lucy ran immediately to find their guidebook to Bath and its surroundings.

"Oh Mama, do let us go. It sounds enchanting. Let me read you the description given by Mr John Collinson only a few years ago,

On the summit of Combedown a mile northward from the church, among many immense quarries of fine free stone, are large groves of firs, planted by the late Ralph Allen, esq; for the laudable purpose of ornamenting this (at that time rough and barren) hill. Among these groves is a neat range of buildings belonging to this parish. It consists of eleven houses built of wrought stone, raised on the spot; each of which has a small garden in front. These were originally built for the workmen employed in the quarries but are now chiefly let to invalids from Bath who retire hither for the sake of a very fine air (probably rendered more salubrious by the Plantation of firs) from which many have received essential benefit. The surrounding beautiful and extensive prospects; the wild, but pleasing irregularities of the surface and scenery, diversified with immense quarries, fine open cultivated fields, and extensive plantations of firs…

I went walking with Marianne and Annabel near there last year in a place delighting in the name of Fairy Wood. You know how we both love the scent of pines, I felt most invigorated after our walk."

A visit was agreed for the following week, which gave Mr Wightwick the opportunity to invite Sam to join the party while at Thursday's cotillion ball at which Sam had – as he now regularly did – already ensured his name was written into Lucy's dance card for two dances, one a cotillion and the other a *dance espagnole*.

Lucy would have been happy to have danced with Sam all evening, but her mother was firm in refusing to allow her to commit such a social *faux pas*. Already her friends were commenting on Mr Lord's marked attention to her daughter; no doubt other, less charitable, people were also, and she had no wish to see Lucy's chances thrown away because of inappropriate behaviour.

So it was with some surprise that Mrs Wightwick learned of her husband's invitation to Sam, but she was nevertheless pleased and resolved to ask him later that evening what he had found out about the young man. Mr Wightwick was somewhat evasive when he visited his wife in her room before going to bed, telling her only that he had put out some feelers to people he trusted and still awaited their responses.

The day of their outing dawned grey and dreary, so the ladies made sure they wore strong boots and warm pelisses, for by now it was early December and very cold. Lucy was wearing a new hat which she thought became her rather well, and only hoped that it would not be spoiled by rain. Promptly at 10.30, Sam rode up to their door on a hired horse. He and Mr Wightwick were to ride to Combe Down while the ladies drove (much to Lucy's frustration; she would have preferred to ride also, but her mother did not care to).

Despite the weather, which remained gloomy, the day was enjoyable. The ladies enjoyed an energetic walk in the woods, while Mr Wightwick took Sam with him on his visit to the paper mill and was pleased that Sam asked several shrewd questions of the mill manager about its prospects. It had been built in 1805 on Viscount Hawarden's land and was owned by John Bally, a bookseller in Milsom Street frequented by Lucy and her mother. The paper it produced – both plain and coloured – was of extremely high quality. Thomas was fascinated by the water wheel which drove the plant, thought to be the largest in England at a diameter of 56 feet.

The gentlemen joined the ladies for a stroll through the picturesque village, where the houses were generally built of beautiful limestone from the Combe

Down mine which was also used for many of the buildings in Bath and elsewhere in England. Cottages had even been built to house the mine and mill workers, whereas previously their shelter had consisted of wooden shacks. Mr Wightwick would have liked to visit the mine to see for himself the 'room and pillar' method by which the stone was extracted (where "pillars" of stone were left to support the roof, and open areas or "rooms" were extracted underground before the pillars themselves were partially extracted), but neither his wife nor his daughter showed any enthusiasm for prolonging their stay and wished to return home for dinner, so he abandoned the idea.

Thomas visited his wife's boudoir that evening before bed, wearing a dark green befrogged dressing gown, together with the matching slippers his daughter had given him the previous Christmas. His wife was having her hair brushed out by her maid, but upon seeing her husband asked the girl to pass over her nightcap then told her she could leave. Tying the strings of the cap under her chin, she turned to face Thomas, then sat placidly with her hands folded in her lap waiting for him to tell her what was on his mind.

"I cannot help liking young Mr Lord," he began, without preamble, "but I remain concerned. I have as yet had no indication that he possesses the wherewithal to maintain a wife and household. I have received a report that he left behind debts of honour when he sailed from Barbados, and if true that worries me on two counts. Firstly, it is unacceptable to leave gambling debts unpaid and, secondly, I have no wish to see Lucy – our only daughter – married to an inveterate gambler. Such a marriage would cause her nothing but heartache, he would run through her settlement in no time, and then where would she be? If they were to live in England, he would be a constant drain on our resources. If Mr Lord wishes to return to his family home, she could end up living the life of a pauper. The plantation owned by the Lords is not, as I understand it, a particularly profitable one – and it is not clear to me whether Mr Samuel Lord has any further claim on it in any case. What would they live on?"

His wife made soothing noises. "Mr Lord is a very pretty behaved gentleman. I have witnessed no evidence of straitened circumstances. He has been paying court assiduously to Lucy – indeed, I have on at least two occasions had to speak severely to her to prevent her spending too much time in his company. To his credit, Mr Lord has never sought to monopolise her, or to stand up with her more than twice in an evening. He is kind to Stubbs, too."

"Of course, we are not yet certain what his intentions are, but Mr Lord is certainly behaving like a suitor and I would not be surprised if he asks to meet me. Are you sure of Lucy's feelings in this matter?"

"She has indicated clearly to me that she would welcome an offer from Mr Lord. I do not believe that she has ever encouraged any man's attentions the way she does with him and am sure she would be quite cast down were she not to receive an offer."

"I still think we should be circumspect, Lucy. I hope to have a report soon on his time in London. I believe he spent two or three years there before coming to Bath, and any information I can glean on that might be instructive. It would be helpful to know where he lodged, so that I can discover if he left any unpaid bills there. Did he come to Bath simply because he was overdrawn in London? He has no connections here, so it seems likely that he is hanging out for a rich wife. That in itself is no crime" – Thomas had, of course, married money when he married Lucy Stubbs – "but I need to be convinced that he will use that wealth wisely."

Mrs Wightwick was able within a few days to provide her husband with the address of Sam's lodgings in London – or rather, the address he chose to provide, for it happened to be one where he had settled up before leaving. Mr Wightwick had taken the trouble to hire a private detective to look into Sam's time in London, so he handed the address over and waited for events to take their course.

As he had predicted, Sam sought an interview with him just before Christmas. He had seized an opportunity when they were walking in Sydney Gardens one day – Lucy's maid, who was an incurable romantic, and sighed soulfully every time she saw them together, following them decorously some ten paces behind – to propose to Lucy. She had blushed, and stammered that he must speak to her Papa, but when Sam pressed her to tell him if she had any feelings for him, she bit her lip, looked up at him and, with her heart beating uncomfortably fast, whispered "yes".

"I shall seek to speak to Mr Wightwick at the earliest opportunity!" declared Sam. "Lucy, you have made me the happiest person on earth."

He did not tell her that he was becoming desperate. His funds, which had seemed immeasurable when he first arrived in England nearly four years previously, were perilously low. He had been very careful to pay all his bills promptly in Bath, and to settle all his gambling debts, but was not sure he could continue to do so for much longer without a big win at the tables – or being able to announce his engagement to a wealthy bride. That would prevent his creditors pressing him for payment.

Thomas had once again been away on business, this time in Wolverhampton. He returned on the 20th of December in order to accompany his wife and daughter back to Hewelsfield, where they planned to spend the festive period. Tipped off by Lucy, Sam knocked at the door of the house in Bathwick early one morning when he knew Thomas would be at home, sent up his card and was duly ushered into Mr Wightwick's study. Sam found his palms were sweating, and he was more nervous than he had expected – but then, a lot hung on the outcome of this meeting.

Thomas invited Sam to take a seat in one of the plush leather armchairs and offered him refreshment, which he declined.

"What can I do for you, Mr Lord?"

Sam had decided that his best approach was to be blunt, and as open as he dared to be about his circumstances. "Well, sir, I have come to ask you for your daughter's hand in marriage."

There was a short silence. Thomas again thought wistfully that if Lucy were still under age, it would be easy for him simply to dismiss the approach and refuse to allow any further contact between the two.

"And can you tell me why I should entertain this request? What will you bring to the union? Where will you live? I need hardly tell you – I am sure you are aware – that I am extremely fond of my only daughter and wish to ensure her future happiness."

"I plan for us to live in Barbados. My father left the Long Bay plantation jointly to me and my brother. It does not, yet, have the standing of one of the major plantations such as Sunbury or Drax, but we have plans to expand it by buying neighbouring estates (or portions of them) as they come to market. We cannot grow sugar at Long Bay and must find suitable land on which to do so. The margins on cane production are far greater than on cotton, as I am sure you are aware, sir."

"As I understand, you sold your inheritance to your brother and I presume that is the money on which you have been living since you came to England. What funds do you have to invest in such a venture?"

Silently, Sam cursed Mr Wightwick's business connections in the West Indies. Clearly, he would need to tread carefully and be inventive.

"I still retain a stake in Long Bay, sir, and that is where I plan we should live initially. Then, as we expand, I would build a separate house on Long Bay land for Lucy and I. I propose, with your agreement and Lucy's, to invest her dowry in that venture."

It was not true that he had any legal stake in Long Bay anymore, but the gambler in him hoped that Thomas would not find that out, rather that his future father-in-law would be impressed by his openness over the use of Lucy's dowry.

Thomas thought wryly that, if he was a rogue, Sam was indeed a very plausible one. "I also understand that you left the West Indies without paying several debts of honour," he said slowly, carefully studying the young man before him. "What is your explanation for this?"

Sam began to break out in a cold sweat, thanking his lucky stars that he had had the forethought to ensure he paid all his bills and debts promptly in Bath. "On my honour, sir, I had no knowledge that I had left any such debts unpaid. I am mortified. May I know how you came by this information? If I knew which debts remained unpaid, I would make every effort to rectify the omission immediately."

Thomas said nothing, looking frowningly at Sam for a long moment. What the young man said could, possibly, be true, but somehow he could not quite believe it. And, although he hid his feelings, he could not help but be surprised that Sam intended to return with Lucy to Barbados. Given the length of his stay in England so far, he had assumed Sam would continue to leave the running of Long Bay to his brother John and live on his share of the profits – assuming there were any – and set up house near the Wightwicks. He was not at all sure he liked the sound of his beloved Lucy being whisked off to the West Indies where he could no longer help her if she encountered any problems.

At last he got up and went over to a side table from which he helped himself to a small glass of madeira, without offering any to Sam. "If you had not known that my daughter's dowry would be large, would you have offered for her?" he asked.

Sam detected a trap. He could express his undying love for Lucy, but he thought her father was too shrewd to fall for that. Or he could nuance the truth and hope that would appeal to him. He took a deep breath,

"It is true, sir, that I could not marry some penniless beauty whatever my feelings might be. As I said, in order to expand the family estate I must take funds back to Barbados. I was lucky enough to meet your daughter and be captivated by her liveliness. I flatter myself that she feels some attraction to me also…"

Thomas, frowning, interrupted him. "I assume you have already spoken to my daughter? I doubt you would have expended so much time and effort without some encouragement from her, however improper in you both such a conversation might be!"

Sam permitted himself to look uncomfortable. "Indeed, sir, I have spoken to Miss Wightwick, and she quite rightly asked me to approach you, which is why I am here today. I do hope you will not forbid the match?"

"I shall not forbid it – but neither shall I countenance it, nor will I countenance an engagement, until I am satisfied as to your prospects, sir. I believe I am correct in thinking your brother is now the head of the family?" Sam nodded. "I shall write to your brother, if you would be so good as to furnish me with his details and will speak to you further on this matter once I have his response. In the meantime, I will not forbid contact between you and Lucy, but I do expect you to behave circumspectly, so that her good reputation is maintained. I shall not invite you to join the family at Hewelsfield; I believe a period of quiet reflection during which you do not see one another could be beneficial, but you may call on us once we return to Bath in January."

Once again, Sam cursed inwardly. There would be no response from Barbados for at least twelve weeks, and by then his financial situation would be desperate. There was little he could do, however, but accept Mr Wightwick's decision with every appearance of good grace. He rose and bowed.

"Thank you, sir. May I take this opportunity to wish you a merry Christmas? And to say that I look forward to seeing you again in the New Year."

"I bid you good day, sir. Until January," said Thomas, ringing the bell for a footman to show Sam out.

Lucy had sent her maid Betty to lie in wait for Sam to leave her father's study and give him a message. Excited to be playing a part in a real-life romance, Peggy was on the lookout from the basement kitchen, and scurried up the stairs as Sam, clapping his hat on his head, descended the main stairs from the front door.

"If you please, sir," said Peggy breathlessly, her hands clasped tightly in front of her apron, dropping a hasty curtsey, "Miss Lucy said to tell you that she would be visiting the library tomorrow morning at around eleven o'clock, sir…" She tailed off uncertainly, thinking that the young master looked like a thundercloud, frowning angrily at her. But Sam answered her pleasantly enough.

"Thank you. Tell your mistress I shall see her there." And with that, as Peggy bobbed another curtsey, he strode off down the hill to the centre of Bath. The maid scurried indoors to report her conversation to her mistress.

"He was scowling, Miss Lucy. If the meeting had gone well with the master he would be smiling, would he not?"

Lucy did not encourage any further conversation but thanked the girl and wondered when would be the best time to approach her father. She waited until she knew her mother was busy with Cook and the housekeeper in the kitchen, then made her way to the study. Timidly, she tapped on the door.

"Come!"

Her father was seated in one of the armchairs, frowning over his spectacles (he had recently found difficulty reading) at some papers covered with intricate figures. When he saw who was standing in the doorway he beckoned to Lucy, although the frown did not lift.

"Come in and close the door." Lucy did as she was told and approached warily. For once she was at a loss to know how to start the conversation, but Thomas put her out of her misery by doing so himself.

"You want to know about my conversation with Mr Lord. Well, Lucy, I will tell you some, though not all, of what passed between us. But first, you must know that I am very displeased with you for speaking to him before he spoke to me, and your mother will be horrified by your behaviour."

"Oh, Papa, you will not tell Mama? I know she will be cross, although she is very fond of Mr Lord. And I did say that he must speak with you…"

"But only after indicating that you would welcome his advances! That is not how a well-bred young lady should behave, and well you know it!"

Lucy blushed, and hung her head. Then, knowing her father could never be angry with her for long, she went over to his chair and sat on the arm, putting her hand on his shoulder. "I am sorry if I was unladylike, Papa, but please tell me what passed between you and Mr Lord?" she wheedled.

"I told him I would not forbid the match…" Mr Wightwick had to stop speaking as his daughter hugged him ruthlessly. "But," he continued, standing and holding Lucy away from him by her wrists, "I also told him that I will countenance no betrothal or announcement unless and until I receive satisfactory information from the head of his family regarding his prospects."

Lucy looked pleadingly at her father. "I may continue to see him, Papa, may I not?"

"When we return to Bath after the Christmas period. He will not be coming to Hewelsfield. I think it best for everyone to put a little distance between the two of you." And then, as his daughter looked crestfallen, he put his hands on her shoulders and gave her a little shake. "It is for a few weeks, Lucy. You are my only daughter, and I do not want you to contract an alliance in haste which you may regret at leisure."

"How could I do that, Papa, when he is the only man for whom I have any real feelings?" she cried, conveniently forgetting that a few weeks earlier she had thought she could be comfortable being married to Adrian Letchworth. "Besides, he inherited a plantation in Barbados so must certainly be able to support a wife – and even if he could not, my dowry is quite large, is it not?"

Thomas looked at her unhappily. He had no desire to share his suspicions with her that Mr Samuel Lord was a fortune hunter and a gambler with little capacity for hard work – or to tell her of the rumours concerning his womanising. So, for once in his life, he took refuge in playing the role of a righteous father.

"That is enough, Lucy," he said sternly. "I will make no decision until I have received the information I require from Barbados. Then, we shall see. I make no promises. In the meantime, you will behave decorously. I begin to think that spending the Season in Bath, which your Mama teased me into agreeing to, is not conducive to good behaviour. You know you have a tendency to be too impulsive. I cannot and will not allow you to ruin your life by marrying someone who may not be quite all that he seems. I expect you to accede to my decision in this, Lucy. I know your mother was disappointed that you did not contract a marriage as a result of your first Season, but I wish to see you happy and saw no evidence that you showed a decided preference for any of the young men that you met so I was content for you to remain unwed a while longer. Now you are showing a decided preference for Mr Lord, I simply wish to ensure, insofar as is possible, that you will be comfortable and cared for should you marry him, for once you are married, there is nothing I can do."

Lucy had been about to burst into a passionate speech to her father about his failure to understand, but his last words gave her pause. Unhappily, she nodded.

"Very well, father. I shall do as you ask and wait until the new year. But," as she lifted her chin defiantly, "I will not change my mind, and nor will Mr Lord!"

When Lucy had gone, Thomas slumped back into the armchair, his business papers abandoned, and fiddled with his spectacles. Although the first report he had received on Sam remained locked away at the Bloxwich property, he knew the wording almost by heart. He had still not received any information about Sam's activities in London and did not expect to for several weeks yet but hoped very much that it would indicate a reformed character. He did not want to forbid his daughter to see Mr Lord but her welfare was at stake, and without comfortable reports from both the private detective and from John Lord he would feel compelled to do so.

Lucy thought she would miss her friends, and most particularly Sam, over the Christmas period, and she moped throughout the entire journey from Bath to Hewelsfield. The weather had turned cold and clear, and frost still lay on the ground when they set out. There was a hustle and bustle around the coach, with the servants heaping fur coverlets and down pillows in for the four Wightwicks, as well a sturdy basket of provisions (hard-boiled eggs, cheese, a fresh loaf of bread, cherry comfits, wine and small ale) to sustain them on the first leg of their journey. They were to rest the first night at Bristol before heading for the Old Passage to cross the Severn for the second and final stage.

However, Christmas was always a busy time in the Wightwick household, as it had become the tradition for several of her mother's family to come and stay with them, and Lucy found it difficult to be miserable for very long in the presence of her cousins Sabrina and Eliza, both lively girls and part of a family of fourteen siblings. She liked their parents, Elizabeth (her mother's sister) and James Rann too, and was only sorry that she would not see their son, her cousin James, this time as he had left – looking proud as punch in his new regimentals, according to her aunt – in the summer to fight in the Peninsular War. The days passed quickly, with rides and several hunt outings across the frozen countryside, games of loo and fish before a roaring fire, impromptu dancing, putting on an amateur play, attending church, and a great deal of eating and drinking, where formality was tossed to the winds. In short, Lucy enjoyed herself.

Meanwhile, her father received a report from the private detective he had hired, and it did not make for comfortable reading. While it was clear from the misspelling that its author was not used to writing and probably had received little education, the message was obvious. Samuel Lord had been no paragon of virtue while in London and had failed to pay his bills on several occasions. He had switched lodgings regularly and left at least two landlords out of pocket; and his tailor had never received a penny from him following the first payment on account. He had returned to his lodgings on more than one occasion late at night following an evening's heavy drinking, and when one of his rather boisterous friends had broken some of the landlady's best glasses and spilt cheap wine all over the carpet – her pride and joy – had become extremely aggressive and belligerent when she suggested he pay for the damage. She had thrown him out the following day. He spent much of his time frequenting gambling dens and brothels, although he also engaged in admirable manly pursuits such as riding in the park, boxing and learning how to fight with a sword-stick, and of course visiting all the sights of London.

Thomas read and re-read the report, which was blotched and written on poor quality paper, then folded it and locked it away in his desk drawer. He thought long and hard about whether he should share its contents with Lucy or his wife, and in the end decided to give Sam the benefit of the doubt by asking him, on their return to Bath, to justify himself. He did not want to see Lucy's gaiety during their time at Hewelsfield dissipated. He knew it was likely he would have to have an unpleasant conversation with his daughter at some point – unless he could persuade Sam to withdraw gracefully on his own account – but he was not at all sure that she would believe any of the negative stories about Sam or, indeed, pay any heed to them if she did. She seemed to be head over heels in love with him.

He found it hard to enter into all the festivities which was unlike him, but his wife put it down to some business transaction that had not turned out the way he had wished. He volunteered to return Stubbs to school and left the women to return to Bath on their own, rather than have to put on a brave front of false gaiety.

Since he went straight from Stubbs' school to Great Bloxwich to meet with his agent, it was not until the third week of January that he re-joined the family in Bath. He was agreeably surprised that Sam appeared to have taken his words to heart and was no longer living in Lucy's pocket or visiting her at home more than once a week, but he was surprised that Lucy seemed to be taking it in her stride. Of course, he was unaware that the two had met in town – when his daughter was ostensibly visiting Annabel – and that Sam had explained that, given the distinctly lukewarm nature of her father's attitude to his proposal, it would be better for them to be extremely careful and give no rise to suspicion that they continued to see rather more of each other than her parents were aware of.

Lucy, while she was uncomfortable with the need for subterfuge, accepted the wisdom of this, but it also – as Sam had hoped – made her rebellious. She was all for confronting her father on his return, but Sam advised her against it, hoping to fan the flames of her rebellion further. For he was already contemplating a very risky idea, a runaway marriage.

In an ideal world, Sam thought crossly, he would have been able to charm Mr Wightwick as easily as he had charmed Lucy's mother and the betrothal of Miss Lucy Wightwick and Mr Samuel Hall Lord would already be a prominent entry in the London and Bath newspapers. As it was, his only option was to manipulate Lucy's sometimes tempestuous nature by persuading her that her father was about to forbid them to see each other again. Sam had not had to try very hard to make Lucy fall in love with him and was convinced that if she thought they were to be parted she would accede to even the most outrageous suggestion to prevent this. And a runaway marriage was extremely outrageous. It would ruin her socially were it to become public knowledge, and could result in her financial prospects being diminished – but Sam was gambling that Mr Wightwick's innate fondness for his daughter made it extremely unlikely that he would cut her off without a penny.

Sam knew that, in law, Lucy's father could not prevent them marrying because Lucy was already of age. He was also aware that, when Thomas received a response from John Lord, he would know that Sam had lied to him about retaining an ownership stake in Long Bay and that he really was the fortune hunter he feared. Thomas would then do everything in his power to stop Lucy making what would be a totally unequal match – and he could easily prevent Sam and Lucy meeting by taking her away to Hewelsfield or Great Bloxwich. Sam was almost broke and could not afford to waste any more time wooing Lucy or on having to start over again in some other town with another eligible, well-dowered girl.

Sam was prepared to gamble that, were there to be a runaway marriage, her parents would quickly come round to accepting the situation with good grace, partly to avoid a scandal but also because their only daughter was clearly so in love with him, and once he was married to the rich Miss Wightwick, he would have little to fear from creditors – and would be able to pay for his lodgings.

Sam had no wish to frighten Lucy away, so he did not mention the idea of a runaway marriage to her but went ahead nevertheless with his plan. Having looked up what was required in the library, he knew that in order to avoid the reading of the marriage banns (which would announce to everyone in Bath what he was up to and might be stopped by Mr Wightwick) he would need to get a marriage licence. He wrote to the office of the Bishop of Bath and Wells to apply for a one according to the 1757 Marriage Act and awaited a reply. A week later, he had a response inviting him to the Bishop's Palace at Wells to make his sworn statement that there was no impediment to the match. He told Lucy that he had to go away for a few days on business, hired a gig – which was as much as he could afford, although he would have liked to drive a curricle – and set off on the twenty-mile stretch for Wells.

Despite its small size, Wells had city status by virtue of its Cathedral. It was a bustling market town, dominated by the Cathedral and Bishop's Palace. Sam found a room at the Crown Inn; he had to share it with three other travellers as the place was extremely busy. He saw his horse stabled, wandered around the town, returned to the inn for supper and went to bed, where he got little sleep as one of his companions snored extremely loudly all night.

The following morning, after a quick breakfast, Sam walked across to the Palace, where he had to ask several times for directions to guide him to the right office. The Bishop's secretary kept him waiting some thirty minutes, but finally he was ushered into a big, light, airy office which looked more like a huge drawing room thanks to the furnishings, the only item to suggest its real purpose being the large walnut bureau behind which the secretary sat.

The business was conducted remarkably speedily. Sam made his sworn statement – to the effect that he and Lucy were not related, that there were no previous marriages, and that both parties were of age – paid his ten shillings and folded the precious paper in his breast pocket. He was informed sternly that the marriage must take place within three months in a church or chapel in an area where either Sam or Lucy had already lived for four weeks. Sam indicated that he understood and took his leave, heading back to the Crown where he called immediately for his gig to be made ready, settled up his bill and set out on his way back to Bath. He was relieved that he had not, as he had half expected, had to go to the expense of an additional night at Wells or, indeed, an additional day's hire of the gig.

By the time he reached his lodgings in Orange Grove, he was cursing the gig and never wanted to set eyes on one again. Gigs were open to the elements, so Sam had taken a gamble on the January weather remaining dry when he chose to hire one for his trip. On the road to Wells he had been lucky, but on the return journey the heavens opened as he drove through Ston Easton, so that both he and the tired horse were soaked and bedraggled by the time he returned the hired equipage. He hoped none of his Bath acquaintance had seen him and shouted for the landlady's son to prepare him a bath as soon as he entered the door to his lodgings.

Sam woke the next morning with a sore throat and a raging fever; clearly his soaking had resulted in a chill. It was a Thursday, and he had hoped to see Lucy at the cotillion ball at the Assembly Rooms in the evening but felt too ill to do anything other than huddle in his room, shivering. The landlady made him a steaming mustard bath and insisted he sit with his feet in it, but he did not take her up on her offer to have her daughter fetch the doctor to him, or even purchase some medicine. he did not want to spend any more of his dwindling money unless he had to.

By Sunday he felt somewhat better. Besides, the landlady had decided he needed mothering and would not leave him alone, which he found trying. So, having ascertained that the day was crisp and cold, he dressed and strolled, with something less than his usual jauntiness, towards the Cathedral, where he expected to see the Wightwicks after they attended Sunday Service.

They were standing among a group of friends near the entrance to the Cathedral, and Lucy was chattering animatedly to Adrian Letchworth. Sam's heart missed a beat. As far as he could see, Adrian was the only possible competitor for Lucy's hand, and it would be too galling to lose her now. He quickened his step and, as he approached the group, bowed to Mrs Wightwick and the lady she was talking to, whom he recognised but whose name he could not quite remember.

"Mr Lord! We quite thought you had abandoned us," Lucy's mother said. "Was your trip a success?"

"Yes, indeed, ma'am; only I got soaked in a rainstorm on the return journey and caught a chill. I have been abed these past few days."

Mrs Wightwick tut-tutted, and tried to persuade Sam to try some of her favourite remedies, but he laughed. "No, no, ma'am. I have no desire to quack myself. I am still feeling very weak but it will pass."

Lucy was still talking to Adrian Letchworth a few yards away and had made no effort to join Sam and her mother. He deduced that she was miffed at his absence and wanted to punish him for it. So he bowed to Mrs Wightwick and walked across to the pair.

"Morning, Letchworth. Miss Wightwick." He bowed slightly in their direction, then realised he was going to sneeze. He pulled a large handkerchief from his pocket and sneezed into it twice.

"Mr Lord, are you unwell?" asked Lucy with concern. She had, in fact, been studiously ignoring his presence, hurt that he had not been to see her all week, but one look at his drawn face, pink nose and puffy eyes made her feel sorry for him.

"I was caught in an absolute downpour earlier this week and suffered a chill. I am on the mend but had to keep to my bed for a few days. You would have thought I would be used to torrential rain – the rain in Barbados is always thus – but then, the island is always warm, and I think my constitution has still not acclimatised to the English weather after all these years."

Both Lucy and Adrian made suitably compassionate noises, and the talk turned to the gossip of Bath since Lucy had last seen Sam. Meanwhile, Lucy cast about in her mind for ways in which she could indicate to Sam where he might meet her for a private conversation. She broke in rather gauchely on the two men's conversation.

"I have just finished reading *Marmion*. Have either of you gentlemen read it? It is a truly exciting poem by Walter Scott, about the Battle of Flodden." When Adrian and Sam exchanged appalled glances, she laughed, "You know, poetry is not only intended for women to read. After all, it is frequently written by men! You should try it. I have just completed *Marmion*, and must return it to the lending library tomorrow, as they say there is a long waiting list for it. Will your sister be in town, Mr Letchworth? Perhaps she would like to meet me at the library after I have finished my chores, at about noon?"

Adrian promised to give his sister the message, while Sam clearly understood that there was an underlying message for him. The little group then broke up, with Sam smiling comfortingly at Lucy as he bowed farewell to reassure her, wordlessly, that he would meet her before noon.

He waited until they had all left the area then made his way inside the Abbey. It was quiet now, the service finished. A verger was trimming the candles after snuffing them out, and the haze and smell of their smoke drifted up around the Gothic arches towards the soaring roof. Sam hesitated for a moment, then squared his shoulders and went up to the man.

"I wish to enquire about arranging a wedding in the Abbey. Could you direct me to the Deacon, sir?"

The verger turned and looked at Sam. "If it is only information you require, sir, I may be able to help you. When would you be wishful for the marriage to take place? And would this be your wedding, sir, or are you making enquiries for a friend, perhaps?"

Sam hesitated, considering briefly whether it would be more sensible to indicate the latter, then he gave a mental shrug and answered firmly, "My own wedding."

"May I congratulate you, sir? Perhaps you would come with me to the vestry, and we can discuss this more privately."

The verger led the way to quite a long, narrow simply furnished room lined with hanging space for vestments along the walls, with a wooden bench and a small table. Once they were both seated, he folded his hands in his lap and asked again when Sam wanted to be wed.

"I would like to arrange it quite soon, within the next three months if possible," Sam answered. He did not want to give the man the impression this was a runaway match, but at the same time his creditors would be all over him if he was unable within a very short period to indicate to them that his financial situation had changed for the better.

The verger dipped his head to acknowledge this. "Well, sir, you must understand that you will need to allow two weeks for the banns to be read…"

Sam interrupted him, "Oh there will be no need. I have obtained a licence."

"In that case, sir, you will need a ring and two witnesses (or I could make myself available as a witness if needs be); and you will need to arrange the ceremony a few days in advance, to ensure that a member of the Abbey's clergy is available to conduct the service."

"Much obliged to you, Sir – Mr…?"

"Russell is my name sir. Just ask for me when you are ready to make the final arrangements and I will ensure all goes smoothly."

Sam tipped his hat to Mr Russell and bade him good day, well-pleased with his morning's work. He decided to repair to the steakhouse for a luncheon, suddenly realising that he was ravenous having eaten very little for the past week.

Sam arrived at the lending library promptly at eleven o'clock the following day but had to kick his heels and pretend an interest in the London newspapers that he did not possess while he waited. One story that did hold a passing interest for him was that the Admiralty had dispatched two vessels, the 32-gun fifth-rate frigate HMS Solebay and the Cruizer-class brig-sloop HMS Derwent, to police the African coast in pursuance of the new Slave Trade Act, which banned 'the Purchase, Sale, Barter, or Transfer of Slaves, or of Persons intended to be sold, transferred, used, or dealt with as Slaves' from any part of Africa.

Sam curled his lip. Did these sanctimonious hypocrites realise what would happen to their supply of cotton and sugar without slave labour? It would diminish as struggling plantations went out of business, and the price of what remained would soar. What was more, the Royal Navy itself used enslaved Africans in its dockyards in Jamaica and Antigua! At least they had only abolished the trade in slaves; Long Bay, like other plantations on Barbados, had foreseen that this might happen and introduced a breeding programme to bring on new slave stock.

Lucy arrived half an hour later. The weather had turned cold and wet again, and both her shoes and the hem of her dress below her pelisse were dark with rainwater. She was breathing hard as though she had been hurrying. She went straight to the library desk and handed over her copy of *Marmion*, then looked around for Sam. He thought she looked a little like a startled faun, eyes darting in every direction.

He folded the newspaper and tossed it on the table before strolling over to meet her.

"Miss Wightwick, how delightful to meet you here," he said as he bowed to her. "I see you have been caught in the rain – your shoes are soaked. Would you care to wait here with me in the hope that the shower will pass, or at least lessen? I could then escort you to your next appointment."

He noticed that she was trembling and hoped that she was not going to fall into a fit of hysterics when he outlined his plan to her. He led her over to the reading area where he had previously been sitting. It was unusually empty, probably because of the inclement weather.

"I spoke to Papa yesterday," Lucy began abruptly, in a low voice. "I hoped he would have seen by now that we really do care for each other and wish to be married, but he said he had not received any positive reports about your behaviour. I don't know what he means, or who he asked, he would not tell me! I do not know what to do, how can we persuade him?"

Sam glanced around quickly to ensure there was no-one within hearing. He took Lucy's trembling hands in his and squeezed them gently then, in an equally low voice, said, "Lucy, you are of age. You do not require your father's permission to wed. We could simply get married and then tell your parents after the fact…"

Lucy's eyes widened as she looked up at him in shock. "Elope, you mean? I would be ruined! Father would never forgive me! Are you mad?"

"It is true that I am madly in love with you, Lucy, but I would not do anything you do not wish for! We do not have to elope. We could be married here, in Bath, by licence. I do not see how else we are going to be together if your father continues to oppose the match."

"Oh – I do not know! I am so miserable. I must speak to Papa again – perhaps Mama can persuade him? We cannot speak more of this now, there is Rebecca arriving."

Lucy raised her gloved hand to wave to Rebecca and invite her over. Sam stayed a few minutes then took his leave, while the two young ladies sauntered arm-in-arm towards Milsom Street.

Sam was not ill-pleased with the morning's activity. He had planted the seed in Lucy's head about a secret wedding, and rather thought that the fact she could be married in Bath rather than eloping to Gretna Green (which he would be unable to afford in any case) might persuade her. He really wanted to tie the knot before Mr Wightwick could receive a response from brother John, as this was likely to indicate that Sam no longer had any legal or financial stake in the Long Bay plantation. Once Mr Wightwick knew that he was just an impecunious younger son, he would redouble his opposition to the match and doubtless forbid Lucy to wed him. The fact that she was already of age would count for nought. She was highly unlikely to fly in the face of a direct order from her father.

Sam rather thought that if he made himself less available to Lucy, she would become increasingly frustrated and more prepared to accede to his suggestion. So Lucy looked for him in vain at the Cotillion Ball that week, and he did not call at the house in Bathampton. When she attended Sunday service at the Abbey, she noticed he was in the congregation at some distance from the Wightwicks, and was glad when he came over to the family afterwards to pay his respects, but of course there was no opportunity for any private conversation. Lucy noticed that her father was very stiff and cold towards Sam and determined to seek her mother's help that evening to change his mind.

During the evening when the tea tray was brought in after supper, the two ladies were alone in the drawing room while Mr Wightwick enjoyed a solitary glass of port in the dining room. Lucy waited until the maid had left, took a deep breath and said, "Mama, I need to talk to you. You like Mr Lord, do you not?"

Her mother turned; her eyebrows raised in surprise. "You know I do, Lucy. Whatever is the matter?"

"Papa appears to have taken a dislike to him but will not tell me why. You know Mr Lord asked Papa for my hand before Christmas? I would very much like to marry him and hope that you may be able to find out the reason for Papa's prejudice and persuade him otherwise."

"I will speak to your father. I thought that he welcomed the fact that you had finally formed an attachment for an eligible young man, but I do know that he commissioned a report on Mr Lord's activities in England before he moved to Bath. He has not told me about its findings. Indeed, I do not know whether he has yet received it. But I am sure he only has your best interests at heart. If Mr Lord is all that he appears to be your father will have no objection."

She nodded to indicate that the subject was closed, and asked Lucy to help her sort the heavy skeins of silks which had that day arrived, so that she could begin her new piece of embroidery.

When her father joined them, Lucy stayed only to drink a bowl of tea then made her excuses and went away to bed. Mrs Wightwick, her fingers still busy with the silks, looked over at her husband who was reading a long letter from Thomas Evans the Chepstow timber merchant.

"Thomas, have you thought any further about the prospect of Mr Lord as a son-in-law? Lucy has remained remarkably steadfast in her attachment to him, and I should so like to see her safely wed by the end of this Season."

Mr Wightwick folded the letter and removed his glasses. "I have not told little Lucy this, but I have now received two negative reports on Mr Lord. I await a letter from his elder brother, to whom he sold his share of the inheritance, which will I hope clarify his status with regard to the West Indies property. I am concerned that Mr Samuel Lord appears to be an inveterate gambler who 'forgets' to pay his debts of honour; a pauper; and possibly a libertine to boot. I believe, my dear, that marriage to such a one could only cause our daughter heartache."

Mrs Wightwick sank back in her chair, shocked to the core. Feeling faint, she groped for her smelling salts on the little table next her and held them under her nose.

"Mr Lord's behaviour in Bath has been impeccable. I have heard nothing to his detriment, and his demeanour is that of a well-bred young man. No doubt he gambles – everyone does. You yourself are fond of a game of cards. Are you sure, Thomas, that these reports do not exaggerate the sins of youth, and that he may have improved with a little maturity?"

"That is why I wish to wait for Mr John Lord's response to my letter before I pass judgment. If he tells me that his younger brother no longer has any status in relation to Long Bay, I will know for a fact that Lucy's would-be husband lied to me, and that he does not have the wherewithal to provide for her. Add to that a questionable character, and he hardly seems to me the sort of prospective beau I would expect you to endorse."

"Lucy will be twenty-three next Saturday. She will end an old maid unless we find her an eligible young man very quickly. I was convinced she had found one in Mr Lord! Oh, Lud!" After having recourse to the smelling salts again, she continued tearfully, "Have you told her any of this? Have you forbidden the match?"

"I have told her only that I have received no favourable reports of Mr Lord. I have not forbidden the match – yet; I thought that likely only to provoke rebellion. Lucy is headstrong, and I do not want her to do something she will regret. She might take it into her head to elope…"

Mrs Wightwick gasped. "I am sure she would do no such thing! She must know that it would ensure she was rejected by much, if not all, of Society. A flight to Gretna Green? The scandal it would create! I should be so ashamed! And there is no need, if you have not forbidden the match."

"Exactly so. If I do have to forbid it, I will tell Lucy everything I have found out about her suitor. I am afraid he is a fortune hunter. Better for her to have a disappointment now – if she does not wed (though I see no reason why she should not do so later), I can provide for her and provide for her handsomely. If she marries this man, I will be unable to do anything. I cannot in all conscience withhold her dowry, but will I get any commitment from him that he will use it for her benefit?"

Mrs Wightwick went to bed a troubled woman. She tossed and turned all night, trying to think how best to break the news to her only daughter that the man they both thought was an eligible suitor (and handsome into the bargain) might be an imposter. When her maid brought her hot chocolate in the morning, she lay back on the pillows and covered her eyes with one arm, trying to fight the headache which resulted from the worry. Eventually she sighed, rose and dressed in the clothes her dresser, Podmore, had laid out for her. She spoke to Cook and the housekeeper, ordering more flowers to replace the ones in the hall which were drooping badly.

When she reached the breakfast table, Lucy was already there. Mr Wightwick had been and gone and was now immersed in his study. As they were served their tea and toast, and Lucy finished her boiled egg, Mrs Wightwick invited her up to her bedroom for a chat.

Lucy laid down her napkin and followed her mother, wondering what it was she wanted to say away from the servants' hearing. She closed the door and sat, a little nervously, on a small cane chair near the dressing table.

"I talked to Mr Wightwick last night about Mr Lord," her mother began without preamble. Lucy looked up, expectant; she was pleased her mother had responded so quickly to her request. "He reiterated to me what he told you, that he has heard nothing positive about Mr Lord concerning his time in England before he came to Bath. As you and I know, his bearing here has been impeccable, but there are apparently some unanswered questions about his prospects, his gambling, and other things."

Mrs Wightwick knew that she was telling her daughter more than Thomas had wished to do at this stage, but she wanted to prepare her. "The question about his prospects will be answered when Mr Lord's brother responds to your father. You would not wish to marry a pauper, would you, Lucy?"

"I do not care if he has no fortune! Papa will settle a handsome dowry on me, will he not? I do not need to marry a rich man! You were wealthier than Papa when you married him, weren't you, Mama?"

"Your father is not and never has been much of a gambler. If Mr Lord were to play fast and loose with your dowry, you would end up with nothing, and your father will be unable to protect you, particularly if you were living in the West Indies. Furthermore, you may find life very difficult if his attention wanders…"

"But, Mama, we love each other! Do you believe Mr Lord's attentions to be purely those of a fortune-hunter?"

"That's as may be, but do not place your confidence in being able to hold his devotion. It is not even fashionable for a husband to be forever in his wife's company, and I am sure it will not be different on Barbados. How will you feel if he flirts with someone else in a few months and spends less and less time in your company?"

"That is cruel, Mama, and unworthy of you!" cried Lucy with tears in her eyes. She got up to leave, and her mother eyed her uneasily.

"Nothing is decided yet, Lucy. I am sure your father will get a satisfactory answer from Mr Lord's brother shortly, and I will then wholeheartedly support your desire to get married, as will your father."

This discussion took place on Friday morning. On Saturday, Lucy had invited her friends to celebrate her birthday: the afternoon would be spent playing the piano, singing, dancing, playing cards, to be followed by dinner, and she was sure Cook would make a sumptuous cake for the occasion. But it was a subdued Lucy who greeted her guests as they arrived, and she looked in vain for Sam who had promised to come. But she was a proud girl with no wish to wear her heart on her sleeve, so she put up her chin and became the life and soul of the party, winning at a silly game of fish, losing pennies heavily in a game of speculation, playing several songs with gusto on the piano for others to sing to, and dancing country dances with every one of the men including her father. To all intents and purposes she was thoroughly enjoying herself, but inside she was desperate to talk to Sam. She was almost ready to acquiesce to his outrageous plan for a secret marriage, but at the same time she wondered why he had failed to come to her party; was he tired of her already?

On Monday, she was walking with Annabel in Sydney Gardens when Sam came hurrying up to join them. Annabel dimpled at him irrepressibly, but his focus did not waver from Lucy. He pressed her hand.

"Miss Wightwick, I am so sorry to have missed your birthday yesterday. I have a present for you, which I hope you will treasure. Open it in private later" – Annabel made a little *moue* of disappointed curiosity – "and tell me then what you think. Did you enjoy your party?"

Lucy smiled her thanks and tucked the small package into her muff while Annabel gave an animated – and embellished – description of the party with all its singing and dancing that Sam had missed. He laughed, and suddenly burst into a rendition of *Comin' thro' the Rye* by Robert Burns, demonstrating that he was rather a fine baritone. Several startled passers-by looked severely at him, but this just set all three-off laughing, a state which lasted until they reached Molland's, the pastrycook's, in Milsom Street.

When she arrived home, Lucy had several packages secreted in her muff, including Sam's. She carried them up to her room and sat on her bed to open his gift. It was a small oval cameo, a very good likeness of Sam. Lucy held it close then kissed it, before placing it carefully on her dressing table. She sat down at her escritoire and wrote to thank Sam for the present. She added his Orange Grove address and affixed a wafer to seal the letter, then rang the bell for her maid.

"Please see this is delivered to Mr Samuel Lord at Orange Grove, Peggy. And tell him that I shall be in Sydney Gardens tomorrow again at noon. You will accompany me." Peggy curtsied and hurried away, delighted to continue the role she of go-between she had allocated to herself.

Lucy was aware that her mother would not wish to accompany her on Tuesday as this was her 'at home' day. So she set off briskly with Peggy as chaperone at half past eleven. The weather continued fine and dry though very cold, and Lucy wore a new blue, fur-trimmed pelisse which she knew became her. Her heart was beating slightly faster than usual and the cold whipped some colour into her cheeks.

She and her maid reached the Gardens before Sam and, as it was too cold a day to sit on a bench and admire the view, Lucy continued walking briskly along the paths, nodding to acquaintances and occasionally stopping to pass the time of day with them. It was not until a quarter past twelve that Sam made his appearance. He was breathless and apologised for having been 'unavoidably detained'. He was not going to tell Lucy that he had had a run in with his landlord over his lackadaisical approach to paying his rent on time.

Peggy stepped back and walked at a discreet distance behind her mistress and Mr Lord. Lucy recounted the discussion she had had with her mother the previous Friday. "I am so worried that Papa will decide to prevent us seeing each other even at public events, and I don't know whether I can continue to have clandestine meetings like this, it makes me nervous. What are we to do?"

Sam took a deep breath and bet his all on one last throw of the dice. "Do you trust me, Lucy?" When she nodded 'yes', he went on, "Have you had time to consider my suggestion? Will you marry me if I arrange for the ceremony to take place at Bath Abbey?"

Lucy blushed; inside her muff she was wringing her hands. Her heart beat painfully fast, and she wondered how she could even be considering such an outrageous suggestion. But she was now convinced that her father would try to stop them marrying, and she could not bear the idea of being parted from Sam.

It was her turn to take a deep breath. "Yes, Sam, I will. But only if you accompany me afterwards to break the news to Mama and Papa."

"Of course! You do not think I would let you go through that ordeal alone, do you? Leave it to me, Lucy. I will make all the arrangements. Shall I see you at the Cotillion Ball this week? I will let you have any news then." Sam put his hands on her shoulders. "I wish I could kiss you, Lucy – kiss away that look of strain on your face. But I do not think it would help our cause if I were to create a scandal in the middle of Sydney Gardens! So I will control myself until the parson has declared us man and wife. Oh – if for any reason you cannot come to the Assembly Rooms on Thursday, give your maid here a note for me, otherwise, I shall see you there!"

"I only hope I can maintain my composure. What if Mama asks me what is wrong? I am afraid I might blurt out the truth. I must be strong. I know. I will keep your beautiful cameo with me at all times, and that will give me strength. Thank you for the best birthday gift I have ever received."

Sam gently caressed her cheek with his forefinger, then stepped back, bowed, and turned away, pushing his hat on his head at a jaunty angle and swinging his cane as he hurried towards the Abbey to find Mr Russell. Lucy, followed by the faithful and incurably romantic Peggy, waited a few moments then walked more slowly to the print shop in Milsom Street, where she bought a small landscape print that she thought would please her father. She was by this time chilled to the bone and shivering, so she had Betty call up a sedan chair to take her back to Bathampton, with the maid walking beside it.

The house was bustling when they reached it. Her Aunt Elizabeth had arrived for an unscheduled visit, and her father was preparing for one of his periodic business trips to Great Bloxwich and Wolverhampton. She handed her outer clothes to Peggy and hurried to the drawing room to greet her Aunt, who exclaimed at how cold she was when she presented her cheek for Lucy to kiss. She pulled her niece – of whom she was very fond – towards the fire which was blazing merrily in the grate, gently pushing her into the seat closest to the flames, and continued her interrupted discourse with her sister. Since this appeared primarily to be an update of all the gossip related to other members of the family and mutual friends, Lucy allowed her thoughts to wander until her father came into the room to bid them farewell.

"I have a gift for you, Papa. Let me fetch it for you – I think it just perfect for Wightwick House." She ran upstairs to her room to collect the package and pressed it into his hands on her return as she stood on tiptoe to kiss his cheek. "Goodbye, Papa. When will you be back?"

"I shall be away no more than a week. I must see Caxton" – Caxton was his agent – "to resolve a problem that has arisen with one of the tenants. Apparently, he has the lawyer lined up to meet me too. And I hope to talk to one or two gentlemen about the potential benefits of investing in a coal mine."

He turned to give his wife a farewell kiss, bowed briefly to Elizabeth and was gone. Unbidden, the thought came into Lucy's head that she might be a married lady the next time she saw him. She sat down hurriedly to still a sudden trembling at the enormity of it all. Her mother regarded her with concern.

"You are still shivering, Lucy. I hope you have not taken a chill by going out on such a cold day. I shall give you spirits of hartshorn[3] and Gascoigne's powder to ensure you do not contract one of your putrid sore throats."

Lucy smiled weakly and made no demur when her mother rang the bell and summoned her maid, Ruth, to fetch the medicines and a shawl for her daughter. Ruth returned bearing the medication and a beautiful India shawl, deep amber in colour, with a rich and variegated fringe and border. It was designed to be drawn negligently through each arm so as to form a flowing drapery on the right side of the body, but Mrs Wightwick wrapped it tightly around Lucy's neck and shoulders to avert the threatened sore throat. Lucy stroked the beautiful fabric and listened dreamily to her mother and aunt gossiping as she gradually thawed out.

---

[3] Smelling salts

She was just beginning to feel hungry when the butler entered to announce that dinner was ready. Mrs Wightwick prided herself on an excellent table whether the family was at Hewelsfield, Great Bloxwich or Bathampton, and there was always sufficient to feed several unexpected guests as well. Today there was fried sole, boiled beef, woodcock in bechamel, roast leg of mutton with sweet sauce, batter pudding and drippings, macaroni and tarts, served with an abundance of the good wines Mr Wightwick liked and which, despite the constant wars with France and Spain, never seemed to be in short supply. By way of dessert there were Chantilly cream, Lucy's favourite apple tart, cheesecakes and some filberts.

Lucy carried the dish of filberts back to the drawing room after the meal, and the three ladies played whist together all evening accompanied by glasses of sweet wine. Tuesday was card assembly day at the Rooms, and Elizabeth would like to have attended; but Mrs Wightwick was reluctant to allow her daughter to become too accustomed to such a pastime because, she felt, the modern attitude to gambling was far too lax so she was steadfast in refusing to go unless Lucy was temporarily under the care of some other matron.

Lucy was on a winning streak, and enjoyed herself so much that for a while she forgot to worry about her promise to Sam and whether she would become a social outcast, but it all came flooding back when she was getting ready for bed and, having tied her nightcap firmly under her chin, she placed Sam's cameo under her pillow, crawled under the bedclothes and burst into floods of tears. She slept very badly and emerged at the breakfast table heavy-eyed, which her mother put down to her catching a chill the previous day which led to further physicking.

She passed the day in a bit of a dream, keeping close to the fire in the drawing room and playing little part in the conversations with a steady stream of visitors. Even Annabel, avid for news of Lucy's relationship with Sam, failed to draw her out, but was pleased to hear that she still planned to attend the Ball the following day. They arranged to meet up before the ball at cotillion practice in the tea room as usual, and Annabel could only hope her friend would be more forthcoming then.

Still in a bit of a dream (probably brought on at least in part by the laudanum drops Mrs Wightwick kept pressing on her), Lucy accompanied her mother and her aunt on a visit to the shops and library on Thursday morning and to the tea room in the afternoon. Worried that she might inadvertently tell Annabel the enormous secret that weighed on her, she told her instead of Sam's birthday gift and discreetly drew it out of her pocket to show the cameo off.

"What a shame that it would not be suitable for you to show it in public! It is an excellent likeness, and shows Mr Lord to be very much attracted to you, do you not think, Lucy? Has he asked you to marry him yet? When will your engagement be announced?"

Lucy hushed her, casting a warning glance in the direction of her mother. "Please say nothing, Annabel. Mama knows nothing yet."

Annabel's eyes danced, and she squeezed her friend's arm. "Of course I would not dream of upsetting anything. But how romantic!"

The girls were called sternly to attention by the dancing master, and they spent the next hour practising the moves of the cotillion for the evening. There was no time for more private conversation, for which Lucy was grateful. She longed to confide in somebody but dared not, she must take the most momentous decision of her life without support. She returned home with her mother and her aunt for dinner and went willingly to her room to rest before the ball.

Lucy had bought a new blue underdress for her white lace, high waisted ballgown, together with matching blue satin slippers, and could not help but be pleased with her appearance when she studied herself in the mirror. It gave her courage, and she felt calmer as she descended the staircase to set out for the Upper Rooms. Elizabeth nodded at her approvingly, and Lucy smiled, but by the time they reached their destination her heart was beating uncomfortably fast. She looked around anxiously for Sam, but they had arrived early and there was no sign of him. She was obliged to dance with two other partners before he appeared.

There was a break in the dancing, and Lucy was sipping lemonade with Annabel. Both girls were fanning themselves vigorously, as the room was very hot. Annabel smiled mischievously at Sam and said that they had quite given him up. Sam promptly begged for a dance with each of them and the three engaged in idle chat until the next set formed – or rather, Annabel and Sam did, Lucy was too nervous to do more than nod and smile.

As they took their places on the dancefloor, Lucy looked up at Sam with pleading in her eyes. He smiled comfortingly at her, but it was not really possible to converse on anything serious in such circumstances. Lucy performed the complicated moves of the dance automatically, longing for it to finish. It seemed to go on forever, but finally Sam was bowing and offering to escort her back to her mother. He took the long way round and managed to find an alcove in which they could stop to have a brief conversation.

"I have arranged everything for Sunday, Lucy. All you need to do is find an excuse to stay in town after Service, and I will meet you at the Abbey."

Lucy went pale. It was the news she wanted but also dreaded. Sam was concerned she might faint and create a scene. He took her fan from her limp hand and fanned her with it. "You do still want to marry me, Lucy, don't you?" he asked softly. "I do hope so. It is certainly my most ardent wish."

"Oh, Sam, I do, but I am frightened. What will people think? Will Mama be very angry?"

"I am sure both your parents only want your happiness and will come to accept our marriage very quickly. Your friends may be surprised by the fact that there has been no announcement, but they will forget about it soon enough. But we cannot linger here, that *will* create a scandal. Will you marry me on Sunday, Lucy? If not, I will think you are not serious about me."

Sam was deliberately putting her under some pressure. He wanted to make sure they tied the knot as quickly as possible, or he would have to leave town without paying his bills which would mean Bath would no longer be open to him. But he was treading a delicate tightrope. He did not want to put her under so much pressure as to frighten her off. Aware of her rebellious streak, it had not occurred to him that she might be nervous despite the danger to her reputation of a secret marriage, yet he had to push her. Given his desperate financial situation it was now or never for him.

Miserably, Lucy nodded. She was torn between her desire to be with Sam, and her fear of doing something improper. Desire won. Sam squeezed her hand and beamed at her.

"I had better return you to your Mama, or she will be thinking I have kidnapped you!" he laughed, starting to thread his way once more through the throng of people. "Who is the lady with her? They look alike."

Lucy explained it was her aunt and introduced them.

"Ah – so this is the famous Mr Lord about whom I hear so much!" exclaimed Elizabeth, appraising him.

"It is a pleasure to make your acquaintance, ma'am," responded Sam bowing. He greeted Mrs Wightwick, then asked if he could fetch drinks for the ladies or whether they preferred to wait until refreshments were served in the tea room at nine o'clock, when he would be delighted to escort them all. Mrs Wightwick answered for all of them, saying they would prefer to wait, so Sam bowed again, smiled at Lucy and sauntered off to find Annabel for the promised dance with her.

"Well!" exclaimed Elizabeth. "He is a handsome man, if rather swarthy. Though that is only to be expected I suppose, coming from the West Indies. You appear to have done well for yourself, Lucy. I am sure you will be the envy of all your friends. What are his prospects?"

Lucy's mother answered firmly, "Mr Wightwick is dealing with that side of things. I know he wants to be sure there is sufficient substance behind the façade to keep Lucy in comfort."

"You are fond of him, are you not? He certainly appears to dote on you," Elizabeth said to Lucy, who blushed.

"Yes, Aunt," she said in a low voice, her eyes cast down.

"I know it is *de rigueur* for unmarried girls to appear modest and retiring, but a smile would be appropriate, Lucy! Is everything alright?" Elizabeth asked.

"Oh – yes, Aunt. I would very much welcome it if he were to ask Papa for my hand in marriage, but I would not want to give people cause to laugh at me were it not to happen." Elizabeth nodded thoughtfully and turned to engage in a good gossip with her sister as Lucy's hand was claimed for the next country dance.

Lucy did not see Sam except at a distance for the rest of the evening. She was in anguish. She so wanted to talk through every aspect of their hurried wedding with him, to seek comfort from him that what they planned was acceptable, that she would not be despised and ignored by Society for – to all intents and purposes – eloping with him. Instead of which she had to contain herself and have all the arguments and counter-arguments go round and round in her head, particularly the old adage 'marry in haste, repent at leisure'. And Sam seemed loving yet impatient. If she did not acquiesce to his wishes, would he leave her? And then where would she be? She had attached herself so thoroughly to him that everyone would laugh at her and she would never find another eligible suitor! Oh, why did Papa seem so unwilling to approve their engagement? As a result, by the end of the evening she was only too glad to go home, for her head was pounding.

It had been arranged that Annabel would come over the following morning for the girls to spend some time together. She arrived full of curiosity, and all agog to learn what was happening between Sam and Lucy. By the time Elizabeth – who was a late riser – looked for Lucy to discuss her situation further, her niece was closeted with Annabel in her room. Lucy had asked for a tray of rolls, hot chocolate and fruit to be taken up so that they could talk and play cards together over breakfast without interruption from her mother or her aunt. She was nervous that Annabel might say something outrageous, such as suggesting a runaway marriage, and Lucy would be unable to lie. The last thing she wanted was for her mother to learn what she was planning.

Lucy had taken some valerian for her headache and, although her eyes were still puffy, was feeling better and decidedly hungry. Annabel's appetite always belied her tiny frame, and initially the girls concentrated on their food. But, having finished her second roll and started on a second helping of chocolate, Annabel wiped her mouth with her napkin and said firmly, "Lucy, I will burst if you do not tell me what is going on! I am sure loads has happened and there is more to this story than the cameo Mr Lord gave you. Why are you not happy? It is clear he is very attached to you."

Lucy got up hastily from the small table at which they were breakfasting and went to the window, fiddling with the cords around the curtains. She had decided she would tell Annabel about the questions her father had raised regarding Sam's prospects, his gambling, and his way of life generally before he came to Bath. Without turning around she recounted what her mother had told her the previous week, then promptly burst into tears. Her friend tried to comfort her.

"Mr Lord is so nicely behaved I am sure there is some mistake? Or perhaps the stories relate to his youth, and he was simply sowing his wild oats? Just think of Peter, Mama has hysterics when she hears of his behaviour, but Papa (although he does get very cross with Peter) says he will grow out of it."

"Do you really think so? What if Mr Lord's brother fails to provide Papa with a satisfactory report – or indeed, if he fails to reply at all? I am sure Sam – Mr Lord – will grow tired of waiting and look for another eligible female! I am not pretty enough to keep his attention long, I fear."

"Why, he has not so much as looked at another woman since he met you! I have tried to flirt with him, but he is either uninterested or does not want to create a breach between us, for which I admire him," declared Annabel.

Lucy sniffed, and started to load their breakfast things onto the tray. Annabel snatched a last pear, then helped her friend carry everything downstairs to the kitchen, before scampering back to Lucy's room where they continued the conversation in a desultory way over a game of loo. Lucy was relieved that Annabel did not suggest a runaway marriage so she was not obliged to lie, but she did worry her friend might say something to her mother and impressed on her the need to keep their conversation secret.

After Annabel left, Lucy sat down to practise the piano until she was interrupted by her aunt. Elizabeth had heard all about the doubts surrounding Sam's suitability from her sister; indeed, she knew more than her niece. Concerned, she sat Lucy down by the fire and pointed out that the Wightwicks had Lucy's best interests at heart, and that no father could be expected to be complacent about the possibility of an undesirable suitor. However, Lucy must be brave, no-one was forbidding the union, yet.

Lucy looked up. "But I love him, Aunt Elizabeth. He is the only man I have ever loved or could ever love. And if I am richer than him, does that matter? Mama was wealthier than Papa."

All this was said very calmly, so Elizabeth's concern that Lucy might be contemplating something as extreme as a runaway marriage was quashed, and she did not ask the question.

The Wightwick ladies spent a quiet day on Saturday, with only a couple of visitors despite the weather continuing to be fine. Lucy spent the morning writing a letter to her father, and also one to Miss Priddy, her old governess. She so hoped neither her father nor her governess would feel ashamed of what she was about to do. Later, she went for a walk with her aunt to enjoy the sunshine and then, as the sun went down, the three ladies played at cards.

Lucy had still not worked out how she was going to manage to get away to join Sam after they had been to church on Sunday. She knew her aunt was leaving later in the day and thought her mother might insist on her being at the house to say goodbye.

As it turned out, her friend Marianne was also attending the Abbey service, and proposed they go for coffee afterwards, promising to send Lucy home in a chair later. So Lucy hugged her aunt farewell and walked away arm in arm with Marianne, keeping an anxious eye out for Sam. As soon as the girls were out of sight of Mrs Wightwick and her sister, he appeared in front of them, doffing his hat and bowing with a flourish.

"And where are these two lovely ladies going?" he enquired. Marianne told him and asked him to join them. "I can only stay a short while, as I promised I would meet Mama at the Pump Room. She is determined that King Bladud's water will cure her of her stomach pains, so she is drinking the horrid stuff every day."

Sam and Lucy exchanged glances. "Then let us go at once," said Lucy, while Sam offered to find a chair for Lucy when Marianne had to leave.

Half an hour later, Marianne set off for the Pump Room and Sam took Lucy's arm, turning her back towards the Abbey. She felt quite exposed as a single woman, walking alone with a man, and was sure everyone was staring at her disapprovingly, but in fact she saw no-one that she knew during their short walk.

As they entered the Abbey, Sam bought her a posy of primrose and crocus from a flower-seller at the door.

"I am sorry I cannot give you a grand wedding, if that is what you desire, Lucy, but at least I can give you some flowers," he said, pressing the small bunch into her hand. Lucy smiled up at him, and he saw the spark of stubbornness in her eyes of which he had grown so fond but which had been absent of late.

Lucy put her shoulders back, straightened her bonnet and said – with a smile that was a little rigid – "I am ready, Sam."

They entered the now-quiet church and Sam looked for Mr Russell. He need not have worried; the verger was on the lookout for him and came up to them almost immediately. "Good morning, sir. Welcome, ma'am. Please to come this way."

He led them briskly to one of the side chapels where a young curate was waiting for them. "If I might trouble you for the Licence, sir?" asked Mr Russell. Sam drew it out from his pocket. "Thank you. And may I confirm that you have the ring?" Sam nodded. "And, as I indicated, sir, you will require two witnesses. I am happy to act in that capacity if you would like me to, but we do need another."

"A friend promised he would be here, but I am afraid he is late... Ah there he is! I shall fetch him over now, since he will not know where to go." And Sam marched towards the entrance where a plump, jolly looking young man in a natty outfit consisting of a dark blue Bath cloth coat, pale yellow skin-tight pantaloons and a beautifully tied cravat was looking around him languidly, leaning on his cane.

"This is Lewis Maddet, and he has agreed to witness the ceremony," said Sam as the two returned. Mr Maddet, who clearly had exquisite manners as well as a tendency to dandyism, removed his hat and bowed deeply to Lucy, who curtsied in return. He then presented her with a tiny, beautifully worked box of coloured glass as a wedding gift, and Lucy thanked him warmly, her smile lighting up her face.

The curate coughed, indicating that time was wearing on and he wished to begin. Thus called to order, Sam and Lucy stood before him, Lucy's hand on Sam's arm, with Mr Maddet standing to one side with the verger.

The service was over more quickly than Lucy had expected. In a daze, she made her vows to love, honour and obey Sam, smiling up at him shyly, put out her hand and had a ring placed on it.

"I now pronounce you man and wife," said the curate. He was not inclined to linger, and fidgeted while Mr Russell opened the register and ushered first the groom and then the bride to sign it – the very last time she would sign herself as 'Lucy Wightwick', Lucy suddenly thought. And then, before the two witnesses had affixed their signatures, he made his apologies, bowed and was off, striding down the Abbey. Mr Maddet signed his name with a flourish; Mr Russell in a more careful hand.

"May I be the first to wish you every happiness, Mr and Mrs Lord?" said the verger, clasping Sam's hand and bowing slightly to Lucy. "Please stay in the

Abbey for a while if you wish, but I must go and attend to some other duties. Goodbye." And he, too, was off.

"Lewis, will you join us for a celebratory toast?" a buoyant Sam said, clapping his friend on the back. "I will indeed," came the response, with a broad grin and Sam finally kissed his bride.

The three of them emerged into the sunlight blinking as their eyes adjusted to the brightness. Lucy was clinging to Sam's arm, still in shock from her first kiss and the depth of feeling it had roused in her.

"Come, Lucy, I shall take you to The Raven public house, where we can have a pie and a pint – not your usual wedding breakfast, I grant you, but we shall enjoy it nonetheless." And they set off, accompanied by Mr Maddet, on the short walk to The Raven.

It was Lucy's first visit to The Raven, and once Sam had found them a corner booth and banged on the table to get the attention of an overworked waitress, she enjoyed looking around her at the noisy crowd of people, amazed at the variety, from well-dressed young bucks to stout merchants and coal mongers, as well as a number of very dubious women in rather revealing costume, which made her blush.

Cushioned as she was in a corner between the two men, Lucy was able to enjoy her pie and pint in comfort, but she did not think she would have ventured in alone. She sat back once she had finished, feeling slightly sleepy, and watched as Sam and Mr Maddet managed to consume several more pints. She hoped Sam would not get too drunk since he was to accompany her to break the news of their marriage to her mother. Eventually she nudged him.

"Sam, I should be getting home. Will you come with me? We need to tell Mama our news."

Sam's eyes were slightly glazed as he turned to her, but his speech was still clear enough. "Indeed, I must carry my bride over the threshold of her parental home, since I have none to offer her! Do you think your mother will be pleased, Lucy?"

She looked down at her hands, twisting the unfamiliar ring. Suddenly she was afraid. What had she done? What would Papa think?

Sam noticed her change of mood and gave her a comforting hug. "I am a fool to have said that! But, Lucy, she likes me, I am sure that once she has got over the shock of our getting married without her knowledge, she will be happy with your choice."

Lucy, unsure, said nothing, and a few minutes later the little party broke up and Sam hailed a hackney cab to take them to Bathampton. Once in the carriage he took Lucy in his arms and kissed her, but she was not as responsive as previously, overwhelmed with concern about what her parents' response might be. Her defiance and courage had all but deserted her, and the journey which she wished could last forever was over all too quickly.

As Sam helped her down and paid off the hackney driver, she looked up at the front door of the house and swallowed convulsively. She was shivering when

Sam escorted her up the steps, but when the door opened, she squared her shoulders and lifted her chin.

"Is Mama in, Roberts?" she asked the footman. "Yes, Miss Lucy. She is in the parlour with Mrs Rann."

Lucy led the way to the parlour and they both entered. "Ah, Lucy, there you are, just in time to bid your aunt farewell. And Mr Lord, so kind of you to escort my daughter home! You have met my sister, Mrs Rann, of course?"

As Sam bowed to the two ladies, Lucy blurted out, "Mama, Aunt, we have something to tell you."

Elizabeth looked up at once and guessed what was coming. Her sister was not really paying attention, however, and had not caught Lucy's tone. So she responded, slightly absently, "And what is that, dear?"

Lucy looked at Sam pleadingly. He held her hand in his, turned towards Mrs Wightwick and said, "Please congratulate us, ma'am. Lucy and I were married this morning at Bath Abbey."

Mrs Wightwick shrieked and fell back on the couch. "Married! But you were to await your father's decision. What have you done, you wicked girl? And what will all our friends think?"

Elizabeth thought back to the conversation she had had with Lucy a few days earlier and wished with all her heart that she had pushed her niece harder and asked outright whether she was contemplating a clandestine marriage. But it was too late now, the deed was done. It was true that the marriage had not yet been consummated – or at least she hoped this was so, she did not want to think Lucy had cast all caution to the winds – so it would in theory be possible to annul and thus overturn it. But this would create a scandal in itself and might not work anyway since Lucy was of age. Best just to accept it and get on with life, hoping that Mr Lord genuinely cared for the girl and was not quite as penniless as Mr Wightwick clearly thought.

"What's done is done," she said firmly, voicing her musings aloud. "Come, Lucy," turning to her sister, "we must decide how best to deal with the situation. There is no point railing against fate. Your daughter is of age, if she finds that she has made an impecunious marriage, she will have to live with it. I am disappointed in you, Lucy," turning to her niece, "and very disappointed in your behaviour, Mr Lord."

Lucy's courage returned and she looked defiantly at her mother and aunt. "I told you, I love him. I am sorry if I have disappointed you, but I hope you can accept the fact that we are married. You are not going to turn me out of our home, are you, Mama?"

Mrs Wightwick had recovered her composure. "Where are you planning to live, Mr Lord?" she asked.

"Well, eventually I plan to return to Barbados with Lucy as my bride. But for now…" Sam tailed off. He hoped that the Wightwicks would indeed accept the *fait accompli* of their sudden marriage and house the newly-weds at one of their properties. He had not given much thought to their immediate accommodation, however.

Elizabeth took charge. "I suggest you return to your lodgings, Mr Lord. Lucy will stay here. Your wedding night will have to be postponed. This offers the best chance of smoothing things over and preventing malicious gossip. Mrs Wightwick and I will speak to Mr Wightwick on his return and suggest that you could spend some time at Great Bloxwich, or one of the other Staffordshire properties. I am sure Mr Wightwick will wish to have a conversation with you, Mr Lord. We will let you know when he arrives."

She stood as she spoke, making it clear that Sam should leave. He bowed with as good grace as he could muster, embraced Lucy and made his way to the front door. Elizabeth closed the door firmly behind him and returned to the parlour. Shutting that door with a snap, she said to her niece, "What possessed you to do such a stupid thing?"

"I thought Papa was going to prevent us from getting married because of some silly scruple about Sam having less money than me, but I would not let that stand in our way."

"Mr Lord has left debts behind him in Barbados, in London. His reputation has been far from spotless in other ways also. Your father simply wanted to make sure you were not marrying a gazetted fortune-hunter who would lose interest in you as soon as he had control of your money! He had not even forbidden the match."

"I know that, Aunt. But there was every chance he would, and I know that he would have been able to keep us apart even though I am not underage. Anyway, I thought you and Mama liked Mr Lord and would be pleased."

"I would have been pleased to see you wed to any man with reasonable prospects who cared for you. Mr Lord is charming, but I am not convinced that he truly cares for you, or that he has any prospects at all. Nor do I think it was at all the thing – and he knows this – to wed you in this secretive manner."

A maid, summoned by the bell rung vigorously by Mrs Wightwick, entered and dropped a curtsey, waiting for her orders.

"Bring the ratafia and three glasses," said Mrs Wightwick.

"And the madeira," added Elizabeth.

While the maid was fetching this Mrs Wightwick, apparently recovered from her initial shock, began laying out plans.

"You will spend the afternoon in your room, Lucy, writing letters to a few of your key friends to let them know of your new status. Think about how you will explain the lack of notice of your betrothal without creating a scandal. I suggest you remove that ring from your finger. I shall have a dinner tray sent up to you. Tomorrow we will carry on as though this secret wedding had not taken place. You are to treat Mr Lord as an acquaintance only when we meet him out. You are only permitted to behave towards him as his wife when in private here. Your father will return on Tuesday or Wednesday, I think. Elizabeth, are you able to stay a little longer to support me when I break the news to him? I know you were planning on leaving now, but do you have anything pressing to attend to?"

Elizabeth, who would not have missed such an exciting event for anything, indicated that she was happy to postpone her departure and when the maid returned with the refreshments, asked her to tell the coachman that she no longer required his services that day.

When they all had a glass in their hands, Mrs Wightwick continued. "I think it would be best, Lucy, if you and Mr Lord had a few days to get used to each other at Hewelsfield. If you then go straight from there to Wolverhampton no one will know for certain when you got married and we can make it look like a quiet wedding rather than a clandestine one."

"Perhaps it had to be quiet out of consideration for Mr Lord, whose family could not be expected to come all the way from Barbados?" suggested Elizabeth, who was enjoying herself.

"Now all we have to do is persuade Mr Wightwick that this is all for the best," said Mrs Wightwick with a sigh.

****

The next couple of days dragged by for Lucy, and she found it very hard that she had to behave as though Sam were a mere acquaintance when they met in public. In fact, they saw little of each other, she spent most of her time at home and he did not visit – although he did write her a very tender note.

Meanwhile Sam made sure that his landlord was aware of his changing circumstances. He had Mr Maddet drop a word in the man's ear that he was to be wed to Miss Wightwick, a wealthy heiress. The effect was immediate, the landlord stopped pushing for immediate payment and became happy to rack up the bills once more. Sam was a mightily relieved man – back on track again, his mission to marry into wealth accomplished. He felt close to Lucy – physically attracted to her even. He felt sure she was attracted to him also, and that he could easily overcome any maidenly shyness and teach her how to enjoy his lovemaking. And within a couple of years he should have one or more sons to inherit the castle he would soon be building at Long Bay.

Chapter 4
Oceanus, 1809

On the eighth of December 1808, Lucy clung to her father on the Falmouth dockside, and the tears flowed freely. The excitement of the adventure ahead of her, her desire to travel to a faraway land with her beloved husband, to see the sights he had so colourfully described to her, to experience the exotic, was subsumed in the sudden realisation that she was leaving behind everything she had ever known and indeed the person she had – until recently – loved most in the world, her father.

She was shaken by doubt, and more than a little fearful. He patted her shoulder and she straightened herself reluctantly. She had chosen her path, against his wishes, and now pride dictated that she must follow it. Perhaps it was just the fact that she was in 'a delicate condition' and feeling somewhat heavy and awkward that was causing her to have the megrims. The baby – she, her husband and her father were all sure it was a boy – was kicking strongly inside her belly, whether in excited anticipation of the voyage or because it had picked up her despondency, she did not know. She smiled at Mr Wightwick a little tremulously and Sam, who had been standing impatiently by, noted this and intervened.

"Come along, my dear. It's time we were going aboard. I think you will love the quarters we have been allocated – I took the liberty of telling the captain that we have not long been married, and he has given us the best there is on the ship."

He held out his hand to her and she took it. "Farewell, Papa," she said in a small voice, and gave her father another smile full of love and tenderness.

"You will come back to visit us – and bring our grandson, too," he said to her, with a meaningful look at Sam.

"To be sure we will, sir," responded Sam smoothly, "and I hope we can look forward to welcoming you to Barbados also."

With a bow to Thomas, he turned towards the companionway, gently pulling Lucy with him. On board, they joined other passengers at the ship's rails, looking down at the small figures below. She was for the moment oblivious to the noise and bustle going on all around her, all her attention fixed on etching a last glimpse of her father into her memory. He waved back at her once more from the dock, bowed in their direction, then abruptly turned and walked towards his waiting carriage, unwilling to give vent to his own emotion at losing his only daughter and leaving her to the vagaries of a man he still mistrusted profoundly. She had made her bed; he could only hope that she would not regret it, and that

Sam would treat her honourably. He made a mental note to contact one or two of his trader friends who travelled to the West Indies regularly and ask them to bring back news of Lucy whenever they could.

Sam put his arm solicitously around the drooping shoulders of the diminutive figure of his wife. "Let me show you our cabin, my dear. I am sure you will like it," he repeated.

They went astern and he helped her down the steep ship's ladder. On the way they met a pleasant, middle-aged woman who was clearly already known to Sam.

"This is Mary, the stewardess, who will look after you since you have no maid," he said, and Mary dropped a curtsy, smiled and promised to bring some tea to the cabin as soon as they were underway.

The cabin was large and well decorated, with a solid-looking mahogany four-poster bed, a clothes press, a table with four chairs, a small escritoire which Lucy immediately recognised as her own from home (she squeezed Sam's hand and smiled her thanks at his thoughtfulness), a delicate cream chaise longue and two washstands. There were bookcases on the pale green walls, and a large window with dark green drapes looking out on the river. Lucy's interest was aroused by the fact that all the large items of furniture were firmly attached to the floor, and Sam pointed out that this was to prevent them sliding around in rough seas. Her spirits rose, and she declared herself delighted with their accommodation.

"I believe we are about to cast off," said Sam. "Let us go up on deck and watch the process – then you can come back here and get Mary to help you unpack our belongings," he gestured to their chests, stowed against the port wall.

She followed him willingly if a little awkwardly into the narrow corridor and back up the stairs, and he found a sheltered bench for them to sit on and watch the crew preparing the packet ship to slip its moorings. The Princess Mary was a 179-ton brig, fitted with ten six-pounder guns. Lucy had never seen a ship from this vantage point and plied him with questions about all that was going on, occasionally having to compete with the noise of the anchor being hauled in and the shouted commands and responses among the crew, her excitement coming to the fore again and her doubts and fears forgotten.

Sam looked down at her homely little face, sparkling now with curiosity, and answered all her questions patiently. They would deal well together, he thought. She was a bright little creature and, though not beautiful, would adapt quickly to Bridgetown society and certainly add to his slightly shaky standing there, particularly when the size of her fortune was known. And that standing would be further enhanced when she produced an heir.

She watched in fascination as the small sails started to fill just enough to enable the Princess Mary packet to thread her way through the water teeming with shipping of all sizes and they moved smoothly away from the dock and down river. Then Sam took her below and left her to the stewardess's ministrations.

"We dine at six with the captain," he said. "I will come and fetch you then." And with a wink to Mary, he was gone.

Lucy spent a pleasant time with Mary arranging Sam's and her possessions and learning how to do so in such a way as to avoid any likelihood of loose objects hurtling about the cabin in bad weather. Then Mary helped her dress for dinner, bobbed a curtsey and hurried off to attend to some of the other lady passengers.

The weather was remarkably calm for December, the air was crisp and cool, but there was no sign of the winter gales her father had gloomily predicted they were likely to face on the passage. So when Sam came to collect her and lead her to dinner, she professed herself very content with her surroundings – and absolutely famished.

"Must be the sea air affecting you already, my dear," he said, laughing. "Master Pocock," he said, as they approached the captain, "may I introduce my wife, Lucy to you?"

The captain's clear green eyes swiftly appraised Lucy. "May I wish you very happy, ma'am?" he said. "I have reason to know your father well in the way of business. We shall take good care of you, I promise – although I am afraid you are likely to spend some uncomfortable hours when we hit the Atlantic storms. It is unusual not to encounter them at this time of year."

Lucy smiled and thanked him for his concern and expressed her pleasure with the cabin they had been allocated.

"I was happy to be able to provide you with the best on board, I really have no need of all that space since my wife is not sailing with us on this voyage."

"Oh – have we taken your cabin, Captain?" cried Lucy. "I had no notion – I am so sorry. I am sure we would have been very comfortable in one of the other cabins – would we not, Sam?"

"It is my pleasure, so let that be an end to it," said the captain, bowing awkwardly, and he showed them to the seats on either side of him at the head of the table. Lucy looked around her, curious about the others at the dinner table. There seemed to be one or two officers of the ship's crew, and the rest were paying passengers like themselves. Sam was already in conversation with one slightly rakish looking character whom he seemed to know; she could see two other women, both much older than herself, and several other men. She wondered what their business was, and whether they were all going to Barbados or leaving at Madeira, or maybe going beyond Barbados to one of the other islands.

****

Much though she had enjoyed the buzz of conversation, Lucy was exhausted and retired earlier than the others from dinner and made ready for bed, Sam escorting her then returning to join the men.

Lucy stood for a while at the porthole, gazing out. The ship was following the English coast and she could see occasional clusters of lights. But they looked very small and far away. Lucy wondered what it would be like to look out and see nothing but water; she would soon know. She took a long, last look at

England and made herself ready for bed. But she could not sleep. Her mind raced around and around. The last, emotionally charged, months had gone so quickly. Meeting Sam, her worried father's disapproval, her mother's shock, the rushed private marriage, even now she wondered at her daring. The wrenching conflict with dear Papa, wanting so much to please him but loving Sam too much to let him go. Papa staring up from the dockside then turning away; she had never seen him cry but she was sure she caught his eyes glistening. Now she was sailing into a new life, at once exhilarating yet unknown.

Their first night in bed together Sam had been so passionate, so powerful. She had cried out with the pain at first and wondered what was happening, for although she knew she must submit to her husband in all things and respond to his bodily needs nobody had ever explained what that actually meant. But Sam had shown tenderness towards her, explaining it was all perfectly normal, and on the second occasion the pain had gone.

Lucy snuggled down into her pillows. She had so much to think about, so much awaiting her. She fell deeply asleep, the ship rocking her gently.

****

The next day at breakfast, a slender middle-aged man with a careworn face bowed to her. She held out her hand for him to kiss and he introduced himself.

"Welcome aboard, ma'am. I am Dr Smith and I am the ship's doctor."

"I am pleased to make your acquaintance, sir. I may have reason to consult with you during the voyage," said Lucy a little shyly.

"Do not worry if you become seasick, ma'am. We all do, even though we travel upon the sea all the time. I will be happy to attend to you but suggest that the best thing is to take to your bed during the worst of it and try to drink tea to avoid becoming dehydrated. And as soon as you are able, go up on deck – the fresh air will revive you, and you will soon get your sea legs."

Lucy smiled her thanks, but it was not of seasickness that she was thinking. Now that she had left all she had ever known, she had to admit that she was more than a little afraid of the changes happening to her body as a result of her pregnancy, and briefly wondered if she had been foolish not to take her mother's advice and remain in England until after the birth. Still, it was too late now to change things and this was apparently the best time of year to sail to the West Indies. It was almost impossible to avoid bad weather but at least their voyage would take place well outside the hurricane season, or so they had been told. She put her worries to the back of her mind, and instead asked the doctor what he knew of the island which was to become her home.

He looked at her for a long moment, then responded, "It is a beautiful island Madam. Though it is small, it encompasses many different characters. Much of it now consists of sugar plantations, but there are still patches of the lush, green forest which was its true nature. The sea is a beautiful, deep turquoise colour, and you will see flying fish leaping from the water, and giant turtles floating in the shallows. I understand you are heading for the east coast, which is somewhat wilder because it faces the Atlantic Ocean. There are steep cliffs and massive natural rock formations, and the winds can be fierce there. I am sure your husband will have provided every comfort for you, though it may take you some little time to adjust to all your servants being Negro slaves."

"I have only ever met one Negro, and he was a little boy with curly hair who had been given to one of my mother's friends," said Lucy. "What are they like? Do they speak English?"

"After a fashion, mostly. They are simple creatures with no learning and heathen beliefs. But they are very strong – you will see women working in the fields as well as men and matching them in bringing in the harvest. The women carry huge burdens on their heads, a custom they brought with them from Africa – you will see them coming into the marketplace in Bridgetown to sell vegetables they have produced, and all will be carried on their heads. They have good singing voices, and love dancing – though it's little enough chance they ever get to do so."

Lucy's eyes had widened in astonishment at Dr Smith's description of the women, but her attention was caught by his last comment and she cast him a look of enquiry. Correctly interpreting it, he responded,

"They are made to work very hard and have little time to themselves. Many owners treat them harshly – I have no doubt swift punishment is often needed for transgressions, but some of the injuries I have seen indicate unnecessary cruelty, in my opinion. Do not repeat what I have said – I would be looked at askance by most Barbadians. But my advice to you Mrs Lord is, treat your slaves firmly but kindly. They will repay you with loyalty, I think."

That night, at the end of the meal the three ladies withdrew leaving the men to enjoy their port, much as they would have done at home. As the stewardess escorted them back to their cabins, Mary's attention was claimed imperiously by one of Lucy's fellow passengers, a gaunt, fierce-looking older woman dressed entirely in stiff, black bombazine. She walked slowly, with a stick, her gnarled fingers showing signs of arthritis, and demanded Mary's assistance in struggling out of her clothes. But Lucy felt wide-awake; she was restless and wanted neither to remain in the cabin nor go to bed. She stripped off her jewellery, pulled a pelisse over her dress, and made her cautious way up on deck alone. A gust of cold wind made her shiver, so Lucy pulled her pelisse tightly about her and manoeuvred gingerly around the shadows she could see on deck to reach the rail. It was pitch black, the only lights those hanging on the ship's masts and some distant twinkling which might have been from others in the convoy. She suddenly felt alone and very small in this vast expanse of nothingness and, as the baby kicked, had a twinge of fear. She had not the faintest idea about the process of giving birth and hoped it would be different from the birth of a foal she had once witnessed; it looked very painful and messy. Who would help her? She hoped there was a good midwife on the island and all of a sudden felt a rush of longing for Nurse's comforting hugs and soothing words.

She turned to go back to their cabin where she shed her pelisse, hanging it up neatly, then took out her new journal and settled at the escritoire to make her first entry. She dipped her pen in the ink then nibbled the end of it, thinking what to write.

She decided to start with a description of the cabin, then moved on to record what the doctor had told her about Barbados. Flying fish, she thought, and women carrying baskets on their heads – but they seemed such strange ideas she could not really imagine it. She wrote for about half an hour, then yawned and stretched. It was still early, but she was beginning to feel sleepy. They had been up early, and she had not slept well the night before. She debated whether to call Mary to help her prepare for bed then decided against it and struggled out of her petticoats as best she could. She was thankful that her hair was short – it meant there was no need to brush it out and plait it for the night. She put on her nightdress and climbed into the bed, leaving just one light burning for Sam when he came in later. She lay on her back, massaging the swell of her belly with her hands, snuggled into the pillows and thought about how fast her life was changing. But it was not long before her eyelids closed and she drifted into sleep.

Sometime later, she was awakened by a muttered oath as Sam – somewhat the worse for wear – staggered into the cabin and bumped into a piece of unmoving furniture. She heard him taking off his clothes and using the chamber pot, then with a groan he fell into bed beside her. She lay unmoving, and almost immediately heard gentle snores from Sam. She was relieved. He could be very insistent when inebriated, and although she knew it was his right to use her body as he wished, she was afraid that if he were too rough, he might harm the baby. She reached out hesitantly and stroked his hair, then turned over and fell asleep again herself.

When she next awoke, it was morning. She lay listening to the creaking and banging sounds around her, and realised the ship was rolling in a way it had not been the previous night. They must have moved away from the English coast into the open Atlantic. She sat up, wondering how she would keep her balance walking around the ship, and whether she would ever get used to the pitching motion. She untied the strings of her nightcap and ran her fingers through her hair. She looked tenderly down at the man sprawled asleep next to her. She would like to get up, but she did not want to disturb him – and she wanted hot water to wash in. She was unsure whether Mary would simply arrive with it, or whether she should have made some arrangement the previous evening. She hesitated, took one more look at Sam, then gently swung her legs out of bed. At that moment, the ship gave an almighty heave, and Lucy grabbed the bedpost nearest her to avoid being flung to the floor. She stood up, and made her way to the window, clinging all the time to fixed objects like the table. She pulled back one of the green drapes and looked out on the tossing grey sea in front of her. Several of the waves slapped against the window, giving the impression they were actually sailing under the sea. Fear rose in her, creating a physical sensation of nausea and claustrophobia which she fought down. She was lucky, she thought, to be travelling astern, she wondered what it must be like travelling at the for'ard end of the ship, as the bow ploughed through the waters. She thought it would in all likelihood be both noisier and rougher than in their comfortable cabin in the stern.

She turned to get back into the bed and heard a light tap on the cabin door. "Come," she called softly.

In came Mary. "Good morning, ma'am. I have brought you tea. Would you like your hot water now?" she asked.

"Yes, please, Mary, though we will leave my husband to sleep longer. I will need your help to dress also – it seems very rough today."

"You will see far rougher weather before we reach Barbados, ma'am. Still, I am glad to see you have not succumbed to seasickness yet as one of the other ladies has! I must look in on her, then I will come back with the hot water and help you."

She looked at Lucy's rounded stomach, more obvious in her nightdress than in her day clothes. Lucy took good care to drape a shawl over her high-waisted dresses so that her pregnancy was not immediately apparent.

"When is the baby due Madam?"

Lucy looked down and blushed. "In February," she answered.

Mary shook her head. "You would have done better to have had it first and travelled later," she said, unconsciously echoing Mrs Wightwick's words. "You are going to find the stairs more difficult over the coming weeks."

By the time she returned with the hot water, Lucy had finished her tea but Sam had still not stirred. Mary poured water into the washstand, then left Lucy to wash while she picked up the clothes Sam had strewn across the floor and hung-up Lucy's crumpled evening dress. She lifted a fresh day dress of blue wool from the clothes press and laid it on the bed. Lucy turned away from the basin and staggered.

"Try to sit down as much as possible while dressing ma'am, that way you are less likely to fall," advised Mary. Lucy sat on the bed to pull on her stockings and her chemise. Mary helped her to lace up her stays and put on her shoes then threw the dress over her head. Lucy pushed her arms into the sleeves and stood a little shakily for the dress to be straightened and fastenings to be done up.

Mary handed her a shawl and looked her over critically. "You do not show much yet. Most will not realise you are having a baby. Shall I tell the doctor?"

"Yes, please do," replied Lucy gratefully. "I was talking to him last night at dinner and he seems a kind man. But naturally I could not talk to him about this at the table."

Having been assured that Lucy could manage her hair herself, Mary hurried off to attend to the other lady passengers, advising Lucy that breakfast was laid out in the wardroom where they had dined the previous evening.

Lucy was surprised that she was again ravenously hungry, and she lingered over a breakfast of bread and butter and some rather tepid coffee. She was joined only by one other passenger who gave her no more than a perfunctory bow then applied himself with equal diligence to his devilled kidneys and the papers he had brought in with him.

When Lucy got back to their cabin, she found Sam shaved and in shirtsleeves. He looked at her with a rueful smile.

"Devil of a lot to drink last night and lost a bit at craps to Dangerfield, if I remember rightly. Let me get some breakfast then I'll take you up on deck to show you the view if you're up to it – and blow away my cobwebs!"

Once Sam had donned his greatcoat, helped Lucy into her pelisse and ensured the hood was firmly in place he led her along the corridor, adjuring her to hold onto the rails, and helping her up the companionway. It was bitterly cold on deck, with an icy wind and sleet falling intermittently. Sam led Lucy into the lee of the bridge, keeping his arm around her shoulders, and together they stared out at the grey sea. They searched for signs of the other ships in their convoy, and Sam pointed with satisfaction at the frigate keeping pace with them at some little distance, which was there, as he explained to her, to deter any attempts by the French or Spanish to seize the British ships. Lucy shivered; she would hate to be taken prisoner, particularly so near the time she would be brought to bed for the birth of her child.

In happier times ships had called at one of the ports on the French coast to pick up wine both for use on the voyage and to sell at later destinations. Because Britain was still at war with Napoleon Bonaparte it was now unsafe for her ships to hug the coast of, or attempt to land anywhere in France or Spain, her ally. Instead the Princess Mary stopped briefly at Lisbon to pick up some supplies and leave some mail, then made for Madeira where they anchored overnight and the passengers were able to go ashore. Lucy could see lush, steep, terraced slopes rising from the harbour, every square inch appeared to be cultivated. As soon as the ship anchored a host of smaller boats, some containing cargo for onward shipment, others selling fresh produce or offering passage to the shore, hurried towards the Princess Mary and the rest of the convoy.

They had now been at sea some two weeks and were delighted to feel solid ground beneath their feet once more. The ship re-provisioned with fresh fruit, salt butter, drinking water (that remaining in the barrels loaded at Falmouth now tasted rather brackish), several casks of eponymous Madeira wine and additional flour. Despite the unceasing light rain which fell during their short stop, Lucy took pleasure in strolling on Sam's arm around the broad streets of Funchal and admiring the beautiful old buildings.

From Madeira the Princess Mary and four of the convoy headed south towards the Cape Verde islands. Lucy detected a different atmosphere among the crew, excitement tinged with nervousness, and asked Sam if he had noticed it too.

"Can't say I have," he responded, "but it is not in the least surprising. We must try to tiptoe around the Canary Islands – far enough out into the Atlantic to avoid Spanish privateers, but not so far out as to delay our voyage or get caught in an Atlantic storm without any chance of reaching port. Captain Pocock will want to ensure his cannon are manned and ready for action just in case."

"Could we not take a different route to ensure the Spanish do not see us?"

"We could have gone straight to the Azores, but at this time of year we would be more likely to encounter storms on the way. If we missed the islands through being blown off course, there is nowhere else to take fresh provisions on board, so the Captain must have decided it was worth running closer to the Canaries instead."

This frightened Lucy and she slept very badly their first night back at sea then stayed on deck most of the following day anxiously scanning the horizon for enemy shipping. The glitter of sun on seawater hurt her eyes and made her tired, and in the afternoon she fell asleep, wedged into a corner of the sheltered bench she and Sam had found when they first boarded at Falmouth. She awoke refreshed and forgot her fears laughing at a pod of dolphins cavorting around the ship. They dipped and jumped as if to attract attention and seemed almost to be winking at her, Lucy thought. Over the following days she saw no ships other than their own convoy nor any glimpse of land, and since the weather was kind she relaxed and enjoyed the voyage.

One evening at dinner the captain turned to Lucy and said, "We shall cross the Tropic of Cancer tomorrow, Mrs Lord, and since we have two sailors aboard who have never been this far south before the crew are keen to conduct the traditional orgies of Neptune. Have you heard of this?"

Lucy shook her head and looked up at Captain Pocock who was seated next to her, his green eyes smiling.

"We have a ritual whereby anyone entering the Tropics for the first time must be introduced to Neptune. As Neptune is the King of the Sea, they are immersed in a tub of seawater."

"And since this is my first time, must I undergo this ordeal?" Lucy asked.

"No, ma'am, we shall exempt you on the grounds of health. I understand from Dr Smith that you are in the family way." Lucy blushed, embarrassed that the fact that she was breeding should be discussed so openly by a stranger. "But you may find the ceremony interesting to observe. The crew take it very seriously. It is considered bad luck if you fail to undergo the ducking. The Bosun and his mate dress in costume that they make themselves – and their dress can sometimes be very amusing – then conduct the ceremony. It will take place at nine o'clock in the morning."

The following morning Sam took Lucy up on deck to view the proceedings. She asked if he had taken part in the ceremony when he left Barbados in 1804.

"I managed to avoid that fate," he answered, laughing. "I think they do not generally involve the paying passengers unless they have for some reason taken a dislike to them. I gave King Neptune some coin and he left me in peace."

A large wooden tub had been placed in the centre of the forward deck and two seamen were busy filling it with pails of seawater. Then two strange figures approached, garbed in patched and billowing robes, one – the bosun's mate – carrying some kind of large implement, meant to represent Neptune's trident Lucy suddenly realised. Three more sailors, barefoot, came forward and approached a small group to one side of the deck, two of whom were no more than boys and each clad only in a pair of ragged short trousers. They looked rather apprehensive.

"An' it please you, may we ask if you have ever before been in these parts of Neptune's dominions?" they were asked. A murmured negative was the only response. "Then if you would be so kind, lads, please to approach the tub set up to mark the occasion."

Reluctantly the boys moved forward and, watched by a group of curious passengers and half a dozen crew (the rest remaining at their stations as commanded by the captain since the ship was still too close to the Canary Islands for him to relax his vigilance against the enemy) were thrown bodily into the tub. After much spluttering they were hauled out dripping wet, and the audience gave them a round of applause. One of them grinned sheepishly, but the other seemed on the verge of tears and was still coughing seawater. The first mate bellowed

"All right, lads, back to work. You've had your fun and King Neptune will be pleased!"

Before the Princess Mary reached the Cape Verde islands almost four weeks into the voyage, a storm blew up.

A south easterly gale made the huge sails flap and shiver, and the masts creaked and groaned ominously. Crew were sent scampering up the shrouds to take in and furl the canvas and the first mate peremptorily ordered all passengers below decks and out of the way. Sam grabbed Lucy by the arm as she lurched about feeling helpless and she was hurried down clinging to him, clutching at handrails, anything to try and steady herself. Safely ensconced in their cabin, Lucy could hear shouts from the men, a rush of bare pattering feet, the slapping of wet ropes flung down on deck, and through it all a growing hissing sound from the sea and the roar of the wind.

The noise frightened her and she sat for several hours at the little table playing cards with Sam to take her mind off the danger they were in. Now she understood only too well why all the furniture was battened down. She remembered how small and helpless she had felt them to be, all alone on the limitless ocean, in the early stage of the voyage and fought down her feelings of panic. She wanted Sam to be proud of her and was desperate not to disgrace herself by hiding her head under the coverlet which was what she felt like doing.

Eventually she took to bed as she began to feel queasy and Sam left to join other hardy souls in the wardroom. For two days the ship was driven north west before the gale rather than south-south-east towards Cape Verde. The captain used all his expertise to keep his barque afloat while avoiding being driven onto the African coast or, worse still, too close to the Canary Islands. Between decks there was a din of smashing crockery, barrels that had broken loose from their lashings and sundry smaller items not nailed to the floor thudding to and fro as the ship heaved and wallowed. It was impossible to stand or sit in safety or comfort, so anyone not involved directly in looking after the boat took to their bunks.

Lucy could not sleep. Her jumbled thoughts grew more lurid. The storm would never end. The ship would be smashed. She would never survive in the water. She was totally in the grip of the wild elements. Hours and hours and still more hours of it, days maybe, she had lost track of time. The ship plunged and heaved, there was no way the Princess Mary could survive, surely?

But the wind eventually did die down. The ship had survived – somehow. *She* had survived – somehow. Unable to sleep properly through it, she had drifted momentarily in and out of consciousness, Sam sometimes attentively with her, sometimes gone. Carrying the baby was tiring enough, but now she was shattered. When it became safe to go on deck once more, Lucy made her cautious, lumbering way up the companionway escorted by Sam.

She was shocked and almost driven to panic again by the height of the waves, having been under the impression that the sea would be almost as calm as before the storm, but the great grey-green mountains of water still towered above the Princess Mary and seemed about to crush her. It appeared to Lucy's eyes that they would be smashed to smithereens and she was amazed to realise that the ship was gamely battling on despite one of her sails having been torn away from the mast and actually riding the waves. This realisation reduced her panic somewhat, but she was still terrified she would be swept overboard by a mountain of water crashing on the deck, terrified of drowning, so would not stay long on deck and certainly had no hesitation in agreeing to his command that she not go up there unaccompanied.

Over the next few hours the sea did grow calmer, the sun came out and they altered course towards the Cape Verde Islands once again, which they should reach in three or four days according to the captain.

At dinner that day (the cooks had somehow salvaged provisions and crockery) the captain, who looked completely exhausted, complimented Lucy.

"I understand you and your husband were almost the only passengers not to succumb to seasickness, Mrs Lord."

"I think I was too petrified to be ill, Captain. And I must confess I did not feel at all well, which is why I took to my bed."

Over the days that followed, Lucy took to going up on deck every morning after breakfast when the weather allowed. The fact that she was pregnant was now clear for all to see and made clambering up and down the stairs laborious and inelegant. She found herself disinclined to do very much other than sit and read and watch the ever-changing ocean. So she would settle herself on a sheltered bench, where the first mate had taken to placing cushions for her, and by the time Sam or the parson's wife came to check how she was doing she would have noted where the remaining ships in their convoy were and picked up a report on their progress from Master Pocock or the friendly first mate.

She never ceased to wonder at the nimbleness of the bare-footed crew swarming up the rigging to the accompaniment of bellows from the bo'sun, and liked to watch the two black seamen in the hope of becoming more accustomed to the way they looked and their manner of speech. She did not want to shame Sam by appearing green and gauche when surrounded by what sounded to be a veritable phalanx of slaves at Long Bay, though she continued to worry that she would be unable to understand them and so lose their respect as soon as she arrived. Besides, she found herself fascinated by their size and strength, the well-toned muscles on permanent show, for they generally wore only a coarse pair of trousers with a rope belt, no shirt or shoes.

She could sit there watching the tendrils of brown weed which were a feature of the Sargasso Sea, looking out for the exquisite little Nautilus or Portuguese man'o'war jellyfish, its rainbow-tinted tail set to the north east trade wind; the leaping shoals of flying fish like flights of silver darts, some of which fell inboard, were grabbed and cooked for dinner. She laughed in delight at schools of dolphins swimming and jumping alongside the ship, and as they sailed ever closer to their destination, she saw black grampuses and giant turtles for the first time. And every evening there were breath-taking sunsets to watch for a few short moments, as the tropical sun sank below the horizon. Now that her terror at the storm was over, she was entranced by an amazing new world.

Sam was not one to sit dreamily beside her for long, nor did he like to read for hours on end if the superior attraction of a game of quadrille with some of their fellow passengers was on offer. But given how keen he had been to shake the dust of Barbados from his feet four years previously, the glimmer of excitement he felt at the expectation of showing Lucy his – their – home surprised him, and he found he was more than happy to answer her questions about the island known as 'Little England' as much for the fact that alone throughout the West Indies it had only ever had one master as for its lush greenness. He even confided to her some of his plans for Long Bay (though he forbore to point out that it was her dowry which would finance them), and she loved the pride and passion that crept into his voice when he did so.

The doctor, with whom she now felt thoroughly comfortable, would also often sit with her, and encouraged her to be in the fresh air as much as possible. She had felt rather shy when he first examined her, but he had put her at ease with his quiet, matter-of-fact manner. He had children of his own – though they were full grown now – and soothed her occasional qualms about the unknown by suggesting that she seek the support of her mother-in-law (whom he described as a quiet, dignified and very pleasant lady) on her arrival at Long Bay. Both he and Sam assured her they would be arriving at the best time of year; it would be the dry season, with pleasant, sunny weather, and she would enjoy watching her first sugar cane harvest.

"At Long Bay there is nearly always a breeze," Sam told her. "It will keep you cool and blow away the smell of sugar which can get a bit heavy."

They anchored at Praia, the Cape Verde island capital on Santiago, just long enough to pick up supplies for the final leg of their voyage, fresh meat, salt, fruit (particularly bananas), coffee, fish and drinking water as well as wine and port.

They were now only a few weeks away from Barbados, and conditions were generally perfect for sailing with a stiff north easterly breeze. Lucy had long ago found her sea legs, but with the pregnancy weighing heavily she was becoming increasingly clumsy and one morning, making her way as usual to the cushioned bench, her eye was caught by the glint of a shoal of flying fish leaping out of the water. She stumbled in her thin shoes and fell awkwardly on one of the many coils of rope. She cried out in pain as her ankle twisted, then trying to get up she felt an even sharper pain in her abdomen. The sound of running feet made her look up. Two of the crew were running towards her, and she bit her lip to stop herself from crying. As they helped her gently to her feet, another stab of pain made her gasp and double over.

"Please – will you fetch my husband?" she asked, as they settled her solicitously to the bench.

By this time, the first mate had arrived. "Back to your posts," he barked at the two sailors, "I will fetch him myself, ma'am." He looked closely at Lucy and decided to fetch the doctor at the same time.

Sam and the doctor arrived almost simultaneously from different parts of the ship, and Sam exclaimed at her already swollen ankle. But the doctor asked gently, "Where else are you hurt, Mrs Lord?" Thoroughly frightened now, Lucy whispered that it was her stomach. "I think your baby may be arriving early," he responded. "Mr Lord, will you help me get your wife below so I can examine her in the privacy of your cabin?"

With some difficulty, the two men half carried, half supported Lucy below deck and along the corridor to the cabin. Lucy could no longer hold back the tears which were coursing down her cheeks, and she was shivering uncontrollably. They laid her on the bed, and the doctor said, "I need to loosen your clothing, ma'am; with your permission?"

Lucy nodded her agreement and hiccoughed on a sob. Then came another strong, sharp pain and she twisted onto her side and moaned.

"It's the child alright," said the doctor with a frown. He glanced at Sam, who was looking worried and rather pale. "You can do no more good here," he told Sam roughly. "Do you go and fetch the stewardess, ask her to get the galley to put water on to boil then come straight here."

"She will be alright, won't she? She's not going to lose the baby, is she?" The doctor shook his head impatiently, then took pity on the young man, turning him gently towards the doorway and promising to let him have any news as soon as possible.

The stewardess arrived with extra sheets and towels and busied herself getting Lucy out of her dress, petticoats and stays and into a nightdress. This coincided with a lull in the pains and she lay still while the doctor examined her.

"Sam wanted our first child born at Long Bay, and so did I," she said wistfully.

"Well, you must both get used to the idea of him being born at sea. I do not believe that you did any major damage when you fell, and I think it will be some hours until the birth. You understand the pains will get worse before that happens?" Lucy looked at him a little blankly. "I will just put a dressing on that ankle of yours, then I will leave you with Mary here who will be able to fill you in on some of the details," he said kindly, realising that she had absolutely no idea of the process of giving birth. Mary nodded at him, then slipped away to fetch some tea for Lucy and tell the galley boy that she would not be needing quantities of boiling water until much later.

When she returned, the doctor left them and went to find Sam to update him, telling Mary to call for him when she thought it necessary. He found Sam with a glass of wine at his elbow, playing three-handed whist with two other passengers, although his heart did not seem to be in it. Meanwhile, Mary helped Lucy sit up in the bed and settled down to enlighten her ignorance about the birthing process, answering her questions as honestly as possible. How big will the baby be? How can it possibly be born from there? Won't it tear me apart? How long will it take? Will the pain get worse? The stewardess's own three surviving children were being cared for by her mother while Mary was away working, so she could speak from experience.

After their conversation – which Lucy found difficult, never having spoken about such intimate matters even with her mother – she felt calmer.

"I would have died of embarrassment if the doctor had talked to me in such a way," she admitted to Mary, "but I am truly grateful to you." The pains had ceased, and Mary encouraged her to get out of bed, to walk around the cabin, to sit at the table.

"There will be plenty of time for lying in bed later," she said with grim humour. "I am very glad you did not have your lying-in during that terrible storm, Madam." She left Lucy, promising to bring her some lunch shortly. She also went to look for Sam, to suggest he visit his wife.

It was several hours before Lucy experienced another contraction, but when she did it was the start of a regular pattern, with pains every thirty minutes or so. Mary looked in on her, found her calm, and promised to return in a couple of hours or earlier if Lucy called for her. Lucy found it difficult to concentrate on her book and started pacing up and down the cabin like a caged animal, but the winds had picked up again with squalls of rain and mountainous waves which made such movement almost impossible.

By the time Mary returned – with the doctor – Lucy's pains were coming every ten minutes. Her cap was askew, and Mary gently removed it. As she did so, Lucy gave a startled cry as her waters broke, her eyes went in miserable embarrassment towards the doctor, who quietly directed Mary to strip the top covers off the bed and place some towels on it. Lucy quickly forgot her embarrassment as the contractions speeded up. Doubled over, she staggered towards the bed and lay down.

For the next few hours, the doctor and Mary were fully occupied supporting Lucy through her first labour. Finally, long after most of the passengers and crew had sought their beds, the baby began to emerge to a final agonised cry from its mother. Lucy had never known such wrenching pain, entrapped by a blur of emotion and confusion, hardly knowing what was happening – to her or the baby. Would it survive – would *she* survive?

Then she was vaguely aware that Mary had taken the infant and laid it on a towel set aside for that purpose; the doctor tying off and cutting the umbilical cord, removing the placenta.

Lucy suddenly became aware that Mary had turned to her, was smiling, saying, "Congratulations. It's a boy!"

The doctor wrapped the baby in the towel and handed him to Lucy. Hot, panting, her hair slick with sweat, Lucy opened her arms for the tiny bundle. It was a magical moment for her, this tiny being staring solemnly at her, its luminous eyes blinking vaguely into the early moments of its new bewildering life.

"I will give the good news to your husband," said the doctor, and left Mary to whisk away the stained sheets and towels, bathe Lucy's face and neck, comb her hair and put her in a new nightdress and cap.

Sam reeled through the door in high good humour. "Let me see my son and heir!" he exclaimed, breathing brandy fumes over wife and child. He studied the red and rumpled-looking creature, now fast asleep, then kissed Lucy tenderly on the forehead.

"Well done, m' dear. How do you feel?" he enquired, as a bit of an afterthought.

Lucy smiled at him. "Tired, but happy. I should like to call him Oceanus, if you please, Sam."

He frowned – then to her relief, smiled. "It is a strange name but given where we are, I can understand. By all means, if that will make you happy," he shrugged. "I will be off to drink a toast to my son – and I will find another bunk for tonight, to let you get some rest." And he staggered from the cabin, his lack of balance due in part to the continuing squally weather and in part to his state of inebriation.

Part 3
Barbados, 1809–1812

Chapter 5
Long Bay

Sam was keen to celebrate the birth of Oceanus – as was the custom – as soon as possible on arrival in Barbados. As they neared the island – and once Lucy was permitted to leave her bed – she basked in the sunshine of his approval, enjoying his pride in their son and the fact that everyone on board the Princess Mary was happy for them.

She felt she had finally come of age, and adored the small scrap of humanity, so dependent on her for his every need. Sam had informed her carelessly that she should have anything and everything she wanted when they reached Long Bay, including a wet nurse for the baby; secretly she hoped to persuade him this was unnecessary, as she got real pleasure from the act of nursing, laughing at the greedy way Oceanus suckled as though he feared he would never get another meal.

She knew it was usual for wealthy women to employ wet nurses as it left them free to continue running their household and live their normal lives, and their figures would not be ruined by breastfeeding. Indeed, her mother had employed a wet nurse for Stubbs and, she assumed, for her too. Yet she was oddly reluctant to hand over her son to another woman to provide him with milk, fearing the bond established between her and Oceanus might be broken.

They would all live together with his elder brother John, his sisters and his mother at Long Bay, at least for the present, Sam had explained. She had been somewhat surprised, and a little fearful, since they would have to defer to John as the elder brother and she was uncertain how either his wife or Sam's mother, the widowed Mrs Lord, would feel about her presence.

Sam reassured her, "Don't worry. You will be first in importance, my dear, since you bring an heir to Long Bay. John may have married five years ago, but his wife seems only to have given him sickly girls. Anyway, I mean to start building our own house as soon as I can agree the site with John and he can spare the slaves from field-work."

Sam had enthused her about his dreams of a great house, set high on the cliffs, strong enough to withstand the hurricanes which sometimes battered the island, and grand enough to impress even wealthy visitors from England. He wanted it to be the biggest, most majestic establishment in Barbados – maybe even in the whole West Indies.

Late one afternoon, Sam came to fetch her from their cabin where she was feeding Oceanus. "Come, Lucy. You must get your first view of Little England and your new home."

She put the sleepy Oceanus carefully into his crib and followed her husband on deck. As the wind whipped at her hair, the shimmering mound that she had first seen mid-morning when the cry of "Land ho!" rang out from a young black sailor way above their heads had now resolved itself into a low-lying gently undulating soft green island with a twisted spine of hills along its north-east corner, off to starboard.

Sam pointed towards the shore. "That is Long Bay Estate," he said, excitedly indicating one of the low cliffs above a white beach. She nodded but could not think of anything to say; they were not yet close enough to see any detail, and there was just a glimpse of a large, low, distinct white house if she strained her eyes, aware of waves crashing against the coast and sending great plumes of spray high into the air. He seemed disappointed that she did not share his enthusiasm, so she squeezed his hand and smiled at him.

As they moved briskly westwards, the emerald water at the base of the south-eastern cliffs sparkled in the sun and set off the gentle browns and greens which were the predominant colours of the land.

She could see a line of brilliant white, and asked Sam what it was.

"Cobblers Reef," he responded grimly. "It is feared by every ship's captain. You would not believe it on a calm day like today, but it is a terrible danger to all seafarers in inclement weather. Many vessels have broken their backs there. Sometimes the sailors make it ashore, to the beach below Long Bay. More often than not they drown."

Lucy shivered. It reminded her how little she really knew of her new home and how much she had to learn. The fact that Sam had called Barbados 'Little England' gave her comfort, but his comments about Cobblers Reef made her suddenly aware how far she was from everything she knew.

As they rounded Needham's Point into Carlisle Bay the sun was setting fast. Lucy could just about make out the white houses dotted about, above and behind the mangrove swamps and low cliffs, then Sam pointed out the lights of the capital Bridgetown, their destination, but it was already too dark for her to be able to make out the buildings there. That would have to be left until tomorrow, for the captain had already told them that, since they would arrive after dark, they would have one more night on board the ship before disembarking by wherry in the morning. He had arranged a farewell feast, with the last of the provisions they had picked up in the Azores; she smiled at her husband and they turned together to go below and change for dinner.

She would be glad of an opportunity to say a leisurely goodbye to the doctor, and she realised with a start that she would miss him. Over the weeks at sea he had become a familiar face, a link with home, and she had come to depend on his calm confidence since he delivered Oceanus. Now she would be alone again, she mused, as, after dinner, she busied herself with their packing, ready for an early start.

The next morning, the 28th February 1809, they were up at dawn, patiently waiting their turn to be ferried across to Bridgetown, already bustling with activity. Bridgetown was an extremely busy but narrow port, not deep enough for the larger ships, so these would anchor in the Bay outside, whilst lighters – or wherries – carried all cargo, whether human, animal or other, to and from the shore. Lucy was helped carefully down the ladder by two sailors, holding her breath as she clung alternately to the rope rails or to one of the agile men. It seemed a very tortuous, long way down, the ladder swaying on the gentle waves. When she was safely ensconced Oceanus was handed to her, and Sam quickly followed them into a wherry in which several kegs and crates, together with half a dozen hens, were already precariously balanced. Two other passengers squeezed in next to them, and the boat turned towards the quay. Lucy looked up and gave a last wave to those she could see way above on the deck of the Princess Mary, then turned her attention towards her new country.

Within no time at all it seemed, one of the sailors was expertly casting a rope around a stanchion to pull them close in; the boat was tied up firmly, and two black men, dressed only in rough trousers and shirts, leapt nimbly down to transfer the baggage to shore. Lucy stared at them curiously, then looked up at the quay and realised with a start that the number of black faces far outnumbered the white ones. She must get used to this, she supposed.

Sam left the boat first, then Lucy was handed up. She staggered, and clutched Sam's arm for support. He laughed.

"I forgot to warn you, my dear. You have become so used to your sea-legs that you have forgotten the land doesn't usually heave and slide under your feet – it will take you a few hours, no doubt, to get your land legs back!" he reassured her.

"You there – fetch us a carriage," he ordered one of the slaves who had just put down one of the chests from the boat.

"Yes, massa," the man responded, eyes downcast.

He soon came back with a dusty-looking vehicle drawn by two rather skinny horses, and Sam entered into some brisk bargaining with the driver about the price for transporting them to Long Bay and, once that was satisfactorily completed, made arrangements for their belongings to be transported separately but as speedily as possible. He helped Lucy in with Oceanus, tossed a small coin to the slave who had fetched the carriage, swung up behind Lucy shutting the door, and banged his cane on the roof smartly to advise the driver to set off.

Their way out of the port and along Bridgetown's main street was necessarily slow because of the jostling throng of people – both black and white, with various horse- or slave-drawn vehicles all contending busily for space. Lucy was glad of their pace, as it allowed her an opportunity to look about her. She noted with interest that the buildings were all in good condition, most with a veranda, none more than two storeys high, most whitewashed although there was also a sprinkling of colour on some of the walls. Along the main street were numerous shops – mostly the open fronts to warehouses, she realised. The notion of properties given over purely to the retail trade was a new one here, and the traditional style of building (living quarters over a jutting veranda which sheltered the shopfront below) prevailed. It reminded Lucy a little of parts of Bath, and she thought she would enjoy exploring here. One dress shop in particular caught her eye and seemed to contain wares of surprisingly good quality.

There was a stark contrast in both the dress and demeanour of the black and white folk she saw. The whites walked with heads held high, the men with a swagger, the women all closely followed by at least one slave generally burdened down with packages or holding a parasol over the mistress's head. The whites were richly dressed, in last season's fashions, but there was clearly no shortage of money. The blacks, on the other hand, moved more slowly, taking care always to make way for the white folk, eyes downcast – she noticed that they never seemed to look into the face of a white person even when speaking to them. Their clothes were generally drab and basic and few had shoes, though she spotted the odd gaily-coloured handkerchief or shawl on some of the women. She saw one or two with their babies strapped to their backs, one hand holding onto a basket carried on their heads, and noticed how gracefully they moved. She sat back against the squabs thoughtfully; she had a lot to learn and to grow accustomed to.

Sam had said nothing since they left the harbour. She looked across at him now and saw him lounging at his ease with an amused smile on his face. "So, Lucy, what do you think?" he asked.

"It is all so completely, utterly different from home. I hardly know what to think of it!" she smiled. "It will take me some time to understand how everything works here, and I will need your help to do so. Are all the black people slaves? They look so sad. And I had no idea they came in so many different colours!"

"Their colour depends on which tribe they're from and where in Africa, and some of the lighter ones of course are mulattos – mixed white and Negro blood. Not all are slaves, they can buy themselves out of slavery, and when some owners die, they bequeath them their freedom. Several run quite lucrative businesses here in Bridgetown."

"What about those born here? Surely slaves marry and have children?" she asked.

"Oh – we encourage them to breed, though they don't need to be married to do that. They breed well enough – we have never had a problem replenishing our stock from within, unlike the other islands. Most slaves aren't Christian so marriage doesn't mean anything to them anyway. Within limits, we encourage black babies; a 'picaninny' born at Long Bay belongs to the plantation and will in time become a worker there, and that's far cheaper than buying more slaves at the market."

Lucy sat still, rigid with shock at her husband's casual, offhand tone. Despite having been aware of the diverse opinions expressed over the Act abolishing the slave trade two years previously, she had never considered slaves as property, though now that she thought about it, she realised that of course that was what it meant. But it was the notion that they were nothing more than a bag of corn or a wooden table – a thing rather than a person – which shocked her deeply. Even more so her husband's rather patronising, dismissive arrogance. Was this a common attitude in Barbados, she wondered? She looked down at the sleeping Oceanus in her arms and determined not to let him develop such a casual disregard for the humanity of others, but she said nothing, just storing her thoughts away.

As they left the outskirts of Bridgetown, the carriage picked up its pace and bowled along in a cloud of dust so that, despite the heat, it was necessary to keep the windows tightly shut. The roads seemed good, often better than those back in England, and Sam explained that each of the eleven parishes was responsible for building and maintaining the main thoroughfares between plantations and to and from the capital Bridgetown and a second busy centre, Holetown.

By now she was perspiring heavily, and Oceanus was grumbling. As the hours passed, Lucy caught glimpses of the occasional grand gateway, lush gardens, spreading, low white houses, as well as lines of what she thought at first were sheds, but discovered later to her surprise were the slave quarters. But most of the route on this agricultural island was dominated by a sea of what Sam told her was sugar cane, tall and thick, light green-brown and swaying slightly in the breeze. Despite the closed windows, she could smell the sweet, cloying odour of sugar mixed with the dust. It all felt very different from neat English fields of wheat, maize, potatoes or turnips, or the lush pastures for fattening livestock that Lucy was used to.

As the carriage moved further east, lurching frequently on the dusty road, the landscape changed and the fields of cane were interspersed with other crops, which Sam pointed out to her as aloe and cotton, together with small areas which appeared dedicated to producing vegetables. In some places there were stands of fustic, redwood, cedar or ironwood – native trees which had covered the island before the advent of white settlers.

It felt as though they were climbing now, and as they slowed, she caught a flash of the sea sparkling below to her right through the trees and scrub. They had reached a kind of plateau, and Lucy noticed with surprise that her view was no longer blocked by whispering sugar cane, the scene now was of flat scrubland, neat fields of aloe, cotton and other crops she did not recognise, interspersed with windmills, low trees and the occasional plantation house with its attendant slave huts.

Before her and to her right was a cliff, with cacti, dense, lush sea-grapes and other low-lying greenery tumbling down it towards a beautiful white beach. The carriage swung left and the horses slowed to a walk, snorting as they recovered from the brisk pace they had kept up for some fifteen miles. They had stopped rarely and for short breaks to relieve themselves and for Lucy to feed Oceanus on the long journey, and like the horses, she was parched. They passed through some gates, and Lucy realised they must have arrived.

Sam rapped again on the carriage roof, the driver stopped and Sam opened the door, turned and held out his arms to lift Lucy down.

"Welcome to Long Bay. Welcome to your new home," he said. "Come and see what you make of it."

Her arms aching from holding the baby for an unusual length of time, she shifted him against her shoulder and looked around her curiously. Immediately aware of the strength of the wind she held tightly onto her hat with her free hand. Taking a deep breath she inhaled the sharpness of the sea mingling with a strong smell of horse sweat, a quite faint smell of sugar and a much richer, lusher scent which came from a beautiful avenue of trees ahead of her. This led to a compact, two-storey house set on a slight rise, white like all the others she had seen, with jalousied windows lit up by a sun which was now at its zenith. The house was entirely surrounded by a wide wrap-around veranda. She was aware of a booming sound apparently coming from behind the house, but there was so much that was new to take in that she thought nothing of it. Lucy turned and smiled at Sam.

"It is beautiful," she said. "It all seems so… so rich; so exotic. Please explain everything to me and tell me the names of all the trees and plants, for I do not recognise any of them."

Sam helped her back into the carriage, told the driver to walk on and wound down the windows. "The trees along the drive are mainly mahogany. My father planted them when John Barrow first introduced them to the island some twenty-five years ago, and we hoped to harvest some elsewhere on the plantation for export to England, it makes beautiful furniture as you know. But it is slow-growing and it is easier to make money from sugar-cane so it hasn't really taken off as a crop."

The long drive was smooth, shady and well-maintained, better even than the road they had just travelled from Bridgetown. As it opened out, Lucy could see a manicured garden, as beautifully maintained as the one at Hewelsfield, but so different in its content. It was clearly laid out to provide as much shade as possible, and at her request Sam pointed out the different trees as tamarind, flame-trees, mango, jacaranda and frangipani. Even the names, she thought, were exotic and other-worldly, the blossom wildly colourful.

Suddenly she spotted something odd running up the trunk of a mango tree; it stopped on a high branch and peered down at them. Sam laughed when she pointed to it and asked what it was.

"One of our dratted green monkeys," he said. "They're everywhere. They even get into the kitchen to steal food, and they love ripe mango."

He pointed to the thick, green hedge which seemed to stretch right around the house and told her it consisted of lime trees. These were grown for two reasons, to provide a key ingredient for the island's famous lime punch, and because their sharp thorns provided a degree of security against unwanted visitors, animal or human.

The carriage swung to a halt before the house. A young slave came running out to let down the steps and open the door. He bowed to Lucy and held his arm for her to steady herself as she got out, still holding Oceanus and, because of the wind, only daring to let go of her hat for as long as it took to alight. As Sam stepped out behind her, the slave looked up.

"Massa Sam!" he exclaimed with surprise.

"Hello, Jonah," responded Sam. "So you're doing house duty now are you? I thought you'd be working in the fields. Is my brother around?"

"Massa John out checking de aloe," responded Jonah.

Sam grunted, took Lucy by the elbow and turned towards the house. They climbed a flight of steep stone steps to the open front door, and stepped into a large vestibule panelled with dark, glossy wood. The booming sound – even louder at the front of the house than at the end of the drive – died to a whisper inside.

After the bright sunshine outside, it appeared gloomy. As Lucy's eyes adjusted to the dim light, she saw that everywhere was spotlessly clean, shining as though it had just been polished (as indeed it had). There was a subtle fragrance, which she later learned was from the frangipani blossom cut daily to fill bowls in all the main rooms. A welcome breeze played around her skirts and she noticed with surprise that she could see straight into all the interconnecting rooms on the ground floor; there appeared to be no doors. Lucy caught sight of herself in a huge, ornate mirror and grimaced. Despite her best efforts this morning, she had not been able to repair the ravages of weeks at sea, and her appearance was somewhat bedraggled. Her dress, too, looked the worse for wear and she longed to change into something fresh.

She had the feeling there were several pairs of eyes looking at her. She looked up, and saw two women slaves busily polishing the wooden banister, studiously not looking directly at her. Turning her head towards the back of the hall, she caught the glint of two pairs of eyes – children, she thought, from the height – and realised they were looking at Oceanus, asleep on her shoulder.

Sam meanwhile had handed his hat and cane to Jonah. "Come, Lucy. I am going to introduce you and our son to my mother," and he indicated that she should climb the stairs. "She is no doubt in her parlour at this hour."

Lucy would have preferred to have her first meeting with her new mother-in-law once she had bathed and dressed in fresh clothes (and, she thought ruefully from his smell, Oceanus could do with being changed too), but since no one had yet suggested showing her to her room she could only acquiesce.

At the top of the stairs, they turned left along a cool, dim corridor with a highly polished wooden floor, and Sam headed straight for an open door about half-way along. He took Lucy by the hand, and fleetingly she wondered in surprise whether he was nervous. But she had no time to find out. As they crossed the threshold she saw his mother at once, dressed in dark grey silk with a white lace cap on her neat, grey hair, and seated in a comfortable-looking rattan armchair stitching at some fine embroidery. Behind her was an ornately carved wooden screen, discreetly hiding the bedroom which lay behind.

"Mother," announced Sam, "may I present my wife, Lucy; and our son, Oceanus?" and, still holding Lucy by the hand, went up to Bathsheba Lord and kissed her cheek.

The widow dropped her needlework, looked up at her son and clasped his left hand in both of hers.

"Samuel! We looked for your arrival some weeks ago – why did you not send a message from Bridgetown and Thomas would have fetched you! It is wonderful to see you. But where are my manners? Welcome to Long Bay, my child." And she stood up to greet Lucy, who dropped a curtsey.

The two women looked each other over carefully. They were of a similar height, but Lucy's dimpled plumpness contrasted with Bathsheba's spare frame and surprisingly dark complexion. Faced with a mother-in-law as neat as a new pin, Lucy felt the need to explain her appearance.

"I am sorry, ma'am, for appearing before you in my travelling clothes..." Oceanus chose this moment to make his presence felt. He opened his eyes, yawned, then started to wail lustily, drawing Bathsheba's eyes to him.

Her mother-in-law started. She had not taken in Sam's introductory words, being too preoccupied with seeing him again after five long years. And, of course, while Sam had sent a letter announcing his marriage to Lucy the previous year, he had seen no reason to write again to tell his mother that his wife was pregnant, believing that the birth would take place only once they arrived at Barbados.

"Your son, you said Samuel? That is excellent news! My fourth grandson – I look forward to becoming properly acquainted with him. Congratulations, my dear," she said to Lucy. The wailing had become a strenuous bawling, and Oceanus' face had turned bright red. "It appears he is demanding to be fed," said Bathsheba with a smile. "I will organise the staff to show you to your rooms so that you can provide for his needs and make yourselves comfortable. I am sure we can arrange a wet nurse among the slaves very quickly." And she rang the little bell on her table.

Before the chimes could die away, it was answered. Presumably, thought Lucy, the crying baby had attracted attention. Two black maids entered, and over Oceanus' screams Lucy heard Bathsheba giving orders before waving Lucy out of the room with them. Sam accompanied them, but sensibly waited to say anything until his son's yells had been silenced by Lucy feeding him. One of Lucy's trunks was already in the room, and she asked one of the girls to unpack a change of clothes for the baby and, in particular, a fresh linen clout as Oceanus' clothing was soaked through with urine, and to bring warm water for a bath for him. Sam sent the other to look for a cot or, if one was not available, to get the carpenter to make one.

He turned to his wife. "No doubt you will want to rest yourself," he said. "My room is just next door. I am going to bathe and change, if enough of the baggage has arrived, then I must go back to my mother for a while. I will come and fetch you in time for lunch. I don't know about you but I am ravenous." And with that he left her.

Lucy wriggled to make her position more comfortable and switched a now contented Oceanus from one breast to the other. She ran a finger over the soft down on top of the baby's head and smiled ruefully. Her introduction to her mother-in-law had not been quite as she had pictured it, but perhaps that had been no bad thing. She had detected a certain reserve in Bathsheba's look initially, which she had been hard put to understand, but Oceanus had clearly been the ticket to instant acceptance. That was helpful; if they were all to live together, she had no wish to alienate her mother-in-law or the head of the family, John, but she was not at all sure how the sudden arrival of a stranger in their midst would go down or, indeed, how they would react if she upset their plans as she meant to do in relation to the suggestion of a wet nurse. She sighed softly. She had a lot to understand, but she thought she could learn to like this place.

The slave returned with a large jug of hot water and an empty metal basin which she placed on the floor near the window. Oceanus, having eaten his fill, did not object to being handed over and the girl lay him on a towel and started to undress him.

"What is your name?" said Lucy.

"Francine, mistress," the girl said, without looking up from her position on the floor.

"Do you have children of your own?" asked Lucy.

"No, mistress, but I help with some of the little ones."

Lucy was surprised to find that it was not that difficult to understand Francine, despite the heavy accent and her way of missing out certain words. And the girl appeared to know what she was doing. Lucy tested the water, and Francine seemed to have got the mix just right, and when the girl lifted Oceanus into the basin she held him competently. Lucy allowed her gaze to wander around the room.

It was spacious, with a heavy four-poster mahogany bed in the centre shrouded in mosquito netting. It was a corner room and had two large windows looking out over the sea and covered with Venetian blinds to allow the air to circulate while blocking out the blazing sun. Two bedside tables and a dressing table of some lighter wood, a large mahogany clothes press, a chaise longue (where she had sat to feed Oceanus) and two of the rattan armchairs she had admired in Bathsheba's room around a low table completed the furniture, and there would be plenty of room for her escritoire when it arrived as well as for the baby's cot.

There was some commotion in the hallway, then Bathsheba Lord stepped briskly into the room, followed by a large black man carrying a wooden crib.

"I told Thomas to fetch the crib my children had from the store-room. You may of course decide to choose another, but I thought it fitting for my grandson to use the same one as his father," said Bathsheba.

Lucy smiled inwardly; her tone indicated that she would view it as an insult if her new daughter-in-law rejected the cot. As Thomas put it down in the corner, she went over to inspect it. It was a solid piece of furniture, set on rockers, with its own mosquito net and lovingly carved from some light wood. It seemed to glow an inner red, so perhaps it was cherry. It had clearly been washed and quickly polished before being brought to the room; she could smell the beeswax.

"It is beautiful, ma'am – thank you," she said, smiling at her mother-in-law. By this time, Francine had dried and clothed Oceanus. Imperiously, Bathsheba held out her arms for her grandson, who yawned hugely and knuckled his eyes. She inspected him closely and appeared to approve. She handed him back to the girl, waving her over to the crib, and Oceanus was laid down to sleep.

"Unpack Mistress Lucy's things and run her a bath, girl," Bathsheba told Francine, and with a nod to Lucy she turned and left.

"Please fetch water for the bath first – then you can find me something to wear while I am washing," Lucy smiled at Francine, who gathered up the towels she had used for the baby and went away to organise the water.

Next came Thomas again, this time carrying an adult-sized tin bath. He took away the baby's bath, full of water, and a few minutes later returned with another man carrying a second trunk. Obviously the luggage had arrived from the ship. When they came again with her escritoire, Lucy showed them where to place it, just as Francine appeared with a large pitcher of hot water, another maid carrying an equally large one of cold water. Oceanus did not stir. Lucy noticed how, even with five adults in the room, it still seemed spacious and airy. Her initial impression about its size was confirmed, while the jalousied windows allowed the air to circulate constantly creating a welcome breeze.

Francine fetched a screen from beside the clothes press and opened it around the tub, then poured the water in. The second maid left with the empty pitchers, only to return twice more with full ones, staggering under their weight, as Lucy was undressing. Lucy asked her to close the door, unwilling to be surprised by any more arrivals while she bathed. The girl seemed surprised but did as she was told.

Francine seemed determined to stay with Lucy while she was in the bath, Lucy tried to send her to unpack the trunks, but surprisingly the girl said firmly, "I help you, mistress."

When she realised Francine was planning to soap her all over, it was Lucy's turn to be firm, she was horrified and embarrassed. "You may wash my hair; that is all," she said.

Again she detected surprise; as she was to discover, wherever you went, whatever you did in Barbados, there was an army of ever-present slaves to do everything for you that you always thought you could do yourself, from picking up a handkerchief to bringing you a glass of water from the other side of the room or washing and dressing you. White Barbadians seemed to do nothing; they told their slaves to do everything for them.

Washed and dried – again she would not let Francine help – Lucy reclined on the chaise longue wrapped in towels, dozing gently while Francine started to unpack. She selected one of Lucy's white muslin dresses, shook it out and lay it on the bed ready for wear. But then she seemed to hesitate, and Lucy realised that Francine had absolutely no idea what all the undergarments were for, or how they should be worn. Clearly, she had not acted as a lady's maid before. Clasping the towels around her, Lucy got up and went over to the girl, who looked up cringing and with fear in her eyes. Lucy was shocked. Did Francine think she would be punished for her ignorance? She smiled encouragement, taking the girl gently by her shoulder.

"Come, let me show you. This goes around my waist and laces at the back to keep me slender." She held the stays up against Francine. "The chemise goes over the top, under the dress; and then of course there are the stockings. Now, please help me to get dressed."

With a few instructions, Francine managed to get Lucy into her underclothes despite a struggle with the stay laces, putting a wrapper around her shoulders, then brushed out Lucy's short hair, already almost dry in the warm air. She twisted a piece of hair around her finger to create a curl across Lucy's forehead, and looked at her anxiously in the mirror to see if she approved. Lucy nodded, then stood up, shedding the wrapper, to have her dress thrown over her head and twitched into place. As Francine was tying the sash, the door opened and Sam came in to escort her to lunch downstairs. Lucy noticed that the girl's eyes had again dropped to the floor.

"Thank you, Francine," she said gently. "Will you watch over Oceanus for me?"

Without raising her eyes, Francine's answer came softly, "Yes, mistress." Lucy turned and went out on Sam's arm.

They descended the wide, panelled staircase and made their way to the dining room, its French windows open onto the shaded lawn. Again there was that mingled scent of brine, sugar, frangipani and beeswax. A number of people were already in the room, and Sam set about introducing Lucy to them. "My brother, John. My sisters, Sarah, Bathsheba and Betty." As Lucy bowed and shook hands with them all, she took covert stock. John looked serious and did not appear totally at ease with his younger brother. Sarah was thin and pale; she looked ill and did not say much. Bathsheba and Betty took after their mother in looks; of the two, the younger one, Betty (who appeared to be the same age as Lucy) seemed the more self-confident and lively. Bathsheba, named after her mother, was older than she had expected, and Lucy realised that she must be a confirmed spinster as she was well into her thirties.

Her mother-in-law swept in with another, younger woman who was noticeably pregnant and walked quietly over to stand at the opposite end of the table to John.

"Ah – I see you have been introduced to some of the family, Lucy. But you have not yet met John's wife, Sarah, I think?" She nodded in the direction of the woman who had accompanied her, who gave a small, stiff bow. Bathsheba continued, "Shall we sit down?" She moved to the centre of the table, and Sam motioned Lucy to sit on his brother's right. As the servants, white-gloved, began to serve the soup, John turned to Lucy.

"I understand you have brought your son with you, so I must offer my felicitations on both your marriage and the birth at one and the same time," he said.

"Thank you. Yes, Oceanus was born while we were at sea. Sam had hoped he would be born here at Long Bay, but that was not to be."

"I am sure he will be a welcome playmate for his cousin John, who is two now. We must have a celebration. A feast always makes the workforce more productive. We should arrange it in the next few weeks, should we not, Mother? We could have both boys baptised together."

The widow nodded. "I shall make the arrangements tomorrow. You can help me Lucy."

"I will do so too, Mama," said Betty. "Oceanus – what a strange name! Did you call him that because he was born at sea, or is it a family name? When can I meet him?"

Lucy smiled and answered both questions. "Because he was born at sea. You can come and meet him after luncheon, if you like."

Sam who had said nothing since they sat down looked up sharply when John mentioned his son but still he made no comment. Looking across the table at her husband, Lucy saw that he was frowning, and pushing his food around his plate. She remembered he had dismissed the idea of anyone taking precedence over Oceanus and realised that it must have come as a rude shock to him that John had a healthy two-year-old heir. There was an awkward silence, broken by the younger Bathsheba, who asked Lucy if she would like to walk in the gardens later, to which Lucy agreed.

The soup, accompanied by roasted small birds like quail and a cheese tart, had been followed by several different fish and a mutton pie, and these were now being removed to make way for fruit. Lucy tried the mango and found the orange fruit delicious. As the meal came to an end, John pushed back his chair.

"I must get back out and check on the cotton harvest, they are working over at Nine Acres field. Will you accompany me, Sam?" Without a word, Sam too pushed back his chair and went out with his brother.

Sam's mother stood up, signalling that it was time for all the company to leave the table. Betty tucked her arm through Lucy's, and went with her to see Oceanus, who was still sleeping – lying on his back, with arms and legs at all angles. Betty exclaimed at the cot, recognising it at once for the one all the Lord children had used, and put her foot on its base to rock the child in it gently. She glanced at Lucy and said in a sudden rush, "I am so glad you have brought Sam back to us. Life is more fun with him around – John is such a sober-sides!"

Lucy frowned slightly, wondering whether to say what was on her mind. She gave a mental shrug and went ahead. "Are Sam and John very close?" she asked.

"Oh no – they have always been at odds, since we were children. They are very different characters. And it got worse after Father died, I think John felt that Sam was not pulling his weight on the plantation, leaving all the work to John. And I think he was right," she added thoughtfully. "John is out every day in the fields; he doesn't leave everything to the overseer as most people do. But Sam was never really interested. He always wanted something bigger and better. He always had grand plans for the future which involved spending a lot of money. But this is not a large sugar estate like Drax Hall, so where's the money going to come from? That was why he went to England, to make his fortune – at least that's what he told us. Did he do so, Lucy?"

Lucy's mind was racing. Had she been completely blind? Had Sam only married her for her money, as her father had gently hinted was his concern? The doubt was like a cold douche of water over her happiness. But then she thought about his attention to her on the long sea voyage, his pride at Oceanus' birth, and felt comforted; surely he must love her at least a little?

"I do not know his situation, Betty. My father dealt with all that side of things when we were married. But he has talked to me too about his plans for a big house here on the island, which he intends to start building as soon as he can, and I am sure that must mean he has sufficient funds to complete the project."

Betty opened her mouth to say something then apparently thought better of it and shut it again. Lucy was glad; she felt they were getting into deep waters, and she did not know anyone here well enough to trust them with her thoughts. To forestall any further confidences, she suggested they went to find Betty's sisters Bathsheba and Sarah for the promised walk, and the two young women went back downstairs.

Armed with parasols to shade them from the afternoon sun, all three sisters set off with Lucy to show her the extensive gardens and – at her request – teach her the names of the local flora, so different from the English countryside. From the front door, they pointed out the extent of the Long Bay estate – which seemed to Lucy, from the slight eminence on which the house stood, to include everything in sight. She remarked on the pleasant temperature, and the girls explained that this was the cool, dry season; she would notice a real difference when July came with the rains, turning the air hot and humid day after day.

They walked between sandalwood, baobab and silk cotton trees, past the entrance to the long drive of mahogany; they watched and laughed at the green monkeys at play in the mango trees; and Bathsheba pointed out some bearded fig trees, which – like the West Indian cedar – had been ubiquitous on the island when the Portuguese first discovered it so they named it after the huge trees in their own language, *los Barbados*. As on her arrival, Lucy was stunned by the technicolour riot of flowers which proliferated in the carefully maintained beds – colours which could only work well together in nature, orange from the birds of paradise harmonised with magenta bougainvillea; white, orange, pink and purple hibiscus teamed with cream frangipani and yellow Christmas candles. Lucy tried to commit to memory their exotic names and decided she must bring her sketchbook out to paint them to send to her mother.

The three women turned to retrace their steps to the house – Sarah had already gone back because she tired easily. Lucy gave a guilty start as she realised, they had been walking for longer than she realised. Oceanus would no doubt be awake and crying.

"Oh, don't worry," said Bathsheba carelessly. "Your girl will look after him."

Lucy said nothing but speeded up and ran straight up to her room on their return. Francine was there, with Oceanus on her shoulder. He was, indeed, crying for food, and Lucy fed him before returning to join the rest of the women for a bowl of tea.

Her mother-in-law, informed by her daughters of Lucy's whereabouts, looked up and said firmly, "I will arrange for a wet nurse so you can avoid the inconvenience of constantly being on hand for your son."

"Thank you, ma'am," responded Lucy, equally firmly, "but I do not wish to put you to the trouble of doing so. I grew used to looking after Oceanus on the voyage and wish to continue in the same way."

There was a moment's silence. Her daughters looked at their mother, and Lucy realised that she was not used to being contradicted. She held her breath, wondering if there was going to be an outburst. There was great relief all round when Mrs Lord simply inclined her head and said, "As you wish," adding, "But it is *most* unusual behaviour."

Then she switched the subject. "You will need to be churched before the christening. I shall make the arrangements with the vicar when we attend service on Sunday." And she nodded dismissal.

Historically, European women were confined to their beds or their homes for extensive periods after giving birth in a custom called lying-in; care was provided either by female relatives (mother or mother-in-law), or by a temporary attendant known as a monthly nurse. 'Churching' was a ceremonial rite performed on women in order to restore ritual purity which served to mark the end of these weeks of separation and re-integrate the new mother into her community. The rite needed to be performed before the woman could attend normal church services, including the baptism of her own child.

Lucy did not see Sam again until the family congregated for drinks before supper on the wooden veranda outside the drawing room. The temperature had changed hardly at all now the sun had set, and a breeze from the sea made it very pleasant. She was introduced to the island's famous rum punch, using limes from the hedge surrounding the house, but she did not much care for it, being unused to strong spirits, preferring instead to drink water flavoured with the lime juice. The water from the island came from huge, natural underground cisterns and was crystal clear, purified further by passing through a limestone dripstone – porous limestone bowls through which the water was filtered.

She noticed Sam was consuming quite a number of glasses of punch. When John was occupied using the spyglass to check on something he could see going on in the slave quarters, she asked Sam how his ride around the estate had gone and received a somewhat non-committal answer.

"I should like one day to go with you to see the fields and learn about what goes on," she said, a little timidly, adding hurriedly, "if you don't think it too much trouble."

Sam looked at her in surprise. "If you don't think you will find it too tiring, of course I will take you," he responded. "Perhaps not tomorrow, but the day after. And I might even show you where I would like to build our new home," and with this he looked challengingly at John, who took no notice.

In the short, tropical twilight, the bats had come out, and were swooping around the house and veranda. Lucy sat back on her comfortable wicker seat and surveyed them somewhat sleepily, contrasting this evening with a typical one 'back home'. *No,* she thought to herself, *I must get used to the fact that this is now my home. Hewelsfield is just a place to visit.* Fleetingly she felt sad, but the warmth of the evening, all the fascinating things she had learned already today, the welcome – even if in some cases ambivalent – she had received from Sam's family meant she could not remain sad for long.

Sam did not visit her in her room that evening and, having lived in such close proximity to him for the last few months, she felt a little uneasy. But she said nothing, things were so different here in many ways that she did not want (as she usually did) to jump to conclusions or be too impetuous. She knew she had a tendency to act first and think later which she must now curb. And once she fell asleep, she slept long and deeply in her canopied bed, waking only to feed Oceanus every few hours – and even he slept for a whole five-hour stretch at one point.

Francine brought her hot chocolate when the sun was already quite high in the sky at seven o'clock. Lucy lay and sipped her drink, watching Oceanus as he gurgled to himself in the crib, which was rocking gently in response to his energetic kicks. Francine brought water for her to wash in once she had fed the baby and helped Lucy to dress for breakfast.

Following the meal, Lucy and Betty were summoned by Mrs Lord senior to help her organise the celebration in honour of the birth of Oceanus. Lucy's mother-in-law dispatched a slave with a message for the local vicar of St Philip's Church, setting the date of 21st March for a double baptism and requesting the vicar to visit Long Bay to discuss the details. Sarah, whose son John would be baptised at the same time as Oceanus, was nowhere to be seen. With a few suggestions from Betty, Mrs Lord senior swiftly wrote out a list of neighbours to be invited to the celebration (necessarily a short one because, as John had pointed out, most would be caught up with the sugar harvest) and told the girls to write out the invitations.

Lucy was surprised, given that from what she had already seen slaves were expected to do everything for their owners, her mother-in-law did not also give this task to them, but Betty explained that most of them could neither read nor write. Mrs Lord then summoned the housekeeper and made arrangements for the provisions needed for the feast. Lucy learned that it was the custom on the birth of a firstborn and male heir for everyone on the estate to be given a day off work and join the festivities and realised that the rest from their labours this entailed must be the reason John had said it would make the slaves more productive afterwards. And they would be able to celebrate (belatedly in one case) the birth of two male heirs and firstborns at once. How coldly functional, how clinically indifferent to their dignity and needs as human beings John's attitude to 'his' slaves was, Lucy thought to herself.

When the day of his christening came, the two-month-old Oceanus was dressed in a new white dress as was his two-year-old cousin, made by one of the house slaves and beautifully embroidered, and the family (without Sarah, who was suffering a very sickly pregnancy) set off after breakfast for St Philip's Church for the baptism, leaving the housekeeper to oversee arrangements for the feast which would begin at lunchtime. Her mother was heard by Betty to mutter that Sarah's weakness was a disappointment.

"So I think," said Betty to Lucy, "that your reputation may have been enhanced by the fact that she is always ailing when she is breeding, but probably even more by the fact that she has failed to produce a second son so you are still on equal footing!" Betty was not fond of her sister-in-law Sarah, and increasingly spent time with Lucy to avoid her.

By this time, Lucy had learned that little John had twin sisters, Mary Elizabeth and Frances Sodbury, born in March 1808, but no mention had been made of having them baptised at the same time as the boys. Lucy wondered a little at this and asked Sam about it, but he had shrugged dismissively and said merely that it would become too complicated and the girls could be christened at any time.

Lucy was surprised to see that the church appeared quite new. Her mother-in-law informed her that some twenty years earlier it had replaced a previous building which had been fatally damaged by storms. It was also smaller than she had expected, but it was solidly built of stone, with crenelations at the top of the wall and a series of Gothic windows set well back in their stone embrasures. The inside was simply whitewashed, and Lucy found it cool and restful.

The vicar, the Reverend Nicholson, who seemed to be in some awe of Sam's mother, conducted the baptismal ceremony efficiently and with a minimum of fuss, and refused a polite invitation to join them for the feast back at Long Bay. Oceanus slept through it all until the cold water was poured onto his head, from which point he cried noisily, which Lucy was by now used to. (Little John, by contrast, had accepted the whole process stoically and uttered not a sound). She noted with an inner smile that her mother-in-law took care to make the return journey in a different carriage from the one in which she herself travelled with the baby – to avoid more of the child's wails she assumed.

Back at the house, they were met by a delicious smell of roasting meat. A pig and a cow had been butchered and barbecued to feed family and visitors, several of whom had already arrived. Lucy hurried to her room to feed Oceanus, who was making it loudly known that he was very unhappy not to have been fed already, and on her return John introduced her to Dr Nathan Lucas and his wife Mary who, it turned out, were frequent visitors to the estate, as long-standing friends of John and Sam's parents as well as Dr Lucas being the family doctor. In discussion, they divulged that they had a daughter – also called Mary – the same age as Lucy and Betty, and expressed the hope that Lucy would get to make her acquaintance in the near future. Lucy rather liked the couple, feeling an affinity with them she was not sure she could have with her own new family.

The slave cooks had supplemented the meat with an array of local delicacies such as candied sweet potatoes, pickled breadfruit and corn seasoned with chilli butter. As she glanced at the trestle tables where the estate's slaves were clustered, Lucy realised that this was probably the best meal they would get all year. Anticipation of this, together with the rum which had been distributed among the workers in preparation for a toast to the children, created a happy atmosphere, and Lucy reflected that the downcast mien and listlessness of the slaves which she had so far only registered in her subconscious was likely to be due as much to poor nutrition as to the ever-present threat of punishment for the slightest petty infringement. She was dimly aware that much poverty and poor living conditions existed in several English towns – for example, Bristol – as a result of their burgeoning industry but she did not think that even in Bristol and Wolverhampton she had ever seen such hopelessness.

Lucy smiled at Francine, who was watching over Oceanus in his crib, which had been brought outside for the occasion. Little John had wandered off with his elder sister Adriana and could be seen a little distance away playing in the dirt with several other small children, watched over by a couple of black nurses. Lucy wondered if she might be able to help Francine gain her freedom, but knew she was still too ignorant of the system to be able to suggest it yet.

At that moment, Sam sauntered over, lifted the child from his crib and held him aloft as family, visitors and slaves alike roared their approval and clinked their glasses and the slaves starting up an impromptu dance.

Chapter 6
Life on the Plantation

Over the coming days and weeks, both Lucy and Sam basked in the warm glow of his mother's approval at their production of a healthy son, and Lucy enjoyed the level of attention and affection Sam continued to show her.

Although the enforced intimacy of shipboard life had given way to the more normal arrangements of the period for a wealthy couple – namely, separate bedrooms – Sam took to visiting her almost nightly for a chat before they went to sleep, and frequently for rather more. She found she increasingly enjoyed and looked forward to his lovemaking; he seemed very knowledgeable about what would be likely to cause her pleasure, and she shyly started to experiment with returning his caresses, embarrassed initially but becoming more confident as he encouraged her. She occasionally wondered in what circumstances and with whom he had gained his expertise but decided not to ask in case she did not like the answer.

She quickly learned that even the most upright white men on the island considered female slaves to be bred for their carnal use and appeared to see nothing reprehensible in bedding them whenever they wished. The feelings of their wives and fiancées, let alone of the girls themselves, were not considered. She had, for instance, stumbled one morning across Juba, a black girl perhaps sixteen years old, leaving John's bedroom clutching a torn bodice to her chest and with a dark welt on her cheek. She looked as though she had been crying. The girl fled when she noticed Lucy but continued her duties about the house as normal. John was a little more cheerful than usual at breakfast that day, but nothing else changed. Lucy wondered what his wife Sarah would have to say about it, and indeed whether she even knew. It was strange, she found herself reflecting, that these white men – maybe even including her husband, although she desperately hoped not – both treated their slave women as lowly sub-humans yet simultaneously bedded them. What strange creatures men were! Was this another exertion of their power or an expression of their sexual lust – or a perverted combination of both?

On some mornings, Lucy rode out with Sam – and occasionally John – beginning to learn her way around the plantation. At her firm but quiet insistence they visited the slave quarters carefully situated, she was told, where the wind would not blow the smell towards the house but the owners could nevertheless keep an eye on their property as she had noted John doing on her first night, using the spyglass on the veranda. Both brothers made it very clear, however, that she must never visit the slave quarters on her own. She found the quarters depressing; nearly all were constructed of wattle and daub, with thatch roofs which would burn fiercely should there be a fire. A few were constructed of limestone like the main house: these were for the families of skilled slaves, who were highly valued and treated better than the others, with a freedom of movement they could only dream of. But all the buildings were sparsely furnished, with cast-off barrels used for tables, a piece of wood laid on a shelf in the wall for a bed and bits of hessian sacking for bedclothes.

They visited the aloe fields, where Lucy was introduced to the method of cultivation. She watched the slaves bending over the base of the plants, removing the aloe 'pups' to propagate the crop; she watched the careful way they cut the leaves for harvesting, to avoid any of the precious juice being exposed to the air. She marvelled at their stoicism, seeing the slaves' hands bleeding despite the cloths they wrapped around them, from the aloes' razor-sharp points. And she visited the small factory, powered by the estate's own windmill, where the aloe was prepared for use, either as a laxative or to tend burns or cuts.

They also visited the cotton fields, where the harvest was in full swing. West Indian cotton, she already knew, was considered to be of very fine quality and fetched a high price in London or Bath. She watched the slaves toiling under the overseer's whip to the backbreaking tasks of picking the cotton, and then later clearing the ground. She was told that cotton rapidly depleted the nutrients in the soil so after harvest an area might be left fallow until the following season, while in other fields the cotton bushes might simply be pruned to get a further harvest the following year. Once harvested, the raw cotton was carried to a big barn, where older slaves – mostly women – who were too slow to work the fields any longer sat and removed the cotton from its husk, picking out as many seeds as they could for replanting before bagging the raw cotton for export. Lucy began to understand why John and Sam were both so keen – for different reasons – to expand their landholdings. If they had land suitable for sugar, or more land available to cultivate for cotton, their revenue would be far greater.

Sam made it very clear to Lucy that he did not want her riding out without a male escort, even if she was accompanied by one or more of his sisters. Her usually rebellious spirit was subdued by an unpleasant incident she witnessed when they visited the cotton fields before breakfast one morning a few months after her arrival. She saw the white overseer, Alexander – whom she thought a cruel brute – apparently leaning against a tree some little way along the path. The wind was blowing in their direction. Faintly, she thought she could hear moaning or sobbing, as though someone were in distress. She was about to turn and mention it to Sam, who was riding slightly behind her, when the overseer moved, and she caught a glimpse of a girl cowering away from him, her back against the tree and her dress askew. The overseer turned towards them, pulling up his trousers as he did so. It was obvious to even the meanest intelligence what he had been up to, but he remained either oblivious to or uncaring of their presence. Sam hailed the man, and pushed his mount past Lucy, spurring towards him. She followed more slowly, and saw the girl stumble off towards the cotton field, her face tear-streaked. Seething with indignation, she gave the overseer a curt nod and as soon as Sam moved away, she grabbed his arm and, stumbling slightly over the words, told him what she had seen and demanded to know what he was going to do about it.

"Why, what do you expect me to do?" Sam replied in surprise. "He has done nothing wrong. Though come to think of it, it is embarrassing for you to catch him at his leisure pursuits. I am sorry if that has distressed you."

Lucy ground her teeth, retorting sharply, "It is not merely that he has not the decency to conduct what you call his 'leisure pursuits' in private, but rather that he was clearly using that girl in a way that she did not welcome. She was crying, Sam! She may be a slave, but surely she has some right to choose to whom she gives her body?"

"She had probably been lazy, wasn't picking the cotton as quickly as she should. It was either the whip or the man," responded Sam.

Lucy gasped. "Have you no feelings for that poor girl? I think this whole system is completely barbaric! I understand now why our Parliament voted to abolish the slave trade. Why can you not pay your servants a wage and provide them with some dignity, as we do at home? They are human beings. Different, yes of course. But just people like us with feelings like us."

His eyes narrowed. "This is your home now, my girl. And this 'barbaric system' as you call it provides you with sugar and cotton and spices at prices you can afford – these are no longer goods destined merely for kings and queens because of their expense. I would have thought you would welcome that. I have told you before, our slaves are well cared for; they are housed and fed. Many of those who gain their freedom come begging for their old jobs back because they cannot survive once they leave the plantation. Slaves are our property, to do with as we wish, it's not in an overseer's interest to damage it, and I am sure that girl was really quite ready to receive his advances."

Lucy was so angry she spurred her horse to a gallop, oblivious to the broken ground along which they rode. She did not slow down until she reached the stables. She dismounted and was already going upstairs to bathe and change when Sam caught up with her again. He gripped her elbow.

"I warn you, madam wife, not to meddle. This is not yet your world, and your interference will not be welcome. Learn to accept what you cannot change."

Lucy did not answer but raised her chin and swept along the corridor to her room which, for once, was empty. Francine, who had taken on the duty of caring for the baby in Lucy's absence, must have taken Oceanus out. She rang the bell for water to be fetched and sat brooding in one of the rattan chairs as she waited for it, twisting the ribbons of her riding hat between her fingers.

By the time she went into breakfast, she was calmer. There was no sign of Sam, she presumed he had already eaten. His invalid sister Sarah was the only person present, and she crept away shortly after Lucy arrived. Lucy ate some guava, a dark and rich pink, the deep taste of which she loved, and sipped at a bowl of tea, staring unseeingly through the windows. Afterwards, with Oceanus fed and resting with Francine, she did what she had been meaning to do since she arrived, and took her paints, sketchpad and easel out into the lush garden to try and capture some of the exotic flora for her mother.

Like all her contemporaries, Lucy had learned to draw and paint watercolours under the tutelage of her governess and when at school in Keynsham, but unlike them Lucy was genuinely talented, and she quickly became absorbed in her work and lost to what was going on around her. She was startled therefore when Betty touched her on the shoulder gently to get her attention, having been standing for some time behind her sister-in-law admiring the bird of paradise flower Lucy had been working on.

"That is truly beautiful, Lucy, I wish I could paint like that," said Betty. "I want to stroke your picture, to feel the petals – it looks so lifelike."

"Thank you. It is for my mother," said Lucy. "I cannot see her ever travelling out here to visit me, and she loves flowers so I thought I would paint some of the beautiful things you grow here and send the pictures to her."

"I came to ask you if you would like to go for a walk," said Betty, "but if you are busy…"

"I would like that very much. If you don't mind waiting until I have finished this one? I won't be long."

Betty flopped down on the lawn in a way Lucy was sure her mother would not approve of, legs apart and her stockinged ankles in full view, while Lucy put the finishing touches to her picture and began to pack up her painting equipment.

"Don't worry about that. One of the girls can take it all in for you," said Betty carelessly. "You, boy," she said somewhat imperiously to one of the gardeners, "go and fetch Mercy from the house and tell her to take the mistress's painting things to her room."

Lucy linked arms with Betty to share her parasol for their stroll among the flowers, Betty stealing a glance at her. "I saw Sam leave the house this morning looking black as a thundercloud. Have you quarrelled?" she asked carefully.

Lucy nodded. Then, a little reluctantly since the subject matter was clearly not suitable for an unmarried girl – albeit one the same age as her – she said cautiously, "We disagreed over the importance of something I saw the overseer doing. I didn't like the way he was abusing a field slave."

"That explains it, then. It's really none of our business what they do in the fields, is it? If Sam saw nothing wrong it was probably that you are just not yet used to our ways. He doesn't like his judgement being called into question, you know. I expect no man does."

Betty must have repeated the conversation to her mother, for Bathsheba took Lucy to one side before they sat down to lunch and said, "I understand you witnessed something unpleasant in the fields this morning. I can guess what it was," and, as Lucy flushed crimson, she nodded briskly. "The *mores* on a working estate are probably very different from anything you have encountered before. You must remember that the slaves belong to us, body and soul. Although I do not condone Alexander for carrying on so publicly, he had every right to take the girl if he wanted her. He, at least, is unmarried; you may have noticed that it is quite common here even for married men to take a slave girl as their mistress. I consider this immoral, but it is the way of the world. You will win no friends if you try to interfere, or even show your disapproval." She patted Lucy's arm in a friendly if slightly distant fashion and moved into the dining room. Lucy wondered if she knew about or condoned John's escapades with Juba, the girl she had seen leaving John's room when she first arrived at Long Bay.

She and Sam were very correct and cold with one another for the next few days. He did not visit her bedroom, nor take her out with him. Lucy – who had thought she was being very dignified but appeared rather to an objective observer to be indulging in a fit of the sulks – began to feel lonely and isolated, and when she noticed a rather beautiful mulatto slave called Grace looking up at Sam from under her long lashes as he lounged, smiling, against the newel post, Lucy decided it was time to woo her husband back. She waited until the dinner hour, then made sure she left her room at the same time as Sam. She put a hand on his arm.

"I am sorry, Sam. I don't like you being so cold towards me. I know I still have a lot to learn, and it is sometimes very difficult…" her voice trailed off, and she looked up at him, a short, plump little figure, her brown eyes looking appealingly up at him. "I would really like to go out riding with you again, I miss our morning excursions. And besides, Oceanus is missing you too."

Sam looked at her in silence, a slight frown on his forehead. "I will not have you losing your temper with me in that way again," he said. "But I suppose it must have been a bit of a shock, seeing nature in the raw as it were. Mother said I should have a word with Alexander and tell him to be more discreet."

She bit her tongue and said nothing, just continued to look beseechingly up at him, her hand still on his arm.

"Tell you what, we'll go out tomorrow and I'll show you where I want to build my castle. It's not too far, and you're a far better rider than my sisters so the rough ground shouldn't bother you."

Lucy brightened and decided not to question his use of such a grandiose term for their new home. Arm in arm, they descended the staircase. Mrs Lord looked at them approvingly, and Betty looked relieved. Lucy realised she had probably been a bit selfish – she was the stranger here; she might feel uncomfortable living with slavery, but the Lord family knew nothing else. She smiled at everyone and went over to talk to Betty.

The next morning she woke at half past five to the sound of the slave bell tolling to call the workers to the fields. She fed Oceanus, handed him over to Francine, dressed quickly in her riding habit and hurried downstairs to meet Sam, who awaited her outside the front door, already astride his big chestnut, Nero. A stable boy held her glossy black mare, Empress, he helped settle her into the saddle, and Sam waited a touch impatiently for her to arrange her skirts around the pommel. She nodded to the boy, smiled at Sam and they set off at a fast trot down the long drive.

Lucy relaxed. She loved riding. Sam was right, she did ride well. Her father, having decided at an early stage that no amount of punishment would stop his beloved daughter being wayward and headstrong, realised he would find it hard

148

to prevent her careering all over the countryside in which they lived so ensured that she had an excellent riding teacher who not only managed to dissuade her from trying to ride astride like a man instead of side-saddle as was proper for a lady, but also to instil in her a real respect for the animal, thus preventing her from carrying out some of her more hare-brained schemes in case she hurt or even killed her horse.

They reached a straight stretch of sandy path which Lucy now knew well. She dropped her reins, urging Empress into a canter, and overtook Sam just for the sheer joy of racing. Taken by surprise, Sam was soundly beaten, and grinned reluctantly at her laughing countenance as he caught up with her at a stand of casuarina trees.

"Don't let my mother see you behaving like a hoyden," he warned her. "You'll fall from grace again. Anyway, come on, I'm taking you to see where I plan to build our castle – once I can sort dear John out." He turned and led her back away from the fields and up a faint track towards the clifftops. Lucy followed silently, wondering as they threaded their way through the scrub along the stony ground what he had meant by his last, somewhat sharp remark.

The north-easterly winds increased in strength as they neared the cliffs, and when Sam finally stopped, Lucy was holding firmly to her hat with one hand to prevent it being blown away. He dismounted and helped her to do so also, tying the reins loosely at the horses' necks to allow them to crop at the scrubby grass. He took her hand and drew Lucy towards the cliff edge. Below her she could see the ubiquitous sea-grape and cacti; to her left Long Bay beach glittered in the sun, and directly ahead but further out she could see the waves breaking on Cobblers Reef, surging white heads on deep turquoise. As she had found out soon after her arrival, the booming sound she had noticed came from the waves crashing on the reef and the beach.

Without thinking, Lucy uttered the first words to come into her head. "Does this wretched wind never let up?"

Sam caught her by both shoulders and shook her. "Why must you always complain?" he shouted angrily, if rather unfairly.

Lucy bit her lip, a little frightened. It occurred to her that, if indeed Sam had only married her for her money, it would be easy for him to push her over the edge of a higher cliff than this one, such as the one at Crane perhaps, and then live exactly as he pleased. There would be no witnesses to the deed, and she would have no chance of surviving such a fall.

"I am sorry, Sam. Show me where you would build. Would the house look out to sea or inland? How big will it be? And why can you not build where you want to?"

Still frowning, Sam moved away from the cliff and walked towards an area where the ground dipped slightly. Lucy followed more slowly and watched as he began to draw almost invisible lines with his whip on the stony, sandy soil to demonstrate the size and shape of their future home.

Lucy noticed that, as before when Sam had spoken to her of his building project, he became extremely animated, his eyes alight with excitement, and he had clearly thought long and hard about what he wanted.

"This must be the grandest mansion on the whole island. I want it to stand proud and welcoming to ships crossing the Atlantic, proof that we in Barbados are not uncouth barbarians, to be despised by the Mother country, but that we relish fine architecture and design," declared Sam. "I will call it Long Bay Castle, and I shall get Charles Rutter, who has been redecorating Windsor Castle, to design the interior."

He had already told her he wanted something far larger than the house they currently lived in, perhaps some fifteen to twenty bedrooms to the current seven. While Lucy could understand him wanting his own house (something she would also prefer), she had not understood why he wanted anything so big. Now, from his comments, she got some inkling that he had suffered a few rebuffs and slights when first in England. Perhaps London had not proved as welcoming as more provincial Bath?

Now he talked to her of a two-storey castle, with walls over two feet thick and a crenelated parapet, the four corners of the building on the four points of the compass. Broad flights of blue and white marble steps would sweep up to open verandas with iron railings on all four sides of the castle, and on both floors, each room would have French windows opening onto the veranda. Inside, the upper floor would be reached by a wide, elegant marble staircase, topped by a beautiful domed ceiling covered in frescoes. The kitchens and service areas would be in the basement. There would be a separate bathhouse and large privy outside the house, fed by water pumped up from the beach below. Sam pointed his stick westwards. "That will be the driveway, with the slave quarters on either side of the gate. That way none of their stench will be blown towards us," he said, and she flinched. "And, just to show you that I do realise I need to compensate for the wind, the drawing room will be on the leeward side, protected from the wind by an enclosed veranda, and looking straight down the drive."

"I think it sounds magnificent, Sam. Why do we have to wait? What did you mean when you said you need to sort John out?"

Lucy was sitting on the ground with her back to a large rock, and Sam moved across to join her. For a few minutes he said nothing, swishing his whip aimlessly at the scrub next to him. At last he looked sideways at her.

"I am not sure how much you know about my circumstances, Lucy, so let me explain. As you have seen, we are a large family. My eldest brother, Richard, died before my father, but you have not yet met my married sister Mary. Father owned one of the biggest stores in Bridgetown at 150 Broad Street, and he bought Long Bay out of the profits. When he died, he left Long Bay jointly to John and me. But the plantation is not profitable enough by itself to provide for all of us. For that, it needs to expand and develop sugar. John wants to buy more land but hasn't the funds to do so." Sam stopped, and looked thoughtfully at Lucy, wondering how she was taking all this and how much more he should tell her.

"John wants me to invest our money in expanding the plantation and won't let me build the castle until I have done so."

Lucy was her father's daughter and had an unusually shrewd head for business. "Is my settlement large enough to cover both?" she asked. "I do not know enough about land prices or the costs of building here."

"It is not. We would have to wait until the estate produced sufficient profit to enable me to finance the building. And that is assuming that John gives me my share... And I'll wager you will find it damnably uncomfortable playing second fiddle to John's wife in the meantime!"

Lucy rather agreed. She had looked forward to being mistress of her own house, and already found it irksome that everything at Long Bay was ordered by Sam's mother. Playing second fiddle not only to her but also to Sarah, John's wife – particularly knowing that Sarah would view Long Bay as her son's inheritance and guard it jealously – might be unbearable.

"I would have thought John would welcome the thought of losing three mouths to feed. We could even offer to take Betty with us until such time as she marries." Fearful that he would get angry, she added diffidently, "If... if you were to build something a little less grand, Sam, would we be able to contribute something towards expanding the plantation? Perhaps that would be sufficient to mollify him?"

"I will not compromise," responded Sam harshly. "It is my... our money. Why should I put it into his plantation? It is his responsibility to provide for the girls."

Lucy looked at him, puzzled. "What do you mean, 'his plantation'? Your father left it to you jointly."

Too late, Sam realised he had let his anger get the better of him and would have to tell Lucy the truth. He looked at her under frowning brows and said curtly, "He did, but I sold my share to John before I went to England."

Lucy's mind whirled. "So – we are living as unwanted guests in your childhood home, with no rights to any share in it either for you or for Oceanus?" she said slowly. "And all we have to live on is my settlement? Then why *are* we living here? Why not purchase a property elsewhere, perhaps a sugar plantation that will produce an income for us to live on?"

"Because Long Bay is and has always been my home. I want it to become a great plantation, to match or exceed those which are the biggest and best now, like Drax, Lascelles and St Nicholas. I want the Lords to be part of shaping Barbados' future, not bit players. John has no real ambition – just wants to make a living – though I think he'd like to be invited to become a Barbados Assembly Councillor!"

"But to succeed, you would need to buy back into ownership of Long Bay with John or purchase other land to add to it," said Lucy, frowning. "So that is why you need my settlement, and why you need John's agreement on where to build your castle. Betty told me you went to England to make your fortune. That was the reason?" Sam nodded. "And did you make your fortune, Sam? Or was that why you married me?" Lucy asked softly and sadly.

There was a long silence. "I did form the intention to marry money, it is true," Sam said carefully, "but" – and he caught her determined little chin in his right hand and turned her face towards him – "that was by no means why I offered for you! I could not have married you had you been penniless, but I was lucky enough to fall for a girl with prospects." He smiled, "An infuriating, wilful creature who also has the passion and strength to help me achieve my ambition, and who has already given me a son and heir."

He hugged her – as a brother rather than a lover might, thought Lucy – then held her by the shoulders facing him, waiting to hear how she would respond. He could not afford for her to turn against him now; while, legally, her matrimonial settlement was already his to spend, he hoped to benefit further financially from her wealthy father's fondness for her in his will. Sam was gambling that Thomas Wightwick would leave a large sum to Lucy or his grandchildren on his death and that he, Sam, would be able to enjoy the proceeds. He needed to keep her sweet.

Lucy looked gravely at him for what seemed like a long time. Then she sighed. And in that moment, she grew up, the romantic notion that her handsome, exotic, debonair husband had fallen as desperately in love with a short, plain English girl as she had with him was shattered for ever.

Perhaps – she hoped – he really was fond of her in his own way, but not in love. He had, she suspected, deliberately swept her off her feet, grateful to have found a personable girl wealthy enough for his purposes, young enough to have a head full of romantic nonsense and with an indulgent father. Now she would have to work hard to retain his affections, for her own and Oceanus' sake, or her life so far from England could become unbearable.

The following Sunday, as Lucy was getting herself ready to accompany the other ladies of the house to St Philip's Church for the service as usual, Sam surprised her by announcing that he would go too. Carelessly, he informed the assembled company that he had met John Barrow while visiting Bridgetown, and he had invited them all to Sunbury for lunch.

"You will like Sunbury, Lucy," he said. "It is a beautiful old plantation house. And now the sugar harvest is coming to an end, it's time to start introducing you into Barbados society."

His mother frowned, and scolded Sam for failing to give them more warning of the visit, but she could never be cross with him for long and – like Lucy – was clearly quite pleased that the somewhat humdrum nature of their days was to be enlivened. Other than the feast for Oceanus' and John's baptism, there had been little in the way of entertaining at Long Bay since Lucy's arrival, nor had they been anywhere apart from the weekly visit to church, which was one reason why Lucy valued her morning rides with Sam so much. There was a palpable air of excitement in the group as they set off (even John's habitually sombre demeanour had lightened) and it had nothing to do with expectations of the vicar's sermon.

They took two carriages to drive the six miles to St Philip's Church. Over the weeks, Lucy had been introduced to a number of the regular church-goers, including John Barrow and his wife Mary. John's wife Sarah's mother, Mrs Marshall, also attended St Philip's, and when John saw her, he hurried over to greet her. Dr Nathan Lucas came over to pay his respects to Mrs Lord senior and, as he had promised, to introduce his daughter, Mary Kingsley, to Lucy.

Mary, of a similar age to Lucy, had her father's smiling eyes and calm demeanour, Lucy thought, and liked her on sight. She had soft brown hair and was of a similar height to Lucy although her figure was more slender. Mary congratulated Lucy on her marriage and on the birth of Oceanus, whom she expressed a desire to meet. Lucy smiled, and opened her mouth to invite Mary to visit Long Bay one day the following week – then shut it again as she remembered her position as guest rather than hostess. Instead she turned to her mother-in-law who was still talking to Dr Lucas and waited for a break in their conversation to ask if Mary might visit.

"We would be delighted," responded Bathsheba. "Perhaps, Nathan, you and your wife could bring your daughter over? Shall we say a week on Wednesday?" Dr Lucas bowed his thanks, and the whole party moved into the church.

Lucy enjoyed the visit to Sunbury, as Sam had told her she would. Like most sugar plantations it was a self-sufficient community, as self-contained and independent as any small town. She thought that many of the large estates in England and Wales, like Clevedon Court or Tredegar House, would have been similarly self-contained in earlier times. As at Long Bay there were the plantation house and slave huts, barns for livestock, stables for the horses and storage sheds for plantation supplies, but there were far more buildings – mainly associated with the production of sugar, such as the boiling and curing houses – as well as a medical post, and a gaol (while at Long Bay they merely had the stocks and a whipping post for meting out punishment to the slaves, along with a couple of makeshift cells below the house). Long Bay used its single windmill to power the aloe distillation; Sunbury had several windmills to power its vast sugar works.

Most of the more than four hundred acres of plantation lands at Sunbury were a sea of tall sugar cane, whispering, singing and shimmering dependent on the weather, and populated by hungry rats. But there were also fields producing the meat, vegetables and fruit to feed such a vast enterprise, pigs, cows and poultry; sweet potatoes, plantains, okra, guavas, oranges, bananas…

Built along standard plantation house lines, Sunbury was grander by far than Long Bay, more imposing but with no more rooms, although the dining room was extremely large - the table could surely seat twenty with ease. Lucy was struck by the fact that Sunbury's main house was so small by comparison with great estate houses in England and wondered about some of the other places she had heard mentioned with reverence, such as Drax and Lascelles. The gardens were truly beautiful and John Barrow himself took her on a guided tour when asked to by Sam, with Betty accompanying her.

"In some parts you can still see the original, sturdy flint walls from the 1660s," Mr Barrow said, pointing to a long wall facing away from the prevailing winds. "My father rebuilt much of it when he bought it more than twenty years ago, after we had had a particularly destructive hurricane season; you may have noticed the jalousie shutters on all the windows which were put in at that time. He added to it, of course, as well. My father-in-law, William Senhouse, describes Sunbury as one of the best built plantation houses on the island."

"Was it your father who planted the first mahogany trees my husband told me about?" asked Lucy.

"Yes, indeed. He is a noted horticulturalist – in fact, he is away on an expedition at this moment. Are you particularly interested in trees, ma'am?"

Lucy explained how fascinating she found the exotic vegetation on the island, and Mr Barrow promised to show her after lunch the stand of three hundred mahogany trees his father had planted, as well as some interesting teak and black willow samples. At first, he viewed this promise as a bit of a chore and wondered why he had not foisted the excursion onto his wife, but he quickly revised his preconception of Lucy as a typical empty-headed, highly strung English girl who would wilt in the Caribbean heat and bemoan her lot so far from English civilisation. He found she had a genuine interest in the island's way of life and quickly grasped the commercial pros and cons in relation to sugar and cotton cultivation. When he expressed surprise, she explained how her father had sometimes allowed her to accompany him to his place of business in Bristol, or to meet with the shipbuilders in Chepstow and had – unusually for the period – wanted her to have a firm grounding in business matters. When he learned that she had given birth on board the Princess Mary during the crossing from England, his admiration grew. She spoke of it so matter-of-factly, yet he thought it must have been quite frightening and traumatic for a gently-bred girl.

By the time they returned to the house, the two were firm friends, and he remarked thoughtfully to his wife later that Sam Lord might have bitten off more than he could chew when he married Lucy, she was no fool and would be unlikely to put up with the sort of wild behaviour Sam had got up to before he left for England. He expected fireworks and wondered how it would end.

As their party left Sunbury, John Lord said, "We shall look forward to returning your hospitality shortly, when you both visit Long Bay to celebrate my twins' christening."

"We are looking forward to it very much, John," responded Mary Barrow. "I only hope that my husband's militia duties do not prevent us from doing so!"

On the way home in the carriage, Lucy asked about the militia. John, who was travelling with Sam and Lucy, answered, "We provide our own military force here. All plantation families have at least one member in the militia, and we train regularly – one Friday a month. Every free man between the ages of sixteen and sixty is expected to serve, apart from clergymen. John Barrow is a colonel and takes his duties seriously. He is a good leader – thoughtful, and not afraid to try new things. I am a member of his unit. In fact, our next training session is in Bridgetown on Friday. You should think about joining up, Sam, now you are back, we need all the able-bodied men we can get."

To both his and Lucy's surprise, Sam responded to the idea with enthusiasm, and agreed to accompany his brother to training that weekend. Lucy thought, resignedly, that there were probably other attractions for Sam in going to Bridgetown and wished she could accompany the two men. The glimpse she had had of a bustling, lively town when she first arrived from England made her yearn to spend some time there, and while Sam probably looked forward to cock-fighting, card games, gambling and ogling pretty girls, she wished she could visit the shops, go dancing and explore a little. The outing to Sunbury had only made her realise how stifled she had begun to feel at the reclusive life she had been leading since her arrival. She enjoyed looking after Oceanus, but she had expected to be running a household, and thought there would be far more social interaction with their peers. Even at Hewelsfield there always seemed to be things to do, and of course during the Season she had spent her time in a social whirl in Bath.

Perhaps the trip to Sunbury had a similar effect on the whole household. The following day as they sat at the lunch table Betty announced abruptly, "Mother, if I am not to disgrace myself at the twins' christening, I simply must visit Bridgetown. Two of my dresses are so shabby that I have given them to my girl, I cannot possibly wear the same dress as when John and Oceanus were baptised, and I do not believe I have anything else suitable to wear. Besides, I think it is time to catch up with the London fashions that Lucy brought with her."

Even the ailing Sarah, normally so quiet, brightened and added her mite to the conversation. "Besides, Mama, Lucy has not yet seen the store that Father established."

Mrs Lord smiled and said she had been planning a visit herself to put in train the provisioning required for the twins' christening in a couple of months. Her daughters cried out at the idea that she might have considered going to Bridgetown without them, and after some discussion it was agreed that all the ladies – all except John's wife Sarah, who was due to give birth again any day now – would spend Friday in town, leaving the previous afternoon and spending the night at the Royal Naval Hotel.

On the Thursday the women of the household were all gathered outside the front door following a light lunch, preparing to get into the carriages, when Lucy was surprised to see Sam trotting along the path from the stables.

"I thought I would accompany you, Mama," he said. "I have some business to attend to in Bridgetown as well as militia training tomorrow – and I want to hear Lucy's views on our capital at first hand!"

Lucy put a hand on Nero's bridle and looked wistfully up at Sam. "May I not ride Empress to town since you are riding Nero?" she asked.

Sam shook his head decisively. "No, m'dear. I shall have to rest Nero more than one night in any case, and I plan to stay on in Bridgetown and meet up with some friends on Saturday after militia training. The long ride would tire you out and you would have no energy left to go shopping. Besides, Empress would need to rest overnight too, and I don't fancy leading her back to Long Bay when I come back after the weekend. I do not believe you have the stamina to ride there and back in such quick succession. Remember, the journey takes at least four hours."

Lucy stifled a sigh but turned to get into one of the two carriages with Betty and Sarah. Mrs Lord and Bathsheba would travel in the other. A couple of house slaves accompanied the party, sitting on the box seats and looking quite as excited as their mistresses. Francine had brought Oceanus to the door to see them off, and Lucy surprised herself by not feeling any guilt for leaving him in the girl's care for the longest period since his birth almost six months previously; she had never left him overnight before. She hoped that Oceanus would not complain too much at being fed cow's milk or pap in her absence; or perhaps Francine would find one of her fellow slaves willing and able to breastfeed him for this short period. She felt torn between her love for her son and her desire to be near him and a longing to be free of all responsibility, however briefly, and enjoy life.

The carriage steps were raised and the doors closed. Sam wheeled Nero and set off at a brisk trot down the drive, the two conveyances following behind him.

Lucy looked at her sisters-in-law. "What do you have it in mind to purchase?" she asked.

Betty's face was alive with laughter. "As much as I can possibly get away with!" she answered firmly. "It's not often that I get such an excuse! I shall buy several lengths of dress fabric; I need a hat, and undergarments and shoes..."

Sarah looked shocked. "How can you be so extravagant, Betty?" she asked. "You know Mama says we must be careful. For my part..."

Betty interrupted her impatiently, "Don't be such a misery, Sarah, you always cast such a damper on things. When do you think we'll have a chance like this again? It's a great opportunity to replenish my wardrobe – even Mama and John can't object – and the twins' christening means I am sure to be able to squeeze another dress in among my purchases!"

"For my part, I plan to buy just a shawl, and maybe a new overdress to go over my cream satin underdress. And I would love a pair of silk stockings, like the ones you have, Lucy," Sarah added wistfully.

Lucy looked at them both thoughtfully. Apart from the day of her arrival, when Betty had referred to Sam's need to make his fortune, money had never been mentioned, and she had received an impression of elegant luxury at Long Bay, underpinned by the army of slaves. It had never occurred to her that it might all be a veneer: the curtains and carpets were not threadbare; the horses were of excellent quality; the food was always plentiful, and because they had so rarely been off the estate there had been no call to demonstrate a large wardrobe. Her in-laws were always dressed neatly, but (as she now realised) they recycled the same two or three dresses week in, week out. She wondered slightly ruefully if her own more extensive choice had rankled with them. She had seen no reason not to wear all the beautiful gowns she had bought before travelling, revelling in the fact that being married gave her greater freedom to be more sophisticated in her dress than when she was single. But if the Lords were genuinely short of cash, the ladies might well have regarded her as flaunting her wealth and been irritated by it. Of course, she thought in some exasperation, if life in Barbados had been as expected, she would have been running her own household away from Long Bay, and the family would not have been subjected to such constant reminders that she came from a rich family.

By now they had turned left onto Six Path and were passing the Jones plantation. She realised that Sarah had asked her something and asked her to repeat it. "I merely wondered what your plans were, Lucy," said Sarah. "You have some beautiful dresses already, will you wear one of them for the christening, or will you buy a new one?"

"I was planning on buying some new undergarments and sandals, but if I see nice lace to trim some of my hems or gold net for an overdress, I will be very pleased. I think I could wear my primrose muslin for the christening party, but I would like some new gold ribbon for a sash and some sandals to match. Do you think that would look right?" she asked her sisters-in-law.

Betty nodded vigorously. "I think it is quite exquisite, and I particularly like the short, puffed sleeves. That was what I meant about the fashions you brought with you. All my dresses have long sleeves."

"At least that way you don't get bitten to death by the mosquitos," Lucy laughed. "You have a good seamstress at Long Bay, don't you?" she went on. "I remember she made Oceanus' christening robe. If we buy some patterns and some lengths of fabric, I'm sure she could make up some new dresses and alter some of your existing ones by changing the sleeves for a fraction of the price you would pay for new outfits in town. And we could use some of the leftover material to make matching reticules. That was something I often did at home."

She regretted the word as soon as she had uttered it. She had promised herself that she would now think of Barbados as home, and this was the first time she had made such a slip. But she quickly realised that was not why Sarah and Betty were looking at her askance.

"How do you make a reticule? Is it not very difficult?" asked Betty. Of course, thought Lucy, they had been brought up with slaves to do everything for them, why should they ever have had to consider making their own reticules?

"It is a little fiddly, but if we can find some card and some glue, I would be happy to show you how to do it," Lucy responded, relieved that they appeared not to have noticed her gaffe. "We should look for some fashion magazines too, because I have no doubt fashions have changed again since I left England!"

Bridgetown had developed in a higgledy-piggledy manner. It was originally built upon a street layout resembling early English medieval or market towns with its narrow serpentine street and alley configuration, and was both a residential and a mercantile district, so houses great and small were interspersed with brothels and taverns. It even had its own cage for containing riotous sailors as well as a ducking stool, situated in the horse pond, to 'cool the ardour of ladies condemned as common scolds'. In the early 1630s Governor Henry Hawley established his Courts of Law and built the Session Houses there, and by the time of Lucy's visit in 1809, the town (or at least the wealthy sections of it) had become neat, orderly and opulent.

It was dark by the time they reached Bridgetown, the rapid sunset taking place an hour before. The first thing Lucy noticed as they approached the bustling streets of the capital was the fetid smell; she wrinkled her nose at its unpleasantness. Betty noticed.

"You can tell the rainy season will shortly be upon us," she remarked. "Bridgetown was built on a swamp, Lucy. You probably didn't notice it when you arrived in February, but the smell gets worse as the weather gets hot and steamy – and it's not very healthy. I'd hate to live in town but it's fun to visit."

"Look, Lucy, there is Government House, where the Governor General, Sir George Beckwith, lives," added Sarah, pointing to the many brightly lit windows they could see off to their right and more animated than Lucy had ever seen her. "Is it not graceful?"

"Have you ever been there?" asked Lucy, looking across at what she could see of the imposing white mansion in beautiful, formal grounds with sweeping lawns and a grand framed, gated entrance.

"No, though Father went there several times, the household bought many items from his store. No doubt they still do, but we have no involvement in it anymore and didn't see our brother Richard very often."

There was a short silence. There was something a little uncomfortable about it, but Lucy could not quite put her finger on what it was. "Tell me about Richard, and the store," she begged.

The two sisters exchanged glances.

"Richard was a businessman through and through. He did very well, and expanded the store when Papa handed it over and moved to spend all his time at Long Bay," said Betty, taking the lead. "Richard lived in Bridgetown until his death; he would have turned forty this year. He married Martha, who now oversees the store, and they had five children." She checked, then looked at Lucy. "He was very different from John and from Sam. He was proud to be in trade and thought Sam frivolous. And as for John – they were always quarrelsome. Richard advised selling Long Bay, for he could never see the value in struggling to maintain a low-profit plantation and did not have the same feel for the house that we all do. I know that he refused to put any of his money into improving it…"

"I did not know that!" interrupted Sarah, clearly surprised. "How do you know? I am sure he would not be so mean-spirited."

"I know because I overheard the two of them arguing about it on the last occasion Richard visited us when he and Papa were both still alive," retorted Betty. "And don't tell me I shouldn't have been listening, for I should think they could be heard in the slaves' quarters they were both shouting so loudly!"

By now, they were travelling at a walking pace. Lucy could see a huge church to the right, with a big, square tower, and asked the sisters to tell her about it.

"That is St Michael's Church, the largest in Bridgetown and, I think, the whole island," Sarah said. "It was built after the 1780 hurricane by public lottery to replace a smaller one which was destroyed and can accommodate three thousand worshippers at a time."

Lucy's eyes widened. "So many? But then, I suppose there are thousands of slaves in Bridgetown, so you would need a very large church – if they are Christian, that is?"

"Oh – black people aren't allowed in, even the Christian ones, only whites," responded Betty carelessly. "The Negroes congregate over there in Amen Alley" – she pointed – "so they can join in the 'Amen' at the end of the service. Oh – and look over there, do you see that big old silk cotton tree? It's called Justice – it's where public hangings are carried out."

Slowly, the carriage made its way past charming balconied houses, gaily painted in bright colours as far as Lucy could tell in the poor light which spilled from their open doors, although not all were in a good state of repair. Lucy recognised the beginning of Broad Street, crammed with warehouses and stores, which she had seen when they first disembarked all those weeks ago.

"Thomas will take us to Father's store first tomorrow after breakfast. It is in the middle of Broad Street," Betty said. "We shall pay our respects then take a look at what products there are on offer. We can put everything on account there. Mama says we are invited to lunch with Martha – then, if there is time, I want to visit Swan Street because textiles are such good value there, with a much wider choice than you can find at the store."

"Oh no – it is so crowded and noisy, and they jostle you so," complained Sarah.

"I should like to see it," remarked Lucy. "Perhaps Sam would go with us?"

Betty looked sceptical and said something about taking one of the house slaves with them, but Lucy was not really listening. She had suddenly been struck by a real concern about how she was going to pay for her purchases – she had been so excited about the trip that she had not previously considered the fact that she had no Barbados coinage and had not thought to ask Sam about this. She had a faint memory of her father bringing back a strange, silver coin some years ago following one of his visits to the West Indies traders in Bristol or Chepstow; she did not think English money was used here – and she only had a few English coins left in any case.

When the carriage stopped at the inn where they were going to stay, Lucy waited impatiently for the step to be let down then hurried over to Sam who remained astride Nero and looked as though he was going elsewhere.

"Sam – I never thought, I have no money!" she exclaimed, standing at his stirrup.

"Don't worry – just put whatever you want from the store on tick," Sam replied.

"But I cannot expect John to pay my bills – we must pay our own way! Besides, what if I go elsewhere? Please can you let me have some pin money?" She felt as though she were begging and was indignant, the anger welling up inside her. Why should she have to ask for spending money when she had brought so much into the marriage? An allowance for pin money must have been included in the marriage contract; it always was.

Sam's eyes narrowed. "I'm coming back to join you all tomorrow for lunch with Martha, Madam wife, I'll give you some money then and explain what's what. Meanwhile, just set up a separate tab in the store – have them send it to me instead of John, if you're so squeamish."

With that, he touched his hat to her, turned Nero and tapped the horse's sides with his heels and the women turned wearily towards the welcoming lights of the inn. They took two rooms, Betty shared the smaller one with Lucy, and Sarah, Bathsheba and her mother the larger one. If the Lords were as strapped for cash as she now thought possible, Lucy wondered how they could afford the expense of this visit.

The following morning Lucy and Betty were up bright and early, washing quickly in the water provided before joining the rest of the party downstairs for breakfast. The distance to the store was so short that Bathsheba had told Thomas to leave the carriages at the stables. He would escort them on foot to 150 Broad Street.

The ladies entered the store, two neatly-uniformed black men standing at the open entrance to guard against thieves and other undesirables. The store manager had already recognised them and sent a young boy to inform Martha Lord of her in-laws' arrival, and Lucy hardly had time to do more than glance hurriedly around the large room in which she found herself before a tall, well-dressed woman, her hair already lightly flecked with grey, was greeting Mrs Lord senior, curtseying gracefully. Lucy bowed and smiled as she was introduced, commenting appreciatively on the size and quality of the store.

"I hope you will find everything you are looking for. I like to think we compare favourably with the shops in London and Manchester, but I have never been and would welcome your comments over lunch, which I have arranged in the Royal Naval Hotel," said Martha.

She beckoned to three black assistants hovering nearby in expectation of the summons and asked them to provide every assistance to the five ladies. She reminded Mrs Lord that lunch would be served in a private room at the Hotel at noon, bowed to them all and moved swiftly away towards a staircase at one end of the store, vanishing upstairs to the living quarters and, presumably, her office.

Mrs Lord left the four younger women to browse the fabrics and accessories while she bustled away to satisfy herself that the provisions ordered for the christening party were all in train. Lucy was determined not to appear careless with money, and quickly located some gold net and lace, adding several lengths of different coloured ribbon, four pairs of silk stockings (an extravagance, but she planned to make a present of them to her sisters-in-law) and some undergarments to the pile being looked after by one of the assistants.

"Please ensure these are put onto Mr Sam Lord's account and not to Mr John Lord's," she instructed.

She then turned her attention to helping Sarah and Betty choose the muslin fabrics and silk shawls they wanted and enjoyed herself hugely. Her sister-in-law Bathsheba's tastes were quite different. She had quickly found some silver-grey silk which, topped with a white lace fichu, would make up into a sober but luxurious gown and set off her dark hair well. All four moved on to the shoe department, trying on a range of sandals, but only Betty and Lucy bought any. Betty then asked the assistant to find some patterns and fashion plates for them all to study, and they spent the next half hour discussing over a bowl of tea which ones to take back to Long Bay to have made up.

Punctually just before noon, a grey-haired, stately black man approached the ladies, bowed deeply and announced in a solemn, gravelly voice that he had come to escort them to luncheon. Standing very erect, he slowly led them through the bustling store to the street, and they walked the short distance back to the hotel. He stood aside at the door for the ladies to enter, and again bowed to them with a flourish. Betty started giggling and whispered to Lucy that he seemed like a character in a very bad play. He then closed the door and they could hear him making his equally stately return to the store.

Betty's mother looked at her youngest daughter – who had collapsed onto a chair, overcome with laughter – and admonished her for being unladylike. However, Martha chose that moment to join them so Betty escaped a severe scold.

As they sat down to a light luncheon of cold meats, preserves and fruit, Lucy took covert stock of Martha while she was engaged in settling her mother-in-law at the table. She seemed grave and business-like, very self-contained, and Lucy unaccountably felt slightly uncomfortable with her.

The meal was informal, and there were no servants present. Martha courteously passed Lucy a dish of cold meats to choose from just as the door opened again to admit Sam, who looked to be in tremendous good humour. He nodded carelessly to the party, poured himself a glass of French wine and sat down to join them, asking at exactly the same moment as Martha whether their morning's shopping had been successful. Betty was full of chatter about the many beautiful things they had seen, and even Sarah added a few comments. Meanwhile Mrs Lord discussed with Martha the household items she had found and those that she still lacked and Lucy thought she had never seen the family so animated. Only lending half an ear to the chatter, she looked around her with interest. She had heard the tale of the previous owner of the hotel, Rachel Pringle, a woman of mixed race, and had also heard that this and other hotels were primarily brothels, yet the room they were in was cool, graceful and beautifully decorated, and Lucy had seen no women loitering near the entrance in hope of attracting business on the Lords' arrival. Perhaps the stories were exaggerated; she must ask Betty, or possibly Sam, later.

Sam asked what their plans were for the afternoon. With a sideways glance at her mother, as though she expected disapproval, Betty told him of the plan to visit Swan Street. Mrs Lord frowned.

"I do not like the idea. It is dirty and cramped, and you will get your pockets picked. In any case, Sarah is too tired and must not go. And you know how difficult it will be for the carriage to get close – you will have to walk and it is very hot."

"But it is to show Lucy a different side of Bridgetown. I am sure she has seen dozens of stores in England but the stalls on Swan Street will be something new," argued Betty.

"I have finished my business for today," said Sam. "I will accompany them, Mother. Together, Thomas and I should be able to keep them safe."

Betty and Lucy turned to him as one in surprise.

"I made sure you would have no interest in coming with us, Sam," said Betty. "Besides, I thought you had militia training all day. But it will be much more fun with you there, thank you."

As they rose from the table, Sam touched Lucy's arm and handed her some bills and coins. "I'm coming with you to make sure you don't get conned by the Jews in Swan Street," he said. "I'll teach you what you should pay for any gewgaws that take your fancy, and also how to barter. I'll wager you never learned to do that in Bath, did you?"

Sam, Lucy and Betty took their leave of Martha, and Mrs Lord seized the opportunity to state particularly firmly that they would of course see Martha again very soon, with the children, at the twins' baptisms the following week. Martha escorted Mrs Lord, Bathsheba and Sarah back to the store and settled them on comfortable settees in the shop to look at fashion plates, so only Betty and Lucy set out with Sam for Swan Street, accompanied by Thomas the coachman with a hefty stick, and a house slave to carry any purchases. Each of the girls unfurled a parasol and took one of Sam's arms, as they all set off along Broad Street.

Their pace was necessarily slow as both girls were keen to look in the shop windows they passed, while Sam seemed content to keep an eye open for any acquaintances or pretty girls. Moreover, since Broad Street was the main shopping street, it was teeming with people. When they turned off Broad Street to make their way towards parallel Swan Street, it became quieter, with fewer stores, looking increasingly less well-kept. Lucy noticed black men sitting on the ground listlessly dozing in the shade of the trees which lined the road. Why were they not working? she wondered. Surely their masters would have them beaten? But perhaps things were different in town and these were free Negroes. The hustle and bustle which had surrounded them only a few moments ago was replaced by a general air of apathy. She thought she understood why Mrs Lord had been reluctant to let them visit Swan Street.

They spent about an hour wandering the cramped spaces between stalls and stores on Swan Street. Quieter than Broad Street, it was nonetheless extremely busy, mainly with Jewish merchants doing business with each other or with other members of their own community, which had been established more than one hundred and fifty years before by Sephardic Jews arriving on the island as refugees from Dutch Brazil when the Portuguese took back control. They had already fled the Inquisition in Spain and Portugal once, and had no desire to be subjected to it again in a Portuguese colony. With their knowledge of the sugar industry, learned in Brazil, and their commercial acumen, they quickly made themselves useful in their new home, Barbados.

The scent of fresh coffee seemed to waft along the whole street, and Lucy was intrigued by the variety and volume of textiles on offer. It seemed very good value, and she quickly bought several ells of fabric suitable for making up into both day and evening dresses, as well as cambric for blouses and a length of sturdy olive-green wool for a new riding habit, as the one she had brought from England was becoming rather worn. Betty seemed untiring in her desire to hunt out bargains, but Sam began to get bored and Lucy was more interested in soaking up the atmosphere than buying anything further, so after Betty had insisted on buying a pair of outrageously brightly coloured slippers which she would never wear they turned to make their way back to the store. Lucy's head had started to ache and she found the heat oppressive.

As they retraced their steps on Broad Street a well-dressed, heavy-set man who would certainly have been classed as part of the dandy set back in England approached them, bowed deeply to the ladies while doffing his hat and addressed Sam.

"Shall I see you at Mortimer's this evening? He is holding one of his card parties, and you know how amusing they always are. You are staying over in Bridgetown, I take it?"

Sam nodded. "May I present my wife, whom I don't believe you have met, and my sister Elizabeth? Lucy, Betty, this is Mr Thomas Daniel of Bristol. Yes Thomas, I am staying over, I was dragooned into attending militia training this morning by John and now plan to enjoy myself. I shall see you at about eight this evening then?"

After bows all-round the Lords continued their progress towards the store and found the rest of their party where they had all taken tea together that morning. Lucy sank into a chair and welcomed the offer by a young black servant of a bowl of tea. Betty was regaling her sisters and mother with her version of their visit to Swan Street and Lucy was content to listen.

"Did you enjoy it, Lucy or did you find it very dirty?" asked Sarah.

"I found it fascinating but you were quite right about it being tiring. Yet it was well worth it to find some good value fabric to replace my riding habit."

"I think it is time we were leaving," said Mrs Lord, rising and smoothing down her skirt. "We are going to be late for dinner as it is – it is already after five o'clock. Boy, fetch your mistress so we can say goodbye," she said to the servant who had brought Lucy her tea.

"I shall take my leave of you now, Mother," said Sam. "I will see you on Monday when I return." He gave Lucy a peck on the cheek, bowed and waved briefly to everyone else, and departed swiftly.

The ladies were not long behind him, piling their packages into the arms of the slaves before strolling along Broad Street back towards the Royal Naval Hotel in the gathering shadows as the sun rushed to meet the horizon. Lamps were being lit, competing with the phalanx of stars in the sky above. By the time they reached the inn it was six o'clock and night had fallen. They had a light meal and went to bed early.

They were all pleasantly tired on the return journey on the Saturday and said little. Lucy contented herself with looking out of the window and drinking in the view. In some places the sugar cane was still standing, a continuous light, bright green shimmering ripple of tall, swaying stems, like a green sea. If the windows had been open, Lucy knew she would be able to hear a constant rustling, as though the canes were whispering together. But the harvest had already begun, so there were large, bare areas, blackened by the burning which took place before the harvest to kill the rats. Interspersed among the cane were windmills, fields for grazing cattle, areas for growing cotton or sweet potatoes, okra, plantains and guava. It underlined the self-sufficient nature of plantation life on the island.

They stopped several times to ease aching muscles and relieve themselves, and for a slightly longer time at Oistins, a small fishing village where the sea air reinvigorated Lucy and they all drank mauby (a brown, bitter-sweet drink made from bark). Betty named the plantations they passed through, such as Sewell and Newton, but they did not stop here as Lucy would have expected them to. Surely the Lords knew these families and must socialise with them sometimes?

They did not reach Long Bay until long after noon, by which time they were all hungry. Lucy and Sarah had dozed much of the way, but Betty still seemed full of life. Lucy thought briefly about Sam and his card party, fervently hoping he would win more than he lost, and envying him his ability to have a broader social life. But she was looking forward to seeing her son and eagerly made her way upstairs to check on him. Oceanus was a little grumpy and, clearly, hungry. He had not taken kindly to being denied his mother's milk. As always, Francine was waiting patiently with him, and Lucy was suddenly stricken with remorse that she had not thought to buy the girl something.

The rest of the weekend passed quietly with Sam away. Lucy was surprised how much she missed him; he had spent the night away before, but no more, and she found herself restless for their morning rides. After church on Sunday, she passed the time with Oceanus, and teaching her sisters-in-law – including John's wife Sarah – to make matching reticules for the new dresses the estate dressmaker had already been put to work on. She also began a charcoal sketch of Francine as a gift.

Sam visited her while she was dressing for dinner on the Monday. He looked somewhat dejected, which was soon explained. He had "lost rather a lot at cards, m'dear, over a bad bottle of brandy".

Lucy was shocked. She knew it made him angry when she took him to task, but she could not help it. "But Sam, we need all the money we've got to build or buy ourselves a home," she blurted in dismay.

He bristled, "Well, a man's got to have some fun. I planned to increase our savings, not deplete them. I need to find a way to give John more for developing the estate if I'm to persuade him to hand over the land I want for my castle. If I could win at cards, I wouldn't have any more worries." Lucy bit her lip and refrained from saying that gambling seemed a very uncertain way to make a return.

"Could you persuade your father to come up with some more cash, Lucy?" Sam asked.

She drew a deep breath and said firmly, "No, I will not, Sam. He made a very generous settlement which could easily provide us with somewhere to live, although we must invest a good portion also to provide income for the future. I do not think he'd take kindly to providing more, particularly if he found out you'd gambled some of it away. He has to provide for Stubbs, who will inherit his properties and must maintain them."

Sam's frown deepened and he looked mutinous. "I must and I will have my mansion," he said. "I don't want to just live anywhere. Why shouldn't I have somewhere here at Long Bay? Father left it jointly to me and John, after all."

Wary of provoking an outburst, Lucy was reluctant to remind him that he had sold his share to John before leaving for England for six years but she was irritated, and once again felt a cold finger of fear about what the future might hold. She did not want to return to her father's house a pauper, or live in Barbados as one, particularly not as the indigent hanger-on at Long Bay, but she was powerless to stop her husband spending her settlement as he pleased.

"Would it help if I spoke to John, do you think?" she suggested hesitantly. Sam thought about it. "He seems to like you," he said. "It can't do any harm. But don't try to talk about finance."

"I'll wait until after the twins' christening. No doubt Sarah will add her mite to any argument we may make about the benefits of us moving out," said Lucy shrewdly.

Chapter 7
Spreading Her Wings

Lucy enjoyed the visit by Mary Kingsley and her parents on the Wednesday. The visitors stayed several hours, eating luncheon with the Lords, and Lucy had no time at all alone with Mary, but her observation of the young woman's liveliness and pleasant manner with all the younger women in the household confirmed Lucy's impression from their initial meeting that they would get on well.

Mary, of course, already knew the three Lord sisters as well as Sarah, John's wife (who was brought to bed of a daughter, Haynes Elizabeth only a few days after the trip to Bridgetown, on 10th May), and was quite at ease with them. Betty's account of her and Lucy's visit to Swan Street made her laugh delightedly and led on to a discussion in which they all joined of the shopping they had done and the dresses they planned to wear for the christening. Over the coming weeks Lucy came to know Mary well through mutual visits and the two became close friends.

The day of the twins' baptism on 25th July 1809 dawned bright and sunny, but the air felt heavy with humidity and Lucy wondered whether the feasting might be spoiled by rain. For the first time she was thankful for the winds which constantly played around the eastern coast of Barbados where Long Bay lay, providing welcome coolness.

The house had been in a ferment for days, with every single inhabitant of the estate put to work cooking, cleaning and preparing. Lucy had enjoyed the activity, welcoming it as a change from her humdrum (if comfortable) existence with its lack of intellectual stimulation or clear role and responsibilities. So she was happy to help open up every room in the plantation house, oversee groups of slaves cleaning and polishing every available surface, chandelier, picture and ornament, advise her sisters-in-law on completing their outfits and – her special responsibility – take charge of the flower arrangements to be placed throughout and outside on the trestle tables.

The house slaves, too, appeared happier than she had seen them, and often sang softly to themselves as they worked, once they realised that Lucy had no objection to them doing so. She learned some of the tunes and would hum along with them, though unable to pick up the words. She realised they were looking forward with anticipation to their day off at the festivities, with plentiful food and drink. It would make a welcome change for them also; while field slaves had Sunday off to socialise and tend their small gardens in the hope of selling such produce as ginger for a few coins, some of the house slaves had to be on duty almost constantly. It was an onerous life, she thought, catching herself wondering for the very first time what it must have been like to be a servant at home in England. But at least they were employees – subservient certainly but their status far superior to slaves treated as objects rather than human beings.

Mrs Lord had made overseeing the kitchens her particular project, ably assisted by her daughter Bathsheba. The house had been redolent for several days with exotic smells in which cinnamon and ginger seemed to prevail, and when Lucy awoke early the day of the ceremony the scent of roasting meats was already wafting through the house. It made her hungry, and she threw off the light cover on her bed, pushed her feet into slippers, pulled a wrap around her and settled down to feed Oceanus who was gurgling in his crib. Then, when there was still no sign of Francine, she rather timidly, knocked on the dividing door between her own and her husband's room, unsure whether he would already be up and about or be angry at being rudely awakened.

The door was opened by Joseph, brandishing a shaving brush in one hand. He bobbed his curly head to Lucy, a shy grin on his face, and he stood back to let Lucy see her husband seated in front of the window, swathed in a towel and clearly mid-way through being shaved. He grunted at Lucy, "You are up early."

"I can smell meat roasting and I am hungry," she replied. "Only I am not sure what the arrangements are for breakfast this morning given all the preparations, or at what time we must be ready to leave for the church. And Francine has not come yet."

Sam frowned. "Why on earth don't you just holler for the girl?" he asked in exasperation. "Joseph, go and fetch the lazy trollop, and be quick about it or my shaving water will be cold." As Joseph turned to go, Sam continued, "I see no reason why we should not have breakfast as we always do, the feasting will take place outside, and the Negroes can clear breakfast away while we are at the church. John wants us to leave at ten o'clock – no doubt he's already prowling the corridors like an omen of doom. I don't understand why everyone's making such a fuss anyway – I don't remember this disruption for my son's baptism!"

Lucy was surprised, she thought the preparations very similar. Perhaps this was just another indication of Sam's jealousy about his brother. So she merely smiled and said, "It's not every day that twins are christened."

Joseph must have found Francine on her way to Lucy's room, for he returned with her almost as soon as he had left. She scurried past Sam's room and Lucy whisked herself back through the dividing door, closing it behind her to prevent Sam's wrath falling on the girl.

Francine was breathing fast, her eyes downcast. "I am sorry, mistress. I not know you already awake." She was clearly afraid of being reprimanded; it was the first time Lucy had heard her speak 'pidgin'.

"Please fetch water, Francine. I will bathe now, and I must see to the flowers before I change for the christening. You can wash and dress Oceanus while I am at breakfast."

The girl hurried out again to do as she was told. Lucy paced about the room, Oceanus first at her breast then on her shoulder, humming one of tunes she had learned from the slaves. Once Francine and another slave had with difficulty brought the heavy pitchers of water for her bath, she handed the baby to Francine, washed and dried herself quickly and put on her dress from the previous day before heading downstairs.

Lucy made her way first to the kitchens, which were in a separate block next to the house to reduce the risk of fire. Here a huge table had been set aside nearby for the flowers. A garden boy was just bringing a large armful as she arrived, and she saw with satisfaction that the pails and vases they had set out the previous night filled with water were now almost all full of blooms. She headed for the breakfast room where she was relieved to find Betty also up and ready to put the final touches to the flower arrangements. The two hurried their meal, and Lucy instructed one of the maids to take a bowl of fruit and some lime-water to her room so she could quench any hunger pangs before changing her dress. It would be a long time before the christening feast.

The two women spent nearly an hour, aided by one of the house slaves, arranging the flowers into every receptacle they had been able to find; Lucy had decided she wanted a vase on every table throughout the ground floor of the house, and on every trestle table outside. The scent of the blooms was almost overpowering in such a small space but would add a welcome freshness for guests once the vases were dispersed over a wider area.

Several house slaves came to collect the finished vases and distribute them around the house. Lucy left Betty to supervise this and went in search of the housekeeper who was in her element. A christening was always an important occasion and she was determined to ensure that everything was perfect and the mistress was pleased with her efforts. Lucy asked her to ensure that the flowers for the trestle tables were only placed outside just before the guests were due to arrive, to prevent them wilting in the humid heat.

The housekeeper's round, ebony-toned face creased into a smile. "Yes, Miss Lucy; you no worry. All will be very well." Lucy hoped she would remember, she seemed to have so much to do. As she turned to leave, the housekeeper was already instructing one of the kitchen girls to bring out more serving dishes from a chest somewhere in the cellars, as there were not enough to be found in the dining room.

She hurried up the main staircase to her room, where Francine had laid out her outfit for the christening. Seeing the silk stockings on the bed, she remembered she had bought additional pairs for Betty and Sarah and asked Francine to find them. She hurried down the corridor to the sisters' room and tapped on the door; a black maid opened it cautiously and bobbed a curtsey. As Betty turned in surprise to welcome her, Lucy said

"I must not stay or I will not be ready on time. But I wanted to thank you for your help this morning – and for being so kind to me since I arrived in February. I have a little gift for you, I remember how much you admired my silk stockings…"

Betty squealed with pleasure and gave Lucy a spontaneous hug as she accepted the present. "Oh! I just love the *feel* of them… I shall dance the night away, I think," she said. "Thank you, thank you, thank you!"

Lucy blushed, and wondered how often Betty received any gifts, it seemed effusive gratitude for such a small thing. She smiled at the excited young woman and turned towards Sarah who was also touchingly grateful, blushing scarlet with pleasure, but not demonstrating her gratitude in quite the same boisterous way as Betty. Lucy returned to her own room, where Francine helped her change into the lemon muslin gown she had decided to wear, brushed out Lucy's hair in the simple, elegant style she had found her mistress liked on the day of her arrival and threaded through it some of the gold ribbon Lucy had bought in Bridgetown.

There was an air of excitement about Francine too. Lucy looked at her thoughtfully, then instructed her to bring out of the clothes press a vividly-coloured shawl which Lucy shied from wearing but which would, she thought, be set off beautifully by the slave's dark skin. Francine shook it out, preparing to throw it over Lucy's own shoulders, but Lucy gently took it and placed it around the girl's shoulders. Francine's eyes widened and she looked a mute question at Lucy.

"For you, Francine, so you will be the prettiest girl dancing tonight," she said, smiling.

Lucy clasped a string of pearls around her own neck, picked up a small, ivory fan which her father had given her and her newly-made reticule and stood to make her way downstairs to meet up with the rest of the christening party.

"You will have Oceanus ready in his best clothes for our return, won't you?" she asked Francine, and noticed that there were tears in the girl's eyes. She was stroking the bright shawl and for the third time that morning, Lucy felt faintly embarrassed at the extreme pleasure such a trifling gift could create. Francine nodded mutely, and bobbed a little curtsey, not trusting herself to speak.

Downstairs, the family was gathering. They were to travel in three carriages, since this would prevent the ladies' gowns becoming crushed. At 10 o'clock precisely (John had been pacing up and down anxiously looking at his pocket watch) the party trooped outside and climbed into the vehicles, setting off at a smart trot. The horses had all been groomed until they shone, their bridles decorated with white satin bows and their tails and manes plaited and threaded with gaily-coloured ribbons. Lucy thought they looked magnificent.

The Reverend Nicholson again performed the baptismal ceremony quickly and efficiently as he had done for Oceanus and little John. Sarah, the twins' mother, looked grey and exhausted as she had done since their birth and carrying even one of her daughters appeared almost too much for her; her husband held the other.

By the time they left the church, Lucy found that the weather had changed quite dramatically. Gone were the blue skies and sunshine of the morning, replaced by dark, rolling clouds promising rain, and squally gusts of wind which caught at the ladies' hats and blew swirls of dust into everyone's faces. John cast an anxious glance at the sky and, taking his wife by the elbow, propelled her towards their carriage instead of lingering for the usual pleasantries. The guests were not slow to follow suit, and soon a cavalcade of carriages was on the way to Long Bay.

They had only just reached the outskirts of the straggling hamlet beyond St Philip's Church when the rain began to fall, a few fat drops followed by such a torrent of water as Lucy had never seen. It thundered on the roof of the carriage, which was stiflingly hot, and shut the flat plateau outside from view.

"Welcome to the rainy season," said Sam, grinning at her.

"Will this last all day?" asked Lucy, used to days of monotonous rain in England.

It was Betty who answered her, "No, no; it will all have stopped in ten minutes!"

Lucy was sceptical, but sure enough the rain soon slackened off and the clouds rolled away, leaving the sun to glitter on the rivulets and steaming puddles left behind. She could hear the horses' hooves splashing through the water now, and their progress was considerably slower than on the journey out, as the animals laboured through the mud and loosened stones.

When Lucy alighted from the carriage at Long Bay, she expected the storm to have cleared the air but the temperature did not seem to have changed at all. If anything, it felt hotter now because of the oppressive humidity. She turned to look up at Thomas the coachman. Water was still dripping off him, but it did not appear to bother him. The horses were in a sorry state, though. Heads hanging, all signs of their earlier festive appearance gone, any bows and ribbons remaining were bedraggled, and their coats were wet and steaming. As guests' carriages started arriving, Lucy hurried up the steps to check on the flower arrangements and find out what impact the sudden downpour had had on preparations for the christening feast.

She need not have worried. The flowers in the house looked and smelt beautiful; the housekeeper had an army of slaves drying the outdoor trestle tables, and the flowers for these were still waiting where she had left them. Having checked with her mother-in-law whether her help was needed with anything, she made her way back outside, a parasol shielding her face, to where the colourful array of guests from the church was gathering. There was no sign yet of the field slaves arriving from their quarters, but perhaps they would only appear when the food was ready.

Lucy had expected to enjoy the day, because it provided one of their rare social engagements, but she was surprised that she felt rather low, and reluctant to enter into the party spirit. A headache, probably brought on by the heat and humidity, was nagging at the back of her skull, and she blamed her lack of enthusiasm on that. With a sigh, she straightened her shoulders and moved purposefully among the throng, smiling and greeting people, many of whom she now knew at least by sight. She saw her friend Mary being bored to death by a rotund, florid-faced planter with an enormous moustache, and went over to rescue her.

The house boys were moving among the guests with trays of lime punch and lemonade, and Lucy gratefully accepted a glass of lemonade, draining it in record time.

Mary gave her a sympathetic glance. "You are unused to our weather, Lucy. Are you finding the heat oppressive?" she said.

Lucy nodded, but said stoutly that she was sure she would accustom herself. They were standing in the shade of one of the tall mango trees, and Lucy glanced upwards as she heard the leaves rustle above her head, thinking that perhaps she would catch a glimpse of one of the playful green monkeys. But it was two small, solemn black faces that looked down at her, wide-eyed, two of the slave children hiding away to watch the festivities from above. She smiled and waved at them, and Mary, following her glance, did the same. Emboldened, they settled themselves in the crook of a tree branch and set to stripping one of the fruits of its skin and devouring it. Seeing the first drops of sticky juice falling through the leaves, Lucy and Mary moved hurriedly away to avoid being spattered. Mary was still laughing as they accepted a second glass of lemonade from a houseboy.

"They are little imps! If any of the men catch those boys, they'll be thrashed for stealing fruit!" she said.

"You won't tell anybody, Mary? After all this is a holiday for everyone, and I cannot believe they often have a chance to eat properly. It would be a shame for them to miss the feast."

"My father always says 'let them get away with stealing something small, and they will go on to rob you blind'. What they are doing is wrong, but it is very difficult to punish someone for making you laugh so no, I will not tell anyone. But if other guests stand under that tree while the boys are finishing their mango, they will soon be found out!"

Lucy was saddened to find her friend – and indeed Dr Lucas, for whom she had the greatest respect – seemed to concur with the general attitude towards slaves, but on reflection realised she should not be surprised; Mary had grown up on Barbados and probably knew little else. So she said nothing more on the subject, and when Mary asked her to visit the following Wednesday, she accepted happily.

The kitchen staff, overseen by the housekeeper who was overseen in turn by John and Sam's mother, had been loading the trestle tables with dishes while the girls had been speaking. The slave tables, set off at the far end of the dining area and upwind from the main guests so that the latter's nostrils would not be assailed by any pungent odour from the workers, groaned just as much under a weight of food as the whites' tables did, but not all the dishes were the same. Lucy learned two new ones that day, *coocoo*, a creamy blend of cornmeal and okra, and another called *privilege*, a mix of rice, okra, hot pepper, pig's tail and onions. These along with chicken were common on the slave tables, although they also had access to the roast pork, salt beef and fried flying fish which were popular with the whites. For everyone, there was plenty of pudding and souse, a spicy mashed sweet potato encased in pig's belly (which Lucy liked), and boiled pig's head served with a 'pickle' of onions, hot and sweet peppers, cucumbers, and lime (which was far too greasy for Lucy's taste and turned her stomach).

There was no shortage of things to drink, either; rum, from the Mount Gay distillery, local frothy beer and mauby were the most popular on the workers' tables; rum punch, rum and beer on the whites' tables.

When the kitchen slaves cleared the remains of the meat and fish dishes away and brought out piles of fruit – papaya, guava, mango, banana – and sticky sweetmeats made with coconut, the music started. It struck Lucy that she rarely heard music, which had been a ubiquitous part of her life before Barbados, at Long Bay. Occasionally some of the girls sang softly, and when she rode out with Sam she heard the field hands singing rhythmically as they went about their backbreaking work, but she had only seen or heard musical instruments (other than the piano she occasionally played) at Oceanus' christening.

Now, as the rum and the punch continued to flow, several of the slaves brought out fiddles and reed pipes (clearly prized possessions, given the care with which they were handled) and began to play – slow, melodious, haunting tunes at first, turning as time progressed to wilder, faster music with a definite beat which got Lucy's feet tapping under the table almost against her will, it urged her to dance, and as the slaves began to get to their feet she watched fascinated and longed to join them, although the style of dancing was totally unknown to her.

She felt eyes upon her and turned quickly, to find John Barrow had come across to where she was seated and was smiling at her. Returning the smile, she motioned to him to join her at the rapidly emptying table. The men were slipping away to enjoy a game of cards and smoke, Lucy thought resignedly, but it was with a start that she realised that apart from three young women chattering animatedly at one end of the table, she was alone.

John Barrow sat down, a glass of lime punch in his hand. "So, what do you make of our celebrations, Mrs Lord?"

"I have enjoyed myself immensely. I have encountered several new dishes today. It is wonderful to see the slaves enjoying themselves. I find their music infectious and am surprised I have not heard them playing instruments before."
Barrow replied carefully "Drums would be their traditional instrument, but they are forbidden by law here in case they are used to pass messages to start an uprising. They fashion the pipes from hollowed-out cane stalks. How they have come to possess fiddles I have no idea; the occasional gift, I imagine, together with their innate ability to recycle anything we may toss out. I think we all find the music infectious – I see some of the younger guests are joining in the dancing!"

As he said it, Lucy saw several matrons hurrying across the grass to remonstrate and drag their daughters away from the dancing slaves. She also noticed that the slave numbers were dwindling. They had been quietly slipping away to their quarters, many of them staggering under the influence of the strong drink they were unused to, but it was clear that the musicians were in their

172

element now and they did not stop playing even as they made their way along the track to their compound.

John Barrow offered Lucy his arm, and they walked together towards the house, blazing with light. Lucy had seen no sign of Sam for several hours and assumed he was playing cards with his cronies.

"Do you not play cards, Mr Barrow?" she asked.

"Indeed I do," he responded, "but I enjoy hearing the Negro music and watching them dance, so I stayed out here as long as I could. You will have it all to enjoy again at Crop Over in a few weeks – it is a huge celebration of the end of the sugar cane harvest."

"But we have no sugar at Long Bay, so I do not know whether we will hold such a celebration, particularly so soon after the christening," said Lucy.

"I had not thought of that. Would you like to come to Sunbury again for Crop Over? You and Mr Lord could stay as our guests. And I shall hope to see you dancing then – we will have real musicians playing the dance tunes you know."

"I should like that very much indeed. Let us go and find Sam and you can repeat your kind invitation directly to him."

All of a sudden, Lucy felt happier than she had in ages. She liked John Barrow, and Sunbury, and looked forward to the visit as a real treat, something more akin to the social life she had been used to before her marriage.

They found Sam, as expected, in the card room, slouched over a baize table with a half empty bottle of brandy next to him. His eyes were heavy and glittering. As Lucy and John Barrow made their way over to him, the rubber had just finished and Sam threw down his cards.

"Damnable luck!" Lucy heard him mutter, and her heart sank as she saw the stack of his IoUs in front of a coarse, leering and dishevelled man she did not know seated at the same table. Nevertheless, she approached him.

"Sam, Mr Barrow has kindly invited us to Sunbury for Crop Over. May we go?"

Sam looked up, frowning. He looked at Lucy's hand resting on John Barrow's arm and leaped drunkenly to the wrong conclusion.

"Unhand my wife, sir!" he said, slurring his words and staggering drunkenly to his feet. He suddenly seemed to realise who it was. "Oh – it's you, John. What's that you say, Lucy?"

She patiently repeated her request.

"Aye let us do so. Perhaps my luck at the cards will change there. I'm losing devilishly." And he slumped back in his seat.

Lucy watched him anxiously, but John Barrow drew her discreetly away, knowing she would get no sense from her husband now.

"Let us go and find my wife and let her know of my invitation to you," he said. As they walked in search of Mary Barrow, he saw Lucy's forehead was still furrowed. "Is there something bothering you, Mrs Lord?" he asked.

"Please call me Lucy. It is just that I…" her voice trailed off, and she could hear her mother's voice in her head, scolding her for impetuosity.

John Barrow looked at her gravely. "It is common for men to drink heavily and lose money at cards here, Lucy. Indeed, I think it is a national pastime."

"I know that," Lucy sighed, "but I worry that we won't be able to fulfil Sam's dream of building a place of our own if he loses everything. And he does seem to be amazingly unlucky at cards. Oh – there is your wife."

Confidences at an end, she greeted Mary warmly and thanked her prettily for John's invitation. Soon afterwards, the Barrows went home, part of a stream of guests calling for their carriages. A diehard few (including Sam) remained in the card-room, but Lucy knew better than to try and coax him away from the tables. She slipped upstairs to find Oceanus being cared for by one of the younger house slaves. Francine had clearly decided to make the most of her gift and was probably dancing in the slave quarters, from which Lucy could still hear music. She dismissed the girl and played with Oceanus for a while, sitting on the floor with him as he sat in front of her, a trifle unsteadily, and looked around him, chewing one little fist. Then, holding the baby on her shoulder for comfort, she looked out of her open window into the gathering darkness, softly singing *Suo Gan* to him, a Welsh lullaby that Nurse had sung to her little brother, Stubbs.

Hunan blentyn, are fy mynwes
Clyd a chynnes ydyw hon
Breichiau mam sy'n dyn amdanat
Cariad mam sy dan fy mron...[4]

She had no idea how long she stood there, rocking the sleeping Oceanus on her shoulder, but finally she became conscious of a sore back, stiffness in her legs and aching arms. She changed and fed her son and placed him carefully in his crib, wearily took off her own clothes, washed perfunctorily in the pitcher of cold water left on her dresser, put on her nightgown and cap and crawled into bed. She felt very low, although she was too tired to think why this should be, she had been looking forward to, and had enjoyed, the party. Slowly she drifted off to sleep, to the strains of the music still coming from the slave quarters.

She awoke suddenly sometime later. The room was in complete darkness, and the music had died. The rain had started again, and she wondered whether that had woken her, but immediately heard a loud bang and a muttered curse, her husband, clearly the worse for drink, bumping into a piece of furniture. He collapsed heavily onto the bed, pinning her legs, breathing hard. She could smell sour wine.

"Where are you, wife? I want you. I will have you," he panted as he groped at the sheet with which she had covered herself.

Kneeling now, he triumphantly pulled the sheet off her with one hand while fumbling with his trousers with the other. There was just enough light from the candle he must have brought with him for her to see that he was dishevelled and had already discarded his coat and shoes. Looking down at her as she lay, rigid

---

[4] To my lullaby surrender, warm and tender is my breast, Mother's arms with love caressing, lay their blessing on your rest

with fear at the leering expression on his distorted face, he suddenly grabbed her breast through the nightgown and squeezed hard in a display of drunken ferocity. She cried out in pain and as he slapped her face hard with his other hand, she felt his signet ring cut into her cheek. In a frenzy he tore at her nightgown and ripped the delicate lawn fabric from her body. He kicked her legs apart with his knee, pinned her arms above her head and pressed himself into her belly, cursing as he fumbled to undo the buttons on the fall front of his trousers.

Lucy bit her lip to avoid crying out – she did not want to wake the baby. As Sam brought his face close to hers, she could not avoid turning her head away from the stench of his breath, earning her another slap on the same bruised cheekbone. He pushed his face into her shoulder and used his hand to thrust his swollen penis hard into her. She cried out now, with the pain of this rough entry and he covered her mouth with his to stifle the sound. She retched at the smell, tears sliding down her face into her hair. He grunted, lifted himself onto his elbows and, with one last painful heave, it was over, he was spent. He collapsed across her body and almost immediately began to snore. The baby was whimpering but she could hardly move under Sam's weight. Indeed, she found it hard to breathe.

She lay for a few moments, feeling the sticky pool between her thighs, gathering her strength, and eventually managed to push her husband's inert body partly to one side and crawl out, naked, from under him.

She groped for her peignoir and pulled it on, then picked up the fretful Oceanus who immediately nuzzled her breast, demanding food even though, at six months old, he was down to one or two feeds a night and would not generally wake for another hour or so. She winced and switched him away from the side bruised by Sam's rough treatment. Suckling the baby calmed her, and she soon stopped trembling, but she felt dirty and ashamed. Was this really what marriage was about?

Oceanus fell asleep again at her breast and after about half an hour she laid him down once more in his crib and moved across to the dresser to wipe herself down with the water she had used earlier. She blew out Sam's candle, tiptoed back to the bed and lay on it, as far away from her husband as she could without falling off, her peignoir wrapped tightly around her. She would have gone instead to her husband's bed next door but was afraid to leave Oceanus. She lay awake for hours, rigid, on her back, feeling the throb and ache of her body and wondering how she was going to face the day. Sam continued to snore, unmoving, where she had left him.

At some point she must have dozed out of sheer exhaustion, for she woke to full light with Sam stirring beside her and staggering off the bed, pushing angrily at the mosquito net.

He groaned. "The devil! My head!" and without a backward glance at Lucy made his way to his own room, pulling the door closed behind him. She heard him collapse onto his own bed and, once she could hear him snoring again, she went over and for the first time turned the key in the lock of the dividing door.

She checked her face in the mirror over the dresser. A black bruise had already appeared on her cheekbone, her eye was swollen half-shut and there was a small crescent cut where Sam's ring had caught her. She crawled back into bed, pulled the sheet up to her chin then curled into a ball and sobbed her heart out into the pillow as she finally allowed herself to give full vent to her wretchedness. For once, she ignored Oceanus when he became restless and cried for food, but her sobs lessened as his wailing grew more insistent.

And there Francine found her when she hurried in, somewhat later than usual and looking tired but happy. She picked a bawling, red-faced Oceanus up first and carried him over to the bed to hand him to Lucy. It was only then she looked at her mistress and when she saw her face, a little exclamation broke from her. She said nothing however, just handed the baby over then left the room with the ewer of dirty water and the empty pitcher. Lucy listlessly let Oceanus feed and did not look up when Francine returned with a fresh pitcher of hot water. She allowed the girl to gently bathe her face, then wrinkled her nose as Francine opened a small pot of strange-smelling unguent which she proceeded to smear on Lucy's bruised cheek.

She said nothing however, but merely allowed Francine to tend to her. The girl returned to the kitchens to fetch more water for a bath. After some coaxing, Lucy consented to get out of bed and clamber into the warm bath Francine had prepared. She winced as she slid into the water, and Francine frowned as she saw the bruises forming on her mistress's ribs and stomach. Still she said nothing, she put the bar of soap in Lucy's hand and turned to wash and dress the baby. That done, she placed him in his crib and went to hand Lucy her towel. For once, she allowed Francine to dry her, standing with her head bowed all the while. Francine once again applied the strange-smelling ointment, and when Lucy raised her head at this, she broke the slave rule of only speaking when spoken to and volunteered some information which she hoped would jolt Lucy out of her listless, abject state.

"This best medicine from obeah man, Mistress Lucy. You will soon be well, nobody will see."

As she had hoped, Lucy's curiosity was aroused. She had not heard the term before, though she would later learn how much the white slave-owners feared the influence of obeah, as many slave rebellions had at their centre an obeah 'priest'. At this point, however, Francine said no more; having piqued her mistress's interest, she hoped she would soon revert to her usual lively self. But when she tried to coax Lucy into a morning dress, Lucy turned mutinous, and peremptorily ordered the girl to find her a clean wrapper and remake the bed. She refused to go downstairs, instead picking up Oceanus (who was enjoying a nap and howled lustily at being so rudely awakened) and pacing up and down the room with him before sitting down again on the chaise longue and placing the squirming child on the floor in front of her.

Francine did as she was told and organised the removal of Lucy's bathwater and the used towels, leaving her mistress to rest and, hopefully, wake refreshed and ready to face the day. As a slave, she was so used to being beaten that it could not have occurred to her that it was not the pain that was upsetting her mistress but rather that Lucy was bitterly ashamed at what had happened and had not the courage to face Sam's family with a black eye. At the same time she felt violated and betrayed, and seethed with anger. How *dare* he behave so appallingly? Had she not proved herself a dutiful wife? More than that, had she not shown him real love and affection, giving herself to him willingly? So why must he use violence? She was no less a piece of property than Francine was, she thought furiously.

When she failed to emerge from her room for luncheon, her mother-in-law paid her a visit. Mrs Lord senior swept in, dressed impeccably as ever in black silk, and imperiously demanded what ailed her daughter-in-law. Lucy, who was seated with her damaged cheek facing the window, slowly turned her head. Bathsheba Lord's eyes narrowed.

"What happened?" she asked.

After a long pause, Lucy replied softly, "Your son, ma'am."

"And your husband, Lucy, do not forget that. What did you do to provoke him?"

This succeeded where Francine had failed. Lucy saw red and for the first time gave her mother-in-law a demonstration of the lack of submissive nature which her own mother had so frequently deplored. Using very unladylike language, she described to Bathsheba what had happened.

"I was asleep, ma'am, when your drunken sot of a son came in and attacked me, forcing himself on me and hitting me when I have always given myself to him willingly. I do not know what provoked him, but it was certainly not I. No doubt, like his brother, he has a violent streak…"

Mrs Lord was clearly furious. "How dare you abuse my sons? You have certain duties as a wife, I assume your mother made you aware of these? Yes, you have given Samuel a son, but that alone is not enough…"

By this time Lucy was beside herself. Tears of anger coursing down her cheeks, she faced her mother-in-law.

"You too are a woman ma'am. Do you condone this behaviour? Your son marries me for my money, brings me thousands of miles from all I am familiar with, then beats me for no reason, treating me no better than your other son treats his slave whore!"

She clapped her hand over her mouth, knowing immediately that she had gone too far and that henceforth she would get no support from Bathsheba.

Her mother-in-law's dark eyes flashed, and incongruously Lucy realised just how beautiful she must have been as a young girl; no doubt Sam took after her.

"You will remain in your room until you are fit to be seen in public," Bathsheba said coldly. "Your meals will be brought here. I will tell the family that you have a fever and are not to be disturbed."

She turned on her heel and left the room.

Lucy found she was trembling and sat down again hurriedly on the rattan chair in the window. She realised she had made a powerful enemy, she could no longer hope for any help from that quarter should her relationship with Sam deteriorate further. She could almost hear her mother tut-tutting at her impetuosity, and never had she felt the lack of her beloved father more keenly. Her last sight of him, staring up at her aboard the ship then turning abruptly to walk away on the quayside, was etched on her memory. But he was far away and could do nothing to help her. Lucy pulled her knees up to her chest and rocked gently in the big chair, the tears flowing unheeded.

Twilight fell, and – after feeding Oceanus – she crept into bed, having checked the connecting door to Sam's room was still locked. She lay watching the stars come out and wondered how such a beautiful place could hold such dark secrets and such cruelty. She was feeling extremely sorry for herself by the time Francine arrived with a tray and some candles, but was so exhausted that she fell asleep almost immediately after the girl had anointed her bruises once more, relieved when Francine whispered "Massa gone to Bridgetown", because she knew this meant he would not return that night – even though, she thought bitterly, it probably also meant he would squander more of their – her – money.

Chapter 8
Storms Gather

Over the next few days, Francine was her only visitor, bringing her meals and water for washing, caring for Oceanus, putting ointment on her bruises. Lucy was amazed at how quickly these faded. By Tuesday the stiffness in her body had vanished and she thought the fading yellow mark on her cheek scarcely visible to the uninitiated. She screwed up her courage and went downstairs for the evening meal.

Betty greeted her with an exclamation of delight. John nodded gravely to her, Mrs Lord coldly. Sarah, always interested in questions of health, asked solicitously how she was feeling. She replied suitably but remained quiet during the family discussion over the meal, retiring again shortly afterwards. Sam, she noticed, made no appearance, presumably he remained in Bridgetown.

This had been a calculated appearance on her part. She had not forgotten the arrangement she had made with Mary to visit her on Wednesday and was worried that Mrs Lord might prevent this if she had not already re-integrated herself into the life of the Long Bay household. She said nothing, however, and after a quiet breakfast the following morning she waited until the family were all out of sight then ordered the carriage to take her to the Lucas' house.

The River Plantation on which the Lucas family lived had come to them through Mrs Lucas. It was a good size, some four hundred acres, and being situated inland suffered far less than Long Bay from the prevailing winds. As a gust threatened to blow Lucy's skirts over her head when she tried to enter the carriage outside Long Bay, she considered this a blessing. She liked the River house, which she found restful. It was typical of Barbados plantation houses, low and white with a veranda all around, always neat and smelling of beeswax. She gave the coachman the command to set off and sat back against the seat for the short journey with a sense of relief.

Mary was walking in the garden when Lucy arrived, and hurried to greet her as she alighted from the carriage.

"Mother is out," she said gaily, "so we can have a comfortable time together and talk of whatever we wish!"

Then, as Lucy turned her face towards her, she gasped, "Oh, you poor thing! Whatever have you done to your face? Come in and tell me all about it!"

They climbed the front steps and Mary ordered tea to be brought to the ladies' room, a light and airy space which gave onto a secluded part of the garden. She pushed Lucy into a comfortable chair, then tilted her chin with her finger, turning her guest's face gently from side to side.

"Lucy, you did not get those marks by falling, so don't try to make me believe it. Whatever happened?"

Lucy's brown eyes filled with tears at the sympathy she could hear in her friend's voice, but she hesitated to tell her the shameful truth. A pause ensued, during which the maid brought in the tea and Mary, waving her away, poured them each a bowl.

As she handed Lucy hers, she said gently, "I will quite understand if you wish to keep your business private, but I will guess at what occurred and you can either confirm it or tell me to go to the devil and I will say no more."

Lucy looked a little startled at her friend's unladylike language but still said nothing. "Well then, Lucy, it looks to me as if someone hit you, and the most likely culprit must be your husband. Am I right?"

Lucy nodded miserably, and now the tears began to flow in earnest, as they had not done since the night of the rape.

"Was he drunk?"

Again Lucy nodded.

"I should like to help, Lucy. We are friends, are we not? And I hope you trust me. If it is of any help, let me tell you some things you may not have guessed about myself. No doubt you have wondered why my husband, Charles Kingsley, is not here with me in Barbados. We married five years ago, but he is an absolute brute and has some very strange desires which I have no wish to accommodate. Besides which, he is a gambler and a spendthrift, and we were well on the way to being penniless, so I came home to Mother and Father. Until he finds himself a useful occupation, I have no plans to return to him. That may make you think me heartless, but I only tell you this – which should remain secret between us – to assure you I would not betray any confidence of yours."

Lucy looked at her friend in surprise. Never having met her husband, she had vaguely assumed he was away on business, and that Mary was on a long visit to her parents. Now she realised that they might have rather more in common than she had thought. And so the story came tumbling out, although Lucy blushed fierily and stumbled over the words when she told of Sam's violent behaviour in the bedroom.

Mary was a good listener. What she had not told Lucy was that her husband took delight in pornography, constantly drew pornographic pictures himself, and that he liked to act out these fantasies. She knew he did so with many other women, at which she felt both shame and relief since she had no similar desires. So she had a good deal of sympathy for Lucy's plight, and especially for the fear that she must feel at being so many thousands of miles from her own family, with no hope of support from her mother-in-law.

She questioned Lucy closely on how frequently Sam had shown her violence and was relieved to hear that this had been the first time, Lucy did not mention some of her earlier fights with Sam, but Mary would in any case have dismissed the punishment he meted out on these occasions as appropriate. It was accepted practice for husbands to chastise their wives physically for any misdemeanours. She suggested tentatively that perhaps it had been the drink talking, together with frustration at having his desire to build his mansion – into which he could channel his energy – blocked. She pointed out that Lucy must try to make the marriage work. A lot of men behaved badly at some point, and it did not necessarily mean they were inherently violent or wicked, and Lucy's position should she return to Britain having left her husband might be very unpleasant, as society would look askance at her. Better by far to do what so many unhappily married women did and put up with frequent physical and mental marital abuse unless it became overwhelming, as it had in Mary's own case although even she had no intention of living permanently apart from her husband.

Mary pointed out what Lucy already knew, that she was quite as much Sam's property as any of the slaves so he could do as he pleased to her in law. If there were no further incidents such as this one, she would do best to put it behind her.

None of this was news to Lucy, but it gave her some comfort to have unburdened herself to her friend, and she promised to return to Long Bay and try to continue with life as before – though she was convinced she had now made an implacable enemy of her mother-in-law. She told Mary that she had suggested to Sam that she should speak to John about obtaining permission to build where Sam wanted, and Mary encouraged her to do so.

Lucy stayed to have luncheon with Mary and her mother, who had returned from whatever errand she had been on. Mrs Lucas stared at Lucy's bruises, but was too well-bred to say anything, making a mental note to question her daughter after Lucy's departure.

As Lucy left, they all looked anxiously at the sky. August was firmly in the hurricane season. Lucy had been told on numerous occasions how lucky they were in Barbados as the island did not suffer these huge storms or hurricanes with the same regularity as much of the West Indies. But it was clear a storm was brewing, and the coachman needed no urging to make the two-hour long journey back to Long Bay as quickly as he could.

On her return – following a longer journey than usual as the horses battled against the wind – she could see feverish activity going on all around the house, teams of slaves, under the supervision of John and Sam, were boarding up windows and doors, drawing water and storing it in monkey jars to see them through the hours – and possibly days – ahead. The thunder which had been rumbling throughout the journey had increased in ferocity, with blinding flashes of lightening becoming increasingly frequent. Finally, to her considerable relief, they pulled up in front of the house, though Lucy was taken by surprise at the strength of the roaring wind when the carriage door was opened for her, so she clung to the arm of the enormous slave who stood there ready to help. She was almost blown up the steps into the house.

Spotting her arrival, Sam shouted that she must get inside quickly, he was going to check the stables were battened down as safely as possible. He strode off, and she thought that he was in his element, facing danger and having something practical to do. It made her more determined than ever to ask John about the piece of land when the time was right.

Inside the house, the women were just as busy, supervising slaves who were stowing away breakable objects such as the nick-nacks and ceramics which decorated the side-tables. She could see why. Even with the shutters closed, the wind gusted through the open-plan rooms and corridors and would surely smash small items if it grew any stronger. Other slaves were carrying bedding, chamberpots and other comforts down to the basement, clearing furniture off the veranda and storing it.

She cast off her hat and asked Sarah, whom she saw first, what she could do to help, and was soon busy overseeing the kitchen staff taking some supplies to the basement and storing others so that they had less chance of being ruined by the incoming storm. Happy to be busy, somewhere at the back of her mind she understood that this was to be a storm like nothing she had ever experienced, that would make the storm at sea pale into insignificance, but perhaps precisely because it *was* an unknown, as yet she felt no fear.

All the time she was aware of the incessant crashing of thunder and the roaring of the wind, although the boards hurriedly nailed up over the windows dimmed the equally incessant lightning inside the house. When the front door opened and John was almost flung to the floor with the force of the gale, however, she gasped in terror at the vicious, brilliant light outside – and could see that the slaves too were absolutely petrified. She pulled herself together and kept them busy, trying to still her trembling, knowing that once the slaves gave way to their fear they could probably not even be beaten into co-operating.

Their tasks finally completed, everyone in the house congregated in two groups, the slaves in the kitchen, the family in the dining room. Lucy found herself looking around anxiously for Sam, whom she had last seen on his way to the stables. She went out into the hall, where she could feel the wind whistling under the front door and hear a booming sound outside. Excited voices were coming from the kitchen, and she thought the slaves might welcome a calming voice. But when she opened the door, she saw Sam, surrounded by a gaggle of female slaves, all hugging and patting him and clearly delighted he had made it back to the house.

Relief flooded through her, her pain and humiliation all but forgotten as she smiled at the sight of him safe and sound. He was shaking the water from his clothes, like a dog, and spraying the slaves as he did so, which made them laugh. He looked up and saw Lucy in the doorway and grinned broadly at her. He strode across and put his hands on her shoulders, his face alight with excitement, and totally unshadowed by any thought of the humiliation he had heaped on her. Lucy wondered if he even remembered what he had done.

Sam smiled down at her and shouted in her ear (for the roar from outside made it impossible now to hear anyone speaking in a normal voice),

"What a lark, eh, wife? Not frightened, are you? No doubt we'll find a lot of damage when this is over, and we'll have lost a few slaves and cattle, but at least the harvests are almost all in so it's not all bad."

Then, as the house shook under the buffeting and the wind roared and screamed, he looked around and said: "Come, it's time to get to the cellars. If the roof does blow off in this hurricane, we'll be safer there and we will have supplies if it's a long haul."

He clapped his hands, to get the slaves' attention. "Down with you," he ordered, and did not have to repeat himself. The frightened slaves scrambled for the trapdoor leading to the basement cellar and started disappearing down the ladder.

Sam took Lucy's hand and pulled her towards the dining-room, where John had begun to usher the family down the ladder beneath another trapdoor. Lucy belatedly realised that the trapdoor was the reason they had all congregated in that room, and moved across, still holding Sam's hand, to join Betty and John who were getting ready to descend.

Once in the cellar, with the trapdoor closed, she realised they could still hear the storm although in a muffled way, as well as the booming sound she now realised must be the waves crashing on the beach; but although the trapdoor rattled occasionally, at least she could no longer feel the house shaking. She realised that even here, in such an extreme situation, the division of blacks from whites prevailed, there was a wall dividing the two parts of the cellars, with a connecting door. Then she thought about the poor field slaves, who were no doubt cowering in their flimsy quarters or in the open fields, terrified out of their wits. But she was careful not to show her concern; instead she asked Sam if the horses were alright.

"Absolutely terrified, rearing and bucking all over the place," he responded, "but there's two or three boys with each of them holding them down so they don't run off and break their legs in this storm."

John heard him and came over. "Thank you for seeing to the horses, Sam. No doubt we'll have to rebuild the stables when this is over. I sent most of the field slaves to the mill and to Union Hall to take shelter, so I hope our losses won't be too heavy."

Lucy realised with a start that she had not given a thought to Oceanus, mortified, she thought, where was he? She went to the connecting door and opened it, hoping to see Francine. The cook was huddled on the floor near the door, and it was pitch black in there. The family had storm lanterns, but there was nothing for the slaves.

"Where is Francine?" she asked the woman, who shook her head.

Lucy turned back for one of the lanterns and moved through the dark crowded slave-side of the cellar, already rank with sweat and other unpleasant odours, searching for Francine and her child. She found them in the far corner, Oceanus asleep on Francine's lap, as the girl sat and hummed a lullaby, though it was barely audible. Seated next to her was a wet nurse rocking Sarah's tiny new-born, Haynes Elizabeth. Seeing Francine so calm, Lucy left Oceanus to sleep with her, hung the lantern on a convenient hook on one of the beams leaving some light, and threaded her way back to her section to a murmured chorus of 'thank yous' from the grateful slaves.

Throughout the long night, they could scarcely hear the thunder for the roar of the wind, but the gratings near ceiling level in the cellar showed vivid flashes of lightning and torrential rain. The ladies sat on chairs brought down for that purpose; the men stood, lounging against the walls, or sat on cushions or blankets on the stone floor. Several times Mrs Lord senior ordered a couple of the slaves to lay out something to eat and drink on the table pushed against one wall; all the ladies were persuaded to drink some wine with their picnic, and Lucy began to feel drowsy. She picked up one of the blankets which had been brought down earlier and curled up in it as far from the light of the lanterns as possible.

At first she watched John and Sam playing a game of cards, but she must have fallen asleep despite the storm, because the next time she looked around, Sam was alone, leaning against a stout wooden strut and casting dice one hand against the other, while everyone else dozed around him. She crept over to the corner where a screen had been erected to hide the array of chamberpots. Wrinkling her nose at the odour, she went behind it, raised her skirts and relieved herself, before making herself comfortable again on her blanket, and fell asleep again for a few hours.

When next she woke, she was sure she could hear a dog barking, then thought she must have dreamt it when a tremendous clap of thunder was followed once more by the roaring wind. Sam was nowhere to be seen, but John noticed she was awake.

"The wind has changed direction slightly; it was probably the lull as it changed that awoke you," he said.

Lucy struggled up in her crushed skirts and shivered slightly. She went to the table and helped herself to a glass of water from the monkey jar. She could hear the occasional moan from the slave section next door, but they were much quieter than when they first arrived, and she could hear no sound of a baby crying. She decided to wait for Francine to bring Oceanus to her, she had no desire to feed him with all these people around her in any case – that would be just too shocking. She hoped Francine had had the forethought – unlike her – to bring water and pap down for the baby.

The storm seemed to continue unabated, and when Francine brought the hungry, yelling Oceanus to her a short while later, Lucy looked about her in despair, wondering how she was going to find some privacy. Sam, who had reappeared as silently as he had disappeared, noticed her distress, and ordered a couple of the slaves to rig up a curtain around her so she could nurse her child in peace. His mother did not miss an opportunity to point out coldly that Lucy would have been better to have availed herself of the offer of a wet nurse.

Just before midday, John went out to investigate whether it was safe for everyone to return upstairs to the main house. The wind was still howling, but the lashing rain had turned to squalls and the thunder was rumbling in the distance.

He returned an hour later with a grim face. "The stables are all but demolished; one horse has had to be shot because of its injuries; another is missing having kicked one of the boys and broken his leg, so that's one Nigger who'll not be good for much for a while. It goes without saying, of course, that the slave quarters will need rebuilding."

"And is it safe to go upstairs?" enquired his mother.

"Yes, Mama. I think you ought to take a look around the house – a tree came down and has done some damage to the roof on the south side, but other than a few broken windows I think we have got off lightly."

Sam got up from the chair in which he had been lounging, half asleep. "I will organise a search for the missing horse and the rebuilding of the stables," he volunteered.

John turned to him in surprise and thanked him. Sam winked at Lucy, gave a cheery wave to everyone else, and was gone.

Feeling a little better about her relationship with Sam, Lucy – carrying the now replete and sleepy Oceanus – followed the ladies of the house and the slaves upstairs where John was already supervising the removal of most of the boards over the windows and doors. Outside was what appeared to be an alien landscape. Trees had been flattened, bushes and flowers uprooted, so for the first time she had an open vista before her instead of the lush, shady garden she had grown used to. There were several dead green monkeys. She thought sadly that there were likely to be many slaves dead on the island too, and that they would be paid almost as little attention.

Over the next few days there was plenty for them all to do around the house and garden, and Lucy proved herself a willing helper. The atmosphere between her and her mother-in-law thawed slightly, and life seemed to return more or less to normal. They sent and received messages to and from nearby friends, all of whom had suffered damage but, as Sam had said so presciently, since the sugar cane harvest was virtually complete, the financial losses were minimal. John, however, was sombre. All the cotton bushes at Long Bay had been torn out of the ground by the ferocity of the gale and while the cotton harvest was also secure, it would mean he would have to replant from seed and there would be little or no harvest next year. Money would be tight.

The Barrows wrote to confirm that Sunbury remained ready to welcome her and Sam for Crop Over (delayed because of the storm), and she looked forward to this with great curiosity and excitement.

The one shadow on her horizon was that Sam had flatly refused to take Oceanus with them.

"We shall only be away one night. Francine can look after him and either find a wet nurse to feed him or give him pap," he said in exasperation. "After all, you were happy enough to leave him behind when you went to Bridgetown shopping!"

Reluctantly, Lucy gave in, having anxiously sought assurances from Francine.

The weather since the night of the storm had been remarkably kind, even the north east wind, always strong during the wet season (and welcome for the coolness it brought to the humid nights) seemed gentler than before. Apart from the occasional shower, it was unusually dry, and Lucy enjoyed the dappled sunshine through which she and Sam passed at a fast trot on the five-mile trip to Sunbury.

The view from the carriage was very different from the last time they had passed this way, the landscape (in part because of the storm, but mainly because the sugar harvest was over) was more open because the tall, rustling canes were gone, along with the cloying smell. The slaves were still hard at work, though, Lucy saw groups of them slashing and burning grass, shrubs and any old cane left after the harvest, while others worked laboriously in pairs, digging holes for the next season's cane plants. She had heard this work was so hard that the slaves generally died within seven years.

Sam and Lucy had timed their visit to coincide with the climax of the Crop Over festival. Each sugar plantation held its own celebration whenever their own harvest was over, centred on the mill yard and paid for by the plantation owners – although Sam told her that the slaves held their own additional celebrations with dancing in their quarters. "Some mumbo-jumbo to do with ancestral spirits," he added dismissively.

Sam was in high good humour, as he always was in anticipation of a social event, and he answered Lucy's questions patiently and teased her gently. She thought sadly that if only she could wipe out the memory of what he had done the night after the baptism of John and Sarah's twins, she could believe once more that they were a young, loving married couple. Perhaps things would come right between them at Sunbury, but then, if Sam got drunk – as he was wont to do – he might again become violent. She shivered, despite the warmth of the carriage, with its windows shut tight against the dust, then resolutely put her fears aside and decided to live for the moment and try to enjoy herself.

From the time of their arrival at Sunbury that was not hard. Mary Barrow, an excellent hostess, had been on the lookout for them and hurried down the shallow steps from the front door to greet them warmly. John Barrow, she told them, was overseeing the finishing touches being put to the processional carts. She whisked them upstairs to their room, their luggage following on the heads of two burly slaves, and suggested they refresh themselves then join her downstairs as soon as possible before heading over to the mill-yard.

When they reached the yard, the windmill towering over it, the place was redolent of party atmosphere and roasting meat. Hundreds of slaves – as Lucy learned, Sunbury owned some two hundred and thirty slaves – dressed brightly in their best clothes, were standing around the edges of the yard, and there was a small group of seats set out at one end – with a slave holding a parasol over each one – for the white people. They greeted their mistress briefly as she passed between them with Lucy and Sam, then returned to their happy chatter. Lucy realised it was the loudest she had ever heard a group of slaves talking.

They took their seats and John Barrow joined them, greeting Lucy in particular very warmly. A house slave, impeccably dressed in breeches, a long-tailed coat and white gloves, bowed and offered Lucy a glass of lemonade from his tray, before doing the same to Sam and the Barrows. John raised his arm as a signal for the formal part of the festivities to begin.

Through the wide entrance to the yard came an immensely tall Amazon of a woman, coffee-coloured and with big, dark eyes, dressed entirely in white and with a complex and very beautiful white headdress covering her hair, a vivid orange flower tucked over one ear providing the only splash of colour. In one hand she held a rope, attached around the neck of an ox pulling a cart beautifully decorated with flowering branches of hibiscus, bougainvillea and oleander, on top of which sat a large mound of what Sam told her were the last canes harvested, tied down with a gaily coloured cloth. Everyone was applauding, with several of the slaves whooping and shouting also. The Amazon's face cracked into a broad grin as John also stood up to applaud her. He turned to Lucy, seated beside him, and explained that she was their best, most productive, cane picker.

Next came a series of other carts, all as beautifully decorated and carrying canes tied down with brightly coloured cloth, each accompanied by a small group of field slaves. Lucy noticed one or two staggering; despite the early hour, she thought they must already be drunk on the rum and beer which had no doubt been flowing throughout the festivities.

The very last cart carried 'Mr Harding', an effigy of the traditionally loathed plantation overseer, made of cane trash stuffed into an old pair of trousers and a coat, with a top hat on its head, signifying the end of harvest time. Overseers were generally poor white men who had been brought against their will to the colony as indentured servants, and having served their time, stayed on. They were known for their cruelty. The procession entered the mill yard and made two or three circuits so that the enthusiastic crowd could get a great view of the beautiful decorations and the workers themselves.

As the procession stopped, an old and respected field slave stepped forward to John as the day's host. With great solemnity, his hat in his hands, the slave gave a flowery little speech thanking his master on behalf of all the revellers. To Lucy's surprise, John bowed to the man and made an equally flowery speech in reply, and she realised this was all part of the ritual.

This apparently was the signal for the real fun to begin. After a final round of applause, the workers started to spill out of the yard, although a few dozen remained behind to set up trestle tables for the feasting. In the field next to the mill-yard, a band was already striking up and a range of stalls and competitions had been put in place. As the Lords and Barrows moved towards the field in the wake of the crowd, Lucy realised with delight that it was very like a country fair at home. There was the greased pole which people tried to climb to reach a money prize at the top; several young boys trying out stilt-walking; here were colourful sweetmeats for sale; there some birds whittled from wood. When she spied a coconut shy, she had to have a go. Egged on by laughing slaves, she did her best and won a little prize, then Sam had a go also and proved he had an astonishingly good aim. For his prize he chose a lacy parasol, which he presented to Lucy with an exaggerated, low bow. The watching slaves loved this gesture and applauded him loudly, laughing all the while. Sam's grin as he stood up was infectious, and Lucy found herself laughing also.

Mary had left them in order to go and oversee the final preparations for the feast, but John continued to accompany Sam and Lucy as they strolled around the field. They went over to where the band was playing, and Lucy was fascinated by the array of instruments, from the traditional fiddle and banjo to bottles filled with water and a strange looking home-made instrument she was told was called a *shak-shak*, made from a hollowed-out gourd filled with dried beans. The tempo of the music was infectious, as she remembered it from the twins' christening.

Many members of the band and the dancers with them had on strange costumes, and John and Sam tried to explain some of them to her. There was 'shaggy bear' – a man dressed in an outfit made of bundles of plantain leaves; the 'mother sally' (from whom Lucy quickly averted her eyes in embarrassment) which was another man dressed up like a woman with exaggerated bosom and buttocks; the 'donkey man' – who danced in a donkey costume with four legs, but which, in silhouette, looked like a man riding a two-legged animal; and the stilt-man who walked and even danced on the slim elevated posts she had watched the boys trying out earlier. It was only this latter character that resembled anything Lucy had seen in England, and she asked what the origin of such strange costumes was. Sam shrugged, uninterested, but John replied that he had heard they derived from the slaves' 'heathen ancestor worship'.

The music the band played enthusiastically was eclectic. Sometimes it was quite recognisable as a dance tune Lucy could as easily have heard in Bath, such as a quadrille (slaves who were good musicians often played for guests in their master's house); others had a beat she did not recognise at all; and, just as she was about to turn away, they started a simple yet rhythmic tune and a man and woman stepped forward from the crowd and began singing. Lucy could not understand the words, but she heard Sam laugh along with the rest of the audience, so it was clear that he did.

He turned to Lucy and said, "I hope you don't understand what they're singing; it's not very polite!"

She smiled, content to see him so relaxed, then jumped as the slave bell rang out. For once the slaves greeted its sound gaily, knowing it was the call to table, and they all began to stream into the mill-yard.

Sunbury had provided a number of animals to be slaughtered, so that there was meat in abundance, made into stews, pudding and souse, and roast pork. There were fragrant pots of peas and rice, as well as coconut bread and cassava bread, or pone. All these dishes were washed down with copious amounts of liquid both alcoholic and non-alcoholic. Swank was a favourite, made from cane liquor diluted with water; fancy molasses, mauby, coconut water, rum and falernum – a cordial made from an infusion of citrus, spices, nuts and, of course, sugar. Lucy had her favourite lime water (as did Mary), while Sam and John drank beer.

When they'd finished eating, John got up to move around the tables, clapping one man on the shoulder, drinking a glass with another, admiring a new baby. Lucy thought that it was far more like a harvest festival at Hewelsfield than anything she had previously seen on Barbados, and that it was the first time that she had seen a white man treating the slaves as they would their labourers in England. Even though she knew it was probably just a way of behaving for the festival period (John Barrow had a reputation as a strict but fair master, so no doubt his slaves were flogged for transgressions like all the others), it made her feel more relaxed.

She asked Sam to take her back to the field so she could watch the stilt-walkers weaving their way between a troupe of acrobats walking on their hands, and laugh at a group of muscular slaves chasing a greased pig, hoping to win a prize but failing to catch it to the great amusement of the watching female slaves. There were barrel dancers, too, wearing barrels with the top and bottom removed. She thought they must be very hot, their black faces glistened with sweat.

The band struck up another tune and she and Sam watched a large group of young slaves start dancing to it. It was nothing she recognised, but Sam told her it was called the treadmill dance. She watched, fascinated, as the music changed to the chigga-foot dance; and next she heard something more familiar, a polka tune. Sam caught her arm and she willingly tried to dance with him, but the steps were somewhat different from what she knew and they both ended up laughing with a crowd of onlookers as she learned the four-knee polka. Sam spied John and Mary coming to take them back to the house so he told the band leader to play a country dance, and the four of them performed it to the applause of the crowd.

They watched a while longer, until Lucy's eyes widened at the suggestive antics of some of the more energetic dancers in front of her.

Mary tut-tutted good-humouredly. "I think it is getting a little too wild for us ladies now. I shouldn't think your dancing master ever taught you the steps to the aptly-named *belly to belly*, did he?" she asked Lucy.

"I shouldn't think he even knew them!" Lucy responded.

"Come and have some of my rum punch," invited John. "These Negroes will keep dancing and singing all night until they drop, or at least while there's any food left. It can get a little boisterous. We will come back out at around 8 o'clock to watch 'Mr Harding' being burnt."

They sat on the veranda with their lime punch – even Lucy had some, slightly diluted – and Sam taught her poker so they could play with their hosts. Lucy proved an apt pupil and revelled in the fact that her husband was such good company, just as he had been on the voyage across eight months previously.

They duly went out to watch the straw effigy of 'Mr Harding' being burnt, at which point John sent the slaves back to their quarters where they would continue to party. Half a dozen of the house slaves joined the Barrows indoors, and John checked all the windows and doors were locked. Lucy, unaccustomed to the alcoholic punch, was growing sleepy. Sam pushed her gently towards the staircase and returned to John for a nightcap and cigar.

That night, he made love to Lucy gently, as he had on so many occasions in the past, and she put aside her fear of that dreadful night of a few weeks previously, hoping against hope that Mary Lucas had been right and that it had been a one-off aberration.

Chapter 9
Long Days

The plantation routine continued as normal, with little to change the leisurely pace as far as Lucy was concerned.

Life seemed rather flat after the excitement of Crop-Over. She sketched and painted, wrote letters to her parents, played with Oceanus, strolled decorously in the garden with her sisters-in-law, went to church on Sundays and rode with Sam on mornings when he was at Long Bay, visited (or was visited by) Mary Kingsley or the Barrows or occasionally Mary Austin.

She had first met Mary, Sam's older sister, and her husband Dr Richard Keen Austin at the twins' christening. They were accompanied by two of their children, Bathsheba and Caroline, around twelve years of age and very well behaved. Lucy liked Mary on sight. She was like an older version of Betty, with the same lively character.

She found herself getting ratty and short-tempered, and knew it was because she was bored. At Long Bay she neither enjoyed the round of social visits she had enjoyed in Bath, nor was she occupied with household duties as she often was at Hewelsfield, and had expected to be once she married Sam. She would have liked to learn more about the plantation business but knew this would be looked at askance both because she was a woman but also because Sam no longer had any ownership stake. She tried on several occasions to speak to John and plead for Sam to be given the plot of land he wanted so that he could start his building project. He was spending more and more time away from Long Bay, and she had a shrewd suspicion that he was drinking and gambling to excess in Bridgetown, and indeed that he probably had a mistress there. She tried to find out how much money he was losing at cards, but he immediately flew into a towering rage, demanding to know what right she had to question his actions. He shook her hard by the shoulders, then flung her away from him with such force that she stumbled and fell backwards, catching her lower back on the corner of a chair seat. Winded and in pain, she sat on the floor of her room with tears coursing down her cheeks as he slammed out of the house.

He did not return for several days, and when he did, he looked more dissipated than ever and smelt of some cloying scent. Lucy thought ruefully that the whole family must be aware that he had some girl set up in town but supposed that this was slightly less embarrassing than him taking up with one of the plantation slaves. In one or two of the houses she visited, she had been appalled by the cruelty shown by some of the ladies to their personal slaves and was indebted to Mary Kingsley for the information that it was not unknown for a plantation owner to take his wife's personal slave (who generally spent more time with the wife than he did) as a mistress, or simply to bed them and drop them. There was little the poor wife could do other than take it out on the girl – who had no choice in the matter either – by being petty and spiteful and constantly disciplining her or having her flogged, despite the potential danger of the slave responding by attempting to poison her mistress.

Lucy did not see Sam again that day until late afternoon, by which time he had shaved, bathed and changed. She was playing with Oceanus, who was a little fretful because – by now nine months old – he was cutting a tooth but could be diverted by crawling all over the floor and being chased by either Lucy or Francine, which caused him to chortle in delight. There came a knock at her door, and Lucy scooped a wriggling Oceanus off the ground to avoid him being crushed by the door opening. She was panting slightly, her face rather pink and her white cap askew, but she was laughing and Sam, opening the door, was struck for the first time in many months by the fact that although she was no beauty, her vivacity was attractive.

"Close the door, Sam, and see how fast your son can move," she said, stooping down to place Oceanus back on the floor.

The baby crawled straight over to his father as fast as the impeding ruffles on his dress allowed, putting his little hands on the glossy surface of his father's hessian riding boots and rocking to and fro as he looked down in fascination at his reflection. Sam scooped him up and held him aloft, at which there was a crow of delight.

The baby grinned and drooled, and Sam swung him back down to the floor, patted him on the rump and said, "Come on, then; let's see you go!"

Oceanus took off for the other side of the room at a speedy, crabwise crawl and Sam laughed.

"I had no idea how much he had grown. Before we know it, he'll be on his first pony!"

Francine came in at this point to help her mistress dress for dinner. She dropped Sam a curtsey, her eyes downcast. Sam crossed to the connecting door to his room and tried to open it, but it was locked.

"What the devil…" he exclaimed, turning to Lucy.

She stood as if turned to stone. "You have been away, Sam, and I was afraid that anyone could come in, so I have taken to locking my doors at night," she said breathlessly.

He nodded carelessly, seemingly accepting her explanation. Unlocking the door he said, "I'll take Oceanus through with me while you get dressed." And, to Francine, "Come and fetch him, girl, when your mistress is ready."

Lucy breathed a sigh of relief and made a mental note to be careful not to leave the door locked as she had been doing. There had been no repeat of his behaviour the night of the twins' christening, and Lucy had no desire to goad him into it again. As she had thought, he clearly had no recollection of what he had done – or, which would be worse, thought nothing of it.

Worried that Sam would become impatient with the baby, she hurried her toilette and sent Francine to fetch him before she had slipped on her shoes. She need not have been concerned, Sam was seated on a stool with his back to his dressing table and had handed one of his hairbrushes to Oceanus who was chewing it with enormous concentration. He threw a temper tantrum when Francine tried to remove it forcibly from his grasp. Sam looked with distaste at the wet, mangled brush and told the girl to clean it and return it to him later when Oceanus was asleep. Husband and wife then descended the stairs together, Lucy teasing Sam gently over the state of his hairbrush so that both were laughing when they emerged onto the veranda.

John's face, in contrast, was like thunder. Lucy looked quickly from him to his wife Sarah, but the latter looked completely unruffled, pale and composed as ever, so Lucy did not think they had quarrelled. She sighed inwardly. Clearly tonight was not going to be the right moment to ask him about the piece of land for Sam's mansion. At dinner, she tried to coax out of him what the problem was, but John's responses were perfunctory, almost curt. At the end of the meal, he scraped his chair back and addressed Sam,

"I wish to speak to you, Samuel. Please join me in my study."

Sam raised one eyebrow, glanced at Lucy – who shook her head to indicate she did not know what was wrong – and lounged away from the table, his hands in his pockets, the ladies quickly following him out of the dining room and making their way to the drawing room.

Despite the fact that the study, to the right of the drawing room, was the only room on the ground floor to have a door (which, at this moment, was firmly closed), it was not long before they heard voices raised in anger.

There was a brief, embarrassed silence, then Mrs Lord senior took charge, suggesting in a voice which brooked no refusal that John's wife should sing for them while Betty accompanied her on the piano. Technically, Sarah's voice was quite good, but she sounded rather wooden, and after two songs Betty turned impetuously to Lucy and suggested she sing them some English folk songs.

Worried as to why the brothers were quarrelling, Lucy had never felt less like singing, but she did as she was asked. Her voice was well suited to the style, and she persuaded all her sisters-in-law to join with her in the chorus; between them, they drowned out the angry sounds from the study. They heard an outer door slam, but neither of the men re-joined them that night.

When Lucy went to bed, she could hear sounds from Sam's room next door, but she could not quite pluck up the courage to enter, not knowing what mood Sam would be in if it was indeed him rather than his man. If Sam did not come to her that night, she resolved to get up for their usual early morning ride, hoping that he would come and she could find out what had occurred.

Sam was reluctant to discuss the quarrel the following morning, but Lucy persevered, pointing out that it could have a bearing on John's decision in relation to the castle project. It transpired that John had discovered that Sam had withdrawn a sum of money from the plantation account with the bank to repay some of his gambling debts. The two of them were trotting along a broad path some way out into the plantation, and Lucy turned to look at her husband, wide-eyed with dismay.

"Surely you can't have spent all the money from my father already, Sam?" she exclaimed.

"Of course not!" came the curt response.

"Then, why…?"

"Why not? It's my money too, I put funds into the plantation account, dammit!" he growled angrily.

This, then, had been Sam's contribution towards purchasing an addition to the Long Bay plantation. No wonder that John was angry, no doubt he felt he could not trust Sam to keep his side of the bargain and would now be even more reluctant to set aside land for his brother to build his beloved mansion. And Sam's contribution would be even more vital following the devastation caused by the recent hurricane. Lucy sighed, and wondered how on earth they were ever going to disentangle themselves from the increasingly stifling atmosphere, living cooped up with the entire family and without any rights or control.

"So what did John say? How was it left?" she asked.

"I must replace the funds at once. Which I shall do when I win some money at cards, which is bound to happen soon; a man can't have bad luck forever. He cannot use it yet anyway, we have no property purchase waiting in the wings. I shall spend the weekend in Bridgetown – I have militia training there, as does John, and I shall stay a few days to recoup my losses."

This was said with such certainty that Lucy did not dare voice her fear that, indeed, a man could have bad luck forever, and she wished he would stop gambling. She thought ruefully that, if she was feeling frustrated at her lack of responsibility or ability to control her daily life, it must be even worse for her husband, who no doubt found it irksome that he had no say in ordering plantation life – hence his enjoyment of the activity engendered by events such as the recent hurricane. She felt helpless at her inability to make him see that gambling away her dowry was rendering his dream (and her life) ever more impossible.

Sam left early the next morning and she did not see him for another four days. Although she was growing used to his absences, she did not like them, and frequently fretted that not only would he gamble away every penny of their money, but also that he was spending too much time with some beautiful quadroon girl in Bridgetown.

When he returned, much to her surprise, he was full of good cheer. It seemed his luck had turned and he had for once won a great deal of money at cards. He had replaced the funds he had withdrawn from the plantation account and bought presents for his wife (a delicate gold chain and locket) and sisters. John remained cold and distant, but everyone else felt that life was a little brighter and less humdrum with Sam back at Long Bay.

The rainy season continued, and Lucy became accustomed to the frequent short, heavy bursts of rain, usually accompanied by squally winds, and succeeded by steamy sunshine. She found it tiring and was grateful she did not have to labour in the fields as the slaves did. Her morning rides became more infrequent as Sam spent longer away from home with his cronies in Bridgetown, but she broke up the monotony of life on the plantation with frequent visits to and by the Lucas family, and occasional ones to the Barrows at Sunbury or visits to other plantations.

Once Sam escorted Martha and her children back to Long Bay for a meal, but Lucy could not warm to her as she had to Betty or to Mary Austin. And John's wife Sarah seemed to grow paler and more aloof by the day; Lucy finally understood and looked on her more sympathetically when she found her retching into a bowl in the scullery off the kitchens and learned that she was already pregnant again despite having given birth to a daughter as recently as May. However, it reinforced her determination to try and talk to John about Sam's castle, but John was absent from the house almost as much as Sam, spending all day, every day out on the plantation to ensure his new cotton plants did not fall victim to the dreaded pink boll worm, and frequently not even returning to eat with the family. Lucy wondered how his wife felt about his absence but did not feel at ease enough with Sarah to ask.

Christmas 1809 came, and with it another feast for the family and a holiday for the slaves. Lucy had gone with the other ladies of the house to Bridgetown to do some shopping for gifts. She had bought Sam a new set of hairbrushes to replace the one chewed by Oceanus, which had never been the same again, and she had the estate carpenter make a frame for her sketch of Francine and another for a painting of a bird of paradise flower for Betty. She had bought gloves, ribbons and slippers for other members of the family and sweetmeats for her friend Mary, who had a sweet tooth.

She puzzled over what to give Oceanus, who was now eleven months old and attempting to stand whenever he could find something to hang onto. Francine told her that one of the plantation slaves was gifted at whittling wood, and Lucy asked her to order a toy green monkey from the man. When it arrived, she was as delighted with it as Oceanus, the slave had made it with a tail that swung when the toy was placed on the edge of a table.

During the festive meal, Lucy thought how different the food was from anything they would be having in Hewelsfield or Stafford. Flying fish, *cocoo*, okra and a dish that was new to her, *jug* (consisting of pigeon, peas, stew and salt beef, onions, Guinea corn flour, and spices), would never be seen in England, although the Christmas dishes they accompanied such as boiled ham and roasted pork would be familiar. She found it strange celebrating Christmas in such hot weather and missed the roaring log fire around which they would sing carols at Hewelsfield. Even the familiar church service they had attended in the morning seemed strange, the brilliant colours and scents of the flowers, not to mention the ever-present sea of black faces wherever you looked outside the confines of the church.

They exchanged gifts after the meal on the veranda, and Lucy seized the opportunity offered as she gave John his gift of dark maroon leather slippers to broach the subject of Sam's longed-for castle.

"I do not think it can be easy for you or Sarah to have us living here permanently with you, John – particularly now she is breeding again. The house will grow very crowded as your family grows, and even more so when there are brothers and sisters for Oceanus too. I do not want us to be a burden on your finances, and I know things will be very difficult without a harvest next year. If we were to live somewhere else close by, we would all have the best of both worlds. We would be able to help each other when needed, and the children could grow up together."

"You are welcome in my house, Lucy," said John, frowning. "There is no possibility of giving Sam what he wants until we have purchased land suitable for a sugar crop and begun to make a profit from it. Besides, I know what Sam will do, he will 'borrow' slaves to help with the construction, use raw materials which I can ill spare from the plantation also, and no doubt he will wildly overspend and come running to me for assistance. I must provide for the girls and Mother. As a result of his actions, she has signed a deed of conveyance on Long Bay to Sam and I so we can borrow funds to expand the business, in return for an annuity which I must honour. Life is too precarious to contemplate his grandiose plans. Can you not persuade him to purchase something smaller and earn a living, since he seems so averse to helping with the aloe and cotton crops here?"

"His heart is set on his castle. And he will be using his money, not yours, so he will take nothing away from your mother or your sisters."

"He will if he tries to use my slaves when they should be in the fields, growing and harvesting the crops, or when he takes timber from Long Bay or uses the brick kiln. And that is what he would do, Lucy."

"Are you ruling out any hope he may have of being able to build within the Long Bay estate? That would break his heart, I think."

"I am not ruling it out, but we must expand the plantation and build the profits before I will contemplate it. If he would spend more time working the fields with me and less gambling in Bridgetown, we might achieve that more quickly." John turned away as he said this, indicating that the conversation was at an end.

It was with a heavy heart that Lucy reported the conversation to Sam later that evening. She was surprised that he took it calmly, having feared that he might lose his temper and take it out on her by hitting her, but he simply shrugged and said he had expected nothing better.

Lucy, however, felt trapped. If Sarah had a son in a few months' time she, Lucy, would feel even more of an interloper here at Long Bay; her relationship with her mother-in-law remained too uncomfortable for her to view with equanimity spending the whole of her married life here with no role or responsibilities of her own. She longed to suggest visiting her parents but dared not as it would deplete their resources still further and push any chance of an independent lifestyle into the distant future. There seemed no way out for her. So she said nothing, thinking that she might discuss it with Mary Kingsley when she saw her in a few days.

She drew some comfort from Francine's ecstatic reception of her portrait when the girl helped her get ready for bed. There were tears in Francine's eyes and she kissed Lucy's hand. As she left Lucy's room to return to the slave quarters, she held the picture tightly to her chest, and it seemed likely she would sleep with it that night.

The days and weeks dragged by. They celebrated Oceanus' first birthday on the 27th of January 1810, for which there were presents sent over by the Wightwicks and a long letter for Lucy from her mother, thanking her for all the flower sketches and paintings she had sent and telling her all the local news. Lucy shed a few tears because it all seemed so distant now, she even found it hard to recall her parents' features. So she wrote and asked for pictures of them, and four months later was delighted when two little cameos arrived with a letter from her father.

30th April 1810

My Dearest Daughter,

Mama and I were pleased to hear that you liked our gift for Oceanus. She has framed the pencil sketch you sent of our Grandson and placed it in the Parlour.

I hope the small pictures enclosed with this letter are all that you had hoped. As Oceanus grows, it will be good for him to know what his English grandparents look like.

One of the ships in which I took a stake arrived recently with an excellent cargo of Cotton from Barbados. I wondered if it came from Long Bay? It will fetch a good price, so I may now invest in a coal mine I have had my eye on for a while.

I hope you are well and happy. Please say all that is proper from me to your family.

With fondest love from your Mama and Papa.

Sam's luck at the tables waxed and waned, and she learned to put a careful guard on her tongue when he had had a run of bad luck as this tended to induce drinking and, although he had not raped her again, he could be violent so she tried not to provoke him. Once, when she was feeling very low and he had been rough with her, she wrote a letter to her father asking if he could see any way to providing some additional funds to purchase a property, but she tore it up without sending it, knowing that Sam would never accept anything he considered inferior to his dream castle and that the money would simply be squandered on dice or cards if it were provided.

She confided some of her frustration to Mary, but there was little she could offer Lucy other than sympathy. Despite everything Lucy still loved Sam and would in any case have shied away from so drastic a step as leaving him. As Mary had pointed out previously, this would mean a return to England and social ostracism, with little or no money. Besides, what would she do about Oceanus?

She could not bear to be parted from her child but knew Sam would not let her leave with his son and would assert his legal rights over the boy. And how would she pay for her passage? And since neither of the women could think of a way to persuade John to change his mind about granting the land to Sam to begin building his castle, Lucy must learn to put up with her generally comfortable, if monotonous existence.

She gritted her teeth and made several pleasant trips to Bridgetown with her sisters-in-law, often met there by Sam and sometimes by Mary Austin, sometimes accompanied by Mary Kingsley, although they usually remained within the confines of Broad Street. Once or twice she accompanied Betty to drink tea with one of her contemporaries at another plantation. Otherwise, one day was very much like another. It was only Oceanus' progress as he learned to walk and talk that gave her any real pleasure or provided any evidence that time was indeed passing. When Sam was at home, he delighted in taking his son on his shoulders for a walk in the grounds. Oceanus would crow with happiness and clap his hands, then point when he saw one of the green monkeys ('monkey' was one of his first words) and ask to be put down so he could chase them.

Lucy marvelled at how patient and tolerant Sam was with not only his own child but also his nieces and nephews, behaviour rarely in evidence with her. She had learned to read his moods gradually and tried to avoid doing or saying anything to arouse his temper, but sometimes she could not resist fighting with him (over money, his constant absences, the way he did not involve her in decisions about their son) and had more or less resigned herself to sporting bruises and aching ribs or buttocks from his beatings. Well, her father had tried to warn her that she was marrying trouble, she had made her own bed and now she must lie in it. Even if she had been living in England she was too proud to admit that she might have made a mistake to the parents she had defied; as it was, there was nothing she could do here in Barbados – nowhere she could go, nobody she could turn to with any power to improve her situation.

The major social event in the calendar was the wedding of Sir Reynold Alleyne to Rebecca Alton in late September 1810. As Betty explained to Lucy, "Sir Reynold Alleyne comes from an old family and is very highly thought of. He has several large plantations on Barbados including Four Hills and Alleynedale Hall. We have been invited to his wedding to Rebecca Alton, which is bound to be a very sumptuous affair, because her family's plantation, Harrow, is very close to Long Bay so we know them quite well although we do not frequent each other's houses much. What a stroke of luck! It provides us with a wonderful excuse to go shopping since we absolutely must look our best for such a grand occasion. I think we must have at least two new dresses each so that we can change for the dancing in the evening."

St Philip's Church was thronged with guests from the plantation hierarchy, all dressed in their best, and Lucy thought that in the shimmering sunlight they looked like a flock of tropical birds or swathe of Barbadian flora. She nodded and waved to acquaintances already seated in the pews as the family moved towards the front of the church, shaking hands warmly with the Barrows and smiling at Mary Kingsley, who remained her only real friend on the island.

Settling herself, she unfurled her fan and looked over it towards John and Sam. Her husband looked extremely handsome and debonair, and Lucy was surprised at the sudden rush of love and desire that coursed through her. Sam appeared to be trying to make John laugh, without much success.

Suddenly everyone was standing, the bride (whom Lucy hardly knew, having only once paid her a courtesy visit at Harrow with Betty) arrived looking very attractive, dressed in light blue silk. She was pale and seemed a little nervous. She walked down the aisle on her father's arm, glancing neither to right nor to left, to stand next to Sir Reynold.

As the ceremony progressed, Lucy compared it wryly with her runaway marriage to Sam two years before. She wondered whether Miss Alton had expectations which would be dashed as hers had been, or whether this was a more prosaic union. And how quickly would she give birth to a son, cementing the proud Alleyne succession?

A rush of jealousy surprised her; this girl's status, like John's wife's, was assured unlike Lucy's. She flinched at this ignoble thought, and unconsciously smoothed her belly, hoping against hope that she was finally pregnant again and would give birth to a second healthy boy. She had missed her monthly period twice, so it seemed likely… but there was no hint of morning sickness – yet.

In December she accompanied the Barrows to Bridgetown in order to visit the newly opened Cheapside Market and do some Christmas shopping. By this time she knew that both she and Sarah Lord were pregnant. Secretly she was pleased that she felt strong and healthy, and that Sam was once again paying her a little more attention, while Sarah was as always suffering from morning sickness and looking grey and miserable – hardly surprising since her last baby, Haynes Elizabeth, had died in August at the age of fifteen months.

As the three shoppers, backed up by two sturdy house slaves, walked briskly along Lower Broad Street, Lucy noticed a derelict area on their right containing what looked like a ruin, and asked John Barrow what it was. "The ruins of St Michael's Church. It was destroyed in the hurricane of 1780," he responded. "They've built a new one now – you probably saw it on the way in." She remembered Sarah telling her about it on her first visit.

"But that was forty years ago," she said. "How is it that nothing else has been built here since?"

John shrugged. "This neighbourhood is not nearly as sought after as Broad Street, and I think the Church probably had enough on its hands building its big new replacement. Besides, part of it's still used as a burial ground for Negroes. No doubt they'll put something else here when it's worth their while."

Lucy stopped to look. Quite a number of black people, men, women and children, were clambering among the broken stones, turning them over, picking some up to carry away. Others were just sitting, staring at nothing, or praying over a grave. The little party moved on, and a faint hubbub of noise came to Lucy's ears on the breeze.

"That's the market!" exclaimed Mary.

"Keep a tight hold on your purses, ladies," said John, and in another hundred yards they reached the marketplace. A riot of colours and smells greeted them as they started to wend their way between the stalls which offered everything from fresh produce to haberdashery, household goods to livestock.

Lucy looked around with interest. The first thing she noticed was that colourful clothing was far more common among the black women vendors than she had seen anywhere else on the island since her arrival. Most of the shoppers were also black, although there was a sprinkling of other white visitors like themselves. Enthralled she watched the graceful, swaying gait of a woman about her sister-in-law Bathsheba's age weaving her way through the throng with a huge tray of cassava on her head.

Lucy would happily have lingered among the food stalls which she found fascinating, but Mary was less interested and was making her determined way in the direction of the haberdashery stalls.

"If you want to buy something, Lucy, don't offer the first price they ask," said John. "They expect you to bargain them down. Start at about a third of what they ask and work your way up a little."

Lucy nodded, but added, "I'm not sure I shall understand what they say to me. I cannot understand any of the conversations going on around us."

"That's because they're using their own barbarous language," laughed John. "They'll talk English to you, don't you worry."

Mary had found a colourful stall with dozens of different ribbons which clearly appealed to her. She pointed to three and asked the stallholder, a tiny, wizened old woman with no teeth and an enormous broad-brimmed hat that completely swamped her, for a price. To Lucy's admiration, she then entered briskly into bargaining and appeared satisfied with the deal she reached.

As they moved on, a stall selling wooden toys caught Lucy's eye and she stopped, her hand on John's sleeve.

"I should like to buy one of these for Oceanus," she said. "He so loves the monkey I gave him last Christmas."

The stallholder was an old black man who continued to whittle his products while waiting for customers. He laid his knife and unfinished toy aside when Lucy bent to look at the items for sale. In the end she chose a small cart, gaily painted red, and a startling green and black bird on a stick. She entered somewhat hesitantly into bargaining with the old man. She would have paid over the odds, but Mary joined in and insisted on a lower price which was eventually agreed. The toys were handed to the houseboy and they moved on.

As with the visit to Swan Street the previous year, it was Lucy who tired first, despite the parasol diligently held over her by one of the slaves. She thought she would love to spend a morning at the market with her easel and paintbox, although not sure she would really be able to capture the sound and smell in a picture.

On their way to have a light lunch at the Roebuck Street tavern, they bumped into John Lord hurrying out. The (all white) members of the Barbados Assembly frequently met there since no dedicated Parliament building existed, although they were shortly to move to the upper floor of the town hall. John had become an Assembly member the previous year and took his duties very seriously; as Sam had prophesied, he enjoyed the role immensely. He agreed to join them for lunch when invited to do so by John Barrow, and over the meal the conversation of the two men turned to their concern over the impact of William Wilberforce's commitment to outlawing slavery.

It was the 10th of December, and John explained that there had been a passionate debate that morning in the Assembly during which members expressed the concerns of most of the white population on the island about an increase of arrogance and vice among the slaves, of which there had been growing evidence since the successful Haitian slave rebellion in 1804. Robert Haynes, a fellow planter-Assemblyman, had voiced for all of them the fear that 'there was something brewing in [the Negroes'] minds', and the House of Assembly had resolved to urge tighter police control[5].

That evening, Lucy repeated the gist of the conversation to Sam. While she had so far not felt any animosity directed at her at Long Bay, she could not but be conscious of the enormous numerical differential between whites and blacks on the island, and she was afraid for Oceanus and her unborn child.

But Sam, characteristically, dismissed her concerns, "John and his fellow Assembly members are old women," was his retort. "The militia will crush any unrest before it ever really gets started. There are always one or two troublemakers, but Barbados is nothing like Haiti. The French are barbaric and have a very high attrition rate among their slaves. Our slaves are well looked after and could not survive on their own. You'll see – they'll increase militia training, make a lot of noise about it, and this'll all die down in a few weeks. Besides, Negroes are like children, they love Christmas because the lazy devils don't have to work. Don't go worrying your head over it."

Although only too well aware of the way whites looked down upon their slaves as sub-human, Lucy nevertheless always felt uncomfortable at references to slaves 'being like children'. They were not. They were more like us than anyone cared to admit, she reminded herself. But what could she do? She was in no position as a dependent woman to say or do anything. Convinced that William Wilberforce would be successful in outlawing slavery just as he had the slave trade, Lucy wondered what its impact would be on the plantocracy. No doubt they would lose both power and wealth. What would it mean for her and Sam, she wondered?

Christmas came and went again, and also Oceanus' second birthday at the end of January 1811. Sam was away in Bridgetown so missed it, but Lucy ordered out the buggy and drove out with their son along the clifftops to watch the surf thundering onto Cobblers' Reef.

February was Lucy's favourite month on Barbados – dry and warm, without the sweltering humidity of later months, and a complete contrast to February in Chepstow or Wolverhampton which would be cold, rainy and windy. Early in

---

[5] *Sugar in the Blood*, pp. 271-2

the month, she returned to the house from a morning ride with Sam, ravenously hungry, but as she sat down at the breakfast table having changed out of her tight-fitting riding habit, she noticed that John, Sam and Mrs Lord senior were looking grave, and both Sarahs were white as sheets.

As a white-gloved slave shook out her napkin, she looked across the table in inquiry. "What has happened?" she asked with a touch of impatience, as no-one said a word.

"We hear there's been an uprising of slaves in Louisiana," replied John heavily. "There have clearly been some deaths, but we don't know the details yet."

Conscious of the slaves present in the room, Lucy said no more but shivered slightly, as the concerns expressed by Assembly members in December echoed in her head.

Over the next few days, the basic facts of the story became known. In the middle of the night of the 8th of January 1811, a small group of slaves had entered the bedroom of plantation owner Manuel Andry. After slaves slung a few axes and other domestic weapons, a wounded Andry managed to escape, but his son did not. The slaves then quickly seized arms and marched to New Orleans, picking up fighters along the way as whites fled in fear. The local militia apparently put down the revolt relatively quickly, and the Louisiana Governor William Claiborne declared that the uprising was caused by 'a simple band of brigands out to pillage and plunder'. But the fact that the unrest went beyond a single plantation and across Louisiana, that copies of the French Declaration of the Rights of Man were found in slave quarters – and that many of their own slaves on Barbados knew about and were clearly excited by the event – caused real concern among the white community.

Night patrols by armed militia, as well as an increased police presence, became the norm. As usual Sam revelled in the excitement, happy to be out and active. Lucy noticed that the slightest transgression by any slave was dealt with extremely harshly, brandings and whippings were carried out almost daily at Long Bay, generally overseen by the sadistic Alexander.

Most of the transgressors were field slaves, and Lucy did her best to avoid attending their punishment, but one day Juba, the girl she had seen soon after her arrival leaving John's bedroom in a battered condition, was dragged back to Long Bay in chains, tied to the back of a cart, and Mrs Lord insisted that all of them were present at her flogging since she was a house slave.

Lucy's stomach heaved as the semi-conscious girl was stripped to the waist, tied to a tree and given twenty lashes. When they untied her, she fell senseless to the ground then screamed as someone threw a bucket of salt water over her back. A muscular black man, eyes to the ground but looking sullen, picked her up and, slinging her over his shoulder, carried her towards the slave quarters.

Rather tentatively, that evening as she dressed for dinner and Francine bathed Oceanus and prepared him for bed, Lucy asked how Juba was.

"She hurt," came the soft answer, and Lucy could draw her out no further.

Lucy was sure in the next few days and weeks that there was an air of foreboding about the house, and more whispering and sullenness among the slaves than previously. None of them ever sang any more. But as her stomach swelled and her movement became more awkward, something else occurred to take her mind off any potential uprising: an outbreak of measles.

Chapter 10
Birth and Death

It started in the slave quarters, as most epidemics generally did, probably brought in by one or more new slaves. John grumbled about the loss of productive workers at such a busy time in the fields, and his mother seemed to take it as a personal affront when several of the housemaids and kitchen staff fell ill.

Sarah, as pregnant as Lucy, became frantic with worry when little John, now four years old, fell ill towards the end of March, and Lucy became paranoid about Oceanus' safety, frequently refusing to let the toddler out of her sight. He had got used to spending time with his cousin John and became fractious at his mother's possessiveness, often wailing that he wanted Francine. But Lucy was afraid Francine would also contract the disease and tried (without much success) to manage without her. She quickly realised that she had adapted completely to the Barbadian lifestyle of total dependence on slaves, and would have to continue to rely on Francine and others to bring her bathing water, wash her clothes, prepare and serve food… She was by now big with her second baby, her legs and feet swollen and aching, and she kept bursting into tears for no reason.

Francine accepted her crotchets patiently, but the family (including Sam) left her alone as far as possible. She would sit in front of the open window of her bedroom, feeling sorry for herself, convinced that Sam had taken dozens of slave mistresses, and wishing herself back at her parents' house. There seemed no-one around she could talk to about her feelings.

Little John began to improve, according to the reports Francine gave her, but about a fortnight after his cousin had come out in spots, Oceanus started to be feverish. At first, Lucy and Francine thought it was just a childish cold, but over the next few days his condition worsened and then the tell-tale spots began to appear on his chest.

Francine wanted to remove Oceanus from Lucy's room, worried that if her mistress contracted the disease her unborn baby would be harmed, but Lucy fell into hysterical sobbing, clinging to the little boy. It was only when her mother-in-law took control of the situation and ordered Francine to take him to another room that she gave up the fight. Bathsheba told her coldly to pull herself together and oversaw the removal of Oceanus' crib and clothes.

Lucy lay on the chaise longue, her face blotched, her eyes swollen with crying, hiccoughing softly and feeling unutterably depressed. Francine slipped in later to let Lucy know that she had been detailed to care for Oceanus and could therefore no longer look after Lucy for fear of infection – nor would Lucy be allowed to see her son until the danger was passed.

"I give him obeah medicine, mist'ss," Francine whispered, "Mist'ss, Lord not know."

Lucy took to her bed. She refused to get dressed or leave her room. Another of the slave girls, Mercy, was detailed to look after her, but was unable to persuade her to eat much or take an interest in anything. Dishevelled and unkempt, she lay in bed continually drafting and redrafting morbid letters to her father about Oceanus' likely death and her wish to follow him quickly.

Bathsheba sent Sam to remonstrate with her, the only time she had seen her husband in about four weeks. He hardly recognised her and on seeing the letters, grew extremely angry, and crushed them into a ball which he hurled across the room. He shook Lucy roughly by the shoulders, yelled for slaves to bring water for a bath and threatened to have them strip her and put her into it if she would not cooperate. Reluctantly, she struggled up, almost losing her balance, but once Sam and the houseboys had left, she climbed into the bath and lay there while Mercy washed her hair and body.

Afterwards she felt calmer and wondered at her own behaviour. Dressed in a fresh nightgown, seated in one of the rattan armchairs while Mercy stripped and remade the bed, she asked the girl how Oceanus was.

Mercy, knowing full well that the little boy was clinging to life by the merest thread but under strict instructions not to tell Lucy, did not raise her eyes but said, "I ask Francine, miss."

That night Lucy went into labour. She tried to remember what she had been told two years before, on board ship, and began pacing her room, holding on to items of furniture to avoid falling over. The pains started coming more frequently, she banged on Sam's door, but there was no answer. She opened the door into the corridor, and almost tripped over Mercy, curled up asleep on a pallet on the floor. The girl hurried off to get help as Lucy doubled over in pain and panted hard, clinging to the birthing stool that had been placed in her room in readiness.

Her mother-in-law swept in and took charge, sending for the midwife before retiring once more to her own room. In the early hours of the morning of 22nd April 2011, as the sun crept over the horizon, Lucy gave birth to a baby girl. Once both she and the baby were clean and presentable, Mercy gave Bathsheba's maid the news, and at around ten o'clock the widow, looking as precise as ever, came to visit.

Lucy was sitting up against a bank of pillows, looking more like her old self, the baby asleep beside her. Bathsheba bent over the sleeping baby, checked her fingers and toes, then turned and sat down.

In a slightly dreamy voice Lucy asked, "How is my son? How is Oceanus?"

"Still poorly. He is being well cared for. It is best if he stays away from you and the baby until he is better," responded her mother-in-law firmly.

Lucy was tired, and simply nodded, it was as she expected. "Where is Sam?" she asked next.

"I have not seen him for several days. No doubt he will return sometime soon," came Bathsheba's response.

Over the next week, Lucy acted as if in a dream. She fed the baby, Emma, when she cried but took no real interest in her. She was a scrawny baby who did not radiate the same zest for life as Oceanus had when he was born. Lucy bathed when told to, ate when told to; she was docile and passive, far from her usual self. Sam visited once only; Lucy thought he looked tired and worried, but she could not summon up the energy to ask him why.

She began having vivid dreams and found it impossible to get comfortable in her bed. Her breasts were hard and they ached. It hurt when Emma tried to suckle, but the baby cried constantly and seemed to be getting no nourishment. John's wife Sarah, now hugely pregnant, came to visit Lucy and, worried by the hectic spots of colour on her cheeks and her strange behaviour, asked their mother-in-law to visit her. Bathsheba found her, standing bent double over the foot of the bed, one hand clutching a bed post and the other pressed to her breast. Both mother and baby were crying. Mercy was hovering in the corner, hands twisted in her skirt, looking worried.

Bathsheba looked sharply at Mercy. "Have you told her?" she asked. She was referring to the fact that little Oceanus had, tragically, died the previous day. The girl shook her head. "Then what is wrong with her?" asked Bathsheba, exasperated.

"Mist'ss hurt. Can't feed baby," replied the girl.

Bathsheba felt Lucy's burning forehead, took in at a glance her swollen, painful breasts and realised what was wrong. Lucy had mastitis. She sent Mercy to fetch her own maid, whom she asked to bring laudanum, then sent Mercy to find a wet nurse among the slaves for little Emma. She pushed Lucy gently into bed, dosed her with the laudanum and wiped her brow with a cool cloth soaked in lavender water until the drug began to calm her.

Over the next few days Lucy's fever mounted, and she slipped in and out of hallucinations and nightmares whenever the effects of the laudanum wore off. She was hardly aware that Emma had disappeared, or that the doctor had come to bleed her, or that Francine had returned to her side, merely asking her once, drowsily, when she would see Oceanus. Francine returned a non-answer, under strict orders from Bathsheba not to tell her mistress that the little boy had died like so many others. Measles was a killer at all levels of society, and in the crowded slave quarters, doubly so.

The funeral was arranged quickly as was the custom by her mother-in-law, but without telling Lucy. On the day it happened, the 5th of May, she woke feeling a little better, and asked Francine quite lucidly for sight of both her children. The girl soothed her, explaining that she had been seriously unwell and must wait until she was out of danger before having the children near her. Tired, Lucy drifted quickly back to sleep, thinking only how quiet the house was.

Lucy continued to improve, but she was exhausted by her illness and it was several days before Dr Lucas thought she would be able to stand the strain of hearing of Oceanus' death. High levels of child mortality were the norm in the

West Indies, and those born and bred there accepted the fact. But neither the doctor, nor Bathsheba or Sam had considered that despite the high infant mortality rates in England also, Lucy might see things differently.

It was Sam who broke the news to her when she asked again to see Oceanus.

"I am afraid we have lost him, my dear. He was too weakened by the measles and he died while you were recovering from little Emma's birth. We buried him at St Philip's a week ago."

Lucy was sitting on her chaise longue, and Sam sat down awkwardly next to her and put an arm around her shoulders. Lucy's gaunt face and black-ringed eyes stared up at him. The tears welled up and slid down her cheeks, but she made no sound. A feeling of total emptiness and desolation overtook her. In Oceanus she had found someone to whom she could give her unconditional love – something she had learned her husband did not want – and now he was gone.

"I am so sorry, Lucy, but we still have little Emma Lucy and we will have other sons," said Sam clumsily.

Lucy wept into his shoulder until exhausted, at which point Sam lifted her onto the bed, patted her hand awkwardly and left her to Francine's ministrations. Still Lucy uttered no sound, just turned her face away. She once again refused to eat and showed no interest in anything – even little Emma when Francine brought her to visit a few days later. Francine continued to tend to her, telling an unresponsive Lucy news of the estate such as the birth on the 10th of May of John and Sarah's daughter, Elizabeth, but was unable to persuade her to swallow more than a mouthful of broth occasionally. Lucy seemed determined to starve herself to death.

Betty and Sam tried to rouse her from the depths of her depression with no success. Sam brought Emma to visit her, but Lucy showed hardly a flicker of recognition. It was Sam, not Lucy, who cradled the baby in his arms and kissed the little, downy head before handing her to Francine.

In desperation, and after a fierce row with his mother who abhorred the idea of washing their dirty linen in public, he begged Mary Kingsley to visit Lucy and see if she could achieve better results. Not that Bathsheba need have worried, Mary's father was the family doctor, and who would Mary tell anyway? But Lucy hardly reacted to her friend's presence, she seemed to float outside herself, looking on those in her room from a long distance.

Eventually Bathsheba lost patience with her daughter-in-law. She marched unannounced into Lucy's room one morning when John and a reluctant Sam were already out on the estate, and vigorously opened the shutters and windows. Lucy, used to the semi-darkness, winced and wearily covered her eyes with one arm. Francine, who had just washed her mistress and put her into a fresh nightgown, stood in the corner of the room, eyes cast down.

"Get up, Lucy, this instant. You are no longer ill, you are deliberately moping yourself into a decline. I am sick to death of your die-away airs. Do you think you are the first woman to lose a child? You attended the funeral of Sarah's daughter last year. Did she behave in this namby-pamby way? No, she dealt with it with dignity – and now she has another healthy girl. Do you think life was plain sailing for me? Or Mrs Lucas? Or Mrs Barrow? We all suffered losses – I too lost a son, Thomas. No doubt your mother did also. It is painful, but you get over it. Now do you see the wisdom of my suggestion that you follow our traditions and find a wet-nurse for your babies? If you had done so for Oceanus, you would have felt his loss far less keenly."

Bathsheba went on, "I admire Samuel's forbearance, I really do. I have no idea why he has been so patient with you. He wants a son, it is your duty to provide him with one. Now, get up and get dressed. You may have luncheon in your room today, but I expect to see you at the dinner table later."

With that, she swept out of the room, ignoring the tears rolling silently down Lucy's cheeks. Francine, afraid for herself and for Lucy of the consequences of not obeying Bathsheba, tried to coax her to sit up and have her hair brushed, but Lucy merely turned over and put a pillow over her head. When the luncheon tray was brought, she refused to swallow a mouthful.

At 4 o'clock, Bathsheba's brisk footsteps could be heard outside the door. Francine quailed, knowing she was likely to be blamed for Lucy's behaviour. True to form, Bathsheba took in the scene at one glance, crossed swiftly to where Francine stood and boxed the poor girl's ears hard. Arms akimbo, she then stood over Lucy.

"I told you to get up. Why have you not done so?" When there was no response, she pulled Lucy up roughly by her arm and slapped her twice, very deliberately, across the face. As two red weals appeared on Lucy's cheeks, Bathsheba noted with satisfaction that her eyes narrowed with real hatred.

"That is better. I don't care if you hate me, girl, but you are not going to disgrace this family or your own. I thought I saw some fight in you when you first arrived, and I rejoiced in that. Do you think a weakling, however wealthy, would hold my son's interest for more than a few days? Do you want to drive your husband into the arms of a slave girl? Because you are doing just that. Men have appetites, he will go elsewhere if you do not take him to your bed. I have seen the way he looks at some of the house girls now. Is that what you want, Lucy? Do you want him to have his sons by this girl?" as she grabbed Francine's arm and pulled her forward. "How will you feel if that happens? You'll get no favours from me – I don't see the point of housing and feeding you unless you contribute in some way. I am sure John and Sarah will agree, this is already a crowded household."

Lucy's eyes widened. Licking her dry, cracked lips she whispered, "You would not recognise his by-blows, would you?"

"Why not? Surely you have seen such situations in England? Where do you think I get my dark skin from?" Bathsheba challenged her. "I thought perhaps you had heard the rumours that my mother or grandmother was the result of a liaison between an English planter and his housekeeper. Once a mulatto or quadroon always one, never acceptable to island society even if born free. I married John when he ran a small trading station. I have no illusions, if he had owned Long Bay then, been a member of the plantocracy, do you think despite my family's good name I'd have been acceptable? Why do you think we go about in society so little? It is because some, believing the rumours, still hold up their noses at me – though they would never have dared to show it while John was alive – and I will not give them the satisfaction of being able to snub me!"

"This is not genteel England, Lucy. Only the strongest survive. I despise your insipid, incestuous, hypocritical, easy white upbringing. Here you will have to earn respect. Show me that you possess some of that inner steel I thought I glimpsed when you first arrived, or I wash my hands of you. Now, get up. And you," turning to Francine, "fetch water for a bath."

Francine hurried first to open the door for Bathsheba, who swept out, then did as she was told and followed to arrange for water to be brought for Lucy's bath.

Lucy lay back on her pillows thinking over what her mother-in-law had said. She remembered when she first emerged from the schoolroom going to an open day at Piercefield House, not far from Hewelsfield. Her mother had been full of curiosity because the owner, Nathaniel Wells, was a black man, a magistrate and church warden at St Arvan's. Lucy realised it was the only time she had ever seen a black man other than as a servant or slave. The freed blacks she had seen in Bridgetown, and the little page boy she had seen years ago in England, did not really count. She remembered her initial shock at the sheer number of slaves on Barbados and the prevailing attitude towards them as nothing more than inanimate objects, and her vow not to let Oceanus grow up with the same hateful attitude. At this poignant memory, the tears welled in her eyes once more, but for the first time in many weeks she fought them back. Her mother-in-law's scorn had cut through her depression in a way the kindness and sympathy of others had not and roused a real fear in her of losing Sam and being alone with no support on Barbados.

When Francine returned with a burly young slave carrying cans of water and the tin bath, she made an effort to get out of bed by herself but stumbled and would have fallen had it not been for Francine putting an arm around her waist. She was weak from so much time in bed and for lack of food. Francine helped her out of her nightgown and into the bath, washed her hair and soaped her body, dried and dressed her like a little child, and Lucy allowed her to do so. Her clothes hung loose on her; her face, looking back at her from the mirror, showed hollow cheeks, grey skin and sunken eyes ringed with dark shadows.

Lucy knew well that she was not beautiful, but rarely had she felt less attractive. With all the competition she faced for her husband's affections, it was clear she would need to regain her health and her looks as quickly as possible. She was glad she was not going to have to face the family until dusk, when the candlelight would be kinder and hide her imperfections.

She asked Francine to place a hibiscus flower in her hair and arrange a pretty silk shawl around her shoulders, then slowly and shakily made her way downstairs on the girl's arm. The family, with the exception of Sam, was already gathered on the veranda, and welcomed her back into the fold in their different ways, Betty with a beaming smile, John with a grave nod, his wife with a preoccupied glance and hurried pat on her arm, then Betty and her sister

Bathsheba took one arm each and helped her towards a comfortable rocking chair. The ever-ailing Sarah offered Lucy one of her many shawls, which she gently declined. It was only then that she squared her shoulders, lifted her chin and glanced in her mother-in-law's direction. A grim little smile and a nod of satisfaction was all the recognition she received, but it was enough, for now.

"Where is Sam?" asked Lucy.

"Oh – he went to Bridgetown a couple of days ago," responded Betty carelessly. "I'm sure he will be so pleased to know that you are better when he returns."

Lucy caught Bathsheba's eye, and interpreted her look as 'see? I told you it was not a moment too soon'.

She managed to swallow a little chicken and some fruit, but her shrunken stomach rebelled at the idea of any more food, her usual robust appetite had deserted her. And when, after the meal, Sarah sent for her children and Lucy saw sturdy little John run to her, followed by a solemn Adriana, she felt the ready tears well up again.

Afraid she would disgrace herself, she pushed herself to her feet and tried to walk to the door unaided, but it was beyond her strength. Blinded by tears, she almost failed to notice that it was Mrs Lord senior who took her elbow before handing her over to one of the slaves to be helped upstairs. But when she thought about it afterwards, she supposed it constituted approval of her effort by Bathsheba.

Sam did not return for several days, and when he did, he looked sleek and pleased with himself. Lucy supposed – rightly – that for once he must have had a run of luck at the gambling tables, and also – with a stab of jealousy – that he had been with some girl in town, as he was very vague about where he had been staying.

The women were increasingly alone in the house, since John's duties as an Assembly Member took him frequently to Bridgetown (occasionally accompanied by his wife, Sarah). Lucy's health and fitness improved slowly, but although she was fond of Betty, she was now finding the atmosphere of the house even more stifling. She had nothing in common with her sickly sister-in-law, the other Sarah, or with her elder sister, Bathsheba; and she resented (although she also respected) her mother-in-law's grip on the household. She wondered idly how John's wife – who, as spouse to the head of the house should by rights have held sway – countenanced it but was not on sufficiently good terms to discuss it with her.

Besides, Sarah now had five healthy children including her son, and Lucy felt insanely jealous every time she saw them. The fact that baby Emma seemed to be thriving in the care of her wet nurse did nothing to assuage this. Lucy continued to feel totally indifferent to the poor little creature, and her behaviour towards Emma was the exact antithesis of what it had been towards Oceanus. Until about six months before his illness, Oceanus had slept in the crib in Lucy's room. She had fed him and played with him every day. She never asked to see Emma, indeed it was Sam who showed far more interest in and affection for her.

As soon as she could, Lucy resumed her morning rides with Sam when he was at Long Bay, both to break up the monotony of the days and to try and bind her husband more firmly to her. Occasionally they rode to the preferred site for Sam's castle, but more frequently they rode inland, straying onto tracks on neighbouring estates whose sugar crops Sam regarded with a hungry eye. On this, he and John were of one mind; they needed more land, and they needed land suitable for cultivating that great wealth-producer, sugar.

One morning as they trotted briskly along, Lucy slightly ahead of Sam, a black shape suddenly leapt up in front of her, causing her horse to rear. Lucy kept her seat with difficulty, then screamed in sheer terror as a horrific vision swam before her eyes. She was hardly aware of Nero trying to bolt behind her, as Sam cursed his mount and laid about him with his whip. She was frozen to the spot, her heart hammering, Empress snorting and rolling her eyes. For what seemed an eternity but was probably no more than a few seconds, Lucy stared from close quarters at the grotesque and bloodied mask of a slave whose nose had recently been slit for trying to escape before a furious Sam, Nero now under control, pushed past her and started laying about the man with his whip.

The commotion attracted the attention of the local overseer, who ran to see what was happening.

"Trying to make a run for it again, are you?" he panted at the slave, whose arms were pouring blood from the lashes they caught which were aimed at his head.

"Sam – stop! Stop! You are killing him!" shouted Lucy, as Sam continued to curse and use his whip. He turned to glare at her.

"Killing's too good for the likes of him, miss. This is the third time he's tried to escape," growled the overseer, before Sam could say anything. "I'm sorry, sir, that he troubled you. I'll take him back and chain him to the others so he can't get away so easy again."

"See you do," growled Sam and then, as the overseer dragged the slave away, "how dare you countermand me, Madam? That Nigger could have killed us both – don't you tell me not to punish him."

Part of Lucy realised that the strength of his anger was due to two things, she had scared him when she screamed and Nero had reared up, and the overseer had heard her telling Sam to stop using his whip on the slave. But she was not used to being spoken to in such a fashion (her father had never raised his voice to her), and all her pent-up emotion poured out as something in her snapped and she lost her temper in return.

"You are an uncivilised brute! These are men, not animals! How can you possibly say they are better looked after here than on the other islands? Of course they run away if you treat them so harshly! He did me no harm – he scared me because he jumped up so suddenly and because of the terrible damage that had been done to his face."

She looked on in amazement as Sam, his face contorted with rage, raised his whip hand to slash at her. She just had enough presence of mind to duck and turn her face away, so the lash caught her ear rather than her cheek, but it fell heavily on her shoulder, causing her to cry out with pain. Empress snorted and backed up. Lucy, tears of anger coursing down her cheeks and blood pouring down her back and neck, wheeled the horse and kicked her into a gallop, not pausing until she got back to the stables. She slid from the saddle and pushed the reins into the hands of a startled groom, then made her way into the house by a side door in the hopes of avoiding meeting Bathsheba or any of her sisters-in-law.

Francine was waiting for her, a warm bath ready. She stole a glance at her mistress' stormy, battered face but said nothing, prudently limiting herself to helping Lucy out of her riding habit. She slipped away while Lucy lay soaking in the water to fetch her little pot of salve.

"I should give you money to purchase one of those for me. I think I am going to need it. But I have no money…" said Lucy.

Francine anointed her bruised shoulder and cut ear with salve and handed Lucy a cotton ball to hold against the latter until it had stopped bleeding. She dressed her hair so it covered the ear and helped Lucy into her muslin day-dress. Lucy, still simmering with anger, sniffed defiantly, looked into the slave girl's dark, serious eyes, put up her chin and moved to the door.

She hesitated before the dining room door, then shrugged and went in. She need not have worried, no-one else was there. She ate some fruit and drank a bowl of tea and wondered what to do with the day. On a whim, she decided to visit the slave quarters, defying the fact that she had been told not to do so. She knew few of the slaves would be there – only the old and toddlers – as they were already at work in the fields or the house, but she decided it was time to look at their living conditions herself, having only paid a fleeting visit on her arrival. She did not pause to wonder why this had suddenly become so important to her, her mother would have said that Lucy always seemed to behave in the most perverse, defiant and wayward fashion when reprimanded, but she pushed that thought away.

Her breakfast finished, Lucy changed her shoes for a slightly sturdier pair, picked up her parasol and walked down the steps from the open front door onto the gravelled driveway and towards the tree-lined avenue leading to the main gates. Even in the welcome shade, Lucy began to feel uncomfortably hot before she had walked half a mile, but she was determined not to let that stop her. As she approached the pathetically flimsy huts which made up the slave quarters, her nostrils were increasingly assailed by a powerful, unpleasant smell of human waste, reminiscent of one she remembered from visits as a child to Bristol Docks with her father, and she noticed steam and swarms of flies rising from what she assumed to be the midden. She could feel the sweat trickling uncomfortably down her back and under her arms, sticking tendrils of hair to her face; the hem of her dress was grey with dust.

There was no-one to be seen at the first hut, but Lucy could see a group of small children playing further along the makeshift path and walked towards them. They stopped playing and fell silent as she approached, looking solemnly up at her from big, nearly black eyes and huddling together for safety. Even at this age they were aware of the power white people had over their lives. An old black woman, leaning on a stick with gnarled, arthritic hands shuffled towards them, eyes cast down in the presence of a white woman as she would have been taught. She waited in silence, and suddenly Lucy felt foolish. What was she doing here? Why had she come? What did she really want?

She cleared her throat, smiled at the children, and asked, "Is Francine here?" knowing very well that Francine was somewhere in the main house.

The children's blank, uncomprehending faces stared back at her; the old woman shuffled her feet but remained silent. Dispirited, and not knowing what to say or do, Lucy turned to go back the way she came; she could feel their eyes following her. Her earlier anger had evaporated and she wished she had not come. She had achieved nothing by her defiance, and now she must walk all the way back to the house and change her dress again.

She had not gone far before she heard horses' hooves pounding along behind her. Sam pulled up sharply next to her in a swirl of dust and gravel and jumped down as a lathered Nero snorted and tossed his head.

"What the devil are you doing here? You know very well that you must stay within the gardens unless you are escorted, and on no account must you visit the slave quarters. These Negroes cannot be trusted. They are already over-excited by stories of the slave revolt in Louisiana, anything could set them off!"

Lucy's anger revived. "Oh – so they cannot be trusted!" she retorted sarcastically. "Yet you all entrust your children to them from the moment they are born. Surely, they must be in danger every minute? Perhaps that is why Oceanus is dead, perhaps they poisoned him, and now plan to do the same to Emma! If we want them to be safe, we should take them to England."

"That is a stupid thing to say. I am as sorry as you are that our son is dead, but he could as easily have died of the measles in England as here. And you know very well that it *was* measles that he died of."

Lucy caught her breath on an angry sob. "What do you care anyway? You only saw our son when it suited you – you did not spend every day with him, feeding him, watching him grow…"

At that Sam slapped her twice, hard. Her accusation touched him on the raw and was unfair. As she well knew, Sam loved little children and had spent more time than most fathers of the era with Oceanus, as well as showing great affection for his nephews and nieces.

"Perhaps you should spend more time with your baby daughter now, it is not I but you that have neglected her, poor little thing. You have become an ill-tempered harpy, wife, caring for your daughter might make you more pleasant company!"

A furious Lucy took an inexpert swing at him, but he easily caught her wrist in his strong grip. He then tossed her ignominiously across his horse's saddle bow, quickly mounting behind her so she had no chance to slip back to the ground.

"If you stop screaming like a fishwife you may sit side-saddle on the pommel. Otherwise I will deliver you to the house bent over Nero's neck like a sack of potatoes and throw you in the root cellar," Sam threatened.

That would be the ultimate indignity. Lucy curbed her instinct to claw and kick her husband and let him pull her roughly into a precarious seated position on the pommel. She glared at him, her face beetroot red, her short hair wild, her parasol abandoned.

Nero trotted sedately towards the house with his double burden. As they approached, Sam warned Lucy once more,

"Do not go anywhere near the slave quarters again. There are always some that are sick, and you could easily catch one of their diseases. And you do not understand what they are capable of; in Louisiana they attacked the planter's family in their beds. By going alone to their quarters you lay yourself open to violence."

He nodded to one of the slaves nearby to help Lucy down, tipped his hat to her and turned Nero towards the stables.

Lucy went to her room and rang for Francine and fresh water, feeling dishevelled and dirty. She managed to undo enough buttons on her dress to allow her to slip out of it, leaving it in a pile on the floor, and pulled on her wrapper. As usual, Francine made no comment, just did as she was told, and Lucy grew calmer as she poured water into the ewer and sponged away the grime, blood and sweat. She remembered that her friend Mary Kingsley was coming with her mother to pay a visit and share luncheon with the Lords and began to feel more cheerful. She did not want to dwell on her behaviour that morning. In her heart of hearts she knew she should not have disobeyed a direct order to avoid the slave quarters but Sam's earlier violence had provoked her, and she tried to dwell on that in order to continue to feel self-righteously aggrieved.

That became more difficult when she found that her friend was aghast at what she had done, and not at all surprised that Sam had been so angry.

"These Niggers must be kept in their place, Lucy. You did not grow up here, they require constant discipline, and when you have a serial escaper like the one who startled you this morning, regular floggings are the only thing they understand, along with branding and nose-splitting. Your husband was saving you from possible attack. I know Papa has stepped up discipline and security among our slaves since we heard about that dreadful business in Louisiana in January. And as for the slave quarters – well, I have never been near them! Pray, why in the world did you want to go there?"

Lucy was distraught and deeply disappointed that Mary did not feel as she did but thought that on the question of slavery she and her friend were, sadly, poles apart because of the way each had been brought up. And Mary had some other, unwelcome, news to impart. She would be returning to England and her husband, the Reverend Kingsley (who had finally found some gainful employment) at the end of the year, and Lucy would lose the pleasure of her company. This was a real blow, since although Lucy was fond of her sisters-in-law Betty and Mary, she had failed to make any other close friendships since arriving on Barbados, and she wondered sadly how she would cope with this new loneliness, particularly if she did not manage to win back Sam's affection. She longed to see her parents and brother again, and wished it were possible to accompany Mary on the journey.

By the time Francine dressed her for dinner, Lucy's shoulder sported heavy bruising from the application of Sam's whip that morning, and they struggled to find an evening dress high enough at the neck to conceal it. In the end, Francine pinned a lace fichu in place around the neckline, and Lucy determined to keep a shawl draped over her shoulders also. The fierce anger that had kept her spirits up was spent; she ached all over from the rough ride on Nero and from Sam's treatment. She felt utterly lost, totally bereft, alone and sorry for herself.

It was therefore a subdued Lucy who joined the family for the ritual of pre-dinner drinks on the veranda. John was away again, so Sam was the only man there. He was in conversation with his mother when Lucy arrived and merely nodded to her. She sat next to Betty at dinner and limited herself to nodding and smiling in all the right places at her vivacious chatter.

When Sarah asked after dinner for the children to be brought in, Lucy raised her head and quietly asked that Emma be brought in too. She was relieved to see Sam's face brighten, and it was he who strode across to take the baby when she arrived in the arms of her wet nurse. After a few moments, Lucy joined them. Sam handed Emma to her without a word, but his face showed approval.

Try as she might, Lucy could not feel any real affection for the baby; indeed, she found herself more interested in the antics of little John with his baby sister, Elizabeth. She certainly felt no compunction about handing Emma back to the wet nurse when Sarah decided she had seen enough of her children. Lucy wondered why her feelings for the little girl were so different from those she had for Oceanus. She was not to know that she was suffering from post-natal depression; such terminology did not yet exist, and neither did any form of treatment.

The party broke up soon afterwards. Sam strolled out onto the terrace to smoke a cigar and Lucy went upstairs with her sisters-in-law. She waited for a while, seated at her window, in case Sam should visit her, but when she had still not heard him coming upstairs an hour later, decided he must be punishing her still. In some ways she was grateful. Her bruised body was throbbing now, and she would have found it difficult to respond to his lovemaking whether it was gentle or rough. But she could not help thinking of what her mother-in-law had said.

Over the coming weeks, they had a visit from Mary Austin (who was pregnant again) and her younger children, and Lucy accompanied by Betty and her mother visited Sunbury. She continued to meet Mary Kingsley once a week and went to church at St Philip's on Sundays, but otherwise life returned to the previous humdrum routine that had existed prior to Emma Lucy's birth – although without the pleasure or the occupation of Oceanus' company. Lucy sketched; she practised the piano rather more often; and she asked her mother-in-law if she might make overseeing the flower arrangements for the house her special task, to which Bathsheba graciously agreed. She still rode occasionally in the mornings with Sam, but both he and John now spent several days a week away, either at the Assembly in Bridgetown (in John's case), in convivial sessions with friends (Sam), or on exercises with the militia, which had stepped up its activities since the Louisiana revolt. Overseeing operations at Long Bay was left increasingly in Alexander's hands, although John would have preferred Sam to take a greater interest in proceedings.

As Lucy had noticed soon after her arrival on the island, plantation life was insular and secluded, in part because the lack of roads made travel difficult, and also because plantations were generally pretty much self-contained, producing most of what they needed by way of food stock and caught up in the relentless toil of running a complex agricultural business. Yet she also knew, from conversations with Mary Kingsley and Mary Barrow, that other plantations maintained a far more active social life, and she longed for such activity even as she remembered Bathsheba's explanation for Long Bay's reclusiveness.

Her letters home became increasingly stilted, what was there to say, other than that the time passed too slowly and that she was lonely? She had poured her heart out in a letter written shortly after Oceanus' death, and been disappointed when her mother's reply arrived some five months later stating matter-of-factly,

Your father and I are sorry that we shall now never know Oceanus, but sadly these foreign climes are not kind to the weak and vulnerable, such as children are. No doubt your new daughter is a great comfort to you.

Lucy had no desire to tell her mother that she continued to have little or no feeling for Emma, nor that she had ceased to fight very hard to retain Sam's attention despite the fact that she was now certain he not only had one or more mistresses in Bridgetown, a common enough occurrence among the white men, but also that he was bedding at least one of the house slaves at Long Bay whenever he did return home.

Apathy once again began to creep over her, she allowed Francine to get her up in the morning, bathe and dress her and reverse the order in the evening, but she had no real desire to do so, and her former liveliness had all but vanished. She took to drifting for hours along the corridors of the house, her fingertips dragging along the walls, silent as a ghost; she rarely had energy or interest for painting, reading or writing her journal, activities which she had taken to with gusto when she first arrived.

She had no idea what her sisters-in-law occupied themselves with. John's wife Sarah oversaw a few of the household duties under Mrs Lord senior's strict instruction; Sam's sister Sarah showed increasing signs of debilitating sickness, spending most of the day lying on a sofa; Bathsheba she saw rarely (she seemed to have several good friends at nearby plantations whom she visited regularly), and even Betty sought Lucy out less often, unsure how to cope with Lucy's depression.

Chapter 11
A Slave Revolt?

As she drifted, she was often sure she heard whispering. Generally, Lucy was not a fanciful woman; indeed, her mother had often suggested that while her practical nature could be very useful, she would do well to disguise it as it might make her appear overly managing to potential suitors. At first she thought apathetically that the wind must be carrying the sigh of the sugar cane fields towards her, but one day as she stepped noiselessly around a corner the whispering stopped abruptly and two slaves, who appeared to have been deep in earnest conversation, moved apart – one of them, a man, darting quickly towards the other end of the corridor and down the stairs towards the kitchen. Faintly puzzled, Lucy looked at the remaining slave, now industriously polishing the banister with beeswax.

"Juba, you will be punished if anyone else catches you loitering here instead of completing your chores," she said as she recognised the girl she had seen leaving John's room in tears what seemed so long ago, then whipped more recently for running away.

As Lucy turned to go back the way she had come, strangely reluctant to pass Juba and continue in the direction the other slave had vanished, she was scared by the look the girl gave her. Juba uttered not a word, but her eyes slid sideways with such a look of hatred that Lucy was shaken out of her apathy.

Impetuously, Lucy turned her steps towards her mother-in-law's parlour, but the room was empty. She stood on the threshold, biting her lip and frowning, twirling a curl of her hair round and round one finger, a childish habit she had never fully grown out of, and which she did unconsciously when deep in thought.

She turned briskly and marched towards her own room with a firm tread. She wanted to consider how she was going to deal with what she had just witnessed, and she certainly did not wish to discuss it with her mother-in-law with other people (particularly slaves) milling around.

As she sat in one of the rattan chairs before her open window, a doubt shook her. Had she imagined the look Juba gave her? Would she simply get the girl in trouble unnecessarily by reporting her for slacking to Mrs Lord? But she pictured that look again and shivered. And she also realised that she had not recognised the slave Juba had been talking to. But if it was someone she did not recognise, then it must have been one of the field hands. And what was he doing in the house? It certainly was not a love tryst, their discussion had seemed too earnest for that.

In the end, Lucy decided to broach the subject with Bathsheba after lunch. She was so preoccupied with what had happened that she was somewhat thrown when, arriving at the ladies' room before the meal, she was greeted with a contemptuous sniff by her mother-in-law, who said sarcastically,

"I am glad to see you appear to have cast off your foolish megrims finally and deign to grace us once again with your presence."

Lucy had been trying to avoid appearing at the lunch table as often as possible, and Bathsheba had once more become impatient with what she saw as her lack of backbone. She saw Betty watching her sympathetically, the younger Bathsheba studiously looking with great interest at a bowl of flowers on the other side of the room. Lucy swallowed her resentment – she could not afford an angry outburst when she had this burning need to unburden herself to her mother-in-law and, if she were honest, she had been behaving like one of those die-away ninnies she herself used to despise. So she bit back a stinging retort and said meekly

"Yes, ma'am; I am feeling much better. I think I will take up my paints again this afternoon in the garden, unless you need me for anything?"

John's wife Sarah came in at that moment, and Mrs Lord contented herself by saying, with a little nod, "Some activity will soon get those crotchets out of you. Betty can accompany you."

Having thus disposed of her youngest daughter's afternoon, she rose and all the women of the household – the two men were absent – sat down to eat.

Luncheon was never a long affair, being a lighter meal than the evening one. As they rose from the table, Lucy intercepted her mother-in-law and asked quietly, "May I speak to you, ma'am? In private?"

Bathsheba looked at her, her gaze raking Lucy's face as if she could read in it the reason behind this unusual request. Then she nodded decisively. "Come to my room in one hour."

Betty was regarding them with frank curiosity. As Mrs Lord left the room, Lucy forestalled any comment from her sister-in-law by suggesting that they might go out for a walk together before she visited Bathsheba or settled down to paint.

Punctually an hour later, Lucy approached her mother-in-law's parlour, still not quite sure what she wanted to say. She hesitated in the doorway, and glanced uncertainly at the ever-present slave girl, Frances. Bathsheba followed her glance.

"Leave us," she dismissed her. Frances, eyes downcast, bobbed a curtsey and scurried out past Lucy, who quietly closed the door behind her.

"Well?" demanded Bathsheba, looking at her daughter-in-law with some curiosity.

Lucy moved across to the window and stood looking out, her back to her mother-in-law. She squared her shoulders.

"I may be making something out of nothing, ma'am, but I saw something today which worried me."

She turned and related the story of her encounter with Juba and the unknown slave as concisely as she could.

"I do not want to create trouble for Juba, but the look she gave me frightened me, and I could not understand why she was whispering so earnestly to a Negro man I have never seen before…"

Lucy thought how feeble this sounded. There might be a perfectly good explanation for the man's presence, and she had not a shred of proof that the two were up to no good, merely her instinct.

Her mother-in-law was frowning.

"There have been increasing signs of unrest among the slaves ever since news of the Louisiana uprising reached them. Juba has tried to run away before and is a troublemaker. Two of the field hands ran off a few days ago, it may be that Juba or the male slave had news of them and was passing it on. The fact that Juba showed you hatred is not surprising, most of the Negroes hate us, but they also fear us, and as long as we ensure their fear is greater than their hate, they will do as they are told. I am more concerned, if you are right and the man was indeed not one of the house slaves, that a slave with no right to be in the house was here. If there is a conspiracy, I need to know more about it. I shall consult with John. In the meantime, keep your eyes and ears open and report anything unusual to me."

She nodded dismissal to Lucy and rang the bell beside her for Frances to return.

As Lucy headed for her own room, her first feeling was one of relief that her mother-in-law had taken her seriously, but then a little frisson of fear struck her. What if a revolt like the one in Louisiana were to take place at Long Bay?

She rang for one of the houseboys to carry her easel and paints out to the garden, and found herself staring at him, trying to work out if he too harboured the sort of simmering resentment evident in Juba, then realised it was almost impossible because the boy's eyes remained downcast.

She put on a straw bonnet, picked up her parasol and followed the slave boy outside, where she directed him to set up her easel under the mango tree where she and Mary had found the two slave children eating the fruit on the day of the twins' christening. The air was hot and still, and although the sun was shining, enormous, dense black clouds were rolling in from the horizon. Lucy thought it would make a beautiful storm scene and set to work to try and complete as much as possible before the impending rain arrived to drench her and her painting.

As always when she painted, Lucy became totally immersed in her work, forgetting the unsettling events of the morning. She painted without stopping for several hours and was startled by a voice at her elbow,

"Miss's Betty sen' me fetch your things. You get wet," said the young black man beside her, eyes downcast.

"Oh – you made me jump, Joshua! But you are right – it is about to rain. Hurry inside with the easel now and be very careful with my painting. I will bring the paints, and you can come back for the stool."

She stood up as she spoke, wincing at the stiffness in her back, and picked up her paints and parasol. Joshua was already on his way, and Lucy followed more slowly. As she reached the house, a few big fat drops of rain began to fall and she hastened up the shallow steps, meeting Joshua as he turned to run back for the stool.

She stood in the hallway and watched, wondering idly if Joshua was part of any conspiracy. When he stood before her again, stool in one hand and dripping water onto the flagstones, he gave her a shy smile, his eyes alight with pleasure at the relief the rain and accompanying wind offered from the prevailing oppressive heat. Lucy decided that whatever was going on, Joshua was not part of it, and smiled in return.

"I don't think you will be popular if you drip water all the way upstairs," she said. "Just leave my things here and go and dry off in the kitchen."

Lucy stayed in the doorway, watching the torrential rain which she knew now from experience would stop as suddenly as it had started in about ten minutes. She could see in the distance, towards the slave quarters, a group of three or four slave children capering about in the rain and clearly enjoying the sensation.

John took Lucy to one side that evening when the family gathered on the veranda for drinks before dinner and asked her to repeat what she had seen that morning. As she did so, in a low voice, she wondered how John felt – if, indeed, he felt anything – at the news that his sometime mistress might be plotting against him.

"What secrets are you keeping from us?" Betty called out from the other side of the veranda.

John failed to erase the worry from his face as he turned towards her but merely waved acknowledgement.

"Thank you, Lucy. I have no need to ask you not to say anything to the others for now?" She shook her head, and they both moved towards Betty, who had been joined by John's wife, Sarah.

When Betty repeated her question, John shook his head at her and said with finality, "No secrets, Betty. Leave it now."

Betty pouted but did as she was told, and Lucy had the bright idea of diverting her by asking if they thought the Barrows might be persuaded to invite all of them to Crop Over Day celebrations following the visit she had so much enjoyed with Sam the previous year.

Betty responded with so much enthusiasm that Lucy laughingly offered to dash off a letter to John and Mary Barrow after dinner, "Unless you would prefer to do so yourself, ma'am?" she added as an afterthought, turning to look at her mother-in-law.

Mrs Lord senior waved her fan languidly in Lucy's direction to gesture her acceptance of Lucy's offer to write to Sunbury.

The letter was duly written and taken over to Sunbury the following morning. Lucy busied herself with her self-ordained task of overseeing the allocation of flowers throughout the house, then called Joshua to carry her easel and paints outside into the garden so she could finalise the storm scene she had begun painting. She heard the rumble of wheels and, shading her eyes, looked along the driveway towards the main gate. The dogcart was being driven briskly away with two passengers, Alexander the overseer's deputy, a scarred, taciturn black man whose name Lucy did not know; and Juba, clutching a small cloth bundle tightly to her. Absorbed as she had been in her painting, Lucy had completely forgotten about the events of the previous morning; seeing Juba brought it all back to her, and she wondered where the girl was going. Deciding she had done enough for the day, she unfurled her parasol and strolled back to the house, where she rang for one of the slaves to collect her things. It was Joshua who answered the summons, and when he returned, her easel under one arm, her paints in a basket over the other and the almost-complete picture carried carefully in front of him, she asked him where Juba was going.

"To market, mist'ss. She moving on," he responded, and Lucy realised that John and his mother must have decided to act quickly to lance the boil of any festering discontent and sell Juba at the slave market.

For a moment she felt guilty that her suspicions had resulted in the girl being uprooted and sold on like a piece of unwanted furniture. At the same time, she was relieved she would not again see the hatred that had filled Juba's eyes and, in any case, the slave could have expected to be whipped or branded at the very least. Fleetingly, Lucy wondered why the Lords had behaved in uncharacteristically lenient fashion and decided she would put the question to John if the chance arose.

Neither John nor Sam put in an appearance that evening, and Lucy had no desire to upset the delicate truce with her mother-in-law so she held her peace about Juba. Betty, too, was staying away with friends for a few days at the other end of the island and the evening dragged, and Lucy found the small-talk which pervaded the dinner table irritating beyond belief. She had to bite her tongue to prevent herself making an acid retort to an anodyne but inane comment made by John's wife, and when her mother-in-law signalled that the tea tray should be brought into the drawing room Lucy hurried over to the French windows which gave onto the veranda and stepped out into the sticky, humid air, unable to sit quietly with the other women.

She excused herself soon afterwards and retired to her room where, having dismissed Francine, she paced around like a caged beast before leaning on the windowsill and trying to calm herself by breathing deeply, inhaling the now familiar scent of mingled frangipani, Lady-of-the-Night jasmine and mango and listening to the muffled booming of waves crashing onto Cobblers' Reef and Long Bay beach mingled with the nearer sound of the ubiquitous tree frogs. It occurred to her that less than forty-eight hours earlier the idea that she should have so much pent-up energy would have been unthinkable; the 'Juba incident', as she thought of it, appeared to have banished her depression and lethargy.

On a whim, she searched out her journal. She had started writing this on the long sea journey to Barbados but had added nothing to it since Oceanus' death. Now she decided to write down what had occurred and make a note of anything unusual or suspicious which she saw in the coming days. She was not entirely convinced that getting rid of Juba would close down any thoughts of insurrection at Long Bay; she could not help remembering that she had come upon Juba talking to an unknown slave so there was at least one other involved.

Lucy deliberately opened the journal at a fresh page and tried to avoid reading her earlier entries; but once she had written up her encounter with Juba and the unknown male slave and sketched them from memory, she could not resist going back to look at what she had penned in earlier, happier times. Tears coursed silently down her face as she read about Oceanus' short life – his first tooth, his first steps, his first words – and she was overcome by longing to hold the little boy again. She barely noticed that she had not written a single word about her daughter, Emma.

She had been sitting at her dressing table, poring over the diary by the light of a candle. She stood up now, stretching cramped muscles, snuffed the candle and returned to leaning on the windowsill, staring unseeingly out into the garden bathed in moonlight. Apart from a whisper of breeze and the ever-present waves, everything was very still, and this calmed Lucy. She started thinking about her future with greater clarity than she had for several years, the voices of her mother and her mother-in-law jostling in her head to give her advice.

In truth there was no way out: she was trapped. She had chosen her husband and her future, for better for worse, was now entwined with his. She was as much his property as any of the slaves, she thought. The only way to bind him to her was to have his children, and to lead him to believe that she could bring him further wealth on top of her dowry to further his dream of building a castle. But this was not a good place in which to bring up children. She must persuade Sam that, while they were small, any children they had must be brought up in her old home. That way they would be less likely to succumb to the diseases which spread like wildfire on the island – dysentery, tuberculosis, cholera, typhoid, yellow fever, mumps, or the measles which had so cruelly taken Oceanus. And they could be sheltered from the appalling brutality of slavery and taught to treat all human beings with decency. She was reminded again of her vow on first arriving in Barbados never to let Oceanus develop Sam's casual disregard for the humanity of his slaves.

For herself, she would like a home of her own to manage; the apathy that overcame her at Long Bay was at least in part a result of having nothing to do. She realised that her mother had instilled in her a wish to be industrious but here she was no more than an unwanted guest, with no role to play. So she must enter into all Sam's plans and do whatever she could to make them come to fruition. If slavery was to continue in Barbados – and the only thing that had changed since the abolition the slave trade in 1807 was that plantation slaves were increasingly encouraged to have children to provide the next generation of workers, instead of buying them in from Africa – she would do what she could to grant her slaves their freedom and ensure they were well cared for. But none of this could or would happen unless she managed to win back Sam's attention; her illness and her melancholy had driven him away, and she was all too aware that he was more than happy to succumb to the temptations of an easy life with one or more pretty slave mistresses, at least until her dowry dwindled to nothing. There was no time to lose, and her programme to attract her husband back must begin tomorrow. As she finally slipped into bed, her last waking thought was that she could probably count on her mother-in-law to further her interests in this at least.

The following morning, she had Francine wash her hair and asked her to arrange for the hairdresser to visit her after breakfast to cut it. She showed an interest for the first time in months in choosing her clothes, and when she anxiously studied her face in the mirror decided that, although she would never be a beauty, she was at least still passable. She hesitated, then she turned to Francine.

"Do you know whether my husband is returning today? Does Joseph know?"

Francine shook her head, but when she brought David, the estate slave who cut the ladies hair, to Lucy's room after breakfast, she said that Joseph thought Sam might return that evening.

"Francine, my dresses need taking in as I have lost weight. Please send for the young girl who made up our clothes last year," she said, while David snipped at her hair.

"Mary gone work in the fields now. I ask if she come tonight."

Momentarily, Lucy was surprised, then she remembered how many female slaves she had seen working the cane plantations along the road. Apparently, women were not only cheaper, they were stronger and lasted longer than the men doing the heavy work.

"Well, if she can't come, there must be someone else who knows how to tailor a dress," said Lucy. "See who you can find."

That afternoon Francine brought along a slave Lucy had not seen before. She looked malnourished and walked with a pronounced limp. Her pidgin English was incomprehensible to Lucy, who asked Francine about her.

Apparently, the woman was another field-worker who had recently given birth. Sometime earlier in her life, she had learnt to sew. Lucy guessed that she would welcome the work because sick slaves or those who could not work for any reason were often poorly fed, but Lucy was not convinced she knew what she was doing. However, having given the girl – who looked at least ten years older than Lucy but was probably a similar age – her oldest dress to take in at the waist, which she did quite competently, Lucy decided to entrust her with several others, and asked her to have one of the evening dresses ready for her to wear for dinner that evening. She then told Francine to ensure the girl, whose name was Prudence, was fed in the kitchen before going back to the slave quarters and dismissed them both.

She penned a careful letter to her mother, hinting at the idea that in future her children should be brought up in Britain until old enough to withstand most of the diseases which flourished in Barbados, and inviting Mrs Wightwick's opinion. She was confident she could persuade her father but for this she needed her mother's support also.

By the time she had finished she needed to dress for dinner. Francine returned with the re-fitted dress, followed by Samuel with a large jug of hot water. Lucy took more care than she had recently over her toilette, added a few drops of the precious French perfume she had brought with her from Chepstow, and asked Francine to place a frangipani flower in her hair. Draping a cream-coloured silk shawl over her shoulders she rose and instructed Francine to bring Emma straight to her on the veranda, crossing her fingers that the effort would be worthwhile and that Sam would return to find her charmingly employed playing with their daughter.

Sure enough, just as the family was about to go into the dining room, Lucy heard Sam's firm footsteps approaching them. He was greeted with pleasure by Betty – who was helping Lucy keep both Emma and Elizabeth amused – and he looked both surprised and pleased to see his wife (who smiled warmly at him) occupied as he felt she should be rather than ailing and depressed as he had last seen her.

Lucy silently breathed a sigh of relief that he had arrived home in a good mood, the tables must have been reasonably kind to Sam. He gave an arm to both ladies as the nursery slaves took the baby girls to bed, and throughout the meal he was the old, charming Sam with whom Lucy had fallen in love, so it was not difficult to be affectionate towards him or keep up – with Betty's help – an amusing flow of small-talk.

As the ladies left to retire to bed after the tea-tray had been brought in, Sam held the door for them, and Lucy gave him what she hoped was a provocative look from beneath her lashes. He smiled at her, pinching her chin, but said nothing.

Lucy had Francine look out her prettiest nightgown and cap and sat up in bed hoping that Sam would decide to visit her tonight and not prefer the attentions of whichever slave girl he was currently seducing. She was gratified, therefore, if also a little frightened, when she heard him enter his room and, five minutes later, open the dividing door.

Arrayed in a damson brocade dressing gown over his white linen shirt, with slippers on his feet, he sat on the bed facing Lucy and took her hands in his.

"Mother tells me you have been busy," he said.

It was clear that he had visited his mother before coming to her, and presumably Bathsheba had told him about Juba. Lucy opened her mouth to say something but he put a finger on her lips to silence her then bent to kiss her. She responded by throwing her arms around his neck and realised with a start that she had been lonely without him, despite having driven him away.

Their lovemaking that night was as satisfying as anything that had happened in the early months of their marriage and, after Sam had left her and returned to his own room, Lucy lay for a while with tears of gratitude trickling down her cheeks. Perhaps she could still make this marriage work for both of them.

The following morning Sam and Lucy resumed their habit of a pre-breakfast ride. Without discussing it, they rode briskly in the direction of the site of Sam's proposed mansion, reining in the horses to look out to sea from the top of the cliffs. Suddenly, Sam wheeled Nero round.

"Come, Lucy. Let us ride along the beach. The horses could do with getting the fidgets out of them, and the tide is out."

He led the way down a winding track to the beach, Lucy following with a degree of caution. When they reached the beautiful white sands below, she smiled and, without warning Sam, urged Empress into a canter. Empress was more than willing, and as she felt Nero draw up alongside her stretched out her neck and increased her speed to a gallop. The two riders only checked their mounts as two miles of smooth sand gave way to rocky debris, clearly the result of a recent rockfall.

As they turned the horses and began to walk back, Sam asked Lucy to describe what had occurred the morning she saw Juba talking to an unknown slave in the house. She did so, then looked at him and asked,

"Sam, why was Juba sent to market? I thought she was likely to be put in the stocks for a day, or flogged, or put in one of the cells for a while."

"Oh, John and m' mother were pretty certain the plot – if there was one – had spread no further, so thought it prudent to get rid of the wretched girl as quickly as possible. If she had stayed here to be punished, she might have won others over to her cause. I've suggested we bring the militia to St Philip's to run some exercises and search a few slave quarters – that should frighten off any more of them with silly ideas."

With no warning, Sam suddenly dismounted and stooped to pick something up from the sand. "Must be my lucky day!" he said grinning, "It has been many months since I had treasure off this beach," and he held up a sovereign to Lucy.

She exclaimed in surprise, "Where did that come from?"

He pointed with his whip out to Cobblers Reef, glittering in the sun. "As I told you, ships sometimes get wrecked on the reef. The tide and currents bring the contents ashore here. The beach is within the curtilage of Long Bay, so any goods which end up here belong to us. We have had some good finds of oil and wine and bolts of silk – although all too often they are ruined by the salt water – but I've rarely found coinage, despite dreaming of doing so! A chest full of gold or jewels would mean I could build my castle – and it shall be a castle, Lucy, mark my words! – without John always pulling a long face."

By this time, Sam had swung himself back into the saddle, and the horses were picking their way with slack rein back towards the foot of the cliff path. Lucy decided there would be no better time to discuss key parts of her plan for the future with Sam.

"I have been thinking about your castle, Sam. John seems no more likely now than he was two years ago to let you go ahead, particularly if it means taking labourers from the fields. He wanted you to dedicate more effort to the family business," and, as Sam turned his scowling face towards her,

"Let me finish! I think we may have been approaching this the wrong way. What if we both immersed ourselves in everything to do with the estate, constantly asking questions, you spending time in the fields and at the mill, I busying myself interfering in household matters? It is my belief they would none of them – your brother or his wife, or your mother – appreciate such interference and they might be more willing to concede it would be best for everyone were we to have our own project to focus on."

She fell silent, waiting not unhopefully for Sam's reaction; his scowl had turned into a more thoughtful frown. He reined Nero in and stared out to sea.

"Call their bluff, you mean, and play them at their own game? It might work. I've heard rumours of a small sugar plantation in the next parish which is likely to come up for sale soon. If I showed an interest in securing and running it, I would wager John would do anything to ensure he had charge of it – it's likely to yield far better returns than Long Bay! But if you try to meddle in running the household, Mother and Sarah will give you short shrift!"

"I thought perhaps I could ask your mother to give me lessons on managing household slaves. It is, I think, very different from managing servants."

Sam nodded. "That might do the trick. It's not a bad plan, Lucy. I'll start annoying John by insisting on inspecting the cotton fields today. Now come on – I'll race you to the path!"

And, kicking Nero into a gallop, he was gone. Lucy did her best to catch him but had to laugh as she pulled Empress up to see Sam with a self-satisfied smile on his face – it was normally she who won their races. She thought he looked a bit like a schoolboy caught in mischief, not at all like a man in his mid-thirties.

They had to climb the low cliff in single file and were too busy watching where the horses put their hooves in the loose sand to talk, but when he reached the top Sam waited for Lucy and they rode on side by side.

"Keep your ears open for any more unrest among the slaves," he said abruptly. "You did well, going to my mother with your concerns. My sisters don't need to know, particularly Sarah who's constantly ailing now. If there's more to this than meets the eye, we need to be alert though. No sign of that with your girl, is there?" Lucy shook her head and felt absurdly pleased to have his praise.

Sam went out again immediately after breakfast in search of John, who had gone to the aloe fields, to put their plan into practice. Lucy had to wait until lunchtime to put her approach into effect as her mother-in-law was nowhere to be found.

"I should like to learn from you, ma'am, about managing slaves in a household," she ventured, while they were seated at the table. John's wife Sarah looked up sharply, and Bathsheba eyed Lucy in some surprise.

"Why this sudden interest?" she asked.

"Because, ma'am, I hope one day to have a house of my own to manage, when Sam's plans come to fruition, and although I know about managing an English household, things are rather different here." It was important to have both women on her side. Sam was right in saying they would resent any suggestion of meddling, and she had no wish to incur her mother-in-law's wrath again.

Bathsheba nodded slowly. "Very well. We shall start tomorrow after breakfast. Come to my parlour. Sarah will help."

"I am sorry, ma'am, but I am to accompany John to Bridgetown tomorrow. When I return, I will be happy to help."

Sarah looked anything but happy, but Lucy hoped her emphasis on leaving to set up house elsewhere might win her over.

When the family gathered for dinner that evening, Sam and John were leaning on the veranda in earnest conversation. Seeing Lucy arrive, Sam winked at her over John's head but continued to talk to his brother. Lucy drifted into conversation with John's wife and Bathsheba, paying little attention as all the while she was wondering how well Sam was managing John. She asked Sarah how long she and John would be away in Bridgetown.

"Only until the end of the week," was the response.

Later Sam told Lucy that he had hit on the idea of suggesting that John arrange the details of the militia exercise around St Philip's as a warning to any rebellious slaves; in addition to his Assembly duties, the militia was now John's primary reason for going to the capital. In the meantime, he had instructed Sam to oversee aloe harvesting activity in the fields.

"So we can't ride tomorrow, Lucy. I'll need to be out there early to discuss what's going on with that scoundrel Alexander. I'll see if he's any inkling of more unrest than usual among the field slaves, too."

The following morning, Lucy presented herself at her mother-in-law's parlour as agreed after breakfast to begin her instruction in slave management.

"The key things to remember, Lucy, are to keep them busy so they have no time to get up to mischief; to be very clear in your orders, leaving nothing to chance; and to ensure they are constantly aware that any deviation from their duties will lead to punishment," said Bathsheba.

Lucy could not believe that the possible descendant of a former slave would show such a callous attitude towards those less fortunate than herself. The rumours Bathsheba had told her about simply could not be true.

"Do you never reward those who do well, ma'am? Does that not encourage them to work better and be more loyal? I am thinking in particular of those who look after the children – if they have cause to hate us, might they not hurt the children?"

Bathsheba shook her head decisively.

"They have a childlike love of all little children, black, white or mulatto, so I have no fear of that. What I have seen, however, is the disastrous results of a white owner being lenient towards his slaves. They view it as a weakness they can exploit."

Lucy thought about Francine, how delighted the girl had been with her gifts of the shawl and the sketch; she had seen no sign that such occasional acts of kindness had had any negative effects, but she held her peace. Bathsheba had been watching her, and said abruptly, "I am sure your mother runs a well-disciplined home and the servants are strictly managed. Here it is only a difference of degree."

227

Lucy smiled. "She does indeed run a well-managed home, but the more senior servants would certainly not respond well to threats of punishment. Mother enters into conversations with Cook and the housekeeper and discusses what must be done. I suppose you could say that orders are couched as requests. And as for Nurse, or Ned – who is now head groom but who taught me to ride – I doubt they would stay silent if threatened with punishment. They are almost part of the family and will be well looked after when they leave my parents' employ."

"Some of the house slaves buy or are given their freedom; most of the field slaves die in service," Bathsheba responded matter-of-factly, and Lucy shivered. Was it any surprise that they dreamt of rebellion? she wondered. She certainly would have done, if she had been one of them, there was no doubt in her mind. But she kept her thoughts to herself, it was no part of her plan to alienate her mother-in-law.

"The cook's mother and I played together as children," Bathsheba continued, "so I have fewer concerns than many that I may be poisoned. I took her on as a favour to her mother. But you can never totally trust any of them. Thomas, the coachman, has been with us many years, and both John and Sam believe he would never do anything to hurt a member of the family. Indeed, his son, also Thomas, is being trained to take his place. My sons may be right, but it always pays to be vigilant nonetheless."

Hesitantly, Lucy asked the question which had been on her mind for many months.

"If you do not mind my asking, are the slaves aware of the rumours about your background? If so, would they not look on you as one of them? Does that not make you feel more secure?"

Bathsheba smiled grimly. "Hardly. Many of them would hate me all the more because I have achieved freedom and a lifestyle they can only dream of. Much as they would like to have what I have, they would see me as a traitor, aping the white man's ways. You, on the other hand, they view as a soft touch because you are an outsider. They know that white women who come from England or France rather than being brought up here are more likely to treat them leniently, and they take advantage whenever they can. So if you ever set up your own house here, you will have to rule them with a rod of iron from the start so they understand you will brook no nonsense. It would be as well for you to start now, then the rumour will spread. One of the maids dropped a whole tray of china this morning; you will accompany me now and you will give the order for her to be placed in the stocks."

Obediently, Lucy rose when Bathsheba did, swallowing her revulsion. From an objective point of view, she could see the sense of what her mother-in-law said, but she could not feel comfortable with it. Her mother would have docked some of the housemaid's pay for a similar misdemeanour – but of course, slaves received no pay. She hoped her distaste was not too evident and thought ruefully that she had only herself to blame, she had asked Bathsheba for these lessons after all.

When they reached the yard where the stocks were located in the full sun, a dejected looking girl of about fifteen was standing in the shade of a banana tree, a burly black man holding her arm so that she did not run away.

Bathsheba nodded to Lucy. "Tell him to place her in the stocks," she instructed.

Lucy squared her shoulders, beckoned to the man and when he approached, pulling the reluctant girl with him, said, "Place her in the stocks for two hours."

She watched as the girl's hands, feet and head were locked in place then, her head high and her shoulders back, she nodded to Bathsheba with all the authority she could muster and turned to go. She could not bear to watch as the young slave suffered in the glaring heat of the midday sun, without food or water, and was afraid that if she stayed her resolution would crumble and she would either be violently sick or order the girl's release.

"She broke a great deal of china. I would have punished her for double the time, but you did well," said Bathsheba with grudging admiration as they approached the house. "You may accompany me today and watch how I handle affairs."

Lucy quickly realised that her mother-in-law had trained the household slaves in such a way that they knew what must be done and did it with little or no further instruction. Bathsheba would come upon them silently and whichever slave noticed her first would increase the zeal with which they were carrying out their tasks. Bathsheba would inspect their work and occasionally demand that it be redone, but otherwise she would sweep out and onto the next group. She had a little conversation with the housekeeper and the cook, otherwise it seemed she ruled, as she had indicated, by instilling fear into her staff. Lucy hoped that she would be able to use more of her mother's methods when she eventually had her own house to run.

She had no opportunity to talk to Sam until the evening but did so when the children were brought in after dinner, under cover of playing with Emma. He had ridden out to the fields and inspected the aloe harvesting, as well as the pruning of many of the cotton bushes for several hours. He had had to tell Alexander to flog two of the slaves who were slacking, after which the work rate among the others had picked up. As she already knew, Sam was not squeamish about meting out physical punishment, being accustomed to the casual cruelty which was common throughout Barbados and, indeed, all slave plantations. He listened to her account of her first lesson with Bathsheba and nodded approvingly when she described how she had handled the maid's punishment.

"Well, it's a bore, but if we're going to keep up this charade, I'd better go out every day this week and come up with a list of annoying questions or suggestions for John on his return, and you'd better do the same with my mother. I really don't know why John feels the need to go out every day – it could easily be left to Alexander with John or I visiting the fields occasionally to make sure there's no slacking. Anyway, it is to be hoped that he manages to organise the militia visit for this weekend. I shall enjoy that."

The following day Sam received a note from his brother confirming that the militia would arrive two days later, on the Friday evening, and spend the whole weekend carrying out a search exercise across St Philip's and St John's, and that Sam should be ready to join them. They would muster outside St Philip's Church, and as few people as possible must know of the detailed plan to avoid the slaves getting wind of it.

At four o'clock on Friday Sam, resplendent in his militia uniform, mounted Nero, waved a cheery farewell to Lucy and Betty and set off at a smart trot down the drive towards the church. Lucy knew none of the details of the search programme and went to bed after dinner with the other women of the household wondering what exactly was going to take place.

Around eleven that night she woke with a start to the sound of distant shouts and several screams and went to her window to look out. There was a flickering light around the slave quarters, which she realised must be fire, and she was just about to raise the alarm when a horseman galloped along the drive to the front door and gave it a thunderous knock. Lucy threw on her peignoir and ran barefoot along the corridor and down the stairs, reaching the front door at the same time as John's wife Sarah. The two of them pulled back the heavy bolt and opened the door to see Sam, in high good humour, never happier than when he was actively engaged in something with an element of danger or violence.

"John sent me to warn you not to worry about anything. We've surprised them in the slave quarters and are turning the place upside down, checking all their belongings. Any seditious material and we make an example of a few of them – that should do the trick. Keep an eye on any slaves you have in the house – don't let them out. We'll be back with a couple of men to search them too shortly."

And with that he sprang onto Nero's back and headed in the direction of the slave quarters.

Bathsheba had been listening from the top of the staircase, and now gave orders to Sarah and Lucy to round up the few house slaves who remained in the big house overnight, sleeping on pallets outside the women's doors, and take them to the dining room with the few belongings they might have with them, such as their hessian blankets, while she checked on her three daughters.

Within ten minutes, the whole household, slaves and mistresses, was huddled in the dining room, the ailing Sarah helped down the stairs by her own maid and one of the two elderly male slaves in the house. They did not have long to wait before John arrived with two men who smelled strongly of smoke.

Having hurriedly greeted the ladies, John watched as they searched the slaves' pathetic bundles. It took them no more than five minutes, and when they had finished John dismissed the men to wait outside with the horses while he quietly told his wife and mother what was happening.

After he had gone, Bathsheba directed one of the slaves to bolt the door again and dismissed them to their sleeping places. She then passed on what John had told her to her daughters and to Lucy.

"This – as I think you are aware, Lucy – is a militia exercise across our parish and St John's. They are searching all slave quarters for any signs of incipient rebellion and are on the lookout for runaway slaves. It's useful training for the militia and an excellent warning to any slave who may be planning mischief. We want to ensure such an event as happened in Louisiana is nipped in the bud before it can happen here. There's nothing more for us to do – you should all go back to bed."

And Bathsheba nodded to them and led the way upstairs.

Francine did not normally sleep in the house – Lucy had said it made her more nervous to have someone outside her door than not – so Lucy did not see her until the next morning. The girl had obviously been crying and would not look at her mistress.

"Francine, what is wrong?" Lucy asked gently. "Did they frighten you, those men who came last night?"

"They burn our t'ings. They burn picture you gave me," came the soft reply.

Lucy was struck again by the casual cruelty meted out to seemingly perfectly innocent people who already had virtually nothing.

She put her arm around Francine's shoulders. "I will draw you another, Francine. I promise. I am sorry they took all you had – do you know why they were here?"

"Looking for books and papers – looking for rebels," she said, wiping the tears from her face with the back of her hand. "But I don' hurt you, Miss Lucy!"

Lucy sighed. "I know you wouldn't, Francine, but I think they did it as a warning. They say there are some slaves who hate us and do want to hurt us. Do you know anything about that?"

Francine looked up at that, then down again, and slowly shook her head. She *does* know something, thought Lucy, but she did not want to scare the girl.

"I am afraid for the children. Will you warn me if you hear anything that might mean harm to them?" she asked.

"On'y talk, mist'ss. Always talk – nothing more."

"But will you tell me if there ever is anything more?" persisted Lucy.

Reluctantly, Francine nodded.

"I will say nothing to anyone about this now, Francine, and I shall make you another picture very soon."

She had no intention of sharing their conversation with any of the household, it could only lead to trouble for Francine, as they tried to force from her what she meant by 'talk', and Lucy was convinced the girl had spoken honestly – she did not wish to lose her goodwill.

They did not see Sam or John again until Sunday evening, but although everything seemed to continue as normal in the house, Lucy was aware of an undercurrent among the slaves. In general, they were more sullen and downcast than before the raid; they seemed deliberately to perform their tasks as slowly as possible; the younger Bathsheba had a jug of lime water 'accidentally' tipped over her silk evening dress; Sarah's maid 'forgot' to set her panoply of medicines within easy reach; hot food arrived at the table cold… Such misdemeanours were harshly punished, and Mrs Lord told Lucy when they discussed it with Sarah during one of Lucy's lessons that such behaviour was to be expected and dealt with, and that soon things would return to normal.

Lucy was resting in her room when Sam returned, but she could hear him shouting for Joseph as he came through the front door. She went to the top of the stairs as he began to bound up them two at a time and laughed out loud at the picture he presented. Normally quite dapper and point-de-vice, he was grubby, crumpled, with a large sooty mark across his nose. He was clearly in need of a bath, as he cheerfully admitted when he saw Lucy.

"Don't come near me, wife, I am not fit for gentle company!" he said gaily. "I have enjoyed the past few days immensely – I shall tell you all about it later, but I must and shall bathe first. Joseph, you old devil, where are you?" he thundered.

At that moment, Joseph appeared from the kitchen quarters and looked up at his master.

"Water for shaving and for a bath and be quick about it man!" instructed Sam, and the slave withdrew to carry out his orders.

When Sam and John joined the rest of the family on the veranda, he happily launched into a colourful account of the weekend's militia exercise and continued to regale the assembled company with the tale over dinner, apparently oblivious of the fact that slaves were continually with them and of the impact such stories might have on them.

"Forty of us *rendez-vous*'d at St Philip's Church on Friday evening. John Barrow had ordered us into two sections, one to cover St John's, the other St Philip's. Our section went straight to Four Square plantation. The slaves were already asleep for the most part, so it was easy to take them by surprise. Two men went up to the house to warn John Simmons, who owns Four Square, and search the slaves there, while the rest of us worked over the slave quarters. We chased them all out into the open and some of the men corralled them there while we searched each hut. One or two had tried to hide, so we took everything from their huts and used the furniture to start a fire to burn anything which shouldn't be there. There were some books, and one slave had a newspaper report of the Louisiana rebellion, which no doubt he'd taken from the house. We burned them all and gave the slaves concerned twenty lashes each. We took the one with the newspaper prisoner and handed him to the overseer for a spell in the plantation jail…"

At this point, John interrupted, "All those we arrested will be taken before the magistrates in Bridgetown later in the week and made an example of."

Sam, having made use of the pause to swallow a generous helping of rum punch, picked up his tale once more.

"We came to Long Bay next and followed the same procedure. We started on the slave quarters then, as you know, I came up to the house to warn you. Only thing we found of relevance was, would you believe it, a copy of the French Declaration of the Rights of Man in one of the huts! A big ugly Nigger with only one eye was from that hut, so he's been punished…"

"He was a good field hand more's the pity, but he's been taken to Bridgetown already," interjected John. "At least he's the only hand we've lost – some of the other farms lost maybe half a dozen!"

"We went on to the Grove plantation, Bayleys, Pool and Kirton then, same process. Didn't find anything there but put the fear of God into them anyway before they went into the fields. We called a halt for breakfast there and revised our tactics."

At this point they all moved into the dining room. Once they were seated, John took up the tale.

"It was daylight by now of course, so we couldn't catch them red-handed by pulling them out of their huts. And doubtless we had lost the element of surprise – it only needed one Negro from somewhere we'd already searched to take a message from the mistress to another estate where we hadn't been and spill the beans. So we organised a forward posse to ride up to each house in advance of the main militia section to alert the household and conduct a search of the house staff who slept there and restrain those who slept in quarters. The rest then swept in behind, searched the main slave quarters and made a note of where anything suspicious was found. When that happened, we'd leave a posse to sort out the problem when the slaves returned from the fields at sundown while the rest of us went on to the next."

"How did they react when they came back to find all their possessions dragged outside?" asked Lucy, thinking of Francine and the ruined portrait.

"As you'd expect, they howled or looked surly depending on their nature," said Sam. "Some tried to run – so we knew they were guilty of trouble-making. We rounded them up for punishment where we could though a few had to be shot. It's a good warning to others."

"And did you find much evidence of a conspiracy?" Bathsheba asked crisply.

"It's mostly in their heads, as you know, Mother," John responded. "But we found a nest of obeah activity at Crane House – put the obeah woman in solitary confinement for Robert Hunter to decide what to do with her. And at Sunbury a list of names was found. John Barrow is personally working on the Negro who had it to find out what that's about."

After the children had been brought in for their nightly visit and the family dispersed for the night, Sam surprised Lucy by accompanying her upstairs. He went to his own room first, where Joseph stood ready to help him out of his jacket and shoes. He donned his dressing-gown and slippers and entered Lucy's room via the dividing door. He lounged at his ease on the chaise longue while Francine brushed Lucy's hair, then said impatiently to her,

"Be off with you, girl. I'll help your mistress now."

Francine gathered up Lucy's discarded gown and fled, closing the door behind her.

"Do you remember what that Nigger looked like, the one you caught plotting on the landing?" Sam asked abruptly as soon as the door shut. He was frowning slightly.

Lucy was in the process of removing her jewellery, seated still at her dressing table, and turned to him in surprise.

"No, Sam, I'm sorry. I only saw him fleetingly with Juba. I just remember thinking I had not seen him previously, which made me think he was a field hand. Is it important?"

"How was he dressed?"

"The way the field hands dress – rough trousers with loose top. I think his feet were bare. He certainly was not dressed like one of the house slaves. Why?"

"I wondered whether it was the one we found at Sunbury, but it was probably just a runaway. No matter. Anyway, I think our exercise will have taught them all a lesson and ensured that any ringleaders we didn't catch find it very hard to recruit any followers in future!"

With that he stood up, shedding his dressing-gown and unbuttoning his shirt as he strode towards his wife, and pulled her to her feet to coax her towards the bed.

In the following weeks, life returned to its routine, although Lucy found herself much more alert to what was going on around her. She noticed the house slaves never sang anymore, and they continued to be more downcast and surly than usual. Francine's face was wreathed in smiles when Lucy presented her with her replacement portrait, and Lucy wondered ruefully if the raids Sam had enjoyed so much had actually done more harm than good by destroying the few poor possessions the slaves owned.

Lucy continued her 'lessons' with Bathsheba and Sarah (who was pregnant again), though she did not think she learned much beyond the apparent need to deal harshly with slave labour at every opportunity. Sam sporadically spent time in the fields, or closeted with John in his study, demonstrating his new-found zeal for the future of the Long Bay plantation as they had agreed, but he could never be industrious for long and would take himself off to Bridgetown for gambling sessions (and, Lucy feared, other nefarious activities) for several days at a time. The one responsibility he did continue to put regular effort into was the militia, probably because – Lucy thought – it offered the lure of occasional danger and adventure.

Shortly before Christmas 1811, Sam returned from one of his periodic visits to Bridgetown and announced to Lucy that he had by chance met Master Pocock, who had been captain of the Princess Mary packet on which they had travelled to Barbados two years previously. Would Lucy like to accompany him to town to do her Christmas shopping and dine with the captain? They could stay overnight at the Clarence.

Lucy was delighted at the suggestion. It was the first time Sam had offered to take her with him to stay in Bridgetown, although Sarah frequently accompanied John, and she felt starved of society and outside stimulus. Messages were sent and the date set for the following Thursday, and when Lucy hesitantly proposed that they ask the Barrows to join them also she was pleased when Sam agreed.

They set off after breakfast, Lucy clutching her hat tightly as she got into the carriage as the weather was squally. Thomas the coachman strapped their valises securely to the back of the carriage and they set off, Francine (who was more excited than Lucy) and Joseph in the dog cart which followed. Little Emma had been left in the nursery with her cousins, and would no doubt be well looked after there. When they reached Bridgetown, Thomas dropped them off at Martha's store then drove on, still followed by the dogcart, to the Clarence Hotel, owned by the notorious Betsy Austin – a free mulatto woman – where they would be staying and dining later.

Sam gave strict instructions to Francine and Joseph to have everything ready for their arrival and gave Lucy his arm. They paid a courtesy call on Martha, then Lucy asked Sam to take her to Cheapside Market, which she had found a useful source of Christmas gifts previously. As they strolled along Broad Street in the sunshine, the earlier squalls having passed, Lucy felt happier and more relaxed than she had for a long time.

However, her contentment was soon ruffled. Sam was clearly well-known in Bridgetown, and they were constantly stopping to exchange greetings with others who were passing along the street, including some whom Lucy knew such as Dr Nathan Lucas, whom she asked for news of Mary who had now returned to England and her husband. Her sister-in-law Mary Austin came into sight from Swan Street accompanied by two slaves, and informed Sam and Lucy that her daughter, born some three weeks earlier on 20th November, was to be named Lucy Wightwick. Lucy was touched, and impulsively invited her to join them at dinner with her husband Richard, exclaiming that the birth of little Lucy was the same date as that of Henry, John and Sarah's most recent child.

As Mary went on her way, Thomas Daniel, to whom Sam had introduced her and Betty on the occasion of her first visit to Bridgetown, doffed his hat and bowed from across the street. Then she noticed a military man in smart regimentals approaching them, a plump and lively-looking dark-haired, coffee-coloured woman on his arm. Sam hailed him and introduced him as Captain Buscome of the York Light Infantry and his wife.

While the men engaged in discussion about the war in Spain, Lucy attempted some small talk with Mrs Buscome, but soon realised indignantly that the lady – whose dress was more revealing than was proper, she thought belatedly – appeared more interested in casting languorous glances under her lashes at Sam than in any conversation with herself. To her dismay, she also noticed that Sam, never averse to the charms of a pretty woman, seemed to appreciate such outrageous flirtation. She glanced at Captain Buscome, but he seemed oblivious to his wife's behaviour – if indeed she really was his wife rather than his mistress, she thought suddenly.

Despite the sun's warmth, Lucy shivered, she had reluctantly accepted, because it seemed inevitable, that Sam had one or more slave mistresses, but naïvely it had never occurred to her that he might be playing the field in Creole or white society. That represented an even more dangerous challenge to her plans to make her marriage work.

The men's conversation ended, and Sam glanced down at Lucy, who looked at him appealingly.

"I have promised to take Mrs Lord to the market so I must not delay longer. I will see you tomorrow, as agreed," he said to the captain.

He then bowed, a little too deeply Lucy thought, to the lady who responded with a roguish smile.

She decided it would be better to say nothing. Sam would probably fly into a rage, which would not help her plans in any way and would be exceedingly unpleasant into the bargain. So she directed his attention to an extremely pretty snuff box in a shop window to divert his attention and when he had admired it determined to return and buy it for his gift later in the day. They reached the market without mishap and Lucy purchased several small items which Sam laughingly refused to carry for her, instead beckoning to a ragged little black boy and promising him a coin for carrying the lady's parcels.

Sam had an appointment with a lawyer that afternoon, so after they had eaten a light luncheon at the hotel Lucy, accompanied by Joseph and a wide-eyed Francine (who had never before visited Bridgetown), went alone to Martha's store to continue her shopping. She gave some money to Francine and sent the two slaves to the shop where she had that morning seen the snuff box, with instructions to buy it and return to find her in the store. Her purchases complete, including some new paints and brushes for herself and a pair of scissors Bathsheba had asked for, she was leafing through a pattern-book when she caught sight of Mrs Marshall, Sarah's mother.

Lucy greeted her politely and was surprised when the older woman invited her to take a bowl of tea with her, since they hardly knew one another. She was more than happy to accept, however, and the two women enjoyed a pleasant half hour together before parting company, when Lucy returned to the hotel accompanied by Joseph and Francine, both laden down with packages. Sam returned while she was changing for dinner and seemed in high good humour, although he was a little vague when she asked him about his afternoon activities.

He had organised a private room in which to entertain their guests, which Lucy thought was unnecessarily extravagant. At least, however, it would mean she could relax without the embarrassment of seeing him flirting with any pretty girl who happened by.

The evening passed pleasantly, and Lucy was delighted to see her friends the Barrows again, and Captain Pocock, who at first seemed a little overwhelmed in the Barrows' and the Austins' company but soon – with the help of a quantity of lime punch – loosened up and had a fund of sea-faring stories to keep them amused.

When he learned of the death of Oceanus, he awkwardly patted Lucy's shoulder to express his sympathy. He assured them all that he would be delighted to welcome all or any of them on board his ship as passengers at any time in the future, and he promised to arrange delivery personally of the packet Lucy had had the forethought to prepare for her parents (containing a letter, some sketches and small gifts) as soon as possible on his return to Falmouth.

Chapter 12
End of an Idyll

Christmas and New Year passed quietly, with occasional visits to and by the Barrows, the Lucases and the Marshalls, and Martha came on Boxing Day with two of her children. By mid-January, Sam was thoroughly bored of demonstrating diligent attention to the state of Long Bay's crops, particularly since John's attitude to his plans for building a big new house appeared to have altered not one iota, and he spent a wild week in Bridgetown with Thomas Daniel and other friends losing money at cards.

This prompted a fierce argument with Lucy. The lack of privacy available in the house invariably led her to remonstrate with her husband when they were out on a morning ride, and this time was no exception. The discussion started reasonably enough.

"I am running out of questions to ask your mother about running a household, Sam. Is John showing any signs of relenting and permitting you to begin building our new home?"

"Shouldn't think so. No idea. I haven't clapped eyes on him in over a week," replied Sam, shrugging. They were trotting back along the beach, riding side by side.

Lucy looked at him in surprise. "Did you not see him even once during your stay in Bridgetown? Not even at militia training?"

"I made very sure to avoid him! I have absolutely nothing in common with the saintly John, he bores me to death. And I felt devilishly unwell on Friday – too much brandy and a late night with Thomas, so I didn't go to training."

Interpreting this correctly, Lucy sighed in exasperation. "Did you win anything at the tables, Sam?"

He scowled. "No," he said abruptly, "I lost about £300 I think."

Without stopping to think about the consequences Lucy blurted out, "Oh Sam, why do you keep wasting my dowry this way? Don't you *want* to build your castle? How can you ever hope to better our situation if you keep losing money at cards?"

Sam immediately lost his precarious hold on his temper. Knowing he was in the wrong did not help.

"How dare you lecture me, woman? It is my money and I shall spend it how I wish! Do you concentrate on giving me sons – and also on persuading your father to leave some of his wealth to us in his will!"

All Lucy's pent-up frustration rose to the surface and for once she made no effort to keep her own temper in check but released all her anger in one blast.

"If you didn't spend so much time away with your precious friends in Bridgetown drinking and gambling away *my* money, perhaps I might start breeding again! And I am more likely to ask Papa to set up a trust for little Emma than to leave me more money for you to waste!" she screamed at him.

Purple with fury, his face contorted, Sam dropped his own reins, grabbed hold of Empress's bridle and yanked Lucy's mount towards him. Gripping Nero with his knees he set about his wife with his whip, beating her on the shoulders and ribs and catching her across one cheek. Not all his blows landed on her, one landed on Empress's flank, causing her to snort and try – unsuccessfully since Sam was still holding the bridle – to rear. So she put her head down as far as she was able and bucked instead, causing Sam to loosen his hold. Lucy, sobbing with anger, was clinging onto the pommel for dear life which was fortunate as Empress took off at once and headed back towards the comfort of her stable.

Lucy managed to regain control of the reins after several minutes at a wild, dangerous gallop and slid from the horse's back to the mounting block in the yard to hold Empress's head against her shoulder while she tried to still both their trembling. Then she handed the horse to one of the stable-boys and went in search of Francine's usual ministrations for her cuts and bruises.

The simmering resentment between them which resulted from this row was soon overshadowed by a far greater concern with an outbreak of typhoid across the island. Such outbreaks happened with some frequency on the plantations and, because of the close quarters in which the slaves lived and their generally poor health, decimated their population, although the whites, too, were not immune.

John's concern was for the reduced productivity of the fields which resulted from slave illness and death; Lucy, screened as she was from its impact in the house, only began to take notice when Emma's wet nurse succumbed and she, Sarah and Sam were anxious that the contagion might spread to the children. Lucy, in particular, was smitten with remorse that she had lavished so little love and attention on Emma. Typhoid was a cruel disease, showing initially like so many other illnesses with fever, headache, rash and diarrhoea, but it was also called 'slow fever' for a reason; these symptoms were followed by haemorrhaging from the bowels and open skin sores.

In the end, none of the whites at Long Bay contracted the disease but Martha did, and within a few short weeks she was dead. They buried her at St Philip's on the 2nd of February and Lucy was shaken to the core, reliving her horror on the death of Oceanus, whose third birthday they should have just celebrated. It weighed on her mind for weeks and led Lucy to raise with Sam rather earlier than she had meant to her plan to bring up any children in England, particularly since she rather thought she might be pregnant again, although she did not disclose this to her husband. Sam's reaction, as might have been expected, was negative.

"This is your home now; it will also be our children's home. They must grow up understanding the ways of this country. Barbados, not England, is where they belong. When they are older, they may travel – may even spend a few years being schooled over there, but I won't have them growing up with any lily-livered, wishy-washy liberal notions!" Sam shouted at her, by which Lucy correctly understood him to mean abolitionist tendencies.

Incensed, Lucy shouted back, "If you insist on bringing up our children on this disease-ridden island, they will never attain adulthood, and you won't have anyone to pass your godforsaken castle onto if it ever gets built!"

Sam slapped her cheek, whipping her head round, and Lucy's hat fell off. They were on their way back to the house from the stables this time after their early morning ride, and Sam grabbed Lucy's arm and pulled her towards the kitchen quarters. Below these were store rooms – where the household had spent the night of the storm – and two jail cells where slaves were often placed in solitary confinement. Sam opened the door to one of these and pushed Lucy inside.

"Let's see what this does to cool your temper, you little shrew!" he threw at her, and slammed the door shut, turning the key in the lock. It was black as pitch, with no window and no light from outside, and it stank, a rank odour of old sweat and musty earth. The air was fetid and stifling.

Lucy took a cautious step forward, her arms outstretched. Her fingertips touched the opposite wall immediately. She turned to the right and stumbled slightly as her foot encountered something hard. She bent down and felt the obstacle, chains to secure any slave being punished here. At least Sam had spared her that, she thought. She finished her exploration of the tiny space. Nowhere to sit, other than the floor; nothing inside the cell other than the chains. Not enough space to lie down even if she wanted to.

Dazed, Lucy sat on the floor, hugging her knees. She was stunned by Sam's behaviour. He had beaten and raped her before when he was angry, but this was a first. She wondered how long she was to remain down here. What if Sam left for Bridgetown – as he was quite capable of doing – without telling anyone where she was? She could die of thirst or starvation before anyone found her! She tried shouting, and banging on the heavy wooden door, but the solid earth seemed to push her voice back in her face, and she was sure no one outside could hear. No doubt the cell was constructed in just such a way to ensure the cries of any slave imprisoned here could not be heard, and to increase their feeling of isolation.

Time passed, but Lucy had no way of knowing whether it was hours or minutes. She was cramped, hot, thirsty and uncomfortable. She stood up to ease her cramped legs, but there was nowhere to pace and she soon sat down again, leaning her head against the dank, sandy wall. She could feel the grit in her hair. Sweat prickled uncomfortably between her shoulder blades, under her arms and in a ridge under her breasts. She started to feel hungry then, worse than that, she wanted to relieve herself. She groped around the cell again but could find no bucket which might be left for such a purpose. Grimly, she struggled to loosen her stays slightly to ease the pressure on her bladder which helped a little.

She must have dozed, for she woke with a start, sweat pouring down her face now and her whole body feeling damp. A raging thirst and a desperate need for a privy were the only things she could think about. She could do nothing about the former, but she must do something about the latter. Cautiously, she stood again on feet numb from being so long in the same position and tested the ground all around the cell to judge if it fell away appreciably in any direction. Miserably, she decided it did not, and shuffling to the corner furthest from the door, she went down on her knees and clawed at the hard earth with her fingernails to try and create a slight dip. The sweat dripped off her nose as she did so, and Lucy wiped her face with the back of one hand. Eventually she gave up. She stood up, turned, pulled up her skirts and squatted down with her bottom against the wall, then let go. For a few blissful moments the relief was such that she did not care if she flooded her cell, but she did not dare to sit down again once she finished. Instead she stood with her back to the wooden door and tried calling out again. A smell of ammonia was added to the already fetid air.

Now, finally, Lucy allowed her emotion to overcome her, and the tears coursed down her cheeks to mingle with the sweat and soil already there. For perhaps ten minutes she wallowed in feeling sorry for herself, then she gave herself a mental shake, sniffed loudly, rubbed her face with her forearms – no doubt smearing dirt across it – and contemplated how she was going to get out of here. She remembered her hat had fallen off. Someone would find it, surely? And start looking for her? But why would they search the slave cells? She veered from hope to despair.

Her legs grew weary and she could no longer stand against the door. She grabbed at the chains and piled them into a heap, which made a dry, if very uncomfortable seat, and lowered herself onto it, hugging her skirts around her legs. She leant back against the wall and once again fell into an uneasy doze.

Eventually, some four hours after Sam first locked her in, she heard the key scraping in the lock and pushed herself to her feet. The door creaked open, and Lucy squinted in the accustomed light. It was Betty who stood there, with Francine. She heard Betty gasp and saw her turn away, no doubt from the smell that emanated from the open door.

"What on earth happened, Lucy? What are you doing here? Who locked you in?" Betty asked questions in rapid succession. Lucy stumbled towards the door and Francine gave her an arm to lean on.

Lucy raised her face to Betty. "Your brother happened," she said bitterly. "I said I wanted our children brought up in England, away from disease, and he threw me in this dungeon."

Betty looked shocked but said nothing – Lucy knew her loyalty to her brother was warring with their mutual friendship. Francine meanwhile was gently guiding her away from her horrible prison towards the house, she took her up the servants' staircase to avoid her being seen by any other members of the family.

When they reached Lucy's room, she helped her out of her clothes and wrapped her in a peignoir, gently pushed her onto a seat and went to organise water for a bath. Lucy slid under the water, revelling in the feel of it on her gritty skin. Once she was dried and dressed in her chemise, she asked Francine how she had found her.

"Found hat, mist'ss. I see Master Sam very angry. Ask Miss Betty to help."

Briefly, Lucy wondered what had caused Francine or Betty even to consider that she might be in the slave cell, but she was too tired to bother to ask, and relaxed as Francine brushed her hair dry. She ate a plate of fruit and drank copious amounts of lime water before falling asleep for several hours. When she awoke, it was time to dress for dinner.

Sam was already on the veranda when she went downstairs. Lucy lifted her chin at him and Sam glowered back at her. Betty looked uncomfortable, but everyone else seemed oblivious. Fights between Lucy and Sam had become so commonplace that most of the family ignored them. Lucy noticed Bathsheba's sharp little eyes darting between the two of them though and was resigned to a difficult discussion with her later. She decided she would raise the subject of the children being brought up in England at her next lesson with Bathsheba on slave household management.

When she did so, she was surprised that her mother-in-law did not give her a dressing-down as normal, but merely looked at her thoughtfully. "Is that really what you want?" she asked. Lucy nodded. "And are you with child now?"

"It is possible but I cannot be sure."

"I will see what I can do. I cannot have this continual strife in my house. I will talk to Samuel and see if we can come to some arrangement. He is right, you know, your place is here as is the children's. Perhaps, though, I could persuade him to let you visit your parents for a few months, if they will furnish the money for your passage."

Lucy bowed her head in apparent submission but said nothing, relieved that her mother-in-law seemed inclined to take her part for once but incensed that she expected Thomas to fund the voyage.

Later that day, she overheard Bathsheba talking to Sam in her parlour.

"Let the chit return to England if she can persuade her father to pay for her passage, but of course you will not allow her to take Emma with her. She will return after a few months, her parents will not want the shame or expense of keeping her permanently. And you could visit her in Bristol or wherever it is they live."

Sam said something Lucy could not catch.

"That's as maybe. She shall not take Emma. Were she to bear you a son you can always get hold of it if you want to and bring it out with you from England. The law is on your side. Perhaps she is right – infant mortality may be lower there. You have Lucy's money – if you have not already squandered it – and that is really what you want. Let her go on a visit to her parents. As I say, I have no doubt they will encourage her to return here!"

Sam left it to his mother to inform Lucy of what had been agreed. This Bathsheba did with characteristic bluntness, informing her daughter-in-law that she might visit her parents for a few months if they provided her passage money. Lucy thanked her courteously, then smiled inwardly to herself. It was amazing, she was being allowed to go home to have her baby, and now everything would be alright. She would write at once to her father, pleading with him to pay for her passage. She would be suitably submissive until she left, and once back in England it would be hard for Sam to force her to return, wouldn't it?

And so Lucy's trip was announced as a visit to her parents, with the possibility that Sam would join her later. While she waited for her father's response, Lucy passed her time writing her journal, writing letters to Mary Kingsley and to her schoolfriend Annabel, sketching the house and – from memory – some of the sights of Bridgetown, and spending more time with little Emma. Lucy felt some guilt about abandoning her daughter (something that it would have been unthinkable to do to Oceanus had he lived), but she had no legal right in any case to demand the baby accompany her.

Sam was clearly sulking, Lucy thought. He was behaving in a cold and distant way to her, yet oddly he also appeared more possessive around her than he had ever done. It was obvious that while it might be alright for him to play fast and loose with his wife, the idea that she should dare to express a wish to be apart from him hurt his pride.

She was determined not to confirm to him that she might be pregnant again for fear he and his mother would change their minds about her going. Whereas Sam would normally have avoided her bed and sought his pleasure elsewhere had he known Lucy was pregnant, his ignorance led him to visit her almost every night during those last weeks before she left, making love to her with a certain desperation as if to remind her that she belonged to him.

Lucy suffered him to do as he wished; occasionally, the spark that had existed between them in the early days was rekindled and both were left panting, exhausted and satisfied, but on other nights he would come to her without warning, throwing Francine out of the room and locking the door before stripping Lucy of any clothing and taking her quite savagely.

As a result, she sported many bruises, not all of which she could hide; but the family made no comment, and she saw no-one from outside so she ceased to worry about them. Perhaps, she thought wistfully, Sam's possessiveness was a sign that some small part of him loved her still? For despite the almost casual violence he visited upon her, despite the destruction of all her illusions about his motivation for marrying her, nothing had quite extinguished the love Lucy had felt for Sam when she first met him four years earlier.

When Mr Wightwick's response to her letter arrived, agreeing to pay her passage and enclosing a banker's draft, she sighed with relief and felt happier than she had since before Oceanus died. Now she could plan in good earnest. In the end it was John who organised her passage. It was as though Sam hoped that if he failed to do so, Lucy's determination to leave could be thwarted. She did not take much luggage with her; she did not want to make it look as though she never planned to return, and in any case, fashions would have changed by the time she reached England and she could buy new clothes there.

So, in late June 1812, Lucy embarked on the Hope bound for Bristol where her father would meet her. Sam had spent a good part of the last night with Lucy, and it was one of the times he forced himself upon her: no tender, farewell lovemaking for her. At some point during the night he had acknowledged her imminent departure. Lucy remembered him grabbing a fistful of her hair to jerk her face towards him and grunting into her ear,

"And how would you like another spell in the cellar, eh, Madam? Perhaps that would make you more accommodating."

Lucy went cold at the thought. She had not forgotten how unpleasant the hours she spent in the slave cell had been, or her fear that no-one would think to look for her there until it was too late. When she did not answer him, Sam let go of her hair, pulling out a clump of it which became caught in his signet ring, and slapped her face hard.

"Well? Would you enjoy that?" he demanded fiercely. "Perhaps I should keep you there all the time, I warrant you'd be more than happy to see me then!"

Her eyes watering from the pain, Lucy bit her lip firmly, determined not to give him the satisfaction of hearing her cry out. With only the tiniest tremor in her voice, she said

"I am always happy to see you, Sam. I just wish that you would be gentler with me, like you were when we were first married. Why do you get such pleasure from hurting me?"

He slapped her again.

"Why do you take such pleasure in thwarting me? You took a vow to honour and obey me, yet I have seen little sign of obedience in you. I tell you – for your own safety, mind! – not to visit the slave quarters and what must you do but go alone? You refuse to ask your father to help me build a house, even though that would give you the status you desire; and now you insist on going back to England to your parents, when your place is here with me!"

Sam flung away from her in a fury, marching stark naked through the dividing door into his own room and slamming the door behind him.

The only person she was truly sorry to leave behind was Francine, who wept inconsolably at the departure of her mistress, convinced she would be sent to the fields and never see Lucy again.

A wave of remorse struck her; this girl had provided Lucy with so much solace and comfort over the past three years, yet she had given no thought to Francine's fate once she left. Too late, she realised that there was nothing she could do. She should have asked Sam to gift Francine to her, that way she could in turn have given the girl her freedom. But Francine belonged to Long Bay.

Lucy scooped together the few small coins she had and poured them into the slave's hands, feeling embarrassed at her selfishness. Her eyes downcast, Francine murmured something Lucy could not catch; Lucy embraced her gently, feeling the thin bones beneath the coarse fabric of her blouse.

"Thank you, Francine, for everything. I wish that I could take you with me, although I do not think you would be happy in England. Would you like me to ask Mrs Lord to let you care for Emma Lucy once I am gone?"

"Please, Miss Lucy," came the soft reply, but Francine would still not look at her.

Lucy sent her to fetch one of the men to cord up the one small trunk she was taking with her and take it down to the carriage, then made her way along the passage to say her farewells to her mother-in-law, who she thought unlikely to wave her goodbye from the doorstep since she disapproved of Lucy's departure. Bathsheba greeted her coolly and waited for Lucy to speak.

"I shall be leaving for Bridgetown shortly, ma'am, and would not wish to interrupt you so have come to pay my respects now."

Her mother-in-law inclined her head but said nothing. Taking a deep breath, Lucy continued, "Would you see to it, ma'am, that Francine is put in the nursery to look after Emma Lucy, please?"

Bathsheba studied her awhile. "I have the impression you are more concerned about the fate of that slave girl than you are of your own daughter, Lucy. I can promise nothing, the deployment of our slaves is in John's hands, not mine."

Lucy was well aware that this was untrue, John would do exactly what his mother told him to, and it made her dread that Francine might be subject to an act of petty revenge and sent to the fields to work, where she stood little chance of survival.

"I will talk to John," Bathsheba went on, "and you may be sure that in any case your daughter will be well cared for, together with her cousins. You will be able to see for yourself on your return here."

At this she looked at her daughter-in-law sternly, as if daring her to announce that she was leaving her husband for good. Lucy felt as though she was being reprimanded by a governess – not that she had ever hated her own governess in the way she frequently did Bathsheba. She felt respect, yes, and grudging admiration for Sam's mother, but she could not like her. So Lucy lowered her eyes, bit her tongue, and bobbed a small curtsey before leaving the room.

When the time came for her departure, Sam had still not made an appearance, having gone out riding very early according to his personal slave, Joseph. So it was a very small group of people who gathered to bid Lucy farewell and God speed on her journey. Betty was there and gave her a fond hug, for once taking in the mass of blue, black and yellow marks on Lucy's face and neck but saying nothing. Francine was there, tears pouring unashamedly down her face, holding little Emma. The little girl wriggled, wanting her freedom, then smiled at her mother and held out her arms. That almost broke Lucy's resolve, she felt a wave of genuine affection for the child for the first time, and kissed her curly, blonde hair before turning away with tears in her own eyes. She looked in vain for her other sisters-in-law, but there was no sign of them, and John, of course, was already in Bridgetown.

Then, as Lucy looked around one last time, Betty said,

"Sam hates goodbyes. I am sure that is the reason for his absence," she loyally defended her brother. "Perhaps he has gone to Bridgetown already and will meet you there."

Lucy nodded, not wishing to cause a rift between Sam and Betty, but suddenly feeling tired and dejected. Betty took pity on her and at the last moment insisted on accompanying her sister-in-law to Bridgetown harbour which Lucy was glad of. She had thought their friendship had cooled somewhat after Sam had locked her in the cellar and she did not want to leave on bad terms since she was fonder of Betty than anyone else in Sam's family apart from Mary Austin.

Thomas, the coachman, closed the carriage door and Lucy opened the window to wave goodbye to the little group as he mounted his seat and gave the horses the off. By the time they reached the end of the long driveway and headed north-west uphill towards the Rick Grenidge plantation, Francine and Emma were pinprick figures, and Lucy sat back in her seat and, having closed the window against the dust, allowed the tears to slide down her cheeks unheeded.

She was not sure whether she was crying with relief or sorrow at leaving, and after a mile or so, gave herself a mental shake, sniffed defiantly and mopped her eyes with a wispy handkerchief, determined only to look forward not back.

Relieved, Betty said, "I do understand why you feel you need to go back to England. Sam was wrong to put you in the cellar, whatever you may have done. But please don't be too angry with him, I think he will be lost without you and go back to his old, wild ways. You will come back, won't you?"

Lucy smiled and said, "I'm only going on a visit to my parents, Betty. I have not seen them for over three years and I miss them, and my brother Stubbs."

"I wish I could come with you, but Mother and John would never waste the passage money on me," sighed Betty. "Perhaps I may still find a rich husband and he will take me to visit England some day!"

"Please see that Francine is taken care of, that she is not sent to the fields," Lucy said in a low, pleading voice. "I have spoken to your mother, but…" She looked at Betty, and it was clear she understood everything that was unspoken.

"I will do what I can," she promised Lucy.

The two women sat in companionable silence for most of the rest of the journey, and Lucy mentally ticked off the estates as they passed them. Jones was on the left, then a long gap before Carringtons hove into view, then Bentleys (also both on the left) and at last Windsor on the right where they stopped briefly to stretch their legs. She felt as though she were in a sort of limbo, and the journey seemed dreamlike, never-ending. She recognised Boarded Hall on the right, and when she saw Hendersons she knew only three miles remained.

When they reached the docks, John was waiting for her but there was still no sign of Sam. John assisted the ladies out of the carriage then organised the disposal of Lucy's baggage to the waiting area for the Hope which was sitting quite low in the water at anchor further out in Carlisle Bay.

"You will be sharing your stateroom with a Miss Kilmer. She has been a governess here but her charges have all outgrown her tuition and she has decided to return to England. She will look after you, and I have asked the captain, Jarrett, to watch out for you also. Miss Kilmer seems a pleasant enough sort," he said gravely.

He hesitated, then took both Lucy's hands gently in his, which startled her.

"Lucy, I know there has been trouble between you and Sam – and I know it is none of my business!" as she stiffened. "All I wish to say is – I know he can be difficult and headstrong, and that he is not good with money, but you have been good for him, you know."

Lucy looked up at him, astonished. Unconsciously John had echoed Betty's earlier comment.

"It is true, and I fear that while you are gone, he will become very wild again. Please come back to us as soon as you can. I and all the family will welcome you back with open arms."

Lucy's mind conjured up a picture of her mother-in-law and she thought that there was one member of the family who probably would not care if she never returned, but she merely smiled her thanks to John for his kind words.

"I have been on board to check your cabin, Lucy," said John. "There will not be much space but if the weather is fine you can spend time on deck."

Lucy was helped down into the little boat by a burly seaman who had already swung her trunk down, and settled herself between a corded trunk and a hen coop towards the back then looked up to wave John and Betty goodbye. As they moved swiftly out into deeper water she continued waving at the brother and sister standing side by side on the quay until they appeared as mere dots on the horizon.

Part 4
Cecilia 1812-1814

Chapter 13
The Quandary

The little boat moved quickly towards the mother ship, The Hope, a square-sailed sloop in which John had booked her passage. She had arrived from England carrying a mixed cargo of coal, cloth, guns and barrels of port wine in April, and her master, Captain Jarrett, had almost completed overseeing the loading of a return cargo of sugar, rum, cotton, tamarinds and castor oil. Perhaps her name was a good omen, thought Lucy.

The deck was in a bustle, with meat carcasses and hogs of wine or water, chicken coops and sacks of grain piled up ready to be distributed in the ship's hold. Lucy stepped carefully around them and over coils of rope to reach the steps – or ladder – leading towards the cabins. She asked a half-naked sailor – averting her eyes – which one was hers but he just shrugged to indicate he did not know and hurried on his way.

Lucy looked around for someone in charge and caught sight of the first mate. Picking her way across the deck once more, she asked again,

"Excuse me, but could you direct me to my cabin? My name is Mrs Lord."

Bellowing a final order to one of the sweating sailors cursing at the weight of the carcasses and sacks of grain which would provide their staple diet for much of the voyage the first mate turned, frowning slightly at being interrupted. His brow cleared when he saw before him a well-dressed woman, and he bowed slightly, indicating the ladder she had been about to descend and saying she would find the steward below. He then turned back and began bellowing orders again.

When Lucy did find her cabin, she sat down on the one chair with a weary sigh and removed her hat, which was giving her a headache. She patted her flattened curls, damp with sweat, trying to give her hair a little more body but gave up.

The cabin was far smaller than the stateroom she and Sam had travelled out in so happily more than three years before. It contained two beds, with barely an inch between them, a chair and a small table with a mirror above. There was just space for Lucy's trunk under one of the beds, and she realised she would have to keep everything in the trunk for there was nowhere else to store her clothes. Suddenly weary beyond measure she lay down, listening to the thuds and shouting going on above her head. She was glad Miss Kilmer had not yet arrived, for she had never felt less like making small talk.

She must have nodded off, for she woke with a start to the door opening and a woman she assumed to be Miss Kilmer, accompanied by a burly seaman carrying her trunk. Lucy struggled up to a sitting position, trying to shake off her grogginess.

Her trunk stowed neatly under the other bed, Miss Kilmer turned and introduced herself. To the twenty-seven-year-old Lucy she seemed old, no doubt worn out by difficult pupils and the heat and humidity of Barbados, but she was in fact no more than fifty. She was dressed neatly in a buttoned-up dark grey dress similar to the ones Lucy's own governess had worn, and very different from Lucy's pale muslin. She removed her bonnet, smoothing out the slender ribbons, and placed it on a high shelf Lucy had not noticed.

There was a slightly awkward pause.

"Do you think it will be safe to go on deck now? I would like to say farewell to Barbados as we set sail," said Lucy.

"I am sure we can find a quiet corner where we will not be in the way," responded Miss Kilmer and, replacing her hat, she led the way back up on deck.

Lucy pulled a shawl from her trunk, remembering how chill the breeze could be once the ship left harbour, and crammed her straw bonnet back on her head, hastily tying the ribbons. The two women found their quiet corner (any supplies that had been there had obviously been stored away already) and sat primly on two coils of rope in the lee of a cannon, looking back towards the island.

Lucy broke the silence. "I understand from my brother-in-law that you are a governess? What is the name of the family you have been with? I wonder if I might know them," she said.

Miss Kilmer answered quietly, "I have spent the last fifteen years with the family of Mr John Marshall Morris. They own a plantation called Belleplaine in St Andrew's Parish, perhaps you know it?"

Lucy shook her head. Despite the tiny size of the island, and the small number of people of quality living there, the plantations were generally so isolated and self-sufficient that although much socialising took place at a local level, it was not unusual for the white plantocracy from different parishes not to know each other. Besides, as her mother-in-law had made clear, the Lords had their own reasons for fraternising less than their peers.

"Are you returning to England to take up another post, Miss Kilmer?" asked Lucy.

"No, Mrs Lord. I am going back to nurse my elderly mother near Bristol. She has a weak heart. I am very grateful to Mrs Morris who kindly paid for my passage. And you are returning to visit your parents, I believe? Mr Lord came to speak to me a week ago, and very courteously asked me if I would act as your companion and chaperone until we reach England. What a kindly, pleasant gentleman! Is he your husband, Mrs Lord?"

Lucy explained that John was her brother-in-law and changed the subject, pointing out the fact that the noise on deck had changed. The anchors were being hauled on board, and several sailors were checking that all the ropes were carefully coiled in exactly the correct place for use as the sails were raised on the sloop. The ship shuddered and, with only one small sail hoisted, began to make its slow way out of Bridgetown harbour towards the open sea. Lucy strained her eyes to look for Long Bay, identifying it by looking above Cobblers Reef; she pointed it out to Miss Kilmer.

The Hope was the first of their little convoy out of the harbour, and as it left shelter and the pilot vessels turned away, the wind picked up and tried to snatch the ladies' hats from their heads – and would have done so had they not been firmly tied on.

Lucy looked back; three other ships were following The Hope, and they were to be joined shortly by the Falmouth Packet returning from Demerara, as Lucy was to learn from Mr Jarrett at dinner. She had given no real thought to their safety when she travelled out with Sam, but it was comforting now to remember how ships generally travelled in convoy to have a better chance against marauding French or American privateers. She had heard stories of the French and the Yankees taking women passengers prisoner and holding them to ransom. That would be no better than living as a virtual (and sometimes actual) prisoner at Long Bay, she thought.

Lucy settled easily back into shipboard life, unlike her companion who spent almost the whole voyage being extremely seasick. This made their small cabin very unpleasant, and Lucy spent as little time as possible there. She tried to minister to Miss Kilmer, but found that made her feel queasy too, so generally left the poor woman to the not so tender mercies of the steward. She spent much of the time on deck, watching the flying fish and bottle-nosed dolphins as the Hope sailed serenely through the Caribbean, and whales and other sea-life as the voyage progressed, or simply watching the sea change colour or mood, from calm to angry and back again.

On one occasion, Lucy was convinced she saw a mermaid, and called out to one of the sailors nearby to tell her if she was correct. They were nearing the Azores at the time, for which she was watching as eagerly as the lookout, feeling that a spell on dry land would benefit both her and her companion. She saw what appeared to be a rock sticking out of the ocean, and on that rock a mermaid, combing out her long, green hair. Lucy was certain that the creature sported a fishtail where her feet should have been. Several passengers and two of the sailors crowded to the rail to strain their eyes in the hope of seeing a mermaid, and when one laughed it off as a figment of Lucy's imagination one of the sailors leaped to her defence.

"Excuse me, master, but it be true. Our third mate saw one a-sunning herself not two year since, off Chatham Island. I can't say as I can see one now – but I'm not saying the lady didn't see her neither."

Three times she and the other passengers were ordered below by the captain, twice when the weather turned stormy (by which time poor Miss Kilmer was spent, and lay on her bunk retching drily, with nothing left in her stomach to bring up), and once when the lookout spotted a French privateer on the horizon and the convoy took avoiding action to keep out of its way, while priming their guns in case they could not outrun it.

The Azores provided some blessed relief from boredom. For the first two weeks Lucy had revelled in not having to answer for everything to her mother-in-law, or watch her step with Sam, but the constrained and routine life on board then began to pall. She wrote long letters to send to her former friends in England, telling of her return, which she would post when she reached Bristol. She even wrote one to her former governess, whom she had not contacted in many years. She resurrected her diary, but there was little new information to write in it each day (except for the sighting of the mermaid). And she borrowed books from the other passengers and read them from cover to cover while sitting up on deck. So when almost three weeks after leaving Bridgetown they stopped at Angra do Heroismo on the island of Terceira, the oldest continuously settled town in the archipelago, to restock their supplies with fresh meat, vegetables, water and wine, Lucy breathed a sigh of relief and stepped gingerly ashore with Miss Kilmer tottering along on her arm.

The poor lady quickly recovered from her seasickness once on dry land, and the two went for a brisk and energetic walk. The Azores was a volcanic archipelago with some lofty white-capped peaks such as Mount Pico, but also some gentler islands like Terceira with steeply wooded and cultivated slopes dotted with windmills above a narrow coastal belt, where the houses came right down to the water. They climbed a gentle hill and stopped to admire the view, Lucy wishing she had brought her easel and paints with her – but these had been left at Long Bay.

After a short rest they made their way back down to the town. Miss Kilmer timidly suggested that they stop to take a meal at a pretty little inn they saw, and Lucy blushed, embarrassed to admit that she had not a penny to her name. Miss Kilmer noted her confusion and, kindly patting her arm, said, "It will be my treat, my dear. You have been very patient with my crotchets. I am sorry I have been so unwell and unable to carry out my duties as I promised, to act as your companion."

Lucy hesitated, then accepted the invitation. It was too good an opportunity to miss – the confines of the small wardroom where they took all their meals on board had become oppressive. She would make it up in some way to the former governess once she, Lucy, returned to her parents; she was sure Miss Kilmer could not possibly have much money to spare.

The two ate frugally but well at the inn on fresh fish and vegetables, washed down with a glass of local wine and followed by fruit. All the produce was grown or caught on the island, and the meal was quite inexpensive so Lucy felt less guilty about accepting Miss Kilmer's invitation.

They strolled back towards The Hope in the warm sunshine, enjoying an absence of the tropical humidity to be found on Barbados. When they reached the port they sat on a low wall, clutching their parasols to safeguard their complexions, and watched the barrels, crates, sacks, boxes and live animals being loaded onto the ship. Miss Kilmer was loth to go on board before she absolutely had to (although Captain Jarrett had informed them that The Hope would spend the night anchored at Angra do Heroismo and only sail in the morning), and Lucy was keen to leave as much time as possible for their cabin to be aired.

At least, thought Lucy, they were over halfway on their voyage. If they were lucky and the summer weather held, they should reach Bristol in about two weeks. She was impatient now to get home (she had already stopped thinking of Long Bay as home) and in particular was longing to see her father again. So once they set sail from Terceira (The Hope the last of their small convoy this time), she kept an anxious eye on the weather, eagerly asking the captain each afternoon at dinner whether he was expecting any storms. But the weather stayed benign, and even Miss Kilmer appeared to have overcome the worst of her seasickness; nor did they encounter any more enemy vessels.

On Friday, the 21st of August, The Hope reached Bristol, and as they approached the English coast (escorted by two navy warships), an air of excitement permeated the ship.

Lucy had abandoned her stays for much of the voyage as they were too difficult for her to tie on her own, but she wanted to be properly dressed when she disembarked and asked Miss Kilmer if she would mind helping her. This the lady did but found she could not tighten them as much as Lucy would have wished.

"Are you breeding by any chance, my dear?" she asked, glancing sideways as Lucy's swelling stomach. She was by this time six months pregnant, so her state was becoming increasingly difficult to hide, despite the high waists of her fashionable muslins.

Lucy nodded. "Yes. I wish to have my next child in England and make sure it is reared there. That way it will have a better chance of survival than it would on Barbados."

She had already told Miss Kilmer the bare bones of Oceanus' short life, and the fact that she had had no choice but to leave little Emma behind; as Miss Kilmer knew, it was a husband's prerogative to dictate whether children should live with him or their mother if they were apart.

"Does your husband know?" Miss Kilmer asked gently.

Lucy shook her head, and Miss Kilmer asked no more questions, having formed a shrewd idea now of what was going on. It was none of her business after all, and she would continue to perform the role she had been asked to – of companion and chaperone – until she parted from Mrs Lord at Bristol.

The ladies finished their toilette, took a last look around the tiny cabin to ensure nothing had been inadvertently left out of their trunks and turned to go up on deck for the last time. Several other passengers were already standing at the rails, scanning the coast, eager to get a first glimpse of their berth in the harbour. Lucy and Miss Kilmer made their way for'ard and stood watching the hustle and bustle of the teeming shipping of all sizes entering and leaving the port. The Hope had been attached to two barges and was being towed down the steep, narrow Avon Gorge to dock (for sails were of little use here), an experienced pilot having swung aboard as they entered the Bristol roads to guide the ship safely to her anchorage.

Lucy was thinking about what lay ahead. John had told her that he had written to her father, asking him to arrange for his daughter to be collected from the quay when the Hope arrived. He had also had a quiet word with Captain Jarrett who, as John thought, knew of Thomas Wightwick through commerce. If there was a carriage waiting, she would offer Miss Kilmer a lift to her destination, thus repaying her debt for their lunch in Terceira. If it was not there, she would have to make her way to her father's office and hope that he was not away on business as she had not a penny to her name and still had many miles to travel before arriving at Hewelsfield.

Her brow furrowed as she worried over how she would get there without the funds to pay postboys, or the ferryman, but there was something of even deeper concern nagging at her, something she had avoided thinking about until now. How would her return be viewed? She thought she could probably still twist her father round her little finger but would her mother welcome her or disapprove of the fact that she had not stayed with her husband and child? And what would her friends think? If her actions were looked at askance, she would have no more social life in England than she had in Barbados, and she yearned for a return to the somewhat frivolous lifestyle she had enjoyed during her two years as a débutante in Bath.

Giving herself a mental shake, Lucy stared unseeingly at the approaching dock. She was not here for frivolity, she was here to ensure her next child – which she was sure would be a boy whom she would love almost as much as Oceanus – had a secure start in life, sheltered from the diseases prevalent in Barbados (she refused to admit that Bathsheba was right about the high level of infant mortality in England), and that she, Lucy, would be free from fear of her husband's erratic behaviour.

The Hope drew into the quay, sails furled, the sailors standing by with grappling hooks and ropes, and as the ship bumped gently into the side two of the men leapt ashore to tie her off and make her secure. All was hustle and bustle, with a precarious-looking gangplank pushed out for the passengers to disembark. The two ladies turned and made their way towards it, their ears full of shouted commands as the men hurried to begin unloading the cargo, oblivious now to the handful of passengers. Lucy stepped cautiously onto the gangplank, gripping the rope handrail firmly as the ship rose and fell in the swell, and breathed a sigh of relief when she reached the quay. She turned to assist Miss Kilmer who had followed her, and was clinging on with both hands, a look of fear in her eyes and her bonnet askew. Jostled by the crew and other passengers, they were forced inexorably away from the water; the quayside was narrow, with the front doors of tiny terraced houses opening directly onto it.

Lucy took a deep breath and squared her shoulders, looking around in the hopes of seeing her father. But there was no-one there that she knew, so timidly she approached the nearest coach drawn up a few yards away and asked the coachman whom he was there to pick up. Before he could answer, one of their fellow passengers pushed his way through the crowd and demanded the door be opened for him. A footman jumped down from the box seat and hurried to comply, letting down the steps. Clearly this vehicle had not been sent by her father. As the man climbed in, he turned and doffed his hat.

"May I give you ladies a lift somewhere?"

"Thank you, but my father is sending a conveyance for me," responded Lucy promptly, then equally promptly regretted it, for what if her father did not come?

Firmly, she turned away, Miss Kilmer still in tow, and checked each of the three other vehicles waiting in line. None was for her. Her shoulders drooped. Miss Kilmer saw her despondency and now took charge, saying brightly,

"Doubtless Mr Wightwick has mistook the date, my dear. We shall take a hackney cab. Where do you wish to go?"

"I think it would be best if I go to his place of work in the city. But you must wish to go at once to your mother. Please do not worry about me."

"I promised Mr Lord I would look after you and now finally I may do so." She beckoned to one of the young boys who always loitered on quaysides.

"Please to call a hackney cab for us and load our trunks onto it. You shall earn tuppence for your pains," she said firmly.

Not knowing what else to do, and very conscious that she had no money, Lucy acquiesced and they were soon seated in a cab that was somewhat the worse for wear, with the straw stuffing poking out of the seats. Lucy gave the coachman the direction of her father's office and they set off.

It took some time to get out of the busy port, past the warehouses into the narrow streets crammed full of businesses of every variety. They were so thronged with people that the horses could go no faster than a walk, although Lucy – having glanced at the poor creatures, bones showing through their skin and heads hanging – thought it unlikely that they had it in them to go much faster in any case. After about fifteen minutes the cab drew to a halt, and peering out, Lucy recognised her father's place of business. At least she hoped it still was his place of business, she thought with a sudden qualm, perhaps he had moved.

The steps were let down and Lucy alighted. She knocked on the door, which was opened almost immediately by a young man she had never seen, who showed some surprise at the sudden appearance of a slightly dishevelled woman in front of him.

"Is Mr Wightwick available? Mr Thomas Wightwick?" she asked.

"Yes ma'am. Who shall I say is calling?"

"His daughter and a friend, arrived from the West Indies," she answered, sudden relief causing her to smile at him. "Please be so good as to pay the hackney cab driver – and there are two trunks to be unloaded. Is my father upstairs?"

Pulling himself together, the young man bowed and Lucy turned to beckon to her companion, who was leaning on the open window frame, before bounding up the stairs in a most unladylike manner. At the top she was greeted with astonishment by Baines, her father's longstanding man of affairs, who hurried to pull out chairs for both ladies in his tiny outer office and shout for tea.

"But, Miss Lucy, we were not expecting you until next week! Mr Wightwick will be delighted to see you sooner, but he is with a client just at the moment. Will you take some refreshment while you wait?"

"Thank you, that will be very welcome. I thought there must be some such explanation when I could find no conveyance sent by my father to meet us," smiled Lucy, happy now that her worst fears had not been realised.

The two ladies sat quietly sipping their tea while he checked that their trunks had been safely stowed away downstairs and as he returned, Thomas' door opened and he came out with Thomas Daniel, Sam's drinking and gambling partner, whom Lucy had met on several occasions.

"Lucy!" exclaimed her father, hurrying forward with his arms held out. Lucy submitted to his hug but was afraid to relax in case the emotion welling up inside should become evident to Mr Daniel, so she pulled away, holding her father's hands and smiling tremulously up at him.

"But – how is it that you are here already? I had not looked for you for several days yet. How did you get here from the docks?"

Lucy introduced Miss Kilmore. "She has been so kind as to look after me on the voyage and brought me here in a hackney cab. Miss Kilmore, this is my father, Mr Wightwick, and this is Mr Daniel," turning and holding her hand out for Mr Daniel to kiss, which he did as he bowed gracefully.

"Mrs Lord, it is always a pleasure to see you. Do you wish me to bear a message to your husband telling him of your safe arrival? I leave tomorrow for the West Indies and will visit him in Barbados."

"I would be grateful to you, sir."

"In that case, I shall take my leave of you all now," said Mr Daniel. "I am sure you have much to discuss and I shall be very much in the way."

No-one made any attempt to detain him, merely murmuring their farewells, while Mr Wightwick gestured for Mr Daniel's hat and coat to be brought for him. Clapping his hat on his head, and throwing his greatcoat over one arm, Thomas Daniel strode out of the room, leaving Lucy to let go of her pent-up tears of relief all over her father's shirtfront. Slightly embarrassed, but with tears of sympathy in his own eyes, he held Lucy and patted her hair.

"But where are our manners? Miss Kilmore, I must thank you for taking such good care of my daughter. Are you staying in Bristol?"

"No, sir, I am travelling to Keynsham, to my mother."

"Then you must have dinner with us, and I shall organise a post-chaise to take you to your destination," said Mr Wightwick firmly. "It is the least I can do for delivering my daughter to me early!"

Lucy looked at him gratefully and mopped her face with a handkerchief, while Miss Kilmer faintly demurred before accepting his offer. As Lucy had suspected, she had very little money, and having someone else defray even the small expense of a post-chaise the short distance from Bristol to Keynsham was a great relief.

In high good humour, Thomas – having assisted them both into their pelisses and waited whilst they put on their bonnets – gave an arm to each lady and led them out to a local hostelry, the Coach and Horses, off Queens Square, to dine. Once settled in a relatively quiet booth, away from a group of rowdy sailors clearly enjoying their leave, Lucy – aided occasionally by Miss Kilmore – recounted the tale of their voyage and descriptions of life in Barbados. She said nothing about the reasons for her return to England or about her troubled marriage, that would have to wait until they were alone; but she had not seen her father for nearly four years, so there was still much to talk about.

Once they had finished a hearty meal of woodcock, oyster patties, saddle of mutton, cabbage, beets and potatoes, with lemon jelly to finish, they returned to Mr Wightwick's place of business, where the excellent Baines quickly organised a post-chaise to carry Miss Kilmer to her mother's house. Her trunk was loaded, and Miss Kilmer said a fond goodbye to Lucy, both ladies agreeing to stay in touch by letter. Miss Kilmer turned to thank her host for his hospitality, and he helped her into the carriage. She opened the window to wave as they set off at a smart trot, and father and daughter were left alone at last.

"Come into my office, Lucy, and tell me all," said Thomas. "Baines, no interruptions if you please."

Once inside, he went over to his drinks' cabinet, unlocked it and poured himself a cognac, offering a small one also to Lucy.

Lucy took it, cupping it in hands which trembled slightly. All through the voyage she had imagined her reunion with her beloved father and it had seemed an easy matter to tell him that her marriage was an abject failure, that she still ached for the loss of her wonderful baby son, Oceanus, that she was at the end of her tether and how difficult life had been with an overbearing mother-in-law in a crowded household consisting entirely of Sam's family; that Thomas was right in his original concerns about Sam, but that in spite of everything, she still loved her wayward husband. Yet now, in the cold light of day, she simply did not know what to say, where to start.

Her father sat in an old, comfortable leather armchair and sipped his cognac, looking over his glass at his daughter, his eyes kindly yet stern. He waited silently for his daughter to begin her story, unwilling to ask a question, preferring to let her find the right words. The minutes slipped past, the only sounds in the room the muffled noises of the street below and the loud ticking of the grandfather clock in one corner of the office.

Finally Lucy sighed, took a sip of the burning cognac (which made her splutter), leant back in her seat and began in a small voice, "You were right, Father. Sam was not the golden hero of my dreams when I first met him. He did marry me for my money, though I believe he does – did – care for me at least a little. But life in Barbados is so very different from life here, and it was hard not having you or Mother to turn to for advice and support… Perhaps that would not have mattered if Sam had been in love with me as I was with him, or if we had had a place of our own, but…"

Her voice trailed off again, and she seemed to be looking into the far distance at something her father could not see. Then she turned to him and said, in a stronger voice, "I am going to have another child soon, so at least you will get to see one of your grandchildren."

Thomas smiled and nodded. Again Lucy's voice trailed off. Another silence.

So Thomas asked gently, "And what of little Emma?"

In response she said, almost inconsequentially, "Sam loves children. Emma will be well cared for."

The conversation was becoming stranger by the moment, thought Thomas, not to mention awkward.

"We will look after you, Lucy. Your mother and I are so pleased to have you back with us for a while, we are grateful to Sam for arranging for you to visit us. Will he be coming here too, perhaps when the new baby is born?"

The hand holding her glass of cognac shook noticeably, spilling a drop of the golden liquid on her skirt. Lucy concentrated on smoothing the stain away. But it was joined by another drop as the tears began to flow.

"I do not know, Papa. I do not know anything anymore. The future is so dark, and I am afraid."

The glass fell from her grasp and she covered her face with her hands, rocking backwards and forwards. Now seriously alarmed, Thomas stood up, stooped to retrieve the glass and set it on a side table, then put his arms around his daughter, holding her head against his stomach and smoothing her hair. He let her cry for a while and, when the sobs lessened, pushed up her chin and looking into the blotched, reddened, tearstained face, said with all the authority he could muster, "Now Lucy, I think you had better begin this tale at the beginning and tell me what has upset you so much."

He returned to his seat and picked up his own glass once again, but Lucy followed him and sat down on the floor next to him, her head on his knee as she used to do so often in the study at Hewelsfield as a child.

Taking a deep breath, Lucy began again, telling her story from the time of her departure with Sam on the Princess Mary. She did not tell him everything, of course, she could not bear to tell him of her rape – that was too embarrassing to talk of to any man, even her father. But she told him how happy she had been at first with Sam, how close they had been on the voyage; she told of the birth of Oceanus and the pleasure of spending so much time with him, of her arrival at Long Bay and the strangeness of being constantly surrounded by so many black people, of the lack of privacy in a house deliberately designed to let the air flow between rooms with few if any doors and full to bursting point with so many members of the family living there. She told him of the whistling tree frogs and the bell that tolled every morning at half past five to call the slaves to work, of Francine and the girl's loyalty and dedication,

"I wish I could have given Francine her freedom, Papa, but it was not mine to give. She did not belong to me."

She told him of the early morning rides with Sam, and the terrible things she had seen – the vicious punishment of slaves for the slightest misdemeanour, the black man with the split nose who had risen up in front of her horse and frightened her, and the time Bathsheba had insisted that she, Lucy, give the order for a slave to be whipped for breaking china. Weeping again, she struggled to tell him of the outbreak of measles which had killed Oceanus and the guilt she felt for not having been able to nurse him herself owing to her pregnancy, and the fact that little Emma had been born as her lovely son was being buried.

She told him of the strained and feverish atmosphere among the slaves following the New Orleans riots, and the conspiracy she had suspected and informed Bathsheba about. She told of her friendship with Mary Kingsley and Sam's sisters Betty and Mary, and the boredom, loneliness and disappointment that resulted from having little to do and no household of her own to run.

At this point, Thomas – who had listened patiently, trying as best he could to piece everything together from what was a far from coherent tale – intervened, "But Lucy, I do not understand. Samuel had plans to build a house for the two of you; are you saying this never happened?"

"No, Papa. He insists he will only live at Long Bay, but that belongs to John now, since Sam sold his share to buy his passage to England, and John would not give Sam the land or the workforce to build his house until their revenues were greater. Cotton is not as profitable as sugar, you see, and John wants to be able to invest in a sugar plantation to put their finances on a sounder footing, and would not give Sam what he wanted until then."

Thomas' frown deepened. "The settlement I made on you was easily large enough to allow him to build a house or, I would guess, to buy a small plantation and live there. What has happened to that money, Lucy?"

So Lucy had to tell her father of Sam's propensity for gambling (of which, of course, Thomas was already aware) and the tension between the brothers.

"Are you telling me that he has wasted the whole of your dowry, Lucy?" Thomas asked sharply.

"No, Papa, I do not think he has wasted all of it, but John insists that he plough at least part of it into the family estate to help increase the revenues before Sam can have what he wants."

She could not bring herself to tell her father of the money Sam had taken from the estate's funds to pay off his gambling debts, creating even more bad blood between him and John, but Thomas was astute enough to read between the lines. He grunted but said no more; the frown now a permanent fixture on his face.

Lucy started to tell him about Sunbury and the friendship of the Barrows to turn his mind to other matters, but Thomas would not be diverted.

"And what did you do in all of this, Lucy? It is not in your nature to sit quietly by and allow things to happen to you, you were never afraid to take up the cudgels!"

He smiled wryly, remembering past battles with a stubborn and often wayward daughter, whether it was over the advent of her governess or, indeed, her decision to marry Samuel Hall Lord.

"I tried to reason with John. And I came up with the idea that we should both take a detailed interest in the running of Long Bay, Sam in the plantation and I in the house. I thought that way John, Mrs Lord – Sam's mother – and Sarah –

John's wife – would become so irritated at our intervention that they would all be happy to get rid of us!"

For the first time Thomas laughed out loud. "You little minx! Yet it does not appear to have had the desired effect. Why not?"

Lucy's face, which had lit up in response to his laughter, grew serious once more. "I… I became ill," she stammered, "and… and Sam thought it was all taking too long and grew restless, and lost money at cards which angered me and so… and so…" She bit her lip and her voice trailed off as she realised, she was about to blurt out the truth about Sam's behaviour.

"Did he beat you, Lucy?" her father asked abruptly. Lucy nodded, sadly, her eyes still cast down. "Frequently?" he probed.

Lucy nodded dumbly, her face red with embarrassment, afraid to say a word in case she blurted out the whole dreadful truth.

"There is more, isn't there?" her father asked gently. And when the bent head nodded again, he sighed and stroked her hair. "No doubt you will talk more freely to your mother about that," he said shrewdly, reading accurately between the lines. "Do you wish to leave your husband?"

At that, Lucy tried to compose herself. She sniffed loudly, in a most unladylike fashion, and blew her nose hard, mopping her eyes with her damp handkerchief.

"I… I don't know, Papa. I still love Sam, he can be very good company – indeed, quite delightful – but sometimes I can't bear it. I believe that if he can build his house, he will have enough to occupy him so that he does not fly into a rage so frequently. He… he threw me in the cellar once, the one they use to punish the slaves. Then I really did think I wanted to leave him. But how would I live? Where would I live? You have already paid out a generous settlement for me…"

Her voice trailed off. Thomas Wightwick looked like a thundercloud. He had been concerned about Lucy's entanglement with Sam Lord, but mainly because he thought Sam was a fortune hunter who would waste Lucy's dowry. Of course, it was every husband's right to beat his wife when it suited him, but he had hoped to find a kind husband for his beloved daughter, whose notion of disciplining her for her impetuosity and fiery spirit would be in the form of a gentle rebuke rather than physical punishment. But Thomas was in a quandary; he knew his wife would not look kindly on Lucy abandoning her husband and child, and he did not have the wherewithal to set Lucy up in comfort in England. She was married, she was now her husband's problem… except she was not, she was still his dearest daughter, and he did not wish to see her unhappy.

Thomas sighed and stood up. "Well, my dear, we are not going to resolve this problem today. Baines has arranged for us to stay at The White Lion for the night. Your trunk should already be there. We shall set off early in the morning for Hewelsfield."

Lucy smiled tremulously, gave a final sniff, and put on her pelisse and hat. The hotel on Broad Street was only a short stroll from Mr Wightwick's place of business, so they walked there arm-in-arm enjoying the warm evening as Lucy's cheeks cooled and she became calmer.

The roads were nowhere near as busy as when Lucy had first arrived; this was primarily a place of trade, and while some small merchants and shipwrights lived there the main residential areas were away from the often-unpleasant smell of the port. They passed two or three public houses, and these were indeed busy, full of extremely drunk men and women whose clothing and behaviour were almost indecent. With sudden sadness, Lucy thought that Sam was probably already consoling himself for her absence by visiting just such women in Bridgetown – although the women there would be more likely to be black or mulatto.

No more was said about Lucy's situation that night. Father and daughter had a light supper of steak pie washed down with porter before retiring to bed. Of the four beds in Lucy's room, one was already occupied by a woman of uncertain age who appeared to have removed only her hat and boots before getting under the covers and who was already snoring stertorously. Lucy was already in her nightgown and washing her face in the cold water provided when another woman arrived. They nodded politely to each other, but neither was inclined to talk. Lucy dried her face, tied a lace nightcap over her short hair and having inspected the sheets to ensure that they were clean, crawled into her bed. She ached all over with tiredness and, despite the emotional turmoil her discussion with Thomas had aroused, and the loud snores emanating from one of her companions, Lucy was soon sound asleep.

She awoke at first light and, having used the chamber pot, went to the door to find a chambermaid to bring fresh water for washing, but there was no-one to be seen. Lucy eyed the water remaining from the previous night, poured the stale contents of the ewer into her chamber pot and used what remained in the pitcher to wash the sleep out of her eyes. She dressed in the same travel-stained garments she had worn yesterday, corded up her trunk and went downstairs to find her father.

Thomas was already discussing a hearty breakfast of beef and ale, but Lucy contented herself with an apple and some coffee. While her father settled the bill and oversaw Lucy's trunk being strapped onto their carriage, Lucy stood in the courtyard revelling in the gentle, early morning sun of an English summer.

The horses set off at a trot on the twelve-mile journey to Redwick, on the banks of the Severn just beyond Pilning, where they would embark, coach and all, on the ferry crossing to Portskewett. They took the Aust toll road, through Westbury and thence eastwards towards Pilning. The road was good, far smoother than the narrow limestone roads Lucy had become used to in Barbados. Since the weather was fine, they reached Pilning within an hour and a half despite having to stop at the turnpikes, and the pair of horses pulling the carriage then picked their way along the lane leading to New Passage.

Lucy was more than happy to alight there to stretch her legs, and they had not long to wait before the ferry approached the bank and the work began to manoeuvre a mail coach and her father's carriage on board. The mail's dozen or so passengers had also alighted so the small craft was heavily laden when it set off, and Lucy was relieved that the weather was fine. Harking back to some of the journeys she had made in previous years, under pouring rain and gale force winds, she knew she would not have been foolhardy enough (nor her father either) to attempt to cross on the same ferry as a full mail coach. As it was, some forty-five minutes later the passengers were all disembarking at Black Rock and waiting for the laborious process of disembarking their conveyances to take place.

They set off at a brisk trot along the narrower roads through Portskewett, into Chepstow and across the bridge northwards toward Hewelsfield. Lucy looked out of the window at the familiar countryside, the fields busy with workers gathering in the last of the harvest, grateful for the warm, dry weather which should spell abundant crops this year. She was hungry now and wished she had eaten more for breakfast – which seemed a very long time ago; her father had his nose buried in the newspaper, apparently oblivious to any hunger pangs.

As they drew closer to Hewelsfield, Lucy's thoughts turned to the reception she might expect, and she grew nervous. What if her mother were not pleased to see her? What if she disapproved of Lucy leaving her husband to give birth to her next child here rather than in Barbados? She had never responded to Lucy's suggestion that the children should be brought up in England, and Lucy was uncomfortably aware that her mother was more likely than her father to side with Sam's view of what her behaviour should be. The hunger vanished and she began to feel a little sick.

As they came to Woolaston Common, she broke the silence. "Papa, what does Mama think about my coming back?"

Mr Wightwick put down his newspaper and looked at his daughter over his *pince-nez*. She was looking rather wild he thought, and worried that she might be about to fall into a fit of hysterics. "Why, Lucy, she will be delighted to see you. You know she is very fond of you, she moped after you for months when you left for Barbados. Not that she ever said as much, but she was quite short-tempered and kept looking around as if she expected you to be there when she was going about her household duties."

"And Stubbs? Will I recognise my little brother? He will be eighteen years old this year – a young man already."

"Indeed he is. He has recently completed his matriculation at Trinity and is now off enjoying life with a group of choice spirits I know not where!" her father answered.

"Then no doubt he will come home when his pockets are to let," Lucy responded with a smile. "I look forward to seeing him again."

Not entirely soothed by her father's description of her mother's feelings, Lucy fell quiet again, twisting her gloved fingers together continually. Thomas, meanwhile, had put aside his paper and was sitting forward in his seat, eagerly looking out of the window. He always enjoyed returning home to Hewelsfield – indeed, despite merely being a tenant, he felt it to be 'home' far more than any of the properties in Staffordshire he owned through his wife.

As Hewelsfield church hove into view he gave a satisfied little sigh and beamed at his daughter. "Welcome home, Lucy!" he said, with feeling.

Lucy smiled back, but her heart was beating very fast, and her palms inside the gloves were damp. Still, it was too late now to have any misgivings. What was done was done, and even if her mother disapproved and shut her away at Hewelsfield, that was a far better option than constantly living in fear of being beaten or thrown in a cellar.

She could see the house now. It looked warm and welcoming in the August sunshine, and Lucy took a deep breath, sat up straight and smoothed down her crumpled pelisse. When they drew up at the front door, her father jumped down from the carriage without waiting for the steps to be let down and ran up the steps to the front door, sounding a loud 'rat-a-tat-tat' on the knocker. Lucy hung back, and took her time descending the steps. She checked her bonnet was straight, once again smoothed down the pelisse, and moved towards the house just as the door was opened by a maid she did not recognise. When she reached her father, he put an arm around her shoulder and introduced her,

"Prudence, this is my daughter, Lucy. She is come to stay with us a while, all the way from the West Indies. Please make her room ready and see to it that her trunk is taken up and unpacked."

Prudence sketched a curtsey, and Thomas handed her his hat, cane and overcoat while Lucy unbuttoned her pelisse and removed her gloves, handing these, also, to the maid.

Lucy glanced down at her dress and grimaced. Two months at sea did nothing to improve the looks of anyone's clothing. Mrs Wightwick – like Bathsheba Lord – would be neat as a new pin, and Lucy would feel positively dowdy by comparison which would do nothing for her confidence. Plus the fact, she thought ruefully, that even with a shawl artfully draped across her elbows, at five months her pregnancy would quickly become clear to a mother's sharp eyes, even if her father had seemingly not noticed.

But when her mother bustled into the parlour, alerted to her husband and daughter's arrival by Prudence, she surprised Lucy by coming straight up to her and enfolding her in a warm embrace. Lucy could remember only a very few occasions in her life when her mother had shown any emotion, and it did much to calm the butterflies in her stomach even if it did make tears – resolutely blinked away – well in her eyes once more.

"Welcome, daughter, how kind of Mr Lord to spare you to us for a visit. I had thought your ship was not expected until next week, you must have encountered favourable winds?" to which Lucy nodded. "Well, you are both arrived in time for dinner, so I must go and talk to Cook about changing the menu. Do you wish to rest, Lucy?"

"No, Mama, I am not tired. But I would dearly like a bath, if that were possible?"

"I will send two of the girls up to your room – it is your old room – with cans of water as soon as it has boiled," Mrs Wightwick promised. "And after dinner you can tell me all your news, I am sure that you have already shared some of it

263

with your father on the journey here, and I mean to catch up! Your letters and sketches were very welcome, but I would liefer by far hear it all directly from you."

While speaking, Mrs Wightwick had moved across to her husband, to be embraced by him in turn. Now she removed herself from the circle of his arm, nodded at both and made her way toward the kitchen, presumably to speak to Cook and order up the water for Lucy's bath.

As the adrenalin stopped pumping through her veins, Lucy suddenly felt weary. She crossed to where her father was standing by a window, fiddling with the curtain sash and frowning slightly, hugged him awkwardly and turned away to go upstairs, pulling off her bonnet as she went.

Two young maids Lucy did not know laboured up the servants' staircase with water for her bath, bobbing little curtsies to her as best they could laden down with the heavy buckets. She smiled tiredly at them and murmured "thank you", briefly startled when they smiled back at her and one of them said, "Welcome home, miss." She had become used to slaves who dared not speak unless spoken to, trained never to look the white man in the face. She asked the girls their names, Mary and Ruth.

"Shall I come back after your bath, Miss Lucy, to help you dress?" asked Ruth. Lucy hesitated, in a quandary. If Ruth helped tighten her stays, the news that she was pregnant would be all around the servants' quarters within a few minutes, and from there would reach her mother's ears. But she could not fasten them without help either, so she decided to accept the inevitable.

She felt revived by her bath, and when Ruth tapped gently on her door to seek re-admittance, Lucy was already arrayed in bloomers and chemise. She held out the stays and Ruth tugged hard on the strings while Lucy held tightly to the dressing-table. The girl stopped suddenly and Lucy looked up at the mirror, watching the face behind her.

"Yes, Ruth, I am with child. Now, I know that is big news for you to spread among the servants, but please allow me to tell my mother first, I have not had a chance to speak to her yet. Will you give me your word not to say anything until tomorrow?"

"Yes, miss. Oooh – Cook will be pleased. She often tells stories of when you and Mr Stubbs was children, miss!"

At that Lucy laughed. "I think we must have been the bane of her life! I know I was forever stealing her apple pie, or warm bread, or hunks of cheese and apples from her pantry!"

While they completed Lucy's toilette, she asked Ruth to tell her about the household since she had been away so long. It appeared only Cook and the housekeeper, Mrs Wardle, remained of the former house staff, and Lucy made a mental note to visit them both once she had talked to her mother.

"I am not sure whether many of my clothes are in a fit state to be worn, Ruth. They must all be laundered and then we shall decide. Will you see to it?"

Nodding to the girl, who bobbed another curtsey, she went along the passageway and tapped on her mother's door. As expected, Mrs Wightwick was putting the final touches to her own toilette, she dismissed her maid and turned from the mirror to look at her daughter, who sat down on the edge of the bed.

Lucy started plaiting the tassels of the bed drapes and looked up to find her mother's eyes upon her. She blushed guiltily, feeling like a naughty little girl again, caught in some childish mischief. "No," she castigated herself angrily, "I am a grown woman now. I have done nothing wrong. My mother should welcome the news that I am to have a child soon." She tossed her head and with a hint of defiance looked straight at her mother, who had said not a word.

"I am with child, Mama," Lucy stated baldly. "I will be brought to bed in November."

"Is Mr Lord aware of this happy event?" she asked stiffly.

Ruefully, Lucy thought that she should have expected her mother to get straight to the point. She had hoped to avoid admitting that she had not told her husband before her departure, because that would lead to other unwelcome questioning. But perhaps, after all, it was as well for the truth to come out now, she had already told her father far more than she had intended and he would discuss all with Mama.

"No, Mama. I was barely four months gone when I left Barbados…"

"Then you must write to apprise him of it. I am sure we would welcome him here on a visit also, and he may then accompany you on your return. I do not like to think of you putting yourself in harm's way by travelling the oceans alone, Lucy. It is very dangerous, one hears every week of English ships being attacked by our enemies."

Lucy bit back a caustic comment to the effect that she was probably safer at the mercy of French privateers than she was in her husband's house. She must win her mother over to her point of view.

"Mama, did you receive my letter suggesting that it might be best for our children to be brought up in England? There are so many diseases rife in the West Indies, and I could not bear to lose another child as I did Oceanus."

"I did receive it, Lucy, and was a little surprised. You did not seem to have thought the idea through very thoroughly, so I doubt you had discussed it with your husband. You always were impetuous, but I thought marriage might cure you of that. First of all, it is a great financial and care burden to lay on us, and neither your Papa nor I are getting any younger. How long would you expect them to remain here, living at our and your brother Stubbs' expense? Or is Mr Lord willing to provide us with an allowance for their upbringing? Besides, the children would have no knowledge of their parents, or of their true home and heritage, Barbados. And there is no saying but what they might succumb to disease here, or once they eventually arrived in Barbados. Unless you can advance some very good arguments as to why I should consider your idea further, I consider the matter closed."

Lucy looked at her mother in despair. How could she make her understand how unhappy her life in Barbados had been? And, even if she did, would Mama not simply tell her that she had made her own bed and now must lie in it? She would try one more roll of the dice…

"And what if I stayed in England too, to look after the children? They would then grow up at least knowing one of their parents…"

"Has that been your intention all along, girl? To remain here indefinitely with your child? No, Lucy. Your place is at your husband's side now. Moreover, that would merely add to the expense to us of bringing up your offspring. Naturally I am delighted to have you visit, and you may stay until after the lying in and return with your husband to Barbados next year, and that should be an end to it. Now, we should go down and join your father for dinner before it is spoiled, or I shall be in for a scold from Cook."

The last was said with finality, and Lucy accepted defeat, at least for now, sliding off the bed and opening the bedroom door for her mother to pass through. Perhaps, if she let Papa speak to Mama and tell her what he had learned from Lucy, Mama might look more kindly on her daughter and unborn grandchild remaining indefinitely in England, but it appeared to be a slim hope.

Over dinner, with the servants bustling in and out, the conversation stayed on safe topics such as Lucy's general observations of Barbados. She had written about them, of course, but both her parents wished to hear at first hand her descriptions of the green monkeys, the whistling tree frogs and the flora of the island.

"Tell us about the great houses, and plantation society, Lucy," Mrs Wightwick requested.

"The houses are of very different construction from ours, Mama. They are far smaller, for one thing, it was a great surprise to me when I first arrived. Most are not even as large as Hewelsfield, and there is nothing to compare with any of the English great houses. Of course, the slave quarters are situated at some little distance from the main house, and the kitchen is constructed separately to avoid the risk of fire. But in general the bedrooms number no more than four to six. And there are very few doors, in order for the air to circulate as much as possible because it is frequently uncomfortably warm. So downstairs, there is only the front door, a door out to the back leading to the kitchen (and that is generally open also) and a door to the plantation office – a bit like your study, Papa."

Shortly after this, the conversation switched to political matters, without Lucy having admitted how little she went about in society in Barbados. And there was much to discuss, and to bring Lucy up to date on: the assassination of the Prime Minister on the 11th of May, in the actual Lobby of the House of Commons, by a man called John Bellingham; America declaring war on Britain; the continued turmoil in France and the Duke of Wellington's battles against Napoleon's brother in Spain.

Lucy realised with hindsight how rarely such discussions took place among the Lords, generally being considered matters for the men only there, and she revelled in being able to ask questions and put forward her opinion. She felt as though her brain had shrivelled and lain dormant and was now beginning to put forth green shoots again, no longer starved of nourishment.

The next few days continued warm and pleasant, and Lucy delighted in revisiting her favourite childhood places around Hewelsfield, though surprised that she had not remembered how small the village was. She accompanied her mother to church on Sunday and was introduced to the new rector. While Mrs Wightwick was talking to a couple of her acquaintances, Lucy slipped away to greet the big, old yew tree which she had so loved to climb as a little girl. She smiled wistfully, she was already beginning to feel cumbersome in her pregnancy, and doubted she could scramble up it anymore, even if she had been unencumbered by petticoats and no-one had been there to see her do so and be scandalised.

At luncheon, her mother reminded Lucy that she should write to Sam to inform him that he was to be a father again.

"And I am sure, Mr Wightwick, that we would welcome Mr Lord on a visit to us at the end of the year? He could then accompany Lucy and take care of his family on the return journey to Barbados."

Lucy looked in her father's direction but failed to catch his eye. She had hoped he would broach the subject of Sam's beatings with her mother, but either he had not yet done so or her mother was unmoved by whatever he had said. So, once the meal had ended, Lucy accompanied her mother to the parlour while Mr Wightwick shut himself away in his study.

Lucy sat down at the table and started sharpening the two quill pens handed to her by her mother, while the latter looked out paper and wafers.

"I shall write to Mr Lord inviting him to spend Christmas here at Hewelsfield with us, Lucy, while you can break the news to him that you expect to be brought to bed in November."

"Mama – he has not always been a kind husband," Lucy blurted out. She hurried on, fearing her mother would interrupt, or that she herself might falter in the telling. "He beat me. He ffforced himself upon me… he llllocked me in the dark in the cellar without water…"

She was stammering now, and the tears were coursing down her cheeks as they had when she had told some of the tale to her father in Bristol.

Her mother turned, and her brows twitched together.

"What caused him to behave in this fashion? Did this happen often? You know, Lucy, that I have often deplored your tendency to be outspoken and obstinate in a way that is unlikely to find favour with even the most indulgent husband…"

"It happened when he was drunk, or had lost money at cards, or was feeling irritated by almost anything," interrupted her daughter. "If John, his brother, reiterated his refusal to set aside a piece of land for Sam to build his mansion, he would get into a rage and frequently take it out on me – or go gambling and whoring in Bridgetown…"

She got no further as Mrs Wightwick slapped her cheek hard.

"You are not to use such language in my house – nor, I should hope, anywhere! If you spoke to your husband in this way and took him to task, I am not surprised he beat you. But it would seem your father's concerns about Mr Lord's excesses were well-founded. If you had but listened, you might have given more weight to our reluctance to permit you to marry a potentially inveterate gambler. But remember, daughter, in your usual impetuous fashion, you married Mr Lord without our approval and now you must find a way to make the marriage work."

By this time Lucy was sobbing unrestrainedly and her mother could not help feeling sorry for her. She sighed and sat down next to her daughter, taking possession of one of her hands and patting it gently until the paroxysm of grief eased, when she stood and moved towards a side-table containing several decanters and glasses. She poured Lucy a small glass of Madeira wine and waited while she sipped it, mopped her eyes and blew her nose.

"I think you had best tell me this tale from the beginning," Mrs Wightwick said, in a gentler tone than she had used thus far.

And so Lucy told her of the voyage across to Barbados, of Sam's care for her during the passage, of their closeness and his pride in their son Oceanus. She told of her arrival at Long Bay and her shock at discovering that Sam owned no part of the estate, that he was a penniless younger son but for the dowry Lucy brought with her, and that she was merely another mouth to feed in an already crowded household, although Oceanus' existence meant she was tolerated. She told of her growing boredom and frustration at not being mistress of her own household, and of Sam's frustration at not being able to build the mansion he craved but, equally, of his obstinacy in not accepting the notion of going elsewhere. She spoke warmly about Francine's devotion to Oceanus, and her care for Lucy when Sam beat or raped her, although even with her mother she did not feel comfortable describing in detail Sam's behaviour.

Lucy told of the horrific brutality meted out to slaves. She told of her friendship with Sam's sisters, Mary and Betty, and with Mary Kingsley and the Barrows, but also of the lack of social life driven, apparently, by Sam's mother's fear of being shunned by the other planters for being thought of as mixed race. Very quietly, the tears again coursing down her face unheeded, she told the harrowing details of Oceanus' death and his sister Emma's birth, as well as Lucy's own subsequent illness. She told of her efforts to help her husband achieve his dream and of his violent reaction to her remonstrations when he wasted their funds on gambling, their argument over where to raise their children which led to her shameful incarceration in the cellar – which was the final straw that made her determined to return to England.

By this time, dusk was falling and neither Lucy nor her mother had written their letters.

"Well, Lucy, you have given me a lot to think about. At the end of the day, it was your choice to marry Mr Lord. You know how much importance I attach to the sanctity of marriage and I have no wish to see you shame our family. You have no independent income and your Papa has already been more than generous – you can expect no more money and must find a way to channel your husband's energy into providing a home and future for you and your children. I feel sure Papa will be able to suggest a legal method to help ensure this, but you will need to deliver it.

"Now, we will leave our letters to your husband until tomorrow – and I shall also write to Nurse, to see if she would come back to help us with the new baby. It is possible she is too old and will not feel able to, but I think it more likely she will pack her bags to come to us as soon as she receives my letter!

"Upstairs with you Lucy, bathe your face and change your dress before supper. You will not wish your Papa to see you as you are now."

Having unburdened herself of the full story of the past four years, and believing that she had won at least a degree of sympathy from her mother for it, Lucy felt immensely relieved and that night she slept better than she had in a long time, untroubled by dreams. She awoke long after her father had left for Bristol, her mother having left instructions with the maid that her daughter was not to be woken.

When she did finally descend the stairs, Lucy found her mother hard at work polishing the silver with one of the housemaids. Silently, she joined them, and by the time they stopped for luncheon they were surrounded by a variety of glistening tureens, mirrors, candlesticks and *épergnes*. After lunch Lucy insisted on donning her pattens and pelisse to walk briskly around the village, despite the fact that the weather had turned and a soft rain was falling.

Invigorated by this activity, she meekly acquiesced to her mother's diktat that she write to Sam. It was a short missive.

Husband: I shall be brought to bed of our child in November or December. My Mother writes separately to you to invite you to stay here with us for Christmas should you wish to see it.

I hope and pray that all is well with you and the family. Please give my especial regards to Betty and to Mary, and kiss little Emma for me.

Your Loving Lucy

Silently, she handed this – unfolded – to her mother, knowing that Mrs Wightwick would want to read it anyway. Her mother scanned it, nodded, and placed it within her own invitation (which she did not show to her daughter), affixing a wafer to the whole before wrapping it in waxed paper to withstand the sea voyage, and sealing the package with more wax.

Lucy was firmly of the view that Sam would be unable or unwilling to find the funds for his passage, which would relieve her of any responsibility, and she was able to look forward with tranquillity to the next few months. She felt better and more energetic than she had in at least two years despite the pregnancy, and happily entered into her mother's household activities.

Some two weeks later, her father returned one day with the mail which included a letter from Mary Austin, Sam's older sister. Surprised but pleased, she tore it open.

Dearest Sister

I do hope your voyage was pleasant and that you arrived safely at your Parents' house. I am writing to inform you that we had a joint Baptism on 25 July: your daughter, Emma, together with my little Lucy Wightwick, named as you know in your honour! I made sure you would not object; indeed, I do hope you will be pleased. You know how fond of you both I and my husband, Richard, are.

I wish I had your talent at drawing, but I can only tell you in words how little Emma does. She is still a little sickly, but she crawls very fast now she is in short petticoats and has begun to pull herself up to standing whenever she can, even trying to walk. Sam sees her every day he is at Long Bay, and she is very fond of him.

Please do paint some pictures of your Parents' home and the surrounds: it would please me very much to know what it is like.

I look forward to seeing you again next year, when Sam says he shall return with you.

With fondest love
Your Sister, Mary

Lucy read and re-read the short letter several times; she had been very touched that Richard and Mary had decided to name their daughter after her. Indeed, her eyes stung with tears at the idea that anyone in Sam's family would be so thoughtful.

On the other hand, she was not sure what to make of Mary's last comment regarding Sam. Secretly, she had believed that her husband would not be able to command the money to pay for his passage to England, but it appeared that he was determined to come, even though he could not yet know that Lucy was pregnant again as her letter would not arrive for at least four weeks. Since her return to the parental home, Lucy had felt safe; the news that Sam appeared likely to come after her even before Mrs Wightwick's invitation had been issued frightened her a little, but she also felt a little *frisson* of excitement. Despite everything that had passed, the tug of attraction was still strong.

"I understand you received a letter today," her mother remarked at dinner. "What news does it contain?"

"It was from dear Mary Austin, Sam's older sister. She wrote to tell me that her daughter and mine were baptised together in July. I am not sure if I told you that she named her daughter Lucy Wightwick, after me! You will be pleased, Papa, that the Wightwick name will be continued even beyond these shores."

Her parents exclaimed suitably, and Lucy avoided mentioning anything about the fact that Sam looked certain to come to England – indeed, might already be on his way.

Chapter 14
To the Lords, a Daughter

Towards the end of September, once all the fruit had been harvested and the preserves prepared for winter, Lucy accompanied her parents on a visit to Great Bloxwich in order to re-acquaint herself with her mother's family. Her brother Stubbs was there, about to go up to Oxford again to continue his studies. Brother and sister were almost strangers to each other now, both because Lucy had been absent for almost four years but also because of the difference in their ages. Stubbs had been a schoolboy of fifteen and she a grown woman of twenty-three when last they met; he was now a young man studying the law and enjoying university life while she was a very pregnant matron of twenty-seven who had already given birth to two children of her own. His future lay in the world of work as a lawyer and following in his father's footsteps running the family estate; hers was expected to lie in the far more confined one of home-making and child-rearing, albeit on the other side of the world. Lucy envied his independence and freedom and had little in common with Stubbs.

Lucy and her mother returned to Hewelsfield in the second week of October for Lucy's confinement. Mrs Wightwick was not about to let her daughter be jolted over bad winter roads so late in her pregnancy, because it could too easily lead to her going into labour early or, indeed, to losing the baby. It was also usual for women to remain closeted at home for the last six weeks of pregnancy, both to ensure safe delivery but also because it was not considered proper for heavily pregnant women to be seen in public.

Unable to go about much beyond the village church, Lucy began to keep her journal again, and to write numerous letters. She had already responded to Mary Austin, thanking her for naming her daughter Lucy Wightwick, now she set about responding to her request for paintings of Hewelsfield, producing several pencil sketches of the mellow old house and the ancient church with its beautiful tree. Lucy also wrote to the Barrows, informing them that she would soon be having another child, and to Mary Kingsley and to Betty. She rekindled her friendship with Annabel (now married and living in Yorkshire with two children of her own), and they corresponded with one another every week. And she wrote to Miss Kilmer and to her own old governess, Miss Priddy.

As November came, Lucy became increasingly lethargic and even stopped walking the few hundred yards to the church. She tried to take an interest in knitting, or sewing, with tiny stitches, new baby garments as her mother took great pleasure in doing so once the evenings drew in, and she was keen to keep her mother on side.

In mid-November, old Nurse arrived in the dog cart, having travelled by boat down the canal from Merthyr Tydfil. She had moved there to live with her son, his wife and their three children in a tiny house in appalling conditions on the edge of a town which had grown exponentially over the past forty years as a result of the ironworks. The boat took her to Taffs Well where she had been given a lift on a dray (which she complained jolted her old bones) almost all the way to the bustling coal town of Newport. There she stayed overnight with her sister's family, and the following morning her nephew gave her a lift to Chepstow on his waggon where he left her at a respectable inn, the Three Tuns, in front of the castle, and ensured a message was sent to the Wightwick household at Hewelsfield, in order that the dog cart might be sent to fetch her.

Nurse was now in her late sixties, wizened and wrinkled, and living on the meagre pension Mr Wightwick had provided for her. But while her physical strength was much reduced, her mind was as lively as ever, and she had responded with alacrity to the welcome suggestion that she leave the squalor of Merthyr Tydfil to assist with Miss Lucy's new-born, and be paid a regular wage for doing so.

She arrived only just in time, Lucy's waters broke and her pains began late in the evening of the 16th of November, and she began pacing her room like a caged bear, stopping every now and then to double over whenever one of the pains came. Her mother tried to persuade her to get into bed at once, but she preferred to stand and pace and only regretted the lack of birthing stool in common use in Barbados. As the pains became increasingly frequent, she permitted Mrs Wightwick and Nurse to push her gently onto her bed having removed some of her garments, and in the early hours of the morning of Tuesday, the 17th, Lucy gave birth to a healthy daughter.

It was only when Mrs Wightwick arose, late and heavy-eyed, that her maid brought her a note which had apparently been delivered at the end of the previous day. She broke the wafer and read a very civil message from her son-in-law,

14th November inst.
Dear Madam,
I have this instant arrived by the Falmouth Packet and am writing to beg leave to visit you and Mr Wightwick as soon as I may. I only hope and pray that you are presently residing at Hewelsfield, and not at Bath or Wolverhampton, but should I find you gone I shall scour the country for you as I am most desirous of seeing my Wife again. Life has been most empty without her, but I know that you have her in your safekeeping.

I hope that you and all the family are well. Please pass on my greetings to your Husband.

Yours Ever
Samuel Hall Lord

Mrs Wightwick folded the note up again and slipped it into her pocket, considering when she should tell her daughter that her husband would be arriving imminently, and long before he could possibly have received Lucy's note telling him she was with child or Mrs Wightwick's own letter inviting him to spend Christmas with the family. There was no telling how Lucy would react to the news, and her mother had no intention of upsetting her during her period of confinement. In her day, of course, this would have extended for a full six weeks, but there had been much debate of late years over whether this was truly best for mother and child, and her niece had been advised to be up and about and take gentle walks only a week after her lying-in. Doubtless Lucy would have her own notions; perhaps it would be best to leave telling her of Mr Lord's arrival in England when she began to get restless, unless he had by then knocked at their door.

She took out the letter again and looked at the date, the 14th of November. It was unlikely that he could or would go to the expense of hiring his own post-chaise, she thought. But if he travelled on the Mail, or hired a horse, he could reach Hewelsfield within a day or two, depending on the state of the river crossing.

Mrs Wightwick decided that she would need some support to ensure the reunion between husband and wife went smoothly, then sighed. Knowing how fond Lucy had been of her aunt, Elizabeth, she wished that that lady might have come to help; but Elizabeth had died the year Lucy left for Barbados. So Mrs Wightwick sat down to write to her sister Mary Slaney, asking her if she could please spare the time to come post-haste to Hewelsfield to help, as well as a letter to Thomas to inform him of the birth and of Sam's imminent arrival.

As with Oceanus, Lucy breastfed her new daughter from the start, a move accepted by her mother and Nurse without demur although the custom in Mrs Wightwick's day was to use a wet nurse – as in Barbados – or, at least, put the baby out to a foster mother after the first few months. However, neither would hear of Lucy leaving her room for the first week after giving birth, which roused her rebellious streak and made her fretful and frustrated.

On the Friday, Mary Slaney arrived in a flurry of valises in a hired post-chaise just in time for dinner. She insisted on seeing her new great-niece immediately, even before putting off her pelisse although she removed her fur muff and bonnet. Much to Mrs Wightwick's annoyance, she took Lucy's side in the matter of leaving her stuffy room (the windows had to remain tightly shut in the view of both her mother and Nurse) but expressed surprise and disapproval that Lucy should be breastfeeding.

"My dear Lucy, surely you are aware that you will be unable to breed again whilst feeding the child, and although it is delightful, it is not a son – and I am sure your husband will wish for sons!"

"My husband is not here, Aunt, and I took pleasure in feeding my firstborn – a son – throughout, as I shall do with this little one," and she stroked the baby's head tenderly. It was odd, she thought idly, how fiercely protective she felt about this daughter, while her motherly instincts seemed to vanish when Emma was born.

"Mr Lord not here? But I thought…" began Mary, puzzled, but stopped when she received a glare from her sister. She raised an eyebrow in surprise but decided she had better put herself in possession of all the facts before saying anything more.

"Will you be joining us for dinner, Lucy?" she said instead.

"If Nurse will help me get dressed, I shall certainly do so. I am heartily sick of eating in my room alone!"

The two ladies left Lucy to the ministrations of Nurse, who helped her wash and dress just as she had done when Lucy was a little girl. The baby was left in her cradle, asleep after feeding, and Nurse helped a slightly shaky Lucy descend the stairs for dinner.

In the meantime, Mrs Wightwick had apprised her sister of at least some of the background to Lucy's visit, and warned her that she had told her daughter nothing of Sam's letter.

"But Mr Lord could appear at any moment, and he has every right to see his wife and child!" expostulated Mary, who had some inkling that there was a whiff of scandal around the marriage of Sam and Lucy but remained unaware of the full story. "The fact that he was ungentle with her is neither here nor there. I have great sympathy for Lucy but there is nothing we can do."

"Of course not!" responded her sister, crossly. "I have no intention of preventing him seeing Lucy and the babe, but neither do I have any desire to give the wretched girl advance notice of his arrival if indeed her strength of feeling against him is as she described to me and to Mr Wightwick, since she is so headstrong she might take herself off somewhere to avoid him."

The sound of Lucy descending the stairs with Nurse cut short any further discussion, and over dinner the three ladies took great delight in a good gossip – Lucy, in particular, always found herself in a ripple of laughter over her aunt's comments, and was keen to hear updates on her cousins John, Morton and Honor, as well as society gossip and news of the war with America, in particular the activity of HMS Royal George (a twenty-gun wooden sloop) at the Battle of Lake Ontario and progress in the British blockade of South Carolina and Georgia.

Lucy was eating the last of an apple from the Hewelsfield orchard when all were startled by a loud knocking on the front door. It was not her father, he was not expected for at least another hour, possibly not until tomorrow. Who could it be?

A murmur of voices in the hall, then the door to the dining room was flung open and her husband, still attired in a greatcoat and mud-spattered boots, and dripping water from the crown of his hat, stood for a moment before striding into the room, punctiliously kissing the hands of Mrs Wightwick and Mary, then turning to his wife who sat stock still in her seat, the apple forgotten on her plate.

"Madam, forgive me for coming to you in all my dirt, but I was so eager to see you again." As he said this Sam kissed first Lucy's hand and then her cheek, and when she did not move, he gently brushed her lips with his.

Mrs Wightwick vigorously rang the little bell at her side and when a servant arrived, asked him to relieve Mr Lord of his wet coat and hat and to request the housekeeper to prepare a room for him immediately.

"Have you dined, Mr Lord? You are welcome to join us or, since we were just concluding our meal, we could withdraw and leave you to enjoy your repast alone if you prefer?"

"Ma'am, it is very kind of you. Indeed, I am famished, having ridden from Bristol, but I would prefer to eat after I have removed these boots and washed some of the mud from my person."

At that precise moment, the housekeeper entered and, curtseying to Sam, she told her mistress that his room could be ready almost immediately.

"And one of the men has taken your valise upstairs, sir," she said to Sam. "Shall I show you the way?"

Sam bowed again to the ladies and followed her out. Thus far, Lucy had not uttered a word, but when he left, she turned to her mother and said accusingly

"Did you know Sam was coming? Why did you not tell me? Had you written to tell him about the baby?"

Mrs Wightwick glanced at her sister before answering.

"I was aware that Mr Lord was in England. He wrote a letter, which arrived the day after your lying-in to say he had arrived. I did not know when he would reach Hewelsfield – there was no time for further correspondence and, indeed, he did not provide me with an address at which I could reach him. So, no, I have said nothing more to your husband than what you heard in this room. Are you not pleased to see him, Lucy?"

"No… yes… I do not know!" exclaimed Lucy on a sob. "I do not wish to see him today. I do not know what to say to him. I hope you have not given him an adjoining room…"

"It is I who am next door to you, Lucy, but I fear I do not understand your unease. He is your husband, whom you were happy to marry only a few years ago. Has something changed, dear?" her aunt Mary said this gently, tacitly complying with her sister's unspoken wish that Lucy believe her visit was spontaneous and nothing to do with Sam's arrival.

Lucy sighed. "A great deal has changed, Aunt. Mama has heard some of it, and no doubt will tell you all. I am very tired, and must see to the baby now, and perhaps things will be clearer in the morning. I shall take breakfast in my room, come and visit me then, and we can talk further. Good night, Mama." She kissed both her mother and her aunt, and quietly left the room.

Mary turned to her sister accusingly. "I think you had better tell me everything!"

"Let me but see to Mr Lord's needs and I will meet you in the drawing room for tea," responded a flustered Mrs Wightwick, ringing the bell again.

Some ten minutes later Mrs Wightwick joined her sister in the drawing room. The tea had arrived, and Mary – who had already served herself – made her sit down in a comfortable chair, gave her a cup of tea from the heavy silver tea urn, and handed her the macaroons. Mary, who was a vicar's wife, proved a sympathetic listener, and Mrs Wightwick poured out Lucy's sad tale. This took quite a while, and Mary refrained from asking questions until she had finished, merely moving to the fireplace occasionally to replenish it with coal.

"I am sincerely sorry for Lucy's plight, but what can I do? If only she had not been so headstrong and had heeded her father instead of rushing headlong into that runaway marriage, she would not be in this position. Mr Lord is her husband, and her place is with him – and, what is more, the children's place is with him! And he doesn't even know yet of the new baby," wailed Mrs Wightwick.

"Does Lucy wish for a divorce?" asked Mary abruptly, finally breaking her silence.

At the sound of slightly unsteady footsteps in the hallway, both ladies ceased speaking and looked up, but the footsteps passed the door and could then be heard on the stairs. Mr Lord had clearly finished his meal (and, no doubt, a large quantity of her stock of Bordeaux and brandy, thought Mrs Wightwick bitterly) and was on his way to his room.

Her sister repeated her question, lowering her voice.

"I do not know," sighed Mrs Wightwick. "I do not believe that Lucy is thinking clearly at the moment. I do hope she is not contemplating such a drastic step. Just think of the scandal!" She added inconsequentially, "Do you think I should check in on Mr Lord? What if he sets fire to the bedclothes with his candle? He sounded very drunk."

Mary soothed her, realising her sister was more upset than she had ever seen her, suggesting that she send up a manservant to check Mr Lord had everything he required for the night and to ensure the candle was placed safely out of reach of the bed curtains. She rang the bell, and when a maid responded it was Mary who asked her to fetch a manservant and, when he came, who gave the man the order.

"There is nothing more to be done tonight, Lucy," she advised her sister. "I will visit my niece in the morning as she suggested and see what I can find out. I doubt Mr Lord will be up early. And she must tell him that he has a new daughter. From what you have told me he will be pleased, I think, since Lucy said he is good with children."

The sisters mounted the stairs together. Mrs Wightwick went to her bed to toss and turn fretfully all night, wondering how this was going to end and wishing Thomas were there to advise her. Mrs Slaney sat down to dash off a brief letter to her husband, the Reverend Jonas Slaney, explaining that she would be needed at Hewelsfield rather longer than she had expected before she, too, sought her bed. She lay for a while considering her niece's predicament and what to say to her, then turned over and slept soundly until the maid brought her a cup of chocolate in the morning.

She washed her face and dressed quickly, pinning a shawl over her shoulders for the morning air was chilly, then quietly made her way next door to Lucy's room. She knocked gently, and the door was opened by Nurse, who dropped a curtsey and let her in. As she began bustling about, clearing away the bowl in which she had clearly been bathing the baby, Lucy spoke.

"Thank you, Nurse. That will be all for now. I wish to introduce baby properly to her great aunt."

Mary made a face. "Such an aging title, don't you think?" she said, as Nurse left the room. "How are you Lucy?"

Lucy was feeding the baby and took a moment to shift her from one breast to the other.

"I am not sure, Aunt. I have been better since I returned to England but seeing Mr Lord last night has put me into some turmoil. Did Mama know he was coming? Why could she not have warned me?"

"She knew Mr Lord was in the country but had no idea he would arrive here so soon," Mary responded carefully. "She did not want to upset you when you were still delicate."

"Well, I do not wish to see him," said Lucy pettishly.

"Now you are being silly," responded Mary calmly. "You know he has every right to see you, and to meet his new daughter – of whose existence he remains unaware. Why did you not tell him you were breeding before you left Barbados, Lucy?"

"Because he would not have let me come home, and I wanted to be sure that this baby had a good start in life. You know that my beloved Oceanus died over there?"

Lucy did not realise how easily she had slipped back into considering Hewelsfield, rather than Long Bay, home.

"Babies do die, Lucy, you know that. Look at your mother – she lost two, or was it three, of her children young, and that was here in England. To tell the truth, when you left for the West Indies, I thought I would never see you again. I think it was very good of your husband to let you return for a visit."

Mary was probing gently, trying to avoid asking a blunt question about Lucy's intentions, but hoping to find out if she was seriously thinking about divorce or when she planned to go back to Barbados.

Lucy fired up. "It was *not* very good of him! Did Mama tell you nothing of what I have been through? I could endure his cruelty no longer!"

Mary, who had perched on the edge of the bed, stood up and fetched the nursing chair from one corner to enable her to sit more comfortably.

"What can you be thinking, Lucy? You cannot stay here indefinitely, you know. Mr Lord is your husband. You should make a home together. From what I have heard, a lot of his behaviour may result from frustration. If you had your own household to run, you would not be bored, and he too would have far more to occupy him."

"That may be true, but Sam will not be moved from his dream of building a grand house – he calls it a castle – at Long Bay, and his brother John (who owns the estate) will not allow him the wherewithal to do so unless and until Sam contributes to the family fortunes rather than being a drain on them! He did show an interest in the running of the plantation when I persuaded him it would be politic to do so, but that did not last very long and he went back to his wild ways, drinking and gambling, beating me and… and… going with other women."

This last sentence was spoken in a very small voice, and Mary saw a tear slide down Lucy's cheek. She looked sadly up at her aunt.

"I did love him – so very much! I do still love him, but he makes it very difficult. I don't know what to do, Aunt."

Mary could not remain unmoved by the pathos of this little speech. To cover her emotion, and give herself time to think, she rose and took the now sleeping baby from Lucy's arms to return her to her crib. She sat down again, arranging her skirts.

"Every marriage goes through difficult moments, Lucy. You must learn to work through them, for doubtless there will be more arguments and stormy moments. The best outcome would be for you – and both your children – to live with your husband, their father. If you decide to take the extreme measure of a divorce, not only will it bring disgrace on our families and leave you far worse off financially, but it will also mean you lose your children, for Mr Lord will no doubt exercise his right to have both your daughters grow up with him in Barbados. And how will that make you feel?"

Lucy was sobbing now. "I could not bear it, Aunt. Oceanus can never be replaced, but this little one – well, I have as much tenderness for her as I did for him, and my heart is full. I do not know why, but I could never feel the same way about my other daughter, Emma. Indeed, she may be better off growing up with her cousins at Long Bay – but my heart would break were I to be parted from this child."

Mary sat down on Lucy's bed again and proffered a handkerchief. When her niece had mopped her eyes and blown her nose a few times, she drew Lucy's head to her shoulder, removed her cap and stroked the short, tousled hair soothingly. After a few strangled sobs, Lucy sat up, her face blotched and puffy, pleating and unpleating the damp handkerchief.

"Well, you have no need to take any momentous decisions for now," said Mary. "The first thing is to tell Mr Lord he has another daughter. Then perhaps he may be persuaded to stay at Hewelsfield for a while, and you may see whether you can deal better together in the future. Was he planning to spend much time in England, do you know?"

"I have no idea, Aunt. I knew he planned to come and fetch me, for his sister Mary wrote as much to me in a letter recently. But I know not how he came by the money for his passage, nor how he will fund any stay here – unless he has been unusually lucky at cards! I do know he will always be drawn back to Long Bay eventually, however."

"Then that is when we will need to take a decision on your future, and not before," said her aunt briskly. "Now, would you like your mother and I to break the glad news to him that he has another daughter? Then you can bring her downstairs to meet him later."

Lucy smiled in grateful assent, and her aunt kissed her on the cheek before turning away to seek her own breakfast.

The breakfast room was empty, for which Mrs Slaney was grateful, as she wanted time to consider what her niece had told her and what she should say to her sister. She ordered boiled eggs and coffee from the maid, who also brought some freshly baked rolls, and revelled in the luxury of being able to linger over her meal instead of hurrying away on household or parish duties.

There was still no sign of Mr Lord when she finished, so she went in search of her sister whom she found, as she expected, in the library doing the household accounts. She briefly summarised her discussion with Lucy, and Mrs Wightwick was considerably relieved that her daughter was not planning an immediate and messy showdown with Sam. She was feeling somewhat calmer this morning in any case as her husband – who should have returned the previous evening – must surely arrive soon and would be able to handle any unpleasantness that arose.

Mary amused herself by choosing *Emerson's Essays* at random from the shelves and settling down to read it while Mrs Wightwick continued working. They were interrupted once by the housekeeper coming in to discuss darning sheets, and shortly afterwards they heard voices in the hall and Mrs Wightwick dropped her quill and sped out to greet her husband.

To his surprise, she led him at once into the library and closed the door. Mary had stood up and he moved across to kiss her chastely on both cheeks, he was fond of his wife's sister, and always happy to welcome her to Hewelsfield.

Without any preamble, Mrs Wightwick announced, "Mr Lord is here. He arrived yesterday evening – indeed, we thought it might be you home early – and is still abed after a full bottle of wine."

"Has Lucy seen him?" enquired her husband.

"She was with us when he arrived. He came upon us as we finished dining. But she has had no conversation with him yet. And he does not know about the baby."

Thomas looked across at his sister-in-law, unsure how much she knew.

"Mary spent some time with Lucy this morning before breakfast and has spoken with her regarding what she plans to do," his wife reassured him.

"Thomas, it seems a shame to spring this upon you as you arrive home for a well-earned rest, but dearest Lucy begged me to come when she received a letter from Mr Lord announcing his imminent arrival. I understand that my niece has found married life – shall we say, less easy than she expected? And I do think she has some grounds for complaint," at which Thomas nodded.

"Well, then, I talked to her this morning and pointed out that Mr Lord has every right to insist on his children staying with him – she would be heartbroken to lose the new baby – and, indeed, to insist that she return to him. She certainly has not made up her mind to a divorce, thank Heaven. So, knowing your wife had already invited Mr Lord to spend Christmas here, I took it upon myself to propose he stay for a while so they may become reacquainted. It would be difficult for him to mistreat Lucy under her father's roof, and it may be that they will be reconciled."

Thomas looked from his wife Lucy to Mary and smiled.

"It would appear that you have arranged everything very well in my absence, then. Are you aware of Mr Lord's intentions yet? Does he plan a long stay, or does he intend to take Lucy and the babe back to Barbados as soon as may be?"

"We had very little discussion with him…" started Mrs Wightwick.

"And it is possible that he will change his plans when he knows about the child," interrupted Mary. "Would you be averse to him staying several months with you?"

"I am sure we can arrange somewhere, perhaps Great Bloxwich, for all three to reside for a while should he plan a long stay," responded Thomas. "And now, let me but wash my face and hands after the journey and we shall have a drink before luncheon."

As he left the room, they heard footsteps coming down the stairs; it was Sam.

"Ah – Mr Lord! What a pleasant surprise. I am sorry I was not here to greet you last night, but I am sure my wife made you welcome. I am but this moment come in from Bristol."

"Sir! It is a pleasure to see you again," said Sam bowing. "I am afraid I arrived with very little notice, although I wrote to Mrs Wightwick from Falmouth port as soon as I came ashore. I hope to spend some time in England with my wife, then accompany her back to Barbados."

"Come through to the parlour and have a glass of something. I shall be with you directly, as will the ladies," said Thomas, escorting him to the parlour door.

Mary joined Sam almost immediately, glad of an opportunity to assess for herself what kind of man he was for she had never met him except on his arrival the previous evening. She found him to be debonair and charming, apparently delighted to make her acquaintance.

Meantime, Mrs Wightwick followed her husband upstairs to tell Lucy that her father had returned, and that they were all gathering in the parlour before luncheon. Lucy brightened at the news and promised to be down as soon as she had finished feeding the baby and tidied her clothes.

By the time she joined the other four, the conversation was flowing merrily. Lucy kissed her father and permitted Sam to kiss her cheek and to sit by her. She was uncharacteristically quiet, but the tension gradually went out of her as the minutes ticked by and she listened to the chatter.

"I should like to propose a toast," said Mary when there was a lull. "I think you cannot yet know, Mr Lord, that congratulations are in order, you are a father again!"

Sam turned to Lucy in consternation. "Is this true, Lucy? But – I had no idea! When did this happen? Do I have a son or a daughter?"

The mixture of emotions on his face made Lucy smile for the first time.

"We have a daughter, Sam. I shall call her Cecilia. You shall meet her after luncheon. She was only born on Tuesday."

"But then – surely you should still be abed? Is it safe for you to be up and about so soon?"

"That is just what I said," intervened Mrs Wightwick. "But she will not hear of staying confined to bed any longer, and both the doctor and Mrs Slaney take her part."

"We plan on taking the greatest care of your wife and daughter, have no fear," chipped in Mary. "A gentle stroll in the fresh air will do her no harm. Perhaps you could walk with her after luncheon."

"First, I wish to see my daughter. Then I will gladly take you for a walk, Lucy, if that is what you would like?"

Really, Mary thought, Mr Lord seemed a very pleasant man, and it was difficult to comprehend the kind of behaviour Lucy had described; but there was no doubt that drinking could bring out the worst in a man and perhaps that, together with frustration, had caused him to be cruel. He was clearly delighted to have another child.

Mrs Wightwick stood, indicating that the meal was at an end. Sam smiled at Lucy.

"Will you take me to see our daughter? Cecilia, I think you said you wished to name her? I like it."

He offered Lucy his arm and they left the room together.

Lucy entered her bedroom quietly and, sure enough, Cecilia was asleep in her crib, looking angelic. Sam walked across to get a good look at her, and Nurse dropped him a slight curtsey and stood, hovering, as he bent over and gently stroked the baby's downy head with his forefinger. Cecilia stirred slightly but did not open her eyes. Watching them, Lucy felt all the love she had ever felt for Sam well up inside her again.

He turned to Lucy. "I should like to hold her, but do not want to wake her."

There was pleading in his eyes, and Lucy replied, smiling, "She will wake soon demanding to be fed again, so it does not matter. Nurse, please give Cecilia to her father."

Tenderly, Sam cradled the baby in his arms, and Lucy marvelled once more at the gentleness he showed with children. If only he had continued to show the same gentleness to her…

Snuffling slightly, the baby woke, knuckling her eyes. She looked up at Sam for a moment, then opened her mouth to wail, demanding food. Lucy settled herself on the nursing chair and held out her arms, and Sam walked over and handed her the baby. As she settled Cecilia on her breast, Nurse ran forward with a shawl and threw it over Lucy's shoulders, to maintain her modesty. She then walked firmly to the door and looked expectantly at Sam.

Lucy laughed. "Nurse does not approve of you being here when I am half naked, even though you are my husband. I think you had better leave us now."

"Shall I await you below? Then, when you are ready, we could go for that walk we discussed earlier."

"I should like that. Yes, please. I will join you shortly."

Once Cecilia was replete, Nurse took over once more and placed her in the crib where she fell asleep at once. Lucy straightened her dress and undergarments, put on her pelisse, found a hat and gloves and went downstairs to find her husband. He was in the library, leafing through the London papers which had not long been delivered, but he rose when he saw Lucy, collected his greatcoat, gloves and hat from the chair where he had placed them, donning them as they moved towards the front door. Lucy stopped to slip her feet into pattens, tied her bonnet on firmly so a gust of wind would not blow it away and stepped through the door which Sam had opened.

She stepped out briskly to demonstrate that she was not ailing and did not need to be closeted indoors or – even worse – confined to bed and smothered with covers. Sam took her arm and matched her pace.

"You will be back on a horse very quickly, I am sure!" he laughed. "Then we can resume our early morning rides and this time you shall introduce me to your land."

Lucy winced at the thought of sitting on a hard saddle so soon after giving birth, but she smiled, "Perhaps by next week I will be well enough, but I must ask Papa to procure me a horse. He sold mine when we left for Barbados. You rode here? Have you a good horse?"

The conversation continued in this way as they walked towards Hewelsfield church. They opened the lychgate and Lucy led the way to her favourite tree. She turned to Sam.

"Mary wrote to tell me our daughter was baptised with hers in July. What other news is there from Long Bay?"

"Mama is well and sends her best wishes. She will be pleased to have another granddaughter, will you write to her, Lucy, or shall I?"

Lucy indicated that he should, and Sam continued,

"My sister Sarah is no better, indeed I believe she is weaker than ever and almost fading before our eyes. Betty sends you her fondest love. She and John are keen for you to return home quickly, as am I."

Lucy looked up into the boughs of the ancient tree and thought nostalgically of the days when she wore short skirts and could scramble up to sit on a branch and watch out for her father's return. Her mind was in turmoil. Before Sam's arrival, she had pretty much convinced herself that she wanted them to live apart, although she shied away from the shame of a divorce. She thought of her friend Mary Kingsley, she had spent many months with her parents before finally re-joining her husband. This was what Lucy wanted. She took a deep breath.

"I cannot travel now, Sam. I think it will be many months before I return to Long Bay. I wish to ensure Cecilia is weaned before I even consider it."

"But – that could be as much as two years!" expostulated Sam. "Your place is at my side, Lucy, and I want you back in Barbados where you belong – as does our daughter."

"I do not want Cecilia to fall victim to the measles as Oceanus did, or to typhoid or cholera or... or any of the other diseases which are rife in the West Indies! She shall grow up here in England and be safe."

"Her place is at Long Bay," Sam repeated angrily. "I do not wish us to discuss this now. You are still in a delicate state following the birth of our daughter, and I comprehend your reluctance to go on a sea voyage with her – although our son did well while we were at sea…"

His voice trailed off, as he realised he was providing Lucy with fuel for her own side of the argument.

"We shall discuss this again, but not now. Your mother has invited me to stay at Hewelsfield for the Christmas period, and I have accepted. Are you tired? Shall we continue our walk, or return to your parents' house?"

Sam's manner since his arrival had won Lucy over and she had begun to relax in his company, but his burst of annoyance, and the way he shut down the conversation she had had to screw up her courage to begin, depressed her and made her wary of him once more. Despondently she turned toward home, tacitly agreeing that there was nothing to be gained by walking further.

It was a subdued Lucy who sat down to dinner as the late November daylight faded. As she had fed the baby, tried to take a short nap herself and written a letter to Mary Kingsley, her mind had kept returning to the question of what she should do, but she was no nearer to an answer. Would Sam's behaviour change once he had the castle he so desired, or was his violent nature incapable of change? If she left him would she be a pariah? What would be the effect on the children's lives? Should she tolerate the beatings for their sake? Would she be able to prevent Sam removing Cecilia from her care? If not, she did not think she could bear the aching loneliness. And how and where would she live apart from her husband? It had already been made clear that even her beloved Papa did not feel able to help her. She felt tired and dispirited and took little part in the dinner-table conversation until she heard her father ask a question about the state of business in Barbados.

"It has been a difficult year, sir. Our cotton at Long Bay is in, and the aloes have produced a good crop, but we have been hit by a typhoid epidemic and many of the sugar plantations struggled to finish their harvest because of the shortage of labour. The typhoid has decimated the slave community, so it will take some time for the workforce to recover. Those who have come through it will get better and their strength will return, but it will take a while for the next generation to replace those we have lost."

"And of course, you can no longer buy in slaves from elsewhere to replenish your stock. I shouldn't wonder if you have to buy in new indentured labour to fill the gap."

Lucy was surprised to hear even her father talk about the slaves as though they were cattle. She started to follow the conversation.

"Buying in new workers will increase the cost of production, and prices here will have to rise as a result. At Long Bay we will try to make do with what we have. We will move some of the house slaves who are young and fit to spend at least some of their time in the fields" – at which Lucy thought of Francine, and wondered whether the poor girl had already been set to the backbreaking work of picking cotton or harvesting aloe – "but others will doubtless need to replenish the workforce somehow. Some plantations will go under, but there are always buyers ready to take them on. My brother John was in discussion when I left with one of our neighbouring plantations with a view to purchasing it. You will know it, Lucy," he turned to her. "It is Pool which was owned by Mr Green."

"Did any of the family fall sick with typhoid?" Lucy asked.

"Since Martha died not one of us. The children had become somewhat unruly when I left as there are fewer slaves to watch over them, but they are all well."

"But does this epidemic not make you understand why I fear to bring up our children in Barbados, and wish them safe in England?" said Lucy in a low, passionate voice.

Mr Wightwick eyed her uneasily; he did not want Lucy to make a scene but she was perfectly capable of doing so.

"My dear, you know that we have terrible cases of typhoid and cholera in our English towns and cities (though not, I am glad to say, here at Hewelsfield). There is no saying but that a child here might catch the measles, or typhus, or some other illness. They are small and weak, and disease loves frailty."

"As you say Papa, not here at Hewelsfield. I would like my children to grow up as Stubbs and I did, here at Hewelsfield…"

"I do not think now is the best time for this discussion, Lucy, let us leave it until after Christmas. I understand you will be staying with us until then, Mr Lord?" and he turned back to his son-in-law, hoping that he had done enough to stave off the storm he could see gathering in Lucy's breast.

Lucy was angry and upset that her father had taken Sam's side in the argument, but she needed him to help persuade her mother to take her part and raging at Papa was not going to achieve that. So she bit her tongue and listened to the rest of the dinner table conversation without playing much part in it.

Afterwards, Thomas bore Sam off for a cigar and a glass of French cognac (still possible to obtain, but at black market prices because of the war with Napoleon dragging on), and the ladies retired to the parlour where there was a roaring fire to keep the chill air at bay. Mrs Wightwick picked up a piece of white needlework and busied herself with setting neat stitches; Mrs Slaney, having tried in vain to coax Lucy to explain why she and Sam were now at outs, shrugged and pulled out a well-worn copy of *Evelina* by Fanny Burney, over which she was soon smiling. Lucy fidgeted and yawned, then abruptly rose and, murmuring that she must feed Cecilia, left the room.

She picked up a candle from the hall table and lit it with the taper left for that purpose, then made her way slowly upstairs. She did not know why she had been reluctant to confide in her Aunt Mary, perhaps it had been her mother's presence. Or perhaps, if she were honest, it was because her feelings were totally conflicted. She longed to be loved by Sam, but she was not convinced that he would change, and she did not want to become the physical butt for his anger again.

Nurse smiled at Lucy as she came in and said quietly, "She is still sleeping, Miss Lucy. Do you wish me to wake her?"

"No, let us wait until she wakes of her own accord."

"But will they not miss you downstairs?"

"My father and husband are smoking a cigar, while my mother and aunt are busying themselves in the parlour. I shall re-join them later."

Lucy was tired, so she lay down on the bed thinking she would rest awhile, but thoughts of a future life with or without Sam were going round and round in her brain. When Cecilia started chuntering – with a view to full-blown yelling if her meal was not immediately available – Lucy rose quickly and crossed to the nursing chair, loosening the top of her dress as she did so.

The baby fed and rested, Nurse cleaned and changed her, and Lucy took the child in her arms and kissed her.

"Thank you. Papa has not seen her yet, I shall take her down and introduce them. I hope she is well-behaved! I shall ring for you if she becomes restless, or bring her up here myself if it is time for her next feed."

Slowly and carefully, Lucy carried Cecilia downstairs, the baby half asleep on her shoulder. One of the maids was in the hallway and hurried to open the parlour door for her.

The parlour was warm, comfortable and elegant – her mother's doing. It was a large room, with several sofas, two bookcases, a range of different chairs, small tables – some covered with nick-nacks, others ready to be used – a piano, and a beautiful mahogany sideboard. The curtains, drawn now against the November night, were dusky rose in colour, and the floor was largely covered with a huge maroon silk rug. When Lucy entered, her aunt was by the piano, leafing through a parcel of songs. Her mother was still at her needlework (the room was well lit, with numerous candles), and the men were nowhere to be seen.

Mary turned towards the door. "Ah! Let me see my great-niece. Will she know me again, do you think?"

Lucy handed Cecilia to her and went to take her place at the piano.

"Where did this come from, Mama? I do not believe I have seen it before," she asked, pulling out a book of songs entitled *Rhymes of Northern Bards*.

"Oh – it is newly published. I thought it would make a change so I sent for it. I have not learned many of them yet, and some are in such a strange dialect I do not think I shall be able to."

Saying this, Mrs Wightwick put away her needlework and went to join her daughter at the piano, leaving Mary to develop her relationship with Cecilia.

Mrs Wightwick was a competent pianist, and she took the book of songs from her daughter and riffled through the pages until she reached one she knew. She sat down and began playing the tune. Lucy sat beside her on the piano stool, looking closely at the page and humming along under her breath. Once her mother had played it a couple of times, Lucy stood up and, still looking at the page, sang the words to *O No My Love No* by John Shield.

"That is a pretty song," said Mary, and moved across to join them, the baby still in her arms. So when Messrs Wightwick and Lord joined the ladies, the three of them were in the middle of singing the song together.

At the end, Sam clapped his hands. "Bravo! Encore!" he said with a smile.

Lucy had already turned to take Cecilia from Mary.

"We shall sing for you again in a moment," said Mrs Wightwick, "but now Mr Wightwick shall be introduced to his granddaughter!"

Lucy carried her over and presented the baby to him. Thomas said everything that was suitable, but it was Sam who held out his arms for Cecilia. Lucy gave her to him willingly, unafraid that he would be anything other than loving towards his new child. Cecilia yawned but did not seem at all concerned at being passed around the different family members.

"I never cease to be amazed by the perfection in such tiny hands," said Sam, showing them to his father-in-law who made a non-committal sound in response.

Cecilia whimpered slightly, "Oh dear – she seemed to enjoy your singing very much. Perhaps you would sing again for us now?" Sam asked.

Nothing loth, all three women returned to the piano and sang *O No My Love No* again. Then Lucy found some sheet music with country songs she knew, so she played and sang an Irish folk song, *I Live Not Where I Love* and an English one, *My Thing Is My Own*, whose slightly risqué wording made Sam laugh and Mary Slaney frown, then a version for piano of the haunting tune *Grenadier and The Lady*. Then she played several country dance tunes, and Mary joined her to play a two-handed *sauteuse*. All the while the baby eyed them solemnly and uttered not a peep.

Mrs Wightwick rang for the tea-tray, and Nurse came in at the same time, curtseying to the assembled company and looking expectantly at Lucy, who nodded in Sam's direction.

Nurse went over to him. "Shall I take the baby now, sir?"

"Yes indeed, Nurse, as long as I am promised that I shall see my new daughter again tomorrow!" and Sam handed Cecilia to her and smiled at Lucy.

The turmoil that Lucy had felt during her discussion with Sam at the church had subsided, and she felt comfortable with him again. She smiled back and went to help her mother serve out the tea.

Shortly after tea, Lucy left the cosy parlour and went upstairs again to feed Cecilia before getting herself ready for bed. She slept well that night, despite having to wake and feed the baby frequently.

Over the following days, Sam was at his charming best, the Wightwicks held several dinner parties, followed by impromptu dancing or card games, and Mary was reluctant to go home. In the end, her sister prevailed on her to write to her husband and invite him (and any of their offspring who planned to be with them) to join the Wightwicks for Christmas at Hewelsfield.

The days turned into weeks, and Lucy felt more alive than she had done for several years. The one cloud on her horizon was that no-one – Papa, Mama, Aunt Mary, Sam, her cousins – would permit her to join the hunting parties, and this bitterly disappointed her. But she was so busy with the baby, with relearning all the household management skills her mother had taught her to cater for such a large and varied party, with singing, dancing and card games – and with rediscovering her husband's ability to love her tenderly, which in turn rekindled her desire for him – that after one blazing row with the father she expected to be able to twist around her little finger she gave in relatively gracefully. She could not bring herself to wave the excited huntsmen and women on their way, but she could offer them sustenance when they returned, soaked to the skin and covered in mud, at the end of the day.

The Slaneys left early in January and, despite the poor weather, Thomas decided to accompany them and visit Great Bloxwich and some of his other properties. Only his wife knew that he was wondering whether to place the Lords in one of these for a few months or rent them a property in Bristol or Chepstow in order to keep his son-in-law close and monitor his conduct.

Those remaining all felt the loss of company – Mrs Wightwick with a mixture of relief that she could now relax and satisfaction that everything had passed off so well, Lucy with regret at the departure of her aunt and relief at the departure of two of her cousins with whom she found she no longer had anything in common. But it was Sam who felt it most of all, finding a house deep in the English countryside in the depths of a wet winter and with only two women for company little to his taste. Lucy thought this somewhat ironic, since she had had to tolerate a plantation house far away from Barbados society, with only his family for company, for four years, but she was not surprised when Sam, a few days after the departure of the Slaneys, announced that he had business to attend to in Bristol with Thomas Daniel. He did not suggest Lucy accompany him, and nor did she wish to go; she needed some time for quiet reflection. He rode away on a rare bright, crisp day, his clothes and shaving brushes neatly packed in two saddlebags, hoping fervently that the dry weather would last until he reached his destination, and that the river crossing would not take many hours.

That evening, for the first time in two months, Lucy and her mother found themselves alone in the elegant drawing-room. Lucy was listless and sleepy, having fed Cecilia and handed her over to Nurse. She tried to copy out some manuscript music, but her heart was no longer in it now the party had left. The air was heavy with the mingled fragrance of lit candles and strongly-scented flowers, drooping slightly in vases placed on side tables. The clock on the chimney-piece chimed eight, as Lucy watched her mother mending the hem of a fine linen tablecloth with perfect tiny stitches. She felt her eyelids drooping.

"Mama, may I call for the tea tray early this evening? I am so tired."

Mrs Wightwick looked thoughtfully at her daughter.

"I don't see why not. I shall ring for it now," she said, folding the tablecloth neatly with the needle left in it exactly where she had finished stitching.

Lucy got up to take it from her and place it in the sewing basket near her mother's chair. The two then sat in companionable silence – punctuated only by Lucy trying to stifle her yawns – until the tea tray arrived, when Lucy once again rose to collect the cup poured for her.

"Did Mr Lord indicate when he means to return?" Mrs Wightwick asked abruptly.

Lucy looked at her mother in surprise. "Do you mean here? Or to Barbados?" she asked. There was a slight hesitation.

"Both," came the firm reply.

"I only know that he thought he might return from Bristol within the week. It was you, Mama, who invited him to stay for Christmas, so I thought he might have been as likely to disclose his plans for returning to Long Bay to you," said Lucy, fully awake now.

"He has said nothing. But I doubt life at Hewelsfield will suit Mr Lord, should he plan to make a long stay in England."

Lucy laughed at that. "Nor I! Although life at Long Bay is extremely humdrum, Sam escapes from it to the bright lights of Bridgetown. And now he has had a taste of society life here over the past few weeks, our everyday existence will seem very tedious!"

"Well, you and I at least will be busy for the next few days. Every room in the house must be thoroughly cleaned and the furniture polished. I shall get in an extra girl from the village to help, and I shall be counting on you also, Lucy."

"Of course, Mama. You have no idea how often I begged Sam's mother to be allowed to help at Long Bay. At least then I would not have been bored!"

Chapter 15
Two Proposals

The next few days were spent in a bustle of cleaning, and by the time Mr Wightwick and Sam arrived back together more than a week later, Sam trotting just in front of the carriage, the carpets had been beaten to rid them of dust, the floors swept then polished by two maids on hands and knees, the furniture buffed until it gleamed and smelled of beeswax, the fire grates all blacked and the silverware polished until it shone. Mr Wightwick sniffed appreciatively when he walked through the front door, handing his hat and coat to the waiting footman.

He was clearly in good humour. As his wife came out of the library to greet him, untying her apron strings and rolling down her sleeves as she did so, he held his arms out and embraced her, kissing her cheek enthusiastically.

"Do you know whom I met on the road, Mrs Wightwick?" he asked, without waiting for an answer, "I came across Mr Lord at New Crossing, so we have travelled hence together."

"And where is Mr Lord?" enquired his wife, returning his kiss, and making no objection to his arm remaining around her waist.

"He has taken his horse to the stables but will be in directly. We are both famished! I see you have been busy in our absence, Lucy."

"With the help of your daughter and two stout housemaids, we have turned the house out and given it an early spring clean," she laughed. "Come into the drawing room and tell me all about your trip."

"And where is our daughter?" Thomas asked. "I wish to discuss some of my findings with you without little Lucy's presence – or that of her husband, come to that."

His wife reassured him and, once he had poured himself a Madeira and his wife a ratafia, he settled down to tell her what he had been up to.

"After I parted from the Slaneys, I went first to Great Bloxwich, as we had discussed. I thought the house looked a little tired – it needs your touch, my dear, you could make it as comfortable and delightful as this house. Since we have no tenants at the moment, we could offer it to Lucy and Mr Lord on condition, naturally, that we could and would visit whenever we chose to.

"I talked to my agent about our other Staffordshire properties and rode the boundaries with him. The tenants appear happy, they pay on time, and none have given notice yet…"

At this point Sam joined them, having removed his riding garb and changed into more suitable clothes. He bowed low over Mrs Wightwick's hand, gave her his charming smile and expressed his pleasure at having returned. Mrs Wightwick had a brainwave.

"My dear Mr Lord, you have not seen your wife or child for over a week! Lucy is with Cecilia upstairs at the moment. Why do you not visit her, and tell her also that her father has returned?"

Sam bowed again and turned towards the door, heeding the unspoken command in the politely phrased request. He did look longingly towards the drinks tray, but Mr Wightwick made no move to offer him any sustenance, so he left the room and ran up the stairs to knock on Lucy's door.

Mr Wightwick resumed his tale, "So, if we send Lucy and Mr Lord north, Great Bloxwich it will have to be – unless you know of any of the rest of the Stubbs estate in need of tenants? The Slaneys have none I know; but what of Sabrina McHutchin, your sister Elizabeth's daughter?

"I have also asked Baines to be on the lookout for a suitable house in Bristol but have heard nothing as yet. But do we know what Mr Lord's plans are?"

His wife shook her head. "Then I shall ask him over dinner," said Thomas decisively. "If he plans on staying long, I think they should run their own household so we can see how he treats our daughter. I'll wager he is on his best behaviour here with us, and will never let down his guard!"

Over a dinner of pheasant and roast beef, pigeon pie, turbot and mushrooms, apple pie and comfits, Mr Wightwick turned to Sam and asked conversationally, "So, Mr Lord, how did your business in Bristol prosper?"

"Very well, thank you, sir. I believe you know Thomas Daniel?"

"Indeed I do, indeed I do. I have done business with him on several occasions. Lucy, you will remember, he was with me in my office when you arrived from the West Indies."

Lucy merely nodded. She wondered whether her husband had truly met Mr Daniel on business, or whether he had gone to Bristol for male company and card-playing. The latter had always been their focus when Sam and he got together in Bridgetown.

Mr Wightwick took a sip of the excellent Bordeaux he was drinking. "And does this mean you will be returning soon to Barbados? Or will you be in England for many more months?"

Lucy blinked and wondered whether Sam would lose his temper with her father in the same way he had with her when she had told him she did not wish to return to Long Bay until Cecilia was weaned. But although Sam frowned, he answered pleasantly enough.

"That all depends, sir, on the extent of your hospitality and my wife's views on when it is safe for the child to make a sea voyage. I would wish to return home soon but Lucy, I believe, has some concerns."

Lucy looked at him challengingly. "My concerns, sir, are entirely for the welfare of our daughter, as you well know! I will neither expose her unnecessarily to the dangers of a sea voyage, nor will I expose her to the dangers of the tropical diseases which are rife in Barbados! You told us only a few weeks ago of the way typhoid decimated the slave population…"

"None of the family – and certainly not our daughter Emma – contracted the disease!" Sam shot back, clearly considerably annoyed.

"Now, now, there is no reason for such heat," Thomas soothed. "Lucy, you well know that disease is rife everywhere. We have suffered ourselves in the past, God knows," and he looked at his wife, both remembering the death of their first son. "But it probably is sensible to wait awhile before taking an infant all the way across the ocean. The question is, do you stay here at Hewelsfield? Or Great Bloxwich? Or," turning again to Sam, "do your business interests require regular attendance in Bristol, London or elsewhere? Indeed, how long can you afford to remain absent from your plantations?"

There, it was out, the dread question to which the honest answer was "I have no business, I own no plantation", but doubtless Mr Lord would avoid that, thought Thomas.

Sam thought quickly. He certainly had no desire to upset Mr Wightwick, particularly when his father-in-law appeared to be offering him the use of a big house in Staffordshire. A few months passed at his expense would be most welcome – and perhaps there would be some large towns nearby to spice life up a little. And Lucy so wanted to run a household, perhaps she would be happier there. So he turned to Thomas and said,

"It is most kind in you, sir, to give so much consideration to my plans. My business interests are not such that I need to spend all my time in any one place – I can always travel should I need to do so. I – we – will be happy to fit in with whatever you advise," and he glanced at Lucy as he said it.

There was silence, into which Mrs Wightwick spoke, "I shall need to go to Great Bloxwich within the next month or so to oversee the spring clean there. Perhaps we could travel together – if you are with us, Mr Lord, Lucy and I will not need to trouble Mr Wightwick if he does not wish to travel north again so soon?"

Lucy still looked angry, but the rigidity evident in her shoulders when she argued with Sam had softened. Thomas looked gratefully at his wife, for she had forestalled a possible storm on the part of their daughter and offered a neat way of re-introducing Sam to Bloxwich society, where he had only spent a brief period more than four years previously.

And so it was that six weeks later, as the first signs of spring were showing despite the continued frosts, Lucy found herself, accompanied by her mother and Nurse carrying Cecilia in her basket, making their way along, initially, the well-paved St Briavels to Chepstow road, recently reinstated by the parish, and then the ancient and rather more rutted road to Lower Redbrook, where they would take a barge northwards. Sam rode ahead, enjoying the freedom and relieved that there had been no room for him in the carriage. The baggage lashed firmly to the outside of the vehicle was slight, consisting only of necessities for the journey. The rest of their belongings would follow more slowly with some of the servants, by a more circuitous road route.

Mrs Wightwick, tired from her exertions overseeing the packing up of Hewelsfield Court, leant back against the cushions and was almost instantly asleep. Nurse was humming to the baby, so Lucy had time to think about a conversation she had had with her father in his study several days earlier, before he left for Bristol.

After discussion with his wife, who was of the belief that Lucy must make the best of things and pointed out that there had been no evidence of harsh behaviour by Mr Lord since his arrival more than three months previously, Thomas had reluctantly decided he needed to talk frankly to his daughter about her future. Summoned by Prudence, she had entered the study to find her father surveying his tropical butterfly collection with a frown on his face.

"Is something amiss, Papa?" she asked.

"No, Lucy. Sit down, I want to talk to you about this visit to Bloxwich and what happens after that," he said, having decided not to beat around the bush. He sat down behind his desk and became busy filling his pipe and tamping down the tobacco, before standing again to go to the fire and light a taper to, in turn, light the pipe. Meanwhile, Lucy sat patiently waiting for him to begin, her heart thumping slightly since, if she were honest, she still had not made up her mind what she wanted from the future and was hoping that she could just let the days slide one into another, living in the warm comfort of her parents' home.

The pipe drawing to his satisfaction, Thomas went to pour himself a drink, looking enquiringly at Lucy who shook her head. Finally, her father sat down again, leant back in his chair and said without further preamble,

"Neither your mother nor I have seen any sign of unpleasantness in your husband, and he has now spent the best part of four months with us. Do you believe he has changed?"

Lucy had not been prepared for her father to be quite so blunt, but she swallowed and answered him honestly. "He has not beaten me while here it is true, Papa, but he has ever generally been kind and considerate when we have been in company – for instance when we used to visit the Barrows at Sunbury. We – we have argued, but…"

"Are those arguments always about your return to Barbados with the baby?" interrupted her father.

"Yes. I do not want her to suffer the same fate Oceanus did!"

"And I am sure, from what I have seen of Mr Lord's fondness for his child, that nothing is further from his desire either," responded Mr Wightwick drily. "But he is right you know, Lucy. He is right in law. Your place is by his side; it is up to him whether that is in England or Barbados (though Heaven knows how he thinks he is going to fund any life here, for I am certainly not prepared to subsidise him), and up to him where your children live."

"Papa, will you not take my part in this?"

"No, Lucy, I neither can nor will. I have absolutely no right to dictate what happens to his children, and nor do you. Moreover, whilst I have no wish to see you hurt in any way, I have no evidence that he has done so (and you corroborate that his behaviour while here has been beyond reproach) for which I am heartily grateful. Were that to be otherwise, as your father I would wish to intervene, but anything I might do would be limited. Remember, Lucy, I told you before you married Mr Lord that once you did so I would be unable to help you. The law is very clear."

Lucy was plaiting and unplaiting the fringe of her shawl with fierce concentration. Without looking up, she asked very quietly,

"If... if Sam becomes violent again and if I were to... to leave him," she was almost whispering now, "would you help me then?"

"Is that what you are planning?" her father said sharply.

"I just need to know."

Thomas took a deep breath. "I could probably house you, but not much more, Lucy – and Stubbs would be under no obligation to do so once I am gone. I have lost my investment in two ships recently because of these dratted wars – one sunk without trace, the other taken by privateers – and I have a duty to leave everything in as good order as possible for Stubbs. Besides, you would lose the children."

He said nothing about the effect such a radical step would have on the family's reputation, which would be felt particularly keenly by his wife, as he judged – rightly – that this argument would carry little weight with his daughter if she were determined to leave her husband. Gently, he added,

"Life could become very hard for you, Lucy. It is not what I, or your mother, would wish for you."

He did not tell her that, even then, he was pondering – most unusually – whether to leave fifty per cent of his wealth beyond his fixed assets to Lucy in his will, should she not be able to work out her differences with Sam. The idea that his beloved daughter might be forced into penury was abhorrent to him.

"Believe me, Papa, I have no desire to be separated from my children, or to cause you and Mama distress. But I am afraid for Cecilia. Could we live with you until she is older?"

"I do not see that that is possible, Lucy. Mr Lord will wish to return to his home in Barbados. From what I have seen, he is unlikely to do so without you – and I will have no hand in persuading him to do so! No," he raised his hand to pre-empt Lucy, who had opened her mouth to respond. "Let me finish. Once your mother returns to Hewelsfield, you will have some time alone with your husband, and I hope that you will realise that your future – and that of your daughter – is best served by returning with him to the West Indies. I repeat, I cannot and will not provide a living for Mr Lord, so unless he can find suitable employment here (and I do not know what he is suited for), he must return to his brother's house until such time as he can buy or build his own."

Thomas rose and came around his desk to take his daughter, who had risen also, by the shoulders and kiss her. Clearly the interview was at an end. Lucy caught her father's hand and nursed it against her cheek.

"I will try to make things work, Papa. But I do not know what Sam is going to find in Great Bloxwich to keep him occupied."

Now as the coach rumbled along Lucy, preoccupied with her thoughts, paid little attention to the route they were travelling. She could hardly see anything out of the windows in any case, as the gloomy fog which had persisted for days blanketed the countryside. But now she realised that they were slowing down, and there seemed to be other travellers passing them in the murk; they had reached Lower Redbrook. When the coach stopped, she pulled down the window and cautiously put her head out, welcoming the blast of icy air. Sam came trotting up.

"I will ascertain how long we must wait for a barge. Do you stay in the carriage – it is bitterly cold out here, and the air is noxious with fumes from the iron and copper works. Then, if we must wait, we can all go into the inn together."

He was soon back. "There is more than an hour to wait until the next barge upstream. Mrs Wightwick, you will not object to waiting in the public bar meanwhile?" he addressed his mother-in-law politely.

"So long as I can descend from this jolting and stretch my cramped legs," she responded with spirit, and he held the door for her.

"Nurse, I must use the privy before I feed Cecilia. Will you wait with her here until I return? Then I can pull the curtain and be quite private." The baby had awoken and was beginning to grizzle.

By the time Lucy had returned and fed Cecilia, and Nurse too had visited the privy, they were being called to the barge. Mrs Wightwick swallowed a last mouthful of scalding coffee – the waiter had been hard-pressed, and she had had to wait a long time after ordering – and followed Sam who strode back to the waiting carriage still holding his tankard, to give Lucy a warming sip of small ale. He then shepherded the three women and the baby to the waiting barge on which several fellow travellers were already huddled, together with a range of livestock and a number of crates.

By the time they reached Monmouth, their next port of call, all (other than the baby, who had nonetheless complained throughout) were cold and wet, and Sam was cursing the ruination of his boots. The ladies' heavy, sodden skirts clung to their legs and made movement difficult, but the knowledge that rooms had been booked for them at the Sloop Inn for the night kept their spirits up as they clambered from the barge onto the wharf, and thence the hundred yards or so to the inn. The Wightwicks were good customers, nearly always staying on their journey to Great Bloxwich, and the landlord himself came out to greet them and ushered them towards the great log fire in the public tap room, tut-tutting all the way. He ordered one of the maids over to show them to their rooms but could not stay himself to talk as he had a full house, despite this being the first week of March.

Lucy had asked for Nurse to share the bedroom allocated to her, the baby and Mrs Wightwick. This way they were unlikely to have a stranger foisted on them. Sam was not so lucky, he was forced to share not only his room but also his bed, the landlord saying apologetically that he "was full to the rafters". His mood was not improved by the fact that his bed-companion snored, or that overnight the Boots failed to return his footwear to its previous lustrous shine. However, in the meantime, Lucy – having fed Cecilia again – and her mother enjoyed a couple of hours of rest while their skirts steamed before a cheery coal fire, and they all dined well off-white fish, baked fowl, roast veal, bacon, salad, greens and potatoes, removed with tarts and cheese and washed down with some very pleasant wine. Sam was comforted with a bottle of very good port (on the house, said the apologetic landlord, since he would have to sleep with a roomful of strangers), at which he brightened considerably and promptly sought out a convivial companion to share it with him over a few rounds of blackjack.

The following day they caught the mail-coach to Hereford (eighteen miles), and thence by stagecoach to Wolverhampton (fifty-seven miles), by which time they were all tired and the baby, suffering from wind or colic, simply would not settle and cried constantly, much to Lucy's chagrin and their fellow passengers' annoyance.

They decided to take rooms for the night at the Talbot, where the coach had deposited them, and send a message to Great Bloxwich for the Wightwicks' own vehicle to meet the women the following morning, while Sam hired a horse from the inn's stables. Lucy could not remember being so tired by the journey before, and when they eventually reached the house went straight to bed – hurriedly aired with a warming pan – for several hours, Nurse having taken Cecilia with her. She warmed some cow's milk and added a few drops of laudanum to quieten the baby, and patiently fed her from a spoon. By the time Lucy woke and rang for her, Cecilia and Nurse were fast asleep together in Nurse's bed according to the young maid who answered her bell. So Lucy asked the girl to take out her spare dress from her valise and press it for her to wear, then lay back on her pillows luxuriating in the quiet, the comfort, and the cessation of rocking and lurching over the road.

In the days that followed Lucy was wholly taken up either with Cecilia or with helping her mother spring clean the house. At the weekend, Mr Wightwick joined them, having travelled very comfortably by mail-coach from Bristol to Wolverhampton. The cleaning activity ceased (all the rooms downstairs had been washed and polished until they gleamed and glittered, although some of the drapes had not yet been re-hung), and Mrs Wightwick decided to hold a small dinner party with some near neighbours the following Monday evening. Sam, who had been showing increasing signs of boredom while the women worked, brightened at the notion of company, although privately he thought the guests lacked town bronze and were not the sort of people he would generally seek out.

Mr Wightwick had decided to stay for the week and bore Sam off to visit the potteries at Longton and Burslem the day after the dinner, and they did not return until the Thursday. Longton was situated in a slight hollow and was crammed with a huge variety of bottle ovens belching smoke from a multitude of chimneys. The air was rank with it, and Sam could not get out of the town quickly enough. He thought it more like hell even than the cotton manufactories he had visited, despite the quality of porcelain produced there.

Burslem, on the other hand, was a pleasant, bustling market town situated on the side of a hill. Its population already exceeded seven thousand. The tall kiln chimneys smoked as much here as at Longton, but the fumes were dispelled and dispersed far more easily. Thomas took Sam to visit Josiah Wedgwood's Brick

House Works in Church Street, and Sam started to take an interest in what was going on. He had admired Wedgwood's work for several years and was keen to explore how it might be used in decorating the interior of his new house at Long Bay. Since Thomas also had a passion for fine porcelain – indeed, he had a beautiful collection which Sam had already admired at Hewelsfield – the two of them were soon in animated discussion about how Sam might incorporate Wedgwood's mantelpiece design into a house which had no need of a fireplace. Both bought items, Thomas bought an urn for his collection, and Sam a slender vase as a gift for Lucy. By the time they returned to Great Bloxwich, Thomas had warmed to his son-in-law and felt sure that frustration was what drove his ill temper towards his wife.

Lucy, delighted with the vase – for she had received no gifts from Sam for almost two years – placed it in her room and insisted on it being filled daily with fresh flowers. The invisible barrier she had built between her and her husband began to thaw, and Sam visited her nightly as he had not done for a long time.

Mr Wightwick, satisfied with his efforts to interest Sam in the potteries, left the following Monday for Bristol. Mrs Wightwick remained a further week, inviting a few neighbours and family members to visit for tea or dinner, and even – when there were enough young people – for an impromptu dance, and encouraging them to keep up the contact after her departure.

The Lords settled into a life of apparent provincial bliss at Great Bloxwich.

When Sam and Lucy spent an evening alone together, he would read to her from the recently published *Pride and Prejudice*, over which they would laugh and marvel. When she was alone, she would read *Castle Rackrent* by Maria Edgeworth, or try to interest herself in the white needlework at which her mother excelled. By May, as the days grew longer and the weather brighter, she would take out the pony and trap, with Cecilia carefully wedged into place in a wicker basket, and visit her old haunts, take tea with a neighbour or visit one of her cousins. Sometimes Sam went with her; occasionally he took her to Wolverhampton, and generally they lived the life of a country squire and his wife.

Sam was not unhappy. He found enough to interest him so that he was not bored; he was gregarious and made friends with some of the people he met, joining them in their forays to see (and bet on) cockfights and boxing matches. The life was easy, he did not have any money concerns as the household bills – even including his horse furniture, which was a large proportion of their expenditure – were covered without question by Mr Wightwick on receipt of Lucy's scrupulously kept accounts. But always there was a hankering to return to his home.

At the end of May he received a letter from his brother John.

Dear Samuel

I make sure that you will be glad to hear that one of our objectives has finally been met. Betty and I have purchased the Pool estate, which neighbours Long Bay and which, as you know, is capable of bearing a sugar crop and has its own mill for crushing cane. Mr Green, the owner, was of course never there and I think the fact that his profit suffered greatly last year, losing many slaves to the typhus as he did, made him open to my offer. The cost was eighteen thousand Pounds, of which I have paid one thousand and eight hundred already and entered into a mortgage for the rest.

I plan, as soon as I have put the main house in order, to remove there with Sarah and the children. Mother and our sisters Bathsheba, Sarah and Betty will remain at Long Bay and will, I know, welcome your return with our sister-in-law Lucy. I hope all is well with you. Please do send word: Mother worries although she says nothing, and our sisters would very much like to receive your news.

Your loving brother
John

P.S: please tell your wife (for I think she will be interested) that Sarah has just been brought to bed of another daughter, to be named Mary Francklin

Sam read the letter twice, re-folded it carefully and put it in his inner pocket. The information John had sent him required some thought. The fact that he and Sarah were moving to Pool Plantation meant that Sam, as the only man in the household, would be in charge of Long Bay when he returned. (He did not for one moment let the fact that he still had no title to the property affect his view of the situation). The fact that John had bothered to write at all conveyed a tacit message, in Sam's eyes, that he could start the construction of his mansion house as soon as he went back, since John had already found somewhere else to live. A triumphant smile curled his lips, and his eyes lit up with excitement. Now all he had to do was find a way to persuade his wife to return with him without daring to contradict him or becoming hysterical.

Over the coming days he was attentive and caring, showing how good he was with little Cecilia (now more than six months old and very happy to be tickled or bounced on his knee which made her gurgle with laughter). He visited Lucy's bed every night and stayed with her throughout on several occasions (although this was a severe sacrifice, he saw no reason why either of them should be woken by the baby needing to be fed, and was exasperated that Lucy was adamant that she would not employ a wet nurse). He was skilled in his lovemaking, gentle and solicitous, and Lucy responded with a degree of passion that sometimes surprised him.

Having noted how contented she was busying herself with running the household at Great Bloxwich, Sam had decided to stress the fact that she would have the running of Long Bay as soon as they returned there – before running his new castle once it was complete.

He had suggested several weeks previously that they should reinstate their morning rides, to which Lucy had agreed with alacrity, and it was when they were walking their horses back to the stables that Sam raised the topic of their return to Barbados.

"I have received a letter from John," he began. "He sends regards from all the family and has a piece of news which will interest you, I am sure, Sarah has given birth to another daughter."

"Lud! I have lost count of the number of children she has had. Is it healthy?"

"John did not say. I had the impression that her lying-in was only just complete."

By now they had reached the stables and a groom had taken the horses' bridles and waited patiently while Lucy fed some pieces of apple to her mount. As he left, Lucy looped the tail of her riding skirt over one arm, put her other hand on Sam's proffered arm, and the two began to walk back towards the house.

"John had another piece of news. He has bought the Pool plantation from Mr Green and plans to move there with Sarah and the children once he has rebuilt the house there to his taste. Indeed, he may already have moved!"

Sam looked sideways at Lucy, waiting to see her response to this news.

"Pool…" she mused. "Ah yes, I remember. We used to pass through it on the way to church. They can grow sugar there, is that right?"

"Yes. It seems that Mr Green had had enough – he had insufficient slaves last year to finish the harvest because a number of them died from the typhoid, so his income must have fallen badly."

Lucy nodded, but said nothing more. Sam grew impatient, surely she must understand that he was eager to return?

"With John moving to Pool, there will no longer be any hindrance to my starting to build Long Bay Castle, Lucy. Don't you see? I will be in charge of the estate, and you will be in charge of the household, just as you always wanted!"

"Is John taking your mother to live at Pool?" Lucy asked.

"No. She will remain at Long Bay, as well as my sisters."

"Then she will be in charge, just as she has always been, just as she is with Sarah!"

"But now I can build the house I want, she can stay in the existing one and we will have our own life," he pleaded.

"Then you must return and realise your dream. I shall stay with Cecilia, since she is not yet weaned…"

Sam ground his teeth, trying to keep his rising temper in check, how *dare* she defy him? She was his *wife*, dammit, and she must go with him. She added to his prestige. Besides, who ever heard of a castle without a chatelaine?

"You *shall* accompany me," he growled, low. "Our son was *born* on board a ship and came to no harm; the baby will be fine, and it is best for her to travel now when she cannot walk, and therefore cannot come to any harm by slipping overboard."

"I have tried to tell you before," Lucy's voice had risen, "I will not expose her to the dangers of disease in Barbados. She needs me, and I shall stay!"

By this time they were in front of the house. Exasperated, Sam turned and shook Lucy.

"That did not seem to weigh with you when you left our first daughter, Emma, at Long Bay more than a year ago! You have not even asked how she is since I told you about John's letter."

"You would never have let me leave with her," Lucy's face was shuttered. "Why do you think I did not tell you I was breeding?"

Realisation dawned. "So – you knew before you left, yet failed to tell me? Do you hate me so much that you would keep from me that we were to have another child? And if I had not gone to Hewelsfield six months ago, would you ever have told me?"

Really angry now, he slapped Lucy's face, causing her head to jerk and her hat to fall off. Equally angry she screamed,

"I had already written to you, as had Mama! I will not go, I say! I will not let Cecilia go!" and she raised her riding crop. Whether she truly intended to hit him with it was not clear, but the move made Sam completely lose his temper. He slapped her across the other cheek with one hand and with the other grabbed the crop, twisting it viciously so that Lucy, who did not let go, cried out as her wrist snapped back with a crack.

Having finally wrested the crop from her, Sam took hold of Lucy's upper arm in a vice-like grip and, with a face like thunder, marched her to the front door of the house and past a surprised maid who, taking one look at him, made herself as small as possible. He threw open the door of the study, dragged Lucy inside and slammed it behind him. Tears were running down Lucy's face now as she held her damaged wrist up to nurse it at her breast, and she bit her lip until it bled to avoid making any sound. Sam pushed her down onto an armchair and stood in front of her, unbuttoning his trousers, then forced her onto her knees in front of him. She knew what was coming now and a sob escaped her, but he simply pushed her sprawling onto the rug and pulled her skirts up over her thighs. Without trying to untie the strings holding her long white drawers in place, he ripped them off and entered her viciously. At that she did cry out, once, then lay there until he had finished.

Sam rose, the rage still evident on his face, and put his clothes back in order. "You are my wife, you *shall* obey me. You *shall* return to Long Bay with me and with Cecilia."

"You cannot make me!" Lucy panted. "How will you pay for my passage? Or even for your own, come to that? It is Papa who pays for our life here, not you, and he will not force me to go with you now you have abused me again!"

"You are my wife," he repeated, "and you will do as I say."

And on that, he turned and left the room. Lucy heard the front door slam again. She wondered if he would go straight to the stables and take his horse out again, or have the gig harnessed and make for Wolverhampton to dull his anger with drink and cards.

She went to get up but tried to put her weight on her damaged wrist and had to bite back a scream of pain. She fell forward and lay weeping bitterly for some minutes. Why had the halcyon weeks of romance been shattered? She had almost made up her mind to return to Barbados with Sam until he hit her; and how was she to explain the torn underwear and facial bruising to Nurse? And what would the other servants think?

Finally, she stood up, collected the ruined drawers, mopped her eyes with them, pulled down her riding skirt and, with difficulty, put the tail of it over her arm. She stood for a few moments looking out of the window into the sunny garden and waiting for her face to cool. She knew Cecilia would be hungry but how to face Nurse? She would simply have to lie and say she had fallen from her horse. Giving a defiant sniff, she left the study and mounted the stairs.

Cecilia was crying lustily when she entered her room, kicking and waving her fists, and her face was as red as Lucy's had been. Nurse looked up to scold, but seeing her mistress' tear-stained face she tut-tutted instead, put the complaining baby back in her cot and said

"Whatever is it, *cariad*? What has happened?"

"I… I fell, and I think I have broken my wrist," responded Lucy, trying out her lie. It was clear from Nurse's face that she did not believe Lucy had simply fallen. She took Lucy's chin in one gnarled hand and turned her head this way and that.

"And what are those bruises on both cheeks? And your nose is bleeding! Unless you fell from your horse…"

"Yes – oh! Yes, that is it, I fell from my horse…"

"And did you tear your underwear when you fell?" asked Nurse in a disbelieving tone, eyeing the offending garment.

Lucy blushed and hung her head, saying nothing. Nurse grunted.

"Sit down and let me take a look at that wrist. We will have to get you out of that fitted jacket first."

Not without difficulty, she helped Lucy shed the jacket with its tightly fitted sleeves, and pulled the ruffles up her arm which was already swelling.

"You just wait there, *cariad bach*, while I fetch my salve, some bandages and a splint," and she hurried away to her room at the back of the house.

Cecilia did not take well to being ignored, particularly when she was hungry. She was now showing signs of a temper to match her father's. Lucy tried to lift her using one arm but failed and had to sit back down again with the baby's howls of rage ringing in her ears.

"Nurse, please lift the baby for me so I may feed her," she asked, as soon as the elderly woman returned. Nurse clucked her tongue, put down all that she was carrying and hurried over.

"Poor bairn! *Pwr dab*! There, there," she crooned, her lilting Welsh tumbling out as she lifted the wriggling creature and placed her gently on Lucy's lap.

Lucy had already loosened her top, and Cecilia found the teat quickly and immediately started to suck greedily, hiccoughing once or twice on a left-over sob.

"Now, give me your arm," said Nurse, and proceeded to wash and dress the swollen wrist, binding thick bandages around two splints. "You'll not be riding for a while, Miss Lucy. I'll fashion you a sling, and you must keep it there as much as possible."

By the time she had finished, Cecilia was ready to switch to Lucy's other breast, so Nurse helped turn the baby then sat down in a rocking chair in the corner of the room and quietly hummed the Welsh lullaby *Suo Gan* that Lucy had sung to Oceanus what now seemed a hundred years ago. She smiled tremulously at Nurse, tears welling in her eyes again but she blinked them back. When Cecilia was ready to be put back in her crib, Nurse lifted her in, tucked her up and said to Lucy,

"Do you get yourself into bed also. I will make you some hot milk and you shall rest awhile."

She bustled away but Lucy, unable to unbutton her skirt, continued to sit where she was and mull over the incident with Sam. Her anger had given way to sadness now, the pleasure of the last weeks – indeed, the past six months – had been ruined by this fight and, if she were to be perfectly honest with herself, he probably had a right to be angry that she had left without telling him she was pregnant. But – to rape her again, after all the gentle yet passionate lovemaking she had become used to, that felt like betrayal and shattered in one fell swoop the trust which had been rebuilding between them.

What on earth was she to do? Sam was right, Papa had warned her that he could not come between her and her husband, and if Sam ordered her to return to Barbados, return she must – or take the plunge and seek a divorce, whatever the cost. But she did not really want a divorce, not while there remained a spark of what they had shared when they first met. And it was still there, recent weeks had demonstrated that time and again, it could not all have been a pretence.

Nurse returned with the cup of warm milk and remonstrated with Lucy when she found her still sitting in the chair.

"But I could not unbutton my skirt or loosen my stays, *Nani*," said Lucy, standing as she did so.

Nurse did both, then helped her mistress out of her blouse and looked closely at the black bruise on her upper arm as Lucy winced.

"Hmm! A fall, was it?" she muttered, for the finger marks were clear.

She drew her own conclusions and pushed Lucy towards the bed, holding the coverlet for her to slip underneath. She held out the milk and Lucy drank it gratefully.

"*Diolch, Nani*," Lucy smiled up at the wizened face and lay back on the pillows with a sigh of relief. She did not think she would sleep, but when Nurse looked in on her and Cecilia an hour later, the baby was stirring but Lucy did not move. So Nurse picked the baby up and took her back to her own room, for 'the rest will do her good' she thought.

Sam did not return at all that day, nor until long after the dinner hour on the following one. He looked dishevelled and unkempt. He had not shaved, his clothes were crumpled and he had lost a button, and he smelled of brandy. Lucy was nowhere to be seen; the mistress had gone to visit a friend in the neighbourhood but was due back shortly according to the maid who opened the door to him.

301

"Water for washing and shaving to my room – and make it quick!" he said, and tossing his hat onto the hall table he mounted the stairs two at a time.

He heard his wife return while he was shaving, but she went to her room at once and stayed there, presumably feeding the baby. Sam was not sure how he felt about seeing her again; he was still angry that she had hidden the fact that she was breeding from him ("What *right* did she have?" he kept saying to himself), but the rage which had caused him to attack her had long since been quenched. He hoped the situation was not irretrievable. He had not intended to alienate her; he still had hopes (particularly since spending time with Thomas in the Staffordshire potteries) of largesse to come from his father-in-law in his will. He dressed himself carefully and studied his reflection in the mirror. He was still a handsome man at thirty-seven – he would woo her back again.

He picked up a lace handkerchief and slipped it into his sleeve, then trod lightly down the stairs and lounged towards the kitchen, slapping the bottom of an unsuspecting serving maid on the way. Cook was somewhat startled to see the master but professed herself happy to prepare something tasty for him by way of supper when he told her, with his winning smile, that he had not eaten since breakfast.

Lucy did not join him for supper so he made his way to the drawing room later to time his entrance with that of the tea-tray. She was sitting in a window seat, reading by the last light of the day. She looked up as he entered and stood, her back pressed against the wall, wary as a wild bird. Even in the fading light he could see the livid bruises on her cheeks, her arm in its sling.

"Light the candles," he ordered the maid who was setting out the tea set.

She bobbed a curtsey and hurried to do so. Everyone in the house had heard that the master had a temper on him, and most had put two and two together as Nurse had and assumed, even if they had not witnessed the incident, that her bruised face was the result of him hitting the mistress. So it stood to reason he would have no compunction about hitting a servant who was slow to obey.

Lucy put her book down on the window seat and moved slowly toward the table to pour the tea. She had still not said a word. When the maid finished, she made so bold as to speak before she was spoken to,

"If you please, ma'am, will you be wanting anything else?"

Lucy looked across at her and smiled. "No thank you, Jane. I can manage."

Sam was unsure whether she was referring to pouring the tea or whether this was a coded message but decided to assume it was the former.

"I will pour, if you like, Lucy."

Jane bobbed a curtsey and left the room, closing the door quietly behind her. She listened for a while at the keyhole but could only hear the indistinguishable murmur of voices so concluded the master and mistress were not about to fight and made her way back to the servants' quarters.

Lucy sat down stiffly, and nodded her thanks when Sam placed her tea on a small table at her left elbow so that it would be easy to pick up. He took his own cup and sat opposite her.

"Will you ring for Cecilia to be brought to us?" Sam asked to break the ice.

"It is too late. She will be abed and asleep."

Lucy gave the answer he knew she would. Sam put down his cup, stood, and approached his wife's chair. She shrank back but looked directly at him, a challenge in her eyes. Now was clearly not the time to re-start the conversation about a return to Long Bay. He reached out his hand – at which she could not refrain from flinching – and touched her face gently with his index finger, tracing the shape and lingering on the bruises.

"Are you in much pain?" he asked, nodding towards her broken wrist.

"Yes, all thanks to you," Lucy hissed, indignant that he could not even bring himself to apologise. "It is most inconvenient when I must feed your daughter."

"Have Nurse feed her on pap, then. I will never understand your objections to hiring a wet nurse."

"Perhaps I might have done, had I known you would break my arm!"

There was fury in Lucy's eyes now. If she had been able to reach the poker, Sam thought she would have no compunction about hitting him with it. He moved out of reach, and spoke softly,

"I do not wish to fight with you, Lucy. We must discuss what is to be done for the future, but now is not the time. You are angry and in pain and cannot think rationally."

"I am perfectly rational! I have told you already, I cannot and will not permit Cecilia to be exposed to the dangers of Barbados, and there is an end to it!"

"That is not for you to decide. If I say she shall go, then go she will. You know only too well that legally I have charge of my children – you have no right to challenge me. But I have a proposition to put to you, when you are calmer. For now, I will bid you goodnight, ma'am!" and, holding his temper well in check, Sam made a dignified exit and shut himself in the study to smoke a cheroot and drink several brandies. He was pleased with the way he had handled the situation, and hoped he had piqued Lucy's interest.

The next day after breakfast, he had his horse brought round, strapped on a saddlebag with a change of clothes and trotted off to make another visit to Josiah Wedgwood's pottery. He thought it best to leave Lucy to think about what he had said for several days.

When he returned, Lucy's cousin Honor Slaney was walking with her in the garden. She thought Sam extremely handsome and dimpled flirtatiously when he approached them. He bowed over her hand and smiled as he greeted her, then kissed his wife gently on both cheeks, holding her by the shoulders so she could not pull away.

"Honor has ridden over to see Cecilia. She is staying with us for dinner," she told him.

"Perhaps you would like a glass of ratafia before we eat?" he asked, and offered the ladies each an arm as they turned back toward the house.

They entered through the French windows, which stood open in the warm sunshine, and he poured them both a ratafia and himself a sherry. Some small talk passed between them about the weather before they moved to the dining room.

"Have you been away on business, Mr Lord?" enquired Honor.

"In a way. Mr Wightwick was kind enough to take me on a tour of the potteries when we arrived here in March, and I was very taken with the beautiful designs of Josiah Wedgwood. I wished to make a return visit to look at some of them more closely, as I mean to incorporate them in the castle I plan to build on my plantation in the West Indies."

"Do you plan to return there soon?"

Honor glanced from Sam to Lucy and back again, but it was clear that she knew nothing of their recent quarrel. Lucy was too proud to broadcast to the world that her marriage was failing. The setting could not be better, thought Sam. Lucy was unlikely to defy him or lose her temper with him in company.

"I had hoped to take ship within the month, but my wife is understandably concerned about taking such a young and delicate child on a long voyage, so I think we will probably postpone our departure for several months – or even into spring next year to have the best likelihood of avoiding storms at sea."

He took a sip from his wine glass and looked over the rim at Lucy to see how she was taking this. Her eyes widened in surprise, but then she looked down at her plate and calmly continued with her meal.

"Oh! I should so like to travel! Lucy has described to me your green monkeys, and I have seen some of her beautiful sketches. I so very much wish to see a mermaid but I am afraid of the sea. I think she is very brave to have crossed the ocean so many times."

Sam laughed. "I think mermaids are an old wives' tale – or rather, an old sailors' tale! I do not believe they exist."

"But Lucy has seen one!"

Sam, still laughing, raised an eyebrow at his wife, who put up her chin.

"I believe I saw one on my last voyage. It was off the Azores I think – and the sailor I asked was not in the least surprised!"

He bowed ironically. "Then let us hope we both see one on our return home."

Nothing further was said about Barbados; the talk turned to news of the battles raging all over Europe and in America until the ladies very correctly withdrew, leaving Sam to enjoy a glass of port in solitary silence before he rejoined them in the drawing room, where Lucy's cousin – an accomplished pianist – was already playing a Mozart concerto.

"Do you wish to see the baby again before you ride home?" he asked Honor.

On receiving assent, he rang the bell, and asked for Nurse to bring Cecilia down. Lucy sat silently while Sam and her cousin admired the baby, who was making every effort to stand when her hands were held, until it was time for Honor to leave.

After Sam had thrown her up into the saddle and he and Lucy had waved her goodbye, Lucy asked abruptly, "Did you mean what you said, about not returning to Long Bay before next spring?"

"I did. The baby will be eighteen months old by then, and much stronger. We cannot live here for ever, Lucy, but do you think your father will be happy for us to remain until then?"

"I do not know. It is costly to keep two households, and I know his business interests have not prospered as he would have wished recently. If you were to defray the expenses of this house…?"

She said this without much hope of a positive response, but Sam was so relieved to learn that his idea had taken hold that he told her magnanimously that he would ask John to send over a banker's draft, since the harvest had apparently been good or he would have been unable to go ahead with the purchase of the Pool Plantation. The pair therefore ended the day in greater harmony than either had thought possible a few hours earlier.

Over the following weeks and months, life continued much as before. Sam and Lucy entertained and were entertained in return; they rode (once Lucy's broken wrist had healed sufficiently) and walked; Sam took himself off to Wolverhampton or Stoke sometimes, and the Wightwicks came to stay in August for several weeks. By this time, Lucy's wrist had mended and her bruises faded, and neither husband nor wife had mentioned the return to Barbados once.

On the evening the Wightwicks arrived, Thomas and Sam lingered over their port in the dining room.

"So," said Thomas. "How do you like Great Bloxwich now that you have lived here almost six months?"

At once Sam was alert and wary. With a smile he responded, "Why, sir, it is delightful, and most kind of you to allow my family and I to spend time here."

"Well, Mr Lord, I am afraid that I am going to require the house for a paying tenant before October. I have a delightful gentleman wishful to move in as soon as possible with his family for the winter, while he assesses whether or not to settle permanently in the area. As you know, as a general rule I keep the house available for the family to use, but this is too good an opportunity to pass up since we will, as always, spend December at Hewelsfield.

"Have you had any further thoughts about your departure for the West Indies? Do you plan to leave before the worst of the winter weather or into spring next year?"

Sam blinked, and stiffened slightly at the blunt tone in which this was uttered. He believed he had achieved an understanding with Lucy's father during their visit to the potteries and had never envisaged that Thomas might put pressure on him to move on. He played with his wine glass, twisting it this way and that and tilting it so that the ruby port caught the glint of candlelight.

"Well, sir, I have discussed this at some length with your daughter. She is reluctant to travel while the babe is so small, and whilst I would happily have returned to my duties at home several months ago, I have no wish to upset her, and most recently we have discussed the option of returning there in spring.

"Naturally we will vacate Great Bloxwich before the end of September so that your prospective tenant can move in at the time of his choosing. Would you be so good as to ask your clerk, Baines, to identify suitable lodgings for Lucy and I for the intervening period October to spring? I would suggest Bristol, but perhaps we should ask my wife for her preference."

Sam had no idea how he would pay for such lodgings, but he had never been one to worry over-much about such matters, finding generally that they sorted themselves out – occasionally he had had to leave town post-haste, but most of the time he had a sudden run of luck at cards which allowed him to pay off the most pressing of bills.

Thomas gave a small, ironic bow in Sam's direction. "An excellent idea, sir. And I should like to thank you for being so amenable to the change, I am only sorry that I could not alert you to the possibility when first you arrived. And I shall be happy to instruct Baines according to your wishes."

Upon this, the two retired to the drawing room to join the ladies. Lucy was playing something melancholy on the piano, and her mother was studiously engaged as always in white needlework, but on the entry of the two men both women looked up and dropped what they were doing, and Lucy moved towards the group of chairs around the fireplace.

"My dear," said Thomas addressing his wife, "I have just been telling Mr Lord of our amazing good fortune in having found a tenant who desires to rent Great Bloxwich over the winter period, and he has agreed that he and Lucy should move out as soon as required."

Sam intervened smoothly. "My dear," he said, addressing *his* wife, "I should not wish to take a decision without consulting you as to where we should go. Should you prefer to rent lodgings in this locality, or near Bristol?"

"Since Mama and Papa will be at Hewelsfield, I would rather stay at Bristol or Chepstow, it is far more convenient," Lucy answered firmly.

"Then I shall instruct Baines to seek lodgings for your household in one of those two locations," said Thomas jovially, and no more was said about it, the conversation turning to general matters until the tea tray was brought in after which the ladies went to bed, followed not long afterwards by the two men. Thomas, as usual, made his way to his wife's room where her maid was brushing her hair. Mrs Wightwick, clearly full of important news, dismissed her as soon as she saw her husband, and turned on her dressing stool to face him.

"Thomas, I had some talk with our daughter before you and Mr Lord joined us. I was sure something was amiss; I had heard whispers among the servants and Nurse confirmed it. I fear Mr Lord has a violent temper; he broke Lucy's wrist in the summer."

Thomas sighed heavily. "There is little I can do, my dear Lucy. So long as he does not kill her, and I am sure he has no intention of doing so," as his wife paled, "he can do as he pleases under the law, as you very well know. But I had hoped that any angry humour was simply the result of boredom and frustration rather than a character defect. When we spent time together at the potteries, he was delightful company. In my view he needs, for both their sakes (and for the sake of my financial well-being!) to return to his home in Barbados and busy himself there, and that means Lucy must go too. You will have to do what you can to persuade her – she seems loth to go because of the child."

"I gather that it was her refusal to accompany him that caused their disagreement. If she would only acquiesce, I believe the violence would end. She was ever headstrong, Thomas, you encouraged her too much to voice her own opinion."

"I shall be interested to see how Mr Lord manages financially without my help. I am glad Lucy chose to live near to us, we shall more easily learn if he falls into debt. By the by, I do not know what funds he has available in England, nor how he is to fund their passage to Barbados…"

"Perhaps we can invite them to stay over Christmas again, to see Stubbs who plans to come down from Oxford. It will be easier to ask Lucy to divulge such information if she is with us for some little time than if we were to see her for just a few hours."

"An excellent notion, Mrs Wightwick! It will be the first time in many years that we will have been all together as a family. And do you invite some of your relations too, it is always a pleasure to see your sister Mary and her husband, Jonas."

The Wightwicks remained at Great Bloxwich for a week, during which time they all went to the harvest festival and Lucy enthusiastically recalled the colourful Crop Over festival with the Barrows, and held several dinner parties and were invited in return. Neither Thomas nor his wife saw any hint of aggressive behaviour or unpleasantness from their son-in-law, and Sam was on his very best behaviour (aware that he was watched) and most attentive to his wife and daughter.

Sam and Lucy scrupulously avoided any discussion of the return to Long Bay and, as a result, rubbed along well together. When at the end of their stay, Mrs Wightwick had some wallpaper delivered to redecorate for the new tenants one of the bedrooms which had grown sadly shabby, Lucy offered to help her to hang it (her mother being unwilling to entrust the task to any of the servants as the paper was costly) and sought Sam's assistance also. They spent a tiring but productive day together while her father was away in Wolverhampton, and Mrs Wightwick found her son-in-law to be both a helpful and amusing companion.

Baines delivered on his instructions and found a pleasant house off Queen Square for the Lords to rent, and once Sam had signed the contract the family moved, together with Nurse, to their new Bristol lodgings, and were met by the very superior footman engaged by Baines. It was by now late September, and Lucy went immediately to work to oversee the unpacking of all their cases and interview the candidates Baines had identified for the positions of cook, housekeeper and lady's maid. Sam, feeling slightly at a loss, decided to take himself off to London for a few days to discover if the bankers' draft he had asked of John had arrived with their man of business, although it seemed unlikely as the man, Turner, was generally punctilious in his dealings and would have written to Sam as soon as he received it.

When he returned, order had been restored. The house was spick and span, there were flowers in every room, and Lucy greeted him with a smile. She was holding a letter.

"I have just received news of Mary Kingsley," she said gaily, holding out the paper. "You will remember, Sam, Dr Lucas' daughter. I had not heard from her in an age, but apparently she has been travelling with her husband who has been touring the country. Should you object if I invited her to stay with us?"

Sam always enjoyed company and, besides, he hoped Mary Kingsley would help persuade Lucy that her place was by his side in Barbados, so he had no hesitation in approving her plan.

Lucy looked slightly anxiously at him. "Did… did the bank draft arrive? I do not wish to incur any unnecessary expense if you do not have sufficient funds…"

"It was most fortuitous. The draft arrived with old Turner while I was in London, so we did the business there and then. So now we certainly have enough to see us through the next few months, so long as you do not spend it all on dresses and fripperies, my dear!"

Lucy was inclined to be indignant, then realised that he was teasing her and laughed instead. They dined together in perfect harmony at home and she once again felt the warm glow that she had experienced in the early days of their relationship. If only it could always be thus.

The next few months passed pleasantly enough. The Kingsleys came to stay for several days; Lucy enjoyed seeing Mary again – and Sam was correct in thinking she would encourage Lucy to stay at his side – but neither Lucy nor Sam cared for her husband, and both were relieved when the visitors left. Thomas developed a habit of dropping in to dine once or twice a week when he was in Bristol and was able to celebrate Cecilia's first birthday with them in November, and the Lords became acquainted with a number of people in the city so that their social life became far more varied than it had been at Hewelsfield or Long Bay.

Lucy subscribed to the library and the Theatre Royal, both on King Street, and the Assembly Rooms at Prince's Street, and entered into copious correspondence with former friends; Sam acquainted himself with all the myriad coffee houses, where his easy charm meant he quickly got to know several individuals who would invite him to accompany them to cockfights, badger baiting, wrestling or boxing matches in the vicinity. They spent a week at Christmas at Hewelsfield and renewed their acquaintance with Stubbs who showed a polite interest in meeting his niece for the first time but who did not have Sam's easy way with children.

The winter of 1813-14 was unusually cold. The Lords returned to Bristol just in time, for thick snow fell in the first week of January and was then iced over by heavy frosts making travel difficult if not impossible. The London papers told of an ice fair held in January on the Thames, and an elephant walking across the river at Blackfriars (Lucy expressed a wistful desire to see such a marvel), but the Severn was also frozen, and the Lords joined their friends in the novel activity of skating on the river, but this soon palled on Sam. He became restless as the deep cold continued into February and started talking again about arranging their return to Barbados. He started gambling heavily with his new friends and frequently stayed out late.

Lucy became more independent in her own social life, and unusually returned home one night later than Sam from the theatre. Sam had been drinking and worked himself up into an irrational rage about her absence, so he picked up a foot stool, beat her with it and left her bruised and weeping on the floor of their parlour, surrounded by shards from his shattered wine glass and broken wood from the stool, before slamming out of the house. She did not see him again for two days.

When he returned, he had clearly had a run of luck at the gaming tables. He brought her and Cecilia gifts and behaved as though nothing untoward had occurred. Lucy, unwilling to provoke another bout of rage, winced in pain when he put his arm around her and kissed her cheek, but decided to say nothing. That night his lovemaking to begin with was gentle, but she was too bruised to respond and lay rigid beneath him, angering him to violence again.

She was by now seriously considering leaving Sam and ignoring the advice she had received from friends and family. As soon as the thaw made travel possible in February, she told Sam she was taking Cecilia to visit her parents at Hewelsfield, and that he could join them there later if he wished.

When she arrived, shivering with cold despite the hot brick at her feet in the carriage and the fur rug tucked around her knees by Nurse who had swathed Cecilia in so many clothes she could hardly move, her mother knew instinctively that Lucy had come for a purpose and not just for a social visit. Her heart sinking, Mrs Wightwick sat her daughter near the roaring fire in the drawing room and began a flow of chit-chat to put off the conversation she rightly thought was coming.

Ignoring this, Lucy broke in abruptly, "Mama, I do not know how I can continue to live with Sam. I am constantly in fear of what he may do to me or, indeed, to Cecilia. He wants us to go back to Long Bay, and I do not think I can bear it!"

Mrs Wightwick was flustered. Nothing like this had happened during her lifetime in the Wightwick family, and she was sure she would never be able to hold her head up again if her daughter divorced Mr Lord.

"Now, Lucy, you know very well that your place is at your husband's side. If you have told him again that you do not wish to return to Barbados, it is no wonder if he is angry with you…"

"He beat me because I was out at the theatre when he returned home from his club, or wherever he went! It is unreasonable, Mama!"

"But you were getting on so well at Great Bloxwich – and, indeed, in Bristol. Mr Lord was very charming while you stayed over Christmas. What did you do to upset him, Lucy?"

"Why do you take his part rather than mine? I did nothing to provoke him, Mama, he had been drinking."

"Then I am sure he regretted hurting you once he was sober again. I think we should discuss this calmly and coolly tomorrow with your father. He has gone to Monmouth to meet with Mr Swift, the shipbuilder, about a new venture. Come, let us talk about other things. How does my granddaughter?"

Lucy swallowed hard. Clearly her mother was not going to permit her to discuss what would be a momentous decision without the supportive presence of Mr Wightwick. She could not afford to alienate her mother so she did as she was told, and turned the conversation to lighter topics, such as the fact that Cecilia was now walking – indeed, running unsteadily – and chattered to herself constantly in some language of her own, sometimes using recognisable words. She asked Mrs Wightwick to ring the bell and call for Nurse to bring Cecilia in, and the next half hour passed with both women laughing at the little girl's antics.

After dinner the next day, Lucy returned to the previous day's discussion, this time with her father as well. They were once again seated in the drawing room.

"Papa, I have already told Mama, I do not know if I can continue to live with a husband who is so cruel to me. Please say Cecilia and I may stay with you at Hewelsfield!"

"Lucy, you know I cannot. Your mother is right, your place is at your husband's side. Unless Mr Lord acquiesces in this decision, it is impossible. But I agree that you cannot continue as you are. The Bristol lodgings were always a temporary fix. Many would consider that Mr Lord had been generous to agree to your staying in England for so long, and I know he is keen to return to his home – which is also yours now, do not forget. I think it is time to have a serious discussion with him and agree when you are to go back to the West Indies."

Lucy knew the law. As a married woman, she must obey her husband, her father could not intervene. Only if she took the extreme measure of divorcing him (even assuming he would agree, which she doubted) would she be free of his control. And she still was not sure she had either the desire or the courage to take such a socially damaging step. What would it do to Cecilia's future, for instance? She had hoped that somehow she could slip into living apart from Sam, but unless he agreed to it, how could she? And why should he? He wanted sons, and to ensure a future income if he could.

So she bowed her head, and agreed to her father's proposal. She knew Sam was likely to follow her to Hewelsfield within a few days, for he would become bored in the Bristol house. When he did so, she must be crystal clear about what she wanted for her, and Cecilia's, future.

Over the next few days she faced the fact that she had shied away from leaving Sam for good. She still hoped the good days would return – as they had done for much of the past year – and she could foresee nothing but loneliness and ostracism if she were a divorced woman. But she also held firm to the belief that it would be better for Cecilia to remain in England with her grandparents than to be exposed to the challenges of life in Barbados.

Sam arrived the following week, full of his usual charm towards both his wife and his mother-in-law. Nothing was said about his previous behaviour (Lucy had no desire to anger him when she hoped to get him to agree to her proposal) and she relaxed a little. Neither of the Wightwicks, watching Sam covertly for any sign of the violence Lucy said she had suffered previously, could see anything amiss between them. After a few days, it was Mr Wightwick who raised the thorny subject of the Lords' return to Long Bay.

"Will you be renewing the lease on the Bristol house, Mr Lord, or do you plan to return to Barbados at the end of the current one?"

"It is high time I returned, sir. I am needed at Long Bay now that John has moved away. My mother says she is getting too old to run the plantation and the house, and I cannot leave it to my sisters. So, my dear," turning to Lucy, "I plan to start searching for a ship that can take us home in the spring."

There was a silence in which you could have heard a pin drop. Everyone present felt the suspense and Mrs Wightwick held her breath. After seconds which seemed like hours, Lucy spoke.

"I will return with you, Sam. I understand your need to go back, and I know you are eager to start preparations for building the mansion you have always dreamed of. But I still do not wish Cecilia to be exposed to the diseases which are rife there, she is too young and tender. I would like her to stay here with Mama and Papa, if they are willing to have her."

Although Lucy had suggested this some months before, her mother had dismissed it and thought the idea had gone away, and she gasped when Lucy suggested it again. She looked across at Mr Wightwick, wondering what he thought of the idea.

"That decision does not lie with us, Lucy," her father said gently. "It is a decision for Mr Lord to take. If, sir," looking at Sam, "you are content with this proposal, my wife and I would be delighted to take care of your daughter until such time as you deem it suitable for her to join you."

Sam scowled. He felt that he was being driven into a corner. He could refuse, and insist that Cecilia accompany them, but this would lead to the sort of confrontation he always tried to avoid in front of the Wightwicks. But if he agreed, he would appear weak and vacillating; besides, he was fond of the little girl and had grown used to her presence. Yet if this was the only way that Lucy would accompany him willingly to Barbados, then he must acquiesce; there would be more children, hopefully a son to take the place of Oceanus, and he could always send for Cecilia later. Neither the Wightwicks nor his wife could do anything to prevent that.

He looked up, realising that all three of the others were looking at him expectantly.

"I fail to understand this obsession of yours that our daughter is more likely to succumb to disease in Barbados than in England, but if that will ease your mind, Lucy, and since Mr and Mrs Wightwick are so generous as to offer a home to her for a while, then I agree. We shall leave in May or June, as soon as I can arrange our departure and we can settle our affairs here."

Lucy breathed a sigh of relief and smiled at him. Mrs Wightwick let out the breath she had been holding, and Mr Wightwick raised his wine glass and proposed a toast.

"To your safe return home!" he said, looking at his daughter and her husband.

****

The next few months passed in a whirl of activity. Both Lucy and Sam ordered clothes in the newest fashions to take back with them. Sam's banker's draft had dwindled considerably and was only sufficient to cover the last few months' rent, but his run of luck at cards continued and it was his winnings which allowed them this extravagance. Lucy, having proposed leaving her daughter behind, now clung to her, savouring the last precious moments before they left, sketching her over and over again, and shedding tears often.

Sam finally secured passage on the Jane, which – having come from Cork – would set sail from Portsmouth at the end of June. He sold their horses and used this money to fund the voyage, for he not only had to pay for their cabin but also for food and drink, and the services on board of a maid for Lucy and a valet for himself together with a share of their passage also.

Several days before they left Bristol in a hired post-chaise piled high with baggage, Lucy and Nurse took Cecilia to Hewelsfield. It was hard for her to leave the little girl, and Lucy's distress made Cecilia cry also, but Mrs Wightwick assured Lucy that Nurse would remain with her daughter and she would be a welcome addition to the household.

"I shall hope that you will come back to see us and find out how Cecilia is getting on. She shall have a childhood like yours, Lucy, I promise you," her mother said to comfort her, and finally Lucy tore herself away, tears pouring down her own cheeks and down Nurse's cheeks, while her little girl sobbed pitifully.

The journey of more than a hundred and twenty miles to Portsmouth took seventeen hours in the post-chaise, and despite an overnight stop at a tolerable quality inn, they arrived towards evening on the second day at the Keppels Head Hotel on The Hard weary and hungry. Lucy rushed to find the privy while Sam strode off to alert the steward to their arrival and make the final arrangements for going on board. When he returned to the inn, Lucy had ordered a meal for them both and Sam, who had worked up an appetite, sat down and devoured it with gusto.

At last he gave a sigh of contentment, stretched out his legs and raised a brimming glass of wine to Lucy.

"Well, Mrs Lord, let us drink to an uneventful voyage home! We shall be very cramped, I fear – no captain's cabin for us on this occasion, but at least we have one to ourselves. There is not enough space for all our luggage, but I have paid the steward to ensure he loads it in the hold on top of some of the cargo, so that it is not washing about in the bilges. At all events, it appears we will not be leaving tomorrow, the Jane still waits for some of its cargo. It is to be hoped she will be ready the day after."

"Well, for my part I am happy that we shall not need to rush to the dockside early tomorrow! I declare I could sleep the clock round, and more. And at least we no longer have to suffer being jolted over bad roads for hours on end," responded Lucy, and she smiled at Sam, a little timorously, but it was the first sign of warmth she had shown him since he had beaten her with the footstool.

Sam drained his glass. "Come, wife. Let us make the most of our spacious apartment in this hotel while we can. I have been promised we shall not be disturbed by other guests joining us!"

The implication was clear. Lucy rose, shook out her skirts and came around the table to where her husband was holding out his hand to her, and they mounted the stairs arm-in-arm, not to be seen again until a late hour the following morning.

Part 5
Endgame, 1814-16

Chapter 16
Francine

The Jane arrived at Bridgetown in early August after a relatively uneventful journey. Sam had played cards a lot, but at least he had not hit Lucy during the long weeks at sea in cramped conditions. She wondered what life would be like at Long Bay with John, Sarah and the children gone. Would she, Lucy, be able to stand up to Sam's mother and take over control of the household, or would she have to suffer in silence as Sarah had done? How relieved and happy Sarah must be now! Lucy decided that she would ride over to see her at the first opportunity.

She stood on deck, watching the ships of all sizes around them jostling for position like children in a nursery. She breathed in the familiar scent of Barbados, salt, sugar, nutmeg, unwashed humanity… All of a sudden, she thought about Francine. Would she still be working in the house? Or had she been sent to the fields? She must find out. If Francine was still around, she would ask for her to come back as her personal maid – and she would ask for ownership of the young woman to be transferred to her so that she could set about making her free.

Their turn to be transferred in the lighter to the dockside arrived, and the Lords (with several items of baggage) climbed down the rope ladder into it. Sam had written to his mother telling her which ship they were sailing in, so it was to be hoped that a Long Bay carriage would await them. As before, when they reached the quay strong arms assisted her to clamber ashore, and she smiled at the black face above her by way of thanks but received no answering smile as the man kept his eyes lowered.

"Thank you," she said softly. At that the man did look up swiftly, startled, but almost at once lowered his eyes again.

Sam had gone off to find their carriage. Lucy looked around then followed him, stepping gingerly as she regained her land legs. Thomas, the coachman, greeted his master with a big smile.

"Welcome home, Massa Sam." The smile encompassed Lucy also.

Once the few small pieces of baggage brought across with them in the lighter had been stowed away safely, the carriage set off along Bay Street on the journey to Long Bay. They passed through Sewell, Newton and several other large plantations; they stopped to rest at Oistins and when they reached Six Path, the main transport artery in the parish, Lucy knew they were on the final approach to the Lord home. She was surprised to find that she had missed some aspects of Barbados, she took pleasure in looking at the wide vistas and the hills in the distance. The whispering of the sugar cane rubbing together when they stopped beside the road for a break to stretch their legs. The pleasant warmth (it was before ten o'clock, when the wind was light or non-existent and the sun had not yet made it far enough above the horizon to make her clothes stick unpleasantly to her). The scent of mingled salt and sugar. The exotic nature of the trees and plants. The quality of the white marl roads they were driving on, so much better than most non-toll roads in England.

When they eventually reached Long Bay, even though the light was starting to fade, they stopped briefly to look out over the white beach below as they had the first time Lucy came here. Then Thomas drove them through the gates and down the mahogany-lined driveway to the house, where the lamps were just being lit. Thomas let down the steps and Sam jumped out, turning to assist Lucy.

"Welcome home, wife. Come, let us pay our respects to Mother, and tomorrow I shall begin to plan my castle – so keep whatever plans you have for prettifying this house for the new one!"

There was a suppressed air of excitement about Sam. He was like a coiled spring, full of energy, but liable to take off in some unexpected direction at any moment. Lucy understood that he believed he could finally bring all his grandiose plans to realisation. She followed her husband across the threshold and prayed silently to the Virgin Mary, asking her to intercede and channel Sam's energy into his project rather than being cruel to her.

Her mother-in-law greeted her coolly, and scolded Sam querulously – to hide her happiness at seeing him again, Lucy thought.

"I should like to bathe and change my dress, ma'am, so I shall leave you now. I wish to visit the kitchen and talk to Cook before we dine."

This last was said with a confidence Lucy did not really feel; she wanted to see how Bathsheba would react. There was a long hard stare, then a curt nod, and Bathsheba turned back towards her son, holding his hand all the while. Lucy, whose heart had been pounding, expelled all the air from her lungs in a sigh of relief as she left the room and turned towards her own – the same she had occupied previously.

She rang for a maid, and almost instantly one appeared out of the shadows. Lucy did not recognise the girl and asked her name. "Agnes, ma'am," came the mumbled reply, eyes downcast as always. Lucy ordered water for her bath and went to uncord the one small trunk she had brought with her. No doubt the rest of their baggage would arrive tomorrow. She shook out two muslin dresses, trying to decide which was the least creased, then burrowed for drawers, a chemise and stockings, and laid them all out on the bed.

Agnes returned with two strong slaves – one of whom was Joshua – all carrying pitchers of water, hot and cold. Lucy greeted Joshua warmly and asked if he knew where Francine was now, but he merely shook his head and would not look at her. She was puzzled; Joshua had always been one of the few slaves who disobeyed the rule that all slaves should not look directly into the white man's face, yet now... Perhaps he had been chastised in Sam's absence, she thought, and that had wrought the change in him. She gave a mental shrug, no matter, she could find out about Francine from Betty – or, if necessary, Bathsheba.

Firmly but gently she persuaded Agnes to erect the screens about her bath and then leave her to soak without interruption. She noted that the girl went to sit on the floor in the doorway, waiting for the mistress' orders. Lucy gave a little moan of pleasure as she slid into the warm water and sloughed off six weeks' worth of travel grime. It had been impossible to bathe on board the Jane, it was too cramped, and in any case Captain Wright rationed the water strictly, permitting each passenger only enough to wash in at the basin.

Once she had dried and Agnes had helped her to dress, Lucy asked her to iron the other clean muslin, wash her travel garments and remove the bath water, while she trod resolutely down the stairs and out of the back door to the cook house, all the while expecting Bathsheba to appear and refuse to let her go and give orders to the cook.

The cook was different from the one who had been here two years before and Lucy wondered what had happened to her predecessor. Bathsheba had set some store by the fact that they had known each other all their lives which made her feel comfortable the cook would not poison the food. Had that changed? Had John taken the cook to Pool? She decided not to ask – she would ask Sarah when she rode over to see the new estate. This cook clearly enjoyed her own creations; she was a huge black woman, as wide as she was tall, with a broad nose, thick lips and at least three double chins who waddled rather than walked. She seemed surprised to see Lucy, but word had obviously spread that Massa Sam and his wife had returned, for she clearly knew who Lucy was. She listened, head bowed and eyes downcast, as Lucy explained that she had come to discuss the menus for the following day, then told her what had been agreed with the mistress earlier.

Lucy had no real intention of changing any of Bathsheba's orders, she merely wanted to indicate that she would, henceforth, be in charge. So she listened in turn, then made some suggestions about what should be served the day after, including some of Sam's favourite dishes, and checked to ensure that both tea and coffee would be available at breakfast, as well as a dish of mango with lime, her own preferred dish at that time of day.

"Yes'm," mumbled the cook, and turned back to dicing vegetables, waving her knife at an underling who had been staring open-mouthed at the new arrival and adjuring her to get on with peeling potatoes.

Satisfied that she had made her point, Lucy made her way back into the house and through to the veranda, where Sam was already stirring a bowl of rum punch. He raised an eyebrow and gestured with the glass he held ready in one hand to ask silently if she wanted any. Lucy decided she would have a glass to keep her courage up, and as she sipped it told Sam about her visit to the kitchen.

"Starting as you mean to go on?" was all he said.

At that moment, Betty came languidly through the door then gave a squeal of delighted surprise as she saw her brother.

"Sam! Lucy! I had no idea you had arrived. How wonderful to have you back. The place has been like a morgue without you – I had no idea how much life John brought to the place, despite being here so rarely, until he had gone! How was your voyage?"

She then hugged them both ruthlessly and began to give them all the family news. Her sister Bathsheba drifted out to join them, greeting Sam and Lucy in a more reserved way. Lucy thought she had aged dramatically since she had last seen her, yet she could only be forty years old. Then their mother arrived. She walked with a cane now, but otherwise appeared as vigorous as ever. Betty turned to her impulsively.

"Mama, we should hold a dinner to celebrate Sam and Lucy's return!"

"That would be a lovely idea," Lucy chimed in, leaving Bathsheba no time to reply. "We must invite Mary and Richard, and the Barrows – oh! And the Lucases, and of course John and Sarah. When shall we hold it?"

She was determined to show her mother-in-law that she, Lucy, and not Bathsheba was now mistress of the house and intended to exercise her authority rather than meekly accept whatever Bathsheba decided as Sarah had done.

When there was a lull in the female hubbub Sam, who had busied himself providing everyone with drinks, announced abruptly,

"I should like to see my daughter." He gestured to one of the slaves standing against the wall of the house, waiting for orders. "Bring Emma here. I wish to see her before we dine."

Lucy jumped guiltily. She had not given a thought to her little daughter, so intent was she on making her mark at Long Bay and ousting Bathsheba from her role as mistress of the house.

There was a long silence, and the slave did not move from his post, appearing frozen in his place.

"Your daughter is dead," Bathsheba stated bluntly. "We buried her in April."

Lucy gasped and clapped her hands to her mouth. Sam looked devastated.

"Did you not know? I wrote to tell you, and Mary wrote too, but perhaps you had already left before the letters could arrive."

The younger Bathsheba spoke gently, and Betty went up to Sam and hugged her brother.

"She contracted a putrid sore throat and although we did everything we could, she was dead within a few days. I am so sorry, Sam, Lucy."

Sam turned away, leaning on the veranda railings and staring out into the tropical night. There was another silence, broken only by the cacophony of tree frogs. Lucy went to Sam and Betty yielded up her place when Lucy put her arm around her husband's waist and leant her head against his shoulder.

"Well, you still have another daughter, and you are plenty young enough to breed again Lucy," said her mother-in-law briskly. "Come, let us go in to dine."

The sisters followed her inside while Sam hung back. He had still said nothing, but now he grasped Lucy by the shoulders and looked down into her face.

320

"Now I have none of my children here, and I still have no sons to follow me. I want a family, Lucy; I want children to fill my new house. Cecilia shall live there with us, and there must be more."

Lucy reached up and stroked his face tenderly. "We will have more children, Sam, I am sure."

"You never showed any fondness for her, but I loved my daughter!" Sam said almost angrily.

"I know you did Sam. I think I was just exhausted grieving for our son, Oceanus, and I had no love left to give her. Poor little Emma, she was only three years old…"

She took Sam's hand, and they entered the dining room together. Lucy noted with surprise that Bathsheba had taken a seat on Sam's right hand, abdicating her habitual place to her daughter-in-law. Lucy sat down, inclining her head to Bathsheba to show she recognised the gesture.

Dinner was a somewhat subdued affair, with Sam morose and uttering hardly a word. The others kept up a flow of gentle small talk, with Bathsheba occasionally interjecting a tart comment, but no more was said about the dinner party. When the ladies left the table, Sam called for a bottle of port, pulled out one of his cheroots and sat there smoking.

The group broke up early, as was customary, and Lucy was glad of it for she felt bone weary. Sam was still seated at the dining table, twirling a glass of port to catch the light of the candles. She wondered whether he would drink himself into a stupor, and whether he would visit her tonight. Perhaps she could give him comfort in her bed, but for now he had withdrawn and erected an invisible wall around himself which no-one dared to try and penetrate. Sadly, she followed the other women upstairs, still feeling guilty that she had given no thought to Emma on their arrival.

Agnes was waiting for her and helped her undress and put on her nightgown, combed out her hair and put on her lacy nightcap. Lucy sank into bed with a sigh of relief, extinguished her candle and lay in the darkness contemplating what the morrow might bring. She was sure Bathsheba would not relinquish her role without a fight; tonight had been a mere skirmish, and she had decided on a tactical retreat for now but Lucy had no doubt she would continue to try and rule the roost.

She was dozing when Sam came in. He unbuttoned his trousers and they dropped to the floor. He climbed into the bed and entered Lucy with little preamble. As he lay above her, Lucy felt something drip onto her face, Sam was crying. He rolled off her when he had finished and Lucy cradled his head on her breast, stroking his hair, and eventually he fell asleep in this position.

Lucy woke to the sound of the slave bell at the usual hour. It was still dark. She was alone in the bed; she had no idea what time Sam had left her, but she could hear his gentle snoring, so he must have crept away to his own room next door. She flung back the covers and padded over to the window, opening it wide. The garden was still; the tree frogs were no longer whistling. She remembered sadly how she had loved to sit here, holding Oceanus, in years gone by. The little boy would have been five years old now had he lived.

The house was beginning to stir. She pictured the slaves starting work in the kitchen, bringing in water from the well, stoking the fire in readiness to boil water for the household, preparing the first meal of the day. Lucy was restless and wished her trunks had arrived, she would like to go for a ride but had not packed her new riding dress in the small valise she had brought with her from the Jane. She opened the press to try and locate her old riding dress, but when she found it decided it was too worn and stained, with patches of mildew on it – it must be thrown out. She found a faded muslin dress and slipped that on, it was old and out-of-date, but serviceable.

By the time she went downstairs the sun was rising. She visited the kitchen and asked for a pair of scissors and a basket and made her way into the garden to cut flowers for the house. On her return, she handed the basket over to one of the slaves, asking him to ensure the faded blooms in the various downstairs rooms were replaced with these fresh ones, and went in search of breakfast.

The luggage arrived from the ship later in the day, and Lucy spent some time with Agnes unpacking her dresses, shaking them out vigorously and putting them away in the clothes press. She did not see Sam again until it was time to dine, when he explained that he had ridden out early on a tour of inspection with the new overseer, Malcolm, put in place by John when he had moved to Pool. She smiled at Sam and suggested that they might reinstate their early morning rides from the following day as she now had her new riding habit. He appeared to have got over his morose mood of the previous evening and kept all the ladies except his mother amused with tales of what he had seen on the estate, which was in good order.

"Malcolm does a good job," interjected his mother. "John chose well. But I am glad you are finally taking an interest in the family business, Samuel!"

The following morning Sam and Lucy rode out together as agreed. Since he was in a good mood, she tentatively broached the subject of the projected dinner party with him again.

"Aye. It is time we brought some life into this morgue – and some male company. The house is too full of women. Make whatever arrangements you will. How's m'mother taking your interference?"

"I was pleasantly surprised that she decided of her own accord not to sit at the head of the table at dinner yesterday. Did you say something to her, Sam?"

"Eh? No. Perhaps when she wrote to say she felt she was getting too old to manage Long Bay she meant it. She hasn't gainsaid any of your orders to the kitchen staff, has she? Take control of arrangements for the dinner – just ask her advice every now and then, and I'm sure she'll soon get used to you being the chatelaine!"

Lucy was not entirely convinced, but as she was determined to do just as he suggested she said nothing more. They got back to the house just in time, as the heavens opened with one of Barbados' sudden and violent rain storms. Having put off her riding clothes, she went to the kitchen to talk to the cook about the most suitable day to hold the dinner, in view of the need to ensure all the ingredients for the menu she wanted to offer would be available. They decided on a date, the following Thursday, and Lucy gave her instructions on which dishes she wanted prepared, asking her to draw up a list of what was available in their stores and what would need to be purchased and to come and discuss this later in the day.

The following days fell into a pattern. Lucy and Sam would ride before breakfast, following which Lucy would give orders for the next day's menus, cut flowers for the house and oversee the daily cleaning. She was aware of Bathsheba keeping an eye on her activity; sometimes the old lady would appear as from nowhere, leaning on her cane, and sweep a finger along a table top to check it had been properly dusted and polished, but she rarely made any comment. Lucy was surprised but pleased at her forbearance. She had asked Bathsheba if she had any suggestions for guests to be added to the invitation list, but her mother-in-law seemed content to leave everything to Lucy, so she and Betty had written all the letters and dispatched them with one of the slaves for delivery. Everyone had agreed to come.

The dinner passed off very well. Fourteen of them sat down at the long mahogany table (even the ailing Sarah joined them), and although Lucy thought it a shame that they had been unable to think of any single men to invite to even up the numbers, she glanced with pride down the burnished table groaning with food and smiled as Sam at the other end raised his glass to her in silent approval. She had interspersed the usual Barbadian festive fare with some English dishes, such as a syllabub (her mother's recipe) which she had taught the cook, hovering over her to ensure that it was done right, and if the empty dishes were anything to go by, these were appreciated by the all the guests.

She was delighted to see her friends, Mary and John Barrow and Mary and Nathan Lucas, again and noted with pleasure that her sister-in-law Sarah was far less reserved now that she was out from under Bathsheba's shadow. Over music provided by several of the slaves in the ladies' room following dinner, she caught up on Mary Austin's news, asking after her namesake who was now three years old. It was clear that Sarah was pregnant again; the baby – which would be her ninth child – was due in December. A wave of sadness swept over Lucy as she remembered Oceanus and she wished that she could tell the family that she too was breeding again but knew with certainty that this was not the case. If only she could give Sam another son, he might be content.

When the men joined them, they all played cards, and Lucy went to the piano to play songs old and new, some of which she sang alone while others they all joined in with. Lucy was pleased to see that her mother-in-law seemed to be enjoying the company too and smiled across the room at her, feeling some fondness for her for the first time.

John and Sarah broke up the party, for they were driving back to Pool that night while the others – apart from the Barrows, who returned to Sunbury – were staying at Long Bay. Lucy arranged to ride over to visit Sarah two days later and having bid John, Sarah and the Barrows farewell went back to join the others.

All in all, she thought it was the most fun she had ever had at Long Bay and was delighted to be able to return the hospitality of the Barrows and Lucases. Before the latter left the following day, both invited Sam and Lucy on return visits, and she felt that finally she would be able to enjoy her life in Barbados despite missing her daughter, Cecilia.

Lucy had not forgotten about Francine. She had asked Betty whether she knew what had become of her, but despite her promise to ensure Francine was not forced to become a field slave, she did not know.

"With John moving to the Pool estate, a lot of the slaves went with him – perhaps Francine was one of them?" she suggested.

She had not felt the time was right to raise the matter with John or Sarah over the dinner party but determined to do so when she visited them. Sam – who left the following morning for Bridgetown to join the militia training – would not hear of her riding over alone, so on Saturday she set out in the dog cart (hoping the rain would hold off) accompanied by an elderly one-armed slave called Jonas with an ugly scar down one side of his face who usually helped in the garden. Sarah welcomed her warmly and, over a dish of tea, Lucy asked her about Francine.

"When I was last at Long Bay, I had a slave called Francine as my maid. Do you know what happened to her, Sarah? Did she accompany you her to Pool?"

Sarah wrinkled her brow. "I cannot recall a slave by that name. Have you asked Mrs Lord?" she replied, referring to their mother-in-law. Lucy shook her head. Sarah regarded her sympathetically.

"Is Mama Lord as overbearing as ever? The relief I felt when we came here and I could finally take control in my own home! She was very amiable when we came to dinner on Thursday but I cannot believe it was her idea. Did she object when you suggested it?"

Lucy explained that it was Betty's idea and that, to her surprise, Bathsheba had allowed her to make all the arrangements without hindrance. Sarah exclaimed at that but thought that it would not be long before she reasserted her authority.

"I shall ask John about your Francine when he returns. He has gone out with Alexander to check on the field work, but he will return this evening."

The talk turned to other matters, and Lucy politely asked to see the children. They all trooped in: Adriana, now nine years old; little John, now seven; the twins Mary and Frances, now six; Eliza, four years old; Henry, almost three and the youngest, Mary Francklin, who was just eighteen months old. Adriana curtseyed gravely, while the others (apart from Henry) simply gazed at this stranger in their lives. They were a remarkably quiet and well-behaved group of children, and Sarah soon sat them down with a puzzle in the corner of the room, which they set about doing under the watchful eye of Adriana and two of the house slaves, hardly uttering a sound.

"I was sorry to hear of little Emma's death, Lucy. I gather you never received the letter informing you of it. But what of your other daughter – Cecilia, isn't it?"

"She is nearly two years old now. I left her with my parents in England. I did not want to expose her to the diseases which are so prevalent here, having lost both my other children. And you have suffered several losses yourself; it is very hard, is it not?"

Sarah bowed her head in acquiescence and the two sat in silence for a few moments watching the children busy with their puzzle. Adriana came over and stood next to her mother.

"If you please, Mama, we have finished our puzzle," she said.

"Then you shall all go and have your milk and biscuits," Sarah said, and the two nursery slaves gathered the children up to take them away.

"I should be going also," said Lucy, standing up.

"But will you not stay and eat with us?" asked Sarah.

"No, I should be getting back. I must take order to several things at Long Bay, but I hope you will allow me to visit you again soon?"

Sarah assured her that she would be delighted to do so and promised to ask John about Francine.

That evening when Lucy was changing her dress before joining the other ladies of the house on the veranda for drinks, she opened her jewellery box and looked in vain for her pearl earrings.

"Agnes, where are my pearl earrings?" she asked. "They are not in my box, where have you put them?"

Agnes looked at her blankly. "Me not know, Mis'tss," she answered.

"Then please search for them. I will wear others this evening, but I expect you to find them before I come up to bed."

But the earrings were nowhere to be found. Lucy was upset, they had been a gift from her father on the birth of Cecilia and were a particularly beautiful pair. She ordered the girl to turn everything out of the closets and look again the following day, with no result. She mentioned it to Betty, who had no hesitation in suggesting that Agnes had taken them, and that a whipping might jog her memory as to where they were, but Lucy was loth to punish the girl without some evidence that this was indeed the case.

They had arranged to visit Sunbury the following Sunday after church, and when they returned and Lucy went to change for the evening, she found a small pendant, of sentimental rather than financial value, was also missing from the jewel case. She turned angrily to Agnes.

"Agnes, a pendant is now missing. Where is it? Have you taken it?"

"No, ma'am," came the mumbled reply, but the girl would not look at her and Lucy thought there was something shifty about her attitude.

"Find it, or I will have you whipped!" she said and swept out of the room.

She told Betty about it when she reached the veranda, and Bathsheba – who had sharp ears – overheard the conversation.

"You must have her soundly whipped. If that does not result in her returning your jewels, she should be sent to the fields!" she snapped. "I do not hold with you being too soft, remember what I taught you, Lucy. They will take advantage of you if you do not rule them with a rod of iron."

325

So the following morning, after she had told Sam about the missing jewellery during their ride and he had heartily agreed with his mother, she reluctantly ordered that Agnes be whipped. Although she loathed the practice, deeming it barbaric, she did not know what else to do. She was now fairly sure that Agnes was the thief. The girl must have known what would happen to her if she was found out, and Lucy would look weak if she did not take action.

Looking stern, she stood as tall as she was able and oversaw the process. Agnes had her bodice pulled down to her waist and was tied to a tree in the yard, Lucy could see old scars on her back from previous whippings. She received half a dozen lashes, and when it was over and another slave threw a bucket of salt water over her back (making her scream in pain), she was dragged back to her hut and Sam oversaw a search of her belongings. He returned triumphantly with the earrings, but the pendant was nowhere to be found. Agnes was banished from the house and sent to join the field slaves.

Reluctant to take on another slave she did not know as her maid, Lucy asked Betty if she could share her maid at least for a while. A few days later a letter arrived for her from Sarah.

Dearest Lucy

I have asked John if he knows anything of your girl, Francine. He has checked with Alexander, and she is indeed here at Pool, and has been working in the fields. John is happy to sell her to you if you would still like her to return. If you would like to see her again before you agree a price, please let me know when you plan to visit and I will ensure she is here for you.

Your loving sister
Sarah

Lucy waited until the following morning when she was on her daily ride with Sam so that she could gauge his mood before broaching the subject with him.

"Sam, now that Agnes has been sent to the fields I am without a ladies' maid. I would like to have Francine back, but she is over at Pool with John and Sarah."

He stared at her blankly.

"You don't remember who she is do you? She was the girl who attended me when we were here before. John is happy to sell her to me, but I do not know how to go about it. I do not even know what state she is in, or how long she has been working outside the house. Would you come with me to assess the situation and advise me how much to offer for her please?"

"Oh, aye, I remember now. You grew quite fond of the little creature didn't you? I'll come with you, but it will have to wait until Sunday. This overseer that John left at Long Bay tends to let things slide unless I keep a firm eye on him. See if John will be there and we'll go over after church."

Lucy was relieved. She had been in somewhat of a quandary about how she should go about the purchase, particularly since she had no money of her own and Sam (or perhaps the estate) would have to bear the cost. She duly wrote back to Sarah, who indicated that they would be very welcome and invited them to stay for luncheon.

Sam and Lucy rode to St Philip's Church, and then on to Pool Estate afterwards, leaving the other three ladies (Sarah was constantly ailing now and never went anywhere) to take the carriage. Lucy was unaccountably nervous, she found that while the idea of negotiating the cost of her passage across the ocean to England did not faze her, the idea of haggling over the value of a human life did. Moreover, she did not know whether Francine would want to return to her service – although, of course, being a slave what she did or did not want did not enter into the equation.

As they trotted along the dusty road towards Pool, she asked Sam to explain how slave pricing worked.

"A strong, new male could be sold for £115 on the open market, before the African trade was abolished," said Sam. "Now, of course, things are a little different, 'new' produce will be those born and raised here, and then there are the others – like your girl – who have already worked for a number of years. The price varies according to health, strength and reputation. If the girl's a troublemaker, John may be more open to a low offer just to get her off his hands; if she's a hard worker in the fields, he'll push a hard bargain. She's breeding age too, ain't she? Well, that will make her more valuable. But until I've checked her over in detail, I can't really say how much I'll have to pay. Maybe as much as £60? But I shall endeavour to spend no more than £40."

Despite her revulsion at people being treated and traded like cattle, Lucy could not help but be interested and the short ride passed quickly as Sam answered her questions. When they arrived and swung down from the horses, Lucy realised they were both covered in a fine film of white dust and was grateful that her riding hat sported a net veil which protected her face. Vigorously she beat the dust off her arms and skirts before catching the tail of her skirt up over one arm and treading up the steps beside her husband.

The door had already been opened by a young black boy impeccably dressed in a suit who with one white-gloved hand proffered a tray of welcome lemonade. Sam downed his glass in one gulp; Lucy sipped at hers in a more ladylike fashion and was still holding it when they were ushered into the parlour. It was cool and shady, the windows standing wide and the shutters pulled across to keep out the sun's rays, and the whole house smelt of beeswax and flowers – great vases of Lucy's favourite frangipani blossoms sat at each end of the room. Clearly Sarah was as meticulous a housekeeper as her mother-in-law.

At that moment Sarah came in to greet them. "John has but this moment returned from seeing Alexander and will join us shortly. I see you have been offered lemonade, Lucy; Sam would you prefer something a little stronger?"

As the young slave who had opened the door to them served Sam with a drink of his choice, John made his entrance. He smiled in greeting and seemed genuinely pleased to see them; Lucy was struck by how much more relaxed both he and Sarah were at Pool than she had ever seen them at Long Bay. After a few minutes of general chit-chat, John rubbed his hands together and, looking at Sam, said, "Well, I understand from Sarah that you are here today to conduct some business. Shall we conclude that before we all sit down to eat?"

"Yes indeed. Is the slave here? I would like to inspect her first."

"Come with me to the office. I shall have her brought there."

Lucy had listened to this exchange in growing indignation. "It is I who wish to purchase Francine. I should like to join you." She stood up, preparing to accompany them.

"It is best if I conduct this business for you," Sam told her firmly and both men crossed over to the office which, as in most plantation houses, was the only room on the ground floor with a door.

As this shut behind them Lucy continued to stand rooted to the spot, her fists clenched. Sarah watched her in surprise for a moment then said gently,

"Do you have much experience of buying and selling slaves? I have none. John conducts all that sort of business here. Why is it so important to you, Lucy?"

Slowly the tension drained out of Lucy. What was the point? Sarah had been brought up in this system. She would never understand that Lucy saw Francine as a person, not an object, or that during the bad times at Long Bay Francine had often been the only one to show her any tenderness or give her comfort, or that Francine alone had known Oceanus almost as well as his mother had. Her fists unclenched.

"Papa brought me up to understand commerce, and I would happily have conducted my negotiations with you or with John. It is true that I have no knowledge of buying and selling slaves, but – since you view them as any other chattels – it cannot be so different from any other purchase."

"I am sure the men will settle it between them. Come, let me show you the house. You have only seen this room so far, I think," and Sarah led Lucy away, explaining proudly what she had done to improve the Pool house since taking it over.

Lucy allowed herself to be persuaded, although she would dearly have liked to see how Francine was for herself, but she only leant half an ear to Sarah's gentle monologue, and hoped she was smiling and nodding in the right places. When they descended the stairs again to the ladies' room, having inspected the bedrooms and the nursery-cum-schoolroom, Sarah sent one of the slaves for more lemonade, and the two ladies sat and sipped it in comfortable silence, while another slave fanned them against the sticky midday heat. Just as Lucy began to feel her eyelids drooping, she heard a door opening and the unmistakeable voices of her husband and brother-in-law. She set down her glass and was about to get to her feet with a view to seeing Francine when Sam strode around the corner.

"Well, wife, it's all settled. Though I think myself that you'd have done a sight better to pick a new young 'un, I'm not sure how long this one will last after more than a year working the cane!"

Lucy paled. It was as she had feared; poor Francine had been made to suffer for her loyalty to her former mistress. "I should like to see her, if you please."

"No need for that," responded Sam. "The deal is done now, you cannot change it. John has agreed to send her over in the dog-cart sometime tomorrow since we have ridden over. What's for luncheon, Sarah? I am famished!"

Nothing more was said about the transaction over the meal, and afterwards John bore Sam off on a partial tour of the estate, while Sarah and Adriana took Lucy on a decorous walk around the gardens. Soon afterwards, Sam and Lucy took their leave in order to return to Long Bay before dark, for it was cloudy and there would be no moon that night.

Sam was in a good mood, so Lucy deduced that he felt he had driven a hard bargain with his brother and decided to take advantage of this. "Did you purchase Francine in my name or in yours, Sam?"

"In yours, since you were so insistent about it – although why it matters so much to you, I really cannot imagine. Even though I managed to beat John down on the outrageous price he asked, it is probably a waste of money. What strange idea have you got into your head now?"

"I wish to purchase her freedom," Lucy responded, outwardly calm although she did wonder if such an admission would lead Sam to lose his temper. To her surprise, however, he remained quite genial, indeed, he gave a shout of laughter.

"So that is it! I might have known it would be something like that. Well, take my advice, and don't waste more money than you must. Send the papers to your father and have him deal with it, it costs far less than going through the process in Barbados! Here it will cost as much as £300, in England, as little as ten shillings. Ask Mama, she has freed several slaves and always arranges it through a man of business in London."

Francine was dropped off at the Long Bay slave compound by one of the Pool Estate slaves on his way to do a job of carpentry work for another plantation owner so Lucy did not see her arrive but found her waiting patiently when she went to her room to put away her paints after an enjoyable few hours sketching in the garden. She greeted Francine warmly, but was shocked by her appearance. Some eight to ten years younger than Lucy herself, she looked at least ten years older, with flecks of grey in her hair, deep lines on her face and calluses on her hands. The girl would not look up but dropped on her knees and clasped one of Lucy's hands to her cheek, bathing it in tears. Lucy rested her other hand on the kerchief Francine had tied over her curls, somewhat embarrassed.

"Why, Francine, whatever is the matter? I had hoped you would be pleased to have me back as your mistress – although I could not blame you if you were not. I only wish I could have regularised your situation before I left for England but it was not possible, you did not belong to me…"

"Oh – thank you, Mis'tss Lucy, thank you! It is wonderful to see you again. I thought I would die in the fields…"

She broke off, unable to continue as the tears came thick and fast. Lucy put her hands on the bony shoulders and raised Francine to her feet, then pushed her gently into one of the rattan armchairs and subsided into the other herself, handing her a lacy handkerchief. Francine made a great effort and her sobs eased; she looked up shyly and tried to smile. Lucy noticed that she had lost several teeth; indeed, there was little left of the pretty young woman she had left behind, and she was stricken with guilt that she had not done more for her maid. She was on the point of telling Francine of her plans to free her, but stopped short. Although Sam had been perfectly pleasant about the idea, there was no telling whether he might change his mind, and she did not want to raise the poor girl's hopes until she had received proof of ownership from Sam. So Lucy merely smiled back at her, then gently asked Francine to lay out a change of clothes and fetch a jug of hot water from the kitchen hut.

Over the next few months harmony reigned between Sam and Lucy, as both found sufficient to occupy them in their new-found roles running Long Bay. They still rode together most mornings, and Bathsheba – although she might snipe from the sidelines – made no real attempt to interfere in Lucy's household arrangements. They entertained far more than had ever been the case during Lucy's first sojourn on Barbados, and both she and Sam thoroughly enjoyed doing so. Sam visited Bridgetown occasionally but was rarely away more than one night, and generally spent a good part of the nights he was at Long Bay in Lucy's bed. They paid return visits to Sunbury and several of the other local plantations, and in her spare time Lucy was happy to return to sketching, walking with her sisters-in-law, writing her diary and penning letters to friends and family.

Sam had been as good as his word. He handed over a document indicating that Lucy was Francine's owner, and she promptly wrote to her father, asking him to make all the necessary arrangements for manumission. She still said nothing to the girl as she knew that it would be several months before she received a response from her father, and probably even longer for the paperwork to be processed.

Chapter 17
Betrayal

Sometime in November, just as she was thinking how sad it was that she could not be present for Cecilia's second birthday, Lucy noted a subtle change. Sam seemed moodier and increasingly restless. After the evening meal, he would go outside to smoke a cheroot or shut himself up in the office and fail to visit her room at night. Several times she caught him being rather too familiar with one of the female household slaves, and her heart sank. She tried to ask him why he was behaving differently on one of their morning rides.

"What right have you to question my actions, Madam?" he scowled. "You have everything you always wanted, do you not? A household to run; slaves at your beck and call. You cannot claim to be bored – you have plenty to keep you busy and a constant whirl of social engagements."

"But *you* do not seem happy, Sam. That is not intended as a criticism, I am merely concerned."

"There are only two things I need, the money to start work on my building plans, and a son! Long Bay does not deliver a sufficient profit to pay for your fripperies and the new house, and neither John nor your father will advance me any funds so I do not know how I am to progress. And you show no sign yet of breeding again despite my frequent visits to your bedchamber. Perhaps I should do as John Barrow does and recognise one of my half-breed offspring. At least then I would have an heir!"

Lucy gasped and blanched, her head whirling and her heart beating tumultuously, she had not been expecting this. "Wh-what do you mean, Sam?" she stammered. She felt as though he had hit her in the solar plexus.

"Do you mean about my half-breed offspring? Or about your sainted John Barrow?" he sneered.

Both of them had pulled up their horses. Lucy, still very pale, simply stared mutely at her husband.

"You cannot surely be such a little simpleton as not to know that John has several by-blows. You can check the register at St Philip's if you don't believe me – he has them all baptised! Or, better still, ask Mary. I neither know nor care if I have sired any but I shouldn't be surprised; and if you don't do your duty by me soon, I will take damn good care to keep my options open!"

Sam tugged his horse's head around and, brushing roughly past Lucy, set off at a trot towards home. Lucy followed behind more slowly, careful to keep out of the way of the dust he kicked up, tears rolling silently down her cheeks. All the contentment she had felt since their return to Barbados had been crushed in this one exchange. As she approached the house, she wiped her face with one gloved hand but only succeeded in smearing the dust across both. Handing her horse to a waiting slave, she kicked her foot free of the stirrup, swung her leg over the pommel and slid down, and walked wearily up the stairs to her room, pulling off her hat as she went.

Francine was not yet there but would shortly arrive with water for her bath. Lucy sat in one of her favourite chairs in the window, staring unseeingly out into the garden and going over the hurtful conversation in her mind again and again. She decided she would ask Betty if she knew if there was any truth in Sam's pronouncement about John Barrow; but although she knew that Sam had had several affairs, for some reason it had never occurred to her that these might have resulted in any children – and she certainly could not ask his sister about that.

Francine took one look at her mistress' face and busied herself with readying Lucy's bath and her clothes for the day, uttering not one word. More unusually, Lucy did everything in complete silence and, once dressed, waved her maid away and sat down again at her escritoire instead of heading to see the cook. She had thought she would record the conversation in her diary while it was still fresh in her memory, but the ink dried on her quill without her putting a word to paper and eventually she stood up and made her way downstairs.

She carried out her various tasks mechanically and only roused herself over the luncheon table, when she felt Bathsheba's sharp eyes on her, to ask Betty if she cared to stroll in the garden afterwards. Once the two women were some distance from the house, parasols unfurled to shade them from the sun, Lucy opened her mouth to ask Betty about John Barrow, then shut it again as she wondered how on earth to raise such a delicate matter. In the end, she broke in on some half-hearted – and half-heard – complaint by her sister-in-law about the clumsiness of a new maid and blurted out baldly,

"Betty, do you know if it is true that John Barrow has had several children by his slaves, and has even had them baptised?"

Betty stopped in her tracks and looked at Lucy in some surprise.

"Why, yes, at least two that I have heard of. I know that as an unmarried woman I am not supposed to know about such things – it must be men who devise such idiot-ish social rules! – but it is very common, you know. It helps to boost the slave population, which has become even more important since the trade was abolished. Some plantation owners even adopt such children and educate them with their real family. As for baptising them – why not? Quite a few planters baptise their mistresses, so why not the offspring too? Are you shocked, Lucy?"

"Oh – I have no quarrel with the children being baptised, indeed, I think it an excellent notion. But... I am surprised at John Barrow's behaviour. He always appears devoted to Mary."

"It doesn't often seem to mean anything. Men have much stronger appetites than we women do – at least, that is what Mama tells me. I have certainly never felt any desire to be mauled and grappled with, as though I were a cow or a filly or some other creature put to stud. Of course, we must breed, that is our role, but

332

I do not think I would welcome a man's advances too regularly. What are your views, Lucy?"

Lucy was already pink with embarrassment. Never had she had such an open conversation on matters which should surely remain private, even with her own mother! She mumbled something incoherent then tried to turn the conversation into more normal channels by exclaiming at the sight of a green monkey scampering up one of the bearded fig trees. Betty seemed quite unconcerned but made no effort to return to the subject of John Barrow, for which Lucy was grateful.

Once back in the house, Lucy mounted the stairs to her room and decided to record this conversation also in her diary. As she thought about it, she realised that she could not, in all conscience, blame Betty for her own embarrassment It had, after all, been Lucy who introduced the topic and she blushed once again to think of having been so bold. But as she had already learned, different *mores* existed here in Barbados, and it was to be hoped that Betty would not think the worse of her sister-in-law for discussing something it would be unthinkable for any lady to do in England.

Did confirmation of John Barrow's extra-marital activity change how she viewed her friend, Lucy wondered? She thought about this while she sharpened her quill pen but came to no real conclusion, other than that she felt profoundly sorry for his wife, Mary. Perhaps she could try to discuss Sam's hurtful comments with Mary both to obtain some worldly-wise advice from another married woman and, in the process, find out how she viewed John's actions. Nodding decisively to herself, she dipped her pen in the standish and added a final few lines to her journal entry before dusting the entry with sand and putting the book away in an inside drawer of the escritoire.

She saw nothing more of her husband for several days. He had left for Bridgetown shortly after returning from their ill-fated ride, ostensibly for the monthly militia training but no doubt also to enjoy playing cards, gambling and drinking heavily with friends such as Thomas Daniel (and probably fleecing some of the unwary young officers stationed on the island into the bargain, she thought). When he returned, he was somewhat stiff and aloof with her, but Lucy had already decided that her best way to deal with any continued animosity was to present a smiling, sunny face to him, which should also have the added benefit of diverting any censoriousness on Bathsheba's part towards Sam. She was right, it was one of the few occasions on which she heard his mother speak sharply to him.

"Samuel, you have not addressed one word to me since your return," she reprimanded him at the dinner table. "You are behaving like a bear with a sore head. What has put that frown on your face? Have you been losing money at dice to Mr Daniel again?"

Sam's lips thinned and his face darkened with a flush. As little as any man did he care to be given a dressing down by his mother in public.

"No, Mother, I did not lose money. I was merely reflecting on a rumour of some concern which is circulating. John Barrow mentioned it following training."

He addressed himself to the food on his plate and did not expand any further on the matter until he joined the women later for tea. He waited until there were no slaves in immediate earshot and said abruptly,

"Keep your eyes and ears open for any signs of malcontent among the slaves. It seems there may be a group of troublemakers trying to stir up a rebellion, no doubt led by those damned obeah-men. Savages must be using their jungle-drum system to pass messages between plantations. It'll probably come to nothing, but Barrow is convinced there's something afoot."

Lucy's thoughts went instantly to that day three years previously when she had found the slave girl Juba whispering with an unknown male slave. By reporting this at once to Bathsheba and John any burgeoning rebellion had been thwarted and Juba was sent to market. While that plot – if indeed there was one – had been prevented from gaining widespread support among the slaves, it sounded as though this time the removal of any single slave would not stop an uprising. Lucy shivered; how glad she was that Cecilia was safe in England!

She voiced this thought when Sam came to her room that night. He had undressed in his own room first and was wearing his brocade dressing-gown over a nightshirt. He was shrugging himself out of the gown and sighed in exasperation.

"Nothing will happen. We'll catch the perpetrators – we always do. The slaves have a good life, they don't need to worry about where to live or how to eat. They know what happens if they don't toe the line. They'll be whipped, their noses slit, and they'll lose everything when they're thrown off the plantation. Very few will risk that. We have never suffered the sort of rioting that occurred in Louisiana and I can't see it happening now. Cecilia would be quite safe here – and she will come out to join us, Lucy, make no mistake. I want her to know her heritage."

He put an end to the discussion by removing his wife's nightdress. The candle was still lit and Lucy turned her head away in embarrassment at the sight of her husband straddling her while raking her body with his eyes. Generally, their physical contact took place in the friendly dark. Then he bent his head and kissed her breasts, and Lucy felt a tingling of pleasure, responding with enjoyment to his lovemaking.

As usual, nothing was said about Sam's cruelty of the previous week. His words had cut Lucy to the quick and were even more painful, if that were possible, than the physical abuse he meted out. But there was nothing to be gained by resurrecting the conversation, and Lucy could only hope that he had said what he did in the heat of the moment and did not really mean it.

The following day, she sent a note to Mary Barrow, asking if she might call by to take tea with her. The slave who went to Sunbury returned with the message that Mary would be delighted to see her. Lucy would have preferred to ride, but mindful that Sam, having warned of possible slave unrest, would no doubt be angered if she went unaccompanied, she ordered out the dog-cart and took Jonas with her.

She had deliberately decided to visit during the working day, when John would probably be out in the fields or closeted in his office, as she wanted a private talk with Mary. For the same reason, she had not taken either of her two sisters-in-law with her. Mary Barrow greeted her kindly, as she always did, and led Lucy into a shady corner of the garden surrounded by exotic, sweet-smelling flowers and towering trees, where a table had been set with everything the ladies might need. It was quintessentially English, with tiny sandwiches, scones and cakes to accompany the tea, which was being prepared in a large silver urn as they arrived, and even a pack of cards on a small salver.

At first, Lucy and Mary chatted about the news coming from England, about fashion and hairstyles, as they sipped their tea and played piquet. Then Lucy laid down her cards, looked around to see where the ubiquitous slaves were (two of them stood under a tree nearby, ready to respond immediately to their mistress' orders), and lowered her voice to say,

"I would like your advice on a personal matter, Mary, if you do not mind the imposition."

Mary looked a little surprised but signalled to the two slaves that they should move further away, then turned back to Lucy and waited.

Lucy quailed inwardly. She was about to open herself up to someone in a way which all her breeding told her was indecorous; her mother's shocked and disapproving face floated before her mind's eye, but she had determined on this course and was not someone to be easily deterred. If Mary Kingsley had still been in Barbados, perhaps she would have found it easier to raise the subject with her. Stammering, she said,

"I – I had a very disturbing and unpleasant conversation with my husband recently which shocked me, and I did not know to whom I could turn for advice. I count you as my friend, Mary, so I hope you will not be upset or embarrassed by what I have to say, but please do tell me if you do not wish to discuss a deeply personal and delicate subject."

Mary clapped her hands to summon the slaves and ordered fresh hot water for tea. When they had cleared the used teacups, the urn and other paraphernalia and walked away towards the kitchen hut, she smiled at Lucy.

"Pray, continue, my dear. I am honoured that you look on me as a friend, I certainly consider you my friend, and I know John does too. Now tell me, what is bothering you?"

Thus encouraged, Lucy related the hurtful things Sam had said to her the previous week, though omitting his comments about John Barrow.

"I will admit I was shocked that Sam would say such things to me – in England it would be the height of impropriety even for a husband to discuss with his wife children born out of wedlock – and yet Sam was suggesting not only that he might have some but also that he was considering bringing one into my household as his heir! That was so hurtful. What must I do, Mary? What *can* I do?"

"The best thing that could happen is for you to start breeding again yourself. That will stop your husband looking elsewhere for a son. What he said is true, a small number of planters have adopted their by-blows (you must forgive my plain speaking, Lucy) but that has happened for centuries among the English royal family so they are in good company! Far more, however, simply take their pleasure among the slave women. Even my own dear John has fathered several half-breed children. We have them all baptised and teach them how to read and write."

"But – do you not *mind*?" Lucy asked with some incredulity.

"Oh – it hurts a little, but he is always so affectionate towards me, and I want for nothing, so I have nothing to complain of. I own I might feel differently should he decide to adopt one of them. You will probably find, my dear, that Sam has no intention of doing so and only said it in the heat of the moment, in a fit of anger. He is used to having his own way and – as I think you are all too aware – he can fly into violent rages if crossed."

Startled, Lucy looked directly at her friend, a question in her eyes. What she saw in Mary's sympathetic expression made her blush again. She looked down at her lap and began to pleat folds of her skirt between her fingers. So Mary knew – or at least guessed – that Sam hit her.

"How did you know?"

"I have sometimes noticed bruises on your arms and face, Lucy, and it has always been clear that you were not some insipid English miss who would submit meekly to any proposal her husband put to her but rather an intelligent young woman with views and opinions of her own who was unafraid to voice them. John said when we first met you that he expected fireworks from your union, and that you would be unlikely to put up with the wild behaviour Sam demonstrated before he left for England ten years ago. It must have been hard for you, so isolated from your family in England. I have often wished to offer you my sympathy but could not be sure you wished for it."

The slaves were walking back towards them, carefully carrying a steaming urn and clean crockery. As they laid this out on the table, Mary smiled and said,

"Shall we resume our card game?"

Lucy inclined her head to signify agreement, and while one of the slaves prepared the tea and another laid out clean tableware, she played her cards and thought about what her friend had said. It was comforting to know that the Barrows were sympathetic, but nonetheless Mary had not really answered Lucy's cry for help at the suggestion that Sam might adopt an illegitimate half-breed son – a notion that was all the more hurtful as it would mean such a child usurping the place of their beloved Oceanus. Lucy still ached with the loss of her son. And she was by no means as sanguine about Sam's intentions in this regard as Mary clearly was.

Nothing further was said on the matter; the ladies' conversation stayed on the mundane and Lucy was content to have it so. She spent a further hour or so in Mary's company, then made her way back to Long Bay.

The weeks leading up to Christmas 1814 continued much as before. The Lords entertained more than they had ever done when Lucy first came to Barbados, and Lucy became acquainted with several planters and their wives whom she had never previously met, both entertaining and being entertained by them.

She discovered that there was just as much social life on the island as there was in the country in England. Even Bathsheba, who had told Lucy she did not want to open herself up to being rebuffed by the plantocracy, appeared to enjoy the reduction in monotony, while Betty positively glowed and allowed her natural vivacity free rein. Sarah gave birth to another boy, Samuel, without mishap on the 8th of December, and there was much to-ing and fro-ing between the Pool and Long Bay estates during the Christmas period.

Nothing more had been said about a possible uprising among the slaves, and when Lucy taxed John Barrow about his fears he told her that he had not had these confirmed. He thought that the field slaves (who, along with their masters, had some time off on Christmas Day and organised their own celebrations) seemed content enough for now, but that he expected any signs of unrest to come to the fore again during the unrelenting sugar harvest period.

Mr Wightwick had written to tell Lucy that he had received her letter about Francine and was looking into the matter. She was disappointed – but not surprised – that she could not give Francine her freedom as a Christmas gift, but still said nothing; she did not want to tempt fate by promising the girl something she might not be able to deliver. Finally, in February 1815 a thick packet, carefully wrapped in waxed paper, arrived from Lucy's father, and this contained the long-awaited manumission deed. Lucy placed it carefully in the inside drawer of her desk, where she kept her diary, planning to tell her maid the good news when she could find a suitable time to do so.

Now that she finally had obtained Francine's freedom, she found herself oddly reluctant to offer it to her. What if Francine decided she no longer wished to stay at Long Bay? She might prefer to move to Bridgetown and set herself up in business there. Or perhaps she might look about for a suitable husband and settle down to have children of her own, now that they would be born free. Lucy was fond of Betty and of Mary Austin but they were members of Sam's family, and Mary Kingsley had returned to England. Lucy realised how little she wanted to lose Francine now that she had found her again, and there was certainly no-one Lucy would rather put in charge of any future children she and Sam might have. She decided to talk to her maid about what she might choose to do if she were ever to obtain her freedom before actually handing over the deed.

She locked the desk and went downstairs to meet the cook, oversee the cleaning, cut flowers for all the rooms and bring her household accounts (the aspect Bathsheba had shown most reluctance to hand over) up to date. It had taken an intervention by Sam to ensure that Lucy had control of the household budget, and she was determined not to make even the smallest error in her figures. As she reached the bottom of the stairs she noticed, among the letters lying ready to be taken to Bridgetown to catch the next packet, one addressed to

Hewelsfield written in Sam's large, scrawling handwriting. Why would Sam be writing to her father? It was surprising that he had not mentioned that he intended doing so – it was to be expected that he might ask if she wished to include a letter of her own with it. She would ask him about it at dinner, if he was in a genial mood.

Lucy was sketching in the garden when she saw Sam galloping towards the house in the late afternoon. As he swung himself down from his horse it was easy to see that he was in a towering rage, and her heart sank. He could be heard shouting for Joseph, cursing as he did so, and she wondered what had angered him. She hoped his rage would be short-lived, but in any case today was clearly not the right time to evince curiosity about his correspondence, he would be bound to call her impertinent and would probably hit her, or worse.

She continued drawing for a further half hour then gathered up her sketchbook and watercolours and made her way towards the house, nodding to one of the young slaves who came running up to collect her easel without being asked, for by now they were accustomed to her ways. Wearily, she took off her hat and shoes and lay down on her chaise longue, hoping to replenish her energy with a sleep before it was time to dress for dinner. But although she closed her eyes, she was kept awake by the thought going round and round in her head, what in the world could Sam be writing to her father about? A loan perhaps, to provide the wherewithal to start his building project? Something to do with Cecilia? But in that case, why had he not said anything to her?

An unwelcome suspicion began to form in Lucy's brain. All hope of sleep vanished, and she sat up slowly and went to sit in her favourite position by the window. Was Sam trying to persuade her parents to arrange for Cecilia to travel to Barbados, possibly with the intention of presenting Lucy with a *fait accompli* when the little girl arrived and it was too late to prevent it? Surely, he could not be so cruel – or could he? Indeed, had he ever actually promised *not* to have their daughter sent out? Revisiting all the conversations they had had on the subject, Lucy was reluctantly forced to admit that she had allowed herself to believe that they had reached agreement whereas in actual fact Sam had always clearly stated that at some point sooner rather than later he wished to see Cecilia on the island.

When she joined the family on the veranda for drinks later, Sam – who had obviously already imbibed copious quantities of punch – was there, talking to his mother and sisters, "… and how three of them managed to get away I have no idea! I've a good mind to tan Malcolm's hide for him, but I want to make sure he puts the fear of God into the rest of those damn' Negroes and finds the runaways first."

He looked up, the scowl still on his face, and saw his wife hesitating in the doorway.

"There you are, wife! You'd best keep an eye on the house slaves in case any of them try to make a run for it. I'm revoking all passes so none of 'em can go off to Bridgetown or any of the plantations without one of us until I get to the bottom of this." Lucy looked an unspoken question at them all, and it was her mother-in-law who answered it.

"Three of our best field slaves have run off, presumably together. They must be found and punished, as a lesson to the rest. You shall advertise their loss in the paper, of course, Samuel?" He growled assent and downed another cup of punch. Lucy's heart sank, but she came forward and said calmly,

"I have not noticed any signs of unrest or sullenness among the house slaves, Sam. Have you, ma'am?" This last question to show courteous deference to Bathsheba, who shook her head.

"We will pay particular attention to them, Sam. It is unfortunate, I believe Jeremiah is doing some carpentry for Harrow plantation. No doubt the Altons will be annoyed at any delay."

"It can't be helped. Write a note to explain – they'll understand. And if it hurts Jeremiah in his pocket, perhaps he will be keen to tell me anything he knows about the three who've gone. I'll speak to him now." Sam sent one of the slaves scurrying to find Jeremiah and bring him to the office and went there himself to wait, slamming the door.

"It is a most inconvenient time for this to happen," said Bathsheba. "February and March are our busiest months, and I know John was counting on some of the Long Bay slaves going to help with the sugar harvest at Pool. Let us hope they are quickly caught."

Over the next few days the search went on. One slave was dragged back in chains, tied behind the dog-cart driven fast by Malcolm, the overseer. He was already bloodied from falling frequently on the road, but the whole plantation was ordered out to see him whipped and his nose slit. Lucy tried to avert her eyes but could not avoid quietly retching at the pitiful sight. His screams rent the air, and he was too weak to move after the flogging so he was left where he collapsed in the middle of the yard as a lesson to the rest. The other slaves looked at the ground and shuffled their feet and Lucy could feel waves of hate emanating from them. She studied the house slaves carefully, but their demeanour was one of sorrowful stoicism rather than anger directed at their owners.

The second was found a week later. His leg had become caught in a snare (some of the planters placed them in the wooded areas around their property for just such an eventuality) and the limb had already become gangrenous so it had to be amputated at the knee. He survived another couple of days, then died.

The third was Agnes, the girl who had been caught stealing from Lucy, and she was never found. Doubtless she was either living in hiding in Bridgetown or had fallen to her death into one of the many deep gullies which riddled the island.

"And a good riddance, too," was Sam's comment. "She was never much use in the field, bone idle."

With all of this going on, it had not seemed advisable to question Sam about the letter Lucy had seen and, indeed, she almost forgot about it until one day in April when the Falmouth Packet brought a letter for her from her mother along with several letters for Sam.

My dearest Lucy,

I was surprised but pleased to learn that you had decided to arrange for Cecilia to live with you at Long Bay. We shall be sorry to lose her. She is a delightful child, and both Papa and I have become very fond of her, but it is only right and proper that you, her parents, take on the responsibility for bringing her up. As you know, I was shocked that you should set yourself up against your husband in this.

I am concerned that she will not be travelling with you, but I understand that Mr Lord has asked your father to locate a suitable woman to have the care of her on the voyage and he, of course, will be with them. Nurse, you know, is getting on in years and it is all too much for her.

I hope that you are well on the way to doing your duty by your husband and will present him with an heir shortly who will be a companion for Cecilia.

Please convey my regards and best wishes to Mrs Lord, your mother-in-law.

We are all well here, although I find that I have a little rheumatism now, not helped by the wet weather. Your brother Stubbs is now undertaking his articles and doing very well according to your Papa.

With my fondest love
Your Mother, Lucy

Lucy read the letter through twice in stunned silence in the privacy of her bedroom. The house was very quiet. Mrs Lord was resting in her room, the ailing Sarah had not appeared downstairs for several days, Betty was staying away with friends in the North of the island and Bathsheba had driven out to visit Sarah at Pool.

An icy rage seized Lucy. She had been right in her suspicions – how *dare* he? How *dare* he? She crumpled the letter in her fist then smoothed the thin paper out and reread her mother's words. Her first thought was that she must confront Sam with his perfidy and demand that he call a halt to his plans. Cecilia was far too young, she would be bound to contract scarlet fever, or typhus, or measles in Barbados. Lucy was not going to submit tamely to her wishes being gainsaid and losing a third child to this disease-ridden hellhole! But then she remembered that Sam had left that morning for one of his periodic visits to Bridgetown to meet Thomas Daniel and other cronies and would not return for several days. She would confront Bathsheba instead. No doubt her mother-in-law was in on this dirty little secret.

She stood up, smoothed her skirts and checked that everything about her appearance was neat and orderly, then walked along the corridor to Bathsheba's room and knocked briskly on the door. This was opened by Bathsheba's maid Rose who looked surprised to see Lucy but stood back to let her in. Bathsheba was sitting by the window sewing.

"I have received a letter from my mother, ma'am and wish to discuss its contents with you," said Lucy without preamble.

Her mother-in-law stretched out one gnarled hand and Lucy put the slightly crumpled paper into it, standing in front of Bathsheba while she read it.

"Were you aware of your son's plans to go behind my back, and against my express wishes?" she demanded, her normally soft brown eyes bright with anger.

Bathsheba looked steadily at her fuming daughter-in-law, something like approval in her eyes at this show of spirit. She handed back the letter, neatly folded.

"I was aware that he planned to have Cecilia brought here as soon as possible – like Mrs Wightwick, I disapproved of you going against *his* wishes – but I did not know that he had already arranged everything. Indeed, I had no knowledge that he intended to go to England himself to fetch her!"

"So you approve of his going behind my back, ma'am? I might have known it!" Lucy almost spat the words out, beside herself with fury.

"It will surprise you to know that I do not condone his behaviour in concealing his plans. I believe he should have told you what he was going to do and brooked no opposition! But that is past praying for now. What do you intend to do?"

"I shall confront him on his return and insist he put a stop to this madness, ma'am," returned Lucy coldly, and turning on her heel left the room with her head held high to return to her own room and there to pen a response to her mother almost commanding her parents to do everything they could to thwart Sam's wishes. She sent one of the slaves to Bridgetown, bidding him to make haste and send the letter by the first ship due to leave for England, and to return at once to let her know the name of the vessel and the date she was to sail.

She had to wait a further three days for her husband to return but, far from cooling her anger, the delay only served to stoke the flames.

Sam was in a cheerful mood. He had won a tidy sum at a game of blackjack during a long night's carouse with his friend Thomas Daniel (who was about to leave for England again on one of his own ships), and his man of business had at last received a positive response from Charles Rutter to Sam's request to discuss the decoration of his planned new mansion at Long Bay. He would meet the man during his visit to England to collect his daughter Cecilia and had already written to Mr Rutter to advise his – Sam's – likely date of arrival in June, asking him to propose to the Lords' man of business in London a suitable date for them to meet.

Lucy did not see Sam return, she had driven over with Betty to visit Sarah at Pool. John was away on Assembly business in Bridgetown, and Sarah seemed to welcome their frequent intrusions on her isolation. The two ladies stayed for a light luncheon, dutifully admired the flock of Sarah's children paraded before them and rode gently back to Long Bay under a darkening sky with lightning flickering on the horizon.

Sam was closeted in his office with the overseer when Lucy and Betty arrived back at the house. Much as she would have liked to burst in on the meeting and throw all his iniquities at Sam's head immediately, Lucy knew that it was quite within her husband's nature to belittle her and throw her out in front of Malcolm, which would put her on the back foot in the argument they were bound to have about Cecilia. So she waited until Sam came out onto the veranda for drinks, and when he greeted her genially said only,

"I should like a word with you, sir – in private if you please."

Sam raised an eyebrow, gave an exaggerated bow and ushered her back into the house before him, lounging behind her as she walked swiftly towards the office. Once inside, she drew her mother's letter from her reticule, turned to Sam and handed it to him saying in a voice which trembled with pent-up anger,

"I should like to know what the *devil* you mean by conspiring behind my back to bring our little daughter here, despite all your promises?"

Sam hardly seemed to notice her unladylike language but stiffened at her tone. He took the proffered letter without a word, taking his time to read it and silently cursing the fact that Lucy's regular correspondence with her mother meant that it was always likely that she would find out about his planned trip before his departure, which was now imminent.

"I know how much you miss Cecilia and, since I must visit England soon on business, thought it would be a pleasant surprise if I returned here with her. I know you would not wish her to travel in some stranger's company…"

"You know very well that I have no wish for Cecilia to come here at all! I wish her to be safe, and to grow up in a gentle, civilised environment. We agreed that she is better off with my parents than here with us. Why are you planning to break that agreement?"

Lucy's voice had risen now and there were two hectic spots of colour on her cheeks. Sam's brows drew together in a frown and all his earlier geniality vanished.

"She is my daughter and I will decide what is right for her. That is the law, as you very well know. To humour you, I agreed to allow Cecilia to remain for a period only with your parents, it was never intended to be a permanent arrangement. She has spent an additional twelve months in England and doubtless will recognise neither of us. I am not prepared for such a state of affairs to continue."

"She is no older than our son was when he died! She would be vulnerable to every disease which is prevalent here – the more so because she has been sheltered from them until now! Surely that is not the outcome you desire, Sam?"

Lucy's attempt to appeal to his better nature had no impact.

"Damn you, woman, of course I do not wish our only child to fall ill or to die! How dare you even suggest such a thing when it was you, not I, who could not have cared less what happened to little Emma! But our children belong here, this is their heritage, whatever their fate…"

Lucy clasped her husband's hands, looking up into his stormy face. "Please, Sam," she begged now, "let Cecilia remain with my parents for a few more years and when she is stronger, we can look again at bringing her out here."

He jerked his hands away from her so roughly that she staggered backwards and almost lost her balance, grabbing the edge of the huge, mahogany office desk for support as Sam lost his temper in earnest and thundered, "I have made my decision, you will accept it. I will not have my daughter grow up without knowing me. I have told you before I want children in our new house – she shall be the first of many. I have been too lenient with you for too long. It is your duty to obey me and obey me you shall! I leave for England in a few days with Daniel on one of his ships and will write to advise you when I plan to return with Cecilia. Now – I want my dinner!"

"But, Sam…"

"Enough, woman! I will brook no more of your defiance. A period in the storm cellar should remind you of your duties as a wife." He had taken a stride towards her as he said this and slapped her face viciously. Now he grasped her arm above the elbow, turning her so sharply towards the door that she twisted her ankle and cried out which merely seemed to anger him further. Having thrown open the door he twisted his free hand around her hair and dragged her towards the back of the house. Their shouting had brought Betty, at least, to the doorway of the dining-room. Lucy was aware of her sister-in-law's shocked face as Sam hauled her out of the house towards the storm cellar, shouting for the cook to come and unlock the door as they passed the kitchen hut.

The cook – who was far too fat to move as fast as Master Sam required her to on this occasion – sent one of her juniors running with the key; his eyes were wide and frightened, shining in the darkness, and his hand trembled so much that he had difficulty turning the key in the lock.

Sam shoved the boy out of the way; he fell without a sound and scrambled up immediately to make a hasty retreat lest his master decide to beat him rather than his wife. As he released his hold on Lucy's hair, a clump of it remained caught in Sam's signet ring and tore away, a sudden sharp pain surging through her. Lucy found herself shoved violently in the back and, tripping over her gown, fell hard and awkwardly onto her knees and one elbow, jarring every bone in her body. Sam aimed a kick at her backside just as she tried to get up, sending her sprawling again and, as he slammed the door shut, said menacingly,

"And there you shall stay, wife, until after I am safely away on my voyage."

Chapter 18
Escape

Lucy sat up. It was pitch black. She put her hand down to feel her twisted ankle. It felt slightly swollen but hurt no more than her other bruises and rather less than her scalp, down which she could feel a small trickle of blood where Sam had inadvertently pulled out her hair. She tried standing but found she could put little weight on the damaged ankle. She would have to hop or crawl to find somewhere to sit. Crawling seemed the safer option.

She turned in the direction of the door and her outstretched hand knocked against the thick wood almost immediately. Now she stood and leaned against it and tried to visualise her surroundings. She thought that Sam had marched her past the usual entrance to the cellar which the kitchen slaves used to collect and store produce; that meant he had once again – as he had two years previously – shut her in that part of the cellar used for punishing slaves condemned to solitary confinement. If she was correct, it was unlikely that she would find any comforting sacks of grain to lie on or tea chests on which to sit. Her prison would be bare of anything other than a bucket for a privy and a jug for water if she was lucky. Slowly, limping but determined to stand if she could, she felt her way around the walls (which did not take long) until she came to another door. If she was right, the presence of a second door would confirm her fears so she set out on her slow journey once again, this time counting corners. There were definitely two doors, as she had feared, she was in the smaller, slave gaol end of the cellar.

She slid down and sat with her knees pulled up to her chest on the cold, uneven stones, leaning her back – with a wince – against the rough wall. Something – a rat? – scurried across her foot, but she was too bruised and tired to pay much attention. Her mind was racing. When was Sam leaving for England? She had absolutely no idea – he had mentioned nothing to her until today – and she therefore could not guess how long she might remain imprisoned. But it was clear that somehow she must escape and make her own way back to her parents' home to try and prevent Sam removing Cecilia from their care and transporting her to Barbados.

This time, she thought, he had gone too far. Despite everything he had done, all the humiliation she had suffered, Lucy had always believed – wanted to believe? – that Sam loved her. She had borne him three children already; was it *her* fault two had died? Was that what had changed his attitude towards her? Or had her father been right about his character all along? Reluctantly, she steeled herself to think objectively about all that had happened over the years since she had met him.

When Sam had first brought her to Barbados, all through the voyage he had been affectionate and even loving, and there had been no mistaking his genuine delight when she gave birth to Oceanus. It was only once they had reached Long Bay – and even then, not immediately – that he had become cruel and violent.

She tried to remember when things had first gone awry. She had quickly learned Sam had a temper and did not like to be crossed, but their arguments had generally centred at first on her behaviour in defying him, or expressing disapproval of what she viewed as barbarism and he had been brought up to believe was the norm. So perhaps she must accept some responsibility for this. Of course, he had also frequently become frustrated by the lack of progress with his dream project, and she supposed it was a wife's lot to provide an outlet for her husband's anger. But then, after the party held to celebrate the twins' christening, he had raped her. She had done nothing to incite such cruelty, so what had made him behave so? Was it a character flaw which she should have recognised while they were still in England? Or simply a moment of madness resulting from too much strong drink, as her good friend Mary Kingsley had believed? It was possible. After all, he could still be kind and attentive, as he had been when they visited Sunbury for Crop Over, or when he was gentle and patient with their children or, indeed, his nieces and nephews.

She supposed the rot had really started to set in when she had become ill towards the end of her second pregnancy and Oceanus had died. Still trying to be objective, she reluctantly accepted that she must have been unbearable to live with and that she could not really blame Sam for seeking his pleasure elsewhere or becoming impatient with her. And she had been wrong to act counter to his express command that she stay away from the slave quarters, but she could not believe that justified his physical violence towards her. Had she been wrong about this, though? Her friend Mary had shown no surprise – was it her own fault for not being suitably submissive? She thought of her mother's strictures about her headstrong behaviour when she was growing up (not to mention her runaway marriage to Sam, she thought ruefully) and sighed. She could not change her nature.

She forced her thoughts towards the good times. There was a pattern to Sam's behaviour, as she had recognised before. When he was busy, when he was faced with danger, he revelled in it. The monotony and lack of independence in life at Long Bay had driven her to depression and Sam to anger. Perhaps she could and should have handled things differently, done more to ensure she was constantly breeding like Sarah in the hope of having more offspring survive the childhood illnesses to which so many succumbed, accepted Sam's inalienable right to decide where their children were brought up… But that too – although normal practice for any married woman – would be against her nature. All in all, she decided, she would have had to be a very different person to accept, as Mary Barrow did, her husband's infidelities, or Sam's continual violence towards her when things did not go the way he wanted. And she could never, ever forgive him for deliberately going behind her back and deciding to put their only surviving child in danger by insisting on Cecilia being brought up in Barbados. As she thought about his duplicity, she felt her own temper flare once more and steeled herself to consider how she might thwart her husband's plan.

First, she needed to get out of her prison. And second, she needed to purchase her passage on a ship destined for England. Neither objective would be easy to achieve. She could not count on Betty helping her out this time. No doubt Sam would have given strict instructions that his wife must remain in the cellar and it was unlikely that she would disobey a direct order from the head of the house. Perhaps Francine? But even if Francine realised where Lucy was, she would be unable to obtain the key to the cellar from the cook. None of the slaves would dare gainsay the master; the punishment would be too severe. Briefly, Lucy considered trying to get a message to her mother-in-law, then dismissed the idea since Bathsheba would almost certainly feel that Sam had been perfectly within his rights to punish his wife, and once she knew Lucy was trying to escape would exercise vigilance on his behalf.

Even when she was released, how would she pay for her voyage? She still had no money of her own and was unsure whether the Lords had an account with any of the ship owners against which she might charge it. She still had a few pieces of jewellery, perhaps a captain might be found who would be willing to accept them in payment – although it was unlikely there would be enough left to buy ship-board necessities like food. Moreover, all this would take time – time she did not have. She needed to arrive at Hewelsfield while Sam was still there or her efforts would be in vain.

Lucy had been sitting in one place for so long that her body had become stiff. She tried to stand and bit her lip in pain as she put too much weight on her injured foot. She probed the ankle gingerly with her fingers, it was swollen, and would no doubt be turning black and blue. She lifted her skirts and, as best she could, loosened her stays to give her bruised ribs some respite.

Since she did not know when he was to set sail, she had no idea whether Sam intended to incarcerate her for hours or days, or indeed whether he would inform anyone else of her whereabouts or tell them to let her out once he had left for Bridgetown. The cook, of course, was aware where she was; she could only hope that Francine would have reason to go to the kitchen hut and would find out what had happened.

The booming sound of the waves, so ubiquitous at Long Bay that she did not notice it anymore in everyday life, was magnified in the cellar, almost as if they were crashing against the very walls. The noise drowned out any other sounds, and Lucy felt incredibly alone. To dispel her anxiety, she limped slowly around the confined space, one hand on the wall, stooping every now and then to look for the latrine bucket. She found it and this removed one concern, she had no desire to do as she had on the previous occasion and relieve herself directly on the floor. She felt better after she had used it but immediately began to feel very thirsty. Another careful turn around her prison failed to locate a jug containing water and she wondered how long she could hold out without a drink.

She started to feel sorry for herself and to stave off any descent into self-pity tried to work out a plan. It all hinged on Francine. If she could speak to her maid, she would promise her freedom in return for her help. She would send the girl to Sunbury and enlist the aid of the Barrows in purchasing passage. Then she remembered that Mary Barrow had told her they were going on a visit to friends at another plantation in the far north of the island. Briefly she considered throwing herself on the mercy of Mary Austin or John and Sarah Lord, but she was reluctant to set any member of the Lord family at loggerheads with Sam. She would have to hope that Francine felt able to locate a suitable ship, either through her own endeavours or, ideally, through one of the go-betweens among the free coloured community Lucy knew the slaves used for their own transactions in Bridgetown, and that the sale of Lucy's jewellery would provide sufficient funds for the purpose.

Lucy stretched and winced. Her whole body ached, her knees and right arm from falling hard on them, her swollen ankle, her head, her backside from Sam's kick – indeed she thought she must be black and blue all over. She staggered upright once again and resumed her stumbling progress around the walls, partly to ease her muscles and partly to while away the time. She wondered how long she had been in the cellar but had no way of telling. After a while she sat down again, this time by the door, and leaning back against it dozed fitfully. In her waking moments she thought with longing about Cecilia and their possible reunion, fiercely determined that Sam should not steal her away. She dreaded the idea that she might arrive in England too late and began to feel a rising tide of panic. If she stayed at Long Bay and waited for Sam's return, how could she ever keep her daughter safe? And if she reached Hewelsfield after his departure, would it be possible for her to come back to Barbados? Even if her father purchased her return passage, her situation at the Lord family home would be untenable, and she would never have another opportunity to leave – nor would she wish to do so without Cecilia.

By now Lucy was consumed with a raging thirst and she began to hallucinate. She was sure she heard voices and banged on the door in the hopes that someone would hear her. She tried to call out but her throat was so parched that she could only emit a faint croak which would never be heard through the thick timbers. A salty tear slid down her cheek and she dashed it angrily away. She thought the booming of the waves would drive her mad, so she got to her feet again and started her painful hobbling around the walls once more. She kicked the latrine bucket with her sore foot and almost doubled over in pain, sobbing drily. She began muttering angrily, scolding herself for her weakness and reciting over and over again why she must escape and what she would say to Sam when she next saw him. This, she told herself firmly, would be at Hewelsfield, where she would prove herself as brave as any savage lioness protecting her cub.

She slid wearily back down the door to a seated position and the whole process – dozing, imagining seeing Cecilia again and arguing with Sam, walking round her prison, hearing voices – repeated itself. Lucy had completely lost track of time, she could have been imprisoned for just a few hours or for several days.

She made use of the bucket again (she could no longer remember if it was only the second time or more) but she was becoming dehydrated, and only a trickle came out. When awake, she was talking almost constantly to herself in the pitch dark. She knew she was doing so because she could hear herself croaking. She ran her tongue across dry, cracked lips and wondered how long she could bear this.

She dozed again and woke certain that she could hear someone knocking at the door. She twisted round onto her knees and banged with both fists on the panels. This time there was no mistaking it, someone knocked back! A fierce exultation seized her and she hit the wood in a frenzy and tried in vain to shout. Silence, apart from the booming waves. She knocked again, nothing. Despairing, she curled up in a foetal position on the hard floor. Whoever it was had not heard her and had gone away – but at least, she thought with a glimmer of hope, it must mean someone was looking for her?

Time passed and Lucy dreamed that she was arriving at her parents' home, only to find it locked up and silent. She knocked on the door in hope of catching the attention of any passing servant left behind as caretaker – and someone knocked back. Rousing herself, Lucy sat up stiffly, there it was again, someone knocking on the door. Dimly she realised that there really was someone at the door to her prison cell and she resumed her frenzied knocking of sometime before. She stopped and listened intently, there was the clear sound of a key grating in the lock. She stumbled backwards, remembering even in her fevered state that the door opened inwards.

The door opened, letting a rush of fresh night air into the fetid cell and with it all the powerful scents of tropical flowers, wood smoke from the kitchen fire and saltiness from the sea. She breathed deeply, took a couple of tottering steps forwards and fell to the ground in a dead faint. When she came to, her head was in someone's lap and her face was being wiped gently with a wet towel. So desperate was she for water that she tried to take the towel in her teeth and suck at it. She felt her head being raised slightly, the towel was removed and a mug held to her lips. She drank greedily and gagged at once, turning her head away as she immediately vomited up the refreshing liquid.

"Gently, Miss Lucy," came a whisper from Francine. "Drink small." Cautiously the slave held the cup to Lucy's lips again, allowing her only a few sips before taking it away.

"Has Master Sam left?" Lucy croaked.

"No, mistress. Massa Sam inside with Massa Daniel."

"Does he know you're here?"

Francine held the cup to her lips again. "No Miss Lucy. I hear Miss Betty say him he must let you go, and he very angry. I think maybe he put you here again."

"How did you get the key?"

"I stole it," Francine answered matter-of-factly.

"Listen, Francine. Master Sam is going to England to fetch my daughter and bring her back here, and I do not wish him to do so. She must not die as Oceanus and Emma did. I have to get to England to stop him doing this. Do you know when he means to leave? Can you find out?"

"Yes, mistress. Thomas or Joseph, they know."

"Good. Now, my husband has said I must stay here until he has left so I will need your help. I must find a ship to take me to England. Will you go to Bridgetown to arrange it for me?"

Lucy felt rather than saw Francine shake her head and was disappointed.

"I not know what to do, Miss Lucy," the girl said in a fierce whisper.

"I will help you but I cannot go myself – at least, not yet and I must arrive before him. But first, will you find out when Master Sam is taking ship, what ship it is and when he will be leaving Long Bay?"

"That I will do, mistress. But I cannot leave you here."

"You must. But please bring some more water and leave it with me. What time is it, Francine?"

"It is night-time. The ladies go to bed, but Massa Sam and Massa Thomas playin' cards."

Carefully, Francine helped Lucy to her feet and when she cried out at the pain of her twisted ankle Francine knelt to feel it and promised to bring some of her obeah ointment when she brought the water. She left the door of the cellar ajar and went off on her errands.

When she returned, she anointed the swollen ankle and bandaged it, handed Lucy a jug of water and a kerchief containing a little food that she had scrounged from the kitchen (the cook had already retired to the slave quarters for the night), and went to fetch the soil bucket to empty its contents. Lucy thanked her profusely and, somewhat reluctantly, Francine locked her mistress in again, promising to return as soon as she could with information about Sam's departure.

Relieved that Sam had not already left, with her ankle aching less abominably and with her thirst quenched, Lucy's spirits rose and she did not mind too much when Francine pulled the cellar door closed and locked it again. She realised she still did not know how long she had been imprisoned, was this the same day Sam had thrown her into the cellar, or the next? She shrugged; it did not matter. She curled up against the door and started to plan exactly what instructions she must give her maid when she returned but, worn out by the day's events, she soon found herself nodding off and lay down on the hard floor. She was fast asleep in minutes.

When she awoke all her aches and pains had returned tenfold; her stays had dug into her ribs and the hard floor into other parts of her anatomy. Groaning, she groped her way to the bucket and having used it located the water jug and took a few sips. Despite her thirst she was aware that she must economise on the water as she had no way of knowing when Francine would be able to return.

She forced herself to limp around the cell a few times, dragging her hand along the wall as she had before, then sat down and resumed thinking about the instructions she would give Francine, if the girl proved willing to try and secure passage for her. Once she had – she hoped – gone over every eventuality in her head, she untied the little package of food Francine had left her and nibbled at a piece of bread. She had not been conscious of any hunger beforehand, but as soon as she started to eat, she realised she was ravenous. Again, she rationed herself. She tried to work out what else was contained in the kerchief: a golden apple, a breadfruit, some meat. She took a few bites out of the golden apple, then wrapped the remainder up with the other items and tied the kerchief securely. She began to feel sleepy and dozed off, leaning against the door. She woke from a vivid dream about Cecilia, watching the little girl at play in the garden at Hewelsfield which unaccountably had sprouted breadfruit and mango trees…

For the next few hours she dozed and walked, had a few sips of water and dozed again. She began to get anxious, what if the cook had found out that Francine had taken the key? Perhaps she was in the stocks and unable to visit her mistress. What on earth would she, Lucy, do then? She tried, not altogether successfully, to persuade herself that Francine's loyalty was such that she would come back, and that perhaps not much time had passed although the hours seemed to drag.

Eventually she heard another knock at the door. She stood up and backed away, a key turned in the lock and Francine opened the door, flooding the dingy cellar with light. She stood there, hopping from one foot to the other in agitation.

"Me no stay, Miss Lucy. Massa Sam, he have passage on the Berwick for day after tomorrow. He leavin' soon now. Here is water, I come back later." And with that, before Lucy could say anything, she pulled the door shut and locked it again. Lucy banged on the wood in frustration, but she understood her maid's fear and, in any case, it would not suit her own plans to get her caught. Miserably, she sat down again and tried to wait with as much patience as she could muster. At least she could now drink her fill.

The next time Francine came it was already dark. Lucy learned that Sam had left Long Bay and given instructions to Betty and his mother that his wife must remain in the cellar until he had set sail on the Berwick. Lucy thumped her fists on the ground with frustration. Even if Francine were prepared to go alone to Bridgetown and attempt to purchase a place for Lucy on another ship, it would all take too long. She hurriedly revised her plans.

"Listen, Francine. Are any of the slaves being sent to Bridgetown on business tomorrow? Could you arrange for me to go with them? And I will need you to come with me – I do not have any money, and you must sell my jewellery so that I can pay for my passage. You can do that, can't you?"

Francine nodded slowly. "I know a woman, yes. And I t'ink Jeremiah, he go work." Jeremiah was one of the plantation carpenters and, as frequently happened with skilled slaves, would sell his skills elsewhere when not needed on the estate, either for his own benefit or for his master's. "But, mistress – the cart no good for you!"

Lucy thought of the picture she must present – dirty, dishevelled, her hair in disarray – and smiled wryly in the darkness. "I do not think I can be too choosy about how I travel, Francine. I feel I must look like a vagabond! Will you find out if he is going and when? And will you come with me?"

The girl hesitated. "What will happen to me, mistress? I be beaten and sent to fields again, and I cannot!" she wailed.

"No you will not, Francine. You are my slave, and I have purchased your freedom. I will give it to you if you will help me do this."

There was a long silence, and Lucy worried that Francine was still too afraid to acquiesce. In fact, it was astonishment that kept her quiet.

"Is this true, Miss Lucy? You do this for me?" in a quavering little voice.

When Lucy confirmed this, she was rewarded with a shuddering sigh. "Oh, t'ank you, t'ank you! I do anything you ask!"

"Then, find out as quickly as you can who is going to town tomorrow and when and come back to let me know. Then we must think how you are going to smuggle me out of here without anyone else in the household knowing."

Francine was so bowled over with excitement at the enormity of what she had just been offered that she almost forgot to lock the door and Lucy had to call her back. The girl scampered off, and Lucy sat back down to wait again.

The next time she visited a few hours later, she told Lucy that Jeremiah was indeed going to Bridgetown with his tools and would be leaving for Oistins before eight o'clock in the morning. It was agreed that Francine would come and fetch Lucy when the slave bell rang and smuggle her up the back stairs to fetch what she needed. Lucy asked wistfully if Francine could take water up for her to wash (she dared not order hot water for a bath as that would arouse suspicion). This time, Francine left the door unlocked. No-one else would visit her mistress in the meantime, and the slave was unsure she would be able to steal the key again as the cook was likely to be busy in the kitchen preparing breakfast.

Lucy spent some time thinking about what she should take with her on the journey. She would only be able to pack a very small bag with perhaps one change of clothes – Jeremiah would be very surprised if told to load one of her trunks on the cart – and her travelling cloak, an absolute must for the sea voyage, would take up a great deal of space. While she pondered, she finished the food – a little dry now, but welcome nonetheless – and washed it down with gulps of water. Oh, how happy she would be to leave this hated cellar! She thought how pleasant it would be to look out at the moon and listen to the tree frogs one last time, but when she tried to open the door, she found there was no handle on the inside. All she could do was wait for Francine to return in the morning, so she curled up on the hard floor to get what sleep she could.

She was awake before her maid arrived, but even though she was listening out for the slave bell, the thick door and booming waves conspired to make sure she did not hear it. Francine had brought no light with her but seemed to be able to see clearly in the dark. She guided a limping Lucy unerringly around the side of the house towards the back door, opposite the kitchen hut, where they waited briefly in the shadows to ensure the cook did not see them. They crept as quickly up the back staircase as Lucy's damaged ankle would allow, and she breathed a sigh of relief when they reached her room. As soon as they were inside Lucy began peeling off her filthy clothes, dropping them on the floor. There were two cans and a large bucket of water awaiting her, so once Francine had poured one can into the ewer, she soaped herself vigorously and rinsed her body off with a cloth provided for that purpose. She knelt and dipped her head in the bucket, then lathered her hair and rinsed the soap off by dunking her head in the bucket once more, relishing the feeling of being clean again. As she stood, Francine wrapped a towel around her. Lucy began to pelt her with questions.

"Have you arranged for us to travel to Bridgetown with Jeremiah? What time does he leave?"

"Yes, Miss Lucy. Him not go without you."

"Did you fetch a valise? I must take clothes with me – and my travelling cloak – but I cannot take my trunk. I must be able to carry the bag myself." When Francine nodded, Lucy went on, "And you, Francine, you will come to Bridgetown with me as we discussed? Do you know whom to approach for help in selling my jewellery and arranging my passage to England? Oh – Francine, look in my jewellery box, you will find the gold necklace Mr Lord once gave me and the pearl earrings from my father. They should bring enough money to cover the voyage. Anything left in the box can go in the valise."

Silently, Francine fetched the jewel case for her mistress to open, then began to lay out clothes for her to wear. She also pulled a somewhat travel-worn valise from under the bed where she must have hidden it the previous evening.

For the next thirty minutes Francine was kept scurrying between helping her mistress to dress and collecting then discarding a variety of items from the clothes press.

"I will need an extra pair of light shoes but also one pair of sturdy ones, for when it rains. Oh – and I will need small clothes, I think three of everything should suffice. Indeed, it must for I will not have room to take more... My hairbrushes, the brush for my teeth... Is there another cake of soap, Francine? I should take one of those also.

"Where is my sketchbook? No, there is no room for my easel or my paints, so I had best leave it behind. But I should like to take one or two of my favourite books, and I will fetch my diary from the *escritoire*...

"Heavens! Where are my wits? You are quite right, Francine – of course I shall need my night attire also," for Francine was already hard at work folding the growing mountain of clothes laid out on the bed and had just pulled a nightgown and cap from the press, preparatory to putting them in the valise.

Of course there was far too much to fit into one small bag, particularly since Lucy would not be wearing her travelling cloak in the humid heat of Barbados and this alone was voluminous enough to take up most of the space. In the end Lucy decided she must take two bags, she would carry one and Francine the other when they went downstairs. So the maid was despatched to unearth another from the store while Lucy herself tackled the contents of her desk. Not only did she need to take out her diary but also a few small items of value, and the deed of manumission for Francine. She searched every nook and cranny and found a handful of English coins but certainly not sufficient to pay for a postchaise should her ship dock in London. They must make every effort to find a vessel to take her to Chepstow or Bristol; besides, that way she might have a chance of arriving at Hewelsfield not long after Sam.

She heard footsteps walking briskly along the wooden floorboards of the passage, a white person's footsteps. She froze in what she was doing, scared that someone was coming to investigate the noises coming from her room when the whole family knew Lucy was locked in the cellar. She thought she could count on sympathy from the sisters but her mother-in-law would be more likely to drag her back down and lock her up again. Then she would never escape, Francine would be punished and sent to the fields, and Sam would bring Cecilia to this pestilential island where she would die of some horrible disease like their other children.

On the verge of panic Lucy bit her lip to stop herself crying out and cowered in the corner between her desk and the window. She relaxed and let out the breath she had been holding, the footsteps had gone past her room. Whoever it was had not heard her rummaging. Francine had still not returned, so Lucy sat down to write a short note to her mother-in-law and Betty explaining her plans. As an afterthought, she added a final sentence stating that Francine was accompanying her and would be given her freedom once Lucy left. She folded the letter and was affixing a wafer when her maid came back with the second valise. This Francine proceeded to pack while Lucy wrote another brief note, 'to whom it may concern', giving permission for her slave to sell her jewels and then, since there was a little room left in the second bag, Lucy decided to take her paints and sketchbook after all.

By now it was already nearly eight o'clock, and she started to fret that Jeremiah would leave without them. Francine had already told her that Betty had gone to stay with the Crichlows at Kirton plantation, so there was only one person they needed to avoid, Bathsheba. Lucy sent Francine to check the lie of the land and she heard Bathsheba in the ladies' room speaking to the housekeeper. So Lucy put on her hat, slipped the letter and the note she had written together with the deed of manumission into the top of one of the bags, strapped her parasol to the top of the other and the two women, each carrying a valise, stole down the back staircase and set off towards the stables.

Lucy's foot, despite the ointment Francine had smeared liberally over it, was still extremely painful, and she made slow progress – particularly carrying the heavy valise. Seeing her struggling, Francine took both bags then when they reached a barn at a little distance from the main house urged her mistress to sit there in the shade while she went to fetch Jeremiah.

In a short while Lucy heard the dull 'clop, clop' of the mule-drawn cart and she stood up, a little shakily. Jeremiah's face showed surprise.

"Lor' Miss Lucy! What you here for? I come git you at de house."

Lucy thought quickly. "Well, you see Jeremiah, I have hurt my ankle out walking and I do not think I could get back to the house without help, so it is best if we leave for Bridgetown from here." Francine, meanwhile, was loading the two valises onto the cart. She helped her mistress up onto the seat beside Jeremiah – having wiped some of the dust off it with her hand – and herself scrambled up into the body of the cart, between the bags. If Jeremiah thought the whole situation strange – his mistress would normally have taken at least the horse-drawn dog-cart – he said nothing but simply cracked his whip and the mule resumed its none-too-speedy progress.

By the time they had passed Ruby plantation and reached Six Path, the jarring and jolting of the cart gave Lucy a headache and she was regretting wearing a hat without a veil, she felt sure her face was plastered with white dust from the limestone track. She gritted her teeth – both against the pain, and to prevent herself screaming in frustration at the slow pace of the vehicle It was difficult to hurry a mule (which on a good day would travel at five miles per hour) and, in any case, Jeremiah was enjoying his day out and saw no reason to rush. Lucy knew that it would take at least another hour to reach Oistins, the busy fishing port on the south coast, where she looked forward with longing to stretching her legs. In the meantime, she concentrated on going over her plan for ensuring Francine was able to buy her cabin space on a ship bound, as soon as possible, for England – and how to avoid being seen by Sam before he left.

Oistins' claim to fame was that the Charter of Barbados (Treaty of Oistins) was drawn up as a result of an English Civil War battle there on the 11th of January 1652 and then signed between locals and the English Crown. The Charter established the Barbados parliament, of which John Lord was now an elected member. As they drove into the little town, Lucy thought it had a sleepy air; unloading the morning's fish catch had finished sometime earlier, and there were a number of poor white fishermen sitting cross-legged on the beach mending their nets for their next trip, along with a handful of black men.

Jeremiah drew the cart to a halt in the shade of a palm tree, indicated the nearby Oistins Tavern with a jerk of his thumb to Francine, and jumped down to hitch the mule's reins over a handy post before hurrying off. Francine slipped down from the rear of the cart to give her mistress a helping hand to dismount, and the two walked along the edge of the sand towards the tavern.

Francine fetched her mistress some water from the drip-stone well next to the tavern, and Lucy drank it down gratefully. She did not relish the notion of a further two or three-hour journey in the mule cart but she said nothing, merely thinking with a mental shrug, *Beggars cannot be choosers.*

When Jeremiah returned, without a word he began to unhitch the mule and hobble it.

"But… Jeremiah, what are you doing? We must continue to Bridgetown at once!" Lucy expostulated. He answered something that she did not understand and she looked questioningly at Francine.

"We go by boat, mist'ss. Jeremiah say it's quicker."

"But how shall we pay our fare? Neither you nor I have any money." Lucy was beginning to panic, she had not expected this, assuming that they would travel the whole way by road. Francine turned to Jeremiah and began a rapid conversation with him that Lucy could not follow.

"No matter Miss Lucy, we pay when we arrive to town." The maid nodded as she said this, and Lucy did not inquire any further, for she was increasingly anxious to reach town and begin searching for a ship. She supposed that Francine must have arranged to give Jeremiah the fare to hand on to the boatman once she had managed to obtain cash for Lucy's jewellery.

Jeremiah picked up the two valises with ease along with his tools and all three made their way to the water's edge, where a number of long, low boats were drawn up presumably waiting for trade. A group of ragged black men with well-muscled arms was sitting under one of the palm trees but got to their feet when they saw a white woman approaching. One of them hailed Jeremiah, who was obviously well-known to them and another conversation of which Lucy understood not a word took place. Two of the men started pushing one of the boats into the water, and Lucy realised they were expected to wade out to it. This was no problem for the two slaves, Jeremiah was wearing short trousers and his feet were bare, and he dropped the bags into the boat in order to push it, while Francine stopped to take off her sandals and hitched up her skirt. Then she looked at her mistress.

Lucy shrugged and bent down to take off her own dainty shoes and wriggle out of her stockings, then followed her maid's lead and hitched up her own, rather more voluminous, skirts and strode forward, enjoying the feel of the warm sand between her toes. The sea was warm and the waves lapped gently so it was no hardship wading in, but she did wonder how she would manage to climb into the boat. She thought wistfully that, as a child, she would have thought nothing of it; her mother would no doubt have deemed her hoydenish but she would have scrambled aboard laughing. She would do the same now.

In the end it did not prove a difficult task, the waves here were gentle, not like those which crashed onto the beach at Long Bay. She told Francine to go first and show her how best to do it, then followed her lead if not gracefully then at least without embarrassing herself too much. Like her maid she had hitched up her petticoats but the water was above her knees so her skirts were drenched. While she made herself as comfortable as possible in the rocking boat, hurriedly pulling the wet skirt down again to cover her ankles, the three men continued to push it further out until they were up to their waists in water, then leapt nimbly aboard. Jeremiah sat right in the stern at the tiller, one took up the oars while the other hoisted a small sail and Lucy, glancing back over her shoulder, was surprised to see how fast they were moving. The current must be with them, she thought.

Thanks to a brisk breeze the journey took a little over an hour, the road trip would have taken double the time in the mule cart. As they approached St Lawrence Gap the coastline grew more rocky and the waves much larger. Lucy clutched Francine, sitting next to her, in fear. This was very different from sailing in the Hope or the Princess Mary, every moment she expected the tiny, frail boat to capsize and toss them all into the water and she had never learnt to swim. Little by little she relaxed, picking up the rhythm of the waves as they ploughed through the water. As they drew closer to Carlisle Bay, there was an increasing amount of traffic, poor fishing boats like their own, slightly larger sailing vessels passing them swiftly and gracefully and, further out in deep water, the largest ships – some anchored, with lighters busily ferrying goods and people to and fro, others approaching or leaving the Bay under very light sail, gingerly finding their way among the flotilla of small boats bobbing on the choppy waters. Lucy and her four companions made their way right into the harbour where the boat tied up near some exceedingly slippery steps leading up to the dock. Francine advised her mistress to climb these with care in bare feet – as it was, Lucy almost fell at one point – and then to sit on a capstan at the top to put her shoes and stockings back on. Embarrassed to be showing her ankles, Lucy hurried to complete this task while Jeremiah took his leave of the two boatmen and placed the valises on the ground next to Francine before hurrying off with his tools to ply his trade. Lucy unfurled her parasol to keep the hot sun off her face and stooped to pick up the smaller bag, but Francine forestalled her.

"I carry both, Miss Lucy. White lady no carry nothing."

It made sense, of course, they did not want to draw attention to themselves by behaving any differently from the norm, and for Lucy to carry a bag when she had her slave with her would occasion comment. So she led the way, Francine trudging behind, until they reached one of the inns just back off the front. Here she sat down on a bench, the two bags beside her, trying to look like any other passenger waiting to board her ocean-going vessel. She had not wanted to go to any of the inns she had frequented with the Lords or the Barrows for fear of meeting John or Sam, and she could only hope that none of their acquaintance saw her at this one, but she could not accompany Francine as the places she must go to exchange Lucy's jewels for money were certainly not places where a well-bred white woman would be seen.

She resigned herself to a long wait, for she did not know whether Francine would be successful immediately or if she would have to try several contacts in different locations. A waiter approached to take her order, but since she had no coins with which to pay him, she waved him away as imperiously as she dared, then sat gazing into the distance, raking the scene with her eyes for fear an acquaintance like Thomas Daniel – or worse still Sam himself – should appear.

It was certainly a lively scene. Although this was a relatively quiet thoroughfare compared to the dockside itself, or Broad Street or Swan Street, it was full of carts piled high with provisions, loud cries of warning to avoid collisions (not always successful) and shouts between barrow boys. There was a constant throng of people – mainly black or mulatto, with a few white soldiers and indentured servants – hurrying along the street and going in and out of the inn.

Lucy was on tenterhooks and found her enforced idleness unbearable. She wanted to scream with vexation and wished she could have accompanied Francine. Her back beginning to ache, Lucy got up and began to pace up and down. She was reluctant to let the two bags out of her sight, or to lose her seat on the bench so took only a few short steps in each direction. After what seemed like hours but was probably only thirty minutes, she took her sketch pad out and began some pencil drawings of the scene. As usual this calmed her; she became utterly absorbed in what she was doing, and jumped in surprise when Francine cleared her throat and said softly, "Mist'ss?"

"Francine! Were you successful?"

"Yes Miss Lucy. I have de money here," handing her a small cloth bag. "I go now to find boat."

The girl looked exhausted. Lucy said, "First you must have something to eat and drink. Here – take this and get yourself something and call the waiter over to me." And she handed Francine a small coin from the bag.

It had been on the tip of her tongue to invite Francine to sit down next to her, but that would never do, best she go to the kitchen or to one of the shacks black people were allowed to purchase food from.

Lucy ordered a jug of lemonade and some fruit from the hovering waiter and downed two glasses at once. Once she had finished her snack and brushed the crumbs from her lap for the waiting sparrows, she took a few hasty turns around the courtyard. She hoped Francine had already set off in her search for a passage for Lucy. While she knew there was nothing she could do to hurry the process her nerves were shot to pieces and she was trembling. She took up her sketch pad once again to calm herself but found it hard to concentrate.

It occurred to her that she would need a bed for the night and she wondered where. She did not want to commit any of her funds, she had no idea how much Francine had managed to obtain, or how much of it she would need for her passage and victuals, and she must pay for their boat trip from Oistins and leave Francine with some money to start her new life as a free woman. It was highly unlikely that she would be able to set sail next day, which was when the Berwick would leave with Sam aboard. Indeed, she might have to wait a week, and such a lengthy stay in Bridgetown would seriously deplete her resources, but she was reluctant to contact Mary Austin because it would set her at odds with her brother should he ever come to hear of it.

The bustle at the inn, and the noise on the street, had died down as the day grew hotter, and Lucy was beginning to feel uncomfortably warm on her bench, even though it was in the shade. She was conscious that there were beads of sweat on her upper lip, trickling down the side of her face and neck. She took another draught of her now warm lemonade and, summoning the waiter, asked for some cold water to drink.

Francine returned as the sun was setting, by which time Lucy was frantic. She could not see her maid's face well enough to gauge whether she had been successful or not. She stood before her mistress, eyes downcast and hands clasped in front of her.

"Well, girl, well?" Lucy spoke unusually sharply, impatient for news and forgetting the ingrained habit that prevented Francine speaking before she had been told to.

"Boat leave in five days' time, Miss Lucy. Go to B'istol?" She was unsure if she had the name of the destination right, but Lucy recognised it easily enough and her spirits rose. If Sam's ship went to London while hers went to Bristol it would matter less that she was leaving later, Sam would have several days' travelling by road once he had docked. He might even stay there for a while in the hope of regenerating his funds by gambling. She must try and find out where the Berwick was headed.

"Will the Captain take me? How much does he ask for my passage?"

"Woman who give money for jewel, she arrange with captain. She say I go back tomorrow to pay."

"Do you know how much it will be? Will I have enough to buy food for the voyage?"

Francine did not answer. It was customary for slaves to avoid trouble by not giving any response their master or mistress might not like; it was clear Lucy wanted to know if the coinage obtained from the sale of her pendant and earrings would be sufficient and since Francine had no idea, she held her peace. Recognising this, Lucy did not push her.

"We must find a bed for the night. Go and ask the innkeeper if he has a room."

Francine came back accompanied by the innkeeper who clearly wanted to be sure the girl's mistress was not an undesirable. When he saw Lucy, he bowed low and quoted a price she thought very high, so looking as haughty as she knew how she said,

"I do not wish to purchase your inn, merely a bed for the night! I have no doubt you are very busy, so I am content to share. My slave shall sleep on the floor next to me."

His face fell, but so did the price. To soften the blow, Lucy made it clear that she also wished to eat at the inn, but the conversation made her realise that she could not possibly afford to stay there until her ship left. She resolved after all to write a note to Mary Austin and ask if she might visit for a few days, which she did before she sat down to eat. After all, Sam would be leaving tomorrow, and by the time he returned there would be no need for him ever to find out that Mary had helped her.

The room was tiny, with two beds – a double and a single pallet – crammed together. In all they were five occupants, including Francine and another slave, who both had to sleep beneath the beds. Lucy wrinkled her nose at the state of the sheets and her sleeping companions then smiled to herself; given that she had spent the last few nights on a dirt floor, she had no right to be too particular.

The message to Mary had been given in the evening to a boy who hung around the inn looking for such odd jobs with instructions to deliver it at first light, and Lucy hoped her sister-in-law was to be found at home and that she would respond positively. Guessing that Sam would have spent his last night on shore drinking and gambling, she thought it unlikely she would be unfortunate enough to meet him early in the morning and, full of nervous energy, set off with Francine as soon as there was enough light to explore this part of the town. This worked up an appetite for breakfast, which she sat down to in the taproom while Francine, armed with the purse, set off to meet her contact with a view to paying for Lucy's voyage.

After her meal, Lucy went back outside armed with her sketch book and sat down in the spot she had occupied most of the previous day. The boy who had taken her message to Mary Austin found her there and stood in front of her, waiting for her to tell him to speak.

"Did Mrs Austin give you a reply for me?"

"Yes, miss. She welcome you today." She handed him a penny which he held tightly in his hand, then raced off to look for other errands he could run.

Her mind relieved of its most immediate care, she settled down again to wait for Francine to return with news of her passage, and while she sketched turned over in her mind what she might be able to purchase for the voyage. She wondered whether she would have to sell the remaining contents of her jewel box but was aware that nothing else would match the value of the pendant and earrings.

When Francine returned, she smiled shyly at her mistress, informed Lucy that she now had a bunk on the Venus leaving for Bristol on the 20th of April and handed her the ticket. Lucy checked the price and winced, the equivalent of £10 English – probably what her earrings had fetched. But it could not be helped.

"Francine, I will need food for the voyage, and a plate and mug and something to cook the food in, and a blanket. But I dare not go shopping until I am sure that Mr Lord has left. Please find out when the Berwick sails and what is its destination."

The girl set off again, this time towards the dock, and came back with the news that the Berwick, bound for London, was due to cast anchor later that afternoon. Lucy decided it would be prudent to leave her shopping until the following day, so she told Francine to settle up with the landlord, fetch the bags and have the boy call up some form of transport to take them both to the Austins.

It was noon by the time they reached the Austins' house on the outskirts of the town, a typical low, white building set in modest but pleasant grounds. Mary greeted her sister-in-law with pleasure and drew her into the shady hallway while Francine slipped away towards the kitchen hut in search of something to eat.

Over a dish of tea, Lucy told Mary that she had decided to return to England on a visit to her parents. Mary said nothing but looked at her a little quizzically. She set down her tea.

"But Lucy, you have not long returned from there. Have you received bad news? Is either of your parents ill? Sam was here last night and said nothing about this – indeed he was due to leave today on the Berwick with his friend Mr Daniel. Are you to accompany him?"

Lucy flushed slightly, realising that the conversation could prove awkward.

"No, Mary, no-one is ill to the best of my knowledge. Sam is not aware that I plan to go. I think I had best tell you what has occurred, though I fear you may not be happy with me."

She proceeded to explain that Sam had made arrangements behind her back to bring Cecilia out to Barbados, and that she herself wished to reach Hewelsfield before Sam removed their daughter from the Wightwicks' care and had just booked herself a place on the next available ship. She drew the letter she had written to her mother-in-law from her reticule where she had placed it.

"Would you be so kind as to have this taken to Long Bay, Mary, in a few days' time? I left in a rush and would not want the family to be concerned so have written a note for your mother…"

Mary was thoroughly surprised now. "To be sure I will, but why did you not leave it at the house before you set off?"

Lucy got up abruptly and walked over to the open window where she stared blindly out, fiddling with the curtain cord. A rustle of silks made her aware that her sister-in-law had moved across to join her. An arm went around her waist.

"Dearest sister, you are limping. What has happened? I think you have not told me everything. I should like to help you – will you not trust me? Has Sam been mistreating you again?"

Tears pricked Lucy's eyelids at the gentle tone. So Mary must have heard – or guessed – about Sam's behaviour towards her too.

"He flew into a rage when I argued with him and threw me in the storm cellar with orders that I was not to be released until he had sailed," she whispered embarrassed, as though the fault had all been hers.

"How did you get out? Does Mama know? Or Betty? Or John?"

"Betty knew. Indeed, she argued with Sam about it I believe but he would not be moved. I could not ask her to help me, Mary, she will continue to live at Long Bay when Sam returns, and it would make life very awkward for her. I had no intention of dragging you into this either, but I am afraid I have very little money left and could not afford to stay at a hotel until my ship departs."

"Who made the arrangements for you? If John did so, surely there can be no problem… Oh – is that why you made your own way to Bridgetown, to ask him to do so?"

Lucy shook her head. "No, I do not wish to set the brothers at odds any more than they are already. Things have been better between them since John and Sarah moved to Pool. My maid found out where I was and brought me food and water, and she helped me to escape. She has sold my jewellery and bought my passage."

"She will be punished severely. Mama will view her behaviour as insubordination and place her in the stocks or have her whipped."

"I have promised her her freedom. I have the deed of manumission with me, my father arranged it, on Sam's advice."

Mary laughed. "What a delightful irony! So you have bought your ticket, but what about what you need for the voyage? Have you arranged that too or can I help you with the arrangements? When does your ship set sail?"

Lucy breathed a sigh of relief and she smiled at Mary. "Thank you. I would very much welcome your assistance but have no wish for you to fall out with your brother. I am truly sorry to involve you but I was at my wits' end, I have a little money left with which to buy provisions but have not had to purchase victuals for a voyage before, and Francine has no experience of doing so either of course."

"I shall send a message to Richard and ask him to have his man of business sort everything out. Which ship do you sail on?"

"The Venus, bound for Bristol in four days' time. But – Mary… Will he do it? He may feel I should submit tamely to Sam's wishes. But if he *is* willing, please only have him purchase the basic necessities for me. I could not afford my own cabin, and it will arouse jealousy and suspicion if I appear better off than those with whom I am to share."

"Leave it to me."

Mary rang the little bell at her side, summoning a slave boy, and sent him for pen and ink. When she had finished writing, she told the boy to take it to her husband in the town and looked across at Lucy.

"I saw that you brought two small bags with you, quite sufficient for a short stay with us but surely not enough for a sea voyage. Will you be able to manage, Lucy?"

Lucy nodded. "There will be no space for anything more. I shall wash my clothes whenever we stay in port along the way and be happy to burn them no doubt once I reach my parents' house! I would like to write to them to let them know when I hope to arrive though. Do you think it would be possible to send it via the Berwick? Or am I too late?"

Mary glanced at the clock on the mantelpiece. "I doubt it will be in time to reach the Berwick before it weighs anchor – but I must admit I think we should try. Just imagine, it could be sitting on the same ship as your husband… Which will reach your parents' house first, do you think? Sam or the letter?" and she laughed again, clearly enjoying the situation to the full.

She settled Lucy down with pen and paper and, as soon as she was done, sent another slave boy scurrying off after the first with orders to locate the Berwick at the dock and ensure the letter was sent aboard or, failing that, to take it to the packet office to go out on the next sailing.

After lunch, the two women strolled in the garden and chatted, with several of Mary's children including Lucy's namesake playing around them. Then Lucy confessed that she was longing for a bath to wash the dirt – and the memory – of the past few days away, so Mary ordered that water be taken to the room which had been hurriedly prepared for her. Lucy found Francine there; she had unpacked everything from the two bags, shaken the creases out of her clothes and placed a muslin dress ready for her mistress to wear. With a sigh of contentment, Lucy slid into the warm water and allowed Francine to wash her hair and scrub her back.

Her hair brushed and her skin glowing, she went downstairs to join her hosts on the veranda. Mary had clearly filled her husband in on her story, and Richard looked at her gravely.

"I hope my presence will not cause you any trouble with Mary's family," she said.

"Do not worry your head over it. I am only sorry that things have come to this pass. What will you do if you do not reach your parents' house in time, Lucy?"

"I do not know. I try not to think about it. If Sam were already to have left with Cecilia… I could not bear to lose her forever, but I do not think my husband would accept my return to Long Bay. He will not condone what he will see as my defiance of his wishes," said Lucy sadly.

Since Richard had been quite shocked by Lucy's actions, he held his peace. He was fond of her, but in his view a wife should obey her husband's wishes – and Sam and Lucy's marriage had always seemed too tempestuous to him. Nevertheless, he did not approve of a man using unnecessary physical force on his wife so he had done as Mary asked and he now assured Lucy that everything would be in order for her voyage. Lucy asked him to render her an account but he waved her away, telling her she would need money for additional supplies at the ports along the way, and when she returned to England. Gratefully, Lucy accepted his help, but was steadfast in refusing the Austins' offer to purchase her a better cabin.

"Please do not mention my presence here to John," she impressed upon them. "In fact, it is probably best if you pretend complete ignorance of this whole affair when you see any of the family."

The next few days passed swiftly despite Lucy's continued nervousness. She suffered nightmares in which her mother-in-law came after her like an avenging angel and dragged her back to Long Bay in chains. When the Austins were entertaining guests, despite their protests she refused steadfastly to emerge from her room not wanting anyone to carry tales to Bathsheba Lord of her whereabouts.

On the day the Venus was to sail, Richard took Lucy up with him on his way into Bridgetown, and she bade a fond farewell to Mary, waving a handkerchief from the carriage window until the house was out of sight.

Earlier, she had been in floods of overwrought tears as she said farewell to her loyal maid. This time she was sure she would never see her again.

"You have been a true friend to me, Francine. I shall never forget you. I shall miss you and I hope you do not suffer any negative consequences as a result of having aided me. Perhaps you would do well to move to the other end of the island, to Speightstown or Holetown, where the Lords are unlikely to find you, or even go to a different island altogether. I want you to have a good life. You should marry and have children, Francine, you are a free woman now so your children will be free also." She embraced Francine and kissed her forehead, their tears mingling for the slave was just as moved as Lucy. Then she solemnly handed the girl the precious deed of manumission, together with as many pieces of eight as she felt she could spare from her little purse.

"Do you have any idea what you would like to do? You will need to work – shall I ask Mrs Austin to help you find employment?" But Francine shook her head firmly.

"I know where I go, mist'ss," she said through her tears. "I will do very well. Thank you, thank you," and she kissed Lucy's hand. Once more they embraced, and Lucy wished her former slave luck with her future life.

Richard took Lucy to the dock despite his disapproval of her behaviour for he was a kindly man and, although he kept his distance as he did not want to be seen associated with her departure, he did not leave until she and the two valises were safely aboard the boat which would take her out to the Venus. Her provisions had already been taken aboard the towering, three-deck ship, other than a small package containing her eating and cooking implements, which she carried with her. As the little boat cast off, she could see him standing back away from the crowd. He raised his hand once in farewell, turned on his heel and strode away.

She was on her own.

Chapter 19
The Reckoning

Every waking hour on board she was obsessed with her mission, hoping against hope that she could arrive before Sam to save Cecilia. She worried about the weather, worried about the strength and direction of the wind, asking at every opportunity the progress the neat little ship was making, whether the average six-week long trip was likely to be achieved.

But, that overarching, haunting preoccupation aside, travelling on the Venus opened Lucy's eyes to the vicissitudes to which life subjected the poorer classes and those who had fallen on hard times. She was in steerage, in a small compartment with four bunk beds; all were occupied, some by more than one person as two of the women had children with them. They must share two chamber pots between them for all their needs and took it in turns to carry them up on deck and empty them overboard – a task that made Lucy retch, especially in rough weather. It was clear to her companions from the beginning that Lucy came from a different world, and they resented it and only grudgingly advised her how she needed to act to survive. No more dinners with the captain, Lucy must cook her own food (something she had never done before, not even at home let alone on a cramped ship) in a tiny galley where all fought for space.

Little care was paid to storing steerage passengers' provisions so they tended to become rancid or get eaten by weevils more quickly than those of 'the Quality' and were subject to pilfering. Water was strictly rationed and there was no thought of using any of it for washing. The whole section began to stink very quickly, exacerbated when the Venus encountered a storm and many got seasick. After a few days Lucy became inured to the smell – indeed, as she ruefully realised, she must be in the same state – but nevertheless spent as much time on deck as she could. She found the daily fight for space in the galley too wearisome to bother very often; she grew thin and her dress hung off her.

What would Cecilia make of her, she wondered, a dishevelled and dirty stranger to the little girl? If, that is, Cecilia was there at all, and had not already been snatched by Sam. In which case what was the point? She was distraught at the very thought, urging the little ship forward.

She was relieved when after eighteen days at sea they finally reached their first port of call, the Azores, where they anchored at Ponta Delgada on Saint Miguel island. Here the Venus would fill up the water casks, obtain fresh fruit and vegetables and replenish its stocks of wheat and meat. Saint Miguel, she had learnt, was the most southerly, bar one, of the Azores; a mountainous island, comprising two volcanic massifs separated by a central low-lying ridge, its highest point, Pico da Vara at three thousand feet.

Wistfully, Lucy remembered her last visit to the Azores with Miss Kilmer and watched as several of the passengers gathered around a guide who promised to take them to visit the giant crater at the centre of the island at the bottom of which the Verde (Green) and Azul (Blue) lagoons coexist, twinned by an arched bridge, which according to legend were formed from the tears of a princess and a shepherd joined by an impossible love. But she could not afford such luxuries. Instead she stayed behind, wandering listlessly through the streets of San Miguel. If by any chance she did make it ahead of Sam, what if Cecilia chose to go with her father rather than stay with her mother? What if both her parents acquiesced to her husband's legal rights over the child and would not fight her corner? She could not bear the thoughts, but they kept circling back to gnaw at her.

Despite concern about depleting her slender supply of coins, she took both her valises ashore and sought out a small unassuming inn in a line of square flat-roofed white-washed houses, where she asked for a room, hot water to wash in and towels. She unpicked a few stitches in the hem of her dress, where she had secreted her little purse, and gave the dress to a slatternly servant along with her small clothes, asking that they be washed and pressed. She unpacked fresh clothes – sadly creased from having spent so long in the valise, for there was nowhere else to put them in the tiny cabin – and gave herself over to the relative luxury of a basin of hot water. She washed her entire body using the soap she had brought and one of the cloths provided, and did her best to wash her hair.

The Venus was taking on fresh supplies, and would no doubt take advantage of the stop to wash down the decks and caulk the seams also, so would be in port at least one night. Lucy took pleasure in sleeping in a proper bed even though she must still share the room, and in dressing in clean clothes. As she strolled along the shady streets of Ponta Delgada under her parasol, she was almost unrecognisable from the woman who had come ashore a few hours before. She took her meal at the little inn and determined to buy some fruit before re-embarking on the Venus the following day. Fresh fruit, which she had taken for granted in her life at Long Bay, was not common to ship-board provisions as it could not be stored. But if she made a few careful purchases, she might at least have a small stock of fruit to last her three or four days.

She returned to the Venus revitalised and more optimistic about the future. She could and would put up with anything to keep her daughter safe. Before she left the inn, she dressed once more in the clothes she wore on arrival, now relatively clean again but stained and faded. She sewed her remaining coins back into the hem of her dress, pricking her finger on the needle as she did so, then folded the dress she had worn in Ponta Delgada and replaced it in the valise. She had made a few pencil sketches of the town and the surrounding green mountains and hoped she would be able to reproduce the vibrant colours once she was settled at Hewelsfield.

Lucy gagged at the fetid smell of the cabin. No effort had been made to clean it, and her previously numbed senses had been re-awakened during her brief stay on shore. She would have to become accustomed once again, but at least the unpleasantness would only last a few more weeks. She stowed her two valises under her bunk bed and turned with relief to go back up on the deck, where the smell was a far preferable one of carbolic and tar. As on a previous voyage, she found herself a coil of rope, out of the way of the sweating, half-naked sailors straining to move unwieldy crates and packs from the untidy piles on deck and place them in the hold. One live pig managed to break his hobble and ran squealing from end to end of the ship, causing mayhem as he went. Lucy could not help herself laughing out loud as she watched a couple of the men trying to tackle the poor creature and wrestle it to the ground. As it was finally driven below her laughter ceased, and she thought a little sadly that this would be the last time the pig had a taste of freedom. All too soon it would be gracing the captain's table as roast pork. As for laughter, would there ever be any in her life again? Everything depended upon getting home first.

The weather was fine and the wind brisk so the master, Captain Phillips, was eager to be under way as soon as possible. The Venus would make next for Portugal and as always in these waters Captain Phillips hoped to God he could avoid coming up against any of the French fleet or at least that his ship could outrun them. Bonaparte had escaped from his prison on the island of Elba at the end of February and although the French navy was much depleted there were still dangerous privateers abroad. When they weighed anchor, Lucy drew her big cloak around her against the full force of the stiff breeze they would encounter once away from the shelter of Ponta Delgada harbour and settled herself more comfortably on the coil of rope. She watched dreamily as the land receded and began imagining her reunion with Cecilia. It was the first time since leaving Bridgetown that she had permitted herself to be optimistic, she realised, superstitiously pushing away the thought. Just focus on getting there as quickly as possible.

She rose reluctantly as the sun was setting to go below to the stinking cabin. She was not sufficiently hungry to face cooking something in the little galley but thought she would eat a piece of the fruit she had bought. But when she reached the cabin, she found that she had failed to secure the paper packet containing the fruit and it had burst and spilled some of the precious content across the floor. She managed to rescue some, but a mango lay squashed and sticky on the wooden boards, while a bunch of grapes had completely vanished. No doubt one of the women or children sharing the cabin with her had helped themselves. There was nothing she could do, she had enough to last her three days if she rationed herself to one item a day. She crawled into her bunk, the bag of sweet-smelling fruit beside her to provide some relief from the stench. Despite the discomfort, she fell asleep quickly and slept through the night, undisturbed by her companions, as the ship made good progress across a quiet sea.

The days slipped by, blending one into the other with little to break the monotony. Occasionally Lucy made a brief entry in her diary. She rarely bothered to cook for herself and her skin grew grey and she became increasingly listless. She had vivid dreams and nightmares, and hallucinated as she crouched

366

quietly in her favourite corner on deck. She did not realise that she was by now severely malnourished – indeed, close to starvation. All she could think of, the scene that played over and over again in her head, was her arrival at Hewelsfield in time to defend her daughter from her husband, who had now assumed ogre-like proportions in her fevered brain.

She revived a little when they docked at Lisbon seven days later and she went ashore again, but she no longer had enough money to take a bed at an inn. She bought some fruit and bread and made a meal of that. She longed only to reach her destination and hoped she would find her father there. Perhaps, if her letter had arrived, he would be waiting for her or send a carriage to meet her at the port. She dreamt often of the pleasure of taking a bath and putting on fresh clothes, of holding, caressing and laughing with her daughter, free of fear and the threat of separation.

Finally the Venus arrived at Bristol on the 4th of June 1815. Lucy had been so haunted about her purpose she had hardly realised that they had had an excellent voyage with favourable winds and no storms. But as the ship crossed the Bay of Biscay towards Bristol, the skies clouded over and by the time they reached the port the rain poured relentlessly from a solid mass of grey. She hoped it was not a bad omen. Lucy pulled her hood up over her hat and wrapped the cloak as tightly about her as she could while laden down with the two valises, but her dress was soaked through and clung to her legs even before she disembarked. Nevertheless, she was not at all sorry to leave the Venus as for her the voyage had been the most unpleasant she had experienced, and once safely on the quay – a little unsteady as she regained her land-legs – she looked around her hopefully for her father or a carriage to collect her.

When it was clear that no-one was coming to meet her she made her way (congratulating herself for her forethought in dressing in stout shoes instead of slippers) to the White Lion, where she and her father had spent the night when she last arrived in Bristol from Barbados. She was in for a rude awakening. She entered and went towards the lounge, still carrying her two bags. She put them down on the floor to undo her cloak and place it over the back of a chair to dry. One of the waiters was passing by with a full tray of hot beverages for other customers, mulled wine and coffee. It smelt very good, and Lucy longed for something to warm her chilled limbs.

"We don't serve your sort in 'ere," the waiter said roughly. "Be off with yer! There's a tavern by the port is good enough for you."

Lucy's jaw dropped. She had never been spoken to in such a tone in all her life, and she was furious. She raised her chin in defiance and plumped down on the big chair close to the roaring fire and beckoned another waiter over.

"I should like a coffee, if you please, and a room so that I can wash and change. And I require pen and paper, I shall write a note for one of the boys to deliver."

This waiter was not quite so abrupt, but the message was the same. "Sorry, miss. I think you want the taproom next door, or maybe the Old Fox on Redcliffe Street."

By this time Lucy was quivering with a mixture of rage and embarrassment. "How dare you! I wish you to send a message at once to my father's place of business on Queen Charlotte Street."

He looked her over doubtfully, eying her stained and faded dress, her drooping bonnet and dirty gloves. Lucy was suddenly painfully aware of the figure she must present after over a month at sea without a bath and only one change of clothes, so she added, "I have but this instant arrived from the West Indies on the Venus."

"That's as may be miss, but I think you will be more comfortable elsewhere. Perhaps you could try the Landoger Trow close by Queen Charlotte Street?"

It was clear that she was not going to get served here and knowing that she had no money to pay for a room or a meal Lucy got up slowly from her seat with what dignity she could muster, donned her wet cloak again and made for the door with her bags.

"I shall tell my father, Mr Wightwick, of your disobliging behaviour. He will be most displeased," was her parting shot.

The waiter merely shrugged and turned away.

Outside again she shivered. She knew her father's office was close by and hoped she could remember the route they had taken in reverse the previous year. Head down, she trudged along, her wet, heavy skirts clinging to her legs and soaked in dirty, muddy water several times by passing carriages careless of pedestrians. With only one wrong turn she found herself before the door she sought and knocked.

There was no answer. The street was more or less deserted. And suddenly it dawned on Lucy, today was Sunday – her father would be at Hewelsfield, and his place of business was closed. As the rain poured down Lucy, utterly dejected, burst into tears. Leaning against the door, her two bags at her feet, she sobbed and sobbed until her throat ached. Eventually she grew angry at her own frailty, sniffed loudly, wiped her nose and eyes on her cloak and considered what to do. She still had a few coins sewn into the hem of her dress, she must hope that there were sufficient to secure her a bed for the night for she had no desire to spend the hours of darkness huddled in a doorway, but she doubted there would be enough to secure a meal as well.

She decided her best option was to make her way to the Llandoger Trow, as suggested by the waiter. Her heart beating fast, she trudged along, head down, no longer paying any attention to the rain or the standing pools of water soaking her from head to foot. When she reached the busy inn she stood just inside the entrance and dropped her bags on the floor, water dripping in a steady stream from her cloak, forming a puddle around her. She kept her hood up over her bonnet. No-one was at the desk, so she rang the bell sharply. A rotund, hot and flustered woman scurried towards her, wiping her hands on her apron.

"I require a bed for the night," said Lucy in her haughtiest tone, drawing herself up.

The woman looked dubious. "We-ell… You'll have to share. We're full."

"I can see you're busy. It's just for one night. I arrived on the Venus from the West Indies, it is most inconvenient that it should be a Sunday or I would have made arrangements to travel on to my destination." She sneezed.

The woman seemed uninterested. "That'll be 1s 6d. Upstairs, at the top, third door on the right. Three to a bed. You'll pay me tonight."

Lucy smiled, so relieved that she had found a place to stay that she did not take exception to the woman's tone or the intimation.

"I shall take my bags upstairs and bring you the money at once."

The room when she found it was tiny, entirely taken up by two large beds. There were signs of occupation – a bag here, a cloak there – but as it was still early, she was alone. This would make it easier to remove her few remaining coins from their makeshift hiding place in her hem. She removed her sodden cloak and ruined bonnet and hung them on a hook provided for that purpose on the door, then slid her two valises under one of the beds and sat down to take out her money.

She counted out the English coins carefully, she had just enough to pay for the bed space and, she hoped, a glass of hot wine to warm her cold bones – nothing more. She clutched the coins tightly and went downstairs again. Having found the woman she paid for the bed, then steeled herself to go into the public tap room and tried to get as close to the fire as possible in the hope of drying out her skirts. She felt very conspicuous and not a little frightened; well-bred ladies did not frequent tap rooms and were likely to be accosted rudely there. And there were some noisy, drunken and ill-bred people – men and women – present, but someone made room for her on the end of a bench at the fireside and, smiling her thanks, she sat down and gave a passing waiter her order. She sat sipping her wine for some 30 minutes, watching the steam rise from her skirt and speaking to nobody, then made her way upstairs, loosened her stays and lay down fully clothed in the second bed as the first was already full with its quota of three.

She lay rigid on the damp and musty sheets, making herself as small as possible next to another occupant, and tried to sleep. But she only managed to doze fitfully, even more so when a third woman joined them, because she was unused to sharing with strangers. Besides, a cacophony of snores from several of them kept her awake, and after an hour or so she began to itch, whether from bed bugs or fleas she could not be sure.

Her snatches of sleep were filled with technicolour nightmares of terrifying carriage chases in which she was trying and failing to catch up with Sam, lashing his horses into a lather and laughing manically because he had already taken Cecilia. Why, oh why had they docked on a Sunday? It was agonising being forced to lie sleepless in an uncomfortable bed (and having to pay for the privilege) when every day mattered and she might even now be too late. Yet what could she do about it? Nothing. She forced down her anxiety, she must be patient. She had come so far, she could not allow herself to fail now. She must be tireless and strong, she could not afford to be ill as she had been after Emma's birth. But as the night hours dragged on, she kept worrying away, becoming more and more depressed. Everything seemed against her. These awful lodgings, time ticking relentlessly away.

Finally she stirred out of her fitful, restless slumber. It was getting light and she dragged herself out of bed, doing her best not to disturb her companions. She pulled her two cases from under the bed, slipped her feet into the still-wet shoes, put on her cloak and stole downstairs to the tap room, now empty but for two men snoring drunkenly at one of the tables. She sat down near the fireplace again, hoping the embers retained some warmth, and scratched unthinkingly at the bites on her arms and legs.

Once the inn began to stir, she decided to leave for her father's place of business, hoping that Baines at least would be there early. She needed to use a privy and could not bring herself to do so at the inn. Leaving behind her ruined hat she pulled her hood over her hair – thinking wryly that she must look an absolute fright – and gathering up her bags quietly left the Llandoger Trow.

The rain was still falling and the streets had turned into rivers. Her shoes and skirts were soon soaked through again, but she kept her head down and trudged along. When she arrived, the door was opened by a young man She gave him no opportunity to close it on her, placing her foot firmly in the way and putting down a valise.

"Good morning. Are my father, Mr Wightwick, or Mr Baines here?"

It was the same young man who had opened the door to her when she arrived with Miss Kilmer. His jaw dropped at Lucy's bedraggled appearance, but he swallowed hard and ushered her in. He was at a loss as to where to put her and Lucy, seeing this, put him out of his misery by announcing firmly,

"I shall wait here. I am soaked through and have no wish to destroy Mr Wightwick's carpets, or to interrupt him if he is with someone. But perhaps you could ask Mr Baines to come down before I catch my death of cold!"

He bowed and hurried upstairs to do her bidding, leaving her in the narrow hall. Lucy shivered and pulled the cloak more tightly about her having dropped her bags in the corner. Almost immediately she heard footsteps descending the stairs and, turning, caught sight of Baines.

"Miss Lucy! Mrs Lord, I should say. Will you not come up? Your father is expected shortly, but the river crossing may have been rough. You are soaked through! What are you doing standing in the hallway?" He glared at the unfortunate young man who had opened the door, who was mightily relieved when she took up the cudgels on his behalf.

"Please do not blame him, Baines. I insisted on waiting here because I did not want to drip all over Papa's beautiful Aubusson rug!"

"Well, you shall come up now. Do you have any fresh clothing in one of those bags? Then you shall change out of your wet things upstairs over a glass of Mr Wightwick's brandy."

Soon she was ensconced by the fire, dressed in clean if crumpled clothes and with a blanket round her shoulders, sipping a glass of fine cognac while her cloak steamed gently over another chairback. By the time her father arrived some two hours later, she was feeling much better but extremely sleepy.

"Lucy! Is that indeed you?" he peered at her myopically, groping for the eyeglass he had taken to wearing since her last visit. "We were not expecting you! Did you write? Is everything alright?"

As he embraced her, Lucy asked with some urgency, "Papa, is my husband arrived yet?"

Thomas Wightwick stepped back in surprise. "No, my dear. I believe we only expect him next week. Did you not travel together?"

When she did not answer he sat down behind his desk and, looking a little stern, asked, "Now, Lucy, tell me what scrape you are in? Why are you so concerned about whether Mr Lord has already arrived? And why are you not either with him or at Long Bay? And why did you not write to warn us of your arrival?"

"He is coming to take Cecilia away from Hewelsfield. He wrote to tell you that, did he not?" Lucy ignored her father's last question.

"Yes, indeed, my dear. We shall be sorry to lose the little girl, but we expected this to happen sooner or later. The child should be with her parents, as your Mama said when you were last here."

"You know my thoughts on this, Papa, and so does Sam. Cecilia is too young and vulnerable to live in Barbados. That is why he never told me that he planned to come and fetch her – I found out by chance. And when I confronted him about it, he beat me and threw me in the slaves' punishment cell without food or water and put the household under orders not to release me until his ship had sailed."

She could feel the anger rising again as she baldly stated what had occurred, and it caused her to look belligerently at Mr Wightwick. He shifted uneasily.

"You know I do not approve of your husband's violence towards you, Lucy, but I can do nothing to prevent him taking Cecilia away, he has the law on his side."

"I know you cannot, Papa, which is why I took passage on the first ship I could in order to do whatever *I* can to prevent him. I prevailed before, and I plan to do so again."

A worried frown creased Thomas Wightwick's forehead, but he wisely decided to deflect the conversation until he had spoken to his wife.

"We will discuss this further once we are comfortable at Hewelsfield. If you are ready, daughter, I should like to leave at once. The crossing may take longer than usual if this wind and rain do not let up," and he went to the door and called for his carriage to be brought round again, telling Baines to cancel all his meetings.

Crossing the River Severn was indeed unpleasant. The rain continued relentlessly, and the waves swept the small boat up to such heights and dashed themselves against it with such ferocity that Lucy became seriously alarmed. Thomas had decided it was not safe to take the carriage across and sent the coachman back to the Boar's Head to await more clement weather or Mr Wightwick's return, whichever happened sooner.

Lucy had rarely crossed under such conditions, usually she had waited until the winds died down and the weather improved. The Severn was always

371

treacherous, and many lives were lost on these crossings every year. But she had no desire to question her father's decision – her experience of storms at sea served to lessen her fear a little and, besides, she wished to be absolutely certain to reach Hewelsfield before Sam did. She kept telling herself that after all her efforts God *could* not be so cruel as to cause her to drown so close to home.

The crossing took two hours, and Lucy had to be helped to disembark for she could hardly stand. Her sodden cloak weighed a ton, and her bonnet was completely ruined. She and her father went into the Old Passage inn and Lucy stood shivering before an enormous fire, creating puddles on the wooden floor, while her father negotiated with the publican for use of a vehicle of some sort to take them to Hewelsfield, since Lucy had no riding habit with her and was, besides, in no fit state to ride the distance. This was clearly demonstrated when she suddenly dropped down in a dead faint, the cloak pooling around her.

The burly innkeeper – who had known her and the Wightwick family for many years – lifted her tenderly onto the settle and called for his wife to minister to her while he bustled off to see whether he had anything in his stables that might suit their needs. He returned within a few minutes, rubbing his hands apologetically.

"Mr Wightwick, sir, I'm afraid all I have left is a small trap or the dog-cart. At least the trap will provide some shelter, sir…"

"Bring us some coffee, and some bread and butter, then have a horse hitched to the trap. We will leave as soon as my daughter has recovered somewhat."

He looked anxiously at Lucy as he spoke, but she had already recovered from her fainting fit and although she still shivered and was very pale, she expressed herself very ready, indeed eager, to continue their journey. She felt unbearably weak but she was not going to be stopped so close to her goal having travelled so far, and with such fortitude. She was a survivor, she told herself, summoning up her spirit to overcome her poor physical state. So Lucy's valises were strapped securely onto the spare seat while she gulped down her coffee, and she and her father set off for the final stretch to Hewelsfield with one of the ostlers driving so that he could return with the trap the same evening.

A large waterproof spread across their knees and the trap's canopy kept the worst of the rain off father and daughter, but they were nonetheless very wet by the time they finally arrived. She was beyond exhaustion, hovering in a semi-state between full consciousness and sleep. Thomas climbed down and offered Lucy a helping hand as she almost collapsed to the ground, nearly pulling him over. He instructed the ostler to unstrap the bags then take the horse and trap to the stables before repairing to the kitchen to get something to eat before his return journey, as this would also allow the horse a brief respite.

The front door opened before Thomas and Lucy had climbed the steps; the maid hurried to help both divest themselves of their sodden outer garments and looked frightened by Lucy's pallor.

"Where is Mrs Wightwick?" asked Thomas.

"She is in the parlour, sir."

"Then we shall join her there. Lucy, do you wish for a bowl of tea, or something stronger?" His daughter was looking very pale again, standing but almost comatose and he suddenly realised how thin she was. Without waiting for an answer, he turned to the maid and said, "Have Hoskins bring lemons, sugar and hot water to the parlour and I shall make a punch to warm us."

Mrs Wightwick must have heard the commotion of their arrival, for she had just risen from her chair when Lucy and her father walked in. She gasped in surprise on seeing her daughter then embraced her and feeling how cold and wet she was, insisting she go immediately upstairs and change.

"You must and shall put on some warm, dry clothing or you will catch your death of cold if you have not done so already. Thomas, what were you thinking of, bringing her all this way in the pouring rain and not using a closed carriage? No, do not try to answer me now. You can both tell me what this is all about – for you have only just left and I did not think to see you, husband, until the end of the week, though I am delighted that you are here – you can both tell me once Lucy is changed out of her wet things. And I must warn Cook to lay more covers..."

By this time she was already shepherding her daughter out of the parlour towards the stairs. But as Lucy mounted them, she could feel her body crumpling underneath her. She could do nothing about it and slithered to the floor in an ungainly heap in a dead faint to her mother's horror.

All was pandemonium as Mrs Wightwick sent a maid scurrying for her smelling salts and Mr Wightwick ordered a sturdy footman to carry Lucy's inert body to her room, where her mother undressed her and wrapped her in blankets at the same time ordering the maid to light the fire. Mrs Wightwick chafed her daughter's hands and sent an order to Cook for a bowl of chicken broth, and by the time this arrived Lucy was showing signs of coming around.

Soon she was dressed in an old though serviceable gown (which hung off her) and a warm wrap, with dry stockings and slippers all from the clothes still remaining at her childhood home. Her mother towelled her hair dry and brushed it. Lucy began to feel better so that when she eventually staggered back down to the parlour on her mother's arm a tinge of colour had returned to her pallid face. Her father was stirring his punch from which a delicious aroma of nutmeg, cinnamon, lemons and cloves arose. Her mother bustled in and out, leaving Cook (who had thought only her mistress was dining at home that day) frantically searching the larder for some additional meat to turn into a fricassee for the master, and the pantry for items to tempt Miss Lucy's appetite.

Mr Wightwick handed each of the ladies a glass of his punch and the three of them sat down by the fire to enjoy it. At last, Lucy could ask the questions most preoccupying her.

"Mama, has Sam arrived yet? Have you heard from him? Where is Cecilia?"

"Why, Lucy, Cecilia is in the nursery having her tea. Mr Lord wrote that he would be here shortly, but we have not seen him yet. Why so agitated?"

"Because Sam is coming only to wrest our daughter from your care and take her back to Barbados! But you already know this, I think."

Mrs Wightwick looked calmly at her daughter. "Lucy, it is his right to make arrangements for his own child. I believe it would be good for her to grow up in the company of her cousins and, it is to be hoped, future siblings rather than living alone with us. Besides, Nurse is now too old to manage and wishes to be with her own family."

"Mama, I have lost two children already who succumbed to disease on that island. I have no wish to lose Cecilia also. She is not yet three years old, and far too delicate to be subjected to a perilous ocean crossing and the frequent outbreaks of measles, typhus, cholera and other fatal illnesses I have witnessed at Long Bay. Besides, there are signs of unrest among the slaves and Barbados may yet face a brutal uprising of the kind experienced in Louisiana not so long ago."

"I have long believed slavery to be barbarous, uncivilised and abhorrent," stated Mr Wightwick firmly. "I had thought, however, that once the trade in slaves ceased those that remained would be treated more humanely because they could not be replaced. What has given rise to this unrest, Lucy?"

"They continue to be whipped, mutilated and degraded – treated as lower than livestock. The only difference is that they are now encouraged to breed, to ensure a constant supply of new slaves. It is no wonder that they consider rebelling. But while I have every sympathy with them, I have no wish to put my daughter in harm's way or to live in fear of her being murdered in her bed. I wish her to spend her childhood, at least, in England – safe and secure, and learning Christian values!"

Thomas was taken aback by Lucy's vehemence, but also rather pleased that she shared his views.

"As your Mama has said, Mr Lord is within his rights to take Cecilia wherever and whenever he wishes. What can you possibly do to prevent him?"

Lucy took a deep breath. "I plan to remain in England and Cecilia shall live with me. I will not return to Long Bay."

The silence which followed this pronouncement was absolute, broken only by the ticking of a clock on the mantel and the crackling of the fire. It was Mrs Wightwick who spoke first.

"Are you all about in your head, girl? You mean to leave your husband? Have you thought of the disgrace? And what will you live on?"

Lucy had been expecting her mother to be horrified.

"Mama, I have thought long and hard about the repercussions of such a course of action. I have no doubt many of our acquaintance will shun me, but so long as my daughter and I are safe I shall not care. I have been made miserable by Mr Lord's unkindness over so many years and I cannot bear it any more. Even his family became used to seeing me covered in bruises, and before his departure from Barbados he threw me in the slave dungeon…"

"I am sure I cannot think what you must have done to enrage him so!" responded Mrs Wightwick unfeelingly.

As his daughter rose hurriedly and began to pace the floor like a caged animal to dampen her anger, Mr Wightwick decided it was time for him to step in. He had been horrified – indeed, mortified – when his beloved daughter had behaved so outrageously by agreeing to a runaway marriage to her profligate husband. Generally when it came to household matters or decisions concerning their children, he left these to his wife. But despite the horrific social scandal Lucy's actions seemed likely to plunge them into (and which he would normally have shied away from) he admired her courage and resourcefulness and he thought it unlikely that Mr Lord would change his ways at this advanced date.

"Enough, my dears. The fact of the matter is that you and I," to his wife, "were all too aware before Mr Lord married our daughter that his reputation was not all we would have wished. His actions since have borne that out. There is no use crying over spilt milk, all we can do now is to make the best of a bad situation."

His wife's mouth fell open. "Thomas! Are you not going to order our daughter to remain with her husband?"

"I have not the right. She is a grown woman now. And, indeed, while I was reluctant for her to take such a grave step as to leave Mr Lord when she was last here, I now think it highly unlikely he will mend his ways. Look at her! Look what she must have endured. I do not believe, as you seem to my dear, that Lucy is to blame for Mr Lord's violent behaviour towards her. She is my daughter – our daughter!" he looked piercingly at his wife. "That is an end to the matter. I shall do what I can to broker a deal agreeable to both parties and which creates as little scandal as possible – as much for little Cecilia's benefit as for yours, daughter, or for ours."

Lucy's shoulders relaxed and she smiled tremulously at her father. She loved him, he was going to help save her and Cecilia. Suddenly everything she had endured seemed worthwhile. The violence. The ugly deprivation of the dungeon. The stress of the escape. The stench and humiliation of steerage. The dirty, freezing drenching weather back on land.

Her mother, meanwhile, was clearly discomfited and fidgeted with the silk of her skirt. Rarely had she heard that note of firmness and finality in her husband's voice. What on earth would the neighbours say? Or her own family? Mrs Wightwick had no desire to be ostracised – nor, to be fair, did she wish her daughter or granddaughter to be. She firmly believed that the worst possible state for a woman to find herself in was divorce (the shame of it!) or, nearly as unpleasant, being unmarried. However difficult relations might be between husband and wife they must find a way to rub along together. But a husband was always right. A wife must not dispute his pronouncements.

"If that is your decision, Mr Wightwick, then of course I shall abide by it. But it is most irregular, and there will doubtless be much unpleasantness, indeed shame for our family. You have brought all your troubles on yourself, Lucy, you married in harum-scarum fashion contrary to your father's judgement and only realised later how right he was in his assessment of Mr Lord's character! You were always far too headstrong and, indeed, you have been much indulged by Papa.

"I shall leave all the arrangements in your capable hands, dear Thomas. I am going to check with Cook that everything is in train for our meal. Perhaps you, Lucy, should visit the nursery and re-acquaint yourself with your daughter."

Mrs Wightwick was already moving towards the door as she said these last words and did not wait for a response. Lucy stood also and embraced her father fiercely, tears streaming uncontrollably down her face, her body shaking, all the tension of the past months pouring out.

"Thank you, Papa, thank you!" she said, and pulling herself away left the room to visit Cecilia. Her father poured himself a large brandy and gulped it down, exhausted by the emotive nature of the preceding conversation.

In the nursery Cecilia was eating her tea. Some was on the floor, and she had liberally smeared the table, her clothes and her face with whatever she had been fed. Nurse – who should have been overseeing the meal – had nodded off in a rocking chair between the table and the fireplace. Lucy was startled to see how old she looked.

"Hello, Cecilia" she said softly.

The little girl looked up but was more interested in slapping her hand into the jelly on her plate and quickly looked down again. Not wishing to stain her fresh gown, Lucy stepped gingerly around her daughter and shook Nurse gently by the shoulder. A rheumy pair of eyes opened and the old woman gave a start.

"Oh! Miss Lucy! Wherever did you spring from? But you are so thin – have you been ill, my dear?"

She struggled to rise, and Lucy helped her up, noting how her hands constantly trembled. She could understand why Nurse would find the care of a lively three-year-old rather too much.

"No-one knew I was coming, Nurse, Papa brought me back with him from Bristol. I mean to stay with my daughter now, I shall not return to the West Indies."

"I'm glad to hear it! A barbarous place and full of foreigners by all accounts. Is your husband here with you?"

"No, but he will be shortly. He plans to take Cecilia away with him, back to Barbados, and I mean to prevent him. Will you help me, Nurse?"

"Well… A woman should not be contrary with her husband, Miss Lucy…"

"But you said yourself Barbados was a barbarous place (although I am sure I do not know how you came by that knowledge!) and, besides, my father has agreed to help."

The Nurse looked surprised. "Are you sure, Miss Lucy? He will defy your husband's will?"

Lucy gave her a truncated version of what had transpired downstairs. "You remember, *Nani*, when you bound up my broken wrist when I was last in England? I did not fall from my horse; it was my husband who caused the hurt. And he has mistreated me often before and since. Papa believes he will not change his ways."

"And Mr Wightwick is the master of the house, so he is clearly right. Oh! It is so good to see you again, dearie," and with tears in her eyes the old woman

376

stroked her former nurseling's hand. Lucy smiled down at the diminutive figure and spoke softly.

"Cecilia and I must get to know one another again. She seems to have spread her tea everywhere so I am not sure how much she has eaten. I think she will need a bath. I will call Prudence and have her send up hot water, and perhaps I can help you get her ready for bed."

Nurse looked in horror at the mess. "I am so sorry, Miss Lucy. I must have dropped off for a few minutes. I am not as young as I was and I find looking after her very tiring. I will clear it up now!"

Laughing, Lucy pushed her gently back into the rocking chair. "No, no, Nurse, you rest there and Prudence can clean it up once she has fetched a can of hot water" and she rang the bell.

By the time the little girl was in her bath, Nurse's pinafore was smeared with jam and other food transferred from Cecilia's clothes and hands. She splashed in the water, totally indifferent to the stranger helping Nurse wash her, and only seemed to acknowledge Lucy's presence when she tried to lift her daughter out. That provoked tears, and she held out her arms to Nurse. Crestfallen, Lucy knew that she should not be surprised or upset, she had not seen the child for a year or more and she was not yet three years old. Once she was dried and, in her nightclothes, Nurse placed Cecilia gently on Lucy's lap.

"Will you sit there now and be a good girl for me? And Miss Lucy shall give you your warm milk. She is your Mama, you know, Miss Cecilia, come back to be with you from far over the sea."

Cecilia looked solemnly at her mother but seemed happy enough now to have Lucy feed her milk as long as Nurse remained nearby. Her eyes began to close before she had finished the cup but when Lucy stood to carry her over to her cot she yelled again for Nurse, wriggling and screaming and working herself up into a frenzy. Only once Nurse had put her to bed did her eyes start to close again. The two women sang a gentle lullaby to her and once the little girl was finally asleep Lucy sent Nurse to have her own dinner, drew up a chair and sat happily watching her sleeping daughter, smoothing her hair, until the maid came to say that the mistress wished her to come downstairs to eat.

Over the following days Cecilia, who had a sunny temperament, accepted Lucy's presence and became used to having her mother look after her; she now asked for Lucy when she was being put to bed. They spent time playing together in the garden at Hewelsfield when the weather was kind; if not, Lucy would take her to the kitchen and spoil her with sweetmeats she cajoled from Cook.

Meanwhile, despite Lucy's pleadings, her father had gone back to Bristol and thence – as he informed his wife in a hastily scrawled note – to London, having heard disturbing rumours about the way the war with Napoleon was progressing and being anxious about his business interests. He did not return to Hewelsfield at the end of the week, merely sending another letter to tell them not to worry and that he would write again to tell them when he would return home. The war seemed very distant to Lucy and of far less concern than her husband's expected arrival. She was surprised – but relieved – that Sam had not yet made an appearance, since his ship had left Bridgetown before the Venus. She was on tenterhooks lest this occur during her father's absence; she slept badly, insisted on checking for herself that all the doors were bolted each night, and started at every unexpected sound.

Relief came in the form of a brief missive from Sam addressed to Mrs Wightwick, informing her that the Berwick had indeed docked in London and that he had some business to attend to before he could travel to Hewelsfield and doubted he would arrive before the 18th or 19th of June. He hoped that he would find her at home and that the delay would not cause her any inconvenience, etc, etc. Mrs Wightwick was inclined to be indignant at his cavalier attitude and apparent arrogance in assuming that she should be at his beck and call but decided she could put this aside if it meant that her daughter would stop behaving in a manner that was setting her teeth on edge.

Seeing her tension drain out of Lucy's face on learning of the reprieve, Mrs Wightwick (who had been somewhat aloof with her daughter since Thomas had taken Lucy's part) took pity on her and the two drove to Chepstow for a morning with the dressmaker, to order two new dresses for her to replace the ancient ones she had found at Hewelsfield and those ruined by travel. At Lucy's insistence, they also visited the reading rooms to find out what the newspapers were reporting. It was clear that different sections of the French armies were on the march in a combined pincer movement against the coalition forces of the Duke of Wellington and General Blücher's Prussian army, but no decisive battles had yet taken place.

Mrs Wightwick, knowing that like nearly every family in the country a number of cousins and nephews were serving in English regiments against 'the Monster, Napoleon', looked worried. Lucy thought wistfully of the bright, gay uniforms which had so enlivened the balls she had attended in Bath before she was married and shivered slightly at the thought that many of the young men wearing them would no doubt soon be lying dead, covered in mud and blood, on some far away battlefield, while others would be grievously injured. She put an arm through her mother's.

"At least there does not seem to have been much fighting yet, Mama. I am sure Papa will send or bring news as soon as he is able as to what is taking place."

The two ladies drove home in sombre mood, but Mrs Wightwick went briskly about her business and Lucy's spirits revived on seeing her little daughter running to greet them. Nothing more was said about the war, and a few days later Lucy's new dresses arrived by carrier in two bandboxes, packed in masses of tissue paper. She rushed to take them out and try them on, the paper rustling in drifting piles unheeded to the floor. There were two for day wear and one for evening. She slipped out of the out-grown, outmoded and faded dress she was wearing and exchanged it for one of the new ones, then twirled in front of the long mirror. Some slight alteration would be needed to the hem, but otherwise it was a perfect fit, the dressmaker had done an excellent job.

"Mama, Mama!" Lucy went to the top of the stairs and called down, then, when her mother appeared wiping her hands on her apron as she had been baking bread in the kitchen with Cook, "Please come up and pin up the hem on my new dress. It is a little too long but I wish to wear it at once."

Mrs Wightwick disappeared into the parlour to search for her pincushion, and by the time she reached her daughter's room Lucy was already trying on the second morning dress, the hemline of which did not need adjusting. It was deep blue with back gathers and long sleeves with some pretty detail at the upper edge.

"What do you think, Mama?" Lucy asked, pirouetting in front of the mirror like a young girl excited by her first grown-up dresses at her coming-out.

Her mother smiled. "Lisette has done a wonderful job. To tell the truth, I did not think she could complete the garments in such a short time. The seamstresses must have worked non-stop! I like the pattern on that calico, it becomes you well. There is no need to raise the hem, Lucy."

"Oh – no; not on this one, but on the other. I suppose, if you were to pin it for me now, I could wear the calico and stitch the hem myself later today. Will you do so, please?"

She was already changing dresses as she spoke, and her question came out a little muffled as she drew the one which needed alteration over her head. Mrs Wightwick obligingly knelt on a cushion at Lucy's feet and for the next fifteen minutes was absorbed in re-pinning the gown's hemline as her daughter turned slowly before her. This one was jonquil muslin, long-sleeved and high-necked. She straightened up to consider her handiwork.

"Yes, that is better. Now, please try on the evening gown and we shall see what alteration that needs."

Obediently Lucy changed clothes once more. The evening dress – a dove grey silk – was very tight at the waist, so Mrs Wightwick unpicked some stitching to loosen it slightly and pinned the sleeves to shorten them as Lucy requested.

"We should send this back to Lisette to alter," she told her daughter.

"No, Mama, that will take several days and I should like to be able to wear all my new clothes at once. There is not much work to do, I shall occupy myself with it after I have finished any tasks you have for me."

By the time they went to bed that evening, both dresses had been altered and mother and daughter were in harmony once more. Mrs Wightwick – who prided herself on her needlework as much as her jam-making – had taken on the job of sewing the waist of the evening gown, while Lucy concentrated on its sleeves and on hemming the muslin dress.

The following day, a Friday, was enlivened by a visit from their neighbour Mr Jane of Haresley Court. Lucy had always been a firm favourite of his and he was delighted to see her, but once the niceties of greeting were out of the way he turned to her mother and said,

"I had hoped for a word with your husband, Mrs Wightwick. Is he here?"

Mrs Wightwick explained that he had gone to London in the hope of obtaining more immediate news of the battles raging on the continent. Mr Jane looked grave.

"So you do not know when to expect him, then?"

Mrs Wightwick shook her head. "No, indeed. Have you any news, sir?"

"Only rumours, ma'am, and reports in the London journals, but they are worrying. It appears the Duke of Wellington and our army may have been routed by Napoleon. I was hoping that Thomas would be able to give the lie to them. It's a bad business, very bad. Will you tell him I called when he does return and ask him to visit me?" He rose and briskly took his leave. As he rode off, Lucy once again noticed the worried frown on her mother's face and asked why she was so concerned.

"We have our landholdings, Lucy, but your father has also been speculating a little and it may well be that we have lost a great deal of our wealth if these rumours are true."

The sombre mood which had prevailed on their return from the shopping trip earlier in the week took hold once more. The weather matched it. Bright and breezy June days had turned into a leaden grey and sodden one, much as when Lucy had returned on the Venus on the 4th of June. As she played with Cecilia on the nursery floor that afternoon – a fire burning in the hearth because it had turned so cold – Lucy wondered what the future held for the little girl and shivered. Still there was no news from her father.

By Monday, Lucy could bear it no longer. She ordered a horse be saddled for her and, donning her old riding dress (Lisette the dressmaker had not yet sent her new one) set off for Chepstow to read the London Gazette in the library. It did not make for pretty reading. Apparently, there had been an enormous battle at a place called Waterloo in Belgium on Saturday the 15th of June, and the lists of dead, missing and injured soldiers seemed never-ending. The Gazette reported that the Allies had won the encounter; if that was the case, Lucy wondered how many losses had been inflicted on Napoleon's army? There was no report of either general being killed or wounded; in that respect, this battle was unlike Trafalgar, with the loss of Lord Nelson himself.

Lucy made her way slowly home, wondering what this news would mean for the family fortunes. She rode to the stables, dismounted at the mounting block and handed the reins to a waiting groom with only a perfunctory pat for the horse, so engrossed was she in her thoughts. The front door to the house was ajar, and as she stepped through she could hear voices. For a moment she went cold, thinking that Sam – whom she had not even considered over the past few days – had finally arrived earlier than he had suggested, but just then the maid came out of the parlour and Lucy saw her father's silhouette through the open door.

She ran towards the parlour and stood in the doorway, glancing from her mother to her father and trying to read their expressions. Her father looked exhausted; her mother's face still wore its worried frown.

"Papa, what has happened? I have been to Chepstow to read the newspapers and there are lists and lists of dead and missing soldiers. Is the war over? Has Napoleon been captured?" She kissed him on the cheek then shook his arm, impatient to hear his take on what had occurred.

"Napoleon was beaten, but at the cost of huge losses to our own side, the extent is not entirely clear yet. At any event, no-one is taking any joy from the Duke's victory."

"And... Mama said your investments may have been affected. Have you lost a lot of money, Papa?"

"I and many others. All the way through most of last week it appeared that the war was going in Napoleon's favour, there was a battle at Quatre-Bras several days before the final one at Waterloo, and that seems to have been a massacre. The markets fell of course, and all the advice was to sell before they fell even further – which I did. Only a very few had the courage or the foolhardiness to ignore the advice and buy. We are not destitute, but we must pull in our horns a bit and live frugally until I can make up the losses." He smiled wearily at his daughter as she thought guiltily about the new dresses she had had made. "And has your husband made his appearance, my dear?"

"Not yet, Papa. I am so glad you have returned. I was dreading having to face him alone when he tries to take Cecilia."

"And I am simply glad that we shall just be immediate family sitting down to dine today. I am bone-weary and have no wish to play the host or to have a difficult conversation with Mr Lord until I am rested!" replied her father.

The evening passed quietly, undisturbed by visitors, but the following morning when Lucy was helping her mother in the stillroom there was a knock at the front door. She thought nothing of it, expecting it to be their neighbour Mr Jane come to discuss the outcome of the war with her father, then she heard the unmistakeable voice of her husband. She paled, and her hands trembled slightly as she wiped them on the apron covering one of her old dresses.

"Mama, Mr Lord has arrived. I am sure it is his voice I heard."

"Go upstairs and change into one of your new gowns – the calico, I think," her mother said calmly. "I shall go to him in the parlour shortly. Your father has gone to Haresley Court but should be back in an hour or so."

Lucy did as she was told, speeding up the servants' staircase to avoid a chance meeting with Sam. She changed her dress, smoothed her hair, put on a fresh cap and draped a shawl across her shoulders, then looked critically at herself in the mirror. She was pleased that she did not look as though her heart were pounding fit to burst out of her chest, but took a few deep breaths to try and stop her trembling. When that did not work, she sat down and thought about Cecilia to shore up her courage.

As she descended the main stairs, she could hear her mother's voice coming from the parlour. She hoped her father would come home soon. She took a deep breath and, steeling herself, put her hand on the door knob and twisted it.

"I see Mama has made you comfortable, Sam. Did you have a good voyage?" said Lucy, pleased that her voice did not waver.

Sam rose hurriedly from the wing-chair in which he had been seated at his ease. His face was a picture of utter shock, which Lucy took great pleasure from.

"Where the devil did you spring from, wife?" he demanded intemperately.

Mrs Wightwick frowned. This was not language used in polite circles and she was just about to chastise him when her daughter took the words out of her mouth.

"I do not think Mama appreciates such coarseness, sir, she looks quite shocked. I should have thought it was obvious where I came from. I, like you, have recently arrived from Barbados; indeed I was surprised not to find you here a week or more ago. I was sure you must reach Gravesend several days before I reached Bristol, for I left after you as you will know."

Sam opened his mouth to retort, and then thought better of it. It might be as well, perhaps, if his in-laws did not hear him confirm that he had locked his wife in a slave cell however much she might have provoked him. His black brows had drawn together in a straight line across the bridge of his nose and his jaw was clenched, but he made Lucy an ironic bow.

"I had no notion you planned to visit England. Had you informed me we could have travelled together."

This was a little too disingenuous for Lucy and she gasped at his effrontery.

"I had no such intention, sir, until I discovered you had secretly plotted to remove my daughter from my parents' care against my wishes and our agreement! And you imprisoned me in filthy degrading conditions in the slave dungeon so you could get away!" She fairly spat this at him.

"That is quite enough!" Mrs Wightwick broke in, using the voice Lucy remembered well from her childhood, a voice which brooked no opposition. "You shall not raise your voices at one another in my parlour. I am shocked that you do not show more decorum!"

Sam, unused to this tone, flushed and looked shamefaced, but Lucy continued to glare at him – though wordlessly now. Mrs Wightwick continued, "Lucy, you will oblige me by ringing the bell. I am sure Mr Lord's room will be ready for him by now, and Prudence will show him to it. We dine at five, sir, as I am sure you will remember, by which time I hope my husband will have returned from Haresley Court. I know that he wishes to speak to you."

The maid had appeared in response to Lucy's summons, and Mrs Wightwick nodded cool dismissal at Sam which left him no option but to bow gracefully and retreat upstairs to cool his temper. Once the door had shut behind him, she turned to her daughter with a look of glacial disapproval.

"And as for you, miss, it is time you grew out of such hoydenish behaviour! I am not at all surprised your husband beats you if that is the way you speak to him! You will behave mannerly in my house in future or you may leave it. You, at least, have no excuse, you were educated to have excellent manners."

Her head held high she sailed from the room to have a discussion with Cook about what might need to be changed in her choice of courses for dinner, without waiting for an answer from Lucy, who slumped down on the nearest chair. She was surprised to find her hands and legs trembling; since she felt no fear, she could only surmise that it was down to the anger that had blazed up in her. She must keep control of her temper. Losing it would not help resolve Cecilia's and her predicament.

After a few minutes Lucy gathered herself, stood and made her way upstairs to dress for dinner. Before doing so she visited the nursery to alert Nurse to Sam's arrival and insist that the old woman stay with Cecilia at all times. Once in her own room she rang the bell and asked for her mother's maid to come and dress her hair. She had noticed that fashions had changed in the past year, hair was now parted in the centre, with tight curls bunched over the ears and any long hair restrained in a bun. Lucy's hair remained fairly short, but she was sure some curls could be coaxed out of it and, sure enough, once the maid had done her work with papers and curling irons, her hair looked very stylish. It gave Lucy confidence to face with a degree of equanimity the tough discussions she knew must surely follow with her father and Sam that evening.

By the time she descended once more to the parlour, in the new evening gown and with her hair dressed differently, she felt calmer and more confident and was able to greet her husband politely. He, it was clear, was still simmering with fury, sitting like a coiled spring, ready to launch at Lucy she thought. But somehow he managed to control his temper in a way he never had in Barbados when in a foul mood. He disciplined himself to behave perfectly correctly and, while mostly ignoring Lucy, did his best to charm Mrs Wightwick once more.

After about half an hour of desultory conversation – Lucy had, most unusually for her, picked up some needlework and sat primly in a corner, stitching away and only speaking when spoken to – there came the sound of the front door and voices in the hall. Her father put his head round the door to the parlour.

"My apologies for my late return, my dear," he said to his wife. "Ah! Mr Lord! A pleasure to see you again! I must not join you in all my dirt" – indicating his riding dress – "but will change as quickly as I can and be with you in a trice."

He turned away and could be heard calling for his manservant as he climbed the stairs.

Sam showed great deference and civility to Mr Wightwick during the meal, and all four engaged in a lively discussion about the recent battles and whether the war with Bonaparte was now over. Mr Wightwick seemed to have recovered his spirits. Lucy wondered whether his losses had been less than feared, or whether it was simply his usual phlegmatic nature re-asserting itself.

When dinner – consisting of artichoke soup, mackerel with fennel and mint, roast beef, mutton pie, cabbage in cream sauce, rhubarb tart and sweetmeats – concluded, Lucy and her mother, as was the custom, stood to leave the men to their port, at which point Thomas looked directly at Sam and said, rather sternly,

"Mr Lord, if you would be so good as to join me in the library, I suggest we take a port or brandy there. I have matters of a serious nature I wish to discuss with you, and you alone."

At this he looked meaningfully at his daughter, as if to pre-empt any outburst from her. She bowed her head, bobbed him a half curtsey and followed her mother from the room.

The two ladies retired to the parlour and Mrs Wightwick picked up *Mansfield Park* which she had begun reading. Lucy tried reading the second volume of

Grimms' Fairy Tales but could not concentrate, and she was too restless to ply a needle. She sat at the piano but broke off after playing only a few bars and began pacing about the room. Her mother looked up.

"I shall ring for Nurse to bring in Cecilia," she said and did so.

As she had hoped this had the desired effect of diverting Lucy, who sat down with the little girl on her lap and looked at a picture book with her, then played 'catch' using a ball of her mother's wool, then took her by the hand and walked out onto the garden path in the watery evening sunshine to look at the flowers. The beautiful colours and the sound of humming bees soothed Lucy, so that when she heard the men's voices as they entered the parlour, she was able to bottle up her impatience to know what had transpired and act as though nothing out of the ordinary was going on.

Cecilia did not recognise her father but went straight to her grandfather, who picked her up and swung her over his head, to the chortling girl's delight. Thomas set her back on her feet.

"Do you remember this gentleman?" he asked her.

Cecilia, finger in her mouth, shook her head.

"This is your Papa, my dear," and he led her gently over to Sam who crouched down to her level and gently stroked her hair.

"Hello, Cecilia," he said softly.

Lucy, watching from just inside the French windows marvelled again at his natural ability with children, for within two minutes their daughter was totally at ease with him, playing and prattling happily. Lucy looked across at her father, a question in her eyes, but he shook his head slightly and sat down next to his wife on the sofa. Lucy could have screamed with vexation, but she knew his ways, he would want to discuss what had been said in the library with his wife this evening before talking to his daughter on the morrow. She sat down again at the piano and played a nursery rhyme she knew Cecilia loved (ring-a-ring-of-roses) and sure enough the little girl ran across to sing it with her, followed by Sam. The tension between husband and wife eased and even after Cecilia had been taken away to bed, they were able to bid one another a polite and formal good night with no sign of the anger and vitriol present earlier in the afternoon. At least he showed no sign of wanting to steal away in the night with their daughter, she thought.

Lucy's father called her to his library after breakfast the following day.

"I am going to put a proposition to you, Lucy, as a result of my discussion with Mr Lord yesterday. He has not agreed to it yet, and I do not want an answer from you immediately either. Troubling situations such as the one you both find yourselves in should not be dealt with in haste but calmly and dispassionately. But your husband is not an unreasonable man, Lucy, and I hope that what I have to say will be acceptable to you also.

"The central issue is what happens to little Cecilia. I think it is fair to say that Mr Lord is very fond of her?" He waited for Lucy's response. Hesitantly she nodded. "And, of course, it goes without saying that you are also. The difficulty lies in the fact that you are reluctant to allow her to live in the West Indies for all the reasons you have rehearsed to me previously; while he, as is his right, wishes her to be brought up at the family home in Barbados."

Mr Wightwick stopped to fill his pipe with tobacco, regarding his daughter all the while to judge her mood. She sat quietly, her face difficult to read, and waited for her father to continue.

"In addition," he continued, "it is important to discover whether your marriage is irretrievably damaged, or whether it is simply a case of two turbulent characters" – Lucy stirred at this and was about to say something but Thomas held up his hand to stop her – "two turbulent characters who need a period of reflection to get themselves back on an even keel. I hope and believe it is the latter, but only time will tell.

"So my proposition is that you both remain here for a few months as husband and wife, allowing Cecilia time to get to know you both better. If that goes well, then you shall all set up house elsewhere in England. You will remember, Lucy, that we were successful with this approach before you went back to Barbados last year."

Again, his daughter nodded, though still hesitantly. After all, Sam had broken her arm then.

"After that it will be for you to decide jointly whether you all return to Long Bay and, if so, when. I must stress, however, that should you decide to seek a divorce from Mr Lord you will find it impossible to retain any say over your daughter's upbringing.

"In the meantime, I propose having a Deed of Agreement drawn up by which Mr Lord shall pay you an allowance and stipulate a bequest in his Will should he predecease you. That way, should you decide to go your separate ways, you will have sufficient funds to live independently and to bring up your daughter."

What Thomas did not say was that it was clear to him that Sam would be extremely reluctant to pay out money to an estranged wife when, if they remained together, he would still be able to use it himself, and that this might cause him to think twice before treating her badly in the future.

"Now, Lucy, I do not want you to respond to this proposition immediately, you must go away and consider it carefully in all its aspects. I have asked Mr Lord to do the same. No doubt he will wish to seek legal advice, so I have suggested he provide me with an answer in two weeks. If you wish to discuss it with me during that time, I will be happy to help you reach your decision."

"What will happen, Papa, if we each come to a different conclusion?"

Mr Wightwick sighed. "I do not know, Lucy. Then we will have to find another way to ensure the best possible future for your daughter. But I do not think it helpful to cloud the issue by considering every possible alternative at this moment, there will be time enough for that. Now, away you go, I have work to do."

Sam had ridden out somewhere on his hired horse, and Lucy did not see him again until dinner time. There was some awkwardness between them, but when Cecilia was brought in to join the adults after the meal her antics had everybody laughing and the atmosphere between husband and wife eased. She was full of chatter, although it was not always easy to comprehend what she was trying to say. It was clear she loved flowers, and she was most insistent that her mother accompany her into the garden to look at them, so Lucy decided to try and teach her their names, while Sam made her a daisy chain crown which earned him an enormous smile.

When Cecilia went to bed, Sam announced he would be leaving for Bristol in the morning and would be away for several days. Lucy thought he must be going to find a lawyer with whom to discuss her father's proposition, so she merely smiled at him.

"Cecilia will miss you, so do not stay away too long."

When he returned a week later, he had obviously spent at least some of his time at the tables and fortune must have smiled on him, for he had bought gifts for everyone. For his mother-in-law, a silk shawl; for Thomas, a new pipe; for Cecilia a little locket and chain which Lucy allowed her to don when she came to join them after dinner but put away for safe-keeping thereafter. Lucy's gift was a delicate comb in the Spanish style.

"I like the new way you have of doing your hair," he said quietly as he gave it to her. Both gift and comment were an olive branch, and Lucy accepted them as such, thanking him prettily and asking her mother to place it on her head.

"Will you ride with me in the morning, Lucy?" he asked, to which she agreed cautiously. She remained wary of him and, since he had already gone behind her back once on the matter of Cecilia, she no longer trusted him. But she loved riding and it would do no-one any good (besides being extremely impolite) for husband and wife to be clearly at odds with one another, so she went along with the suggestion. But if he thought he could change her decision about their daughter he had another think coming. She just hoped he would think twice before imposing his will.

They rode out before breakfast, as had been their habit at Long Bay. Lucy's mount was fresh and full of fidgets, and she was fully occupied for the first half hour in proving she rather than the horse was boss. They found a track at the edge of some fields where they could canter, and when they reined in Sam drew alongside her. He wanted to talk.

"I understand your father put the same proposition to you as he did to me. I have considered it this past week. I believe we can make it work; after all, it is my wish to have Cecilia live at Long Bay that you object to. I shall have to make longer term arrangements for the management of the plantation, I dismissed Malcolm but I think the new overseer is capable of running the place profitably for me for the next six months or so. I must put plans for building the new house on hold since I wish to oversee that personally. So what say you, Lucy? And where shall we go? Chepstow? Bristol? Wolverhampton?"

Lucy had reached the conclusion that she had no real choice but to agree to her father's proposal on the morning he put it to her. Knowing that she had no legal right to decide the future of her daughter, she was terrified of losing even the power of persuasion over Cecilia, so for the sake of her daughter she would try again to live with her husband – but not the other side of the ocean. After all, there had been good times in between the beatings and cruelty; was there a chance they might live civilly together again?

And so began a summer in which the whole country, not just Sam and Lucy, seemed to be starting again. The great enemy, Bonaparte, was vanquished which meant the Continent was once more open to English visitors, and in July the Wightwick household (without Cecilia, who stayed behind with Nurse) undertook the long journey to Paris which neither Lucy nor her husband had ever seen because of the long years of war.

On their return in August, Mr and Mrs Wightwick travelled north to visit family in Wolverhampton, leaving the Lords alone at Hewelsfield. Both Sam and Lucy were on their best behaviour and no fights occurred to mar their serenity; Lucy even tentatively welcomed Sam back into the conjugal bed. In September they were invited as house guests by Lucy's Aunt Mary, who expressly requested that they bring Cecilia with them.

In the meantime, Thomas Wightwick had had a Deed of Agreement drafted by his lawyer. This stated that Lucy was to be paid £300 a year by Sam for life (or £500 should he predecease her); that she gave up all entitlement to her dowry; and that she should have absolute guardianship of Cecilia. All elements must be agreed by both parties or the Agreement would be null and void. Thomas was intent on ensuring Lucy had the rights she so desperately wanted over her daughter, while dangling the carrot in front of Sam that he might retain Lucy's dower apart from a modest sum each year for her upkeep. As long as they remained together this would not be an issue in any case but should they part, Thomas suspected that Sam would rather abandon guardianship of his daughter than his wife's money.

The Agreement was signed by Sam, Lucy and Thomas on the 5th of October 1815, in Sam's case very reluctantly and against all his instincts; but after all, he reasoned to himself, it was preferable to an outright breach with her father, with no possibility of receiving any further financial support which that would emphatically mean. The couple continued to live at Hewelsfield through December but in January moved to rented accommodation in Liverpool. Sam had become restless and bored of country life, and Thomas decided that a life of idleness would only lead him into trouble. So, hoping to avert another descent into gambling, debt and wife-beating, he found occupation for his son-in-law with John Swire, a Yorkshireman who had recently set himself up as a merchant in Liverpool dealing in cotton and wool.

Lucy accompanied Sam to Liverpool with extreme reluctance. Although she welcomed the notion of running her own household once again, she suspected Sam would not settle happily in a northern industrial town with its cramped, smoke-filled streets and leaden skies. Neither of them had any acquaintances in Liverpool; as a result, they rarely had anyone other than themselves for company. To cap it all, the weather was atrocious, the winter was particularly cold, with heavy snow falling as late as April and May, giving rise to much suffering across the country.

It was not long before Sam once again lost his precarious hold on his temper and let fly with his fists at Lucy. Cecilia had been unwell with croup, and Lucy had taken the little girl into her own room to sleep. Sam, having had rather too much to drink, took exception to Lucy (as she increasingly did) refusing him entry to her bed on this pretext. He shook her hard, boxed her ears and bruised her arms, leaving her angry but determined not to let him have his own way, so he slammed out of the house and was away all night.

The second time occurred after Cecilia had recovered. Once again Sam – as was his right – demanded Lucy take him to her bed but he was drunk and the smell of sour wine repulsed her. Her reluctance enraged him so he forced his way into her bedroom and raped her, leaving her bruised and aching and with – she suspected – at least one broken rib.

It was the same old circuitous behaviour. He would never change and she could never accept a life of wanton beatings and rape. She may have no rights as a wife. But she refused to accept that she be treated with as little consideration as Francine, Frances or Juba; she might be a chattel she thought, but never a slave.

Lucy began hoarding coins wherever she came across them. Sam regularly tossed them on the hall table when he came in so it was not difficult, and she thought she might need them to pay for her and Cecilia's passage back to Hewelsfield or at least to her Aunt Mary's in Staffordshire.

Sam's increasingly erratic behaviour saw him dismissed from his employment. The tradesmen's bills began piling up unpaid; they were a month behind with the rent. Lucy took Sam to task over it, pointing out that she had no way of paying for anything since he had not yet paid her the promised allowance. Sam lost his temper, grabbed his wife by the upper arm, yanked open the front door and threw her down the steps onto the road below.

Lucy was lucky that no carriage with a high-stepping team was passing or she might have been trampled, and perhaps even luckier that, despite the fact it was mid-May, a heavy snowfall had blanketed the ground. So she suffered no broken bones, only bruising and wounded pride. She might have frozen to death if the maid had not been peering out of the kitchen basement window and seen her fall; as it was she hurried out and helped Lucy back into the house.

This incident was the final straw for Lucy. Enough was enough. She had no alternative now. She had to leave Sam. It would be very difficult of course – she knew that only too well. But she was not going back. Better to survive as a social outcast than to submit.

As usual after such outbursts of anger, Sam had shut himself away in the dining room with a bottle of wine so Lucy made her way upstairs and crawled wearily between the sheets having locked the bedroom door. She slept only fitfully and rose early to count out the coins she had secreted away. There was insufficient to get her all the way to Hewelsfield on either the stage or the mail, let alone in a postchaise, so she decided on her second option, to make her way to her Aunt Mary.

She donned her cloak, boots and a muff and made her way gingerly to the Golden Lion on Dale Street to buy for seventeen shillings a ticket on the Mail to the Star and Garter on Cock Street in Wolverhampton later that morning for herself and Cecilia. On her return she visited the nursery and asked the nursemaid (old Nurse had finally retired for the second time when the Lords left Hewelsfield) to pack some of Cecilia's things for a journey, then packed a small bag for herself. She sat down to write a note to Sam.

13 May 1816

> *Husband: I am taking Cecilia on a visit to my parents. Sadly, I do not think we can continue to live together. This last attempt has shown me that you cannot change and I will not live-in constant fear of injury to myself or to our daughter.*

> *I have packed only a few things. Please order that the remainder of our belongings be sent by carrier to Hewelsfield.*

> *Should you wish to see Cecilia in the future, please write to advise me when you will visit. When you return to Long Bay, please pass my warm regards to your family, and in particular to Betty and Mary. I shall write to them.*

Yours
Lucy

She could not help shedding a few tears at this sad end to her youthful romance, but in all honesty, she had known it would come to this for a long time. It was her parents' horror at the social stigma of separation and divorce which had made her hesitate, and even now she herself shied away from the notion of divorce. But she had endured too much, her life simply was not worth living anymore if they remained together. Besides, while she had to acknowledge Sam was good with children, what of the time when Cecilia grew to womanhood? Would he show his daughter violence then too? They would have to live apart. Surely that would not be too difficult for people to accept if Sam was in Barbados?

There was still no sound from Sam's room. Lucy cast a last glance around the room, donned her outer clothes again and, picking up her valise, crept downstairs. She propped the letter for Sam on the hall table, listening all the while for any sign to indicate he was awake, and rang for the maid to fetch Cecilia and call a hackney cab. On the short journey, she told her daughter that they were going on a visit to her great aunt, at which Cecilia grew very excited. They reached the inn in good time and their bags were stowed away. Lucy thought it unlikely that Sam would have noticed their departure (and even when he read her note he would assume she had made her way directly to Hewelsfield) but could not relax until they were on their way and clutched her daughter's hand tightly, afraid she might be snatched away at any moment. She breathed a sigh of relief when the coachman, appearing enormous in his gigantic great coat, climbed ponderously onto the box, the guard blew his yard of tin and the Mail rumbled out of the courtyard.

The journey to Wolverhampton, passing by Warrington, Stoke-on-Trent and Stafford took four hours. When they arrived at the Star and Garter Hotel Cecilia was whimpering and fretful having been cooped up for longer than she was used to and seated all the while on her mother's lap. But she soon recovered her spirits when she discovered the publican had a large, shaggy, friendly dog. Lucy dashed off a note to her aunt, and requested it be conveyed to her at once, hoping against hope that Mary would not be away from home for she was not sure she had sufficient funds to pay for a night's lodging. She ordered a bowl of tea for herself and some milk for Cecilia and settled down to wait.

To Lucy's immense relief, her answer came in the shape of her aunt's carriage, so they were transported the last few miles to Rushall, where the Reverend Jonas Slaney had his vicarage, in comfort. Mary sensibly waited to pelt her niece with questions until Cecilia had been taken off to the kitchen for a meal; she then thrust Lucy into one wing chair, handing her a glass of ratafia, and sat down in one opposite her.

"Now, Lucy, tell me all. To what do I owe this unexpected pleasure?"

"I have left him, Aunt. It is over. I could not take the beatings anymore. Last night he threw me out on the street. I had not enough money to travel all the way to Hewelsfield, so I am afraid I am forcing our presence on you – I apologise profusely especially because I must beg a loan of you to get back to my parents' house as well. But this time I will not go back, I will not put up with a life of beatings. One day he will kill me in a drunken rage, and then where will Cecilia be? None of you will persuade me to change my mind."

"Then I shall not try," responded her aunt. "I cannot pretend to approve, and you may be sure my husband will certainly not do so. You are old enough to know your own mind now. But we do need to work out how to limit the social damage such a move will create – not just for yourself or for Lucy and Thomas, but also for Cecilia. You need to think of her future now."

So relieved was she that Mary simply accepted her decision that Lucy burst into tears. A handkerchief was passed silently to her, and she quickly regained her composure.

"I am sorry, Aunt. I have been very selfish. Are you entertaining this evening? If so, I can easily have my dinner on a tray in my room, with Cecilia."

"We are not entertaining, and Jonas will be delighted to see you. I think we will merely tell him that you are on your way to Hewelsfield and decided to pay us a visit. Since we are to be informal, there is no need to change your dress, I doubt you had space to pack an evening gown so we shall all sit down as we are."

Lucy and Cecilia spent two days with the Slaneys, and then the long-suffering Jonas was left to fend for himself while Mary announced that she planned to accompany them to Hewelsfield and would therefore need the carriage and their coachman for up to two weeks.

They broke their journey at Tewkesbury and spent the night at The Bell, with the latter part of their journey to Hewelsfield the following day on the Gloucester to Chepstow turnpike road. They stopped at the Feathers Inn at Lydney for a light luncheon before driving the final few miles to Lucy's childhood home, arriving shortly before two o'clock.

The weather had still not improved, the rain was cold and relentless and the sun never seemed to shine. The fields were sodden; some had not even been ploughed yet, and it had been impossible to sow many crops. There would be hunger among the country folk come harvest-time. But even the weather during this infamous 'year without a summer'[6] could not dampen Lucy's spirits as the carriage finally turned into the road leading to Hewelsfield Court. She let down the window and smelled the familiar scents of home and turned to smile at her daughter and her aunt.

"For the first time in a long while I feel free, Aunt!" she exclaimed. "No matter what happens now, it cannot be worse than the last few years."

And she hugged her wriggling little daughter tightly to her.

---

[6] In April 1815 an Indonesian volcano, Mount Tambora, erupted leading to unusually wet, cold conditions across Europe in 1816: hence the 'year without a summer'

Epilogue: 1861

The carriage slowed, the clip-clopping of the horses' hooves changing their monotonous regularity. Jane Haywood peered out of the window eagerly, they were on the outskirts of Chepstow, and soon she would see Grandmother's little house which she had heard about but never seen.

It had been a long journey from Wilncote, her father's home near Tamworth and although she had enjoyed the adventure of travelling on her own for the first time, she had become heartily sick of being cooped up in the carriage. Indeed, she would have preferred to travel by train or perhaps by canal boat, but Papa had not considered it suitable. Instead she had stayed overnight with her cousins in Worcester.

The carriage stopped, the steps were let down and Jane gratefully took the arm proffered by the stable lad as she climbed out She felt quite stiff, and looked forward to a brisk walk later, after she had greeted Grandmama. She would climb to the top of the hill and visit Chepstow Castle.

Jane's grandmother, Lucy Lord, had lived with the family (Jane's mother Cecilia and father James Haywood and their six children). That was, until Cecilia had died seven years before. Their family house had been on Hagley Road in Edgbaston where Jane, now eighteen years old, had been born. Papa had married again and they had moved to Dosthill House at Wilncote; now there was another Haywood child to add to the original six. Grandmother had chosen to return in her declining years to the area where she had been brought up, on the border between England and Wales, and settled at Hardwick Cottage. Jane had the impression that Grandmama had fallen out with Papa over his decision to remarry; not that she had ever heard this discussed, just that the family had not seen very much of her since her daughter Cecilia's death.

Jane (whose second name was Lucy, after her grandmother) was on a mission. She hoped that the old lady would be happy to tell her tales of her time in Barbados with the grandfather Jane had never known, for Samuel Hall Lord had died in 1844, shortly after she was born. Growing up, Jane had been entranced by the occasional tale she heard about the island. Grandmama Lucy must have led a very exciting life, the girl thought with a sigh. Her own life at Wilncote seemed very limited and rather boring – she would love to travel to exotic places. Perhaps Grandmama would tell her how she might meet an eligible foreign gentleman; otherwise no doubt Papa and Mama would find her a suitable young man from among their own acquaintance in the Birmingham area. Since

Papa was a solicitor, her future husband would probably belong to that circle, and whoever heard of a solicitor interested in travelling the world?

While these thoughts had been chasing through her head, Jane had been admitted to Hardwick Cottage's rather dark hallway by an elderly servant, her cases had been brought in from the carriage which had driven away to a nearby livery stable, and she had removed her coat and hat.

"If miss would be so good as to follow me?" the servant said and led the way towards a door which she opened for Jane. "I will just tell the mistress that you have arrived, miss. Please to wait here."

She closed the door behind her and Jane could hear the servant climbing slowly and heavily upstairs, wheezing as she went.

Jane walked slowly round the small parlour, over-stuffed with furniture and nick-nacks, doubtless collected by her grandmother throughout her long life. The room was neat and clean, with antimacassars on the arms of the chairs, but the curtains were faded and the carpets worn. This surprised Jane; surely Grandmama had received a sizeable inheritance from her husband on his death? She remembered tales of a fabulous castle in Barbados, tales from her childhood when her father James would come to the nursery and tell them all stories at bedtime. Jane shifted uncomfortably, she really needed to use the privy. She wondered whether the house had a modern water-closet, such as those that Papa had had installed at Dosthill House, or whether she would have to use a communal ash-pit privy like the one they had had at Edgbaston. Papa was very strict about hygiene and fascinated by any new invention in the field. He had particularly impressed upon his family that the causes of the mass outbreak of cholera in crowded English cities in 1858 had been caused by poor sanitation.

To take her mind off her desperate need, Jane walked around the parlour again, studying the paintings on the walls. There were some very fine watercolours of exotic flowers; she wondered if they had been painted by Grandmama, for Mama always said that she had been an excellent artist. Oh – there were so many questions she would like to ask Grandmama!

Just then came a knock at the door. The servant entered.

"If you would like to come with me, miss? Mrs Lord is awake and ready to see you now. I will take you up to her."

"If… if you please, I should like to visit the water-closet before I go to her. Perhaps you could show me where it is?"

The woman smiled. "Of course, miss. You have been travelling a long while. Please to follow me." Puffing, she led the way up the stairs and turning sharp right inclined her head towards another door and motioned for Jane to enter. One glance told Jane that this was not a modern water-closet but she was beyond caring and sat down hurriedly on the wooden seat having bunched her skirts about her waist. The privy consisted of a ceramic chamber pot encased in a wooden seat which the servant would have to empty daily.

Feeling greatly relieved, Jane exited the privy. On the landing outside was a pitcher of water and a basin. She washed her hands, and the servant held a towel to dry them on. Jane smiled her thanks.

"Now I feel ready to greet Grandmama! Is she quite well, Mrs...?"

"Cheadle, miss. The name is Cheadle. Mrs Lord is as well as can be expected, miss," was the slightly Delphic reply.

A couple more steps along the corridor, past the staircase, and she knocked on another door. Without waiting for a reply she opened it and motioned for Jane to enter.

"I will bring some tea upstairs for you both in an instant," she said and withdrew, closing the door behind her.

The room was bright and airy, dominated by a huge mahogany four-poster bed which quite dwarfed the little old lady, dressed entirely in black with a lace cap on her whispy white hair, seated in front of it in a chintz-covered armchair. Everything looked well-worn but clean. Jane went up to her grandmother and bent down to plant a kiss on her cheek.

"Dear Grandmama! How pleased I am to see you again. I have missed you very much since you moved back here. Thank you for allowing me to come and stay with you."

Lucy peered short-sightedly at her. "Cecilia?" she asked uncertainly.

Jane's eyes widened with shock. Did Grandmama not know who she was? She knelt on the floor and, clasping one of Lucy's hands in hers said gently,

"It is I, Jane, Cecilia's eldest daughter, Grandmama. Perhaps you do not recognise me, for I was still a child when you last visited us. But I am eighteen now and a grown woman," this was said proudly. "Do you think I look like Mama?"

There was a little silence.

"Jane. Yes, yes, I remember. Poor Cecilia is gone, isn't she? They are all gone now. Tell me, how many brothers and sisters do you have?"

"There are seven of us, but you have not met the youngest, Christine. Elizabeth is most envious of me for she wished to come too; but she is only fifteen and Papa would not permit it. He sent you his best wishes, Grandmama."

Lucy gave what sounded suspiciously like a snort.

"Did he indeed?" she said in a stronger voice. "So why were you so desirous of visiting an old woman like me? Most girls of your age wish to spend all their time at dances and picnics, I remember that I did."

"Because I wanted to hear from you about your life – where you have been and what you have done – and especially about Barbados, and the castle, and the sugar plantation, and the slaves. I want to know what it was really like, Grandmama. Papa – and sometimes Mama – used to tell us stories when I was little, but since Mama died, he has been reluctant to talk about it. It all sounds so romantic! I do not believe I know much about my mother's family history and I wish to learn about it from your lips."

She looked hopefully up into her grandmother's face.

"I fear I shall disappoint you. In truth my story is neither romantic nor glamorous." A small wistful smile creased her worn face, replaced almost at once by – Jane was sure – a flash of anger.

"But of course it is true that you should know something of your heritage. We shall see." Then, more briskly, "Now – where is that dratted woman? Did she offer you any refreshment? You must be hungry and thirsty after your journey!"

Correctly interpreting that Lucy was referring to Mrs Cheadle, Jane responded, "She said she was bringing us tea, Grandmama."

As she said it, there was a knock at the door and the servant came in bearing a silver tray with a steaming urn perilously perched on it, together with cups and saucers and a plate of macaroons.

"Ah! There you are, Matilda. I am sure my granddaughter must be parched. Just put it down on the table, Jane shall serve us. Thank you," and she nodded dismissal.

Jane stood up and went to serve the tea. She brought a cup for her grandmother, together with the sugar bowl and the plate of biscuits and placed them on the little table next to Lucy's chair, then pulled another seat across so that they could sit next to one another. Lucy had said nothing more and appeared unaware of her granddaughter's presence. "It is so lovely to see you, Grandmama," Jane repeated, smiling.

The old lady's face brightened up. "And I am pleased to see you again too. Now my girl. Remind me what brought you here?"

"Tell me about my grandfather please, Grandmama. I never knew him. What was he like? How did you meet?"

Lucy took a sip of her tea. Her gnarled hands trembled as she held the cup, and she set it down again on the table, waving away the offer of a macaroon.

"Your grandfather Sam Lord was a handsome ne'er-do-well who cheated a great many people out of money and wasted your mother's inheritance."

Jane gasped. This was completely unexpected.

"There is a picture of him over there, next to one of your mother."

Lucy nodded towards her dresser. Like the surfaces in the parlour, it was cluttered with ornaments. Jane searched among them and recognised the picture of Cecilia immediately. She lifted the one next to it; a dark, handsome man stared out at her, dressed in the fashion of the day with a beautifully tied cravat. Jane looked up at Lucy.

"Did you fall in love with him, Grandmama? Where did you meet?" she asked gently.

"You are persistent and impertinent, girl! I would never have dared question my elders this way when I was your age!"

But Lucy did not really seem angry so, emboldened, Jane smiled at her.

"I am sure you were very daring and very dashing when you were my age, Grandmama!"

Lucy's mouth twitched, and there was a gleam in her eye. It was clear that she did not object to a show of spirit, recognising approvingly something of her younger self in the girl. She relaxed visibly.

"My mother always told me I was too impetuous. No doubt you have inherited some of my bad traits, but at least you are not a foolish miss with no spark of character! I met your grandfather at a ball in Bath. All the débutantes were drawn to him. My friend Annabel was most envious. I was flattered by his attentions, and he turned my head."

"So it was a love match?" Jane was captivated. "How I wish I could meet a handsome foreigner who would whisk me away to travel the world!"

Lucy glared at her. "You know nothing about it. You have too many foolish, romantic notions in your head."

Startled at this sudden reprimand, Jane came back and sat at her grandmother's feet.

"Then please do tell me how it was, Grandmama, if I am not tiring you."

For a moment Jane thought Lucy might refuse to say any more. She waited patiently, holding her breath, not daring to move even though she was starting to get pins and needles in her legs because of her awkward position.

"If you must sit on the floor like a hoyden, fetch yourself a cushion and lean back against my chair."

Jane smiled and relaxed. It looked as though she would get her story after all. She did as she was told and fetched a cushion, but instead of leaning against her grandmother's chair she simply sat on the cushion half facing her. She smiled encouragingly up into Lucy's face, but still the old lady said nothing, her eyes fixed on something long ago and far away.

"Was Grandfather a good dancer?" Jane asked at last.

"Oh yes. He was very dashing. We danced waltzes and cotillions and the minuet. It made the other girls quite jealous. I was not pretty, you understand, so having a handsome man pay me attention made me feel special. My Mama thought him very charming. So did my aunt Elizabeth."

Another silence.

"Mr Lord possessed a large estate in Barbados, did he not? I know Papa travelled there after his death, and he described the big house he built. I remember he said the locals called it Sam Lord's Castle. It must have been wonderful! I would have loved to live in a castle!"

The old lady winced. "He built that house later. I know what he wanted it to look like and he often called it his castle, but it did not resemble any of the historic castles we have in England. When I first went with Sam to Long Bay we lived in another house, the one he had grown up in. Houses there are far smaller than country houses in England, and a great many of us lived there together. Their mother, three of Sam's sisters, and of course his elder brother John with his wife and children. Life was not easy. I had thought I would be running my own household but that was not the case."

Jane looked up at her puzzled. "I – I do not understand Grandmama. Was that arrangement not unusual?"

"I thought so. But then, I believed my husband co-owned Long Bay with his brother, John, and that he planned to build a new house for us to live in. It was true that he wanted a big, new mansion but he did not own the estate. He had inherited half of it, but unbeknownst to me he had sold his share to John to finance the trip to England on which we met."

"So you were as guests in what you believed to be your home?"

Lucy nodded. "I discovered soon after I arrived that he needed my dowry to fund his future lifestyle. He was very extravagant, you know, and preferred gambling and parties to running the plantation. We could have lived anywhere on the island, but Sam was determined to remain on the Long Bay estate and John was equally determined that he must help grow the family fortunes before starting his *grand projet*."

"What was Barbados like, Grandmama? I saw some watercolours of exotic flowers on the walls downstairs – did you paint them? The colours are beautiful!"

"So you like my sketches?" Lucy looked pleased, for the first time. "Then you shall choose one to take home with you. I took great pleasure in painting the island's flora and fauna. The colours are vibrant and rich, the scents too… I believe there may be a drawing of one of the little green monkeys locked away in a drawer somewhere but, although I can still remember the sound of the tree frogs in the evening, I never saw one to be able to sketch it."

"Did you enjoy living there? It all sounds so very different from England! I think I should like it very much."

Lucy took a moment before answering, "It was very different, certainly from anything I had ever known. There was much to like there but also much cruelty. Have you ever seen a black man, Jane?"

"Once or twice, when I visited the docks with Papa. But I have never met one."

"When I lived in Barbados slavery was still legal. There must have been ten times as many slaves as white men there, and they were treated worse than dogs, whipped and mutilated for the smallest fault, yet expected to make their owners rich by working the fields for them while being paid nothing themselves. I believe your grandfather had some six hundred poor wretches to his name when England abolished slavery. I know he received a handsome sum from the Government in recompense, near £14,000 as I recall. Not that your mother or I ever saw a penny of it!" This was said with some bitterness.

"Were you still living in Barbados then? I know Grandfather died in London, but I do not know how long you had been back in England."

"I returned to bring up your mother here in 1815. Sam continued to live at Long Bay, although he visited England from time to time."

Her eyes as round as saucers, Jane said in a shocked, hushed tone, "Were you divorced, Grandmama? There always seemed to be some mystery around you and Mama – was that it?"

"No, child. We lived separate lives but we never divorced. My parents could not contemplate the shame of it. And I did not want your mother to be damaged by my actions."

Jane battled with herself. She would dearly have liked to ask her grandmother what had caused the rift with her husband, but it was not acceptable to pry into one's elders' private lives. So she put this to one side, hoping to return to it in some oblique way later, and returned to her original question.

397

"Please tell me more about Barbados, and about Grandfather's family. Did you go to many parties? Did you have many friends there? Were you sorry to leave it all behind?"

Lucy seemed to be considering what to say. "There were some I was sorry to leave. I was very fond of two of Sam's sisters, Mary and Betty. Mary was married and did not live with us. She named one of her daughters after me and was always very kind. She looked after my other daughter, Emma, until she died." She stopped, her thoughts once again very far away.

"And Betty?" prompted Jane.

"Betty was the first person to show me real friendship when I arrived. We would walk together in the gardens, and she was the liveliest sister. We did not go out and about in Society much, and she seized on every opportunity that did present itself to enjoy herself to the full. And she was fond of Oceanus..." the quavering voice tailed off, but not before Jane's sharp ears recognised the tenderness in Lucy's voice when she uttered her dead son's name.

"Who was Oceanus, Grandmama?"

"He was my only son. I miss him to this day. He was born on board the ship we took to Barbados. Disease claimed him, as it took so many children. The heat, and our proximity to all those poor black wretches toiling in the fields who were forever getting sick."

"I did not know you had any children other than Mama. Was that why you wanted her to be brought up in England?"

"Indeed it was. So you see, Jane, it may sound exotic but life across the ocean is not near so desirable as you seem to think."

Jane bowed her head for a moment, but her curiosity was insatiable.

"Did you have any friends outside the family, Grandmama? It seems very odd to me that you did not make any acquaintances!"

"Well, there were the Barrows, who lived at the Sunbury Estate which we visited quite often, and Dr Lucas, his wife and their daughter Mary Kingsley who was the same age as me. For a while I was close friends to Mary, but she was only on the island for a long visit to her parents and returned to her husband in England and I rarely saw her after that. The person I saw most was a slave girl, Francine. She cared for me and for the children. I bought her freedom before I left the last time, but I do not know what happened to her. But none of these names can mean anything to you, Jane."

"Then please tell me about Mama's childhood. I know she went to France to finish her education, but that is all. Where did you live?"

"While my parents were alive, we lived with them at Hewelsfield; also Wolverhampton and Great Bloxwich. After your great grandfather died, of course, your great uncle Stubbs inherited all the properties, so we moved to lodgings in Bristol and Bath. Cecilia went to school at Miss Webb's Seminary in Clifton."

"Did you not wish to remain living with Uncle Stubbs, Grandmama? That would have been more comfortable, would it not?"

"No!"

Jane jumped, as Lucy's response came out like an explosion. She looked up to see real anger in her grandmother's face.

"I – I am sorry, Grandmama, I did not mean to be presumptuous."

Lucy sighed. "I am not angry with you, child. You were not to know. My brother and I quarrelled, indeed I brought a case against him in the Chancery court. He did not treat me well. I was left half of our father's income, but Stubbs ensured I never saw a penny of it. Indeed" – the querulous voice rose again in anger – "it is all of a pattern, my husband's debts ensured that Cecilia and I lived in penury (for he never paid me the allowance he had promised), then my brother took everything following our parents' death! That was certainly not what my dear Papa wanted for me."

Jane was a little embarrassed, having been brought up to believe that it was rather vulgar to discuss money. But this conversation had cleared up one mystery; the faded carpets and hangings, and the small size of her grandmother's house, must be down to the fact that she was living in genteel poverty and was not the wealthy widow of a Barbados nabob as Jane had fantasised.

She looked up, planning to ask Lucy whether she had brought much back with her from Barbados, but her grandmother's eyes had closed, she had fallen into a doze as old people so often seemed to do. Carefully Jane stood up from her cushion. She was stiff, hungry and thirsty. Lucy had not stirred, so Jane decided to go downstairs to the kitchen and see if Mrs Cheadle would provide her with a plate of cold meat. She stole out of the room and shut the door gently behind her.

****

Over the days that followed, Jane spent many hours in her grandmother's room, gradually achieving a better picture of the life she had led – a life about which, as children, they had woven many fantastical stories. She wrote to her father, asking him about the Chancery case Lucy had mentioned[7]. A few days later she received a response.

My dearest Daughter,

I was pleased to learn that you are enjoying the company of your Grandmother, although I was surprised that she had raised the subject of her legal quarrel with her brother, Stubbs Wightwick. I would not have thought it was a suitable topic of conversation for a young girl. However, I will endeavour to explain it to you as simply as possible.

When their father, Thomas Wightwick, died his Will stated that he wished his Daughter to have an equal yearly income with his Son during her lifetime to be paid from the profits of his mining interests. This was in addition to an annual allowance of two hundred Pounds, the total not to exceed six hundred Pounds[8].

---

[7] National Archives ref. C107/55, Lord v. Wightwick

[8] To provide some context, a middling family with 2 servants on £200 pa had c. £14 discretionary spend pa; £500 pa was needed to 'live like a gentleman'

He also left a sum to your Mother. However, Mr Wightwick died much in debt. His son repaid a large portion – some ten thousand Pounds as I remember – from his own money and claimed this back from the mines revenue which was only forthcoming after several years. Your Grandmother took your Great-Uncle to Court for refusing to honour the terms of the Will.

The Judge agreed with your Great-Uncle that having kept the debts alive he should be repaid from the profits and, moreover, that he was owed interest on the repayment of his Father's debts from his own money. So your Grandmother's share remained two hundred Pounds per annum but I do not know whether she ever received it, and since she had never received any money from her Husband she felt aggrieved that her income was much reduced from what she had expected.

I believe the rift between them was never healed, and your Great-Uncle died five years after the judgement when you were fifteen years old.

I shall send the carriage to collect you on the Thirteenth of August. Please give my best wishes to your Grandmother and offer her all the support that you can. I enclose a draft on my bank for Twenty Pounds for any expenses you may incur at Chepstow or on your return journey.

Your Brothers and Sisters send their fondest regards to you also.
Your ever loving, Papa.

On some days, Lucy's mind wandered and she believed she was talking to her daughter Cecilia. On others, her brain was sharp and she was able to describe events and places vividly. The weather was warm and sunny and Jane coaxed Lucy to accompany her to see some of the local sights such as Tintern Abbey, using some of the large sum her father had sent to hire a chaise in which to travel. They visited Hewelsfield; the house where Lucy had spent her childhood was much altered, but the church where she was baptised, and Cecilia baptised and married, remained the same.

"Were you not married here, Grandmama?" Jane asked.

Lucy looked sideways at her, then smiled a little mischievously.

"I was married in Bath Abbey. Your grandfather persuaded me to run away with him. I know," seeing Jane's stunned expression, "shocking, was it not? I was very much in love and determined to have my own way, and Papa had concerns about my future husband."

Jane came to respect and admire her grandmother's spirit and courage in adversity. She had hoped to have confirmed the fairy tales she and her siblings had weaved around Lucy, and instead she heard sometimes far more exciting real-life stories. She wondered if she would ever dare, as Lucy had, to be a runaway bride, or to give birth on board ship in pirate-infested waters, or cope with the deaths of her children far away from the loving arms of her family, or live in constant fear of a slave revolt. Regretfully she came to the conclusion that she had not inherited her grandmother's robust attitude to life, reflecting that she would never be able to endure the pain and heartache Lucy had suffered.

Mrs Cheadle had aired and dusted the musty parlour, and when Lucy was not too tired Jane would sit with her there following their evening meal and listen to her grandmother talk.

"Tell me about the castle Grandfather built in Barbados," Jane pleaded.

"I cannot. I never saw it. He built it after I had returned to England. You should ask your father about it. He went to Barbados to lay claim to Long Bay and the other plantations after my husband's death. Cecilia should have inherited everything but Sam made no provision for her in his will although he did set up a trust for your brother's benefit. James did all he could in law to amend this, but I believe Sam's debts were such that there was nothing left. That was not unexpected, he had always liked to spend well beyond his means."

Jane only had vague memories of the story her father had told her as a child about the fabulous castle her grandfather had built and resolved to get him to recount it once more when she returned home.

On another occasion she asked Lucy whether she had ever considered returning to Barbados to live with Sam since life had clearly been uncomfortable for her in England. Lucy hesitated before answering.

"My father had forced Sam to commit to paying me an allowance and to paying for Cecilia's education, but we never received a penny. I saw him occasionally because he spent a great deal of time in England but he could be very cruel and I had no wish to make myself vulnerable to suffering again at his hands. He threw me in a dungeon, you know." This was said in a perfectly normal tone of voice as though Lucy did not realise the enormity of her statement. Jane's jaw dropped in astonishment as she gasped, but Lucy was lost in her story and took no notice. She continued, "Society does not look kindly on estranged wives – unless you happen to be fabulously wealthy – and as Cecilia grew, I became worried about how she would fare if she were unable to meet people, or indeed how she would ever find a husband. When she was about fourteen your grandfather came to visit us in Bristol and I told him of my fears and offered to return to live with him for the sake of our daughter, whom he loved very much. He was always kind to children, even if not to me."

She fell silent. "What happened, Grandmama?"

Lucy sighed. "He told me it would not suit his present habits. I was so mortified at being rejected that I made no further inquiry, but Betty – his sister, with whom I continued to correspond – said that his way of life was immoral. I believe he had taken a mistress – one of the slaves on his estates – by whom he had several children. Later that year, after Papa had died, he came to visit me again. I was staying with Stubbs at Wightwick Manor in Wolverhampton then. This time *he* asked *me* to return to him. I was at a very low ebb and seriously considered doing so, but in the end decided it was too late for us. I was fairly sure he had heard the terms of my father's will and thought I was about to become wealthy and could therefore be useful to him again. That did not seem to me a good basis on which to resume our marriage, so I refused him. I took your mother to France to finish her education instead."

Another silence ensued, and Jane realised her grandmother had nodded off again. She walked around the parlour studying the paintings and deciding which one she would ask Lucy to give her as she had promised the first day. When the old lady woke up, Jane rang for the tea tray and they talked a little more before retiring to bed.

The following day the weather turned sultry and there were frequent downpours. Lucy was very confused and seemed to think she was going to visit her parents at Hewelsfield. Recognising that she was tired, Jane withdrew to the parlour and settled down to record everything her grandmother had told her. In vain she searched the drawers and cupboards for the sketch of a green monkey Lucy had mentioned, or for anything which might give her greater insight into her grandfather.

Late in the afternoon the sky cleared and Jane, who had grown bored and restless, decided to walk down the hill into Chepstow town. For the first time she wished she had friends nearby, or that her sister Elizabeth was with her and was surprised to realise how absorbed she had become in coaxing tales out of her grandmother.

The day before Jane was due to return home, she hired a carriage to take them both to Piercefield Park. Nathaniel Wells, the black son of a St Kitt's planter who had owned it in Lucy's childhood was long gone and the place was up for sale, but the beautiful walks were again open to the public after several years when they had been closed. Mrs Cheadle packed a picnic lunch for them, and Jane and Lucy sat in the open carriage admiring the view – for now aged 75 Lucy could no longer walk far – the hamper between them on the seat.

"Who does own Long Bay and the other plantations now, Grandmama?"

"The property should have passed to your brother Walter, but there were so many debts and mortgages when your grandfather died – and your cousin Frances, John's daughter, also had some claim to it… In any event, even your father could not resolve the disputes surrounding it all. I do know that when Frances married, she handed her share to Sam during his lifetime, in return for an annuity of £1,000 a year which I doubt she was ever paid. Her family, the Trollopes, tried to get possession of Long Bay and Pool through purchase of the outstanding mortgages but to my knowledge they never lived there. They even threw poor Betty out of the house! I do not know what happened."

Jane made a mental note to have a long discussion with her father once she was back in Wilnecote. Not all Lucy's warnings could dispel her longing to visit the Caribbean island which she might, conceivably, have called home in other circumstances, and she was determined to obtain satisfactory answers to her questions somehow.

"How did Grandfather die, Grandmama?"

"Not at all pleasantly. I understand he died of the bloody flux which he no doubt caught in Barbados before travelling to England. He was gambling in a gentlemen's club in Jermyn Street in London when he was taken violently ill. That was what his coachman, Rolstone (who married one of Sam's illegitimate children) told me. He had accompanied Sam from Long Bay and was very upset."

That evening, unprompted, Lucy told Jane the tale of her escape from Barbados in 1815. While she did not dwell in detail on the rough treatment she had received from Sam, for it would have been unseemly to do so, she did explain the reason behind their dispute and the fact that he had imprisoned her, and went on to set out the sequence of events which followed. Her memory was a little hazy on some aspects, and Jane had to use a degree of patience to unravel the astounding story; once she felt she understood what had happened – including the brutality to which she had been subjected – she sat staring at her grandmother in amazement.

"You were so brave, Grandmama! The ultimate survivor. I would never have dared take passage all alone across the ocean. And I would have no idea how to begin to find a passage other than to ask Papa's man of business! I wish I could have met Francine, I should like to thank her for keeping you safe."

Lucy smiled, and became lost in her memories. Jane had a shrewd suspicion she was thinking of Francine and Oceanus and early, happier days following her runaway marriage. She went over to Lucy and hugged her, then knelt in front of her and clasped her hands.

Lucy came out of her reverie.

"Have you decided which picture you would like to take home with you, child?"

Jane pointed to a delicate, detailed watercolour of frangipani blossom. "Then you shall have it. Go and lift it off the wall. Frangipani was my favourite flower there, you know. The scent is so strong…"

Jane did as she was told and stood holding the frame and studying the brushstrokes. "Thank you, Grandmama. I shall treasure it always. And Grandmama…" she hesitated.

"Well? What is it?"

"I would very much like to have the two miniatures of my mother and grandfather that are in your room. Would you leave them to me, please?"

"You may have any pictures you wish when I am gone. It will not be long now, I feel my age more and more every day. I am glad to have had this opportunity to get to know you, Jane. Thank you for taking the trouble to visit an old woman."

"May I visit you again Grandmama?" Jane asked, tears welling up inside her.

Lucy smiled. "I should like that very much."

Jane did not want to leave but Papa had sent the carriage so the following day, Jane found herself pulling down the carriage window to wave a white handkerchief to her grandmother, who stood at the door to Hardwick Cottage leaning on Mrs Cheadle's arm and a stout stick. When the carriage turned a corner and she could no longer see Jane, there were tears coursing down Lucy's cheeks. She knew it was unlikely they would see each other again, and she had so much enjoyed the girl's company, she had reminded her of Cecilia. And in spirit rather of her own younger self too.

She turned wistfully and went back inside, her mind on her escape with the help of Francine, how she had somehow survived all the bad times and enjoyed bringing up Cecilia – in hardship, yes, but without fear of Sam. Come to think of it, Jane was right. Some of her life had indeed been different and exciting. She hoped her granddaughter had learned something from their conversations, if only that a runaway marriage was definitely not a good idea.

Helped to her favourite armchair by Mrs Cheadle who noticed a far-away smile on the old lady's face, Lucy quickly fell asleep there accompanied by dreams of frangipani, whistling tree frogs and three healthy children playing together in a Caribbean garden watched over by a smiling black maid, Francine.

****

Lucy Lord died on 25 October 1863 at home at the age of 77, of 'softening of the brain'. Jane married a Naval Officer, Captain James Lenon, 10 years later.

Afterword

As a child I remember my imagination being fired by my father's tales of a wicked ancestor who lived in a castle in a far-off land luring unsuspecting ships onto the rocks to steal their treasure and whose end was suitably unpleasant. When I was eight years old, my grandfather travelled to Barbados on a banana boat (literally, a Geest ship) to research and, hopefully, disprove the story that Samuel Hall Lord had been a wrecker and another tale (which I was unaware of at the time) that Sam was a wife-beater. He documented his findings in an article[9]. He managed to disprove the wrecker theory, but not that Sam Lord mistreated his wife.

I have always loved historical biographies and novels and when I reread his article many years later it occurred to me that true stories can be just as exciting as fiction, but also that nothing much had been written about Sam's wife, Lucy, so I decided to write her story.

I quickly discovered the truth of the author Philippa Gregory's statement that it's hard to find evidence about the lives of most women in history. So the research for this project took four years, with visits to Bath, Bristol, Wolverhampton, Chepstow, Hewelsfield and Barbados. The bare bones of Lucy's life were included in my grandfather's article, and my research corroborated some of these facts but failed to uncover much additional evidence. There were a few little nuggets, for example, it was news to me that Mary Austin, one of Lucy's sisters-in-law, had named a daughter after her. This implied a close relationship which I have woven into my book. And since my grandfather was writing about Sam rather than Lucy, he mentioned nothing about the dispute over Thomas Wightwick's will. But it has proved impossible to verify which ships Lucy and Sam travelled on because passenger lists were not kept until several decades later, so the names and dates I have used are 'guesstimates' based on the 1963 article and detailed examination of Lloyds List and Lloyds Register records. Nor was it possible – despite discussions with the Barbados Museum and exhaustive searches of online sources which would have been unavailable to Colonel Haywood – to verify (or disprove) my grandfather's assertion that Lucy's final escape was enabled by two enslaved people, or the online innuendo that there was an element of mixed race to Sam's family.

As far as possible I have used real characters and historical facts in Lucy's incredible story but like all historical novels it contains a dose of fiction as the

---

[9] *Sam Lord and His Castle* by Col. Austin Haywood, Journal of The Barbados Museum & Historical Society 1963, pp. 114-26

glue to hold it all together, to make it believable and ensure it flows. As John Le Carré said, 'fact is the writer's raw material, not his taskmaster but his instrument, and his job is to make it sing'.[10] So the Napoleonic Wars, the abolition of the slave trade, the assassination of a British Prime Minister, the Louisiana slave uprising all help to provide context. Most characters in addition to Lucy's family – the Lucases and Mary Kingsley, Mary Ann Chaworth, the Murray brothers, the McConnels – did indeed exist although I cannot say for certain (other than Thomas Daniel) that they met either Sam or Lucy. The only major character who is entirely fictional is Francine. I hope, however, that some distant relative I have not managed to contact has a stack of documentary evidence which will fill in the gaps – even if it does contradict what I have written!

On only one occasion have I deliberately tweaked a historic fact. Barbados suffers only infrequent hurricanes, unlike other Caribbean islands. A major one occurred in 1810 but for the purposes of the story I have it happening in 1809.

I have only hinted at the language of the time, and this is merely to give a sense of different place and period. I did not feel it would add to the story to try and write in the vernacular of Georgian England or Barbados patois and I would in any case have been bound to get it wrong!

I have, however, used the term 'Negro' and some of the other pejoratives only in direct speech (and very occasionally in thoughts) to make the dialogue more authentic of its era. We now live in a very different time, when #BlackLivesMatter has quite rightly forced society to face up to the enduring iniquities our white ancestors heaped on our black ancestors and adjust our language and attitudes accordingly. Consequently, for descriptive passages I use modern language stripped of its historic racism.

---

[10] *The Pigeon Tunnel*, John Le Carré, 2016

Bibliography

Sam Lord and His Castle, Col. Austin Haywood, Journal of the Barbados Museum & Historical Society, 1963

The Representation of Western European Governesses and Tutors on the Russian Country Estate in Historical Documents and Literary Texts, Ulrike Lentz, University of Surrey, June 2008

Female Education, Reading and Jane Austen, Kathryn Sutherland, British Library

The Last Great Dance on Earth, Sandra Gulland, Review 2000

Sugar in the Blood, Andrea Stuart, Portobello 2013

Peregrinations of a Pariah, Florah Tristan, Virago 1986

A Regency Rascal, Lt Col W P Drury, Macmillan 1980

The Falmouth Packets, Tony Pawlyn, Truran 2003

A Record of Bristol Ships 1800–1838, Bristol Record Society publication (Vol. XV)

A Training in Docility by Fay Weldon in *Jane Austen: Critical Assessments*, ed. Ian Littlewood 1998

A Change of Style at the Theatre Royal, 1805-20, Mac Hopkins-Clarke, Bath Spa University

A Perfect Match, Rachel Knowles – Sandsfoot Publishing 2015

Jane Austen's England, Roy and Lesley Adkins – Viking 2013

Manchester: An Architectural History, John J Parkinson-Bailey – Manchester University Press 2000

Wellington: A Journey through My Family, Jane Wellesley – Weidenfeld & Nicolson 2010

Mary Barton, Elizabeth Gaskell, 1848

The Severn District Sea Fencibles 1803–1810, John Penny – Regional Historian (Issue 6) 2002

The Value of Money in Eighteenth-Century England: Incomes, Prices, Buying Power— and Some Problems in Cultural Economics, Robert D. Hume – Huntington Library Quarterly Vol. 77, no. 4, 2015

A Voyager Out: The Life of Mary Kingsley, Katherine Frank – Houghton Mifflin 1986

Evelina, Fanny Burney, 1778
In the Castle of My Skin, George Lamming – Michael Joseph 1953

http://www.ucl.ac.uk/lbs/claim/view/4581: University College London's database of slave compensation